OIL i

Fiction reprints published by Robert Bentley
in clothbound library editions

Nelson Algren
The Man with the Golden Arm

A. Anatoli
Babi Yar

John Brunner
Stand on Zanzibar

Donn Byrne
Messer Marco Polo

Erskine Caldwell
Tobacco Road

Joseph Conrad
Almayer's Folly
Lord Jim

Jack Conroy
The Disinherited

Marcia Davenport
East Side, West Side
My Brother's Keeper
The Valley of Decision

John Dos Passos
Manhattan Transfer

Theodore Dreiser
An American Tragedy
Sister Carrie

Daphne DuMaurier
Frenchman's Creek
Hungry Hill
The Loving Spirit
Mary Anne
My Cousin Rachel
The Parasites

Erle Stanley Gardner
The Case of the Deadly Toy
The Case of the Gilded Lily
*The Case of the Mythical
    Monkeys*
The Case of the Singing Skirt

André Gide
Lafcadio's Adventures
The School for Wives
Strait is the Gate

Nicholai V. Gogol
*The Overcoat and Other Tales
    of Good and Evil*

Ivan Goncharov
Oblomov

Jaroslav Hasek
The Good Soldier Svejk

Evan Hunter
The Blackboard Jungle

Christopher Isherwood
The Berlin Stories

Charles Jackson
The Lost Weekend

Shirley Jackson
The Lottery

Sinclair Lewis
Elmer Gantry

Jack London
*John Barleycorn;
    or, Alcoholic Memoirs*

Frank Norris
McTeague
The Octopus
The Pit

John Powers
The Last Catholic in America

Jean-Paul Sartre
Nausea

Budd Schulberg
Waterfront
What Makes Sammy Run?

André Schwarz-Bart
The Last of the Just

Clifford Simak
Way Station

Upton Sinclair
Boston
The Jungle
Oil!

Wilbur Smith
Shout at the Devil

Josephine Tey
Brat Farrar
The Franchise Affair
The Man in the Queue
Miss Pym Disposes

B. Traven
The Treasure of the Sierra Madre

H. G. Wells
The Invisible Man
The Island of Dr. Moreau
The Time Machine

Sloan Wilson
The Man in the Gray Flannel Suit

OIL!

A Novel by

UPTON SINCLAIR

ROBERT BENTLEY
Cambridge, Massachusetts

Library of Congress Cataloging in Publication Data

Sinclair, Upton Beall, 1878-1968.
  Oil!

  Reprint of the ed. published by A. & C. Boni,
New York.
  I. Title.
PZ3.S616Oi 1980   [PS3537.I85]   813'.5'2   79-24682
ISBN 0-8376-0444-3

FIC

Shuffle the cards, and deal a new round of poker hands: they differ in every way from the previous round, and yet it is the same pack of cards, and the same game, with the same spirit, the players grim-faced and silent, surrounded by a haze of tobacco-smoke.

So with this novel, a picture of civilization in Southern California, as the writer has observed it during eleven years' residence. The picture is the truth, and the great mass of detail actually exists. But the cards have been shuffled; names, places, dates, details of character, episodes—everything has been dealt over again. The only personalities to be recognized in this book are three presidents of the United States who have held office during the past fifteen years. Manifestly, one could not "shuffle" these, without destroying all sense of reality. But the reader who spends his time seeking to identify oil magnates and moving picture stars will be wasting time, and perhaps doing injustice to some individual, who may happen to have shot off his toe to collect accident insurance, but may not happen to be keeping a mistress or to have bribed a cabinet official.

CONTENTS

OIL!

A Novel by Upton Sinclair

CHAPTER I

THE RIDE

I

The road ran, smooth and flawless, precisely fourteen feet wide, the edges trimmed as if by shears, a ribbon of grey concrete, rolled out over the valley by a giant hand. The ground went in long waves, a slow ascent and then a sudden dip; you climbed, and went swiftly over—but you had no fear, for you knew the magic ribbon would be there, clear of obstructions, unmarred by bump or scar, waiting the passage of inflated rubber wheels revolving seven times a second. The cold wind of morning whistled by, a storm of motion, a humming and roaring with ever-shifting overtones; but you sat snug behind a tilted wind-shield, which slid the gale up over your head. Sometimes you liked to put your hand up, and feel the cold impact; sometimes you would peer around the side of the shield, and let the torrent hit your forehead, and toss your hair about. But for the most part you sat silent and dignified—because that was Dad's way, and Dad's way constituted the ethics of motoring.

Dad wore an overcoat, tan in color, soft and woolly in texture, opulent in cut, double-breasted, with big collar and big lapels and big flaps over the pockets—every place where a tailor could express munificence. The boy's coat had been made by the same tailor, of the same soft, woolly material, with the same big collar and big lapels and big flaps. Dad wore driving gauntlets; and the same shop had had the same kind for boys. Dad wore horn-rimmed spectacles; the boy had never been taken to an oculist, but he had found in a drug-store a pair of amber-colored glasses, having horn rims the same as Dad's.

1

There was no hat on Dad's head, because he believed that wind and sunshine kept your hair from falling out; so the boy also rode with tumbled locks. The only difference between them, apart from size, was that Dad had a big brown cigar, unlighted, in the corner of his mouth; a survival of the rough old days, when he had driven mule-teams and chewed tobacco.

Fifty miles, said the speedometer; that was Dad's rule for open country, and he never varied it, except in wet weather. Grades made no difference; the fraction of an ounce more pressure with his right foot, and the car raced on—up, up, up— until it topped the ridge, and was sailing down into the next little valley, exactly in the centre of the magic grey ribbon of concrete. The car would start to gather speed on the down grade, and Dad would lift the pressure of his foot a trifle, and let the resistance of the engine check the speed. Fifty miles was enough, said Dad; he was a man of order.

Far ahead, over the tops of several waves of ground, another car was coming. A small black speck, it went down out of sight, and came up bigger; the next time it was bigger yet; the next time—it was on the slope above you, rushing at you, faster and faster, a mighty projectile hurled out of a six-foot cannon. Now came a moment to test the nerve of a motorist. The magic ribbon of concrete had no stretching powers. The ground at the sides had been prepared for emergencies, but you could not always be sure how well it had been prepared, and if you went off at fifty miles an hour you would get disagreeable waverings of the wheels; you might find the neatly trimmed concrete raised several inches above the earth at the side of it, forcing you to run along on the earth until you could find a place to swing in again; there might be soft sand, which would swerve you this way and that, or wet clay which would skid you, and put a sudden end to your journey.

So the laws of good driving forbade you to go off the magic ribbon except in extreme emergencies. You were ethically entitled to several inches of margin at the right-hand edge; and the man approaching you was entitled to an equal number of inches; which left a remainder of inches between the two projectiles as they shot by. It sounds risky as one tells it, but the heavens are run on the basis of similar calculations, and while collisions do happen, they leave time enough in between for universes to be formed, and successful careers conducted by men of affairs.

"Whoosh!" went the other projectile, hurtling past; a loud, swift "Whoosh!" with no tapering off at the end. You had a glimpse of another man with horn-rimmed spectacles like yourself, with a similar grip of two hands upon a steering wheel, and a similar cataleptic fixation of the eyes. You never looked back; for at fifty miles an hour, your business is with the things that lie before you, and the past is past—or shall we say that the passed are passed? Presently would come another car, and again it would be necessary for you to leave the comfortable centre of the concrete ribbon, and content yourself with a precisely estimated one-half minus a certain number of inches. Each time, you were staking your life upon your ability to place your car upon the exact line—and upon the ability and willingness of the unknown other party to do the same. You watched his projectile in the instant of hurtling at you, and if you saw that he was not making the necessary concession, you knew that you were encountering that most dangerous of all two-legged mammalian creatures, the road-hog. Or maybe it was a drunken man, or just a woman—there was no time to find out; you had the thousandth part of a second in which to shift your steering-wheel the tenth part of an inch, and run your right wheels off onto the dirt.

That might happen only once or twice in the course of a day's driving. When it did, Dad had one invariable formula; he would shift the cigar a bit in his mouth and mutter: "Damn fool!" It was the only cuss-word the one-time mule-driver permitted himself in the presence of the boy; and it had no profane significance—it was simply the scientific term for road-hogs, and drunken men, and women driving cars; as well as for loads of hay, and furniture-vans, and big motor-trucks which blocked the road on curves; and for cars with trailers, driving too rapidly, and swinging from side to side; and for Mexicans in tumble-down buggies, who failed to keep out on the dirt where they belonged, but came wabbling onto the concrete—and right while a car was coming in the other direction, so that you had to jam on your foot-brake, and grab the hand-brake, and bring the car to a halt with a squealing and grinding, and worse yet a sliding of tires. If there is anything a motorist considers disgraceful it is to "skid his tires"; and Dad had the conviction that some day there would be a speed law turned inside out—it would be forbidden to drive less than forty miles an hour on state highways, and people who wanted to drive spavined horses to tumble-down buggies would either go cross-lots or stay at home.

II

A barrier of mountains lay across the road. Far off, they had been blue, with a canopy of fog on top; they lay in tumbled masses, one summit behind another, and more summits peeking over, fainter in color, and mysterious. You knew you had to go up there, and it was interesting to guess where a road might break in. As you came nearer, the great masses changed color— green, or grey, or tawny yellow. No trees grew upon them, but bushes of a hundred shades. They were spotted with rocks, black, white, brown, or red; also with the pale flames of the yucca, a plant which reared a thick stem ten feet or more in the air, and covered it with small flowers in a huge mass, exactly the shape of a candle flame, but one that never flickered in the wind.

The road began to climb in earnest; it swung around the shoulder of a hill, and there was a sign in red letters: "Guadalupe Grade: Speed limit on curves 15 miles per hour." Dad gave no evidence that he knew how to read, either that sign, or his speedometer. Dad understood that signs were for people who did not know how to drive; for the initiate few the rule was, whatever speed left you on your own half of the highway. In this case the road lay on the right side of the pass; you had the mountain on your right, and hugged it closely as you swung round the turns; the other fellow had the outside edge, and in the cheerful phrase of the time, it was "his funeral."

Another concession Dad made—wherever the bend was to the right, so that the mass of the mountain obstructed the road, he sounded his horn. It was a big, commanding horn, hidden away somewhere under the capacious hood of the car; a horn for a man whose business took him on flying trips over a district big enough for an ancient empire; who had important engagements waiting at the end of his journey, and who went through, day or night, fair weather or foul. The voice of his horn was sharp and military; there was in it no undertone of human kindness. At fifty miles an hour there is no place for such emotions—what you want is for people to get out of the way, and do it quick, and you tell them so. "Whanhnh!" said the horn—a sound you must make through your nose, for the horn was one big nose. A sudden swing of the highway—"Whanhnh!"—and then an elbow jutting out and another swing—"Whanhnh!"—so you went winding up, up, and the rocky walls of Guadalupe Pass resounded to the strange new cry—"Whanhnh! Whanhnh!" The birds looked about in alarm, and the ground squirrels dived into their sandy entrance-holes, and ranchmen driving rickety Fords down the grade, and tourists coming to Southern California with all their chickens and dogs and babies and mattresses and tin pans tied onto the running-boards—these swung out to the last perilous inch of the highway, and the low, swift roadster sped on: "Whanhnh! Whanhnh!"

Any boy will tell you that this is glorious. Whoopee! you bet! Sailing along up there close to the clouds, with an engine full of power, magically harnessed, subject to the faintest pressure from the ball of your foot. The power of ninety horses—think of that! Suppose you had had ninety horses out there in front of you, forty-five pairs in a long line, galloping around the side of a mountain, wouldn't that make your pulses jump? And this magic ribbon of concrete laid out for you, winding here and there, feeling its way upward with hardly a variation of grade, taking off the shoulder of a mountain, cutting straight through the apex of another, diving into the black belly of a third; twisting, turning, tilting inward on the outside curves, tilting outward on the inside curves, so that you were always balanced, always safe—and with a white-painted line marking the centre, so that you always knew exactly where you had a right to be—what magic had done all this?

Dad had explained it—money had done it. Men of money had said the word, and surveyors and engineers had come, and diggers by the thousand, swarming Mexicans and Indians, bronze of skin, armed with picks and shovels; and great steam shovels with long hanging lobster-claws of steel; derricks with wide swinging arms, scrapers and grading machines, steel drills and blasting men with dynamite, rock-crushers, and concrete mixers that ate sacks of cement by the thousand, and drank water from a flour-stained hose, and had round steel bellies that turned all day with a grinding noise. All these had come, and for a year or two they had toiled, and yard by yard they had unrolled the magic ribbon.

Never since the world began had there been men of power equal to this. And Dad was one of them; he could do things like that, he was on his way to do something like that now. At seven o'clock this evening, in the lobby of the Imperial Hotel at Beach City, a man would be waiting, Ben Skutt, the oil-scout, whom Dad described as his "lease-hound"; he would have a big "proposition" all lined up, and the papers ready for signature. So it was that Dad had a right to have the road clear; that was the meaning of the sharp military voice of the horn, speaking through its nose: "Whanhnh! Whanhnh! Dad is coming! Get out of the way! Whanhnh! Whanhnh!"

The boy sat, eager-eyed, alert; he was seeing the world, in a fashion men had dreamed in the days of Haroun al Raschid—from a magic horse that galloped on top of the clouds, from a magic carpet that went sailing through the air. It was a giant's panorama unrolling itself; new vistas opening at every turn, valleys curving below you, hilltops rising above you, processions of ranges, far as your eye could reach. Now that you were in the heart of the range, you saw that there were trees in the deep gorges, towering old pine trees, gnarled by storms and split by lightning; or clumps of live oaks that made pleasant spaces like English parks. But up on the tops there was only brush, now fresh with the brief spring green; mesquite and sage and other desert plants, that had learned to bloom quickly, while there was water, and then stand the long baking drought. They were spotted with orange-colored patches of dodder, a plant that grew in long threads like corn-silk, weaving a garment on top of the other plants; it killed them—but there were plenty more.

Other hills were all rock, of an endless variety of color. You saw surfaces mottled and spotted like the skins of beasts—tawny leopards, and creatures red and grey or black and white, whose names you did not know. There were hills made of boulders, scattered as if giants had been throwing them in battle; there were blocks piled up, as if the children of giants had grown tired of play. Rocks towered like cathedral arches over the road; through such an arch you swung out into view of a gorge, yawning below, with a stout white barrier to protect you as you made the turn. Out of the clouds overhead a great bird came sailing; his wings collapsed as if he had been shot, and he dived into the abyss. "Was that an eagle?" asked the boy. "Buzzard," answered Dad, who had no romance in him.

Higher and higher they climbed, the engine purring softly, one unvarying note. Underneath the wind-shield were dials and gauges in complicated array: a speedometer with a little red line showing exactly how fast you were going; a clock, and an oil gauge, a gas gauge, an ammeter, and a thermometer that mounted slowly on a long grade like this. All these things were in Dad's consciousness—a still more complicated machine. For, after all, what was ninety horse-power compared with a million dollar power? An engine might break down, but Dad's mind had the efficiency of an eclipse of the sun. They were due at the top of the grade by ten o'clock; and the boy's attitude was that of the old farmer with a new gold watch, who stood on his front porch in the early morning, remarking, "If that sun don't get over the hill in three minutes, she's late."

III

But something went wrong and spoiled the schedule. You had got up into the fog, and cold white veils were sweeping your face. You could see all right, but the fog had wet the road, and there was clay on it, a combination that left the most skilful driver helpless. Dad's quick eye noted it, and he slowed down; a fortunate thing, for the car began to slide, and almost touched the white wooden barrier that guarded the outer edge.

They started again, creeping along, in low gear, so that they could stop quickly; five miles the speedometer showed, then three miles; then another slide, and Dad said "Damn". They wouldn't stand that very long, the boy knew; "Chains", he thought, and they drew up close against the side of the hill, on an inside curve where cars coming from either direction could see them. The boy opened the door at his side and popped out; the father descended gravely, and took off his overcoat and laid it in the seat; he took off his coat and laid that in the same way—for clothing was part of a man's dignity, a symbol of his rise in life, and never to be soiled or crumpled. He unfastened his cuffs and rolled up the sleeves—each motion precisely followed by the boy. At the rear of the car was a flat compartment with a sloping cover, which Dad opened with a key; one of a great number of keys, each precisely known to him, each symbolical of efficiency and order. Having got out the chains, and fastened them upon the rear tires, Dad wiped his hands on the fog-laden plants by the roadside; the boy did the same, liking the coldness of the shining globes of water. There was a clean rag in the compartment, kept there for drying your hands, and changed every so often. The two donned their coats again, and resumed their places, and the car set out, a little faster now, but still cautiously, and away off the schedule.

"Guadalupe Grade: Height of Land: Caution: Fifteen miles per hour on curves." So ran the sign; they were creeping down now, in low gear, holding back the car, which resented it, and shook impatiently. Dad had his spectacles in his lap, because the fog had blurred them; it had filled his hair with moisture, and was trickling down his forehead into his eyes. It was fun to breathe it and feel the cold; it was fun to reach over and sound the horn—Dad would let you do it now, all you wanted. A car came creeping towards them out of the mist, likewise tooting lustily; it was a Ford, puffing from the climb, with steam coming out of the radiator.

Then suddenly the fog grew thinner; a few wisps more, and it was gone; they were free, and the car leaped forward into a view—oh, wonderful! Hill below hill dropping away, and a landscape spread out, as far as forever; you wanted wings, so as to dive down there, to sail out over the hilltops and the flat plains. What was the use of speed limits, and curves, and restraining gears and brakes?—"Dry my spectacles," said Dad, prosaically. Scenery was all right, but he had to keep to the right of the white-painted line on the road. "Whanhnh! Whanhnh!" said the horn, on all the outside curves.

They slid down, and little by little the scenery disappeared; they were common mortals, back on earth. The curves broadened out, they left the last shoulder of the last hill, and before them was a long, straight descent; the wind began to whistle, and the figures to creep past the red line on the speedometer. They were making up for lost time. Whee! How the trees and telegraph poles went whizzing! Sixty miles now; some people might have been scared, but no sensible person would be scared while Dad was at the wheel.

But suddenly the car began to slow up; you could feel yourself sliding forward in your seat, and the little red line showed fifty, forty, thirty. The road lay straight ahead, there was no other car in sight, yet Dad's foot was on the brake.

The boy looked up inquiringly. "Sit still," said the man. "Don't look round. A speed-trap!"

Oho! An adventure to make a boy's heart jump! He wanted to look and see, but understood that he must sit rigid, staring out in front, utterly innocent. They had never driven any faster than thirty miles per hour in their lives, and if any traffic officer thought he had seen them coming faster down the grade, that was purely an optical delusion, the natural error of a man whose occupation destroyed his faith in human nature. Yes, it must be a dreadful thing to be a "speed-cop", and have the whole human race for your enemy! To stoop to disreputable actions—hiding yourself in bushes, holding a stop-watch in hand, and with a confederate at a certain measured distance down the road, also holding a stop-watch, and with a telephone line connecting the two of them, so they could keep tab on motorists who passed! They had even invented a device of mirrors, which could be set up by the roadside, so that one man could get the flash of a car as it passed, and keep the time. This was a trouble the motorist had to keep incessant watch for; at the slightest sign of anything suspicious, he must slow up quickly—and yet not too quickly—no, just a natural slowing, such as any man would employ if he should discover that he had accidentally, for the briefest moment, exceeded ever so slightly the limits of complete safety in driving.

"That fellow will be following us," said Dad. He had a little mirror mounted in front of his eyes, so that he could keep tab on such enemies of the human race; but the boy could not see into the mirror, so he had to sit on pins and needles, missing the fun.

"Do you see anything?"

"No, not yet; but he'll come; he knows we were speeding. He puts himself on that straight grade, because everybody goes fast at such a place." There you saw the debased nature of the "speed-cop"! He chose a spot where it was perfectly safe to go fast, and where he knew that everyone would be impatient, having been held in so long by the curves up in the mountains, and by the wet roads! That was how much they cared for fair play, those "speed-cops"!

They crept along at thirty miles an hour; the lawful limit in those benighted times, back in 1912. It took all the thrill out of motoring, and it knocked the schedule to pot. The boy had a vision of Ben Skutt, the "lease-hound", sitting in the lobby of the Imperial Hotel at Beach City; there would be others waiting, also—there were always dozens waiting, grave matters of business with "big money" at stake. You would hear Dad at the long distance telephone, and he would consult his watch, and figure the number of miles to be made, and make his appointment accordingly; and then he had to be there— nothing must stop him. If there were a breakdown of the car, he would take out their suit-cases, and lock the car, hail a passing motorist and get a ride to the next town, and there rent the best car he could find—or buy it outright if need be—and drive on, leaving the old car to be towed in and repaired. Nothing could stop Dad!

But now he was creeping along at thirty miles! "What's the matter?" asked the boy, and received the answer: "Judge Larkey!" Oh, sure enough! They were in San Geronimo County, where the terrible Judge Larkey was sending speeders to jail! Never would the boy forget that day, when Dad had been compelled to put all his engagements aside, and travel back to San Geronimo, to appear in court and be scolded by this elderly autocrat. Most of the time you did not undergo such indignities; you simply displayed your card to the "speed-cop", showing that you were a member of the Automobile Club, and he would nod politely, and hand you a little slip with the amount of your "bail" noted on it, proportioned to the speed you had been caught at; you mailed a check for the amount, and heard and thought no more about it.

But here in San Geronimo County they had got nasty, and Dad had told Judge Larkey what he thought of the custom of setting "speed-traps"—officers hiding in the bushes and spying on citizens; it was undignified, and taught motorists to regard officers of the law as enemies. The Judge had tried to be smart, and asked Dad if he had ever thought of the possibility that burglars also might come to regard officers of the law as enemies. The newspapers had put that on the front page all over the state: "Oil Operator Objects to Speed Law: J. Arnold Ross Says He Will Change It." Dad's friends kidded him about that, but he stuck it out—sooner or later he was going to make them change that law, and sure enough he did, and you owe to him the fact that there are no more "speed-traps," but officers have to ride the roads in uniform, and if you watch your little mirror, you can go as fast as you please.

IV

They came to a little house by the road-side, with a shed
that you drove under, and a round-bellied object, half glass
and half red paint, that meant gasoline for sale. "Free Air,"
read a sign, and Dad drew up, and told the man to take off
his chains. The man brought a jack and lifted the car; and the
boy, who was always on the ground the instant the car stopped,
opened the rear compartment and got out the little bag for
the chains to go in. Also he got out the "grease-gun", and
unwrapped that. "Grease is cheaper than steel," Dad would
say. He had many such maxims, a whole modern Book of
Proverbs which the boy learned by heart. It was not that Dad
was anxious to save the money; nor was it that he had grease
to sell and not steel; it was the general principle of doing things
right, of paying respect to a beautiful piece of machinery.

Dad had got out, to stretch his legs. He was a big figure
of a man, filling every inch of the opulent overcoat. His cheeks
were rosy, and always fresh from the razor; but at second
glance you noted little pockets of flesh about his eyes, and a
network of wrinkles. His hair was grey; he had had many
cares, and was getting old. His features were big and his whole
face round, but he had a solid jaw, which he could set in ugly
determination. For the most part, however, his expression was
placid, rather bovine, and his thoughts came slowly and stayed
a long time. On occasions such as the present he would show
a genial side—he liked to talk with the plain sort of folks he
met along the road, folks of his own sort, who did not notice
his extremely crude English; folks who weren't trying to get
any money out of him—at least not enough to matter.

He was pleased to tell this man at the "filling station" about
the weather up there in the pass; yes, the fog was thick—
delayed them quite a bit—bad place for skidding. Lots of cars
got into trouble up there, said the man—that soil was dobe,
slick as glass; have to trench the road better. Quite a job that,
Dad thought—taking off the side of the mountain. The man
said the fog was going now—lots of "high fog" in the month
of May, but generally it cleared up by noon. The man wanted
to know if Dad needed any gas, and Dad said no, they had got
a supply before they tackled the grade. The truth was, Dad was
particular, he didn't like to use any gas but his own make; but

he wouldn't say that to the man, because it might hurt the man's feelings.

He handed the man a silver dollar for his services, and the man started to get change, but Dad said never mind the change; the man was quite overwhelmed by that, and put up his finger in a kind of salute, and it was evident he realized he was dealing with a "big man." Dad was used to such scenes, of course, but it never failed to bring a little glow to his heart; he went about with a supply of silver dollars and half dollars jingling in his pocket, so that all with whom he had dealings might share that spiritual warmth. "Poor devils," he would say, "they don't get much." He knew, because he had been one of them, and he never lost an opportunity to explain it to the boy. To him it was real, and to the boy it was romantic.

Behind the "filling station" was a little cabinet, decorously marked, "Gents." Dad called this the "emptying station", and that was a joke over which they chuckled. But it was a strictly family joke, Dad explained; it must not be passed on, for other people would be shocked by it. Other people were "queer"; but just why they were queer was something not yet explained.

They took their seats in the car, and were about to start, when who should come riding up behind them—the "speed-cop"! Yes, Dad was right, the man had been following them, and he seemed to scowl when he saw them. They had no business with him, so they drove on; doubtless he would take the filling station as a place to hide, and watch for speeders, said Dad. And so it proved. They had gone for a mile or two, at their tiresome pace of thirty, when a horn sounded behind them, and a car went swiftly by. They let it go, and half a minute later Dad, looking into his little mirror, remarked: "Here comes the cop!" The boy turned round, and saw the motor-cycle pass them with a roaring of the engine. The boy leaped up and down in the seat. "It's a race! It's a race! Oh, Dad, let's follow them!"

Dad was not too old to have some sporting spirit left; besides, it was a convenience to have the enemy out in front, where you could watch him, and he couldn't watch you. Dad's car leaped forward, and the figures again crept past the red line of the speedometer—thirty-five—forty—forty-five—fifty—fifty-five. The boy was half lifted out of his seat, his eyes shining and his hands clenched.

The concrete ribbon had come to an end; there was now a

dirt road, wide and level, winding in slow curves through a country of gentle hills, planted in wheat. The road was rolled hard, but there were little bumps, and the car leaped from one to another; it was armed with springs and shock-absorbers and "snubbers", every invented device for easy riding. Out in front were clouds of dust, which the wind seized and swept over the hills; you would have thought that an army was marching there. Now and then you got a glimpse of the speeding car, and the motor-cycle close behind it. "He's trying to get away! Oh, Dad, step on her!" This was an adventure you didn't meet on every trip!

"Damn fool!" was Dad's comment; a man who would risk his life to avoid paying a small fine. You couldn't get away from a traffic-officer, at least not on roads like this. And sure enough, the dust clouds died, and on a straight bit of the highway, there they were—the car drawn up at the right, and the officer standing alongside, with his little note-book and pencil, writing things. Dad slowed down to the innocent thirty miles and went by. The boy would have liked to stop, and listen to the argument inevitable on such occasions; but he knew that the schedule took precedence, and here was the chance to make a "get-away." Passing the first turn, they hit it up; the boy looked round every half minute for the next half hour, but they saw no more of the "speed-cop." They were again their own law.

V

Some time ago these two had witnessed a serious traffic accident, and afterwards had appeared to testify concerning it. The clerk of the court had called "J. Arnold Ross," and then, just as solemnly, "J. Arnold Ross, junior," and the boy had climbed into the witness-chair, and testified that he knew the nature of an oath, and knew the traffic regulations, and just what he had seen.

That had made him, as you might say, "court-conscious." Whenever, in driving, anything happened that was the least bit irregular, the boy's imagination would elaborate it into a court scene. "No, your honor, the man had no business on the left side of the road; we were too close to him, he had no time to pass the car in front of him." Or it was: "Your honor, the man was walking on the right side of the road at night, and

there was a car coming towards us, that had blinding lights.
You know, your honor, a man should walk on the left side of
the road at night, so that he can see the cars coming towards
him." In the midst of these imaginings of accidents, the boy
would give a little jump; and Dad would ask, "What's the
matter, son?" The boy would be embarrassed, because he
didn't like to say that he had been letting his dreams run away
with him. But Dad knew, and would smile to himself; funny
kid, always imagining things, his mind jumping from one thing
to another, always excited!

Dad's mind was not like that; it got on one subject
and stayed there, and ideas came through it in slow, grave
procession; his emotions were like a furnace that took a long
time to heat up. Sometimes on these drives he would say
nothing for a whole hour; the stream of his consciousness would
be like a river that has sunk down through rocks and sand, clean
out of sight; he would be just a pervading sense of well-being,
wrapped in an opulent warm overcoat, an accessory, you might
say, of a softly purring engine running in a bath of boiling oil,
and traversing a road at fifty miles an hour. If you had taken
this consciousness apart, you would have found, not thoughts,
but conditions of physical organs, and of the weather, and of
the car, and of bank-accounts, and of the boy at his side.
Putting it into words makes it definite and separate—so you
must try to take it all at once, blended together: "I, the
driver of this car, that used to be Jim Ross, the teamster, and
J. A. Ross and Co., general merchandise at Queen Centre,
California, am now J. Arnold Ross, oil operator, and my breakfast is about digested, and I am a little too warm in my big new
overcoat because the sun is coming out, and I have a new well
flowing four thousand barrels at Lobos River, and sixteen on
the pump at Antelope, and I'm on my way to sign a lease at
Beach City, and we'll make up our schedule in the next couple
of hours, and 'Bunny' is sitting beside me, and he is well and
strong, and is going to own everything I am making, and follow
in my footsteps, except that he will never make the ugly blunders
or have the painful memories that I have, but will be wise and
perfect and do everything I say."

Meantime the mind of "Bunny" was not behaving in the
least like this, but on the contrary was leaping from theme to
theme, as a grass-hopper in a field leaps from one stalk of grass
to another. There was a jackrabbit, racing away like mad; he

had long ears, like a mule, and why were they so transparent and pink? There was a butcher-bird, sitting on the fence; he stretched his wings all the time, like he was yawning—what did he mean by that? And there was a road-runner, a long lean bird as fast as a race-horse, beautiful and glossy, black and brown and white, with a crest and a streaming tail. Where do you suppose he got water in these dry hills? There on the road was a mangled corpse—a ground squirrel had tried to cross, and a car had mashed it flat; other cars would roll over it, till it was ground to powder and blown away by the wind. There was no use saying anything to Dad about that—he would remark that squirrels carried plague, or at least they had fleas which did; every now and then there would be cases of this disease and the newspapers would have to hush it up, because it was bad for real estate.

But the boy was thinking about the poor little mite of life that had been so suddenly snuffed out. How cruel life was; and how strange that things should grow, and have the power to make themselves, out of nothing apparently—and Dad couldn't explain it, and said that nobody else could, you were just here. And then came a ranch wagon in front of them, a one-sided old thing loaded with household goods; to Dad it was just an obstacle, but "Bunny" saw two lads of his own age, riding in back of the load and staring at him with dull, listless eyes. They were pale, and looked as if they hadn't enough to eat; and that was another thing to wonder about, why people should be poor and nobody to help them. It was a world you had to help yourself in, was Dad's explanation.

"Bunny," the every-day name of this boy, had been started by his mother when he was little—because he was soft and brown and warm, and she had dressed him in a soft, fuzzy sweater, brown in color with white trimmings. Now he was thirteen, and resented the name, but the boys cut it to "Bun," which was to stay with him, and which was satisfactory. He was a pretty boy, still brown, with wavy brown hair, tumbled by the wind, and bright brown eyes, and a good color, because he lived outdoors. He did not go to school, but had a tutor at home, because he was to take his father's place in the world, and he went on these rides in order that he might learn his father's business.

Wonderful, endlessly wonderful, were these scenes; new

faces, new kinds of life revealed. There came towns and villages—extraordinary towns and villages, full of people and houses and cars and horses and signs. There were signs along the road; guide-posts at every crossing, giving you a geography lesson—a list of the places to which the roads led, and the distances; you could figure your schedule, and that was a lesson in arithmetic! There were traffic signs, warning you of danger —curves, grades, slippery places, intersections, railroad crossings. There were big banners across the highway, or signs with letters made of electric lights: "Loma Vista: Welcome to Our City." Then, a little farther on: "Loma Vista, City Limits: Good-bye: Come Again."

Also there were no end of advertising signs, especially contrived to lend variety to travel. "Picture ahead; kodak as you go," was a frequent legend, and you looked for the picture, but never could be sure what it was. A tire manufacturer had set up big wooden figures of a boy waving a flag; Dad said this boy looked like Bunny, and Bunny said he looked like a picture of Jack London he had seen in a magazine. Another tire manufacturer had a great open book, made of wood, and set up at a turn of the road leading into each town; it was supposed to be a history book, and told you something about that place— facts at once novel and instructive: you learned that Citrus was the location of the first orange grove in California, and that Santa Rosita possessed the finest radium springs west of the Rocky mountains, and that on the outskirts of Crescent City Father Junipero Serra had converted two thousand Indians to Christianity in the year 1769.

There were people still engaged in converting, you learned; they had gone out on the highway with pots of vari-colored paint, and had decorated rocks and railway culverts with inscriptions: "Prepare to meet thy God." Then would come a traffic sign: "Railroad crossing. Stop. Look. Listen." The railroad company wanted you to meet your God through some other agency, Dad explained, because there would be damage suits for taking religious faith too seriously. "Jesus waits," a boulder would proclaim; and then would come, "Chicken Dinner, $1." There were always funny signs about things to eat—apparently all the world loved a meal, and became jolly at the thought. "Hot Dog Kennels," was an eating-place, and "Ptomaine Tommy," and "The Clam-Baker," and the "Lobster-Pot." There were endless puns on the word inn—"Dew Drop

Inn" and "Happen Inn," "Welcome Inn" and "Hurry Inn."
When you went into these places you would find the spirit of
jollity rampaging on the walls: "In God we Trust, All Others
Cash." "Don't complain about our coffee; some day you
may be old and weak yourself." "We have an arrangement
with our bank; the bank does not sell soup, and we do not
cash checks."

VI

They were passing through a broad valley, miles upon miles
of wheat fields, shining green in the sun; in the distance were
trees, with glimpses of a house here and there. "Are you
looking for a Home?" inquired a friendly sign. "Santa Ynęz
is a place for folks. Good water, cheap land, seven churches.
See Sprouks and Knuckleson, Realtors." And presently the
road broadened out, with a line of trees in the middle, and there
began to be houses on each side. "Drive slow and see our city;
drive fast and see our jail," proclaimed a big board—"By Order
of the Municipal Council of Santa Ynez." Dad slowed down
to twenty-five miles; for it was a favorite trick of town marshals
and justices of the peace to set speed-traps for motorists coming
from the country, with engines keyed up to country rates of
speed; they would haul you up and soak you a big fine—and
you had a vision of these new-style highwaymen spending your
dollars in riotous living. That was something else Dad was
going to stop, he said—such fines ought to go to the state, and
be used for road-repairs.

"Business zone, 15 miles per hour." The main street of
Santa Ynez was a double avenue, with two lines of cars parked
obliquely in the centre of it, and another line obliquely against
each curb. You crept along through a lane, watching for a
car that was backing out, and you dived into the vacant place,
just missing the fender of the car at your right. Dad got out,
and took off his overcoat, and folded it carefully, outside in,
the sleeves inside; that was something he was particular about,
having kept a general store, which included "Gents' Clothing."
He and Bunny laid their coats neatly in the rear compartment,
locked safe, and then strolled down the sidewalk, watching the
ranchers of Santa Ynez valley, and the goods which the stores
displayed for them. This was the United States, and the things
on sale were the things you would have seen in store-windows

on any other Main Street, the things known as "nationally advertised products." The ranchman drove to town in a nationally advertised auto, pressing the accelerator with a nationally advertised shoe; in front of the drug-store he found a display of nationally advertised magazines, containing all the nationally advertised advertisements of the nationally advertised articles he would take back to the ranch.

There were a few details which set this apart as a Western town: the width of the street, the newness of the stores, the shininess of their white paint, and the net-work of electric lights hung over the centre of the street; also a man with a broad-brimmed hat, and a stunted old Indian mumbling his lips as he walked, and a solitary cowboy wearing "chaps." "Elite Café," said a white-painted sign, reading vertically; the word "Waffles" was painted on the window, and there was a menu tacked by the door, so that you could see what was offered, and the prices charged. There were tables along one side of the wall, and a counter along the other, with a row of broad backs in shirt-sleeves and suspenders perched on top of little stools; this was the way if you wanted quick action, so Dad and the boy took two stools they found vacant.

Dad was in his element in a place like this. He liked to "josh" the waitress; he knew all kinds of comic things to say, funny names for things to eat. He would order his eggs "sunny side up," or "with their eyes open, please." He would say, "Wrap the baby in the blanket," and laugh over the waitress' effort to realize that this meant a fried egg sandwich. He would chat with the rancher at his other side—learning about the condition of the wheat, and the prospects of prices for the orange and walnut crops; he was interested in everything like this, as a man who had oil to sell, to men who would buy more or less, according to what they got for their products. Dad owned land, too; he was always ready to "pick up" a likely piece, for there was oil all over Southern California, he said, and some day there would be an empire here.

But now they were behind their schedule, and no time for play. Dad would take fried rabbit; and Bunny thought he wouldn't—not because of the cannibalistic suggestion, but because of one he had seen mashed on the road that morning. He chose roast pork—not having seen any dead pigs. So there came on a platter two slices of meat, and mashed potatoes scooped out in a round ball, with a hole in the top filled with gluey brown gravy; also a spoonful of chopped up beets, and a leaf of lettuce with apple sauce in it. The waitress had given him an extra helping, because she liked this jolly brown kid, with his rosy cheeks and hair tumbled by the wind, and sensitive lips, like a girl's, and eager brown eyes that roamed over the place and took in everything, the signs on the wall, the bottles of catsup and slices of pie, the fat jolly waitress, and the tired thin one who was waiting on him. He cheered her up by telling her about the speed-cop they had met, and the chase they had seen. In turn she tipped them off to a speed-trap just outside the town; the man next to Bunny had been caught in it and fined ten dollars, so they had plenty to talk about while Bunny finished his dinner, and his slice of raisin pie and glass of milk. Dad gave the waitress a half dollar for a tip, which was an unheard-of thing at a counter, and seemed almost immoral; but she took it.

They drove carefully until they were past the speed-trap; then they "hit it up," along a broad boulevard known as the Mission Way, with bronze bells hanging from poles along it. They had all kinds of picturesque names for highways in this country; the Devil's Garden Way and the Rim of the World Drive, Mountain Spring Grade and Snow Creek Run, Thousand Palm Cañon and Fig Tree John's Road, Coyote Pass and the Jackrabbit Trail. There was a Telegraph Road, and that was thrilling to the boy because he had read about a battle in the civil war for the possession of a "Telegraph Road"; when they drove along this one, he would see infantry hiding in the bushes and cavalry charging across the fields; he would give a start of excitement, and Dad would ask, "What is it?" "Nothing, Dad; I was just thinking." Funny kid! Always imagining things!

Also, there were Spanish names, reverently cherished by the pious "realtors" of the country. Bunny knew what these meant, because he was studying Spanish, so that some day he would be equipped to deal with Mexican labor. "El Camino Real"— that meant the Royal Highway; and "Verdugo Cañon"— that meant "executioner." "What happened there, Dad?" But Dad didn't know the story; he shared the opinion of the manufacturer of a nationally advertised automobile—that history is mostly "bunk."

VII

The road was asphalt now; it shimmered in the heat, and whenever it fell away before you, a mirage made it look like water. It was lined with orange-groves; dark green shiny trees, golden with a part of last year's crop, and snowy white with the new year's blossoms. Now and then a puff of breeze blew out, and you got a ravishing sweet odor. There were groves of walnuts, broad trees with ample foliage, casting dark shadows on the carefully cultivated, powdery brown soil. There were hedges of roses, extending for long distances, eight or ten feet high, and covered with blossoms. There were wind-breaks of towering thin eucalyptus trees, with long wavy leaves and bark that scales off and leaves them naked; all the world is familiar with them in the moving pictures, where they do duty for sturdy oaks and ancient elms and spreading chestnuts and Arabian date-palms and cedars of Lebanon and whatever else the scenario calls for.

You had to cut your speed down here, and had to watch incessantly; there were intersections, and lanes coming in, and warning signs of many sorts; there was traffic both ways, and delicate decisions to be made as to whether you could get past the car ahead of you, before one coming in the other direction would bear down on you and shut you in a pair of scissors. It was exciting to watch Dad's handling of these emergencies, to read his intentions and watch him carry them out.

There were towns every five or ten miles now, and you were continually being slowed up by traffic, and continually being warned to conform to a rate of movement which would have irritated an able-bodied snail. The highway passed through the main street of each town; the merchants arranged that, Dad said, hoping you would get out and buy something at their places; if the highway were shifted to the outskirts of the town, to avoid traffic congestion, all the merchants would forthwith move to the highway! Sometimes they would put up signs, indicating a turn in the highway, attempting to lure the motorist onto a business street; after you had got to the end of that street, they would steer you back to the highway! Dad noted such tricks with the amused tolerance of a man who had worked them on others, but did not let anyone work them on him.

Each town consisted of some tens, or hundreds, or thousands

of perfectly rectangular blocks, divided into perfectly rectangular lots, each containing a strictly modern bungalow, with a lawn and a house-wife holding a hose. On the outskirts would be one or more "subdivisions," as they were called; "acreage" was being laid out into lots, and decorated with a row of red and yellow flags fluttering merrily in the breeze; also a row of red and yellow signs which asked questions and answered them with swift efficiency: "Gas? Yes." "Water? Best ever." "Lights? Right." "Restrictions? You bet." "Schools? Under construction." "Scenery? Beats the Alps."—and so on. There would be an office or a tent by the roadside, and in front of it an alert young man with a writing pad and a fountain-pen, prepared to write you a contract of sale after two minutes conversation. These subdividers had bought the land for a thousand dollars an acre, and soon as they had set up the fluttering little flags and the tent it became worth $1675 per lot. This also Dad explained with amused tolerance. It was a great country!

They were coming to the outskirts of Angel City. Here were trolley tracks and railroads, and subdivisions with no "restrictions"—that is, you might build any kind of house you pleased, and rent it to people of any race or color; which meant an ugly slum, spreading like a great sore, with shanties of tin and tar-paper and unpainted boards. There were great numbers of children playing here—for some strange reason there seemed to be more of them where they were least apt to thrive.

By dint of constant pushing and passing every other car, Dad had got on his schedule again. They skirted the city, avoiding the traffic crowds in its centre, and presently came a sign: "Beach City Boulevard." It was a wide asphalt road, with thousands of speeding cars, and more subdivisions and suburban home-sites, with endless ingenious advertisements designed to catch the fancy of the motorist, and cause him to put on brakes. The real estate men had apparently been reading the Arabian Nights and Grimm's fairy-tales; they were housed in little freak offices that shot up to a point, or tilted like a drunken sailor; their colors orange and pink, or blue and green, or with separately painted shingles, spotted with various colors. There were "good eats" signs and "barbecue" signs—the latter being a word which apparently had not been in the spelling-books when the sign-painters went to school. There were stands where you got orange-juice and cider, with orange-colored wicker chairs out in front for you to sit in. There were fruit and vegetable stands kept by Japs, and other stands with signs inviting you to "patronize Americans." There was simply no end of things to look at, each separate thing bringing its separate thrill to the mind of a thirteen-year old boy. The infinite strangeness and fascinatingness of this variegated world! Why do people do this, Dad? And why do they do that?

They came to Beach City, with its wide avenue along the ocean-front. Six-thirty, said the clock on the car's running-board—exactly on the schedule. They stopped before the big hotel, and Bunny got out of the car, and opened the back compartment, and the bell-hop came hopping—you bet, for he knew Dad, and the dollars and half dollars that were jingling in Dad's pockets. The bell-hop grabbed the suit-cases and the overcoats, and carried them in, and the boy followed, feeling responsible and important, because Dad couldn't come yet, Dad had to put the car in a parking place. So Bunny strode in and looked about the lobby for Ben Skutt, the oil-scout, who was Dad's "lease-hound." There he was, seated in a big leather chair, puffing at a cigar and watching the door; he got up when he saw Bunny, and stretched his long, lean body, and twisted his lean, ugly face into a grin of welcome. The boy, very erect, remembering that he was J. Arnold Ross, junior, and represent-ing his father in an important transaction, shook hands with the man, remarking: "Good evening, Mr. Skutt. Are the papers ready?"

CHAPTER II

THE LEASE

I

The number of the house was 5746 Los Robles Boulevard, and you would have had to know this land of hope in order to realize that it stood in a cabbage field. Los Robles means "the oaks"; and two or three miles away, where this boulevard started in the heart of Beach City, there were four live oak trees. But out here a bare slope of hill, quite steep, yet not too steep to be plowed and trenched and covered with cabbages, with sugar beets down on the flat. The eye of hope, aided by surveyors' instruments, had determined that some day a broad boulevard would run on this line; and so there was a dirt road, and at every corner white posts set up, with a wing north and a wing east—Los Robles Blvd.-Palomitas Ave.; Los Robles Blvd.-El Centro Ave.; and so on.

Two years ago the "subdividers" had been here, with their outfit of little red and yellow flags; there had been full-page advertisements in the newspapers, and free auto rides from Beach City, and a free lunch, consisting of "hot dog" sandwiches, a slice of apple pie, and a cup of coffee. At that time the fields had been cleared of cabbages, and graded, and the lots had blossomed with little signs: "Sold." This was supposed to refer to the lot, but in time it came to refer to the purchaser. The company had undertaken to put in curbs and sidewalks, water and gas and sewers; but somebody made off with the money, and the enterprise went into bankruptcy, and presently new signs began to appear: "For Sale, by Owner," or "Bargain: See Smith and Headmutton, Real Estate." And when these signs brought no reply, the owners sighed, and reflected that some day when little Willie grew up he would make a profit out of that investment. Meantime, they would accept the proposition of Japanese truck-gardeners, to farm the land for one-third of the crop.

But three or four months ago something unexpected had happened. A man who owned an acre or two of land on the top of the hill had caused a couple of motor-trucks to come toiling up the slope, loaded with large square timbers of Oregon pine; carpenters had begun to work on these, and the neighborhood had stared, wondering what strange kind of house it could be. Suddenly the news had spread, in an explosion of excitement: an oil derrick!

A deputation called upon the owner, to find out what it meant. It was pure "wild-catting," he assured them; he happened to have a hundred thousand dollars to play with, and this was his idea of play. Nevertheless, the bargain signs came down from the cabbage fields, and were replaced by "Oil Lot for Sale." Speculators began to look up the names and addresses of owners, and offers were made—there were rumors that some had got as high as a thousand dollars, nearly twice the original price of the lots. Motor-cars took to bumping out over the dirt roads, up and down the lanes; and on Saturday and Sunday afternoons there would be a crowd staring at the derrick.

The drilling began, and went on, monotonously and uneventfully. The local newspapers reported the results: the D. H. Culver Prospect No. 1 was at 1478 feet, in hard sandstone formation and no signs of oil. It was the same at 2,000, and at 3,000; and then for weeks the rig was "fishing" for a broken drill, and everybody lost interest; it was nothing but a "dry hole," and people who had refused double prices for their lots began to curse themselves for fools. "Wild-catting" was nothing but gambling anyhow—quite different from conservative investments in town lots. Then the papers reported that D. H. Culver Prospect No. 1 was drilling again; it was at 3059 feet, but the owners had not yet given up hope of striking something.

Then a strange thing happened. There came trucks, heavily loaded with stuff, carefully covered with canvas. Everybody connected with the enterprise had been warned or bribed to silence; but small boys peered under the canvas while the trucks were toiling up the hill with roaring motors, and they reported big sheets of curved metal, with holes along the edges for bolts. That could be only one thing, tanks. And at the same time came rumors that D. H. Culver had purchased another tract of land on the hill. The meaning of all this was obvious: Prospect No. 1 had got into oil sands!

The whole hill began to blossom with advertisements, and real estate agents swarmed to the "field." A magic word now —no longer cabbage field or sugar-beet field, but *the* field!

Speculators set themselves up in tents, or did business from automobiles drawn up by the roadside, with canvas signs on them. There was coming and going all day long, and crowds of people gathered to stare up at the derrick, and listen to the monotonous grinding of the heavy drill that went round and round all day—"Ump-um—ump-um—ump-um—ump-um"—varied by the "puff-puff" of the engine. "Keep out—this means you!" declared a conspicuous sign; Mr. D. H. Culver and his employees had somehow lost all their good breeding.

But suddenly there was no possibility of secrecy; literally all the world knew—for telegraph and cable carried the news to the farthest corners of civilization. The greatest oil strike in the history of Southern California, the Prospect Hill field! The inside of the earth seemed to burst out through that hole; a roaring and rushing, as Niagara, and a black column shot up into the air, two hundred feet, two hundred and fifty—no one could say for sure—and came thundering down to earth as a mass of thick, black, slimy, slippery fluid. It hurled tools and other heavy objects this way and that, so the men had to run for their lives. It filled the sump-hole, and poured over, like a sauce-pan boiling too fast, and went streaming down the hillside. Carried by the wind, a curtain of black mist, it sprayed the Culver homestead, turning it black, and sending the women of the household flying across the cabbage-fields. Afterwards it was told with Homeric laughter how these women had been heard to lament the destruction of their clothing and their window-curtains by this million-dollar flood of "black gold"!

Word spread by telephone to Beach City; the newspapers bulletined it, the crowds shouted it on the street, and before long the roads leading to Prospect Hill were black with a solid line of motor-cars. The news reached Angel City, the papers there put out "extras," and before nightfall the Beach City boulevard was crowded with cars, a double line, all coming one way. Fifty thousand people stood in a solid ring at what they considered a safe distance from the gusher, with emergency policemen trying to drive them further back, and shouting: "Lights out! Lights out!" All night those words were chanted in a chorus; everybody realized the danger—some one fool might forget and light a cigarette, and the whole hill-side would leap into flame: a nail in your shoe might do it, striking on a stone; or a motor-truck, with its steel-rimmed tires. Quite frequently these gushers caught fire at the first moment.

But still the crowds gathered; men put down the tops of their automobiles, and stood up in the seats and conducted auction rooms by the light of the stars. Lots were offered for sale at fabulous prices, and some of them were bought; leases were offered, companies were started and shares sold—the traders would push their way out of the crowd to a safe distance on the windward side, where they could strike a match, and see each other's faces, and scrawl a memorandum of what they agreed. Such trading went on most of the night, and in the morning came big tents that had been built for revival meetings, and the cabbage fields became gay with red and black signs: "Beach Co-operative No. 1," "Skite Syndicate, No. 1, ten thousand units, $10."

Meantime the workmen were toiling like mad to stop the flow of the well; they staggered here and there, half blinded by the black spray—and with no place to brace themselves, nothing they could hold onto, because everything was greased, streaming with grease. You worked in darkness, groping about, with nothing but the roar of the monster, his blows upon your body, his spitting in your face, to tell you where he was. You worked at high tension, for there were bonuses offered—fifty dollars for each man if you stopped the flow before midnight, a hundred dollars if you stopped it before ten o'clock. No one could figure how much wealth that monster was wasting, but it must be thousands of dollars every minute. Mr. Culver himself pitched in to help, and in his reckless efforts lost both of his ear-drums. "Tried to stop the flow with his head," said a workman, unsympathetically. In addition the owner discovered, in the course of ensuing weeks, that he had accumulated a total of forty-two suits for damages to houses, clothing, chickens, goats, cows, cabbages, sugar-beets, and automobiles which had skidded into ditches on too well-greased roads.

II

The house numbered 5746 Los Robles Boulevard belonged to Joe Groarty, night watchman for the Altmann Lumber Company of Beach City. Mrs. Groarty had "taken in" washing to help support her seven children; now that they were grown up and scattered, she kept rabbits and chickens. Joe usually left for his job at six p. m.; but on the third day after the "strike" he had got up the nerve to give up his job, and now he was on his front-porch, a mild, grey-haired old fellow, wearing a black suit, with celluloid collar and black tie, his costume for Sundays and holidays, weddings and funerals. Mrs. Groarty had had no clothing suitable for this present occasion, so she had been driven down-town in her husband's Ford, and had spent some of her oil expectations for an evening gown of yellow satin. Now she felt embarrassed because there was not enough of it, either at the top where her arms and bosom came out, or below, where her fat calves were encased in embroidered silk stockings, so thin as to seem almost nothing. It was what "they" were wearing, the saleswomen had assured her; and Mrs. Groarty was grimly set upon being one of "them."

The house was in the conventional "bungalow style," and had been built by a wealthier family, in the days of the real estate boom. It had been offered at a sacrifice, and Mrs. Groarty had fastened upon it because of the wonderful living-room. They had put their savings into a cash payment, and were paying the balance thirty dollars a month. They had got a deed to the property, and were up to date on their payments, so they were safe.

When you passed the threshold of the house, the first thing you saw was shine; the most marvelous gloss ever seen on wood-work—and to heighten the effect the painter had made it wavy, in imitation of the grain of oak; there must have been ten thousand lines, each one a separate wiggle of a brush. The fire-place was of many colored stones, highly polished and gleaming like jewels. In the back of the room, most striking feature of all, was a wooden staircase, with a balustrade, also shiny and wavy; this staircase went up, and made a turn, and there was a platform with a palm-tree in a pot. You would take it for granted that it was a staircase like all other staircases, intended to take you to the second story. You might go into the Groarty home a hundred times, and see it both day and night, before it would occur to you there was anything wrong; but suddenly—standing outside on some idle day—it would flash over you that the Groarty home had a flat roof over its entire extent, and at no part was there any second story. Then you would go inside, inspired by a new, malignant curiosity, and would study the staircase and landing, and realize that they didn't lead anywhere, their beauty was its own excuse for being.

Mrs. Groarty stood by the centre-table of her living-room, awaiting the arrival of the expected company. There was a bowl of roses in a vase on this table, and immediately in front of it, conspicuous under the electric lamp, was a handsome volume bound in blue cloth and stamped with gold letters: "The Ladies' Guide: A Practical Handbook of Gentility." It was the only book in the Groarty home, and it had been there only two days; an intelligent clerk in the department-store, after selling the satin robe, had mentioned to the future "oil-queen" the existence of this bargain in the literature department. Mrs. Groarty had been studying the volume at spare moments, and now had it set out as an exhibit of culture.

The first to arrive was the widow Murchey, who had only to come from the end of the block, where she lived in a little bungalow with her two children; she was frail, and timid of manner, and wore black wristbands. She went into raptures over Mrs. Groarty's costume, and congratulated her on her good fortune in being on the south slope of the hill, where one could wear fine dresses. Over on the north side, where the prevailing winds had blown the oil, you ruined your shoes every time you went out. Some people still did not dare to light their kitchen fires, for fear of an explosion.

Then came the Walter Blacks, Mr. and Mrs. and their grown son, owners of the southwest corner lot; they were in real estate in the city. Mr. Black wore a checked suit, an expansive manner, and a benevolent protective gold animal as watch-fob on his ample front. Mrs. Black, also ample, had clothes at home as good as Mrs. Groarty's, but her manner said that she hadn't put them on to come out to any cabbage-patch. They were followed by Mr. Dumpery, the carpenter, who had a little cottage in back of the Groarty's, fronting on Eldorado Road, the other side of the block; Mr. Dumpery was a quiet little man, with shoulders bowed and hands knotted by a life-time of toil. He was not very good at figures, and was distressed by these sudden uncertainties which had invaded his life.

Next came the Raithels, who had a candy-store in town, a very genteel young couple, anxious to please everybody, and much distressed because it had so far proven impossible; they were the owners of one of the "little lots." Then Mr. Hank, a lean and hatchet-faced man with an exasperating voice; he owned the next "little lot," and because he had been a gold miner, considered himself an authority on oil leases. After him came his enemy, Mr. Dibble, the lawyer, who represented the absent owner of the northwest corner, and had made trouble by insisting on many technicalities difficult for non-lawyers to understand; he had tried hard to separate the north half of the block, and was regarded as a traitor by those of the south half. Then came Mr. Golighty, one of the "medium lots." His occupation was not known, but he impressed everyone by his clothing and cultured manner; he was a reconciler, with a suave, rotund voice, and talked a great deal, the only trouble being that when he got through you were a little uncertain as to what he had said.

The Bromleys arrived, an elderly couple of means, driving a big car. They brought with them the Lohlkers, two little Jewish tailors, whom ordinarily they would have talked with only in the tailor-shop; but with these allies they controlled four of the "medium lots," which was sufficient for a drilling site, and cutting right across the block, had enabled them to threaten the rest with a separate lease. Behind them came the Sivons, walking from their house on the northeast corner; they were pretentious people, who looked down on the rest of the neighborhood—and without any cause, for they drove a second-hand car, three years out of date. They were the people who had got this lease, and everyone was sure they were getting a big "rake-off" on the side; but there was no way to prove it, and nothing you could do about it, for the reason that all the others who had brought leasing propositions had been secretly promised a similar "rake-off."

With them came Mr. Sahm, a plasterer, who lived in a temporary "garage-house" on the "little lot" adjoining the Sivons. His dwelling amounted to nothing, nevertheless he had been the one who had clamored most strenuously that the houses should be moved at the lessor's expense; he had even tried to put in a provision for compensation for the rows of beans and tomatoes he had planted on his lot. The others had sought to hoot him down, when to their dismay the silent Mr. Dumpery, the carpenter, arose, declaring that it seemed to him a quite sensible request; he had seven rows of corn, himself, and beans in full blossom, and he thought the contract should at least contain a provision that the first well should be drilled on some lot which was not planted, so as to give the gardeners time to reap the benefit of their labor.

III

It was seven-thirty, the hour set for the meeting; and everybody looked about, waiting for somebody else to begin. At last a stranger rose, a big six-footer with a slow drawl, introducing himself as Mr. F. T. Merriweather, attorney for Mr. and Mrs. Black, owners of the southwest corner; by his advice, these parties wished to request a slight change in the wording of the lease.

"*Changes in the lease?*" It was the hatchet-faced Mr. Hank who leaped up. "I thought it was agreed we'd make no more changes?"

"This is a very small matter, sir—"

"But Mr. Ross is to be here in fifteen minutes, ready to sign up!"

"This is a detail, which can be changed in five minutes."

There was an ominous silence. "Well, what is your change?"

"Merely this," said Mr. Merriweather; "it should be explicitly stated that in figuring the area for the apportioning of the royalty, due regard shall be paid to the provision of the law that oil-rights run to the centre of the street, and to the centre of the alley in the rear."

"*What's that?*" Eyes and mouths went open, and there was a general murmur of amazement and dissent. "Where do you get that?" cried Mr. Hank.

"I get it from the statutes of the State of California."

"Well, you don't get it from this lease, and you don't get it from me!" There was a chorus of support: "I should think not! Whoever heard of such a thing? Ridiculous!"

"I think I speak for the majority here," said old Mr. Bromley. "We had no such understanding; we assumed that the area of the lots to be taken was that given on the maps of the company."

"Certainly, certainly!" cried Mrs. Groarty.

"I think, Mrs. Groarty," replied Mr. Dibble, the lawyer, "there has been an unfortunate accident, owing to your unfamiliarity with the oil-laws of the State. The provisions of the statute are clear."

"Oh, yes, of course!" snapped Mrs. Groarty. "We don't need to be told what you would say, seeing as you represent a corner lot, and the corner lots will get twice as much money!"

"Not so bad as that, Mrs. Groarty. Don't forget that your own lot will run to the centre of Las Robles Boulevard, which is eighty feet wide."

"Yes, but your lot will run to the centre of the side street also—"

"Yes, Mrs. Groarty, but El Centro Avenue is only sixty feet wide."

"What it means is just this, you make your lots ninety-five feet lots, instead of sixty-five feet lots, as we all thought when we give up and consented to let the big lots have a bigger share."

"And you were going to let us sign that!" shouted Mr. Hank. "You were sitting still and working that swindle on us!"

"Gentlemen! Gentlemen!" boomed the voice of Mr. Golighty, the conciliator.

"Let me git this straight," broke in Abe Lohlker, the tailor. "Eldorado Road ain't so wide as Los Robles Boulevard, so us fellers on the east half don't git so much money as the others."

"That amounts to practically nothing," said Mr. Merriweather. "You can figure—"

"Sure I can figger! But then, if it don't amount to nothin', what you comin' here bustin' up our lease about it for?"

"I can tell you this right now!" cried Mr. Hank. "You'll never get me to sign no such agreement."

"Nor me," said Miss Snypp, the trained nurse, a decided young lady with spectacles. "I think us little lots have put up with our share of imposition."

"What I say," added Mr. Hank, "let's go back to the original agreement, the only sensible one, share and share alike, all lots equal, same as we vote."

"Let me point out something, Mr. Hank," said Mr. Dibble, with much dignity. "Am I correct in the impression that you own one of the little lots adjoining the alley?"

"Yes, I do."

"Well, then, have you figured that the law entitles you to an extra fifteen feet all along that alley? That puts you somewhat ahead of the medium lots."

Mr. Hank's lantern jaw dropped down. "Oh!" he said.

And Mrs. Groarty burst into laughter. "Oh! Oh! That changes it, of course! It's us medium lots that are the suckers now—us that make up half the lease!"

"And us little lots that ain't on the alley!" cried Mrs. Keith, the wife of a baseball player. "What about my husband and I?" "It looks to me we're clean busted up," said Mr. Sahm, the plasterer. "We don't know who we belong with no more." Like most of the men in the room, he had got out a pencil and paper, and was trying to figure this new arrangement; and the more he figured, the more complications he discovered.

IV

It had been the Walter Browns who had started the idea of a "community agreement" for this block. Two or three lots were enough for a well, but for such a lease you could only get some small concern, and like as not you would fall into the hands of a speculator, and be bartered about, perhaps exploited by a "syndicate" and sold in "units," or tied up in a broken contract, and have to sit by and watch while other people drained the oil from under your land. No, the thing to do was to get a whole block together; then you had enough for half a dozen wells, and could deal with one of the big companies, and you would get quick drilling, and more important yet, you would be sure of your royalties when they were earned.

So, after much labor, and pulling and hauling, and threatening and cajoling, and bargaining and intriguing, the owners of the twenty-four lots had met at the Groarty home, and had signed their names, both husbands and wives, to a "community agreement," to the effect that none of them would lease apart from the others. This document had been duly recorded in the county archives; and now day by day they were realizing what they had done to themselves. They had agreed to agree; and from that time on, they had never been able to agree to anything!

They met at seven-thirty every evening, and wrangled until midnight or later; they went home exhausted, and could not sleep; they neglected their business and their house-keeping and the watering of their lawns—what was the use of working like a slave when you were going to be rich? They held minority meetings, and formed factional groups, and made pledges which they broke, more or less secretly, before the sun had set. Their frail human nature was subjected to a strain greater than it was made for; the fires of greed had been lighted in their hearts, and fanned to a white heat that melted every principle and every law.

The "lease-hounds" were on their trail, besieging their homes, ringing the telephone, following them in automobiles. But each new proposition, instead of satisfaction, brought worry, suspicion and hate. Whoever proposed it, must be trying to cheat the rest; whoever defended it, must have entered into league with him. No one of them but knew the possibilities of treasons and stratagems; even the mildest of them—poor, inoffensive Mr. Dumpery, the carpenter, who, dragging his steps home from the trolley, with fingers sore and back aching from the driving of several thousand shingle-nails on a roof, was met by a man driving a palatial limousine. "Step in, Mr. Dumpery," said the man. "This is a fine car, don't you think? How would you like to have me get out and leave you in it? I'll be very glad to do that if you'll persuade your group to to sign up with the Couch Syndicate." "Oh, no," said Mr. Dumpery, "I couldn't do that, I promised Miss Snypp I'd stick by the Owens plan." "Well, you can forget that," said the other. "I've just had a talk with Miss Snypp, and she is willing to take an automobile."

They had got into a condition of perpetual hysteria, when suddenly hope broke upon them, like the sun out of storm-clouds; Mr. and Mrs. Sivon brought a proposition from a man named Skutt, who represented J. Arnold Ross, and made them the best offer they had yet had—one thousand dollars cash bonus for each lot, one-fourth royalty, and an agreement to "spud in" the first well within thirty days, under penalty of another thousand dollars per lot, this forfeit to be posted in the bank.

All of them knew about J. Arnold Ross; the local papers had had articles telling how another "big operator" was entering the new field. The papers printed his picture, and a sketch of his life—a typical American, risen from the ranks, glorifying once more this great land of opportunity. Mr. Sahm, the plasterer, and Mr. Dumpery, the carpenter, and Mr. Hank, the miner, and Mr. Groarty, the night watchman, and Mr. Raithel, the candy-store keeper, and Messrs. Lohlker and Lohlker, ladies' and gents' tailors, felt a glow of the heart as they read these stories. Their chance had come now, it was the land of opportunity for them!

There was another agonizing wrangle, as a result of which

the big and medium lots decided to drop their differences; they voted against the little lots, and drew up a lease on the basis of each lot receiving a share of royalty proportioned to its area. They notified Mr. Skutt that they were ready, and Mr. Skutt arranged for the great Mr. Ross to meet them at a quarter to eight the following evening and sign the papers. And now, here they were, exactly on the minute appointed—and they were in another mess! Here were four of the "little lots," set unexpectedly above the "medium lots"; as a result of which, four "big lots" and four "big little lots" were in favor of the lease, and four "little little lots" and twelve "medium lots" were against it!

Here was Miss Snypp, her face brick red with wrath, shaking her finger at Mr. Hank. "Let me tell you, you'll never get me to put my signature on that paper—never in this world!" And here was Mr. Hank, shouting back: "Let me tell you, the law will *make* you sign it, if the majority votes for it!" And here was Mrs. Groarty, forgetting all about the Practical Handbook of Gentility, glaring at Mr. Hank and clenching her hands as if she had him by the throat: "And you the feller that was yellin' for the rights of the little lots! You was for sharin' and sharin' alike—you snake in the grass!" Such was the state to which they had come, when suddenly every voice was stilled, clenched hands were loosened, and angry looks died away. A knock upon the door, a sharp, commanding knock; and to every person in the room came the identical thought: J. Arnold Ross!

V

Not many of these men would ever read a book on etiquette; they would learn about life from action—and here was an occasion, the most instructive that had so far come to them. They learned that when a great man comes into a room, he comes first, preceding his subordinates. They learned that he wears a majestic big overcoat, and stands in silence until he is introduced by a subordinate. "Ladies and gentlemen," said the lease-agent, Skutt, "this is Mr. J. Arnold Ross." Whereupon Mr. Ross smiled agreeably, taking in the entire company: "Good evenin', ladies and gentlemen." Half a dozen men arose, offering him a chair; he took a large one, quite simply, and without wasting time in discussion—realizing, no doubt, how he would be embarrassing the hostess if he called attention to a shortage of chairs.

Behind him stood another man, also big. "Mr. Alston D. Prentice," said Skutt, and they were doubly impressed, this being a famous lawyer from Angel City. Also there had entered a little boy, apparently a son of Mr. Ross. The women in the room many of them had little boys of their own, each one destined to grow up into a great oil-man; therefore they watched the Ross boy, and learned that such a boy stays close by his father, and says nothing, but takes in everything with eager roving eyes. As soon as possible he gets himself a perch in the window-sill, where he sits listening, as attentively as if he were a man.

Mrs. Groarty had got all the chairs her neighbors could spare, and had visited the "morticians" and rented a dozen camp-chairs; but still there was a shortage, and the etiquette book did not tell you what to do. But these rough and ready Western men had solved the problem, having sought out the wood-shed, which was behind the garage, and fetched some empty "lug-boxes," such as you got when you bought peaches and apricots and plums for canning. Set up on end, these made satisfactory seats, and the company was soon settled.

"Well, folks," said Mr. Skutt, genially. "Everything ready?"

"No," said the acid voice of Mr. Hank. "We ain't ready. We can't agree."

"What?" cried the "lease-hound." "Why, you told me you had got together!"

"I know. But we're busted open again."

"What is the matter?"

Half a dozen people started to tell what was the matter. The voice of Mr. Sahm prevailed over the rest. "There's some people come here with too good lawyers, and they've raked up what they claim is laws that the rest of us won't stand for."

"Well now," said Mr. Skutt, politely, "Mr. Prentice here is a very good lawyer, and perhaps he can help clear up the matter."

So, more or less in chorus, they explained, and made known their protests at the same time. Then Mr. Ross' lawyer, speaking ex cathedra, advised them that the statement of the law was absolutely correct, the lease as it stood would be interpreted to mean the area to the middle of the streets and alleys; but

of course there was nothing to prevent their making a different
arrangement if they saw fit, and so specifying in the lease.

And then the fat was in the fire; they began to argue their
rights and wrongs, and their animosities flamed so hotly that
they forgot even the presence of J. Arnold Ross, and of his
eminent lawyer. "I said it once, and I'll say it again," declared
Miss Snypp—"Never! Never!"

"You'll sign if we vote it!" cried Mr. Hank.

"You try it and see!"

"You mean you think you can break the agreement?"

"I mean I've got a lawyer that says he can break it any
day I tell him."

"Well, I'll say this," put in Mr. Dibble; "speaking as a
lawyer—and I think my colleagues, Mr. Prentice and Mr.
Merriweather will back me—that agreement is iron-clad."

"Well, at least we can tie you up in the courts!" cried Mr.
Sahm. "And keep you there for a year or two!"

"A fat lot o' good that'll do you!" sneered Mr. Hank.

"Well, we'd as soon be robbed by one set of thieves as
another," declared Miss Snypp.

"Now, now, folks!" put in Ben Skutt, hastily. "Surely
we're none of us goin' to cut off our noses to spite our faces.
Don't you think you better let Mr. Ross tell you about his
plans?"

"Sure, let's hear Mr. Ross!" cried Mr. Golighty; and there
was a chorus—yes, by all means they would hear Mr. Ross. If
anyone could save them, it was he!

VI

Mr. Ross arose, slowly and gravely. He had already taken
off his big overcoat, and folded it and laid it neatly on the rug
beside his chair; the housewives had made note of that, and
would use it in future domestic arguments. He faced them
now, a portly person in a comfortable serge suit, his features
serious but kindly, and speaking to them in a benevolent, almost
fatherly voice. If you are troubled by the fact that he differs
from you in the use of language, bear in mind that it is not
the English but the south-western American language that he
is using. You would need to play the oil game out in that
country, in order to realize that a man may say, "I jist done
it onst, and I'm a-goin' to do it again," and yet be dressed like

a metropolitan banker, and have the calm assurance of a major-general commanding, and the kindly dignity of an Episcopal bishop. Said Mr. J. Arnold Ross:

"Ladies and gentlemen, I traveled over jist about half our state to get here this evenin'. I couldn't get away sooner, because my new well was a-comin' in at Lobos River, and I had to see about it. That well is now flowin' four thousand barrel, and payin' me an income of five thousand dollars a day. I got two others drillin', and I got sixteen producin' at Antelope. So, ladies and gentlemen, if I say I'm an oil man, you got to agree.

"You got a great chanct here, ladies and gentlemen; but bear in mind, you can lose it all if you ain't careful. Out of all the fellers that beg you for a chanct to drill your land, maybe one in twenty will be oil men; the rest will be speculators, fellers tryin' to get between you and the oil men, to get some of the money that ought by rights come to you. Even if you find one that has money, and means to drill, he'll maybe know nothin' about drillin', and have to hire out the job on contract—and then you 're dependin' on a contractor that's tryin' to rush the job through, so as to get to another contract jist as quick as he can.

"But, ladies and gentlemen, I do my own drillin', and the fellers that work for me are fellers I know. I make it my business to be there and see to their work. I don't lose my tools in the hole, and spend months a-fishin'; I don't botch the cementin' off, and let water into the hole, and ruin the whole lease. And let me tell you, I'm fixed right now like no other man or company in this field. Because my Lobos River well has jist come in, I got a string of tools all ready to put to work. I can load a rig onto trucks, and have them here in a week. I've got business connections, so I can get the lumber for the derrick—such things go by friendship, in a rush like this. That's why I can guarantee to start drillin', and put up the cash to back my word. I assure you whatever the others promise to do, when it comes to the showdown, they won't be there.

"Ladies and gentlemen, it's not up to me to say how you're a-goin' to divide the royalty. But let me say this; whatever you give up, so as to get together, it'll be small compared to what you may lose by delay, and by fallin' into the hands of gamblers and crooks. Ladies and gentlemen, take it from me as an oil man, there ain't a-goin' to be many gushers here at Prospect

Hill; the pressure under the ground will soon let up, and it'll
be them that get their wells down first that'll get the oil. A field
plays out very quick; in two or three years you'll see all these
here wells on the pump—yes, even this discovery well that's
got you all crazy. So, take my word for it, and don't break
up this lease; take a smaller share of royalty, if you must, and
I'll see that it's a small share of a big royalty, so you won't
lose in real money. That, ladies and gentlemen, is what I had
to say."

The great man stood, as if waiting to see if anyone had
anything to answer; then he sat down, and there was a pause
in the proceedings. His had been weighty words, and no one
quite had the courage to break the spell.

At last Mr. Golighty arose. "Friends," he said, "we have
been hearing common sense, from a gentleman in whom we
all have confidence; and I for one admit myself convinced, and
hope that we may prove ourselves a group of business people,
capable of making a wise decision, in this matter which means
so much to all of us." And so Mr. Golighty was started on
one of his long speeches, the purport of which appeared to be
that the majority should rule.

"But that's just the trouble," said Mr. Sahm; "what *is* the
majority?"

"We take a wote," said Mr. Chaim Lohlker, "and we
find out."

Mr. Merriweather, the lawyer, had been consulting in
whispers with his clients. "Ladies and gentlemen," he now
declared, "I am authorized by Mr. and Mrs. Walter Black to
say that they have been greatly impressed by what Mr. Ross
has said, and they wish to make any concession necessary to
harmony. They are willing to waive the point which I raised
at the beginning of this discussion, and to sign the lease as
it stands."

"But what does that mean?" demanded Mrs. Groarty. "Are
they to get a royalty on a ninety-five foot lot?"

"Our offer is to sign the document as it stands, and the
question of interpretation may be decided later."

"Oho!" said Mr. Groarty. "A fine concession that—and
when we've just heard Mr. Prentice tell us that the law reads
your way!"

"We agreed to sign it," said Mr. Hank, doing his best to
make his voice sound pleasant.

"Oh, listen to who's talking!" cried Miss Snypp. "The gentleman that was saying, less than a half an hour ago, that we should go back to our original arrangement—'the only sensible one, share and share alike, all lots equal, same as we vote.' Have I quoted you correct, Mr. Hank?"

"I agreed to sign this lease," declared the ex-goldminer, stubbornly.

"And for my part," said the trained nurse, "I said it once and I'll say it again, never on this earth!"

VII

Old Mrs. Ross, Bunny's grandmother, was accustomed to protest strenuously against a boy being taken about on these business trips. It was enough to destroy all the sweetness of his nature, she declared; it would make him a hardened cynic in his childhood, all this sordidness and hatefulness of money-grabbing. But Bunny's father answered that that was life, and there was no good fooling yourself; Bunny would have to live in the world some day, and the quicker he learned about it the better. So there the boy sat, on his perch in the window sill, watching, and recalling his grandmother's words.

Yes, they were a mean bunch, sure enough; Dad was right when he said you had to watch out every minute, because somebody would be trying to take something away from you. These people had simply gone crazy, with the sudden hope of getting a lot of money in a hurry. Bunny, who had always had all the money he could use, looked down with magnificent scorn upon their petty bickering. You couldn't trust such people around the corner, he decided; there was nothing they wouldn't do to you. That fat old woman in the yellow satin dress, with her fat red arms and her fat legs cased in silk— it wouldn't take much more to have her clawing somebody's face. And that hatchet-faced man with the voice like a buzz-saw—he would be capable of sticking a knife into you on a dark night!

Dad wanted his son to understand every detail of these business arrangements: the terms of the lease, the provisions of the law, the size of the different lots, the amounts of money involved. He would talk about it afterwards, and it would be a kind of examination, to see how much the boy had really understood. So Bunny listened attentively, and put this and that together, remembering the points of the lease as he had heard his father going over them with Ben Skutt and Mr. Prentice while they were driving out to the field in the latter's car. But the boy could not keep his mind from going off to the different personalities involved, and their points of view, and the hints one got of their lives. That old fellow with the stooped shoulders and the gnarled hands—he was some kind of poor workingman, and you could see he was unhappy over this arguing; he wanted somebody he could trust, and he looked this way and that, but there was no such person in the crowd. That young woman with the nose-glasses, she was a hard one— what did she do when she wasn't quarreling? That elderly couple that looked rich—they were very much on their dignity, but they had come to get their share, all the same, and they weren't having any generous emotions towards the "little lots"!

The old gentleman drew his chair over beside Dad and began a whispered conversation. Bunny saw Dad shake his head, and the old gentleman drew away. Dad spoke to Skutt, and the latter rose and said: "Mr. Ross wishes me to make clear that he isn't interested in any proposition for leasing a portion of the block. He wouldn't put down a well without room for offset wells. If you people can't agree, he'll take another lease that I've found him."

This struck a chill to them, and stopped the wrangling. Dad saw it, and nodded to his "lease-hound," who went on: "Mr. Ross has an offer of a lease on the north side, which has very good prospects, because we believe the anticline runs that way. There are several acres which belong to one party, so it will be easy to agree."—Yes, that scared the wits out of them; it was several minutes before they were quarreling again!

Where Bunny sat in the window-sill, he could see the lights of the "discovery well," now shut off and awaiting the building of tanks; he could hear through the open window the hammering of the riveters on the tanks, and of carpenters building new derricks along the slope. His attention was wandering, when suddenly he was startled by a whispered voice, coming from the darkness, apparently right alongside him: "Hey, kid!"

Bunny peered around the edge of the window, and saw a figure, flattened against the side of the house. "Hey, kid," said the whisper again. "Listen to me, but don't let nobody know you're listenin'. They mustn't know I'm here."

Bunny's thought was, "A spy! Trying to find out about

the lease!" So he was on the alert; he listened to a steady, persistent whisper, intense and moving:

"Hey, kid! I'm Paul Watkins, and the lady what lives here is my aunt. I dassn't let her know I'm here, see, cause she'll make me go back home. I live on a ranch up in the San Elido, and I run away from home 'cause I can't stand it, see. I got to get a job, but first I got to have somethin' to eat, 'cause I'm near starved. And my aunt would want me to have it, 'cause we're friends, see—only she'd want me to go back home, and I can't stand it. So I want to get somethin' to eat out of the kitchen, and when I earn some money, I'll mail it to her, so I'll just be borrowin', see. What I want you to do is to unlock the kitchen door. I won't take nothin' but a piece of pie, and maybe a sandwich or somethin', see. All you got to do is, tell my aunt to let you go into the kitchen and get a drink of water, and then turn the key in the door and go back into the house. You come out the front door if you want to, and come round and make sure it's all like I tell you. Say kid, be a good scout, 'cause I'm up against it, it's sure tough not to have a meal all day, and I been hitch-hikin' and walkin' a lot o' the time, and I'm done up. You come out and I'll tell you about it, but don't try to talk to me here, 'cause they'll see your lips movin', see, and they'll know there's somebody out here."

Bunny thought quickly. It was a delicate ethical question—whether you had a right to unlock somebody else's back-door, so that a possible thief could get in! But of course it wasn't really a thief, if it was your aunt, and she would give it to you anyhow. But how could you know if the story was true? Well, you could go out, like the fellow said, and if he was a thief you could grab him. What decided Bunny was the voice, which he liked; even before he laid eyes on Paul Watkins' face, Bunny felt the power in Paul Watkins' character, he was attracted by something deep and stirring and powerful.

Bunny slid off the window-sill, and walked over to Mrs. Groarty, who was wiping the perspiration from her forehead after a vicious tirade. "Please, ma'am," he said, "would you be so good as to excuse me if I go into the kitchen and get a drink of water?"

He thought that would cover the case, but he failed to allow for the fact that Mrs. Groarty was preparing for a career of elegance, and losing no chance of observing the ways of the wealthy, even to the drinking of a glass of water. Her

heart warmed to the son of J. Arnold Ross, and all the vinegar
went out of her voice. "Certainly, dear," she said, and rose
and led the way to the kitchen.

Bunny looked about. "My, what a pretty room!" he exclaimed—which was true enough, because it was all enameled
white paint.

"Yes, it is nice, I'm glad you think so," said the mistress
of it, as she took a glass from a shelf and set the faucet to
running.

"A real big kitchen," said Bunny; "that's always a comfort."
He took the glass of water with thanks, and drank part of it.
So polite and natural! thought Mrs. Groarty. Not a bit stuck
up!

And Bunny went to the back door. "I suppose you've
got a big screen porch here. Kind of hot indoors, don't you
think?" He unlocked the door, and opened it, and looked out.
"The breeze feels good," he said. "And you can see all the
wells from here. Won't it be fun when they get to drilling
right on this block!"

What a friendly little fellow! Mrs. Groarty was thinking;
and she said yes, and it would be soon, she hoped. Bunny said
that perhaps she'd catch cold, with that lovely evening dress
she had on; so he shut the door again; and his hostess was so
charmed by the agreeable manners of the aristocracy that she
failed to notice that he did not lock the door. He put the
empty glass on the drain-board of the sink, and said no thanks,
he didn't wish any more, and followed Mrs. Groarty back to
the crowded living-room.

"What I say is this—" it was the voice of Mr. Sahm, the
plasterer. "If you really want to sign the lease as it was, sign
it as we all understood it; let's figure the land we own, and
not the street we don't own."

"In other words," said Mrs. Walter Black, sarcastically,
"let's change the lease."

"In other words," said Miss Snypp, even more sarcastically,
"let's not fall into the trap you big lots set for us."

VIII

It was to be expected that a thirteen-year old boy would
grow weary of such a wrangle; so no one paid the least
attention when J. Arnold Ross, junior, made his way to the

front door and went out. He reached the back door just as Paul Watkins was closing it softly behind him. "Thanks, kid," whispered the latter, and stole away to the wood-shed, with Bunny close behind him. Paul's first sentence was: "I got a piece of ham and two slices of bread, and one piece of pie." He already had his mouth full.

"That's all right, I guess," said Bunny, judiciously. He waited, and for a while there was no sound, save that of a hungry creature chewing. The stranger was only a shadow with a voice; but outside, in the starlight, Bunny had noted that the shadow was a head taller than himself, and thin.

"Gee, it's tough to be starvin'!" said the voice, at last. "Do you want any of this?"

"Oh no, I had my supper," said Bunny. "And I'm not supposed to eat at night."

The other went on chewing, and Bunny found it mysterious and romantic; it might have been a hungry wolf there in the darkness! They sat on boxes, and when the sounds of eating ceased, Bunny said: "What made you run away from home?"

The other answered with another question, a puzzling one: "What church do you belong to?"

"How do you mean?" countered Bunny.

"Don't you know what it means to belong to a church?"

"Well, my grandmother takes me to a Baptist church sometimes, and my mother takes me to a 'Piscopal one when I'm visiting her. But I don't know as I belong to any."

"My Gosh!" said Paul. It was evident he was deeply impressed by this statement. "You mean your father don't make you belong to no church?"

"I don't think Dad believes in things like that very much."

"My Gosh! And you ain't scared?"

"Scared of what?"

"Why, hell fire and brimstone. Of losin' your soul."

"No, I never thought about it."

"Say, kid, you dunno how queer that hits me. I just been makin' up my mind to go to hell, and not give a damn. Do you cuss?"

"Not very often."

"Well, I cussed God."

"How do you do that?"

"Why, I said, 'Damn God!' I said it half a dozen times, see, and I thought sure the lightnin' would come down and strike me. I said: I don't believe, and I ain't a-goin' to believe, and I don't give a damn."

"Well, but if you don't believe, why should you be scared?" Bunny's mind was always logical like that.

"Well, I guess I didn't know whether I believed or not. I don't know now. It didn't seem like I could set my poor frail mind up against the Rock of Ages. I didn't know there was anybody had ever been that wicked before. Pap says I'm the wickedest boy was ever born."

"Pap is your father?"

"Yes."

"What does he believe?"

"The Old Time Religion. It's called the Four Square Gospel. It's the Apostolic Church, and they jump."

"Jump!"

"The Holy Spirit comes down to you, see, and makes you jump. Sometimes it makes you roll, and sometimes you talk in tongues."

"What is that?"

"Why, you make noises, fast, like you was talkin' in some foreign language; and maybe it is—Pap says it's the language of the arch-angels, but I don't know. I can't understand it, and I hate it."

"And your father does that?"

"Any time, day or night, he's liable to. It's his way of foilin' the tempter. If you say anything at meal times, like there ain't enough to eat in the house, or you mention how the interest on the mortage will be due, and he hadn't ought to give all the money for the missions, then Pap will roll up his eyes, and begin to pray out loud and let go, as he calls it; and then the Holy Spirit seizes him and he begins to jump and shake all over, and he slides down out of his chair and rolls on the floor, and begins to talk in tongues, like it says in the Bible. And then Mom starts to cry, 'cause it scares her, she knows she's got things to do for the kids, but she dassn't resist the Spirit, and Pap shouts, Let go, let go—real loud, in the Voice of Sinai, as he says, and then Mom's shoulders begin to jerk, and her mouth pops down, and she begins to roll in the chair, and shout for the Pentecostal Baptism. And that turns the kids loose, they all begin to jump and to babble; and gee, it scares you, somethin' starts to grab you, and make you jerk whether you want to or not. I rushed out of the house, and

I shook my fist up at the sky and I yelled: 'Damn God! Damn God!' And then I waited for the sky to fall in, and it didn't, and I said, I don't believe it, and I ain't a-goin' to make myself believe it, not if I get sent to hell for it."

"Is that the reason you ran away?"

"That's one of the reasons. You can't get nowhere, livin' like we do. We got a big ranch, but it's mostly rocks, and we'd have a hard time anyhow; you plant things, and the rain fails, and nothin' but weeds come up. Why, if there's a God, and he loves his poor human creatures, why did he have to make so many weeds? That was when I first started to cussin'—I was hoin' weeds all day, and I just couldn't help it, I found myself sayin', over and over: 'Damn weeds! Damn weeds! Damn weeds!' Pap says it wasn't God that made 'em, it was the devil; but then, God made the devil, and God knew what the devil was goin' to do, so ain't God to blame?"

"It seems like it to me," said Bunny.

"Gee, kid, but you're lucky! You never knew you had a soul at all! You sure missed a lot of trouble!" There was a pause, and then Paul added: "I had a hard time runnin' away, and I 'spose I'll go back in the end—it's tough to think of your brothers and sisters starvin' to death, and I don't see what else can happen to 'em."

"How many are there?"

"There's four, besides me; and they're all younger'n me."

"How old are you?"

"I'm sixteen. The next is Eli, he's fifteen; and the Holy Spirit has blessed him—he has the shivers, and they last all day sometimes. He sees the angels, comin' down in clouds of glory; and he healed old Mrs. Bugner, that had complications, by the layin' on of his hands. Pap says the Lord plans great blessings through him. Then there's Ruth, she's thirteen, and she had visions too, but she's beginnin' to think like I do; we have sensible talks—you know how it is, you can sometimes talk to people that's your own age, things you can't ever say to grown-ups."

"Yes, I know," said Bunny. "They think you don't understand anything. They'll talk right in front of you, and what do they think is the matter with your brains? It makes me tired."

"Ruth is what makes it hard for me to stay away," continued the other. "She said for me to go, but gee, what'll they all do? They can't do hard work like I can. And don't you think I'd run away from hard work; it's only that I want to get somewhere, else what's the use of it? There ain't any chance for us. Pap hitches up the wagon and drives us all to Paradise, where the Pentecostal Mission is, and there they all roll and babble all day Sunday, most, and the Spirit commands them to pledge all the money they've got to convert the heathen—you see, we've got missions in England and France and Germany and them godless nations, and Pap'll promise more than he's got, and then he's got to give it, 'cause it don't belong to him no more, it's the Holy Spirit's, see. That's why I quit."

There was silence for a space; then Paul asked: "What's that big crowd of folks in there for?"

"That's the oil lease; didn't you know about the oil?"

"Yes, we heard about the strike. We're supposed to have oil on our ranch—at least, my Uncle Eby used to say he'd come onto signs of it; but he's dead, and I never seen 'em, and I never expected no luck for our family. But they say Aunt Allie here is a-goin' to be rich."

A sudden vision flashed over Bunny—of Mrs. Groarty, in her shiny robe of yellow satin, and her large bare arms and bosom. "Tell me," he said, "does your aunt roll?"

"Gosh, no!" said the other. "She married a Romanist, and Pap calls her the Whore of Babylon, and we're not supposed to speak to her no more. But she's kind, and I knew she'd gimme some grub, so when I found I couldn't get a job, I come here."

"Why couldn't you get a job?"

"'Cause everybody lectures you and tells you to go back home."

"But why do you tell them about it?"

"You have to. They ask where you live, and why ain't you at home; and I ain't a-goin' to lie."

"But you can't starve!"

"I can before I'll go crooked. I had a fuss with Pap, and he says, if you depart from the Holy Word, the devil gets you, and you lie and cheat and steal and fornicate; and I says, 'Well, sir, I'll show you. I think a fellow can be decent without no devil.' I made up my mind, and I'm a-goin' to show him. I'll pay back Aunt Allie, so I'm only borrowin' this grub."

Bunny held out his hand in the darkness. "You take this," he said.

"What is it?"

"Some money."

"No, sir, I don't want no money, not till I earn it."

"But listen, Paul, my Dad's got a lot of money, and he gives me what I ask him for. He's come here to lease this block from your aunt, and he won't miss this little bit."

"No, sir, I ain't a-goin' to turn into no bum; I didn't run away for that. You think 'cause I took some food out of my aunt's pantry—"

"No, I don't think that at all! And you can call this a loan, if you want to."

"You put up your money," said the other, with a note of harshness in his voice. "I ain't a-goin' to call no loans, and you done enough for me already; so forget it."

"Well, but Paul—"

"Do what I say, now!"

"But then, you'll come to the hotel tomorrow and have lunch with me?"

"No, I can't come to no hotel, I don't look decent."

"But that don't matter, Paul."

"Sure it matters! Your Dad's a rich man, and he wouldn't want no ranch-boy at his hotel."

"Dad wouldn't care—honest, he wouldn't! He says I don't know enough boys, I stay by myself and read too much."

"Yes, but he don't want no boys like me."

"He says I've got to work, Paul—honest, you don't know Dad. He'd like to have you come; he'd like us to be friends."

There was a pause, while Paul weighed this proposition, and Bunny waited, as anxiously as if it were the sentence of a court. He liked this boy! He had never met any boy he liked so much as this one! And did the boy like him?

As it happened, the sentence of the court was never pronounced. Paul suddenly started to his feet, crying, "What's that?" Bunny also sprang up. From the direction of Mrs. Groarty's house had come a clamor of voices, rising above the pounding of hammers and the sounds of labor in the neighborhood. The yells grew louder, and yet louder, and the boys dashed to the open window of the house.

Everybody in the room was on his or her feet, and all seemed to be shouting at once. It was impossible to see many in the crowd, but two men close by the window made a little drama all by themselves. They were Mr. Sahm, the plasterer, owner of one of the "little little lots," and Mr. Hank, the ex-gold-

miner, owner of one of the "big little lots"; they were shaking
their fists at each other, and Mr. Sahm, the party of the first
part, was shouting at Mr. Hank, the party of the second part,
"You're a dirty, lying, yellow skunk!" To which the party
of the second part answered, "Take that, you white-livered
puppy!" and hit the party of the first part, Biff! a crack on the
nose. The party of the first part countered with a nasty upper-
cut to the jaw of the party of the second part, Bang! And so
they went to it, Biff, bang! Bang, biff!—and the two boys gazed
through the open window, horrified, enraptured. Whoopee!
A scrap!

IX

There was a general appearance as if everybody in the
room were fighting; but that could not have been the case, for
there were several left to separate Messrs. Sahm and Hank,
and to shove them into opposite corners. Before this process
was entirely completed, Bunny heard a voice calling his name
from the front of the house. "All right, Dad!" he answered,
and ran to meet his father.

The three men of the Ross party were descending the front
steps, and proceeding down the walk. "Come on," said the
father; "we're a-goin' back to the hotel."

"Gee, Dad! What happened?"

"They're a bunch of boobs, and you can't do anything with
them. I wouldn't take their lease if they offered it as a gift.
Let's get out of here."

They were walking towards their car, which was parked a
little way down the road. Suddenly Bunny halted. "Oh, Dad,"
he cried; "wait just a minute! Please, Dad, there's a boy I
met, and I want to tell him something. Wait for me, please!"

"Well, be quick," said Dad. "I got another lease to see
about tonight."

Bunny raced back, as fast as his legs could move. A panic
had seized him. "Paul! Paul!" he shouted. "Where are you?"

There was no sound, and no sign of the other boy. Bunny
ran to the wood-shed, he ran all the way round the house,
shouting, "Paul! Paul!" He dashed into the screen-porch,
and opened the back door, and peered into the empty, white-
enameled kitchen; he ran back to the wood-shed, and then
to the garage in front of it; he stood gazing across the dark

cabbage fields and calling at the top of his lungs: "Paul! Paul! Where are you? Please don't go away!" But there was no reply.

Then Bunny heard his father's voice again, in a tone that was not to be neglected; so he went, with sinking heart, and climbed into his place in the automobile. All the way back to the hotel, while the men were discussing the new lease they planned to make, Bunny sat in silence, with tears stealing down his cheeks. Paul was gone! He might never see Paul again! And oh, such a wonderful boy! Such a wise boy—he knew so many things! A clear-sighted boy, and so interesting to talk to! And an honest boy—he wouldn't lie or steal! Bunny was ashamed, recollecting several times in his life when he had told lies—nothing very serious, but little things, that seemed so petty and mean, in the sudden clear light of Paul's uprightness.

And Paul wouldn't take any of Dad's money! Dad thought that everybody in the world would be glad to get his money; but this boy had refused it! He must have been angry with Bunny for pressing it upon him, else he wouldn't have run away like that! Or else, for whatever reason, he didn't like Bunny; and so Bunny would never see him again!

CHAPTER III

THE DRILLING

I

Once more the valleys and gorges of Guadalupe Grade resounded to the flying echoes of honking horns. This time it was not one car, but a whole fleet of them, a dozen seven-ton trucks, broad and solid, with broad and solid double wheels, and trailers on behind, that carried even more tons. The first load towered high, a big stationary engine, held in place by heavy timbers bolted fast at the sides; that truck went carefully round the curves, you bet! Behind it came the "mud-hogs" and the "draw-works"; and then the "string" of drilling tools, hollow tubes of the best steel, that were screwed end to end and went down into the earth, a mile or more, if need be. These tubes extended over the end of the trailers, where red flags waved in warning; on the short curves they swept the road, and if you met a car coming in the opposite direction, you had to stop while the other car crept carefully by; if there was not room enough, the other car would have to back up to a place where the road was straighter. All this required continuous clamor of horns; you would have thought some huge flock of prehistoric birds—did the pterodactyls make noises?—had descended upon Guadalupe Pass, and were hopping along, crying: "Honk! Honk! Honk!"

What they were really saying was: "Dad is waiting for us! Dad has signed his lease, and the derrick is under way, and his 'rig' must be on time! Clear the road!" Dad would not trust to railroads for a rush job like this; they switched your stuff onto sidings, and you spent a week telephoning and interviewing dumb officials. But when you hired motor-trucks, you owned them for the time being, and they came right through. There was insurance to cover all possible accidents—including the value of any man you might chance to send rolling down a mountain-side in a Ford car!

So here came the dozen valiant tooters, toiling slowly up the grade, at far less than the ordained speed of fifteen miles per hour. Their radiators were hissing with steam, and every mile or so they would have to stop and cool off. But they got to the summit all right; and then came the slow crawl downwards, a man going ahead with a red flag, warning other cars into safe pockets on the road, to wait till the whole fleet had got by. So they got out of the pass, and onto the straight road, where they could go flying like any other cars; then it was a mighty roaring and a jolly sight. "Honk! Honk! Get out of the way! Dad is waiting!"

Perched on top of the drilling-tools were young fellows in blue-jeans and khaki, giving abundant evidence that their last well had not been a dry hole, but had given its due yield of smeary treasures. However, they had got their faces clean, and they met the sunny landscape with no less sunny smiles. They sang songs, and exchanged jollifications with the cars they passed, and threw kisses to the girls in the ranch-houses and the filling-stations, the orange-juice parlors and the "good eats" shacks. Two days the journey took them, and meantime they had not a care in the world; they belonged to Old Man Ross, and it was his job to worry. First of all things he saw that they got their pay-envelopes every other Saturday night—and that the envelopes contained one dollar per day more than anybody else nearby was getting; moreover, you got this pay, not only while you were drilling, but while you were sitting on top of a load of tools, flying through a paradise of orange-groves at thirty miles an hour, singing songs about the girl who was waiting for you in the town to which you were bound.

II

Dad had signed up with the man on the North slope, Mr. Bankside, a gentleman who knew what he wanted, and didn't waste your time. It was not so close to the discovery well, therefore Dad would have to pay only a sixth royalty, and a bonus of five thousand dollars on the two and one-half acres.

Dad and Bunny called at the offices of the Sunset Lumber Company, and had a very special private interview with the president of this concern. Mr. Ascott was a heavy gentleman with flushed checks and a manner of strenuous cordiality; he rumpled Bunny's hair, and swapped cigars in gold-foil, and discussed the weather and the prospects of the new field, so that you'd have thought he and Dad were life-long chums. Until at last Dad got down to business, and said that he positively had to have the lumber for a derrick delivered on the ground within three days; whereupon Mr. Ascott threw up his hands and declared that such an order could not be filled for God Almighty himself. The demand for derrick material had simply emptied all the yards, and orders were piling up a score a day. But Dad interrupted—he knew all that, but this was something special, he had jist got himself into a contract with a big forfeit posted at the bank, and he didn't believe in steel derricks, but the lumber men would sure have to help him, unless they wanted to lose him for good. He wanted to place an order for half a dozen more derricks, to be delivered in the course of the next three months; and moreover, Mr. Ascott must understand that this well Dad proposed to drill was going to extend the field, and lead to new developments, and a big increase in the lumber business, so it was really a public service Dad was performing, and they must all stand together and help him. Moreover, Dad was forming a little syndicate to handle a part of this first well—jist a quiet affair for a few people that knew a good thing when they saw it, and would appreciate getting in on the ground floor; and Mr. Ascott knew Dad for a man of his word, and no piker.

Mr. Ascott said that yes, he did; and Dad said that he had come to that field to give most of his time to it, and he was a-goin' to make a big thing there, and he wanted to get a little organization together—they would all stand by one another, and that was the way to make things go in this world. Mr. Ascott said that of course, co-operation was the word in modern business, he granted that; and he wrinkled up his forehead, and studied some papers on his desk, and did some figuring on a pad, and asked at just what hour Dad had to have that lumber. And Dad explained that his cement-man had the cellar and the foundations half done, and his boss carpenter was a-gettin' a crew together—in a matter like this he wouldn't trust no contractor. It would suffice if Mr. Ascott would have the sills there by Thursday night.

Mr. Ascott said they were having a lot of trouble because the roads about Prospect Hill were in such bad condition; and Dad said he knew that, and something would have to be done about it quick, he was jist a-goin' to see the county superintendent of roads. So then Mr. Ascott said all right, he would do his part; and Dad invited him to come down and look the field over, and let Dad put him onto a few good things down there;

and they shook hands, and Bunny had his hair rumpled again—
something which in the course of business he had to pretend
that he didn't mind.

So that was that. And as they got into their car and drove
away, Dad repeated his maxim that grease is cheaper than
steel. Dad meant by that, you must let people have a share
of your profits, so they would become a part of your "organization," and do quickly whatever you said. And meantime they
had come to the office of the superintendent of roads, where
they had another very special private interview. This official,
Mr. Benzinger, a sharp little man with nose-glasses, was not
dressed like a man of money, and Bunny knew it by the difference in the tone Dad took. There was no exchanging of gold-
foil cigars, and no talk about the weather; but Dad got right
down to business. He had come to Beach City to put through
a job that would employ hundreds of men, and mean millions
of dollars to the community; the question was, would the road
authorities co-operate to make this possible.

Mr. Benzinger answered that of course, the authorities
wanted to do everything to that end—it was the purpose for
which they were in office; the trouble was that this "strike"
at Prospect Hill had caught them without any funds for
rush work. Dad said that might be, but there must be
some way to handle such a situation, everybody'd ought to get
together.

Mr. Benzinger hesitated, and asked just what it was that
Mr. Ross wanted. So Dad explained that he was jist about to
drill on such and such a tract, and he drew a little map showing
the streets that he needed to have graded, and the holes filled
up with crushed rock, so his sills could be delivered on Thursday
night. Mr. Benzinger said that might be arranged, perhaps,
and asked his secretary, the only other person in the room, to
step out and ask Mr. Jones to come in; Dad caught the meaning
of that, and as soon as the secretary was gone, he pulled a little
roll of bills out of his pocket, remarking that Mr. Benzinger
would have to work overtime on the matter, and be put to
extra trouble and expense, and it was only fair that Dad should
make it up to him; he hoped Mr. Benzinger would understand
that they would have many dealings in future, as Dad believed
in taking care of his friends. Mr. Benzinger put the bills
quietly into his pocket, and said that he understood fully, and
the county authorities wished to give every help to men who

came in to build up the community and its industries; Dad might count upon it that the work on those streets would start in the morning.

So then they shook hands, and Dad and Bunny went out, and Dad told Bunny that he must never under any circumstances mention what he had seen in that office, because every public official had enemies who were trying to take his job away, and would try to represent it that Dad had paid him a bribe. But of course it wasn't anything of the sort; it was the man's business to keep the roads in repair, and what Dad gave him was jist a little tip, by way of thanks, so to speak. You wouldn't feel decent not to give him something, because you were going to make a lot of money yourself, and these here poor devils had to live on a beggar's salary. No doubt Mr. Benzinger had a wife and children at home, and they were in debt; maybe the wife was sick, and they had no way to pay the doctor. The man would have to stay late at his office, and go out tonight and hustle up some men to do that job, and maybe get scolded by his superiors for having acted without authority; the superiors were doubtless in the pay of some of the big companies, which didn't want roads built except to leases of their own. There was all kinds of wires like that being pulled, said Dad, and you had to be on the watch every minute. Never imagine that you'd be allowed to come into a new place and take out several million dollars worth of wealth from the ground, and not have all kinds of fellers a-tryin' to get it away from you!

That all sounded reasonable, and Bunny listened while Dad impressed his favorite lesson: take care of your money! Some day an accident might happen to Dad, and then Bunny would have the whole thing on his shoulders; so he could not begin too early to realize that the people he met would be trying, by devices more or less subtle, to get a hold of his money. Bunny, not thinking of opposing his father's arguments, but merely getting things straight in his own mind, was moved to remark: "But Dad, you remember that boy Paul? He certainly wasn't trying to get our money, for I offered him some, and he wouldn't take it; he went away without my seeing him again."

"Yes, I know," said Dad; "but he told you his whole family is crazy, and he's jist crazy a little different, that's all."

III

This was a moral problem which Bunny debated within himself: was Paul Watkins crazy, because of the way he behaved? If so, there must be a crazy streak in Bunny also, for he had been enormously impressed by Paul, and could not help thinking about him. He had paid a tribute to Paul's sense of honor, by resolving that he, Bunny, would permit himself the luxury of not being a liar—not even in trivial things. Also, the meeting with Paul had caused Bunny to become suddenly aware what an easy time he was having in life. The very next morning, when he opened his eyes, lying in the deep soft mattress of the hotel-bed, with its heavy linen sheets so smooth and white, and its warm blankets, soft as fleece, and striped the color of ripe strawberries—at once his thought was: how had Paul slept that night, without shelter and without cover? Had he lain on the ground? But grandmother, if she saw you even sitting on the ground in the evening, would cry out that you would "catch your death!" And down in the spacious dining-room of the hotel, the thought of Paul without breakfast had quite ruined the taste of grape-fruit in crushed ice, and cereal and thick cream, and bacon and eggs, and wheat-cakes with maple syrup. Paul would be going hungry, because he was too proud to eat food until he had earned it; and some strange perversity caused Bunny, in the midst of comfort, to yearn toward this fierce anchorite who spurned the flesh!

The morning after the meeting at Mrs. Groarty's, Bunny had sat under a palm-tree in front of the hotel, hoping that Paul would come by. Instead, there had come Mrs. Groarty and her husband, bringing Mr. Dumpery, and followed by Mr. and Mrs. Bromley, with their temporary friends the Jewish tailors. It was a deputation from the "medium lots," explaining that they had continued their meeting until one o'clock that morning, and had decided to rescind their community agreement, and go each man for himself; now the "medium lots" wanted Dad to take their lease. Bunny told them that Dad was out in the field with the geologist; they might wait for him, but Bunny knew how emphatic Dad was about off-set wells, so there was no chance of his taking a small lease.

After which Bunny took a seat on the bench next to Mrs.

Groarty, for the purpose of finding out whether Paul had revealed himself to her. Bunny confessed to her that he had done something very wrong the previous evening; he had failed to lock the kitchen door after looking out on the porch. Following his program of telling the exact truth, he stated that somebody had gone into her kitchen and taken some food; Bunny had promised not to tell who it was, but it was someone who was very hungry, and Bunny had felt sorry about it. If Mrs. Groarty would let him—and he hauled out his little purse.

Mrs. Groarty was all aglow with pleasure at the delicacy of feeling of the aristocracy; she had quite fallen in love with this strange little fellow, who was so pretty to look at, with sensitive red lips like a girl's, and at the same time had the manners of an elderly marquis, or something like that, as Mrs. Groarty had come to know such persons in moving pictures. She refused his money, at the same time thinking what a shame her own fortune had not been made earlier in life, so that her children could have worn such lovely clothes, and learned to express themselves with old-fashioned elegance!

Two or three days later, while Bunny was poking about the "field," watching the interesting sights, he happened to pass the Groarty home, and saw the future oil-queen feeding her rabbits. "Oh, little boy!" she called; and when Bunny had come near, she said: "I had a letter from Paul."

"Where is he?" cried Bunny, in excitement.

"The letter was mailed in San Paulo. But he says not to look for him, because he's hitch-hiking, and he'll be gone."

"And how is he?"

"He says he's all right and not to worry. The poor child, he sent me two-bits in stamps, to pay for that food he took! He says he earned the money—bless him!" Tears ran down the lady's ample cheeks; and Bunny learned the difficult lesson that human nature is a complicated thing, so that the same fat lady can be at one moment a hyena of greed, and at the next a mater dolorosa.

These two sat down on a rabbit-hutch, and had a good talk. Bunny told Mrs. Groarty just how it had happened, and it was a relief to get it off his conscience. Mrs. Groarty in turn told him about the Watkins family, and how they had moved from Arkansas, traveling in the old fashion, by wagon, when Mrs. Groarty was a girl; before that, she had been driven, as a baby in arms, from the mountains of Tennessee. Their place at Paradise, in the San Elido country, was a goat-ranch, with a spring in a little rocky valley; there was only a couple of acres you could cultivate, and for part of that you had to pump irrigating water by hand. It was a desert country, and she didn't see how they could possibly get along without Paul's work; she would send them a little of her oil money, but she didn't know whether Abel—that was her brother, Paul's father—would take anything from her, he was so crazy with his religion.

Paul asked whether he had always been a "roller"; and the other answered no, it was a notion he had taken up, just a few years ago. As for Mrs. Groarty, when she had married her present husband, three years back, she had found her home in the one true faith which had never changed through the ages; it was a comfortable faith, and let you alone, and you weren't always getting crazy new notions and splitting up into sects. They had a lovely church in Beach City, and Father Patrick had such a kind heart and a big, splendid voice— had Bunny ever been to a Catholic service? Bunny said he hadn't; and Mrs. Groarty might perhaps have found a handsome and wealthy convert, had it not been that she was just then being so sorely tempted by the powers of this world.

Yes—Satan had brought her there, and set her on a rabbit-hutch, and was showing her all the kingdoms of the earth! Right across the street, at number 5743 Los Robles Boulevard, the Couch Syndicate had set up a big tent, plastered with red signs, and there were automobiles driving up all day, with people to buy "units" at ten dollars each. Mrs. Groarty's group of "medium lots" had not yet leased, she explained; they had several offers—the best from Sliper and Wilkins, and had Bunny ever heard anything about these operators? And was Dad really quite decided that the best oil prospects lay on the north side? Mrs. Groarty and her husband were thinking of putting their bonus money, when they got it, into some units of "Eureka Pete"—the Eureka Petroleum Company—which was promising a quick drilling on the north slope. And Bunny found himself suddenly recollecting Dad's warning: "Look out for people who mistake you for an oil-well, and try to put you on the pump!"

IV

Mr. Benzinger had sent two truck-loads of Mexicans and fixed up the roads; and Mr. Ascott had kept his promise and delivered the lumber for the derrick; and Dad's boss carpenter had got his gang, and they had cut mortise-joints in the sills, and drilled holes through them, and set them with bolts; then stage by stage the towering derrick had come into being, 122 feet high, straight and true and solid. There was a ladder, and a platform halfway up, and another place to stand at the top; it was all nice and clean and new, and Dad would let you climb, and you could see the view, clear over the houses and the trees, to the blue waters of the Pacific—gee, it was great! And then came the fleet of motor-trucks, thundering in just at sunset, dusty and travel-stained, but full of "pep"—judging by the racket they made, tooting a greeting to J. Arnold Ross and his son. The ditch by the roadside had been filled with crushed rock, making a place where they could drive in to the field; and there they stood, twelve of them lined up in a row.

There were bright electric lights on the derrick, and men waiting, the sleeves of their khaki shirts rolled up. They went to it with a will; for they were working under the eye of the "old man," the master of the pay-roll and of their destinies. They respected this "old man," because he knew his business, and nobody could fool him. Also they liked him, because he combined a proper amount of kindliness with his sternness; he was simple and unpretentious—when the work was crowded, you would have him eating his beans and coffee on a stool in the "eats" joint alongside you. He was a "real guy"; and with this he combined the glamour of a million dollars. Yes, he had "the stuff," barrels of it—and what is a magician who pulls rabbits and yards of ribbon out of his sleeves, compared with one who can pull out a couple of dozen oil-derricks, and as many miles of steel casing, and tanks, and fleets of motor-trucks, and roads for them to run on?

Also they liked the "kid," because he put on no more airs than his Dad, but was jolly, and interested in what you were doing, and asked sensible questions and remembered your explanations. Yes, a kid like that would learn the business and carry it on; the old man was teaching him right. He knew all the crew by their first names, and took their joshing, and had a suit of old clothing, duly smeared with grease, which he would put on, and tackle any job where a half-sized pair of hands could get a hold.

But there was no joshing now; this was a time for breaking records. There was a big cement block for the engine, and a wooden block on top of that, to take up the vibration; and now the truck with the engine on was backed into place, and blocked firm, and the skids made solid, and in a jiffy the engine was slid into place and ready for business. At the same time another crew had got the big steam boiler ready. There was a tank of fuel oil at hand, and the feed-pipe was hitched up, and she was ready to make steam. And meantime the next truck was backed into place, and the skids put under the "draw-works"; when Bunny came back the next morning he found the big "drum" bolted into place, and the running tackle up in the derrick, and they were unloading the "drill-stem." They would fit a steel chain about three of the heavy pipes at once, and a pulley with a steel hook would come down and seize the chain; the engine would start thumping, and the chain and the steel cable would draw tight, and the pipe would slide off the truck. These pipes were twenty feet long, and weighed nineteen pounds to the foot, and when you had your well a mile deep, you could figure it for yourself, there was fifty tons of steel, and your derrick had to carry that weight, and your steel cables had to lift it, and your drum and engine had to stand the strain. People kicked at the price of gasoline, but they never thought about the price of drill-stem and casings!

All these things Bunny had heard a hundred times, but Dad never tired of telling them. He was never entirely content unless the boy was by his side, learning the business. You mustn't fool yourself with the idea that you could hire experts to attend to things; for how could you know that a man was an expert, unless you knew as much as he did? Some day your foreman might drop dead, or some other fellow would buy him away from you, and then where would you be? Be your own expert, said Dad!

The machinery which did the turning was called a "rotary table"; it was connected with the engine by a steel chain, exactly like the sprocket-chain of a bicycle, except that the links were as big as your fist. The rotary table had a hole through the centre, where the drill-stem went through; there was a corresponding hole in the derrick-floor—and soon there would be one in the ground! The hole in the rotary-table was square, and the top drill-stem, known as your "Kelly joint," was square, and fitted this hole; you lowered it through—but first you screwed in your "collar" and "bit," the tool which did the actual cutting. They were starting with a "disc-bit"—it had two steel things like dinner-plates, set opposite each other, and as they went round and round, the weight of the pipe caused them to chew their way into the earth. You started with an eighteen-inch "bit," and as it flopped round, it cut you a hole two feet across.

Well, the time came when the last tool was on hand, and the last bolt made tight, and the drilling-tools ready for their long journey into the bowels of the earth. This was a great moment, akin to the launching of a ship, or the inauguration of the first president of a republic. Your friends gathered, and the workers from nearby jobs, and a crowd of sightseers. The crew had been hustling for three weeks, with this as their goal, and now they stood, both the day shift and the night shift, proud of their past, and eager for their future. The engineman had his hand at the lever, and his eye on Dad; Dad gave him a nod, and he shoved the lever, and the engine started, and the gears made a roaring racket, and the bit hit the ground—"Spud! Spud!" At least that is what men imagine they hear, and so they call the operation "spudding in." "All aboard for China!" sang the foreman; and everybody who had clean hands shook hands with Dad—including Mr. Bankside, whose land they were drilling, and Mrs. Bankside and the whole Bankside family. They carried Dad and Bunny to their home, which was on the lease, and they opened a bottle of champagne, and drank a wee sip to the health of the Ross-Bankside Number 1, which was already a half dozen feet down in the ground.

V

It was cool at the beach in summer, and back at Lobos River it was hot as the original fires; so the family was going to move. Dad wasted very little time on such a matter; he dropped in at a real estate agent's, and asked for the best furnished house in town, and drove out to an imitation palace on the ocean front, and looked it over, and went back to the office and signed a six month's lease for twenty-five hundred dollars.

Outside, this house was plaster applied to chicken-wire, or something that looked like it; inside, it was shiny like the home of Mrs. Groarty, only it was imitation mahogany instead of imitation oak. There was a big entrance hall, and a drawing-room on one side, and on the other a dining-room, with elaborate up-to-date "built-in" features. To these the owner had added furniture regardless of expense or period: spindley-legged gilded French things, done in flowered silk; mid-century American black walnut, with roses and rosettes; black Chinese teak-wood, carved with dragons. There were statues of nude ladies, in highly polished marble, and also a marble clergyman in a frock coat and a string tie. Upstairs were six bed-rooms, each done in a different color by a lady from the best department-store in town. Some people might have found the place lacking in the elements of home, but Bunny never thought of such a thing—he had learned to be happy in a hotel room, with the use of the lobby. All his life that he could remember, home had been a place which you rented, or bought with the idea of holding it as a real estate speculation. As the Indians in the Hudson Bay country kill a moose in the winter-time, and move to the moose, so Dad started an oil-well, and moved to the well.

First came Mr. Eaton, the tutor; he was used to getting a telephone-call, informing him where the carcase of the moose was to be found. He would pack his two suit-cases and his steamer-trunk, and take the train or the motor-bus to his pupil. He was a rather delicate young man, very retiring, with pale blue eyes, and pockets that bagged because he put books in them. He had been engaged with the express restriction that oil was to come before culture; in other words, he was to teach his pupil at such times as Dad was not doing it. Dad was not quite clear on the subject of book knowledge; at times he would say it was all "bunk," but at other times he would pay it a tribute of embarrassment. Yes, he was a "rough-neck," of course, and Bunny would have to know more than he; but at the same time he was jealous of that knowledge, troubled by fear it might be something he would disapprove of. He was right in this, for Mr. Eaton told Bunny quite shamelessly that there were things in the world more important than oil.

Then came the family limousine, with grandmother and Aunt Emma, driven by Rudolph, who was a combination of chauffeur and gardener, and would put on a frock coat and be a butler at parties. Beside him on the front seat rode Sing, the Chinese cook, who was too precious to be trusted to motorbus or train. Nellie, the house-maid, could be more easily replaced, so she brought herself. A truck brought the trunks and miscellaneous belongings—Bunny's bicycle and Aunt Emma's hat-boxes, and grandmother's precious works of art.

Old Mrs. Ross was seventy-five years of age, and her life had been that of a ranch-woman, in the days before automobiles and telephones and machinery. She had slaved in poverty, and raised a family, and seen one daughter die in child-birth, and a son of typhoid in the Spanish war, and another son as a drunkard; now "Jim" was all she had left, and he had made a fortune late in his life, and lifted her to leisure at the end of hers. You might have been a long time guessing what use she would make of it. Out of a clear sky she announced that she was going to be a painter! For sixty years, it appeared, she had cherished that dream, while washing dishes, and spanking babies, and drying apricots and muscat grapes.

So now, wherever they lived, grandmother had a spare room for a "studio." A wandering artist had taught her the handling of crude and glaring colors. This artist had painted desert sunsets, and the mountains and rocky coasts of California; but old Mrs. Ross never painted anything she had ever seen. What she was interested in was gentility—parks, and lawns, and shady avenues with ladies in hoop-skirts, and gentlemen with wide-bottomed trousers. Her masterpiece was six feet by four, and always hung in the dining-room of the rented home; it showed in the background an extremely elegant two-story house, with two-storied porches having pillars on which you could see every curlicue. In front ran a circular drive, with a fountain in the middle, and water which was very plainly splashing. Around the drive rolled a victoria—or maybe it was a landau or a barouche—with a lady and a gentleman being driven by a Negro coachman. Behind the vehicle raced a little dog, and playing on the lawn were a boy, and a girl in wide skirts, having a hoop in her hand. Also there were iron deer on the lawn—you never got tired of looking at this picture, because you could always find something new in it; Dad would show it to visitors, and say: "Ma painted that; ain't she a wonder, for an old lady seventy-five?" Agents who had come with leasing propositions, or lawyers with papers to be gone over, or foremen coming for orders, would examine it carefully, and never disagreed with Dad's judgment.

Aunt Emma was the widow of the son who had died a drunkard; and to her also prosperity had come late in life. Dad set no limits—the ladies charged anything they wanted, and even drew checks on Dad's account. So Aunt Emma went to the fanciest shops and got herself raiment, and went out to uphold the prestige of the Ross family in the town or city where they were staying. There were ladies' clubs, and Aunt Emma would attend their functions, and listen to impressive personalities who rose and said, "Madam Chairman," and read papers on the Feminine Element in Shakespeare's Plays, and the Therapeutic Value of Optimism, and What Shall We Do for Our Youth? Once every month the two ladies gave a tea-party, and Dad always managed to be "spudding in" a new well, or seeing to a difficult job of "cementing off" on that afternoon.

Aunt Emma particularly patronized the drug-store counters where they sold cosmetics, and she knew by name the fashionable young ladies who presided there; also she knew the names of the latest products they handled, pronouncing these names in quite naive and shameless American—"Roodge finn dee Theeayter" and "Pooder der Reeze ah lah corbeel flurry"— which, it must be added, was the only way she could have got the sales-ladies to know what she meant. Her dressing-table was covered with rows of delicate little boxes and jars and bottles, containing paints and powders and perfumes and beauty clays and enamels, and she alone knew what else. One of Bunny's earliest memories was of Aunt Emma, perched on a chair, looking like an enlarged parokeet in a harness. She was only half dressed, paying no attention to him, because he was so little; so he observed how she was laced and strapped up in armor—tight corsets and dress-shields and side-garters and tightly laced little boots. She sat, erect and serious, putting things on her cheeks and eye-brows, and dabbing herself with little puffs of pink and white powder; and at the same time telling Bunny about her husband, deceased many years ago. He had had many virtues, in spite of his one tragic weakness; he had had a kind heart, so sweet and generous—"yes, yes," said Aunt Emma, "he was a good little man; I wonder where he is now." And then, dab, dab, she was patting the tears away from her cheeks and making them pink again!

VI

Far down in the ground, underneath the Ross-Bankside No. 1, a great block of steel was turning round and round. The under surface of it had blunt steel teeth, like a nutmeg-grater; on top of it rested a couple of thousand feet of steel tubing, the "drill-stem," a weight of twenty tons pressing it down; so, as it turned, it ate into the solid rock, grinding it to powder. It worked in the midst of a river of thin mud, which was driven down through the center of the hollow tubing, and came up again between the outside of the tubing and the earth. The river of mud served three purposes: it kept the bit and the drill-stem from heating; it carried away the ground-up rock; and as it came up on the outside of the drill-stem, it was pressed against the walls of the hole, and made a plaster to keep the walls rigid, so that they did not press in upon the drill-stem. Up on the top of the ground was a "sump-hole," of mud and water, and a machine to keep up the mixture; there were "mud-hogs," snorting and puffing, which forced it down inside the stem under a pressure of 250 pounds to the square inch. Drilling was always a dirty business; you swam in pale grey mud until the well came in, and after that you slid in oil.

Also it was an expensive business. To turn those twenty tons of steel tubing, getting heavier every day as they got longer—that took real power, you want to know. When the big steam engine started pulling on the chain, and the steel gears started their racket, Bunny would stand and listen, delighted. Some engine, that! Fifty horsepower, the cathead-man would say; and you would imagine fifty horses harnessed to an old-fashioned turn-table with a pole, such as our ancestors employed to draw up water from a well, or to run a primitive threshing-machine.

Yes, it took money to drill an oil-well out here in California; it wasn't like the little short holes in the East, where you pounded your way down by lifting up your string of tools and letting them drop again. No siree, here you had to be prepared to go six or seven thousand feet, which meant from three hundred to three hundred and fifty joints of pipe; also casing, for you could not leave this hole very long without protection. There were strata of soft sand, with water running through, and when you got past these you would have to let down a cylinder of steel or wrought iron, like a great long stove pipe; joint after joint you would slide down, carefully rivetting them together, making a water-proof job; and when you had this casing all set in cement, you would start drilling with a smaller bit, say fourteen inches, leaving the upper casing resting firmly on a sort of shelf. So you would go, smaller and smaller, until, when you got to the oil-sands, your hole would have shrunk to five or six inches. If you were a careful man, like Dad, you would run each string of casing all the way up to the derrick-floor, so that in the upper part of the hole you would have four sets of casing, one inside the other.

All day and all night the engine labored, and the great chain pulled, and the rotary-table went round and round, and the bit ate into the rock. You had to have two shifts of men, twelve hours each, and because living quarters were scarce in this sudden rush, they kept the same bed warm all the time. A crew had to be on the job every moment, to listen and to watch. The engine must have plenty of water and gas and oil; the pump must be working, and the mud-river circulating, and the mixing-machine splashing, and the drill making depth at the proper rate. There were innumerable things that might go wrong, and some of them cost money, and some of them cost more money. Dad was liable to be waked up at any hour of the night, and he would give orders over the telephone, or perhaps he would slip into his clothes and drive out to the field. And next morning, at breakfast, he would tell Bunny about it; that fellow Dan Rossiger, the night-foreman, he sure was one balky mule; he jist wouldn't make any time, and when you kicked, he said, "All right, if you want a 'twist-off'." And Dad had said, " Twist-off' or no 'twist-off,' I want you to make time." And so, sure enough, there was a "twist-off," right away! Dad vowed that Dan had done it on purpose; there were fellows mean enough for that—and, of course, all they had to do was to speed up the engine.

Anyhow, there was your "twist-off"; which meant that you had to lift out every inch of your two thousand feet of pipe. You pulled it up, and unscrewed it, four joints at a time— "breaking out," the men called that operation; each four joints, a "stand," were stood up in the derrick, and the weary work went on. You couldn't tell where the break was, until you got to it; then you screwed off the broken piece, and threw it away, and went to your real job, "fishing" for the remainder of your drill-stem, down in the hole. For this job you had a device called an "overshot," which you let down with a cable; it was big and heavy, and went over the pipe, and caught on a joint when you pulled it up—something like an ice-man's tongs. But maybe you got it over, and maybe you didn't; you spent a lot of time jiggling it up and down—until at last she caught fast, and up came the rest of your stem! Then you unscrewed the broken piece, and put in a sound piece, and let it all back into the hole, one stand at a time, until you were ready to start again. But this time you went at the rate Dan Rossiger considered safe, and you didn't nag at him for any more "twist-offs!"

Meantime Dad would be spending the day at his little office down in the business part of the town. There he had a stenographer and a bookkeeper, and all the records of his various wells. There came people who wanted to offer him new leases, and hustling young salesmen to show him a wonderful new device in the way of an "underreamer," or to persuade him that wrought casing lasts longer than cast steel, or to explain the model of a new bit, that was making marvelous records in the Palomar field. Dad would see them all, for they might "have something," you never could be sure. But woe to the young man who hadn't got his figures just right; for Dad had copies of the "logs" of every one of his wells, and he would pull out the book, and show the embarrassed young man exactly what he had done over at Lobos River with a Stubbs Fishtail number seven.

Then the postman would come, bringing reports from all the wells; and Dad would dictate letters and telegrams. Or perhaps the 'phone would ring—long distance calling Mr. Ross; and Dad would come home to lunch fuming—that fellow Impey over at Antelope had gone and broke his leg, letting a pipe fall on him: that chap with the black moustache, you remember? Bunny said, yes, he remembered; the one Dad had bawled out. "I fired him," said Dad; "and then I got sorry for his wife and children, and took him back. I found that fellow down on his knees, with his head stuck between the chain and the bull-wheel—and he knew we had no bleeder-valve on that engine! Jist tryin' to get out a piece of rope, he said—and his fingers jammed up in there! What's the use a-tryin' to do anything for people that ain't got sense enough to take care of their own fingers, to say nothing of their heads?

By golly, I don't see how they ever live long enough to grow black moustaches on their faces!" So Dad would fuss—his favorite theme, the shiftlessness of the working-class whom he had to employ. Of course he had a purpose; drilling is a dangerous business at best, and Bunny must know what he was doing when he went poking about under a derrick.

There came a telegram from Lobos River; Number Two was stuck. First, they had lost a set of tools, and then, while they were stringing up for the fishing job, a "rough-neck" had dropped a steel crowbar into the hole! They were down four thousand feet, and "fishing" is costly sport at that depth! Seemed like there was a jinx in that hole; they had "jammed" three times, and they were six weeks behind their schedule. Dad fretted, and he would call up the well every couple of hours all day, but nothing doing; they tried this device and that, and Dad 'phoned them to try something else, but in vain. The hole caved in on them, and they had to clean out and fish ahead, run after run. They had caught the tools and jarred them out, but the crowbar was still down there, wedged fast.

The third evening Dad said he guessed he'd have to run over to Lobos River; it was time to set a new casing anyhow, and he liked to oversee those cement fellows. Bunny jumped up, crying, "Take me, Dad!" And Dad said, "Sure thing!" Grandmother made her usual remark about Bunny's education going to pot; and Dad made his usual answer, that Bunny would have all his life to learn about poetry and history—now he was going to learn about oil, while he had his father to teach him. Aunt Emma tried to get Mr. Eaton to say something in defense of poetry and history, but the tutor kept a discreet silence—he knew who held the purse-strings in that family! Bunny understood that Mr. Eaton didn't mind about it; he was preparing a thesis that was to get him a master's degree, and he used his spare time quite contentedly, counting the feminine endings in certain of the pre-Elizabethan dramatists.

VII

Well, they made the trip back to the old field; and Bunny remembered all the adventures of the last ride, the place where they had had lunch, and what the waitress had said, and the place where they had stopped for gas, and what the man had

said, and the place where they had run into the "speed-cop."
It was like fishing—that is, for real fish, like you catch in
water, not in oil-wells; you remember where you got the big
fish, and you expect another bite there. But the big fish always
come at a new place, said Dad, and it was the same with
"speed-cops." A cop picked them up just outside Beach City,
passing a speed-trap at forty-seven miles; and Dad grinned
and chaffed the cop, and said he was glad he hadn't been really
going fast.

They got to Lobos River that evening; and there was the
rig, fishing away—screwing the stands of pipe together and
working down into the hole with some kind of grabbing device
on the end, and then hauling up and unscrewing—stand after
stand, fifty or sixty of them, one after another—until at last
you got to the bottom one, only to find that you had missed
your "fish!"

Well, Dad said his say, in tones that nobody could help
hearing. If he couldn't find men who would take care of their
own bones, it was doubtless too much to hope they would take
care of his property. They stood there, looking like a lot of
school-boys getting a birching—though of course the "rough-
neck" who was wholly to blame had been turned loose on the
road long ago.

There was a salesman from a supply house there with a
patent device which he guaranteed would bring up the obstacle
the first run; so they tried it, and left the device in the hole—
it had held on too tight! Evidently there was a pocket down
there, and the crowbar had got wedged crossways; so they'd
have to try a small chunk of dynamite, said Dad. Ever listen
to an explosion four thousand feet under the ground? Well,
that was how they got the crowbar loose; and then they had
a job of cleaning out, and drilling some more, and setting a
casing to cover the damaged place in the hole.

Thus, day by day, Bunny got his oil lessons. He wandered
about the field with Dad and the geologist and the boss driller,
while they laid out the sites for future wells; and Dad took
an envelope and pencil, and explained to Bunny why you
place your wells on the four corners of a diamond, and not
on the four corners of a square. You may try that out for
yourself, drawing a circle about each well, to indicate the
territory from which the oil is drained; you will see that the
diamond shape covers the ground with less overlapping.

Wherever you overlap, you are drilling two holes to get the same barrel of oil; and only a dub would do that.

They drove back to Beach City, and found that Bertie had come home. Bertie was Bunny's sister, two years his senior, and she had been visiting the terribly fashionable Woodbridge Rileys, up north. Bunny tried to tell her about the fishing-job, and how things were going at Lobos River, but she was most cruelly cutting—described him as a "little oil gnome," and said that his fingernails were a "dead give-away." It appeared that Bertie had become ashamed of oil; and this was something new, for of old she had been a good pal, interested in the business, and arguing with Bunny and bossing him as any older sister should. Bunny didn't know what to make of it, but gradually he came to understand that this was a part of the fashionable education Bertie was getting at Miss Castle's school.

Aunt Emma was to blame for this. She had granted Jim's right to confine Bunny's training to the making of money, but Bertie at least should be a young lady—meaning that she should learn how to spend the money which Dad and Bunny were going to make. So Aunt Emma got the name of the most expensive school for young female money-spenders, and from that time on the family saw little of Bertie; after school she went to visit her new rich friends. She couldn't bring them to her home, there being no real butler—Rudolph was a "farm-hand," she declared. She had picked up some wonderful new slang; if she didn't like what you said, she would tell you that you were "full of prunes"—this was away back in history, you understand. She would give a pirouette and show off her fancy lingerie, with violet-colored ribbons in it; she would laugh gleefully: "Aren't I a speedy young thing?"— and other phrases which caused grandmother to stare and Dad to grin. She would be pained by her father's grammar: "Oh, Dad, *don't* say 'jist'!" And Dad would grin again, and reply: "I been a-sayin' it jist fifty-nine years." But all the same, he began a-sayin' it less frequently; which is how civilization progresses.

Bertie condescended to drive out to the field, and see the new derricks that were going up. They went for a walk, and whom should they meet but Mrs. Groarty, getting out of her elderly Ford car in front of her home. Bunny was naively glad to see her, and insisted upon introducing Bertie, who displayed her iciest manner, and, as they went on, scolded Bunny because of his horrid vulgar taste; he might pick up acquaintance with every sort of riff-raff if he chose, but certainly he need not make his sister shake hands with them! Bunny could not understand—he never did succeed in understanding, all his life long, how people could fail to be interested in other people.

He told Bertie about Paul, and what a wonderful fellow he was, but Bertie said just what Dad had said, that Paul was "crazy." More than that, she became angry, she thought that Paul was a "horrid fellow," she was glad Bunny hadn't been able to find him again. That was an attitude which Bertie was to show to Paul all through Paul's life; she showed it at the very first instant, and poor Bunny was utterly bewildered. But in truth, it was hardly reasonable to expect that Bertie, who was going to school in order to learn to admire money—to find out by intuition exactly how much money everybody had, and to rate them accordingly—should be moved to admiration by a man who insisted that you had no right to money unless you had earned it!

Bertie was following her nature, and Bunny followed his. The anger of his sister had the effect of setting Paul upon a lonely eminence in Bunny's imagination; a strange, half-legendary figure, the only person who had ever had a chance to get some of Dad's money, and had refused it! Every now and then Bunny would stop by and sit on a rabbit-hutch, and ask Mrs. Groarty for news about her nephew. One time the stout lady showed him a badly scrawled note from Ruth Watkins—Paul's sister, whom he loved—saying that the family had had no word; also that they were having a hard time keeping alive, they were having to kill a goat now and then—and Mrs. Groarty said that was literally eating up their capital. Later on there was another letter from Ruth, saying that Paul had written to her; he was up north, and still on the move, so no one could get hold of him; he sent a five-dollar bill in a registered letter, and specified that it was to go for food, and not for missions. It wasn't easy to save money when you were only getting a boy's pay, Paul said; and again Bunny was moved to secret awe. He went off and did a strange secret thing—he took a five-dollar bill, and folded it carefully in a sheet of paper, and sealed it up in a plain envelope, and addressed it to "Miss Ruth Watkins, Paradise, California," and dropped it into a mail-box.

Mrs. Groarty was always glad to see Bunny, and Bunny,

alas, knew why—she wanted to use him for an oil-well! He would politely pay her with a certain amount of information. He asked Dad about Sliper and Wilkins, and Dad said they were "four-flushers"; Bunny passed this information on, but the "medium lots" went ahead and signed up with this pair—and very soon wished they hadn't. For Sliper and Wilkins proceeded to sell the lease to a syndicate, and so there was a tent on the lot next to the Groarty home, and free lunches being served to crowds of people gathered up in the streets of Beach City by a "ballyhoo" man. "Bonanza Syndicate No. 1," it was called; and they hustled up a derrick, and duly "spudded in," and drilled a hundred feet or so; and Mrs. Groarty was in heaven, and spent her thousand dollars of bonus money for a hundred units of another syndicate, the "Co-operative No. 3." The crowds trampled her lawn, but she didn't care—the company would move her home when they drilled the second well, and she was going into a neighborhood that was "much sweller"—so she told Bunny.

But then, on his next visit, he saw trouble in the stout lady's features. The drilling had stopped; the papers said the crew was "fishing," but the men said they were "fishing for their pay." The selling of "units" slowed down, the "ballyhoo" stopped, and then the syndicate was sold to what was called a "holding company." The drilling was not resumed, however, and poor Mrs. Groarty tried pitifully to get Bunny to find out from his father what was happening to them. But Dad didn't know, and nobody knew—until six months or so later, long after Dad had brought in his Ross-Bankside No. 1 with triumphant success. Then the newspapers appeared with scare headlines to the effect that the grand jury was about to indict D. Buckett Kyber and his associates of the Bonanza Syndicate for fraudulent sales of oil stock. Dad remarked to Bunny that this was probably a "shake-down"; some of the officials, and maybe some of the newspaper men, desired to be "seen" by Mr. Kyber. Presumably they were "seen," for nothing more was heard of the prosecution. Meantime, the owners of the lease could not get anyone to continue the drilling, for the block next to them had brought in a two hundred barrel well, which was practically nothing; the newspapers now said that the south slope looked decidedly "edgy."

So Bunny, in the midst of his father's glory, would pass down the street and encounter poor Mr. Dumpery, coming home

from the trolley with dragging steps, after having driven some
thousands of shingle-nails into a roof; or Mr. Sahm, the
plasterer, tending his little garden, with its rows of corn and
beans that were irrigated with a hose. Bunny would see Mrs.
Groarty, feeding her chickens and cleaning out her rabbit-
hutches—but never again did he see the fancy evening-gown
of yellow satin! He would go inside, and sit down and chat,
in order not to seem "stuck-up"; and there was the stairway
that led to nowhere, and the copy of "The Ladies' Guide: A
Practical Handbook of Gentility," still resting on the centre-
table, its blue silk now finger-soiled, and its gold letters
tarnished. Bunny's eyes took in these things, and he realized
what Dad meant when he compared the oil-game to heaven,
where many are called and few are chosen.

VIII

Scattered here and there over the hill were derricks, and
the drilling crews were racing to be the first to tap the precious
treasure. By day you saw white puffs from the steam-engines,
and by night you saw lights gleaming on the derricks, and day
and night you heard the sound of heavy machinery turning,
turning—"ump-um—ump-um—ump-um—ump-um." The newspapers reported the results, and a hundred thousand speculators
and would-be speculators read the reports, and got into their
cars and rode out to the field where the syndicates had their
tents, or thronged the board-rooms in town, where prices were
chalked up on blackboards, and "units" were sold to people
who would not know an oil-derrick from a "chute the chutes."

Who do you think stood first in the newspaper reports?
You would need to make but one guess—Ross-Bankside No. 1.
Dad was right there, day and night, knowing the men who were
working for him, watching them, encouraging them, scolding
them if need be—and so Dad had not had a single accident, he
had not lost a day or night. The well was down to thirty-two
hundred feet, and in the first stratum of oil-sand.

They were using an eight-inch bit, and for some time they
had been taking a core. Dad was strenuous about core-drilling;
he insisted that you must know every inch of the hole, and
he would tell stories of men who had drilled through paying
oil-sands and never known it. So the drill brought up a cylinder
of rock, exactly like the core you would take out of an apple;

and Bunny learned to tell shale from sandstone, and conglomerate from either. He learned to measure the tilt of the strata, and what that told the geologist about the shape of things down below, and the probable direction of the anticline. When there were traces of oil, there had to be chemical analyses, and he learned to interpret these reports. Every oil-pool in the world was different—each one a riddle, with colossal prizes for the men who could guess it!

Dad guessed that he was right over the pool, and so he had ordered his "tankage." There was going to be a rush for this, as for everything else, and Dad had the cash—and still more important, the reputation for having the cash! He would get his "tankage" onto the lease, and if he were disappointed in his hopes for oil—well, somebody else would get it, and they would be glad to take the "tankage" off his hands. So there came a stream of heavy trucks, and stacked up on the field were flat sheets of steel, and curved sheets, all fitting exactly.

You may be sure the buyers of "units" did not fail to make note of that! They were hanging round the derrick day and night, trying to pick up hints; they followed the men to their homes, and tried to bribe them, or to get into conversation with their wives. As for Bunny, he was about the most popular boy in Beach City; it was wonderful how many kind gentlemen, and even kind ladies there were, anxious to buy him ice-cream, or to feed him out of boxes of candy! Dad forbade him to say a word to strangers, or to have anything to do with them; and presently Dad banned discussions at the family table—because Aunt Emma was chattering in the ladies' clubs, and the ladies were telling their husbands, besides gambling "on their own!"

The core showed more signs, and Dad gave orders to build the foundations of the tanks; then he ordered the tanks put up, and the clatter of riveting machines was heard, and magically there rose three ten thousand barrel tanks, newly painted with flaming red lead. And then—hush!—they were in the real oil-sands; Dad set a crew of Mexicans to digging him a trench for a pipe line; and the lease-hounds and the dealers in units discovered that, and the town went wild. In the middle of the night Dad was routed out of bed, and he called Bunny, and they jumped into their old clothes and went racing out to the well, and there were the first signs of the pressure, the mud was beginning to jump and bubble in the hole! The drilling

had stopped, and the men were hastily screwing on the big
"casing-head" that Dad had provided. He wasn't satisfied
even with that—he set them to fastening heavy lugs to the
head, and he hustled up a couple of cement men and built great
blocks of cement over the lugs, to hold her down in spite of
any pressure. There wasn't going to be a blow-out on Ross-
Bankside No. 1, you bet; whatever oil came through that hole
was going into the tanks, and from there into Dad's bank
account!

It was time for the "cementing-off," to make the well water-
proof, and protect the precious oil-sands. Down there under the
ground was a pool of oil, caught under a layer of impermeable
rock, exactly like an inverted wash-basin. The oil was full of
gas, which made the pressure. Now you had drilled a hole
through the wash-basin, and the oil and gas would come to you
—but only on condition that you did not let any surface water
down to kill the pressure. All the way down you had been
tapping underground streams and pools of water; and now
you had to set a big block of cement at the bottom of the hole,
solid and tight, filling every crevice, both inside and outside
your casing. Having got this tight, you would drill a hole
through it, and on down into the oil sands, thus making a
channel through which the oil could flow up, and no water
could leak down. This was the critical part of your operation,
and while it was going on the whole crew was keyed up, and
the owner and his son, needless to say.

First you put down your casing, known as the "water-
string." If you were a careful man, like Dad, you ran this
"string" all the way up to your derrick-floor. Next you began
pumping down clean water; for many hours you pumped, until
you had washed the dirt and oil out of the hole; and then you
were ready for the cement-men. They came with a truck, a
complete outfit on wheels, ready to travel to any well. Another
truck brought the sacks of cement, a couple of hundred of them;
the job called for pure cement, no sand. They got everything
ready before they started, and then they worked like so many
fiends—for this whole job had to be put through in less than
an hour, before the cement began to set.

It was an ingenious scheme they had, very fascinating to
watch. They fitted inside the casing a cast-iron "packer,"
having rubber discs at the top and bottom, so that it floated
on the water in the casing; the cement went on top of this.

The sacks were jerked open, and dumped into the hopper of the mixing machine, and the mixer began to revolve, and the river of grey liquid to pour into the hole. It ran fast, and the heavy pumps set to work, and drove it down, stroke after stroke. In half an hour they had filled several hundred feet of the casing with cement; after which they put on a rubber "packer," fitting tight to the casing; and again the heavy pumps went to work, and drove the mass of cement, between the two "packers," down into the hole. When they came to the bottom, the bottom packer would drop, and the cement would pour in, and the pressure of the top packer would force it into every cranny of the hole, and up between the outside of the casing and the earth—one or two hundred feet high it would rise, and when it set, there you would have your "water shut-off."

What could be more fun to watch than a job like this? To know what was going on under the ground; to see the ingenuity by which men overcame Nature's obstacles; to see a crew of workers, rushing here and there, busy as beavers or ants, yet at the same time serene and sure, knowing their job, and just how it was going!

The job was done; and then you had to wait ten days for your cement to get thoroughly set. The state inspector came and made his tests, to be sure you had got a complete "shut-off"; if you hadn't, he would make you do it over again—some poor devils had to do it twenty or thirty times! But nothing like that happened to Dad; he knew about "cementing off"—and also about inspectors, he added with a grin. Anyhow, he got his permit; and now Ross-Bankside No. 1 was drilling into the real oil-sands, going down with a six-inch hole. Every few hours they would test for pressure, to be sure they had enough, but not too much. You were right on the verge of triumph now, and your pulse went fast and you walked on tip-toe with excitement. It was like waiting for Christmas morning, to open your stocking, and see what Santa Claus had brought! There were crowds staring at the well all day, and you put up rude signs to make them keep their noses out.

Dad said they were deep enough now, and they proceeded to set the last casing—it was known as the "liner," and had holes like a sieve, through which the treasure would flow. They were working late into the night, and both Dad and Bunny had old clothes on, and were bathed in oil and mud. At last they had the "liner" all ready, and the tools out, and they started to "wash" the well, pumping in fresh water and cleaning out the mud and sand. That would go on for five or six hours, and meantime Dad and Bunny would get their sleep.

When they came back, it was time to "bail." You understand, the pressure of the gas and oil was held down by the column of water, two thirds of a mile deep. Now they had what they called a "double-section bailer," which was simply a bucket fifty feet long. They would let that down, and lift out fifty feet of the water-column, and dump it into the sump-hole. Then they would go down for another fifty; and presently they would find they didn't have to go down so far, the pressure was shoving the column of water up in the hole. Then you knew you were getting near to the end; one or two more trips of the bailer, and the water would be shot out of the hole, and mud and water and oil would spout up over the top of the derrick, staining it a lovely dripping black. You must drive the crowds off the lease now, and shout "Lights out!" to the fools with cigarettes.

There she came! There was a cheer from all hands, and the spectators went flying to avoid the oily spray blown by the wind. They let her shoot for a while, until the water had been ejected; higher and higher, way up over the derrick—she made a lovely noise, hissing and splashing, bouncing up and down!

It was just at sundown, and the sky was crimson. "Lights out!" Dad kept calling—nobody must even start a motor-car while she was spouting. Presently they shut her off, to try the valve of the casing-head; they worked on, late into the night, letting her spout, and then shutting her off again; it was mysteriously thrilling in the darkness. At last they were ready to "bring her in"—which meant they would screw up the "flow-line" between the casing-head and the tank, and let the oil run into the latter. Just as simple as that—no show, no fuss, you just let her flow; the gauge showed her coming at the rate of thirty thousand gallons every hour, which meant that the first tank was full by noon the next day.

Yes, that was all; but the news affected Beach City as if an angel had appeared in a shining cloud and scattered twenty-dollar gold pieces over the streets. You see, Ross-Bankside No. 1 "proved up" the whole north slope; to tens of thousands of investors, big and little, it meant that a hope was turned into glorious certainty. You couldn't keep such news quiet, it just didn't lie in the possibility of human nature not to tell;

the newspapers bulletined the details—Ross-Bankside was flowing sixteen thousand barrels a day, and the gravity was 32, and as soon as the pipe-line was completed—which would be by the end of the week—its owner would be in possession of an income of something over twenty thousand dollars every twenty-four hours. Would you need to be told that the crowds stared at Dad and at Bunny, everywhere they went about the streets of the city? There goes the great J. Arnold Ross, owner of the new well! And that little chap is his son! Say, he's got thirteen dollars coming to him every minute of the day or night, whether he's awake or asleep. By God, a fellow would feel he could afford to order his lunch, if he was to have an income like that!

Bunny couldn't help but get a sense of importance, and think that he was something special and wonderful. Little thrills ran over him; he felt as if he could run up into the air and fly. And then Dad would say: "Take it easy, son! Keep your mouth shut, and don't go a-gettin' your head swelled. Remember, you didn't make this here money, and you can lose it in no time, if you're a light-weight." Dad was a sensible fellow, you see; he had been through all this before, first at Antelope, and then at Lobos River. He had felt the temptation of grandeur, and knew what it must be to a boy. It was pleasant to have a lot of money; but you must set up a skeleton at the feast, and while you quaffed the wine of success, you must hear a voice behind you whispering, "Memento mori!"

CHAPTER IV

THE RANCH

I

Soon after this it was time for Bunny to visit his mother.

Bunny's mother did not bear Dad's name, as other boys' mothers do; she was called Mrs. Lang, and lived in a bungalow on the outskirts of Angel City. There was an arrangement whereby she had a right to have Bunny with her one week in every six months; Bunny always knew when this time was approaching, and looked forward to it with mixed emotions. His mother was sweet, and gave him the petting which he missed at other times; "pretty little Mamma," was her name for herself. But in other ways the visit was embarrassing, because there were matters supposed to be kept hidden from Bunny, but which he could not help guessing. Mamma would question him about Dad's affairs, and Bunny knew that Dad did not wish his affairs talked about. Then too, Mamma complained that she never had enough money; Dad allowed her only two hundred dollars a month, and how could a young and charming grass-widow exist on such a sum? Her garage bill was always unpaid, and she would tell Bunny about it, and expect him to tell Dad—but Dad would evade hearing. And next time, Mamma would cry, and say that Jim was a tyrant and a miser. The situation was especially difficult just now, because Mamma had read about the new well in the papers, and knew just how much money Dad had; she unfolded to Bunny a plan, that he should try to persuade Dad to increase her allowance, but without having Dad suspect that she had suggested it. And this, right after Bunny had renounced the luxury of small lies!

Also there was the mystery about Mamma's friends. There were always gentlemen friends who came to see her while Bunny was there, and who might or might not be agreeable to Bunny. When he came home, Aunt Emma would ask him questions, from which it was evident that she wanted to know about these gentlemen friends, but didn't want Bunny to know that she wanted to know. Bunny noticed that Dad never referred to such matters; he never asked any questions about

78

Mamma, and Aunt Emma always did her asking out of Dad's presence.

All this had a peculiar effect upon Bunny. Just as Dad kept a safe-deposit box at the bank, into which nobody ever looked but himself, so Bunny kept a secret place in his own mind. Outwardly, he was a cheerful and frank little fellow, if somewhat too mature for his years; but all the time he was leading a dual life—picking up ideas here and there, and carrying them off and hiding them, as a squirrel does nuts, so that he may come back at a later season and crack them open and nibble them. Some nuts were good and some were bad, and Bunny learned to judge them, and to throw away the bad ones.

One thing was plain: there was something which men and women did, which they were all in a conspiracy to keep you from knowing that they did. It was a dark corner of life, mysterious and rather hateful. In the beginning, Bunny was loyal to his father, not trying to find out what his father didn't want him to know. But this could not continue indefinitely, for the mind automatically seeks understanding. It was not merely that the birds and the chickens and the dogs in the street gave you hints; it was not merely that every street-boy knew, and was eager to explain; it was that the stupid grown-ups themselves persisted in saying things which you couldn't help getting. It was Aunt Emma's fixed conviction that every lady was after Dad; "setting her cap at him," or "making sheep's eyes at him"—she had many such phrases. And Dad always showed a queer embarrassment whenever he had been the least bit polite to any lady; he seemed to be concerned lest Bunny should share Aunt Emma's suspicions. But the truth was, Bunny was irritated by his aunt, and learned to evade her questions, and not tell what Dad had said to the nice lady in the hotel at Lobos River, and whether or not the lady had had dinner with them. These worldly arts Bunny acquired, but all the time he was in secret revolt. Why couldn't people talk plainly? Why did they have to be pretending, and whispering, and making you uncomfortable?

II

Within a week after bringing in Ross-Bankside No. 1, Dad had a new derrick under way on the lease, and in another week he had it rigged up, and the old string of tools was on its way into the earth again. Also he had two new derricks under way, and two new strings in process of delivery. There would be four wells, standing on the four corners of a diamond-shaped figure, three hundred feet on the side. It was necessary to call house-movers, and take the Bankside homestead to another lot; but that didn't trouble Mr. Bankside, who had already moved himself to an ocean-front palace near Dad, and bought himself a whole outfit of furniture, and a big new limousine, also a "sport-car," in which to drive himself to the country club to play golf every afternoon. The Bankside family was accustoming itself to the presence of a butler, and Mrs. Bankside had been proposed at the most exclusive of the ladies' clubs. Efficiency was the watch-word out here in the West, and when you decided to change your social status, you put the job right through.

Dad and Bunny made another trip to Lobos River, and not without some difficulty they conquered the "jinx" in Number Two, and brought in a very good well. There were to be two more derricks here, and more tools to be bought and delivered. That was the way in the oil business, as fast as you got any money, you put it back into new drilling—and, of course, new responsibilities. You were driven to this by the forces inherent in the game. You were racing with other people, who were always threatening to get your oil. As soon as you had one well, you had to have "offset wells" to protect it from the people on every side who would otherwise get your oil. Also, you might have trouble in marketing your oil, and would begin to think, how nice to have your own refinery, and be entirely independent. But independence had its price, for then you would have to provide enough oil to keep the refinery going, and you would want a chain of filling-stations to get rid of your products. It was a hard game for the little fellow; and no matter how big you got, there was always somebody bigger!

But Dad had no kick just now; everything was a-comin' his way a-whoopin'. Right in the midst of his other triumphs it had occurred to him to take one of his old Antelope wells and go a little lower, and see what he found; he tried it—and lo and behold, at eight hundred feet farther down the darn thing went and blew its head off. They were in a new layer of oil-sands; and every one of these sixteen old wells, that had been on the pump for a couple of years, and were about played out, were ready to present Dad with a new fortune, at a cost of only a few thousand dollars each!

But right away came a new problem; there was no pipe-line to this field, and there ought to be one. Dad wanted some of the other operators to go in with him, and he was going up there and make a deal. Then Bunny came to him, looking very serious. "Dad, have you forgotten, it's close to the fifteenth of November."

"What about it, son?"

"You promised we were going quail-shooting this year."

"By gosh, that's so! But I'm frightfully rushed jist now, son."

"You're working too hard, Dad; Aunt Emma says you're putting a strain on your kidneys, the doctor has told you so."

"Does he recommend a quail diet?"

Bunny knew by Dad's grin that he was going to make some concession. "Let's take our camping things," the boy pleaded, "and when you get through at Antelope, let's come home by the San Elido valley."

"The San Elido! But son, that's fifty miles out of our way!"

"They say there's no end of quail there, Dad."

"Yes, but we can get quail a lot nearer home."

"I know, Dad; but I've never been there, and I want to see it."

"But what made you hit on that place?"

Bunny was embarrassed, because he knew Dad was going to think he was "queer." Nevertheless, he persisted. "That's where the Watkins family live."

"Watkins family—who are they?"

"Don't you remember that boy, Paul, that I met one night when you were talking about the lease?"

"Gosh, son! You still a-frettin' about that boy?"

"I met Mrs. Groarty on the street yesterday, and she told me about the family; they're in dreadful trouble, they're going to lose their ranch to the bank because they can't meet the interest on the mortgage, and Mrs. Groarty says she can't think what they'll do. You know Mrs. Groarty didn't get any money herself—at least, she spent her bonus money for units, and she isn't getting anything out of them, and has to live on what her husband gets as a night watchman."

"What you want to do about it?"

"I want you to buy that mortgage, Dad; or anything, so the Watkinses can stay in their home. It's wicked that people should be turned out like that, when they're doing the best they can."

"There's plenty o' people bein' turned out when they don't meet their obligations, son."

"But when it's not their fault, Dad?"

"It would take a lot of bookkeeping to figger jist whose fault it is; and the banks don't keep books that way." Then seeing the protest in Bunny's face, "You'll find, son there's a lot o' harsh things in the world, that ain't in your power to change. You'll jist have to make up your mind to that, sooner or later."

"But Dad, there's four children there, and three of them are girls, and where are they to go? Paul is away, and they haven't any way to let him know what's happened. Mrs. Groarty showed me a picture of them, Dad; they're good, kind people, you can see they've never done anything but work hard. Honest, Dad, I couldn't be happy if I didn't help them. You said you'd buy me a car some day, and I'd rather you took the money and bought that mortgage. It's less than a couple of thousand dollars, and that's nothing to you."

"I know, son; but then you'll get them on your hands—"

"No, they're not like that, they're proud; Mrs. Groarty says they wouldn't take money from you, any more than Paul would. But if you bought the mortgage from the bank, they couldn't help that. Or you might buy the ranch, Dad, and rent it back to them. Paul says there's oil on that ranch—at least his Uncle Eby had seen it on top of the ground."

"There's thousands of ranches jist like that in California, son. Oil on top of the ground don't mean anything special."

"Well, Dad, you've always said you wanted to try some wild-catting; and you know, that's the only way you'll ever get what you talk about—a whole big tract that belongs to you, with no royalties to pay, and nobody to butt in. So let's take a chance on Paradise, and drive through there and camp out a few days and get some quail, and we'll see what we think of it, and we'll help those poor people, and give your kidneys a rest at the same time."

So Dad said all right; and he went away thinking to himself: "Gosh! Funny kid!"

III

The San Elido valley lay on the edge of the desert, and you crossed a corner of the desert to get to it; a bare wilderness of sun-baked sand and rock, with nothing but grey, dusty desert plants. You sped along upon a fine paved road, but the land was haunted by the souls of old-time pioneers who had crossed it in covered wagons or with pack-mules, and had left their bones beside many a trail. Even now, you had to be careful when you went off into side-trails across these wastes; every now and then a car would get stuck with an empty radiator, and the people would be lucky to get out alive.

You could get water if you sunk a deep well; and so there were fruit ranches and fields of alfalfa here and there. There came long stretches where the ground was white, like salt; that was alkali, Dad said, and it made this country a regular boob-trap. The stranger from the East would come in and inspect a nice fruit ranch, and would think he was making a good bargain to get the land next door for a hundred dollars an acre; he would set out his fruit-trees and patiently water them, and they wouldn't grow; nothing would grow but a little alfalfa, and maybe there was too much alkali for that. The would-be rancher would have to pull up the trees, and obliterate the traces of them, and set a real-estater to hunting for another boob.

Strapped to the running board of Dad's car, on the right hand side where Bunny sat, was a big bundle wrapped in a water-proof cover; they were camping out—which meant that the mind of a boy was back amid racial memories, the perils and excitements of ten thousand years ago. Tightly clutched in Bunny's two hands were a couple of repeating shot-guns; he held these for hours, partly because he liked the feel of them, and partly because they had to be carried in the open— if you shut them up in the compartment they would be "concealed weapons," and that was against the law.

Near the head of the valley a dirt road went off, and a sign said: "Paradise, eight miles." They wound up a little pass, with mountains that seemed to be tumbled heaps of rock, of every size and color. There were fruit ranches, the trees now bare of leaves, with trunks calcimined white, and young trees with wire netting about them, to keep away the rabbits.

The first rains of the season had fallen, and new grass was showing—the California spring, which begins in the fall.

The pass broadened out; there were ranch-houses scattered here and there, and the village of Paradise—one street, with a few scattered stores, sheltered under eucalyptus trees that made long shadows in the late afternoon light. Dad drew up at the filling station, which was also a feed-store. "Can you tell me where is the Watkins ranch?"

"There's two Watkinses," said the man. "There's old Abel Watkins—"

"That's the one!" exclaimed Bunny.

"He's got a goat-ranch, over by the slide. It ain't so easy to find. Was you plannin' to get there tonight?"

"We shan't worry if we get lost," said Dad; "we got a campin' outfit."

So the man gave them complicated directions. You took the lane back of the school house, and you made several jogs, and then there were about sixteen forks, and you must get the right one, and you followed the slide that took the water down to Roseville, and it was the fourth arroyo after you had passed old man Tucker's sheep-ranch, with the little house up under the pepper trees. And so they started and followed a winding road that had apparently been laid out by sheep, and the sun set behind the dark hills, and the clouds turned pink, and they dodged rocks that were too high for the clearance of the car, and crawled down into little gullies, and up again with a constant shifting of gears. There was no need to ask about the quail, for the hills echoed with the melodious double call of the flocks gathering for the night.

Presently they came to the "slide," which was a wooden runway carrying water—with many leaks, so that bright green grass was spread in every direction, and made food for a big flock of sheep, which paid no attention to the car, nor to all the tooting—the silly fools, they just *would* get under your wheels! And then came a man riding horseback; a big brown handsome fellow, with a fancy-colored handkerchief about his neck, and a wide-brimmed hat with a leather strap. He was bringing in a herd of cattle, and as he rode, his saddle and his stirrup-straps went "Squnch, squnch," which was a sort of thrilling sound to a boy, especially there in the evening quiet. Dad stopped, and the man stopped, and Dad said "Good evening," and the man answered, "Evenin'." He had a pleasant, open face, and told them the way; they couldn't miss the arroyo, because it was the only one that had water, and they would see the buildings as soon as they had got a little way up. And as they went on Bunny said, "Gee, Dad, but I wish we could live here; I'd like to ride a horse like that." He knew this would fetch Dad, because the man looked jist the way Dad thought a man ought to look, big and sturdy, colored brown and red like an Injun. Yes, it wouldn't take much to persuade Dad to buy the Watkins ranch for his son!

Well, they went wabbling on down the sheep-trail, counting the arroyos, whose walls loomed high in the twilight, crowned with fantastic piles of rocks. The lights of the car were on, and swung this way and that, picking out the road; until at last there was an arroyo with water—you knew it by the bright green grass—and they turned in, and followed a still more bumpy lane, and there ahead were some buildings, with one light shining in a window. It was the ranch where Paul Watkins had been born and raised; and something in Bunny stirred with a quite inexplicable thrill—as if he were approaching the birth-place of Abraham Lincoln, or some person of that great sort!

Suddenly Dad spoke. "Listen, son," he said. "There might be oil here—there's always one chance in a million, so don't you say nothin' about it. You can tell them you met Paul if you want to, but don't say that he mentioned no oil, and don't you mention none. Let me do all the talkin' about business."

It was a "California house," that is, it was made of boards a foot wide, running vertically, with little strips of "batting" to cover the cracks. It had no porch, whether front or back, nothing but one flat stone for a step. The paint, if there had ever been any, was so badly faded that you saw no trace of it by the lights of the car. On the other side of the lane, and farther up the little valley, loomed a group of sheds, with a big pen made of boards, patched here and there with poles cut from eucalyptus trees. From this place came the stirring and murmuring of a great number of animals crowded together.

The family stood in the yard, lined up to stare at the unaccustomed spectacle of an automobile entering their premises. There was a man, lean and stooped, and a boy, somewhat shorter, but already stooped; both of them clad in faded blue shirts without collar, and denim trousers, very much patched, held up by suspenders. There were three girls, in a descending row, in nondescript calico dresses; and in the doorway a woman, a little wraith of a woman, sallow and worn. All six of them stood motionless and silent, while the car came into the yard, and stopped, and the engine fell to a soft purring. "Good evening," said Dad.

"Howdy, brother," said the man.

"Is this the Watkins place!"

"Yes, brother." It was a feeble, uncertain voice, but it thrilled Bunny to the depths, for he knew that this voice was accustomed to "babble" and "talk in tongues." Suppose the family were to "let go," and start their "jumping" and "rolling" while Bunny was there!

"We're huntin'," Dad explained, "and we was told this would be a good place to camp. You got good water?"

"None better. Make yourself to home, brother."

"Well, we'll go up the lane jist a bit, somewheres out of the way. You got a big tree that'll give us shade?"

"Eli, you show 'em the oak-tree, and help 'em git fixed."

And again Bunny was thrilled; for this was Eli, that had been blessed of the Holy Spirit, and had the "shivers," and had healed old Mrs. Bugner, that had complications, by the laying on of hands. Bunny remembered every detail about this family, the most extraordinary he had ever come upon outside of a story-book.

IV

Eli moved up the lane, the car following. There was a big live oak tree with a clear space underneath, and Dad placed the car so that the lights streamed upon the space—you never needed to worry about darkness, when you were camping with a car! They stopped, and Bunny slid over the top of his door, and went to work on the straps which held the big bundle to the running-board. He had it off in a jiffy, and unrolled it, and quite magical were the things which came out of it. There was a tent, made of such light waterproofed silk that a structure eight feet square rolled up to a bundle which might have been a suit of clothes. There were the tent poles, made in several joints which screwed together; and the stakes, and a little camp hatchet to drive them with. There were three warm camping-blankets, besides the water-proof cover, which also made a blanket. There were two pneumatic pillows, and a pneumatic mattress, which you sat and puffed at until you were red in the face—it was great sport! Finally there was a canvas bag containing a set of camp utensils, all made of aluminum, and fitting one into another, everything with detachable handles; and aluminum boxes with several compartments for grub. When all these things were set in order, you could be as comfortable in the midst of a desert or on top of a mountain as in the best hotel room.

Mr. Watkins told Eli to help, but Dad said never mind, they knew jist what to do, and it was easy. So then Mr. Watkins told Eli to fetch a pail of water; and next he asked if they'd like some milk—they had only goat's milk, of course. Dad said that was fine; and Bunny was transported to the Balkans, or whatever exciting places he had read about, where the people live on goat's milk. Mr. Watkins said for Ruth to go git some; and Bunny was thrilled again, because Ruth was the sister that Paul loved, and that he said had "sense." Mr. Watkins called after her to fatch some "aigs" too; and Dad said they'd like some bread—and then Bunny got a shock, for the old man said they didn't git no bread, they hadn't room to raise grain, and corn didn't fill out good up here in the hills, so all they had was taters. And Dad said potatoes would do jist as good, they'd boil some for supper; and Mr. Watkins said they'd git 'em quicker if the missus was to bile 'em on the stove —thus showing a complete misapprehension of the significance of a camping-trip. Dad said no, they'd want a fire anyway; and Mr. Watkins said they was gettin' a nip o' frost every night now, and for Eli to rustle 'em up a lot of wood. This was easily done, for as soon as you went a few feet up the side of the arroyo you came upon desert brush, much of which was dead and dry, and Eli tore some of the bushes loose and dragged them down and broke them to pieces over his knee. Then he fetched a couple of stones—that also was easy, for you could hardly walk a dozen feet on the Watkins ranch without hitting your toe on a stone.

Very soon they had a fire going, and the potatoes boiling merrily in the pot, and a jar of bacon open and sizzling in the frying pan. Dad did the cooking—it was a dignified occupation, while Bunny hustled about and set the plates and things on the waterproof cover which served as a table cloth without a table. When the bacon was done, Dad cracked the eggs on the side of the pan, and fried them "with their eyes open." And there was the goat's milk, rich and creamy, cold from the "spring-house;" you didn't mind the strong flavor, because you per-suaded yourself it was romantic. The milk was served in aluminum cups which were part of the camping outfit; and also there was a plate of honey and comb—sage-honey, brown, and strong of flavor—which Ruth had brought.

Dad invited the family to come and have something, but the old man said no thanks, they had all et. Dad said would they please at least sit down, because they didn't seem comfortable jist standin' there; so Eli and the three girls, and their mother, who had joined them, all sat down on stones at a modest distance from the light, and Mr. Watkins sat on a stone a little closer, and while they ate Dad talked with him about the state of the weather, and of the crops, and about their way of life up here in the hills.

And when Dad and Bunny were done, and stretched them-selves on the blankets, feeling fine and comfortable, Mr. Watkins offered to have the tent put up by Eli, but Dad again said not to mind, it was very simple and would only take a few minutes. Then Mr. Watkins said that one of the gals would wash up for them, and Dad said all right, he'd like that; so Bunny got the pans and plates together, and the middle-sized girl, who went by the name of Meelie, carried them off to the house. And then they chatted some more; and Bunny saw that Dad was skilfully finding out about the family, and getting their confidence.

Suddenly came a critical moment in the acquaintance; there was a pause, and in a voice different from his usual one, solemn and burdened with feeling, Abel Watkins said: "Brother, may I ask a personal question?"

"Yes, sure," said Dad.

"Brother, are you saved?"

Bunny caught his breath; for he remembered what Paul had said about Mr. Watkins' way—if you said anything contrary to his religion, he would roll up his eyes and begin to pray out loud and "let go." Bunny had told Dad about this; and evidently Dad had figured out what to do. He replied in a tone no less solemn: "Yes, brother, we are saved."

"You been washed in the Blood?"

"Yes, brother, we been washed."

"What is your church, brother."

"It is called the Church of the True Word."

There was a pause. "I dunno as I know that there message," said Mr. Watkins.

"I am sorry," said Dad. "I should like to explain it, but we're not permitted to talk about our faith with strangers."

"But brother!" Mr. Watkins was evidently bewildered by that. "We are told in the Book that 'The Lord has called us for to preach the Gospel unto them;' and also, 'the Gospel must first be published among all nations.'"

"Brother," said Dad, still with the utmost earnestness, "I understand that; but according to our faith, we get to know men in friendship, and talk about our religion later. We all have to respect the convictions of others."

"Yes, brother," said Mr. Watkins; and his voice sort of faded away, and you could see he did not know what to say next. He looked at the members of his family, as if seeking support from them; but they hadn't yet said anything, except "Yes, Pap," when he gave them an order.

So it was up to Dad to relieve the embarrassment. "We come here to look for quail," he said. "I hear aplenty of 'em about."

V

It was growing so cold that the little fire no longer sufficed for comfort; so the Watkins family took their departure, and Dad and Bunny set up the tent, and stowed their goods in it, and Bunny did his job of puffing at the mattress until it was full. The stars were shining, so they made their bed in the open. After spreading the blankets, they took off their shoes and outside clothing, and laid them in the tent, and crawled under the blankets in a hurry—gee, but that cold made you jump! Bunny snuggled up into a ball, and lay there, feeling the night breeze on his forehead; and he remarked: "Say, Dad, what is the Church of the True Word?"

Dad chuckled. "The poor old crack-brain," he said; "I had to get some way to shut him up."

They lay still, and pretty soon Dad was breathing deeply. But the boy, though he was tired, did not go to sleep at once. He lay thinking: Dad's code was different from the one which Bunny had decided to follow. Dad would lie, whenever he considered it necessary; he would argue that the other person could not use the truth, or had no right to it in the

particular circumstances. And yet, this also was plain, Dad
didn't want Bunny to follow that same code. He would tell
Bunny to say nothing, but he would never tell Bunny to lie;
and as a rule, when he had to do any lying, he would do it
out of Bunny's presence! There were lots of things like that;
Dad smoked cigars, and he took a drink now and then, but he
didn't want Bunny to smoke or to drink. It was queer.

Bunny's head and face were cold, but the rest of him was
warm, and he was drifting, drifting off; his thoughts became a
blur—but then suddenly he was wide awake again. What was
that? The mattress was rocking; it rolled you from side to
side, so that you had to put out your elbows. "Dad!" cried
Bunny. "What's that?" And Dad came suddenly awake; he
sat up, and Bunny sat up—putting his two hands out to keep
himself steady. "By jiminy!" cried Dad. "An earthquake!"

Sure enough, an earthquake! And say, it was queer to feel
the solid ground, that you counted on, shaking you about like
that! The tree began to creak over their heads, as if a wind
were rocking it; they jumped up and got out from under.
A clamor arose, a bleating and moaning—the goats, who liked
this sensation even less than the humans, having no ideas of
earth structures and geological faults to steady their minds.
And then came another kind of clamor—from the Watkins
family, who apparently had rushed out of their cabin. "Glory
hallelujah! Jesus, save us! Lord, have mercy!"

Dad said, "It's all over now; let's crawl in, or we'll have
them folks up here praying over us."

Bunny obeyed, and they lay still. "Gee, that was a terrible
earthquake!" whispered the boy. "Do you think it knocked
down any cities?"

"It was likely jist local," answered Dad. "They have lots
of them up here in this hill country."

"Then you'd think the Watkinses would be used to them."

"They enjoy makin' a fuss, I guess. They don't have so
much excitement in their lives." And that was all Dad had to
say. He had plenty of excitements in his own life, and was
not specially interested in earthquakes, and still less in the
ravings of religious maniacs. He was soon fast asleep again.

But Bunny lay and listened. The Watkins family had
"let go," and were having a regular holy jumping service, out
there under the cold white stars. They shouted, they prayed,
they laughed and sang, they cried "Glory! Glory!" and

"Amen!" and "Selah!" and other words which Bunny did not understand, but which may have been Greek or Hebrew, or else the speech of the archangels. The voice of old Abel Watkins dominated, and the shrill screams of the children made a chorus, and the bleating of the goats was like a lot of double basses in an orchestra. Cold chills ran up and down Bunny's back; for, after all, the scientific mind in him, which knew about earth structures and geological faults, was only a century or two old, while the instinctive mind which pronounces incantations, is thousands and perhaps hundreds of thousands of years old. Priests have wrought frenzies and pronounced dooms, and because the priests believed them and the victims believed them, they have worked, and therefore they were believed more than ever. And now here was an incantation against earthquakes—and people down on their knees, with their hands in the air and their bodies swaying—

"Chariots to glory, chariots to glory,
Chariots to glory with the Holy Lamb!"

Bunny dozed off at last; and when he opened his eyes again, the dawn was pink behind the hills, and Dad was slipping into his khaki hunting-clothes. Bunny didn't stop to rub his eyes, he popped out of bed and got his clothes on quick—that cold just froze your bones!

He clambered up the hillside and began pulling dead brush, and got a fire going and the saucepan on. And then came Eli, bringing the clean plates and things, and asking whether they wanted last night's milk, which was cold, or this morning's milk, which was warm. "And say, did you feel that yearthquake!" asked Eli, in excitement. "Say, that was a terrible yearthquake! Does you-all have yearthquakes in you-all's parts?"

Eli had pale yellow hair, which had not been cut for some time, and had not been combed since the "yearthquake." He had pale blue eyes which protruded slightly, and gave him an eager look. He had a long neck with a conspicuous Adam's apple. His legs had grown too fast for the pair of worn trousers which were supposed to cover them, and which revealed Eli's shoes without socks. He stood there, staring at every detail of the equipment and clothing of these city strangers, and at the same time attempting to probe their souls. "What does this yere True Word teach about yearthquakes?"

Dad was busy frying the bacon and eggs, and he said they would like some of this morning's milk—which was a way to get rid of Eli. But it didn't take Eli long to come back, and he stood and followed every morsel of food as it went into their mouths; and he told them that the family had "prayed a mighty power" over that yearthquake, and yearthquakes meant the Holy Spirit was growing weary of fornications and drunkenness and lying in the world, and had they been doing any of them things? Bunny had but a vague idea concerning fornications, but he knew that Dad had told a whopping big lie just a short time before that "yearthquake," and he chuckled to himself as he thought what a portent the Watkinses would make out of that, if they knew!

The old man came, to make sure they were all right. Mr. Watkins was a bigger and taller edition of his son, with the same prominent pale blue eyes and large Adam's apple; his face was weather-beaten, heavily lined with care, and you could see he was a kind old man, honest and good, for all his craziness. He too talked about the "yearthquakes," and told about one which had shaken down brick and concrete buildings in Roseville a couple of years ago. Then he said that Meelie and Sadie were going out to school, and they would bring in some bread if the strangers wanted it. So Dad gave him a dollar, and they had a little argument, because Mr. Watkins said they wouldn't take only the regular price what they got for the eggs and the milk and the taters at the store, and they didn't want no pay for the camping out, because that wasn't no trouble to them, they was glad to see strangers; it was a lonely life they lived up in these here hills, and if it wasn't for the Lord and His Gospel, they would have very little pleasure in life.

VI

Dad and Bunny strapped on their cartridge belts, which went over their shoulders, and they loaded up the repeating shot-guns, and set out up the little valley and over the hills. Bunny didn't really care very much about killing quail, he was sorry for the lovely black and brown birds, that had such proud and stately crests, and ran with such quick twinkling legs, and made such pretty calls at sundown. But Bunny never said anything about these ideas, because he knew Dad liked to hunt, and it was the only way you could get him away from his work, and out into the open, which the doctor said was good for his health. Dad was quick as lightning to swing his gun, and it looked as if he didn't aim at all, but apparently he did; and he never made the mistake that Bunny did, of trying to shoot at two birds at the same time. Also Dad had time to watch Bunny and teach him—to make sure that they travelled in an even line, and didn't get turned so that one was out in front of the other's gun.

Well they tramped the hills and the valleys, and the birds rose, flying in every direction—a whir, and a grey streak— bang, bang—and either they were gone, or else they were down. But you didn't run to pick them up, because there would be others, they would hide and run, and you moved on, and banged some more, until finally you gathered up all you could find, bundles of soft warm feathers, spotted with blood. Sometimes they were still alive, and you had to wring their necks, and that was the part Bunny hated.

They filled their bags, and then they tramped back to camp, tired and hungry—oh gosh! Eli came, offering to clean the birds for them, and they were glad to let him, and gave him half the birds for the family to eat—it was pitiful to see the light in the eyes of the poor, half-starved youth when he heard this news. It isn't easy to live altogether in the spirit while you are not fully grown!

Eli took the birds to the house, where there was a chopping-block and pails of water handy; and meantime Bunny stretched out to rest, with his feet up in front. Suddenly he sat up with an exclamation. "Dad! Look at that!"

"Look at what?"

"At my shoe!"

"What is it?"

Bunny pulled his foot up close. "Dad, that's oil!"

"Are you sure?"

"What else could it be?" He got up and hopped over, so Dad could see for himself. "It's all up over the top."

"You sure it wasn't there before?"

"Of course not, Dad! It's still soft. I couldn't pack up my shoes like that and not see. I must have stepped into a regular pool of it. And oh, say—I'll bet you it was the earthquake! Some oil came up through a crack!"

Bunny took off his shoe, and Dad examined the find. He said not to get too much excited, it was a common thing to find oil pools close to the surface; as a rule they were small, and didn't amount to anything. But still, oil signs were not to be neglected; so after lunch they would go out again, and retrace their steps, and see what they could find.

It was easy for Dad to say not to get excited; so little did he know about his boy's mind! This was Bunny's dream, that he had had for years. You see, Dad was all the time talking about how he was going to get a real oil-tract some day—one that belonged to himself alone. He would figure up and show that when you paid a man a sixth royalty, you were really giving half your net profits—for you had to pay all the costs, not merely of the drilling, but of the upkeep and operation of the well, and the marketing of the oil. The other fellow got half your money—and didn't do a thing but own the land! Well, some day Dad would get a tract of his own discovery, and have it to himself, so that he could develop it right, and build an oil-town that he could run right, without any interference or any graft.

How was he to find that tract? That was Bunny's dream! He had lived the adventure in a score of different forms; he would be digging a hole in the ground, and the oil would come spouting up, and he would cover it over to hide it, and Dad would buy the land for miles around, and take Bunny into partnership with him; or else Bunny would be exploring a cave in the mountains, and he would fall into a pool of oil and get out with great difficulty. There were many different ways he had pictured—but never once had he thought of having an earthquake come and split open the ground, just before he and Dad were starting out after quail!

Bunny was so much excited that he hardly noticed the taste of that especially delicious meal of quail and fried potatoes and boiled turnips. Just as soon as Dad had got his cigar smoked, they set forth again, keeping their eyes on the ground, except when they lifted them to study the landmarks, and to figure whether they had taken this opening through the hills or that. They had walked half a mile or so, when a couple of quail rose, and Dad dropped them both, and walked over to pick them up, and then he called, "Here you are, son!" Bunny thought he meant the birds; but Dad called again, "Come over here!" And when the boy was near he said, "Here's your oil!"

There it was, sure enough; a black streak of it, six or eight inches wide, wiggling here and there, following a crack in the ground; it was soft and oozy, and now and then it bubbled, as if it were still leaking up. Dad knelt down and stuck his finger into it, and held it up to the light to see the color; he broke off a dead branch from a bush and poked it into the crevice to see how deep it was, and how much more came up. When Dad got up again he said, "That's real oil, no doubt of it. I guess it won't do any harm to buy this ranch."

So they went back. Bunny was dancing, both outside and inside, and Dad was figuring and planning, and neither of them bothered about the quail. "Did Mrs. Groarty ever tell you how much land there is in this ranch?" asked Dad.

"She said it was a section."

"We'll have to find out where it runs. And by the way, son, don't make any mistake, now, not a word to any one about oil, not even after I buy the place. It won't do any harm to get a lot of land in these here hills. You don't have to pay much for rocks."

"But listen, Dad; you'll pay Mr. Watkins a fair price!"

"I'll pay him a land price, but I ain't a-goin' to pay him no oil price. In the first place, he'd maybe get suspicious, and refuse to sell. He's got nothin' to do with any oil that's here—it ain't been any use to him, and wouldn't be in a million years. And besides, what use could a poor feeble-minded old fellow like that make of oil-money?"

"But we don't want to take advantage of him, Dad!"

"I'll see that he don't suffer; I'll jist fix the money so he can't give it away to no missionaries, and I'll always take care of him, and of the children, and see they get along. But there's surely not a-goin' to be no oil-royalties! And if any of them ask you about me, son, you jist say I'm in business—I trade in land, and all kinds o' stuff. Tell them I got a general store, and I buy machinery, and lend money. That's all quite true."

They walked on, and Bunny began to unfold the elements of a moral problem that was to occupy him, off and on, for many years. Just what rights did the Watkinses have to the oil that lay underneath this ranch? The boy didn't say any more to his father, because he knew that his father's mind was made up, and of course he would obey his father's orders. But he debated the matter all the way until they got back to the ranch, where they saw the old man patching his goat-pen. They joined him, and after chatting about the quail for a bit,

Dad remarked: "Mr. Watkins, I wonder if you'd come into the house and have a chat with me, you and your wife." And when Mr. Watkins said he would, Dad turned to Bunny, saying: "Excuse me, son—see if you can get some birds by yourself." And Bunny knew exactly what that meant—Dad thought that his son would be happier if he didn't actually witness the surgical operation whereby the pitiful Watkinses were to be separated from their six hundred and forty acres of rocks!

VII

Bunny wandered up the arroyo, and high on the slope he saw the goats feeding. He went up to watch them; and so he got acquainted with Ruth.

She sat upon a big boulder, gazing out over the rim of the hills. She was bare-headed and bare-legged, and you saw that she was outgrowing the patched and faded calico dress which was her only covering. She was a thin child, and gave the impression she was pale, in spite of her brownness; it was an anaemic brown, without much red in it. She had the blue eyes of the family, and a round, domed forehead, with hair pulled straight back and tied with a bit of old ribbon. She sat tending the flocks and herds, as boys and girls had done two thousand years ago in Palestine, which she read about in the only book to be found in the Watkins household. One week out of three she did this, ten or twelve hours a day, taking turns with her sisters. Very seldom did anyone come near, and now she was ill at ease as the strange boy came climbing up; she did not look at him, and her toes were twisted together.

But Bunny had the formula for entrance to her heart. "You are Ruth, aren't you?" he asked, and when she nodded, he said, "I know Paul."

So in a flash they were friends. "Oh, where?" She clasped her hands together and gazed at him.

Bunny told how he had been at Mrs. Groarty's—saying nothing about oil, of course—and how Paul had come, and just what had happened. She drank in every word, not interrupting; Ruth never did say much, her feelings ran deep, and made no foam upon the surface. But Bunny knew that her whole soul was hanging on his story; she fairly worshiped her brother. "And you never seen him again?" she whispered.

"I never really saw him at all," said Bunny; "I wouldn't know him now, if I was to meet him. You don't know where he is?"

"I've had three letters. Always it's a new place, and he says he ain't stayin' there. Some day, he says, he'll come to see me—jest me. He's scairt o' Pap."

"What would Pap do?"

"Pap would whale him. He's terrible set agin him. He says he's a limb of Satan. Paul says he don't believe what's in the Book? Do you believe it?"

Bunny hesitated, remembering Dad and his "True Word." He decided he could trust Ruth that far, so he told her he didn't think he believed quite everything. And Ruth, gazing into his eyes with intense concern, inquired: "What is it makes yearth-quakes?"

So Bunny told what Mr. Eaton had taught him about the earth's crust and its shrinking, and the faults in the strata, that were the first to yield to the strain. He judged by the wondering look on her face that this was the first hint of natural science that had ever come to her mind. "So you don't have to be scairt!" she said.

And then Bunny saw the signs of another idea dawning in her mind. Ruth was gazing at him, more intently than ever, and she exclaimed, "Oh! It was you sent that money!"

"Money?" said he, innocently.

"Four times they come a letter with a five-dollar bill in it, and no writin'. Pap said it was the Holy Spirit—but it was you! Warn't it?"

Thus directly attacked, Bunny nodded his confession; and Ruth colored, and began to stammer her embarrassed thanks—she didn't see how they could ever repay it—they were having such a hard time. Bunny stopped her—that was all nonsense, Dad had more money than he knew what to do with. Bunny explained that Dad was offering to buy the ranch from her parents, and pay off the mortgage, and let them live there for as long as they wanted to, for a very small rent. The tears began to run down Ruth's cheeks, and she had to turn her head away; she could not control herself, and it was embarrassing, because she had nothing with which to wipe the tears away, every bit of her dress being needed to cover her bare legs. She slid off the boulder, and had a little sobbing fit out of his sight; and Bunny sat troubled, not so much by this display of emotion, as by the ethical war going on in his soul. He told himself, it was really true that his motive in getting Dad to come here had been to help the Watkinses; the oil had been merely a pretext to persuade Dad. For that matter, Dad would have bought the ranch, just to help the family, and without any oil; it might have taken some arguing, but he would have done it! So Bunny comforted himself; but all the time he was thinking of that surgical operation going on down in the cabin, while he sat here letting Ruth think of him as a hero and a savior.

Dad had said, "What use could a poor feeble-minded old fellow like that make of oil-money?" Dad would argue the same way about Ruth, Bunny knew: she was healthy and happy, sitting out there in the sun with her bare brown legs; it was the best thing in the world for her—far better than if her legs were covered with costly silk stockings. And that was all right; but then—some little imp was starting arguments in Bunny's mind—why should other women have the silk stockings? There was Aunt Emma, at her dressing table, with not only silk stockings, but corsets imported from Paris, and a whole drug-store full of fixings; why would it not be good for Aunt Emma to sit out here in the sun with bare brown legs and tend the goats?

VIII

There was Dad's voice, calling Bunny; so he said good-bye, and ran down the arroyo. Dad was sitting in the car. "We're a-goin' in to Paradise," he said. "But first, change them oil shoes." Bunny did so, and put the shoes away in the back of the car. He hopped in, and they drove down the lane, and Dad remarked, with a cheerful smile, "Well, son, we own the ranch."

Dad was amused by the game he had just played, and told Bunny about it, overlooking the possibility of complications in Bunny's feelings. Dad had tactfully begun talking to Mr. and Mrs. Watkins about the family's lack of bread, and that had started Mr. Watkins telling the whole situation. There was a sixteen hundred dollar mortgage against the ranch, with nearly three hundred dollars interest overdue, and they had got a final notice from the bank, that foreclosure proceedings would begin next week. So Dad had explained that he wanted a place for summer camping, where his boy could have an outdoor life, and he would buy the ranch at a fair price. Poor Mrs. Watkins began to cry—she had been born on this place, it seemed, it was her homestead. Dad said she didn't need to worry, they might stay right on, and have all the farming rights of the place, he would lease it to them for ninety-nine years at ten dollars a year. The old man caught Dad's hand; he had known the Lord would save them, he said. Dad decided that was a good lead, so he explained that the Lord had sent him, according to the revelation of the True Word; after which Mr. Watkins had done jist whatever the Lord had told Dad to tell him to do!

And J. Arnold Ross had put the affairs of that family in order, you bet—there would be no more nonsense of giving away their money to missionaries! The Lord had told Dad to tell Mr. Watkins that he was to use his money to feed and clothe and educate his children. The Lord had furthermore told him that the equity in his land was not to be paid in cash, but was to consist of certificates of deposit in a trust-company, which would pay them a small income, about fifteen dollars a month—a lot better than having to pay the bank nearly ten dollars a month interest on a mortgage! Moreover, the Lord had directed that this money was to be held in trust for the children; and Bunny's friend Paul could thank Dad for having saved him a share. Mr. Watkins had said that one of his sons was a black sheep, and unworthy of the Lord's care, but Dad had stated it as a revelation of the True Word that there was no sheep so black but that the Lord would wash it white in His own good time; and Mr. Watkins had joyfully accepted this revelation, and he and his wife had put their names to a contract of sale which Dad had drawn up. The purchase price was thirty-seven hundred dollars, which had been Mr. Watkins' own figure—he had said that this hill land was worth five dollars an acre, and he figured his improvements at five hundred. They weren't really worth that, they were a lot of ruins, Dad said, but he took the old man's valuation of them. The contract provided that Mr. Watkins was to have water sufficient to irrigate two acres of land, which was jist about all he had under cultivation now; of course, Dad would give him more, if he could use it, but Dad wouldn't take no chance of disputes about water-rights. In the morning Mr. and Mrs. Watkins would drive out to Paradise, and Dad would hire a four-passenger car there, and drive them to some other town, where they could put the matter into escrow without too much talk.

In the meantime, Dad was on his way to Paradise, to set the town's one real estate agent to work buying more land for him. "Why don't you send for Ben Skutt?" asked Bunny; but Dad answered that Ben was a rascal—he had caught him trying to collect a commission from the other party. And anyhow, a local man could do it better—Dad would buy him with an extra commission, let Bunny watch and see how it was worked. Fortunately, Dad had taken the precaution to bring along a cashier's check for three thousand dollars. "I didn't know jist how long we might camp," he said, with his sly humor.

So they came to an office labelled, "J. H. Hardacre, Real Estate, Insurance and Loans." Mr. Hardacre sat with his feet on his desk and a cigar in his mouth, waiting for his prey; he was a lean, hungry-looking spider, and was not fooled for an instant by Dad's old khaki hunting-clothes—he knew that here was money, and he swung his feet to the floor and sat right up. Dad took a chair, and remarked on the weather, and asked about the earthquake, and finally said that he had a relative who wanted to live in the open for his health, and Dad had jist bought the Abel Watkins place, and he jist thought he'd like to raise goats on a bigger scale, and could he get some land adjoining? Mr. Hardacre answered right away, there was a pile of that hill-stuff to be had; there was the Bandy tract, right alongside—and Mr. Hardacre got out a big map and began to show Dad with his pencil, there was close to a thousand acres of that, but it was mostly back in the hills, and all rocks. Dad asked what it could be bought for, and Mr. Hardacre said all that hill-stuff was held at five or six dollars an acre. He began to show other tracts, and Dad said wait now, and he got a paper and pencil and began to jot down the names and the acreage and the price. Apparently everything around here could be bought—whenever the man failed to include any tract, Dad would ask "And what about that?" and Mr. Hardacre would say, "That's the old Rascum tract—yes, I reckon that could be got." And Dad said, "Let's list them all," and a queer look began to come over Mr. Hardacre's face—it was dawning upon him that this was the great hour of his life.

"Now, Mr. Hardacre," said Dad, "let's you and me talk

turkey. I want to buy some land, if it can be got reasonable. Of course as soon as people find you want it, they begin to boost the price; so let's get that clear, I want it jist enough to pay a fair price, and I don't want it no more than that, and if anybody starts a-boostin' you jist tell 'em to forget it, and I'll forget it, too. But all the land you can buy reasonable, you buy for me, and collect your commission from the seller in the regular way, and besides that, you'll get a five percent commission from me. That means, I want you to be my man, and do everything you can to get me the land at the lowest prices. I don't need to point out to you that my one idea is to buy quick and quiet, so people won't have time to decide there's a boom on. You get me?"

"Yes," said Mr. Hardacre. "But I'm not sure how quietly it can be done; this is a pretty small place, there's lots of talk, and it takes time to put through a deal."

"It won't take no time at all if you jist handle it my way and use good sense. You don't mention me, you do the buyin' for an unknown client, and you buy options for cash—that means, if the people are hereabouts, you close the deals right off."

"But that'll take quite a bunch of money," said Mr. Hardacre, a little frightened.

"I got a little change in my pocket," said Dad, "and I brought a cashier's check for three thousand, that I can turn into cash in the mornin'. You see, Mr. Hardacre, I happen to be jist crazy about quail shootin', and I had the idea that if I found plenty of quail, I'd get a little land to shoot over. But get this clear, I can shoot quail on one hill jist as good as on the next—and I don't let nobody mistake me for a quail!"

Dad took out of his card-case a letter from the president of a big bank in Angel City, advising whomever it might concern that Mr. James Ross was a man of large resources and the highest integrity. Dad had two such letters, as Bunny knew— one in the name of James Ross and the other in the name of J. Arnold Ross; the former was the one he used when he bought oil lands, and no one had ever yet got onto his identity in time!

Dad's proposition was this: He would make a contract with Mr. Hardacre, whereby Mr. Hardacre was authorized to buy ten-day options upon a long list of tracts, of specified acreage and at specified prices, paying five percent upon the purchase price for each option, and Dad agreeing to take up all these options within three days, and to pay Mr. Hardacre five percent on all purchases. Mr. Hardacre, torn between anxiety and acquisitiveness, finally said he guessed he'd take a chance on it, and if Dad threw him down, it would be easy for him to go into bankruptcy! He sat at his rusty typewriter and made two copies of the agreement, with a long list of tracts that were to cost Dad something over sixty thousand dollars. They read that over twice, and Dad signed it, and Mr. Hardacre signed it with a rather shaky hand, and Dad said fine, and counted out ten one hundred dollar bills on the desk, and said for Mr. Hardacre to get to work right away. He would do well to have his options all ready for the other party to sign, and Dad thought he had some blanks in the car—he wasn't jist sure, but he'd see. He went out, and Mr. Hardacre said to Bunny, quite casual and friendly-like, "What is your father's business, little man?" And Bunny, smiling to himself, answered, "Oh, Dad's in all kinds of business, he buys land, and lots of things." "What other things?" And Bunny said, "Well, he has a general store, and then sometimes he buys machinery, and he lends money." And then Dad came back; through a stroke of good fortune he happened to have a bunch of option blanks in his car—and Bunny smiled to himself again, for he never yet had seen the time when Dad did not happen to have exactly the right document, or the right tool, or the right grub, or the right antiseptic and surgical tape, stowed away somewhere in that car!

IX

They drove back to camp, and it was coming on to sunset again, and the quail were calling all over the hills. They passed the horseman bringing in the cattle, and he stopped and had a chat about the earthquake, and then he rode on, his saddle and stirrup-straps going "Squnch, squnch." And Dad said, "We'll maybe buy that fellow out before night, and you can ride his horse." And they went on, and presently came another fellow, this time on foot. He was a young chap, tall and lanky, but stooped as if he had hold of plow-handles; he was wearing country clothes and a straw hat, and he strode rapidly by them, staring hard at both of them, barely nodding in answer to Dad's friendly "Good evening." Dad remarked, "Queer-looking chap, that," and Bunny retained an impression of a face, very serious, with a large prominent nose, and a broad mouth drooping at the corners.

They went on, and came to their camp, and built a fire, and got themselves a gorgeous supper, with a panful of quail and bacon, and hot cocoa, and toast made of the bread which Meelie and Sadie had brought in, and some canned peaches which Bunny had bought. And after supper Bunny saw Ruth down by the goat-pen, and he strolled over to meet her; she gazed about timidly, to make certain no one else was near, and then she whispered, "Paul was here!"

Bunny started, amazed. *"Paul?"* And then suddenly the truth flashed over him. "That was Paul we passed on the road!" He described the figure to Ruth, and she said yes, that had been Paul; he had taken a "hitch-hike" to see her, as he had promised, and he had brought her fifteen dollars saved from his earnings. "I told him we didn't have no need for it now; but he left it."

Then Bunny cried: "Oh, why didn't he stop and talk to Dad and me? He barely nodded to us!"

Ruth was evidently embarrassed; it was hard to get her to talk about Paul any more. But Bunny persisted, he was so anxious to know Paul, he said, and it seemed as if Paul didn't like him. Only then was Ruth moved to tell him what Paul had said. "He was mad because Pap had sold the ranch. He says we hadn't ought to done it."

"But what else could you do?"

"He says we'd ought to sell the goats, and pay the bank, and raise strawberries, like some o' the folks is doin' here. We could git along and be independent—"

"Paul is so proud!" cried Bunny. "He's so afraid of charity!"

"No, it ain't exactly that," said Ruth.

"What is it then?"

"Well—it ain't very polite to talk about—" Ruth was embarrassed again.

"What is it, Ruth? I want to try to understand Paul."

"Well, he says your Pap is a big oil man, and he says there's oil on this ranch, and you know it, for he told you so."

There was a silence.

"Is your Pap an oil man?"

Bunny forced himself to answer. "Dad's a business man;

he buys land, and all kinds of things. He has a general store, and he buys machinery, and lends money." That was what Dad had ordered him to say, and it was strictly the truth, as we know; and yet Bunny considered himself a liar while he said it. He was misleading Ruth—gentle, innocent, trusting Ruth, with the wide, candid eyes and the kind, sweet features; Ruth, who was incapable of a hateful thought or a selfish impulse, whose whole life was to be one long immolation in the cause of the brother she loved! Oh, why did it happen that he had to practice deception upon Ruth?

They talked about Paul some more. He had sat up in the hills most of the afternoon and told his sister about himself. He was getting along all right, he said; he had got a job with an old lawyer who didn't mind his having run away from home, but would help him to keep hidden. This lawyer was what was called a free-thinker—he said you had a right to believe whatever you chose, and Paul was his gardener and handy man, and the old lawyer gave him books to read, and Paul was getting educated. It sounded wonderful, and terrible at the same time—Paul had read a book about the Bible, that showed it was nothing but old Hebrew history and fairy-tales, and full of contradictions and bloody murders and fornications, and things that there was no sense calling God's word. And Paul wanted Ruth to read it, and Ruth was in an agony of concern—but Bunny noticed it was Paul's soul she was afraid for, and not her own!

Then Bunny went back to Dad, and told him that was Paul they had passed on the road; and Dad said "Indeed?" and repeated that he was a "queer looking chap." Dad wasn't interested, he had no slightest inkling of Bunny's distress of soul; his thoughts were all on the great discovery, and the deals he was putting through. He lay on his back, with a pillow under his head, gazing up at the stars. "There's one thing sure, son"—and there was laughter in his voice; "either you and me move up to front row seats in the oil game, or else, by golly, we'll be the goat and sheep kings of California!"

CHAPTER V

THE REVELATION

I

Bunny was going to school. Aunt Emma and Grandmother and Bertie had got their way by incessant nagging, and he was no longer to be a "little oil gnome," and devote his time to learning to make money; he was going to be a boy like other boys, and have a good time, and wear athletic sweaters, and shout at football games, and be part of a great machine. Mr. Eaton had been spurred to a last suicidal effort, and had patched up the weak spots in the mental equipment of his charge, and Bunny had passed some examinations, and was a duly enrolled pupil in the Beach City High School.

This school occupied two blocks on the outskirts of town, and consisted of several buildings arranged on three sides of a square; elaborate and ornate buildings, a great pride to the city, as well as a strain upon its purse. The school was free, and to it came the sons and daughters of that part of the population which did not have to go to work before the age of eighteen or twenty. This meant all the moderately well-to-do people; and the boys and girls, thus constituting an economic stratum, proceeded to arrange themselves in sub-strata upon the same principle. Their "secret societies" were forbidden by the teachers, but flourished none the less; the basis of admission being wealth and the pleasant things which wealth buys—well-nourished bodies, and fashionable clothing, and easy manners, and a playful attitude towards life.

The young people were collected into small herds, and rushed about from room to room, where culture was handed out to them in properly measured doses. It was an enormous education-factory, and the parents had paid for the best possible equipment, but by some process impossible to explain, it was gradually being taken away from the teachers, and turned over to the pupils. Every year the young people seemed to be less interested in work, and more absorbed in what were called "outside activities"—the athletic-field, the tennis and basket-ball courts, the big swimming pool and the dancing floor. The boys and girls were making for themselves a separate world, having its own standards, its own secret life. They wore pins and badges, and had pass-words and grips with esoteric significance; they had elaborate codes, having to do with the wearing of flowers, or the color of your neck-tie, or the ribbon on your hat, or the angle at which you affixed a postage stamp to an envelope.

It was a herd life, based in part upon money-prestige, like the life of the adults, and in part upon athletic prowess. It consisted in rushing about from one mass-event to another mass-event. You pitted the powers of your team against those of some other team, and the ability of your mob to shout louder than the other mob; you got together and rehearsed these shoutings, while the teams rehearsed the battles over which you were to shout. It was all practice for the later and more real glories of college and university, where the financially and athletically more powerful students would be taken up by the great fraternities, and would perform their social and athletic functions with skill and grace made perfect.

Bunny, as we know, possessed the requirements of a fraternity career; he had Anglo-Saxon features, and plenty of big sweaters, and drove to school in a car of that year's model. He was taken up by an exclusive society, and was soon in demand for whatever was going on. He was enormously interested in everything; he had never imagined there were so many young people in the world before, and he wanted to know them all. He raced about with them from one thing to another, and watched with open eyes and listened with open ears to everything that came from either the teachers or the pupils. But all the time there was something which set him apart from the rest—something sober and old-fashioned and "queer." It came, no doubt, from his knowing so much about the oil business; Bertie was right in her cruel remark that he had oil stains under his finger-nails. He would never share the idea of other darlings of luxury, that "money grows on trees;" he knew that it comes by hard and dangerous work. Also, Bunny had to meet the situation at home, which he understood quite clearly; his father wasn't at all sure that high school was the best place for a boy, and was watching and listening all the time, to see what sort of ideas Bunny was getting. So the boy was always comparing the school's kind of education with Dad's kind, and which was really right?

Before starting out in his new career Bunny received what parents know as a "serious talk"; and that was curious and puzzling. First, Dad was going to give him a car, and there must be rules about it. He must give his word never to exceed the speed limit, whether in the city or outside; and that was certainly a curious case of the double standard of morals! But Dad met it frankly; he was mature, and could judge about speeds; moreover, he had important business for his excuse, but Bunny was to start for school early, and the rest of the time he would be driving for pleasure. He might take out others in his car, but he must never let anyone drive the car but himself; Dad had no money to run a free garage for a high school fraternity, and it would be convenient for Bunny to be able to say, once for all, that his father had laid down the law in that matter.

Furthermore, Dad wanted Bunny to promise him not to smoke tobacco or drink liquor until he was twenty-one. Here again was the "double standard," and Dad was frank about it. He had learned to smoke, but wished he hadn't; if Bunny wanted to acquire the habit, it was his right, but Dad thought he ought to wait until he was old enough to know what he was doing, and until he had got his full growth. And the same applied to liquor. Dad drank very little now, but there had been a time in his life when he had come close to becoming a drunkard, and so he was afraid of it, and Bunny's being allowed to go to college—at least on Dad's money—would have to be dependent upon his promising to avoid the drinking-bouts. Bunny said all right, sure; that was easy enough for him. He would have liked to ask more about Dad's own story, but he did not quite like to. He had never seen Dad drunk; and it was a startling idea to contemplate.

Finally there was the matter of women; and here, apparently, Dad could not bring himself to be frank. Two things he said: first, Bunny was known to have a father with a pile of money, and this exposed him to one of the worst perils of young men. All kinds of women would be a-tryin' to get a-hold of him, jist in order to get him to spend money on them, or to blackmail him; and Bunny would be disposed to trust women, so he must be warned about this. Dad told him dreadful stories about rich young men, and the women into whose hands they had fallen, and how it had wrecked their lives and brought shame upon their families. And then, there was the matter of disease;

loose women were very apt to have diseases, and Dad told something about this, and about the quacks who prey upon ignorant and frightened boys. If one got into trouble of that sort, one must go to a first-class doctor.

And that was all Dad had to say. Bunny took it gratefully, but he wished there might have been more; he would have liked to ask his father many questions, but he could not bring himself to do it, in the face of his father's evident shrinking. Dad's manner and attitude seemed to say that there was something so inherently evil about sex that you jist couldn't bring yourself to talk about it; it was a part of your life that you lived in the dark, and never dragged out into the light. Bunny's idea was that his father's discourse didn't apply very much to himself. He knew there were dirty boys, but he was not one, and never expected to be.

The matter was made easier for Bunny by the fact that he very soon fell severely in love. There were such swarms of charming young feminine things in the school, it was simply not possible to escape them, especially when your possessions and social standing were such that so many of them set out after you! Some young misses were too bold in their advances, or too obviously coy, and repelled the shy lad; the one who secured him was very demure and still, so that his imagination could endow her with romantic qualities. Rosie Taintor was her name, and she had hair that made a tail halfway down her back, and was fluffy on her forehead, with golden glints; she was even more shy than Bunny, and had little conversation, but that was not necessary, for she had a great power of admiration, and had a phrase by which she expressed it: things were "wonderful"; they grew more and more "wonderful," with soulful, mysterious whispers; the oil business was especially "wonderful," and Rosie never tired of being told about it, which pleased Bunny, who had much to tell. Rosie's father, and also her mother, were dentists, and this is not an especially romantic occupation, so naturally the child thought it thrilling to dash about the country as Bunny did, and direct armies of labor, and command vast treasures to flow out of the earth.

Bunny would take her for rides; and when they were out in the country, where it was safe, Bunny would drive with one hand, and the other hand would rest on Rosie's, and truly "wonderful" were the thrills that would steal over both of them. They were content to ride that way for hours; or to get out and wander in the hills, and gather wild flowers, and sit and watch the sunset. Bunny was full of reverence, and when once or twice he dared so far as to place a kiss upon his adored one's cheek, it was with almost religious awe. When the weather was not suitable for outdoor courtship, he would visit her home, where the mother and father had a hobby, the collecting of old English prints; these were framed on all the walls, and there were stacks of them you could look at, quaint eighteenth-century scenes of hunting gentlemen in red coats with packs of hounds, and red-cheeked barmaids serving pots of ale to topers with big pipes. Bunny would look at these for hours—for it took only one hand to turn them over. What is there that is not "wonderful," when you are so young, and at the same time so good? It made Bunny walk on air, just to buy a new straw-hat, and meet his chosen one upon the street, and anticipate her comments!

II

When Dad took his business trips now he took them alone; that is, unless he could arrange them for week-ends and holidays. He didn't like going alone; and Bunny for his part, always had a part of his mind on Dad, and when Dad got back, he would hear all the details of how things were going.

There were six wells now at Lobos River, and they were all "paying big." Dad had four more drilling, and had deepened eleven of his old Antelope wells, and had a pipe line there, through which a river of wealth was flowing to him. On the Bankside lease he had six wells, all on production, and he had paid Mr. Bankside something over a million dollars of royalty, and had only got started, so he said. He had a good well on the next lease, the Ross-Wagstaff, and three more drilling, and out about half a mile to the north he was opening up new territory with the Ross-Armitage No. 1.

It was amazing to see what had happened to the Prospect Hill field. All over the top of the hill and the slopes a forest of oil derricks had arisen, and had started marching across the fields of cabbages and sugar beets. Seeing them from the distance, in the haze of sunset, you could fancy an army of snails moving forth—the kind which have crests lifted high in the air. When you came near, you heard a roaring and a grumbling, as of Pluto's realm; at night there was a scene of

enchantment, a blur of white and golden lights, with jets of
steam, and a glare of leaping flame where they were burning
gas that came roaring out of the earth, and which they had no
way to use.

Yes, when you drove past, sitting in a comfortable car, you
might mistake it for fairyland. You had to remind yourself
that an army of men were working here, working hard in
twelve hour shifts, and in peril of life and limb. Also you had
to remember the pulling and hauling, the intrigue and treachery,
the ruin and blasted hopes; you had to hear Dad's stories of
what was happening to the little fellows, the thousands of investors who had come rushing to the field like moths to a
candle-flame. Then your fairyland was turned into a slaughter-
house, where the many were ground up into sausages for the
breakfast of the few!

Dad had a big office now, with a manager and half a dozen
clerks, and he sat there, like the captain of a battle-ship in his
conning tower. Whatever might happen to the others, Dad
took care of himself and his own. He had come to be known
as the biggest independent operator in the field, and all sorts of
people came to him with propositions; new, wonderful, glowing
schemes—with Dad's reputation for solidity, he could organize
a ten or twenty million dollar company, and the investing public
would flock to him. But Dad turned all such things down; he
would wait, he told Bunny, until Bunny was grown up, and
through with this here education business. They would have
a pile of cash by that time and would do something sure enough
big. And Bunny said all right, that suited him. He hoped the
"something big" might be at Paradise, for then he would have
a real share in it. Dad said, sure, the Watkins ranch was his
discovery, and when they come to drill there, the well would
be known as the Ross Junior.

They had made no move there; they were waiting, because
of an unfortunate slip-up in the negotiations for the land. An
unkind fate had willed that Mr. Bandy, owner of the big Bandy
tract, had been away from home on the day that Mr. Hardacre
had collected his options; and when Mr. Bandy got back, and
learned about all the sudden purchases, he became suspicious,
and decided that he would hold onto his land. At least, it
amounted to that, for he raised his price from five dollars an
acre to fifty! What made this especially bad, the Bandy tract
lay right next to the Watkins section; it was over a thousand

acres, and ran near to where Dad and Bunny had found the oil—in fact, Dad thought the streak of oil was on Mr. Bandy's land, he couldn't be sure without a survey. They would wait, Dad said, and let Mr. Bandy stay in pickle for a few years. It was like a cat watching a gopher hole, and which would get tired first. Bunny asked which was Mr. Bandy, the cat or the gopher; and Dad replied that if anybody ever mistook Jim Ross for a gopher, he would jist try to show them their mistake.

So they were waiting. Some day that mythical relative of Dad's, who was an invalid, was coming into those rocky hills and tend a few thousand goats; and meantime most of the ranches were rented to the people who had formerly owned them. Three or four were vacant, but Dad didn't worry about that; he would leave them to the quail, he said, and told Mr. Hardacre to put up a thousand "No Trespassing" signs over the whole twelve thousand acres he had bought, so as to impress Mr. Bandy with Dad's gluttonous attitude toward small game.

III

The greater part of the civilized world had gone to war. The newspapers which Dad and Bunny read turned themselves into posters, with streamer-heads all the way across the page, telling every day of battles and campaigns in which thousands, and perhaps tens of thousands of men had lost their lives. To people in California, so peaceful and prosperous, this was a tale of "old, unhappy far-off things," impossible to make real to yourself. America had officially declared neutrality; which meant that in the "current events" class, where Bunny learned what was going on in the world, the teacher was expected to deal with the war objectively, and to rebuke any child who expressed a partisanship offensive to any other child. To business men like Dad it meant that they would make money out of both sides; they would sell to the Allies direct, and they would sell to the Central powers by way of agents in Holland and Scandinavia, and they would raise a howl when the British tried to stop this by the blockade.

The price of "gas" of course began to mount immediately. It seemed to Bunny a rather dreadful thing that Dad's millions should be multiplied out of the collective agony of the rest of the world; but Dad said that was rubbish, it wasn't his fault that people in Europe insisted on fighting, and if they wanted things he had to sell, they would pay him the market price. When speculators came to him, showing how he, with his big supply of cash, could make a quick turn-over, buying shoes, or ships, or sealing-wax, or other articles of combat, Dad would reply that he knew one business, which was oil, and he had made his way in life by sticking to what he knew. When representatives of the warring powers invited him to sign contracts to deliver oil, he would answer that nothing gave him more pleasure than to sign such contracts; but they must change their European bonds into good American dollars, and pay him with these latter. He would offer to take them to the little roadside restaurant where they could see the sign: "We have an arrangement with our bank; the bank does not sell soup, and we do not cash checks."

On the basis of his father's reputation for unlimited re-sources and invincible integrity, Bunny had been chosen treasurer of the freshman football team, a position of grave responsibility, which entitled him to sit on the side-lines and help the cheer-leaders. While on the other side of the world men were staggering about in darkness and mud and snow, blind with fatigue, or with their eyes shot out, or their entrails dragging in the dirt, the sun would be shining in California, and Bunny would be facing a crowd of one or two thousand school children, lined up on benches and shrieking in unison: "Rah, rah, rah, slippery, slam!—wallibazoo, bazim, bazam! Beach City." He would come home radiant, with barely enough voice left to tell the score; and Aunt Emma would sit beaming— he was being like other boys, and the Ross family was taking its position in society.

The Christmas holidays came; and Dad was working too hard, everybody declared; and Bunny said, "Let's go after quail!" It wasn't so hard to pull him loose now, for they had their own game-preserve—it sounded most magnificent, and it would obviously be a great waste not to use it. So they packed up their camping outfit, and drove to Paradise, and pitched their tent under the live oak tree; and there was the ranch, and the Watkins family, the same as before, except that the row of children was a couple of inches taller, and the girls each had a new dress to cover their growing brown legs. Things were a whole lot easier with the family, since they had an income of fifteen dollars a month from the bank, instead of an outgo of ten dollars.

Well, Dad and Bunny went after the quail, and got a bagful; and incidentally they examined the streak of oil, now grown dry and hard, and covered with sand and dust. They went back to camp and had a good feed, and then came Ruth, to get their soiled dishes; she was taking Eli's place, she explained, because Eli had been called to attend Mrs. Puffer, that was ill with pains in her head. Eli had been doing a power of good with his healing, it had made a great stir, and people were coming from all over to have him lay hands on them. Bunny asked if Ruth had heard from Paul, and she answered that he had come to see her a couple of months ago, and was getting along all right.

She seemed a little shy, and Bunny thought it might be on account of Dad lying there listening, so he strolled back to the house with her, and on the way Ruth confided to him that Paul had brought her a book to read, to show her she didn't have to believe the Bible if she didn't want to; and Pap had caught her with that book, and he had took it away and threw it in the fire, and had whaled her good.

Bunny was horrified. "You mean he beat you?" And Ruth nodded; she meant that. "What did he use?" cried Bunny, and she answered that he had used a strap off'n the harness. "And did he hurt you?" She answered that he had hurt right smart, it had been a week afore she was able to sit down. She was a little surprised at his indignation, for it didn't seem to her out of the way that a girl almost sixteen years old should be "whaled" by her Pap; he meant it for her good, he thought it was his duty to save her soul from hell-fire. And Bunny could see that Ruth wasn't sure but her Pap might be right.

"What was the book?" he asked, and she told him it was called "The Age of Reason"; it was an old-time book, and maybe Bunny had heard of it. Bunny never had; but naturally, he resolved to find a copy, and read it, and tell Ruth all that was in it.

He went back to his father, and poured out his indignation; but Dad took much the same view of the matter as Ruth. Of course it was a shame for a child to be whipped for trying to get knowledge, but old Abel Watkins was the boss in his own family, and had the right to discipline his children. Dad said he had heard of the book; it was by a famous "infidel" named Tom Paine, who had had something to do with the American Revolution. Dad had never read the book, but it was easy to understand how Mr. Watkins had been outraged by it; if Paul was reading such things, he had surely traveled far.

Bunny couldn't rest there; it was too horrible that Ruth should be beaten because she tried to use her mind. Bunny kept talking about it all afternoon, there ought to be a law to prevent such a thing. Dad said the law would only interfere in case the father had used unusual and cruel punishment. Bunny insisted that Dad ought to do something, and Dad laughed, and asked if Bunny wanted him to adopt Ruth. Bunny didn't want that, but he thought Dad should use his influence with the old man. To this Dad answered, it would be foolish to try to reason with a crank like that, the more you argued the more set he would become; what influence Dad possessed, he had got by pretending to agree with the old man's delusions.

But Bunny wouldn't drop the subject—Dad could do something if he would, and he absolutely must. And so Dad thought for a bit, and then he said: "I'll tell you, son; what you and me have got to do is to get a new religion." Bunny knew this tone—his father was "kidding" him, and so he waited patiently. Yes, Dad said, they would have to elaborate the True Word; they must make it one of the cardinal points in this Word that girls were never to be beaten by men. There would have to be a special revelation, jist on that point, said Dad; and so Bunny began to take an interest. Dad asked him questions about Paul, what Paul believed, and what Paul had said about Ruth, and what Ruth had told him about herself. Bunny realized that Dad was going to try something, and he waited.

They shot some more quail, and came back and built a big camp-fire, and had a jolly supper, and then Dad said, "Now let's go start that there religion." So they strolled down to the cabin, Dad in deep thought, and Bunny on tiptoe with curiosity—for you never could tell what Dad would do when he was in a mood of mischief. In after years the boy used to look back upon this moment and marvel; what would their emotions have been, had they been able to foresee the consequences of their jest—a "revival" movement that was to shake the whole State of California, or at any rate the rural portion of it, and of several states adjoining!

IV

Well, old Mr. Watkins invited them cordially to come in; and Sadie and Meelie gave up their chairs and sat on a box or something in a corner of the room. It was the first time that Bunny had been inside the Watkins' home, and it gave him a shuddering sense of poverty. It was bare boards inside, the same as out; there was a big, unpainted table, and six unpainted chairs, a few shelves with crockery, a few pans hanging on the wall, and a stove that rested on a stone where one leg was broken. That was everything, literally everything—save for a feeble kerosene lamp, which enabled you to see the rest. There were two other rooms to the cabin, one for the husband and wife, and the other for the three girls, who slept in one bed. Attached to the back of the house was a shed with two bunks against the wall, the top one occupied by Eli, and the other vacant, a reminder of the sheep that had strayed.

Eli was in the room, having come back from his expedition. Eli was now eighteen, and had attained the full stature of a man; also his voice was that of a man, except that now and then it cracked and went up in a way that would have been comical, if anybody that listened to Eli ever had a sense of fun. Just now he was telling his parents and wondering sisters how the Holy Spirit had blessed him again, the shivers had seized him, and old Mrs. Puffer had been instantly relieved of her pains. Mr. Watkins said "Amen!" three or four times, very loud, and then he turned to Dad, remarking, "The Lord blesses us in our children." Dad said yes, that was true, possibly more true than they knew; he asked, had Mr. Watkins ever thought of the possibility that the Lord might send a new revelation into the world? And instantly you could see the family sit up, and fix their eyes upon Dad, the whole six of them, as rigid as so many statues. What did their visitor mean?

Dad explained: there had been two revelations so far, to be found in the old and the new testaments; why mightn't it be that the Holy Spirit was preparing another? For a long time the followers of the True Word had awaited this fulfillment; the promise was in the Book, for anyone to read. This New Dispensation would supersede the others, and naturally would have to be different from the others, and the followers of the old message might fail to recognize it, jist like the previous case. Didn't that seem reasonable? Dad asked; and Mr. Watkins answered promptly that it did, and for Dad to go on. So Dad said that this True Word was to be revealed through the minds of men, and would be a message of freedom; the Holy Spirit wanted us to seek boldly, and not be afraid; and presently out of the seeking of many minds the Truth would come—perhaps from some one who had been despised and rejected, that would become the corner stone of the new temple. Dad said all this with the deepest solemnity, and Bunny listened, not a little bewildered; he had never had any idea that Dad knew so much Bible-talk—as much as any preacher!

So it seemed to the Watkins family also. The old man drank in every word, and insisted that Dad should reveal to them all he knew. And Dad told them that they had one son, whose words had been reported to him, and seemed to him to bear the true spirit of the Third Revelation. Dad had met this son, and been struck by his appearance, for he looked jist like what followers of the True Word had been taught to expect— he was tall, and had fair hair and blue eyes, and his look was grave and his voice deep. So Dad believed that the bearer of this message of freedom, to which they were charged to listen, was their eldest son, Paul, whom they mistakenly had driven from among them.

Well, you should have seen the sensation in that family! Old Mr. Watkins sat with his jaw dropped down, as thunder-struck as if Dad had sprouted a pair of angel's wings before his eyes. Mrs. Watkins' thin face wore a look of utter rapture, and her two stringy hands were clasped together in front of her chin. As for Ruth, she seemed just about ready to slide off her chair and onto her knees. Everybody seemed to be pleased but one, and that was Eli. Eli was glaring at Dad, and suddenly he sprang from his chair, his face contorted; he shouted, and his voice cracked, and went up shrill and piercing: "Can he show the signs?" And as Dad delayed to answer, he shouted again, "I say, can he show the signs? Has he healen the sick? Has he casted out devils? Do the lame rise up and walk? Do the dying take up their beds? Tell me that! Tell me!"

Well, sir, it floored Dad; for Eli was the last person in the room from whom he would have expected an onslaught. Dad thought of Eli as a gawky farm yokel, who came, with no socks on, and pants that did not reach his shoe-tops, to bring the milk and take away the dirty dishes; but here was Eli, transformed into a prophet of the Lord, and blazing, after a fashion not unknown to prophets, with a white flame of jealousy! "*I* am him who the Holy Spirit has blessed! *I* am him who the Lord hath chosen to show the signs! Look at me, I say—look at me! Ain't my hair fair and my eyes blue? Ain't my face grave and my voice deep?"—and sure enough, Eli's voice had gone down again, and Eli was a grown man, a seer of visions and pronouncer of dooms. "I say beware of he that cometh as a serpent creeping in the night, to tempt the souls of they that waver! I say, beware the spawns of Satan, that lure the soul with false doctrine, and blast away the Rock of Ages! I give the signs, that all men may know! I stand by the Four Square Gospel, that was good enough for my fathers and is good enough for me! Glory Hallelujah, and Salvation unto they that has washed their sins in the Blood of the Lamb! Hallelujah! Hallelujah!"

Eli flung up his hands with a mighty shriek, and old Mr. Watkins rose from his chair, and shouted "Glory! Glory!" And then a horrible thing began to happen, right there before your eyes; a kind of convulsion seized upon Eli, his eyes rolled up, and foam appeared at his lips, and a series of wriggles started at his shoulders and ran out at his finger tips; and his knees began to knock together, and his features to work in a kaleidescope of idiocy. He began to bellow, in an enormous voice, that you would never have dreamed could be contained in a body of his size; and what he said was—but you couldn't reproduce it, because no one can recollect a jabber of syllables, and anyhow, it would look too silly on a printed page. But it had some kind of spell for old Mr. Watkins, it caused him to throw his two hands up into the air, and jerk his arms as if he were trying to jump up to heaven with them. "Let go!' Let go!" he shrieked, and began to double up and straighten out again as if he had been shot through the middle; and old Mrs. Watkins—poor frail little woman, made of nothing but bones and whipcord covered with skin—began to rock and sway in her chair, and the two little girls slid off onto the floor and wallowed on their stomachs, and Ruth sat white-faced and terrified, gazing at the two strangers, and from them to Eli,

bellowing his jabber of syllables like a furious malediction
at Dad.

And that was the end of it. Dad backed out, and Bunny
with him, and the two of them crept away through the darkness
to their camp; and all the way Dad whispered, "Jesus Christ!"

V

The next day was Sunday, or the Sabbath, as the Watkinses
called it; and by the time Dad and Bunny had got their breakfast in the morning, the family had hitched up their one old
horse to their one old wagon, and departed—the father and
mother riding, and the four young people walking ahead, on
their way to the weekly debauch at the Apostolic Church of
Paradise.

That left Dad and Bunny to hunt quail, undisturbed by
public opinion; and in the afternoon they got into their car,
and rode about to make an inspection of the domain they had
purchased, and to meet some of the neighbors, now their tenants.
Dad had a map, showing the various tracts, and as they drove
he was laying out roads and other improvements in his mind;
some day this country would all be settled, he said—and the
thing to begin with was a rock-crusher! There came riding
along the fellow on horseback whom they had met the first
time; they knew now that it was young Bandy, the son of
their enemy, and they exchanged greetings—the cat and the
gopher being polite!

They rode up into one of the arroyos where there was a
vacant ranch, the Rascum place. They were surprised to find
a charming little bungalow, with a good porch in front,
completely buried under a bougainvillea vine, which would be
a mass of purple blossoms in the spring. "Gee, Dad," exclaimed
Bunny, "this is where we ought to come and stay!" The other
answered, there should be somebody to keep it up; there was
a well here, and with a little fixing it would be quite a place.
There was even a cat, and she looked contented; there were
plenty of gophers, Dad said, and it was a good sign for victory
over Mr. Bandy! They laughed together.

They followed the "slide" down to Roseville, and saw the
old mission there, and had supper, and came round by way
of Paradise in the evening; and on the outskirts of the town,
just after turning off the highway, they came on a building,

standing in a grove of trees, with lights shining in the windows, and a murmur of voices within. One voice rose above the others, a bellowing voice which needed no identifying. It was the "holy jumpers'" church, and Eli was preaching. "Oh, Dad," exclaimed Bunny, "let's hear him!' So they parked the car and got out, and stood in the shadow of the trees; and this is what they heard:

"—for the days of your trials is ended. Come unto me all ye that travels and is heavy ladened and I will refreshen you. For I am the bearer of the True Word! I bring the signs— the sick shall be healen, and the devils shall be casted out— the lame shall walk and the dying shall take up their beds! Brethren, I am sent for to announce unto you the Third Revelation! Once moreover the Holy Spirit disclothes Himself, the New Gospel is unfolded to you, according to the prophesies hithertofore explained. There was an Old Dispensation, and it was outgrowed and supercedened, and now the New Testament is outgrowed and supercedened in the same way, and the True Word of freedom is handed unto you, and I am him that is sent to make it known. And woe unto they that doth not heed, for he shall be casted down into the bottomless pit, and it were better that a millstone was hanged about his neck and he was drowned in the sea. Woe unto he that cometh as a serpent creeping in the night, to tempt the souls of they that waver! I say, beware the spawns of Satan, that lure the soul with false doctrine, and blast away the Rock of Ages! I give the signs that all men may know; and he that follows me will I bless, and his pains shall be healen, and he shall see the glory of God and receive the gifts of the Holy Spirit, the talking in tongues! Glory Hallelujah, and Salvation unto they that has washed their sins in the Blood of the Lamb! Hallelujah!"

The bellowing voice of Eli was drowned in a chorus of acclamation, shouts and shrieks and groans, as if the whole congregation of the Apostolic Church of Paradise were jumping in their seats or rolling on the floor. As a matter of fact, it was but a little while before that very thing was happening; but Dad wouldn't let Bunny go near to see it, it was too degrading, he said, and they got into their car and drove off. "Gee whiz, Dad!" exclaimed the boy. "Eli was saying every word that you taught him! Do you suppose he really believes it all?"

Dad answered that only the Holy Spirit could tell that. Eli was a lunatic, and a dangerous one, but a kind that you couldn't put in an asylum, because he used the phrases of religion.   He hadn't wits enough to make up anything for himself, he had jist enough to see what could be done with the phrases Dad had given him; so now there was a new religion turned loose to plague the poor and ignorant, and the Almighty himself couldn't stop it.

There came next day a man riding out from Paradise, bringing a telephone call for Dad; Ross-Armitage No. 1 was in trouble, and Dad was needed at once.   Before they started for home Bunny managed to have a talk with Ruth, and told her a wonderful plan that had occured to him: Dad said there ought to be some one to live on the Rascum place and keep it up, and Bunny suggested that Dad should buy some goats and stock the place, and rent it to Paul, and let Ruth go there to keep house for him; then Ruth could read all the books she pleased, and there would be nobody to beat her.

Ruth looked happy, but she said Paul would never do that, he wouldn't take anybody's charity.   Bunny insisted that it wouldn't be charity at all—Dad really wanted some one on the ranch, and he would make a business arrangement, Paul would work the place, and pay Dad part of the money.   But Ruth sighed, and said anyhow, Pap would never let her go; he was more than ever set against Paul, on acount of Eli, who was jealous of Paul, and of Paul's claim to know things.   Eli had always been that way, but now he was worse, because the city people had backed Paul, and so Pap didn't even want her to talk with Bunny or his father, for fear she would lose her faith.

Ruth was just Bunny's age, almost sixteen, and Bunny said it wouldn't be but two years before she would be of age, and then she could go where she pleased, Dad said; she could join Paul, or she and Paul could run the Rascum ranch.   Bunny told her not to be afraid, but to wait, and not bother with that fool jumping business; it was hateful nonsense, and it wouldn't hurt her the least bit to think for herself, and use her common-sense, and wait till she was grown up.   Dad would be glad to help her get an education, and get free from Eli and his prophesying—for Ruth might be sure Dad didn't like Eli any better than Eli liked Dad!

VI

Three months passed, and Dad brought in the Ross-Armitage No. 1, and made another big success, and proved up a lot of new territory, and was hailed again as a benefactor to the Prospect Hill field. But once more the doctor said he was overworking; it was time for the Easter holidays, and Bunny studied the maps, and brought Dad a proposition—the Blue Mountains were only ten miles from Paradise, and there was no end of trout fishing there, so why not make their headquarters at the Rascum ranch, and get some trout? Dad smiled; Bunny couldn't keep away from Paradise! To which Bunny answered that Paradise was his discovery; and besides, he wanted to see how Ruth was getting along, and to hear about Paul, and about Eli and his Third Revelation.

Right on top of that came a letter from Mr. Hardacre, the agent, telling how the elder Mr. Bandy had gone out into a field and been attacked by a bull and was badly crippled; Mr. Hardacre didn't believe that young Bandy wanted to work the ranch, but move to the city, so it might be possible to buy the place, if Mr. Ross still wanted it. Bunny was all on pins and needles at that, but Dad told him to keep his shirt on, that young gophers were a lot easier to catch than old ones; and he wrote Mr. Hardacre he wasn't specially keen for the land, but he would take it at the same price as the rest; he was coming up fishing in a few days, and would see about it.

So then Dad wrote a letter to Mr. Watkins, asking him to be so good as to have one of the children go and clean the house at the Rascum ranch and get it ready for them. And Dad told Bunny to go with Aunt Emma to a furniture store in Beach City and get a little stuff, including crockery and kitchen things, and have them put it on a truck and run it out to Paradise; Bunny had better put in some canned food, too, everything they'd need, so the place could be ready when they got there. You can imagine what fun Bunny had with that commission; in his thoughts he was fitting out this house, not merely for Dad and him to camp in, but for Paul and Ruth to settle down and make a home!

When you happen to be the son of a successful oil operator, you can make your dreams come true. Dad and Bunny motored out, arriving just at sundown, and went directly to the Rascum place, and there, standing on the front porch, with the bougain-villea vine now in full blossom, making a glorious purple arch above her head, was Ruth; and alongside her was a man—at a distance Bunny thought it was old Mr. Watkins, but then he saw it was a young man, and Bunny's heart went up into his mouth. He looked at this big, powerful figure, clad in a blue shirt and khaki trousers held up by suspenders, and with a mop of yellowish touselled hair. Could it be—yes, Bunny could never mistake that sombre face, with prominent big nose and mouth drawn down at the corners; he whispered, excitedly, "It's Paul!"

And so it was. The pair came forward, and Ruth introduced her brother to Dad, and Paul said, "Good evening, sir," and waited to be sure that Dad wished to shake hands with him. Then Paul shook hands with Bunny—and it was a strange sensation to the latter, who had lost all at once the Paul he had been dreaming, the boy who might have been a good chum— and had got instead this grown man, who seemed ten years older than himself, and forever out of his reach.

"Did the furniture come?" asked Dad; and Ruth answered that it had, and everything was in order, they'd have had supper ready, if they'd been sure that Mr. Ross would arrive; they'd get it ready right off. Meantime Paul was helping Bunny carry in the bags, and oh, gee—there was the loveliest little bungalow you ever laid eyes on, everything spick and span, even to a pink paper shade over the lamp, and flowers on the center table! Evidently Ruth had put her heart into that job. She asked Dad very shyly what he'd like for supper, and Dad said everything in the place, and very soon the bacon was sizzling in the pan and making a nice friendly smell; and Paul, having emptied the car, stood waiting, and Bunny started in right away to find out all about him, and how he came to be here.

Paul explained that he had turned up yesterday, having come to see Ruth. He had had things out with his father this time; being nineteen now, he thought he was old enough to be allowed to take care of himself. Bunny asked if his father had "whaled" him, and Paul smiled and said his father wasn't in condition to whale anybody, he was getting worse with rheumatism. He was as bitter and implacable as ever, but told Paul to go his own way to hell, and his father would pray for him. Bunny noticed right away that Paul no longer referred to his father as "Pap," and that he no longer murdered the

English language like the rest of the Watkins family; he talked like an educated man, as indeed he was.

Well, they had supper. Paul and Ruth expected to wait on the table, but Dad made them sit down, and they had a little party, the four of them, and it was great fun. Bunny bombarded Paul with questions about himself and his life; and incidentally told Paul how he had hunted for him that night at Mrs. Groarty's, and why had he run away? They talked about Paul's aunt, and the tragedy of her lease, and of the worthless "units" she had bought. Paul had learned from Ruth how Bunny had sent money to her, and Paul expressed his gratitude, and said he would pay it back; he still had that stubborn pride—he would never ask a favor, and he never thrust himself forward, but held back until he was called upon.

He told how he had lived, and how the old lawyer, his benefactor, had died just recently, and had left him a part of his library, all but the law books. It was a most wonderful treasure, a lot of scientific books, and the best old English literature. For nearly three years Paul had had the use of this library, and that had been his life, he had seldom missed an evening reading until after midnight; also he had studied a lot during the day, for he had really had very little work to do, Judge Minter had made a sort of pet of him—having no children of his own, and being stirred by the idea of a boy who wanted to educate himself. The Judge had had an old microscope, and Paul had worked with that, and had made up his mind to a career; he was going to spend a couple more years reading science, and then he would get a job in some laboratory, a janitor's job, if necessary, and work his way up to do microscopic work.

The things that Paul had learned about! He had read Huxley and Spencer, and he talked about Galton and Weissmann and Lodge and Lankester, and a lot of names Bunny had never even heard of. Poor Bunny's pitiful little high school knowledge shrank up to nothing; and how silly seemed foot-ball victories all of a sudden. Dad didn't know about these matters either; he was a man well into his fifties, but he had never met a student of science before! It was interesting to see how quickly he took hold of these things. Paul told how investigators were trying to find out whether acquired characteristics could be transmitted by heredity; it was a most important question, and Weissmann had cut off the tails of mice, to see if the next generations would have tails. But Paul said that was silly, because there wasn't any real change in a mouse when you cut off its tail, no vital quality; the thing to find out was, how long it took the tail to heal up when you cut it off, and whether the new generations of mice could heal up quicker.

Paul said the way to settle the question of inheritance of acquired characteristics was to stimulate the animals to develop some new faculty, and see if new generations would develop it more easily. Dad got the point at once, and said you might learn something by studying trotting horses and their pedigrees; to which Paul replied, exactly. Dad would like to know more about such questions; and Paul had a book with him, which Dad was welcome to read. Ruth was washing the dishes, and Paul went out to get some more wood, and Dad looked at Bunny and said, "That's a fine young fellow, son"; and then Bunny felt a glow of pride, right up to the roots of his hair— because, you see, Paul was his discovery, just like the Paradise oil-field, that was some day going to occupy this spot!

So then Dad settled down to talk business with Paul. Dad wanted some one to occupy this ranch, and Paul said he had thought it over, and would do it if they could make a fair arrangement. Dad asked how he could get along, and Paul said he had saved up three hundred dollars from his wages, and he would get a few goats, and put in some beans this spring, and some strawberries that would bring an income next year; he would pay Dad one-half whatever he got for the crops. They had an argument over that, for Dad thought he ought to pay Paul to act as care-taker, but Paul said he wouldn't take it on that basis, he would insist on going shares, in the regular way they rented land in these parts. And when Mr. Ross came on hunting or fishing trips, Paul of course would move out into the tent. But Dad said no, he was planning to build himself a shack, a better place than this, and Paul might help the carpenter and earn wages if he wanted to. Paul said he could do the building himself, if Dad said so—everything but hanging the doors and windows; a fellow learned to do about all the jobs there were on a ranch. And Dad asked if Ruth would stay with Paul, and Paul said he would settle here in the house, and go easy, and Ruth would come to see him, until gradually their father got used to the idea. It wouldn't be possible to keep Paul and Ruth apart—especially now since Eli was away from home nearly all the time.

So Dad asked about Eli, and the development of the Third Revelation. Only three or four days after Eli had made his announcement in the Paradise Church, there had come a deputation from the church at Roseville, saying that they had heard the fame of Eli's miracles, and would he come and preach to them. And Eli preached, and the "signs" were manifested, and so the new prophet grew bolder. Now he was being driven about the country in somebody's costly limousine, and in the back part of the car was a stack of the crutches of people who had been "healen." These crutches would be set up in sight of each new congregation, and nearly always they were added to; and there fell over the head of the prophet a shower of silver dollars and half dollars, and coins, wrapped in banknotes. Eli had now given himself a title; he was the Messenger of the Second Coming, and the hour of Christ's return to earth was to be made known through him. Sometimes whole congregations would be swept off their feet and converted to the True Word; or again, some would be converted, and there would be a split, and a new church in that place.

"How do you suppose he works it?" Dad asked.

"He really does cure people," said Paul; "there are some about here you can talk to. I've been reading a book on suggestion; it seems that kind of thing has been going on for thousands of years."

"Does he send any money home to his folks?" Dad asked.

And Paul smiled, rather grimly. "The money is sacred," he said; "it belongs to the Holy Spirit, and Eli is His treasurer."

VII

Next morning they set forth after trout; and on the way they stopped to see Mr. Hardacre. Before they went in, Dad cautioned Bunny, "Now don't you say a word, and don't make any faces. Jist let me handle this." They entered, and Mr. Hardacre said that he had an offer from young Bandy, speaking for his father, to sell the ranch for twenty thousand dollars. Bunny's heart leaped, and it was well that Dad had warned him, for he wanted to cry out, "Take it, Dad! Take it!" But he caught himself, and sat rigid, while Dad said, "Holy smoke, what does the fellow take us for?"

Mr. Hardacre explained, there was about twenty acres of good land on this tract; and Dad said all right, call that a hundred an acre, and the improvements, say four thousand, that meant young Bandy was trying to soak them fourteen dollars an acre for his thousand acres of rocks. He must think he had a sucker on his hook.

"To tell the truth, Mr. Ross," said the agent, "he knows you're an oil man, and he thinks you're going to drill this tract."

"All right," said Dad. "You jist tell him to hunt round and find somebody to drill his own tract, and if he gets any oil, I'll drill mine. Meantime, the land I got now will raise all the quail the law will let me shoot in a season."

The end was that Dad said he would pay twelve thousand cash, and otherwise he'd forget it; and after they had got into the car and started the engine, Bunny whispered, "Gee whiz, Dad, aren't you taking a chance?" But Dad said, "You let him stay in pickle a while. I got all the land I can drill right now."

"But Dad, he might get some one else to drill it!"

"Don't you worry! You want that land, because you got a hunch; but nobody else has got any hunches around here, and young Bandy'll get tired after he's tried a while. Let's you and me go a-fishin'."

So they went, and drew beautiful cold shiny trout out of a little mountain lake, and late in the evening they got back to the Rascum place, and Paul fried the fish, and the three of them had a gorgeous supper, and afterwards Dad smoked a cigar and asked Paul all sorts of questions about science. Dad said he wished he had-a got that kind of education when he was young, that was a sort of stuff worth knowing; why didn't Bunny study biology and physics, instead of letting them fill his head up with Latin and poetry, and history business about old kings and their wars and their mistresses, that wasn't a bit of use to nobody?

Next morning they said good-bye to Paul, and went back into the mountains, and spent most of the day getting fish; and then they set out for Beach City, and got in just about bedtime. Bunny went back to school, and his new duties as treasurer for the base-ball team; and Dad set to work putting four more wells on the Armitage tract, and three on the Wagstaff tract. And meantime the nations of Europe had established for themselves two lines of death, extending all the way across the continent; and millions of men, as if under the spell of some monstrous enchantment, rushed to these lines to have their bodies blown to pieces and their life-blood poured out upon the ground. The newspapers told about battles that lasted for months, and the price of petroleum products continued to pile up fortunes for J. Arnold Ross.

Summer was here, and Bertie had plans for her brother. Bertie was now a young lady of eighteen, a brilliant, flashing creature—she picked out clothing shiny enough for a circus dancer. Her trim little legs were sheathed in the glossiest and most diaphanous silk, and her fancy, pointed shoes were without a scratch. If Bertie got a dress of purple or carmine or orange or green, why then, mysteriously, there were stockings and shoes, and a hat and gloves and even a hand-bag of the same shade; Dad said she would soon be having sport-cars to match. Dad was grimly humorous about the stacks of bills, and not a little puzzled by this splendid young butterfly he had helped to hatch out. Aunt Emma said the child was entitled to her "fling," and so Dad paid the charges, but he stood as solid as Gibraltar against Bertie's efforts to push him into her social maelstrom. By golly, no—he was scared to death of them high muckymucks, and especially the women, when they glared at him through their law-nets, or whatever they called them—he felt the size of a potato-bug. What could he say to people that didn't know an under-reamer from a sucker-rod rotator?

This vulgar attitude had been taken up by Bunny, who thought it was "smart"—so his sister jeered. Of course a young lady of eighteen hardly condescends to be aware of the existence of a kid of sixteen; but there were younger brothers and sisters of Bertie's rich friends, and she wanted Bunny to scrape the oil from underneath his finger-nails, and come into this fashionable world, and get a more worth-while girl than Rosie Taintor. Bunny, always curious about new things, tried it for a while, and had to confess that these ineffable rich young persons didn't interest him very much; he couldn't see that they knew anything, or could do anything special. Their talk was all about one another, and they had so many cryptic allusions and so much home-made slang that it amounted almost to a new language. Bunny didn't like any of them well enough to be interested in deciphering it, and he would rather put on his oil clothes and drive out to the wells that were drilling, and if there was no other job for a "roughneck," he would help the cathead-men and the tool-dressers to scrape out the mass of sand and ground-up rock that came out with the mud, and that was forever choking the way to the sump-hole.

Meantime Bunny was thinking, and pretty soon he had a scheme. "Dad," said he, "what about that cabin we were going to build at Paradise?"

"Well, what?" asked Dad.

"Paul writes that Ruth has come to stay with him. So next fall, when we want to go after quail, there won't be any place for us. Let's go up there now, and have a holiday, and build that cabin now."

"But son, it's hot as Flujins up there in summer!" Bunny didn't know where or what "Flujins" might be; but he answered that Paul was standing it, and anyhow it was good for you to sweat, Dad was getting too heavy, and he could sit under the bougainvillea vine in a Palm Beach suit while Bunny did carpentry work with Paul, and it would be a change, and Bunny would call up Dr. Blakiston and have him order it. Whereupon Dad grinned, and said all right, and he might jist as well adopt that Watkins pair and be done with it.

So they went up to the Rascum ranch, taking their tent along—and Paul and Ruth insisted on giving up the house, and Ruth slept in the tent, and Paul made his bed in the empty hay-mow. Paul had hired a horse and plow, and had a flourishing vegetable garden and big patch of beans, and had set in strawberries which he was tending with a little hand cultivator; they had half a dozen goats, and plenty of milk, and some chickens which Ruth took care of.

And most amazing of all, Paul had got the books from Judge Minter's library. Most of them were still in boxes, because there was no place for them; but Paul had made some shelves out of a packing-box, and there stood Huxley and Haeckel and Renan, and other writers absolutely fatal to the soul of any person who reads them. But "Pap" had given up, Ruth said, she had got too growed up all of a sudden, too big to be "whaled;" and besides, Pap's rheumatix was terrible, and Eli couldn't heal it. Dad said that when they were ordering the lumber for the cabin they would get some stuff for bookshelves, and Paul could build them during the winter. Dad and Paul had another argument, and Dad said this was his house, wasn't it, and he sure had a right to put some bookshelves in it if he wanted them; Paul could lend him some books when he come up here, and jist help him get a bit of education, even now, as old as he was.

It was a happy family, and a fine place to be, because it took Dad's mind off his wells, and his trouble with one of his best foremen, that had gone and got married to a fool flapper, and didn't have his mind on his work no more. They got the lumber from the dealer at Roseville, and Paul was the "boss-carpenter," and Bunny was the "jack-carpenter," and Dad kind of fussed around until he got to perspiring too hard, and then he went and sat under the bougainvillea blossoms, and Ruth opened him a bottle of grape-juice, that was part of the fancy stuff he had brought in.

And then in the evening they would drive into Paradise and get the mail, and there came a little local paper that old Mr. Watkins took, and Bunny began to look it over, and gosh amighty, look at this, Dad—a story on the front page, about the marvelous meeting that Eli had held at Santa Lucia, and how frenzied the worshipers had got, and Eli had made the announcement that he had been commissioned to build the Tabernacle of the Third Revelation, which was to be all of snow-white marble, with a frieze of gold, and was to occupy one entire block in Angel City, and be of exactly the dimensions which had been revealed to Eli in a dream. The dimensions were given, and Dad said they were bigger than any block that Eli would find in Angel City, but no doubt they'd find a way to get round that, and call it a new Revelation. The Roseville "Eagle"—that was the name of the paper—was boastful of Eli, who was "putting the San Elido valley on the map," it said. The Apostolic Church of Paradise was to be rebuilt out of the "free will offerings" at Eli's meetings; but the old structure would be preserved, so that pilgrims might come to visit the place where the True Word had been handed down.

And then came Mr. Hardacre, meeting them on the street. He said that young Bandy had got tired of his idea that Dad was going to drill; he wanted to take his parents to the city and be a business man, so the family would take Dad's offer if it was still open. Dad said all right, to let him know, he'd come in any time, and they'd put it into escrow. Next day Mr. Hardacre drove out to the Rascum place, and said he'd taken the escrow officer out to the Bandy place, and old Mr. Bandy and his wife had signed the agreement to deliver the deed; and so Dad and Bunny got into their car, and drove to the bank, and Dad put up four thousand dollars, and signed a contract to pay eight thousand more when the title search was completed. Then, when they were out of the bank, he grinned and said, "All right, son, now you can drill your tract!"

Of course, Bunny wanted to go right to it—wanted Dad to telephone for his head foreman, and get a road contractor at work! But Dad said they'd finish the cabin first, and meantime he'd be thinking. So Bunny went back to work, nailing shingles on the roof, and he was happy as a youngster could be—except for one uncomfortable thought that was gnawing like a worm in his soul. How could he tell Paul and Ruth about their decision to drill, and would Paul and Ruth consider that Dad had got the Watkins ranch upon false pretences?

Fate was kind to Bunny. Something happened—you could never guess it in a thousand years! Only three days had passed since they put through the Bandy deal, and Dad was still thinking matters over, when Meelie Watkins came walking from her home—with a big blue sun-bonnet to protect her from the mid-day sun—and brought an amazing piece of news. Old Mr. Wrinkum, driving in from town, had stopped by, and told Pap that a big oil concern, the Excelsior Petroleum Company, had leased the Carter ranch, on the other side of the valley, about a mile west of Paradise, and was going to start drilling for oil! Meelie gave this news to Dad, who was sitting under the bougainvillea; and Dad shouted to Bunny and Paul, who were up laying the floor of the cabin. The two came running, and Ruth came running from her chicken-yard, and when they heard the news, Bunny cried, "Excelsior Pete! Why, Dad, that's one of the Big Five!"

They stared at each other, and suddenly Dad clenched his hands and exclaimed, "By golly, them people don't drill unless they know what they're doin'. Bunny, I believe I'll try a well here on our place, and see what we get!"

"Oh, Mr. Ross!" exclaimed Ruth. "You ought to do it— my Uncle Eby always used to say there was oil here!"

"Is that so?" said Dad. "Well, I'll take a chance then, jist for fun." And he looked at Bunny, with just the flicker of a smile. It told Bunny a lot, when he came to think it over; Dad had guessed that Bunny was worried, and exactly what was his dilemma with the Watkinses; and Dad had had the wit to save Bunny's face, and avoid the need of confessing. Dear, kind old Dad, that was anxious to do everything for his boy— that would even do his lying for him! How could any boy refuse to be content with such a happy solution of his ethical problems?

CHAPTER VI

THE WILD-CAT

I

Dad had thought things over, and studied his bank account, and given his decision; they would drill the Ross Junior-Paradise No. 1, and do it quick, and give the "Excelsior Pete" crowd a run for their money; there was no use letting the Big Five think they owned the whole oil industry. Dad would stick here and see things started; so he phoned for his geologist, and hunted up a contractor to figure over a well for water.

Mr. Banning, the geologist, came next day, and gave Bunny's hopes a knock over the head at the very outset. He said Dad was right in his idea that you couldn't count very much on that streak of oil on the top of the ground. You might come on oil sands one or two hundred feet down, but they wouldn't be likely to amount to much; if that was all you were looking for, you might bring in one of those little drilling-rigs on wheels such as they used back in Pennsylvania! But out here, said Mr. Banning, the real oil sands lay deep, and you never knew what you'd find till you got there. But he liked the looks of the district, and thought it worth a chance; he spent a couple of days wandering over the hills with Dad and Bunny, studying the slope of the strata, and finally he and Dad chose the side of a hill on the Watkins ranch, not far from the place where Bunny had sat and talked with Ruth while she tended the goats.

The water-well man came, offering to drill a four-inch well for $2.12 a foot; and Dad signed a contract with him, on the basis of his making so many feet a day, and getting a bonus if he went above that, and paying a forfeit if he fell below it. After which Dad and Bunny drove over to pay a visit to Mr. Jeremiah Carey, a rancher near Roseville, who was chairman of the county board of supervisors, which had to do with the all-important question of road construction.

A great part of the road passed through Dad's own property; and it had been Bunny's naive idea that Dad would call in a contractor, and pay the price, as in the case of the water well. But Dad said no, that wasn't the way you did with roads; it

132

was a public road, running from Paradise to Roseville, down along the slide, and it would be graded and paved at public expense. To be sure, Dad would use this road more than anyone else, but also he would pay some of the taxes; all the people owning property along the slide would pay a share, and the new road would increase the value of their property.

All this Dad explained, first to Bunny, and then to Mr. Carey, a friendly old fellow who grew apricots and peaches on the slopes of a ridge overlooking the San Elido valley. Mr. Carey was evidently pleased to meet a famous oil operator, and he took them up to the house and made them sit comfortable in big porch chairs, and called to Mrs. Carey to bring some lemonade for Bunny. Dad produced his gold-foil cigars, and told the chairman of the county board of supervisors what a great thing it was going to mean for this whole section if oil developments came in; he told about the Bankside lease at Prospect Hill, and the million and more which he had paid to the Bankside family, and the palace on the beach front which Mr. Bankside was now occupying; you could see the eyes of Mr. and Mrs. Carey open wider and wider, as Dad visioned this slope covered with a forest of oil derricks. Absolutely, the whole thing depended upon one problem, that of roads. Manifestly, you couldn't bring in derrick materials and drilling tools and heavy machinery over that sheep-track which they now had, and which had jist broken a spring on Dad's new motor-car; nor could the county expect Dad to improve a public road at his own expense, in order to have the privilege of paying tens of thousands of dollars of new taxes into the county treasury. To all of which Mr. Carey agreed.

Dad went on to say that it was a question of time; if the county authorities were going to dilly-dally along, and keep him waiting—why then, he had plenty of other tracts he could drill, and he would keep this here Paradise place for a quail-preserve. Mr. Carey looked worried, and said he'd do his best, but of course Mr. Ross understood that public affairs didn't move in a hurry, you had to issue bonds to pave a new road, and there would have to be a special election to vote them. Dad said that was what he had come to find out about; if that was the case, it was all off so far as he was concerned. Wasn't there some way this work could be done at once, on the basis of its being repairs to an old road, instead of new paving? And Mr. Carey said of course, they had funds for repair work, he didn't know just how much, he'd have to consult his associates on the board.

Mr. Carey got up and strolled down to the car with Dad and Bunny; and as they stood there chatting, Dad took out an envelope from his pocket, and said: "Mr. Carey, I'm asking a lot of your time, and it ain't fair you should work for nothing. I hope you won't take offense if I ask you to let me pay your gasoline and tire-cost while you're running about a-seein' to this." Mr. Carey hesitated, and said he didn't know whether that would be exactly proper or not; and Dad said it would be understood, it was jist for Mr. Carey's time, it wouldn't change his judgment as to what should be done; they would have other dealings, no doubt, and perhaps some day Dad would come wild-catting on Mr. Carey's ranch. The other put the envelope into his pocket, and said Dad would hear from him soon.

Now Bunny had been taking a course in school which was called "civics," and had learned all about how the government of his country was run. There had been many discussions in class, and among other things they had mentioned "corruption of public officials." Bunny—of course without any hint that he had ever had personal knowledge of such a thing—had asked the lady teacher about the possibility of a business man's paying a public official extra sums for his time and trouble in public matters; and the lady teacher had been shocked by such a suggestion, and had declared that it would be bribery without question. So now Bunny told Dad, and the latter explained. It was the difference between a theoretical and a practical view of a question. The lady-teacher had never had to drill an oil well, her business didn't depend on moving heavy materials over a sheep-trail; all she did was jist to sit in a room and use high-soundin' words, like "ideals" and "democracy" and "public service." That was the trouble with this education business, the people that taught was people that never done things, and had no real knowledge of the world.

In this case it all came down to one question, did they want to drill the Watkins tract or not. Of course they might wait ten years, till in the course of the county's development somebody else come in and did what Dad was now a-doin'—put skids under the public authorities, and "greased" the skids. In a great many cases the authorities were greedy, they went out on purpose to hold you up and make you pay; in other cases they was jist ignorant and indifferent; but anyhow, if you wanted things done you had to pay for them. Dad explained the difference between public and private business; in your own business, you were boss, and you drove ahead and pushed things through; but when you ran into public authorities, you saw graft and waste and inefficiency till it made you sick. And yet there was fools always rooting for public ownership; people who called themselves Socialists, and wanted to turn everything over to the government to run, and when they had their way, you'd have to fill out a dozen application blanks and await the action of a board of officials before you could buy a loaf of bread.

Dad said that Bunny would get a practical course in civics, that he could take back to his teacher; they wasn't going to get their road, jist by paying a tip to one apricot-grower. And sure enough, they didn't! A couple of days later Dad got Mr. Carey on the phone, and learned that he had interviewed the other board members, and feared there would be some opposition; the board came up for re-election this fall, and there had been a lot of grumbling over the waste of road funds, and nobody wanted to take on any more troubles. There was to be a meeting of the board next week, and meantime, if Dad had any influence, it would be a good time for him to use it. Dad repeated this to Bunny, and explained, he was supposed to call on the other board members and distribute some more envelopes. "But I'll do it wholesale," said Dad, "and I'll do it quick—before the Excelsior Pete crowd wake up to what's happening. That's our only chance, I've an idea."

So Dad strolled into the office of Mr. Hardacre, the real estate agent, and through the smoke of a gold foil cigar he put to that knowing gentleman the problem of what people he, Mr. Hardacre, would call on, in case he wanted to get a road built in San Elido county. Mr. Hardacre laughed and said that first he'd go to see Jake Coffey, and after that he'd go home and rest. Further questions elicited the fact that Jake Coffey was a hay and feed dealer in the town of San Elido, the county seat; also, he was the Republican boss of the county. Dad said all right, thanks, and he and Bunny were soon in the car, and headed for San Elido at Dad's customary speed. "Now, son," said he, "you'll finish your lesson in civics!"

II

Jacob Coffey, Hay, Feed and Grain, Lime, Cement and Plaster, sat in the private office behind his store, with his feet on a center table from which the remains of a poker game had not yet been cleaned. He was a hard-bitten individual with tight-shut mouth and other features to correspond; his skin was tanned to leather, and all his teeth were gold, so far as they showed. He got his feet off the table and stood up; and when he heard Dad's name, he said: "I was rather expecting you'd call." Dad said: "I only jist heard about you. I came at fifty miles an hour." So they were friends, and Mr. Coffey accepted a gold foil cigar instead of his half-chewed one, and they sat down to business.

"Mr. Coffey," said Dad, "I am an independent oil man; what the Big Five call one of the 'little fellers'—though not so little that I won't show here in San Elido county. I've bought twelve thousand acres, and want to prospect for oil. If there's any here, I'll put a couple of hundred wells on the tract, and employ a thousand men, and pay a few million dollars in wages, and double real estate values for five or ten miles around. Now, Excelsior Pete is here; and of course they'll fight to keep me or anyone else out. The thing I want to show you political fellers is that these big companies never put up the dough unless they have to, and it most all goes to the state machine, anyhow. Like everything else, they need a little competition to keep them softened up. Us independents pay more, and we make the big fellows pay more too. I assume I'm talking to a man who knows this game."

"You may assume it," said Mr. Coffey, drily. "Exactly what do you want?"

"For the present, jist one thing—a road to Paradise. It's a case of no road, no drilling, and that's no bluff, but a fact you can understand, because you haul heavy material yourself, and you may have tried to deliver over that there sheep-trail."

"I have," said Mr. Coffey.

"Well, then, no words needed. I want a road, and I want it without no red tape—I want the county to start work within the next ten days, and jist push the job right through, so that I can get in here and drill my well, now while I got a rig to spare. Maybe that's never been done before, but it's what

I want, and I've come to ask what it's worth. Do I make myself clear?"

"Perfectly," said Mr. Coffey, and his hard face yielded to a slight smile. It was evident that he liked Dad's business methods.

He told his side of the case; and Bunny understood that he was bargaining, drawing a fancy picture of the tremendous difficulties involved. The county machine had been having a peck of trouble of late, some damned fool had stolen some money—a silly thing to take the county's money, said Mr. Coffey, when you could make so much more in legitimate ways. Also there had been criticism of road contracts; they had a crank in this town that published a weekly paper, the "Watch-Dog," and filled it with reckless charges. Well, the long and short of it was that to use the emergency repair funds of the county to build a road for an oil-operator, would be bound to stir up a lot of fuss, and lose votes which the county machine needed. As Mr. Ross had said, the Excelsior Pete crowd, who already had a road to their tract, wouldn't favor Dad's road; they might furnish material for the crank's weekly paper, and they might make a kick to the state committee, and make Mr. Coffey's life a little hell.

Dad listened politely—as the process of bargaining required. He said that he appreciated all these troubles, and would expect to make up for them. In the first place, there would be the job of carrying the county supervisors into office. Would it seem a fair proposition if Dad were to contribute five thousand dollars to the war chest of the campaign committee? Mr. Coffey blew a big cloud of grey-blue tobacco smoke into the air, and sat gazing fixedly at the figure 5 and three 0's written in these clouds.

"You understand," Dad added; "that's a party matter, and separate from any proposition I make to you personally."

"Let's have your whole idea," said Mr. Coffey, quietly.

So Dad gave his "spiel" about believing in co-operation, and how he always got a little organization together wherever he worked, and stood by his friends and gave them a share of what he made. He told about his Ross-Bankside No. 1, and how he had formed a syndicate for that well, and, in order to make sure of getting his derrick material on the spot, he had let the president of a big lumber company have two percent of it—jist a little friendly service, and the well had earned so far nearly six hundred thousand dollars net profits, and the president of this company had made over twelve thousand, jist for his trouble in seeing that Dad always got his lumber the day he asked for it.

And now here was the same thing; if Dad could get a road, he would gamble on the Paradise tract, and Mr. Coffey might gamble with him. Dad offered to "carry" him to the amount of two percent of the well; the cost would run over a hundred thousand dollars, so Mr. Coffey would be getting a two thousand dollar investment, and if the well became a producer, he might get five or ten, or even thirty or forty thousand dollars; such things had happened many times, and were to be reckoned on. Of course, Dad would expect this to mean that he and Mr. Coffey would be friends; they would work together, and help each other with any little favors that might be needed.

And Mr. Coffey puffed several more clouds of smoke, and studied them, and said he felt friendly to Dad; but he thought it would be better if Dad would contribute two thousand dollars to the campaign fund, and carry five thousand for Mr. Coffey personally. And Dad, looking him in the eye, inquired, "Can you deliver the goods?" Mr. Coffey said yes, he could deliver them all right, Dad needn't have any worries. So it was a bargain, and Dad took out his check book and wrote out two thousand dollars to the order of the treasurer of the county campaign committee of the Republican party. Then he asked Mr. Coffey whether he held any public office, and the latter replied no, he was just a plain business man; so Dad said all right then, the agreement could be in Mr. Coffey's name; and he wrote a memorandum to the effect that he had received the sum of one dollar and other good and valuable considerations, in return for which Mr. Coffey was owner of five per cent interest in the net profits of a well to be drilled on the Abel Watkins ranch near Paradise, to be known as the Ross Junior-Paradise No. 1. But it was understood and agreed that the said well was not to be drilled until there was a good hard road completed from the main street of Paradise to the entrance of the Abel Watkins ranch, and if the said road were not completed within sixty days the said J. Arnold Ross was under no obligation to drill the said well, nor to return to the said Jacob Coffey the said one dollar and other good and valuable considerations. And Dad handed that to the said Jacob Coffey, and smiled, and remarked that he hoped it wouldn't fall into the hands of the "Watch-Dog." Mr. Coffey smiled, and laid his hand on Bunny's shoulder, and said he hoped this young man wouldn't make any mistake and talk about it; and Dad said that Bunny was learning the oil business, and the first lesson he had learned was never to talk about his father's affairs.

So then they shook hands all round, and the two got into their car, and Bunny exclaimed, "But Dad, I thought you were a Democrat!" And Dad laughed and said that he wasn't deciding the tariff on hyperchlorides, nor the independence of the Philippine Islands, he was jist gettin' a road to the Watkins ranch. Bunny said, "There's one thing I don't understand; how can Mr. Coffey do all that, if he hasn't any office?" To which Dad answered that the big fellows as a rule avoided holding office for that very reason, so they were free to do business. Mr. Carey could be sent to prison if it were proven that he had taken money from Dad, but nothing could be done to Coffey, he was jist the "boss." The office-holder, said Dad, was either a poor devil who needed a fifth rate salary, or else he was a man actuated by vanity, he liked to make speeches, and be applauded by the crowd, and see his picture in the papers. You would never see pictures of Jake Coffey in the papers, he done his work in his back office, and never in the lime-light.

Bunny, of course, remembered what he had been taught in the "civics" class, and asked if that was the way the business of government was always run. Dad said it was about the same everywhere, from the county up to the state, and on to the national government. It wasn't really as bad as it seemed, it was jist a natural consequence of the inefficiency of great masses of people. It was all right to make spread-eagle speeches on "democracy," but what was the fact? Who was the voters here in San Elido county? Why, the very boobs that Bunny had seen "jumping" and "rolling" and "talking in tongues" at Eli's church; and could anybody pretend that these people could run a government? They were supposed to decide whether or not Dad should have a road and drill a well! It was a sure thing they couldn't do it; and Jake Coffey was the feller that done the deciding for them—he provided that promptness and efficiency that business men had to have, and that couldn't be got under our American system.

III

The water well men got to work, and the telephone line-men; and Dad said it was time to figure on living quarters for their crew. They would get along with a bunk-house while they were prospecting; then, if they found oil, they'd put up nice cabins for the families of the men. Dad said to Paul that he was foolish to waste his time on beans and strawberries, which would keep him a pauper all his life; he had better turn carpenter and do this building job, and after that he could learn oil-drilling. Dad would have his boss carpenter come and figure the materials for the bunk-house, and see to the foundations and the sills, and after that Paul could finish the job with carpenters he'd pick up in the neighborhood, and Dad would pay him five dollars a day, which was jist about five times what he'd get working this old ranch by himself.

Paul said all right, and they sat down one evening and made out the plans of the house. It was going to be real nice, Dad said, because this was Bunny's well, and Bunny was turning into a little social reformer, and intended to feed his men on patty de far grar. Instead of having one long room with bunks, they'd have little individual cubby-holes, each with its separate window, and two bunks, one on top of the other, for the day man and the night man. There would be a couple of showers, and besides the dining-room and kitchen and store-room, a nice sitting-room, with a victrola and some magazines and books; that was Bunny's own idea, he was a-goin' to have a sure enough cultured oil-crew.

Dad and Bunny took a drive to Roseville, to get some furniture and stuff for their own cabin, which was now complete. Dad purchased a copy of the "Eagle," fresh off the press, and he opened it, and burst into a roar of laughter. Bunny had never seen him do that in his life before, so he looked in a hurry, and there on the front page was a story about one Adonijah Prescott, a rancher who lived near the slide between Paradise and Roseville; some three months ago his wagon had been overturned and his collar-bone broken, and now he was filing suit against the county for fifteen thousand dollars damages; more than that, he was suing each and every member of the county board of supervisors, alleging neglect of their public duties in leaving the road in an unsafe condition! On the editorial page appeared a two-column discourse on the dreadful condition of the aforesaid road; there were mineral springs nearby, and it had been proposed to develop them, but the project had been dropped, because of lack of transportation; and now there were possibilities of oil, but these also were in danger, because of bad roads, which kept San Elido one of the most backward counties of the state. The "Eagle" stated that a public-spirited rancher, Mr. Joe Limacher, was circulating a petition for immediate repairs to the road along the slide, and it was to be hoped that all citizens and tax-payers would sign up.

Next day along came Mr. Limacher, in a rusty Ford, and asked Dad to sign! Dad looked very thoughtful, and said it would cost him a hell of a lot of taxes. The public-spirited Mr. Limacher—who was being paid three dollars a day by Jake Coffey—argued a while with Dad, and in the end Dad said all right, he didn't want his neighbors to think him a cheap-skate, so he'd sign along with the rest. Four days later came the news that the supervisors had held a special meeting and voted immediate repairs to the slide road; and two days after that came the grading gang, teams of big horses with heavy plows—you'd never have guessed there were so many in the county, there must have been a score of them on that two mile stretch. They tore up the ground, and men with crow-bars rolled the boulders out of the way, and more teams with scrapers slid the dirt this way and that, and pretty soon it began to look like a highway. And then, beginning at the Paradise end, came countless loads of crushed rock, in big motor trucks which tilted up backwards and slid out their burden. There were machines to level this material, and great steam-rollers to roll it flat—gee, it was wonderful to see what Dad's money could do!

They had ordered the lumber for the bunk-house, and got it in by small loads, and Paul was at work with half a dozen men from the neighborhood. He had engaged them himself, telephoning from Paradise; and if any of them felt humiliated at working under a nineteen year old boss, Dad's twenty-two dollar check salved their feelings at twelve-thirty every Saturday. Even old Mr. Watkins, Paul's father, was impressed by this sudden rise of his "black sheep," and no longer said anything about hell-fire and brimstone. It was on his ranch, you understand, that all this activity was taking place; the carpenters' hammers were thumping all day, and up near the head of the arroyo the artesian well was flowing, and a gang of men and horses were leveling a road up to the drilling site. It seemed to the Watkins family as if the whole county had suddenly moved to their ranch. It meant high prices, right on the spot, for everything good to eat they could raise. You could not help being impressed by so much activity, even though you knew it was the activity of Satan!

Best of all was the effect upon Ruth, who fairly shone with happiness over Paul's success. Ruth kept house for Dad and Bunny, besides what she did for Paul and herself; but it seemed to agree with her, she filled out, and her cheeks grew rosy. She had money to buy shoes and stockings and clean dresses, and Bunny noticed all of a sudden that she was quite a pretty girl. She shared Bunny's idea that his father was a great man, and she expressed her admiration by baking pies and puddings for him, regardless of the fact that he was trying to keep his weight down! The four of them had supper together every evening, after the day's work was done, in the Rascum bungalow with the bougainvillea vine; and then they sat out under the vine in the moonlight and talked about what they had done, and what they were going to do, and the world was certainly an interesting place to be alive in!

IV

It was time for Bunny to go back to school; but first he had to pay his semi-annual visit to his mother.

Bunny had seen a notice in the paper, to the effect that Mrs. Andrew Wotherspoon Lang was suing for divorce on grounds of desertion. Now Mamma told him about it—her second husband had basely left her, two years after their marriage, and she had no idea where he was. She was a lonely and very sad woman, with tears in her eyes; Bunny could have no idea how hard it was, how every one tried to prey upon defenseless women. Presently, through the tears, Bunny became aware that his "pretty little Mamma" was tactfully hinting something; she would have to have a new name when she got the divorce, and she wanted to take back Dad's name, and Bunny wasn't quite sure whether that meant that she was to take Dad back along with his name. She asked how Dad was, and mustn't he be lonely, and did he have any women friends?

That bothered Bunny, who didn't like to have people probing into his father's relations with women—he wasn't sure himself, and didn't like to think about it. He said that Mamma would have to write to Dad, because Dad wouldn't let him, Bunny, talk about these matters. So then some more tears ran down the pretty cheeks, and Mamma said that everybody shut her out, even her own daughter, Bertie, had refused to come and stay with her this time, and what did that mean? Bunny explained, as well as he could; his sister was selfish, he thought, and wrapped up in her worldly career; she was a young lady now, flying very high, with a fast set, and didn't have time for any of her family.

But Bertie had found time recently for a talk with her brother; telling him that he was old enough now to know about their mother. Bertie had got the facts long ago from Aunt Emma, and now she passed them on, and many mysteries were solved for the boy, not merely about his mother, but about his father. Dad had married after he was forty, being then the keeper of a cross-roads store; he had married the village belle, who thought she was making a great conquest. But very soon she had got ideas beyond the village; she had tried to pry Dad loose, and finally had run away and left him, with a prosperous bond-salesman from Angel City, who had married her, but then got tired and left her.

Mamma's leaving had done what all her arguments had failed to do—it had pried Dad loose. He had thought it over and realized—what everybody wanted was money, and he had lost out because he hadn't made enough; well, he'd show them. And from that time Dad had shut his lips and set to work. Some of his associates in the village had proposed to drill for oil, and he had gone in with them, and they had made a success, and pretty soon Dad had branched out for himself.

Bunny thought that story over, and watched his father, and pieced things together. Yes, he understood now—that grim concentration, and watchfulness, and merciless driving; Dad was punishing Mrs. Andrew Wotherspoon Lang, showing her that he was just as good a man as any bond-salesman from the city! And Dad's distrust of women, his idea that they were all trying to get your money away from you! And his centering of all his hopes upon Bunny, who was going to be happy, and to have all of his father's virtues and none of his faults, and provide that meaning and justification which Dad couldn't find in his own life! When Bunny thought of that, he would have a sudden access of affection, and put his arm across Dad's shoulders, and say something about how his father was working too hard, and how Bunny must hurry and grow up and carry some of the load.

He ventured very timidly to broach the matter of his mother's debts, and her plea that her income be increased; and so he got his father's point of view about his mother. There was jist no use a-givin' her money, Dad said; she was the type that never lives upon an income, but always has debts and is discontented. It wasn't stinginess on Dad's part, nor any wish to punish her; she had money enough to live like she had bargained to live when she married him, and that was his idea of justice. She had had nothing to do with his later success, and no claim upon its fruits. If she once found out that she could get money from Bunny, she would jist make his life miserable, and that was why Dad was so determined about it. The tradesmen could sue his mother, but they couldn't collect anything, so in the end they'd learn not to give her credit, and that would be the best thing for her. It was a painful subject, but the time had come when Bunny must understand it, and learn that women who tried to get your money away from you would even go so far as to marry you!

Bunny didn't say so, but he thought Dad was a little too pessimistic about one-half the human race. Bunny knew there were women who weren't like that, for he had found one—Rosie Taintor, who had been his sweetheart now for a year or more. Rosie always tried to keep him from spending money on her, saying that she didn't have any money, and it wasn't fair; she would ride in his car, but that was all. She was so gentle and good—and Bunny was very unhappy about what was happening to their love-affair. But his efforts to deny the truth to himself had been futile—he was beginning to be bored by it! They had looked at the eighteenth-century English prints until they knew them by heart; and Rosie's comment on everything was still the same—"wonderful!" Bunny had gone on to new things, and he wanted new comments, and could not help wanting them, no matter how cruel it seemed. Therefore he did not take Rosie driving so often, and once or twice he took some other girl to a dance. And little Rosie was gentle and demure as ever, she did not even cry, at least not in his presence; Bunny was deeply touched, but like all male creatures, he found it an immense convenience when old loves consent to die painlessly, and without making a fuss! Without realizing it, he got ready to fall in love with some new girl.

V

The new road was done, and the bunk-house was done, and occupied; Dad's boss-carpenter had gone up there, and Paul was working with him on the derrick. Then came the fleet of motor trucks, with the drilling tools, and they were rigging up, and Paul was helping with that. Bunny was in school, and missing all the fun, but Dad got a report almost every day from his foreman, and passed it on to Bunny at supper-time. They were behind in their race with Excelsior Pete, which had already spudded in, having had the advantage of a road from the start; but Dad said not to worry, it would be a long way to the bottom of those wells.

Bunny's great hour came; it happened to be a Friday, and he begged off from school—it wasn't often that a boy had such an excuse, that he had a "wild-cat" named after him, and had to go to press a lever and start the drilling machinery! They set out early in the morning, and arrived in mid-afternoon; and rolling over that new road, hard and smooth and grey, how proud they felt! They came to the Watkins arroyo, and the new road leading into it—their own private road, so marked! There was no one at the Watkins place, everyone had gone up to the well; you could see a crowd gathered about the derrick— the nice new shiny derrick of yellow pine, built on a little shelf, half way up the slope—the Ross Junior-Paradise Number One!

They drove up, and the foreman welcomed them; everything was ready, the last bolt tight, and full steam up—they could have started a couple of hours ago. Bunny looked about; there was Paul among the other workmen, keeping himself in the background. And Ruth—she was with her family; Bunny went up to them, he was glad to see them all, even old Mr. Watkins, in spite of the jumping and the rolling and the rheumatix and other troubles. The whole neighborhood was there, and Bunny knew many of them by name, and spoke to them, whether he knew them or not; they all liked this eager lad— the young prince who had a well named after him. Some of them in their secret hearts were "sore," because they had sold their land so cheap, and if they had held on, they too might have become rich and famous; but nothing of that showed now, this was a great hour, a ceremony about which they would talk for many a day.

Dad looked things over, and asked a few questions, and was about to say, "Go," when he noticed another car coming up the road. It was a big shiny limousine, and it rolled up fast, and the crowd parted, and it stopped, and from it descended—gee whiz, could you believe your eyes?—a young man, tall and rather gawky, stoop-shouldered, sun-tanned, with pale blue eyes and a mop of corn-colored hair; Eli Watkins, Prophet of the Third Revelation, transfigured and glorified in a stiff white collar and black tie and black broadcloth suit, ill-fitting but expensive, and with a manner cut to the same pattern, that peculiar blend of humble pride which the divine profession generates. He was followed by an elderly rich gentleman, who assisted from the car two ladies with costumes, as you might say the feminine gender of Eli's; they were some of the prophet's new converts, or those whom he had "healen." The neighbors stared respectfully, and for a minute or two the well was forgotten, the spiritual power took precedence over the temporal.

Dad came forward, and shook hands with the prophet; bye-gones were to be bye-gones, and all disharmonies forgotten in this great hour. Bunny was amazed by what happened, for he had never known Dad to make a speech unless he was made to. But there was a whimsical streak in J. Arnold Ross, which bubbled up once in a while, and caused these queer turns of events. Dad faced the crowd, and clearing his throat, said: "Ladies and gentlemen, we are drilling this here well on the ranch where Mr. Eli Watkins was born, so perhaps he would like to say jist a few words to you on this occasion." There was a round of hand-clapping, and Eli colored, and was obviously very much flattered; he took a step or two forwards, and folded his hands in front of him in the fashion of a blessing, and lifted his head, and half closed his eyes, and the booming voice rolled out:

"Brethren and sisters: Upon these hills have I tendened my father's herds, like the prophets of old, and have harkened unto the voice of the Holy Spirit, speaking to me in the storms and the thunders. Brethren and sisters, the Lord unfoldens Himself in many ways, and gives precious gifts to His children. The treasures of the yearth are His, and when in His Mercy

they are handened unto mankind, it is His Will that they be
used in His service and unto His Glory. The things of the
body are subjected unto the things of the spirit; and if in God's
wisdom it should happen that this well should bring forth
treasure, may it be used in the service of the Most Highest,
and may His Blessings rest upon all they that own or labor
for it. Amen."

There was a chorus from the audience, "Amen!" And so
there you were, a regular consecration! All the lies that Dad
had told to the Watkins family and to others, the bribes that
he had paid to Messrs. Carey and Coffey—all these were
abrogated, nullified, and remitted, and the Ross Junior-Paradise
No. 1 was from that time forth a sanctified well. And so Dad
turned and looked at Bunny, who was standing by the engine
with the lever in his hand. "All right, son!" And Bunny
moved the lever, and the engine gave a thump, and the chain
gave a pull, and the gears gave a rattle, and the rotary-table
gave a turn, and down underneath the derrick floor you heard
that exciting sound which the oil-men report as "Spud!"

VI

At less than two hundred feet they struck the sands which
accounted for Bunny's "earthquake oil;" there proved to be
two feet of them, and Dad said it would give them enough oil
to run their own car for a year! They were going deeper, still
with an eighteen inch bit, through hard sandstone formation;
they were working in an open hole, with no casing, because the
ground was so firm. Paul was working as a general utility
man, mainly carpentry. "Dad, we're going to make Paul our
manager some day," Bunny had said; but Paul had smiled and
said that he was going to be a scientist, and he wouldn't fool
himself with the idea that the jobs at the top were easy—
he'd not exchange his eight hour job for Dad's eighteen hour
job. This was a subtle kind of flattery, and gave Dad a
tremendously high opinion of Paul!

Thanksgiving Day was coming; and Bunny's soul was
torn in half. It was a great occasion at the school, the annual
foot-ball battle with a rival institution known as "Polly High,"
located in Angel City. And what was Bunny, a real boy or
an oil gnome? He fought it out within himself, and announced
his decision, to the dismay of Rosie Taintor and of Aunt

Emma—he was going to Paradise with Dad! It was the quail season, and Dad needed a change, the boy told his aunt; but the sharp old lady said he could fool himself, but he couldn't fool her.

They didn't have to take any camping things now, for they had their cabin on the Rascum place, with a telephone and everything comfortable. There was an extension phone in the bungalow, and all they had to do was to call up Ruth, and there would be a jolly fire in the cabin, and a supper on the table at the bungalow, with all kinds of home-made good things, the eating of which would make it necessary for Dad to walk miles and miles over the hills next day! First, of course, they would stop at the well, and inspect things, and have a talk with the foreman. There were traces of oil again, and Dad had told them to take a core, and he asked Mr. Banning to come up next day and study it with him.

They came in sight of the derrick. The drill-stem was out of the hole, they could see the mass of "stands" setting in place. When they got nearer, they saw that the crew had a cable down in the hole; and when Dave Murgins, the foreman, saw them, he came out to the car, and it was plain that something was wrong. "We've had an accident, Mr. Ross."

"What's the matter?"

"There's a man fell in the hole."

"Oh, my God!" cried Dad. "Who?" And Bunny's heart was in his throat, for of course his first thought was Paul.

"A roughneck," said the foreman. "Fellow by the name of Joe Gundha. You don't know him."

"How did that happen?"

"Nobody knows. We was changing the bit, and this fellow went down into the cellar for some reason—he had no business there that we know of. Nobody thought about him for a while."

"You sure he went down?"

"We been fishing with a hook, and we got a bit of his shirt."

Bunny was white about the lips. "Oh, Dad, will he be alive?"

"How long has he been down?"

"We've been fishing half an hour," said Murgins.

"And you haven't heard a sound?"

"Not one."

"Well then, he's drowned in the mud. How far down is he?"

"About fifty feet. The mud sinks that far when we take out the drill-stem. He must have went down head first, or he'd have been able to keep his head above the mud and make a noise."

"My God! My God!" exclaimed Dad. "It makes me want to quit this business! What can you do to help men that won't help themselves?"

Bunny had heard that cry a thousand times before. They had a cover for the hole, and any man who went down into the cellar was supposed to slip it into place. Of necessity the dirt caved in about the edges, so that the top of the hole was a kind of funnel, its edges slippery with mud, and in this case with traces of oil; yet men would take chances, sliding around on the edge of that yawning pit! What could you do for them?

"Has he got any family?" asked Dad.

"He told Paul Watkins he'd got a wife and some children in Oklahoma; he worked in the oil fields there."

Dad sat motionless, staring in front of him; and nobody said a word. They knew he really was interested in his men, taking care of them was a matter of personal pride to him. Bunny had turned sort of sick inside; gee, what a shame— in his well, of all places, his first one, that was to start off the new field! It was all spoiled for him; he wouldn't be able to enjoy his oil if he got it!

"Well," said Dad, at last, "what are you doin'? Jigglin' a hook up and down in there? You'll never get him up that way. You'll have to put down a three-pronged grab."

"I thought that would tear him so—" explained Dave Murgins, hesitatingly.

"I know," said Dad; "but you've got it to do. It ain't as if he might have any life in him. Bend the prongs so they fit the hole, and force them past the body. Go ahead and get it over with, and let's hope it'll teach the rest of you something."

Dad got out of the car, and told Bunny to take their things down to the Rascum place, and break the news to Ruth; she'd be upset, especially if she knew the fellow. Bunny understood that Dad didn't want him around when that torn body came out of the hole; and since he couldn't do any good, he turned the car in silence, and drove away. In his mind he saw the men screwing the "grab" onto the drill-stem—a tool which was built to go over obstacles that fell into the hole, and to catch hold of them with sharp hooks. They might get Joe Gundha by the legs and they might get him by the face—ugh, the less you thought about a thing like that, the better for your enjoyment of the oil-game!

Dad came to the cabin after a couple of hours, and lay down for a while to rest. They had got the body out, he said, and had telephoned for the coroner; he would swear in several of the men as a jury, and hear the testimony of others, and look at the body, and then give a burial permit. Paul had been to the dead man's bunk and looked over his things, and put them all into a box to be shipped to his wife; Dad had in his pocket half a dozen letters that had been found among the things, and because he didn't want Bunny to think that money came easy, or that life was all play, he gave him these letters, and Bunny sat off in a corner and read them: pitiful little messages, scrawled in a childish hand, telling how the doctor said that Susie's heart would be weak for a long time after the flu, and the baby was getting two more teeth and was awful cross, and Aunt Mary had just been in to see her, and said that Willie was in Chicago and doing good; there were cross-marks and circles that were kisses from mamma, and from Susie and from the baby. One sentence there was to cheer up Dad and Bunny: "I am glad you got such a good boss."

Well, it made a melancholy Thanksgiving evening for them; they ate a little of the feast which Ruth had prepared, but without real enjoyment. They talked about accidents, and Dad told of something which had happened in the first well he had drilled—they were down only thirty feet, when a baby had crawled down into the cellar and slid into the hole. It had taken a couple of able-bodied men to hold the mother back, while the rest of them tried to get the child out. They fished for it with a big hook on the end of a rope, and got the hook under the baby's body and lifted it gently a few feet, but then the body got wedged somehow, and they were helpless. The child had hung there, not screaming, just making a low, moaning sound all the time, "U-u-u-" like that, never stopping; they could hear it plainly. They started twenty feet from the well and dug a shaft, big enough for two men to work in, breaking the ground with crow bars, scraping it into buckets with big hoes, and the men on top hauling the buckets out with ropes. When they got below the baby, they ran in sideways, and got the baby out all right. The hook had sunk into the flesh of the thigh, but without breaking the skin; the bruise had healed, and in a few days the child was all right.

A strange thing was life! If Bunny had stayed home that day, he'd have taken Rosie Taintor to the foot-ball game, and at the moment when poor Joe Gundha had plunged to his doom, Bunny would have been yelling his head off over a few yards gained by his team. And now, in the evening, he'd have been at a dance; yes, Bertie actually was at a dance, at the home of one of her fashionable friends, or at some fancy hotel where they were giving a party. Bunny could see, in his mind's eye, her gleaming shoulders and bosom, her dress of soft shimmering stuff, her bright cheeks and vivid face; she would be sipping champagne, or gliding about the room in the arms of Ashleigh Mathews, the young fellow she was in love with just now. Aunt Emma would be all dressed up, playing at a card-party; and grandmother was painting a picture of a young lord, or duke, or somebody, in short pants and silk stockings, kissing the hand of his lady love!

Yes, life was strange—and cruel. You lived in the little narrow circle of your own consciousness, and, as people said, what you didn't know didn't hurt you. Your Thanksgiving dinner was spoiled, because one poor laborer had slid down into a well which you happened to own; but dozens and perhaps hundreds of men had been hurt in other wells all over the country, and that didn't trouble you a bit. For that matter, think of all the men who were dying over there in Europe! All the way from Flanders to Switzerland the armies were hiding in trenches, bombarding each other day and night, and thousands were being mangled just as horribly as by a grab in the bottom of a well; but you hadn't intended to let that spoil your Thanksgiving dinner, not a bit! Those men didn't mean as much to you as the quail you were going to kill the next day!

Well, the coroner came, and they buried the body of Joe Gundha, on a hill-top a little way back out of sight, and with a wooden cross to mark the spot. It was a job for Mr. Shrubbs, the preacher at Eli's church; and Eli came along, and old Mr. Watkins and his wife, and other old ladies and gentlemen of the church who liked to go to funerals. It was curious

—Dad seemed glad to have them come and tell him what to do; they knew, and he didn't! Obviously, it didn't really do the poor devil any good to preach and pray over his mangled corpse; but at least it was something, and there were people who came and did it, and all you had to do was jist to stand bare-headed in the sun for a while, and hand the preacher a ten dollar bill afterwards. Yes, that was the procedure—in death, as in life; you wanted something done, and there was a person whose business it was to do that thing, and you paid him. To Bunny it seemed a natural phenomenon—and all the same, whether it was Mr. Shrubbs, who prayed over your dead rough-neck, or the man at the filling station who supplied the gas and oil and water and air for your car, or the public officials who supplied the road over which you drove the car.

Dad had sent a telegram to Mrs. Gundha, telling her the sad news, and adding that he was sending a check for a hundred dollars to cover her immediate expenses. Now Dad wrote a letter, explaining what they had done, and how they were sending her dead husband's things in a box by express. Dad carried insurance to cover his liability for accidents, and Mrs. Gundha would be paid by the insurance company; she must present her claim to the industrial accident commission. They would probably allow her five thousand dollars, and Dad hoped she would invest the money in government bonds, and not let anybody swindle her, with oil stocks or other get rich quick schemes.

So that was that; and Dad said they might jist as well go quail shooting, and forget what they couldn't help. And Bunny said all right; but in truth he didn't enjoy the sport, because in his mind somehow the quail had got themselves mixed up with Joe Gundha and the soldiers in France, and he couldn't get any fun out of mangled bodies.

VII

Christmas was coming; and Bunny had his program all laid out. He was going to take Dad to the Christmas Day foot-ball game, and next morning they would leave for Paradise, and stay there until it was time to go back for the New Year's Day foot-ball game. The well was going fine; they were down over two thousand feet, in soft shale, and having no trouble. Then, a couple of weeks before Christmas, Bunny came home from school, and Aunt Emma said, "Your father just phoned; he's got some news about Excelsior Peter." That was a joke they had in the family—"Excelsior Peter;" Aunt Emma had guessed that "Pete" was a nick-name, and she would be real lady-like and use the full name! So, of course, they teased the life out of her.

"What is it?" cried Bunny.

"They've struck oil."

"At Paradise?" Bunny rushed to the phone, in great excitement. Yes, Dad said, Dave Murgins had jist phoned down; "Excelsior-Carter No. 1," as the well was called, had been in oil sands for several days, and had managed to keep it secret. Now they were cementing off, something you couldn't hide.

Bunny jumped into the car and rushed down to the office. Everybody was excited; the afternoon papers had the news, and some of Dad's oil friends dropped in to talk about it. It meant a new field, of course; there would be a rush to Paradise. Dad was the lucky one—to think he had got twelve thousand acres up there, owned them outright! How had it happened? Dad said it wasn't his doings; he had spent a hundred thousand dollars jist to amuse his boy, to get him interested in the business, and perhaps teach him a lesson. But now, by golly, it looked as if the boy had done the teaching! Mr. Bankside, who had got to be quite an oil-man now, and was drilling a well of his own, said that he always hoped his sons would lose when they started gambling, so they'd not get the habit; Dad said yes, but he'd risk Bunny's soul this once, there was too much money at stake!

After that, of course, Bunny was on pins and needles to get to Paradise; he wanted to quit school, but Dad said no. Bunny decided he didn't care about that old Christmas Day foot-ball game; what did Dad think? To which Dad answered that he'd managed to get along to the age of fifty-nine without ever seeing a foot-ball game! So Bunny said he'd write and tell Ruth, they'd run up on Christmas eve, starting after school, and have dinner late, in regular society style. It would be hard for Ruth to believe that fashionable people in the cities ate their dinner at eight or nine o'clock at night!

Meantime, the bit was grinding away in the well; they were down to 2300 feet, and it was known that Excelsior-Carter No. 1 had struck the sands at 2437 feet. Bunny was so much excited that he would run to the phone in between classes at school, and call up his father's secretary at the office, to ask if there was any news. And so, three days before Christmas, he got the magic word; Dad was on the phone, and said that Bunny's well was in oil-sands. It was too early yet to say any more, they were taking a core, that was all. As soon as he got free from class, Bunny went flying over to the office, and there he listened to a conversation—Dad had put in a long distance call, and was talking to the man from whom he got his machinery. He was ordering a patent casing-head, the biggest made, to be shipped to the well; it was to be put on a truck and start tonight. And then Dad was talking to Murgins again, telling him at what hour the casing-head was due, and they must set to work and break out the drill-stem, and put that casing-head on tight, with lugs on the side, and jist bury it with cement, not less than fifty tons, Dad said; they were away off from everything, out there at Paradise, and if they was to have a blow-out, it would be the very devil.

Well, they got their core, eight feet of it, and it was high gravity oil—a fortune waiting for them, down underneath those rocky hills, where the feet of goats and sheep had trod for so many years! Dad ordered his "tankage," and then he ordered more. Then they learned that the casing-head had arrived; it was screwed on, and the "lugs" were on, and when the cement had set, all the gas under Mount Vesuvius couldn't lift that there load, said Dad. They started drilling again, and took another core, and found the oil heavier yet. So finally Dad gave way, and said it was too important, he guessed Bunny would have to beg off a day in school. Dad gave orders to "wash" the well, and he called up the cement man, and arranged for the big truck to set out for Paradise; Dad would meet them there, and they would do the job the day before Christmas, and if they got their shut-off, they'd celebrate with the biggest turkey in that famous turkey-raising country. So, early the next morning, Dad and Bunny chucked their suit-cases into the car, and set out to break the speed records to Paradise. Three hours later they stopped to telephone, and the foreman said they were "washing;" also that the Excelsior Pete well had got a water shut-off, and had drilled through the cement, and was going down into the oil sands, the final stage of making a well.

They got to San Elido; and Dad said, "We'll jist stop and shake hands with Jake Coffey." They drove up to the store, and Bunny jumped out, and there was a clerk and he said,

"Jake's gone up to Paradise to see the well. Have you heard the news? Excelsior Pete has got a gusher, there's oil all over the place!" Bunny ran out and shouted to Dad, and leaped into the car, and gosh-amighty, the way they did burn up that road across the desert! Dad laughed, and said the speed-cops would all be up at the well.

They got to Paradise, and the town was deserted, not a soul on the streets, and not a car, except those that were hurrying through, like the Rosses. A burglar could have made off with the whole place—but any burglar would have been watching the gusher, along with the speed-cops! You had to park your car a quarter of a mile away from the well, and you could hear the gusher roaring like Niagara Falls! And then, walking, you came round a turn in the road, and you could see the valley, and everything in sight was black; there was a high wind blowing, and it was a regular thunder cloud, a curtain of black mist as far as you could see. The derrick was hidden altogether—you had to make a detour, behind a little ridge, and come over the top to windward, and there the crowds were gathered, staring at the great black jet that came rushing up out of the ground, a couple of hundred feet into the air, with a sound like an endless express train going by. You could see men working, or trying to work, under the derrick; you could see a bunch of them with picks and shovels, throwing up a sort of dam to hold the oil; they wouldn't save much, Dad said, it evaporated too fast.

Dad could watch this scene philosophically; it wasn't his "funeral." If it had been one of the independents, like himself, he'd have offered to help; but this was a dirty crowd, Excelsior Pete, they didn't think the little fellows had any business on earth, there was nothing too mean for them to do. Of course, it was a shame to see all that treasure going to waste; but you couldn't be sentimental when you were playing the oil game. What you had to watch out for was that the wind didn't shift suddenly and ruin your good suit of clothes!

VIII

They watched for a while, and then they remembered they had a well of their own, and drove back to Paradise, and across the valley to the Watkins ranch. They had a long talk with the foreman; Dad examined the core, and the report of the chemist who had tested the oil; he saw that the "washing" was going all right, they would be ready for the cementing off in the morning. Everybody was on tiptoe; they were going to do their job better than the "Excelsior Pete" crowd, and not smear all the landscape with crude petroleum. The tankage was at the railroad depot, and they inspected the foundations, just completed for the tanks.

Everything "hunky-dory," said Dad. They drove over to the Rascum place and saw Ruth, and Bunny got on his hunting clothes, and got a few quail before sun-down; and then they had supper, and Paul told them all the gossip about the well, also how much money Eli had collected for his temple. After supper they went back to the well—they just couldn't keep away! It was a crisp cold evening, a new moon in the sky, a big white star just over it—everything so beautiful, and Bunny so happy, he owned a "wild-cat," and it was "coming in," it was going to yield him a treasure that would make all the old-time fairy tales and Arabian Nights adventures seem childish things. They were lifting the "water-string" now— a process necessary to cementing off; the casing at the bottom had to be raised, so that the cement could be forced under. It was difficult, for the casing was wedged, and they had to put down a tool known as a "jar," which struck heavy blows and shook the casing loose. Standing on the derrick platform, Bunny listened to these blows, far down in the earth; and then suddenly came a sound, the like of which had never assailed his ears in all his life, a sound that was literally a blow on the side of his head; it seemed as if the whole inside of the earth suddenly blew out. That tremendous casing-head, with its mass of cement, which Dad had said would hold down Mt. Vesuvius, went suddenly up into the air; straight up, with the big fourteen inch casing following it, right through the top of the derrick, smashing the crown block and tackle as if these had been made of sugar candy!

Of course Bunny turned and ran for his life, everybody scattered in every direction. Bunny looked once or twice as he ran, and saw the casing-head and a long string of casing up in the air, for all the world like a Dutchman's pipe, only it was straight. When this pipe-stem got too long, it broke off, and crashed over sideways, taking part of the derrick with it; and out of the hole there shot a geyser of water, and then oil, black floods of it, with that familiar roaring sound—an express train shooting out of the ground! Bunny gave a yell or two, and he saw Dad waving his arms, and presumably calling; he started toward his father—when suddenly, most dreadful thing of all, the whole mass of oil up in the air burst into flame!

They were never to know what did it; perhaps an electric spark, or the fire in the boiler, or a spark made by falling wreckage, or rocks blown out of the hole, striking on steel; anyhow, there was a tower of flame, and the most amazing spectacle —the burning oil would hit the ground, and bounce up, and explode, and leap again and fall again, and great red masses of flame would unfold, and burst, and yield black masses of smoke, and these in turn red. Mountains of smoke rose to the sky, and mountains of flame came seething down to the earth; every jet that struck the ground turned into a volcano, and rose again, higher than before; the whole mass, boiling and bursting, became a river of fire, a lava flood that went streaming down the valley, turning everything it touched into flame, then swallowing it up and hiding the flames in a cloud of smoke. The force of gravity took it down the valley, and the force of the wind swept it over the hill-side; it touched the bunk-house, and swallowed it in one gulp; it took the tool-house, everything that was wood; and when there came a puff of wind, driving the stream of oil and gas to one side, you saw the skeleton of the derrick, draped with fire!

Bunny saw his father, and ran to join him. Dad was rallying the men; was anybody hurt? He got the crew together, one by one; they were all there, thank God! He told Paul to run down to the ranch-house and get his family up into the hills; he told Bunny to go with him, and keep away from the fire—a long way, you never could tell in which direction it would explode. So Bunny went flying down the arroyo at Paul's heels; they found the family down on their knees, praying, the two girls hysterical. They got them up, and told them where to go; never mind their few belongings, cried Bunny, Dad would pay for them. Paul shouted to see to the goats, and they ran to the pen, but they weren't needed; the panic-stricken creatures flung themselves against the side of the pen and broke through, and away they went down the arroyo; they would take care of themselves!

Bunny started back; and on the way, here came Dad in his car. He was going after dynamite, he called to them; they were to keep away from the fire meantime; and off he went

in the darkness. It was one time in his life that Bunny knew
his father to be caught without something he needed; he hadn't
thought to carry any dynamite around with him on his drives!

Of course Bunny had heard about oil fires, which are the
terror of the industry. He knew of the devices ordinarily used
to extinguish them. Water was of no use—quite the contrary,
the heat would dissolve the water into its constituents, and you
would merely be feeding oxygen to the flames. You must have
live steam in enormous quantities, and for that you needed
many boilers, and they had only one here, this fire would go
on burning all the while they were fetching more; Bunny had
heard of a fire that burned for ten days, until they made a
great conical hood of steel to slide over the well, with an
opening in the top through which the flames rushed out, and
into which was poured the live steam. And meantime all the
pressure would be wasted, and millions of dollars worth of
money burned up! Bunny realized that, as a desperate
alternative, Dad was going to try to plug up the hole by a
dynamite blast, even at the risk of ruining the well.

The two boys skirted the slopes, and got back to the well,
on the windward side, away from the flames. There they found
the crew engaged in digging a shaft, as close to the fire as they
could get; Bunny understood that it was in preparation for the
dynamite. They had set up a barrier against the heat, a couple
of those steel troughs in which they mixed cement; upon this
they had a hose playing, the water turning to steam as it hit.
A man would run into the searing heat, and chop a few strokes
with a pick, or throw out a few shovelfuls of dirt, and then
he would flee, and another man would run in. Dave Murgins
was working the hose, lying flat on the ground with some wet
canvas over his head. Fortunately, they had pressure from the
artesian well, for their pump was out of commission, along with
everything else. Dave shouted his orders, and the hole got
deeper and deeper. Paul ran in to help, and Bunny wanted
to, but Dave shouted him back, and so he had to stand and
watch his "wild-cat" burning up, and all he could do was to
bake his face a little!

They got down below the surface of the ground, and after
that it was easier; but the man who worked in that hole was
risking his life—suppose the wind were to shift, even for a
few seconds, and blow that mass of boiling oil over him! But
the wind held strong and steady, and the men jumped into the

hole and dug, and the dirt flew out in showers. Presently they were tunneling in towards the well—they would go as close as they dared, before they set the dynamite.

And suddenly Bunny thought of his father, coming with the stuff; he wouldn't be able to drive up the road, he'd have to come round by the rocky hill-side, carrying that dangerous load in the darkness. Bunny went running, as fast as he dared, to help.

There were cars down on the road; many people had seen the glare of the fire, and come to the scene. Bunny inquired for his father; and at last there came a car with much tooting, and there was Dad, and another man whom Bunny did not know. They drove as far up as they dared—the Watkins house had been long ago swallowed by the flames. They stopped and got out, and Dad told Bunny to take the car back to a safe place, and not come near him or the other man with the dynamite; they would make their way to the well, very carefully. Bunny heard Dad telling the other man to go slow, they'd not risk their lives jist to save a few barrels of oil.

When Bunny got back to the well again, Dad and the man were already there, and the crew was setting the dynamite. They had some kind of electric battery to explode it with, and presently they were ready, and everybody stood back, and the strange man pushed down a handle, and there was a roar and a burst of flame from the shaft, and the geyser of oil that was rushing out of the well was snubbed off in an instant—just as if you stopped a garden hose by pinching it! The tower of oil dropped; it leaped and exploded a few times more, and that was the end. The river of fire was still flowing down the arroyo, and would take a long time to burn itself out; but the main part of the show was over.

And nobody was hurt—that is, nobody but Bunny, who stood by the edge of the red glare, gazing at the stump of his beautiful oil derrick, and the charred foundations of his home-made bunk-house, and all the wreckage of his hopes. If the boy had been a little younger, there would have been tears in his eyes. Dad came up to him and saw his face, and guessed the truth, and began to laugh. "What's the matter, son? Don't you realize that you've got your oil?"

Strange as it may seem, that idea came to Bunny for the first time! He stared at his father, with such a startled expression that the latter put his arm about the boy and gave him a hug. "Cheer up, son! This here is nothin', this is a joke. You're a millionaire ten times over."

"Gosh!" said Bunny. "That's really true, isn't it!"

"True?" echoed Dad. "Why, boy, we got an ocean of oil down underneath here; and it's all ours—not a soul can get near it but us! Are you a-frettin' about this measly little well?"

"But Dad, we worked so hard over it!"

Dad laughed again. "Forget it, son! We'll open it up again, or drill a new one in a jiffy. This was jist a little Christmas bonfire, to celebrate our bustin' in among the big fellers!"

CHAPTER VII

THE STRIKE

I

A year had passed, and you would hardly have known the town of Paradise. The road was paved, all the way up from the valley, and lined with placards big and little, oil lands for sale or lease, and shacks and tents in which the selling and leasing was done. Presently you saw derricks—one right alongside Eli's new church, and another by that holier of holies, the First National Bank. Somebody would buy a lot and build a house and move in, and the following week they would sell the house, and the purchaser would move it away, and start an oil derrick. A great many never got any farther than the derrick—for subdividers of real estate had made the discovery that all the advertising in the world was not equal to the presence of one such structure on the tract. You counted eleven as you drove to the west side of the valley, where the Excelsior gusher had spouted forth; and from the top of the ridge, you could count fifty, belonging to a score of different companies. Going east, there were a dozen more before you reached the Ross tract, and now some one was prospecting on the far side of this tract, along the slide to Roseville, where the Mineral Springs Hotel was being built.

The little Watkins arroyo was the site of a village. You counted fourteen derricks here and there on the slopes, and big tanks down below, and tool-houses and sheds, and an office. Dad had built the new home of the Watkins family near the entrance to the place; they had sold their goats, and they now irrigated a tract and raised strawberries and garden truck and chickens and eggs for the company mess. In addition to that, they had a little stand by the road-side, and Mrs. Watkins and the girls baked pies and cakes and other goodies, which disappeared down the throats of oil-workers with incredible rapidity, assisted by "soft drinks" of vivid hues. But you couldn't buy any "smokes" at the stand, these being contrary to the Third Revelation, and obtainable at the rival stand across the road.

The new bunk-house stood a little way back, under the

shelter of some eucalyptus trees. It had six shower-baths, which were generously patronized, but to Bunny's great sorrow you seldom saw anybody in the reading-room, despite the pretty curtains which Ruth had made; the high-brow magazines were rarely smudged by the fingers of oil-workers. Bunny tried to find out why, and Paul told him it was because the men had to work too long hours; Paul himself, as a carpenter, had an eight hour day, and found time for reading; but the oil-workers were on two shifts, twelve hours each, and they worked every day in the year, both Sundays and holidays. When you had put in that much time handling heavy tools, you wanted nothing but to get your supper and lie down and snore. This was a problem which Dad was too busy to solve just now.

Paul was boss-carpenter, having charge of all the building operations; quite a responsibility for a fellow not quite of age. So far they had completed forty shacks for the workers' families, costing about six hundred dollars each, and renting for thirty dollars a month, with water, gas and electric light free. No one knew exactly what these latter services cost, so Bunny could not determine whether the price was fair or not, and neither could the oil-workers; but Dad said they were glad to get the houses, which was the business man's way of determining fairness.

But there was one point upon which Bunny had interfered with energy; he didn't see why everything about the oil industry had to be so ugly, and certainly something ought to be done about these shacks. He asked Ruth about it, and they drove to a nursery in San Elido, and without saying anything to Dad, incurred a bill for a hundred young acacia trees, each in a tin can, and two hundred climbing roses, each with its roots tied up in a gunny sack. So now at every shack there was a young tree with a stake beside it, and all along the road there were frames made of gas pipe, with a rose vine getting ready to climb. It was Ruth's duty once a month to pull one of the laborers off his job and make him soak the trees and the vines, and next day cultivate them and dig away the grass and weeds. For this service Ruth was compelled to receive a salary of ten dollars a month, and bore the imposing title of "Superintendent of Horticultural Operations." Bunny would inspect the growing plants, and sit in his reading room, and persuade himself that he had made a start as a social reformer, resolving the disharmonies between capital and labor, about which he was being taught in the "social ethics" class in school.

Bunny was now almost eighteen, slender, but well built, and something of a runner. He was brown as ever, and his hair was still wavy, and his lips red and pretty like a girl's; he was merry on the surface, but serious underneath, trying most conscientiously to prepare for the task of administering some millions of dollars of capital, and directing the lives of some thousands of workingmen. If the people who wrote books about these matters, and taught them in school, had any useful suggestions, Bunny wanted to get them; so he listened, and read what he was told to read, and then he would come home and ask Dad about it, and when he visited the field, he would ask Paul. The teachers and the text books said there was no real disharmony between capital and labor; both were necessary to industry, they were partners, and must learn to get along together. And Dad said that was all right, only, like everything else, it was theory, and didn't always work out. Dad said that the workingmen were ignorant, and wanted things the industry couldn't afford to give; it was from this the quarrels grew. But Dad didn't know what to do about it, and apparently wasn't trying to find out; he was always too busy getting some new tract developed; and Bunny couldn't very well complain—having got Dad into this latest pile of work!

It seemed a shame, when you came to realize it. This ranch had been a place where Dad could come to rest and shoot quail; but now that they had struck oil, it was the last place in the world where he could rest. There were new wells to be planned and drilled, and pipe lines to be run, and oil to be marketed, and financing to be seen to, and houses and roads, and a gas-plant, and more water—there was something new every day. The books showed that nearly three million dollars had gone into the place so far, and now Dad was talking about the absolute necessity of having his own refinery; his mind was full of a thousand technical details along this line. There was a group of men—really big capitalists—who wanted to go in with him, and turn this into one of the monster oil fields, with a company capitalized at sixty million dollars; there would be a "tank-farm," and several distilleries, and a chain of distributing stations. Should Dad follow this course, or should he save the business for Bunny? The boy would have to decide pretty soon, did he want to shoulder an enormous burden like this, or to let other people carry it for him? Did he want to study all kinds of things, like Paul, or did he want to buckle down to the oil-game, and give his attention to the process of cracking distillation, and the use of dephlegmators in connection with tower stills?

II

Bunny's speculations upon the problem of capital and labor were not destined to remain academic. Spending his Christmas holidays at Paradise, he found Paul looking very serious, and asking what would be Dad's attitude towards the matter of unions in this field. There was an organizer for the carpenters here, and Paul had talked with him, and decided that it was his duty to join. Some of the men had joined secretly, but Paul wouldn't have any concealment in his relations with Mr. Ross. Bunny answered that his father didn't think much of unions, but he certainly wouldn't object to Paul's joining, if Paul thought it was right; anyhow they'd talk it out. So that evening they had a session, which wasn't quite the same as a class at high school.

Dad believed in organization; he always said that, and his formula would apply to workingmen—at least in theory. But in practice Dad had observed that a labor union enabled a lot of officials to live off the work of the real workers; these officials became a class by themselves, a sort of vested interest, and they looked out for themselves, and not for labor. They naturally had to make some excuse for their own existence, and so were apt to stir up the workers to discontent which otherwise the workers wouldn't feel.

Paul said that was one way to look at it; but as a matter of fact, it was just as apt to work the other way—the men would be discontented, and officials would be trying to smooth them down. The officials made bargains with the employers, and naturally wanted the workers to fall into line. Didn't it seem more reasonable to account for disputes in industry by the fundamental fact that one group was selling labor, and the other was buying it? Nobody was ever surprised that a man who was buying a horse didn't value it so high as the owner.

You could see Dad didn't like that, because it was a view that made his business more difficult. He said that what troubled him about unions was, they deprived a man of his personal liberty; he was no longer a free American citizen, he was jist a part of a machine, run by politicians, and often by grafters. What had made this country great was individual enterprise, and we ought to protect that. And Paul said yes, but the employers had set the men a bad example; they had joined a "Petroleum Employers' Federation," which ruled the industry very strictly. Paul had been told that in his early days Mr. Ross had paid his men a dollar a day more than the regular scale, so as to get the best labor; but when he had got into the Prospect Hill field, he had had to join the Federation, and now wasn't allowed to pay more than the regular scale.

That was true, Dad admitted, but he hastened to explain, he hadn't reduced anybody's wages; his business had grown so fast, he had put his men into higher classifications, and when he engaged new men for the old jobs, they had got the regular price. But when Paul pinned him down, Dad admitted that it really was a union he belonged to, and he had sacrificed his personal liberty to that extent. It was clear enough, there had to be some order among the employers, to keep them from cutting one another's throats; and Dad was fair enough to admit that maybe if he were a laborer, he'd see the same necessity.

Paul pleased Dad by saying that if all the employers were as fair as Mr. Ross, it would be easy to deal with them; but the fact was plain that many of them would respect only power, and the workers had no power except as a group. Why was it the carpenters were working only eight hours? Because they were organized all over the country, you couldn't get a lot of good carpenters on any other terms. But the oil workers were poorly organized, so here was this two-shift arrangement, an inhuman thing, and the reason why Bunny couldn't get the men to make use of his reading-room. Paul said that with a smile, to take the sting out of it; he knew it would hurt Bunny, and that Dad wouldn't feel comfortable over it, either. Dad couldn't give his oil-workers an eight hour day, even if he wanted to— because the Petroleum Employers' Federation had taken away his personal liberty and initiative in that respect. Paul added that the Federation would have to face this issue very shortly, because the oil-workers were organizing—right in this Paradise field, as Mr. Ross no doubt knew.

Dad said he had heard it; he went so far as to admit that the Federation had sent him bulletins to keep him posted. But he wasn't worrying, he said; if his men wanted a union, he

guessed he'd find a way to get along with it—he had tried
to be fair all his life, and the men knew it, most of them. Paul
answered that Mr. Ross ought to understand the fundamental
fact, which was that the cost of everything had been going up,
ever since the war in Europe had begun; the price of oil was
going up also, but the Employers' Federation held to the old
wage schedule, and that was not fair, and was making the
trouble. The employers who fought the unions were short-
sighted, for what they really did was to turn the men over to the
I. W. W. Dad looked startled at that, for the "wobblies," as
they were called, had the reputation of being dangerous people,
almost Anarchists, who wanted to seize the wells and run them
for the workers; you heard terrible rumors of a thing called
"sabotage," which meant that the men, if they didn't get what
they considered a square deal, would punish the employers by
damaging the property, even setting fire to wells. Were
I. W. W. really in the field? Paul answered that it wouldn't be
fair for him to report on the men, that would be making him a
spy; but as a matter of fact the wobblies were in every field, and
in every industry—you could never keep them out, and the only
thing to do was to keep their influence down by a policy of
fair play.

Paul had been studying this question of capital and labor,
as he studied everything that came his way. He had been
reading books of which Bunny had never heard even the
names—they were not taught in the high school courses, because, so Paul declared, they gave the labor side. Paul had
been talking to an organizer who was here for the Oil Workers'
Union, an especially intelligent man, who had been working in
oil fields for several years, and knew conditions thoroughly.
Bunny was tremendously interested at that, and said he'd like
to meet the man, and wouldn't Dad like to? Dad made the
answer he always made now-a-days, he was jist too crowded
with business over the new pipe-line, and the problem of a
refinery, but later on, perhaps, he might be interested. Dad
was always fooling himself that way; there was going to be
some time in the future when he would be free!

However, he hadn't any objection to Bunny's meeting all
the union organizers he pleased; he'd no doubt have to bargain
with a lot of them during his life. Paul said that Tom Axton
was supposed to be here secretly, but as a matter of fact the
bosses all knew him, he had been kicked off the Excelsior Pete

property only yesterday. He'd no doubt be willing to talk with Bunny, provided it was made clear that this wouldn't affect his right to organize the men in Mr Ross' employ.

The upshot of it was that Axton was invited to meet Bunny one morning in the reading-room; and that was the biggest sensation this Watkins tract had known since the discovery well had busted loose and caught fire. The men of the night-shift forgot to go to sleep; they waited round to see the sight, and you saw faces pass by doors and windows—and always turned inwards as they passed! The union organizer was supposed to be a mysterious and terrible person, who came onto the tract at night, and met you and your friends somewhere out in the hills; but here he was, being publicly entertained by the Old Man's son! Great kid, that Bunny Ross, said the men—agreeing with Dad on this point!

Tom Axton was a big fellow, slow spoken, soft of voice, with a trace of Southern accent; he looked powerful, and had need to be, considering the treatment he got. Of course, he couldn't swear that it was the Employers' Federation which sent thugs to beat him up and try to cripple him; but when the same thing happened to him in several different fields in Southern California, and didn't happen to anybody else, he naturally drew his own conclusions. Bunny was aghast at this; he had never heard anything like it, and didn't know what to answer—except that he hoped Mr. Axton knew that his father didn't have anything to do with such dirty work. The organizer smiled; he had evidently had a talk with Paul, for he said, "Your father thinks that labor unions are run by grafters and parasites. Well, I wish you'd ask him how much he really knows about the Employers' Federation, and the kind of men who run it, and what they're doing to us. You may find that your father has been neglecting the affairs of his union, just as most of the workers neglect theirs." Bunny had to admit that was a fair point, and when he asked Dad, and found that Dad had never attended a meeting of the Federation, but merely paid its assessments without question—why naturally, that made Bunny have more respect for Tom Axton, and believe what he said about conditions here in Paradise, and in the other fields, and how rapidly discontent was spreading among the men.

Only yesterday the Victor Oil Company had fired fourteen who had signed up with the union; the bosses had a spy among

them, and had waited to give everybody a chance to hang
himself! "You're surely going to have a strike before long,"
said the organizer. "It will be a strike for the three-shift day,
among other things; and when it comes, your father will have
to consider whether to deal separately with his own men, or
to stand by his employers' union, and let a bunch of big business
rowdies drag him into trouble." You can imagine how much
that gave Bunny to think about, and how many discussions he
had with his father, and with Paul, and with the teacher of
the class in "social ethics" at the Beach City High School!

III

The Allies, having control of the sea, were engaged in
starving out Germany; and the Germans were replying with the
only weapon they had, the submarine. The United States
had forced the German government to agree not to torpedo
passenger vessels without warning; but now, early in the winter
of 1917, the Germans gave notice that they would no longer
follow this policy, and everybody was saying that America
would have to go into the war. The German ambassador at
Washington was sent home, and after that the spirit of
neutrality was no longer dominant in the "current events"
classes at school.

To the oil operators it seemed most unpatriotic on the part
of workers, to demand the eight hour day and an increase of
wages at this crisis. What?—when the country was about to
defend itself, and would need oil as never before in history!
But the workers replied that the employers did not make
concessions because they wanted to, but because they had to, and
this might be the only time they would have to. It was not
necessary to assume that the employers were giving the oil
away; they were getting a fancy price for it, and would get the
same price, or better, if the country went to war. The workers
claimed a share, proportioned to the price of everything they
had to buy. They were holding meetings all over the field,
and in the latter part of February their union officials wrote
to the various companies, asking for a conference. When this
request was ignored, they served notice on the employers that
there would be a strike.

Three men came to see Dad; one of them an old employee,
the others new men. All three were young in years—indeed,

you almost never saw an oil worker over thirty-five, and they were all white Americans. This committee held their hats in their hands, and were somewhat pale, embarrassed but determined. They all liked Mr. Ross, and said so; he was "square," and he must know that their demands were reasonable. Wouldn't he set the example to the other employers, granting the new schedule, so that his work could go on without interruption? The strike, if it came, would be bound to spread, and the cost of oil would go up at once; Mr. Ross would gain far more than he would have to pay to the men. But Dad answered that he had joined the Federation, and agreed to stand by its decisions; what would become of his reputation for "squareness," if he were to go back on his associates in a crisis? What he would do was to work within the Federation for an agreement with the men; he would drop everything else, and go down to Angel City and see what he could accomplish. He thought the eight hour day was fair, and he would favor a wage scale adjusted to the cost of living, so that the men's income would not be subject to fluctuations. The committee was cheered by these promises, and there was hand-shaking all around.

Left to himself, you understand that J. Arnold Ross would probably never have taken this advanced position. His mind was on his money—or on the things he wanted to do, and that his money enabled him to do; he would probably have gone with his crowd, as he had done hitherto. But there was Bunny, a "little idealist"; Bunny liked the men, and the men liked him, and Dad was proud of that mutual liking, and could be sentimental for Bunny, where he would never have dreamed of being for himself. Furthermore, there was Paul, who knew the men's side at first hand; and Bunny persisted in bringing Paul into their life, in plying Paul with questions, and making him say, right out, the things he might not otherwise have felt free to say. So Paul had become a force in Dad's consciousness; and so Dad promised to try to help the men.

He attended for the first time a meeting of his own trade union. It was at night, and lasted till one o'clock in the morning; and the next day being Saturday, Bunny came up to town and met his father at the hotel, and heard the story of what had happened. Most of the oil employers, it appeared, were exactly like J. Arnold Ross, in that they left the running of their union to others; there had been not more than forty men at this critical meeting, and the dominant group consisted of representatives of the "Big Five." The chairman, and obviously the man who ran the organization, was an attorney for Excelsior Pete, who owned a small well, presumably to give him standing. He had a group which took the cue from him and voted with him. It had been rather a steam-roller affair, said Dad.

Bunny wanted all the particulars, and plied his father with questions. Dad had pleaded the men's side, as tactfully as he could, and had found exactly two operators in the gathering who were willing to agree, ever so timidly, with his point of view. To the ruling group he had seemed something of a renegade, and they had hinted as much. "You know how it is, son," Dad explained, "this is an 'open shop' town; that's the way the crowd feels, and you might jist as well butt your head against a stone wall as argue with them about unions. There's everything to be said for them—they've had trouble with organized labor, and it's made them bitter. They say"—and Dad went on to detail the arguments that had been hurled at him; unions meant graft, unions meant "hold-ups," unions meant disorder, unions meant strikes, unions meant Socialism.

"What are they going to do, Dad?"

"They're jist not a-goin' to let the men have a union— that's all. I said, 'It looks as if the Federation has turned into a strike-breaking organization.' And Fred Naumann—that's the chairman—snapped back at me, 'You said it!' They'll be a strike-breaking organization, if and when and so long as there's strikes in their field—that's the way Raymond put it, the vice-president of Victor. And then Ben Skutt put in an oar—"

"Ben *Skutt?*"

"Yes, he was there; it seems he's been doing some 'investigation work' for the Federation—a polite name for spyin. He knew jist exactly what I'd said to our men the day before; and he wondered if I realized the unfortunate effect of my attitude—it amounted to givin' the strikers moral support. I told Ben that I usually took the liberty of saying what I thought; I was taking it in this meeting, and I'd take it in the newspapers if they asked me. Naumann smiled sarcastically: 'I really don't think they're going to ask you, Mr. Ross.'"

And sure enough, they didn't—either then, or later! The meeting was supposed to be secret—which meant that individual members were not allowed to be quoted, but the chairman or somebody gave to the press an official story, telling how the meeting had voted to stand firm against the threats of the union. It was a time for all lovers of America to uphold the country's welfare against enemies without and within—so ran the statement in both the morning newspapers.

"What are you going to do?" asked Bunny.

"What can I do, son?" Dad's face was grey, and deeply lined; he was not used to staying up so late, Bunny knew, and he had probably lain awake until morning, worrying over this situation.

And yet Bunny could not help making it harder for him. "Are we going to let those fellows run our business, Dad?"

"It looks as if we'd have to, son. I'm in no position financially to buck the game."

"But with all the oil you've got!"

"I've got a good deal of oil, but it's mostly in the ground, and what I'd need for this job would be a couple of million dollars in the bank."

He went on to explain how modern affairs were conducted. A man never had enough money, no matter how much he had; he was always reaching out, doing business with the future, so to speak. He put money into the bank, and that gave him the right to take out more than he had put in; the bank would take his "paper," as it was called. Here Dad was drilling a lot of new wells, he was buying machinery and materials, and paying for labor in advance—all on the certainty of the oil he was going to get next month and the month after; he knew he was going to get it, and the banks trusted him, on the basis of his reputation, and the known value of his property. But if Dad were to set out to fight the Federation, he might jist as well forget there was such a thing as a bank in the State of California; he'd have to pay cash for everything, he'd have to stop all his development work, and even then, he mightn't be able to meet his notes when they fell due.

Bunny was appalled; for he had thought of his father as one of the richest men in the state, and one of the most independent. "Why, Dad, we don't own our own business! We don't even own our souls!"

That started the other on one of his stock themes. Business was business, and not the same as a tea-party. Property was hard to get, and, as he had told his son many times, there was always people trying to take it away from you. If there was going to be any security for wealth, there had to be discipline, and men of wealth had to stand together. It might seem harsh, if you didn't understand, but it was the way of life. Look at that war over there in Europe; it was a horrible thing—jist made you sick to think about it; but there it was, and if you was in it, you was in, and you had to fight. It was exactly the same with the business game; there was no safety for you, unless you stood with the group that had power. If you stepped out of the reservation, the wolves would tear you to pieces in short order.

But Bunny was not satisfied with general principles; he wanted the details of this situation. "Please tell me, Dad, just who are these men we have to work with?"

Dad answered: they were a group, it was hard to define them, you might say the "open shop crowd;" they were the big business men who ran Angel City, and the territory which lived upon the city, or supported the city, according as you looked at it. They had several organizations, not merely the Petroleum Employers' Federation, but the Merchants' and Manufacturers' Association, the Chamber of Commerce, the Bankers' Club. They were interlocked, and a little group ran them all—Fred Naumann could call a dozen men on the telephone, and turn you into an outcast from business society; no bank would lend you a dollar, and none of the leading merchants would give you credit, some would refuse to do business with you even for cash.

To the hour of his death, the elder Ross never really understood this strange son of his. He was always being surprised by the intensity with which Bunny took things, which to the father were part of the nature of life. The father kept two compartments in his mind, one for things that were right, and the other for things that existed, and which you had to allow to exist, and to defend, in a queer, half-hearted, but stubborn way. But here was this new phenomenon, a boy's mind which was all one compartment; things ought to be right, and if they were not right, you ought to *make* them right, or else what was the use of having any right—you were only fooling yourself about it.

"Listen, Dad," the boy pleaded; "isn't there some way we could break that combination? Couldn't you stop your new developments, and put everything on a cash basis, and go slow? You know, that might be better, in a way; you're trying to do too much, and you need a rest badly."

The other could not help smiling, in spite of the pain he read in Bunny's face. "Son," he answered, "if I set out to buck that game, I'd never have another hour's rest, till you buried me up there on the hill beside Joe Gundha."

"But you've got the oil, and if you settle with the men, it will go on flowing. It will be the only oil from this whole district!"

"Yes, son, but oil ain't cash; it has got to be sold."

"You mean they wouldn't take it from you?"

"I can't say, son; I've never known such a case, and I don't know jist what they'd do. All I say is this—they wouldn't let me lose their strike for them! They'd find some way to get me, jist as sure as tomorrow's sunrise!"

IV

Dad went back to the field and got the representatives of his men together. He did not tell them the whole story, of course, but said that he had tried his best to bring the employers to his views, and had failed. He was bound by agreements that he could not break, but he would be very glad to meet the men's terms if the Federation would do so. If there was a strike, he would make no attempt to work his properties for the present. It would mean heavy losses to him, the shutting down of his best paying wells, but he would try to stick it out, and his men might consider they were taking a vacation, and come back to him when the strike was over. Meantime, he would not turn them out, they might continue to occupy the bunk-house, provided they would keep order, and not injure the property. That was, of course, a very unusual concession, and he hoped the men would appreciate it. The committee answered that the men undoubtedly would do so; they were deeply grateful to Mr. Ross for his attitude. The members of the committee were embarrassed, and very respectful; you see, it is hard for humble working-men to confront their employer, a "big" man, and armed with the magic power of money.

The strike was called for noon on Wednesday, and the men all marched out singing songs. Not more than ten percent had joined the union, but they quit to a man—the few who might have liked to stay were not enough to work the wells, anyhow. They shut off the flow, and left everything in good order, and marched in to Paradise, where they held a mass meeting. There were nearly three thousand workers in this field, and they all came, and most of the townspeople, and a number of the ranchers; the sympathy of the community appeared to be all with the workers.

Tom Axton made a speech, in which he set forth the grievances of the men, and told them, out of his previous experience, how a strike must be conducted. One thing above all others, they must keep public sympathy with them, by obeying the law and avoiding every suggestion of disorder; this would not be easy, because the Employers' Federation knew this, as well as the strike leaders, and would do everything possible to provoke the men to violence; that was the purpose for which the "guards" were coming, the strikers' difficulty would be to keep out of the way. That was generally the case in strikes, if you could believe Axton; he said that the guards were men of a low type, hired by the big detective agencies out of the city's underworld, and supplied with a gun on their hip-pocket. Whether the whiskey-bottle on the other hip-pocket was supplied by the employers, or got by the men themselves, was something Tom Axton did not know. Anyhow, they were brought here by the truck-load, and on the way they stopped at the sheriff's office in San Elido—kept open day and night for the purpose—and were sworn in wholesale as "deputy-sheriffs," and supplied with a silver shield to wear on their coat-lapels, and after that, anything they did was according to law. A few of these deputies were standing about, listening to Axton's speech, and needless to say, they did not appreciate it.

The president of the union, who had come to the field to conduct the strike, also made a speech; and the secretary of the union, and the organizer of the carpenter's union—there could not be too many speeches, for the men were full of enthusiasm, and their minds were open to ideas; it was an education in the meaning of solidarity. They signed up by hundreds, and paid their assessments out of their scanty savings. Committees were appointed, and these got down to work in an old barn which had been hired for headquarters, the only vacant place of any size to be found in the midst of this oil boom. The place was crowded with men, coming and going, and there was not a little confusion, officials and volunteer helpers working as if such things as rest and sleep were unknown to the human organism. There were temporary lodgings to be found—for not many oil operators were being so generous as to provide shelter for strikers! The union had ordered a lot of tents, and would need more yet, when leases expired on shacks which had been rented on company property. Fortunately, not many of the men had families in this field; your oil worker is a migratory bird—he moves to a new field, and has to work quite a while before he gets enough money to bring his wife and children from the last field.

Bunny drove up on Saturday morning; by which time the first flush of excitement had passed. It was a rainy day, and the men had no meeting place, and you saw bunches of them crowded into doorways, or under awnings, wherever there was free shelter; they looked rather melancholy, as if they found being on strike less romantic than they had expected. In front of the oil properties, especially those of the big companies, you saw men pacing up and down, wearing rubber coats and hats, from under which they eyed you suspiciously; some of them carried rifles on their shoulders, like military sentries. Bunny drove up to his father's tract, and there he saw the same sight, and it cut him to the heart—the very personification of that hatred which so pained him in the industrial world, and which he had fondly dreamed he might exclude from the "Ross Junior" field. But the truth was, the "junior" aspects of the business were fading temporarily; the "senior" aspects were in control, and giving the impress to events.

Sitting in the office on the tract, Bunny pinned his father down on the matter of guards; did they really have to have guards against their own men?

"But surely, son," protested Dad, "you can't be serious! Leave three million dollars worth of property unprotected?"

"Where did we hire these guards, Dad?"

"We didn't hire them, son; the Federation is handling that."

"But couldn't we have got guards of our own?"

"I don't know any guards, or where to get them. I'd have had to go to some agency, jist the same."

"And we couldn't have used our own men, that we know?"

"Turn strikers into guards? Why, son, you must know that wouldn't do!"

"Why not?"

"Well, for one thing, the insurance companies—imagine how quick they'd jump to cancel my fire insurance! And then, suppose I was to have a fire, I'd be ruined. Don't you see that?"

Yes, Bunny saw; it appeared as if the whole world was one elaborate system, opposed to justice and kindness, and set to making cruelty and pain. And he and his father were part of that system, and must help to maintain it in spite of themselves!

"Do we pay for these guards, Dad?"

"We're assessed for it, of course."

"Then what it comes to, is this: we have to put up the money for Fred Naumann to break the strike; and even though we may not want the strike broken!" To this Dad remarked, it was devilish inconvenient to have all those paying wells shut off all of a sudden. He turned to some papers on his desk, and Bunny sat in silence for a while, thinking his father's thoughts. They were elemental thoughts, not requiring any subtlety to interpret. There were eleven producing wells on the tract, which on last Thursday morning had been flowing at a total rate of thirty-seven thousand barrels of oil per day. That meant, at present boom prices, a gross income of close to two million dollars a month. Dad's mind had been full of all the things he was going to do with that money; and now his mind was full of problems of how to get along without it. His face was still grey and lined with care, and Bunny's heart smote him. He, Bunny, wanted the men to win; but did he want it at the cost of having his father carry this extra burden?

V

Paul had gone with the strikers, so Bunny learned. Mr. Ross had offered to keep him on, for there was some building that needed to be done, and the carpenters were not on strike. But Paul had thought it over and decided that his duty lay with the oil workers; they hadn't many educated men among them—that was one of the burdens the twelve hour day put upon them; so Mr. Ross would have to accept Paul's resignation, permanently or temporarily, as he might think best. Dad had said there would be no hard feelings, and Paul might come back when the strike was over.

Bunny went up to the Rascum place to see Ruth and ask her about it. The "Superintendent of Horticultural Operations" had gone on strike with the boss carpenter, but they were still occupying the bungalow, and Ruth did the work for Dad, whenever he occupied the cabin. Ruth said that Paul couldn't get out here any more, he was sleeping on some sacks of straw in the union headquarters, where he worked about twenty hours

a day. So Meelie was staying with her sister, and they spent
all their spare time baking things, and old Mr. Watkins came,
with the same old horse hitched to the same old wagon, and
carried the things to Paradise, where they were sold to the
strikers. They had closed up their stand at the Watkins tract,
because there wasn't nobody there but guards, and they wouldn't
feed no guards, not if they starved. So spoke Meelie, who
was a little chatter-box; and Ruth looked at Bunny with some
embarrassment, thinking that wasn't proper talk before him.
But Bunny said he wasn't strong for guards himself, it had
made him sort of sick to see them on the place that was supposed
to be his. And Meelie said the man that was in charge at their
place wasn't a bad fellow, he had been a forester and fire-
guard; but some of them others was awful mean, and Pap was
a-scairt for the girls to go on the road at night, they cussed
something fierce, and they had liquor all the time.

There was an alluring odor of hot gingerbread in the
kitchen, and Bunny had not yet had his lunch; so the girls
set the little table, and the three sat down, and had a meal of
scrambled eggs and potatoes, and bread and butter, and goat's
milk and gingerbread and strawberries—for the plants which
Paul had set out had been diligently tended by Ruth, who
couldn't bear to let living things suffer, even green ones. Ruth
was now a young lady of almost eighteen, the same age as
Bunny, but she felt a lot older, as girls do. Her fair hair was
done up on the top of her head, and you saw her bare legs
no longer. She always looked nice working in the kitchen,
because then her cheeks were rosy; she was competent in her
own domain, and told you to sit down and not mess things
up trying to help. She had the bright blue eyes of all the
Watkins family; in her case they went with a candid, quiet
gaze that seemed to go to the depths of you, and make both
deception and unkindness impossible.

Bunny at this time was just beginning an intense experience
back at home—his first serious love affair, about which we
shall be told before long. Eunice Hoyt was a rich girl, and
complicated; to know her was sometimes pleasure and sometimes torment. But Ruth was a poor girl, and simple; her
presence was soothing, calm and still like a Sabbath morning.
The basis of Ruth's life was the conviction that her brother
Paul was a great and good man. Now Paul had given up
his ten dollar a day job to help the strikers, and Ruth was

baking food for the strikers, and while they had money she would sell it to them, and when they had no more money she would give it to them.

Meelie, likewise, was delighted to bake for the men, but that was not her only interest in them. The coming of oil to the Watkins tract had meant vast changes in Meelie's life, she was no longer to be recognized as a goat-herd, but had blossomed out, acquiring sophistication and conversation, and a bright colored ribbon in her hair and a necklace of yellow beads about her neck. Meelie had been to town the evening before, and it had been so exciting! Eli was a full-fledged preacher now, with a church of his own, and was holding services every evening for the glory of the Lord, and great numbers of the strikers had come, and grace had been abounding; and in between the pentecostal manifestations, Meelie had picked up news of the strike—there had been a fight on Main Street because a drunken guard had been rude to Mamie Parsons; and Paul had been one of a committee to see the sheriff and demand that he take either the liquor or the guns away from his deputies; and tomorrow Meelie was going to church again— there would be three services all through the day; and it was said that on Monday the operators were going to bring in strike-breakers, and start the wells flowing on Excelsior Pete; and the men were getting ready to stop that if they could—it would be terrible!

Bunny drove to town and wandered about to see the sights, but none of them brought happiness to him. He could not see Paul, for Paul was hard at work in the strike headquarters, and Bunny could not go there, because it would not look right, somebody might think he was spying. No longer was Bunny the young oil prince, flattered and admired by all; he was an enemy, and read hostility in men's glances, even where there might be none. He was in the position of a soldier in an army, who feels that his cause is unjust, and has no stomach for the fight—yet it is hard to wish one's self defeat!

On Sunday morning the sun was shining, and never had Bunny seen such crowds in Paradise. Eli was holding a service in the grove alongside his new "tabernacle," and was telling the strikers that if only they would have faith in the Holy Spirit, they need not worry about their wages, there was the miracle of the loaves and fishes, and was not their Heavenly Father able to feed them if they would trust him? Some believed this, and shouted "Amen"; others jeered, and went off to the playground at the school-house, where the union was holding a meeting for those who believed that wages were necessary. Bunny went there, and heard Paul make his first speech. It was a great sensation to Bunny, and in fact, to the whole town; a picturesque situation, you must admit—the two Watkins boys, the rival prodigies of the neighborhood, making speeches at the same time, and preaching somewhat opposite doctrines!

It must be said on behalf of Eli that he did not deliberately oppose the strike, and probably never clearly understood how his doctrine was likely to aid the Employers' Federation. His sisters were baking bread for the strikers, working hard with their physical hands kneading physical dough—and all the while Eli was proclaiming that he could make magical miraculous bread, whole baskets of it, by the agency of prayer. Why didn't he do it, jeered the skeptics; and Eli answered that it was because of their lack of faith. But they said it was up to him to begin; and the production of one single loaf of bread by the Bible method would multiply faith a million-fold, and bring the whole organized labor movement into the Church of the Third Revelation!

Paul had a deep, mature voice, and a slow, impressive way of speaking. He was a good orator, for the very reason that he knew none of the tricks, but was entirely wrapped up in what he had to say. There was a struggle impending over the issue of the re-opening of the wells, and Paul had been consulting lawyers, and told the strikers exactly what they had a right to do, and what they must refrain from doing. They would maintain their legal rights, but not weaken their case by committing the least breach of the law, and giving their enemies a chance to put them in the wrong. Their whole future was at stake, and the future of their wives and children; if they could win the three-shift day, they would have leisure to study and think, and raise their own status, and keep their children longer in school. That was the real issue in this strike, and if democracy did not mean that, it had no meaning, and talk about patriotism was buncombe. The vast throng cheered Paul, and Bunny could hardly keep from cheering also, and went away feeling cheap, and utterly out of harmony with life. He had time to think it over on the long drive back to Beach City by himself; he did not get in until midnight, and all the way he

heard Paul's voice above the hum of the engine, challenging
everything that Bunny thought he believed!

VI

Back in school, Bunny had to get his news about the strike
from the papers, and these did not give him much comfort.
The papers thought the strike was a crime against the country
in this crisis, and they punished the strikers, not merely by
denouncing them in long editorials, but by printing lurid accounts of the strikers' bad behavior. On Tuesday morning you
read how several truck-loads of oil workers—the despatches
did not call them strike-breakers—had been brought into
the Excelsior Petroleum Company's tract, and how, at the
entrances, they were met by howling mobs, which cursed them,
and called them vile names, and even threw bricks at them.
The Employers' Federation issued a statement denouncing this
rule of a peaceful community by riot, and the statement was
published in full.

Next day it was the turn of the Victor Oil Company, which
concern had brought a train-load of men to Roseville, and
from there to Paradise by automobiles, with armed guards to
defend them. There had been more mob scenes; and also
fights between the deputies and strikers at various other places.
It was not long before several strikers were wounded, and a
couple of deputies badly beaten. The Federation issued an
appeal to the governor to send in militia to protect them in
their rights, which were being jeopardized by lawless criminals,
organized to defy the State of California, and cripple the
country on the eve of war.

Nine people out of ten read these things in the papers
and believed them. Practically everyone Bunny knew believed
them, and thought he was some kind of freak because he
hesitated and doubted. Aunt Emma, for example; she just
knew the strikers were born criminals, and German agents
besides, or at any rate in league with German agents, and what
difference did it make? The ladies in the clubs had inside information, right from headquarters, for many of them were
the wives of influential men, who learned what was going
on, and told their wives, and the wives told Aunt Emma, who
was thrilled to be on the inside, as her brother-in-law's financial position entitled her.

And Bertie, who was still worse, the very princess of all
the tight little snobs you ever knew! Bertie went round with
the younger set, and these likewise knew everything, but without having to wait for anyone to tell them. Bertie had condescended to visit one of her father's oil wells now and then,
and there she had noted a race of lower beings at their appointed
tasks—creatures smudged with black, who tipped their caps to
her, or forgot to, but in either case stared with dumb awe,
and beneath their lowering brows showed signs of intelligence
that was almost human, and filled Bertie with uneasiness. She
had visited Paradise once, and spent a night at the cabin, and
patronized Paul and Ruth while they waited upon her, and
both of them, sensing this, had been frozen to silence, and
Bertie had condescended to admit that they were very decent
working people, but she couldn't comprehend why her brother
persisted in making intimates of such. "My God," stormed
Bunny, in a rage, "what are we?" And that, of course, was
disgusting of him—to remind his sister that their father had
been driving mule-teams in a construction camp once upon a
not very long time, and why was it any better to drive mules
than to build houses? Bertie said with dignity that her
father had raised himself by innate superiority; she knew
he had "good blood," even though she could not prove it.
Bunny answered that Paul and Ruth might have "good
blood" too, and they were certainly on the way to raising
themselves.

It was a subject about which the two would never cease to
quarrel. Bertie insisted that Paul patronized her brother, and
presumed upon his good nature, taking towards him an intolerable attitude of superiority. Paul had taken to calling him
"son," as he heard Dad doing, and such impudence was that!
Bertie referred to her brother's friend as "your old Paul;" and,
said Bertie, "your old Paul has gone and turned traitor to Dad,
and it's just what I told you all along, you can't trust such
people." And when Bertie found that Bunny was half-heartedly
sympathizing with Paul, and yearning towards the "mob" himself, she called him a perfect little wretch, an ingrate, and what
not. Their father was risking his life, staying up there among
those outlaw mobs, something which none of the other operators
did—they remained in their offices in Angel City, and let their
agents break the strike for them. But Dad, of course, was
influenced by Bunny, with his silly, sentimental notions; and

if anything were to happen to him up there, Bunny would carry the responsibility all his life.

Dad came home after a few days, and made Bertie still more indignant by telling the members of the family they would have to go slow on expenditures until the strike was over; he was going to have a hard time with his financing. Bertie suggested sarcastically that Bunny might like to sell his car to help his father out in the pinch. Dad told how there had been a little fuss on the property, one of the strikers had got into a fight with a guard at night; it wasn't clear just whose the blame was, but the captain of the guards had threatened to withdraw them all if Dad did not turn the strikers out of the bunk-house and off the property. They had finally compromised by Dad's putting up a fence between the rest of the property, and the part near the road which was occupied by the bunk-house and the homes of the men. It was a fence of barbed wire, eight feet high, and Bertie remarked sarcastically that it would be another place where Bunny and "his Ruth" could grow roses. This jibe hurt, because it summed up to Bunny the part he was playing in this struggle—growing roses on the barbed wire fence which separated capital from labor.

Dad rebuked Bertie, saying that the men were not criminals, they were decent fellows, most of them, and good Americans; the Germans had nothing to do with it at all. The trouble was, they were being misled by agitators just now. But that didn't help matters with Bertie, because "Bunny's old Paul" was one of the worst of these agitators. And Bertie didn't think her father ought to sleep up there in that lonely cabin, and let those Watkins people cook for him. She had heard a wild tale about some restaurant workers on strike who had put poison in the soup; and when Dad and Bunny burst into laughter at that, she said she didn't exactly mean Paul or Ruth would do such a thing, but they certainly couldn't enjoy cooking for both the strikers and for Dad at the same time, and Dad ought to be indignant with them for deserting him in a crisis. Bunny took occasion to declare that Ruth was a true-hearted girl; and his sister broke in, oh yes, of course, she knew Bunny's admiration for the wonderful Miss Ruth, the next thing they'd be hearing he was in love with her—or would it be with Meelie, or what was the other one's name?

Bunny got up and walked out of the room. Bunny was in

love with somebody else, and his sister was hateful in this attitude of class-bigotry. And yet, he had to remind himself, within her own circle Bertie was generous, and sometimes tender-hearted. She was loyal to her friends, she would help them if they got into trouble, and would work and scheme to entertain them. You see, Bertie knew these people; they were all rich, and so she considered them her equals, and was willing to enter into their lives. But the oil-workers Bertie did not know; they were a lower order of beings, created for her pleasure, and owing her a debt of submission, which they were trying to get out of paying.

And what was Bertie, that the oil workers should support her? She was a dashing and brilliant young person, who knew how to spend a great deal of money in super-elegant ways, in the company of other young persons possessing the same accomplishment; she was racing about with them, and her talk was of what they said and what they did and what they owned. Bertie was going a fast pace, seldom in before the small hours of the morning, and if she was up before lunch, it was because she had an engagement to rush away. What was the use of having a lot of money if you didn't have a good time with it? That was the doctrine Bertie hammered into her younger brother; and Aunt Emma echoed it; and now came Eunice Hoyt, who had chosen Bunny, and had the most powerful leverage of all. Be young, be young! everybody cried. Why should you carry all the burden of the world upon your shoulders? Especially since there was not a thing you could do—since the world was fixed and ordained, and would not let you touch the least of all its vested and endowed and chartered disharmonies!

VII

The German submarines had sunk one American vessel too many, and America was going to war; Congress had been summoned, and the whole country was on tiptoe with belligerency. The newspapers had pages of despatches from Washington and New York, and from the capitals of Europe; so it was not surprising that the news of the Paradise oil strike got crowded out. Once in a while you saw an inch or two buried in a back page; three strikers had been arrested, charged with beating up a strike-breaker on a dark night; it was declared by the operators that the strikers had attempted to set fires in the district, and that German agents were active among the trouble-makers: some little thing like that, to remind you that three thousand men, and the wives and children of many of them, were waging a desperate struggle with starvation.

Dad of course had daily reports of what was happening, and so Bunny got the news. Little by little the operators had gathered up a supply of men, paying them extra wages, and bringing them to the field. They were seldom skilled men, and there were many accidents; nevertheless, a number of the wells were back on production, and in two or three cases some drilling was being done. But on the Ross tract everything stood idle; and Bunny could see that his father was irritated by this situation. He was losing a fortune every day—and at the same time losing caste with his associates, who thought he was either crack-brained, or a traitor, they could not make out which. Of course, the Big Five were glad enough to see one of the independents cutting his own throat; but they pretended to be indignant, and spread rumors and propaganda against their rival, and magnified the trouble he was causing in the field.

Bunny could see all this, and he got the sting of it from the gossip which Aunt Emma brought home from the clubs, and Bertie from her house-parties and dinner-dances. And then he would think of the men, clinging pitifully to their hope of a better life, and his heart would be torn in half. There was only one thing that could justify Dad's course, and that was for the men to win; they must win, they must! It was the way Bunny felt when he sat and watched a foot-ball game, and cheered himself hoarse for the home-team. He had an impulse to jump into the arena and help the team—but alas, the rules of the game forbade such action!

There had been more trouble with the guards at the Ross tract, and Dad was going up to the field, and Bunny went along for a week-end. It was springtime now, and the hills were green, and the fruit-trees in blossom—oh, beautiful, beautiful! But human beings were miserable, millions of them, and why could they not learn to be happy in such a world? It was springtime all over the country, and yet everybody was preparing to go to war, and form vast armies, and kill other people, also groping for happiness! Everybody said that it had to be; and yet something in Bunny would not cease to dream of a world in which people did not maim and kill one another, and destroy, not merely the happiness of others, but their own.

They came to Paradise, and there was the strange sight of idle men, hanging about the streets; and of guards at the entrances to all the oil properties. There was somebody making a speech on a vacant lot, and a crowd listening. It was a great time for all sorts of cranks with things to teach—itinerant evangelists, and patent medicine venders, and Socialist orators—the people heard them all impartially. Bunny found that his reading room was being patronized now, there were men who had read all the magazines, even to the advertisements!

Dad interviewed a committee of his men. It was an impossible situation, they reported, the guards were deliberately making trouble, they were drunk part of the time, and didn't know what they were doing or had done. Therefore the union had put up some more tents, and the men in the bunk-house were about to move out. Those who had families, and occupied the houses, would try to stay on, if Mr. Ross would permit it; there was no place for the families to go, and they dared not leave the women and children alone in the neighborhood of the guards. Dad interviewed the captain of the latter, and got the information that the men had liquor, of course; how could you expect men to stay in a God-forsaken hole like this without liquor? Dad had to admit that was true; men were like that, and when you had your property to protect in an emergency, you had to take what you could get. Bunny wasn't satisfied with this argument, but then, Bunny was an "idealist," and such people are seldom satisfied in this harsh world.

Bunny went up to see Ruth and Meelie—the place to get the news! The girls were hard at work baking, but that didn't occupy their tongues, and from Meelie's there poured a stream of gossip. Dick Nelson was in hospital with a part of his jaw shot away—that nice young fellow, Bunny remembered him, he had worked on Number Eleven well; he had knocked a guard down for dirty talk to his sister, and two other guards had shot him. And Bob Murphy was in jail, he had been arrested when they were bringing the strike-breakers into the Victor place. And so on, name after name that Bunny knew. Meelie's eyes were wide with horror, and yet you could see that she was young, and this was more excitement than had ever come into her life before. If the devil, with his hoofs and horns and pitchfork and burning smell, had appeared at a meeting of the Tabernacle of the Third Revelation, Meelie would have enjoyed the sensation; and in the same way she enjoyed this crew of whiskey-drinking, cursing ruffians, suddenly vomited out of the city's underworld into her peaceful and pious and springtime-decorated village.

Bunny asked about Paul, and learned that he had been put on the strike committee, and was editing a little paper which the union was publishing; it was lovely, and had Bunny seen it? They produced a copy—a double sheet, mimeographed on both sides for economy, and with a little oil-derrick at the top of the first sheet, alongside the title, "The Labor Defender." It was full of strike news, and exhortations, and an appeal to the governor of the State against the violence of the deputies and the refusal of the sheriff to take their whiskey away; also there was a poem, "Labor Awake, by Mrs. Weenie Martin, a Tool-dresser's Wife." Paul had just got back from a trip to some of the other fields, where he had gone to persuade the men to join the strike; in Oil Center they had tried to arrest him, but he had got a tip and got away by a back road.

America was going to war, and everybody was thrilled about it; at school they were singing patriotic songs and organizing drill corps. This oil war was so little in comparison that nobody heeded it; but it got hold of Bunny, and came to seem the big war to him. All this arrogance of power, this defiance of law and decency, this miserable lying about workingmen! Here Bunny got the truth, he got it face to face with the men and women whom he knew; and then he would remember the tales he had read in the newspapers—and would hate himself, because he lived upon money which had been obtained by such means! His father was paying the "assessments" of the Federation, and thus paying the salaries of these black-guards—paying for their guns and ammunition, and for the bottles of whiskey without which they would not stay!

What did it mean? What was back of it? One thing—the greed of a little ruling group of operators, who wouldn't pay their men a living wage, but would work them twelve hours a day. They were driving the men with revolvers and rifles, holding them away from the wells, their only source of liveli-hood, and starving them back to work on the old unfair terms. That was the story, just that simple; and here, in Ruth's little kitchen, you saw the process from the inside. The girls had had to reduce the price of the bread they sold, because some people couldn't afford it otherwise! Oil-workers never do save much, because they have to move about, and to bring their families, or to send them money. And now their savings were used up, and the contributions which came from other fields were not enough, and Paul, who had been saving money to study and become a scientist, was using it to support hungry families, and Ruth and Meelie were giving all their time, and even old Mrs. Watkins was helping when she could!

Bunny carried this anguish back to his father. What were the people going to do, when they no longer had food to keep alive? Dad gave the answer, they'd have to go back to work! "And lose the strike, Dad?" Yes, he said, if they couldn't win, they'd have to lose—that was the law of strikes, as of everything else. Life was stern, and sooner or later you had to learn it. They must give up, and wait till a time when their union was stronger. "But, Dad, how can they make it stronger, when the operators boycott them? You know how they weed out the union men—right now, if they give up, most of the companies won't take back the active ones." And Dad said he knew that, but the men would have to keep on trying, there was no other way. Certainly *he* could not support the strike by keeping his wells idle! The men must understand that he couldn't stand the gaff much longer, they had no right to expect it; they must either close the other wells, or see the Ross wells opened. And Bunny turned sort of sick inside, and went about hiding a thought like a dirty vice: "We're going to bring scabs into our tract!"

VIII

There was really only one place where Bunny could be happy, and that was up at the bungalow. He spent his Saturday afternoon there, helping Ruth and Meelie—the one kind of aid he was permitted to give to the strike! Part of the time they talked about the suffering of which they knew; and part of the time they were jolly, making jokes like other young people; but all the time they worked like beavers, turning flour belonging to the union into various kinds of eatables. At supper-time Mr. Watkins came with the wagon, his second trip, and they loaded him up, and Meelie drove off with him to headquarters, while Bunny stayed with Ruth, and helped clean up the place, and tried to explain the predicament of his father, and why he, Bunny, could not really help the strike.

On Sunday he went in to the meetings, and heard Paul make another speech. Paul, always sombre looking, was now gaunt from several weeks of little food and less sleep, and there was a fury of passion in his voice; he told about his trip to the other fields, and how there was no justice anywhere—the authorities of town and county and state were simply pawns of the operators, doing everything possible to hold the men down and break their organization. In this white flame of suffering Paul's spirit had been tempered to steel, and the crowd of workers shared this process, and took new vows of solidarity; Bunny felt the thrill of a great mass experience, and yearned to be part of it, and then shrunk back, like the young man in the Bible story who had too many possessions.

Paul had seen him in the crowd, and after the meeting sought him out. "I want to talk to you," he said, and they strolled away from the others, and Paul, who had no time to waste, came directly to the point:

"See here, I want you to let my sister alone."

"Let her alone!" cried the other, and stopped short in his tracks, and stared at Paul. "Why, what do you mean?"

"Meelie tells me you've been up there at the place a lot—you were there last evening with her."

"But Paul! Somebody had to stay with her!"

"We'll take care of ourselves; she could have come to father's place. And I want you to understand, I won't have any rich young fellows hanging round my sister."

"But Paul!" Bunny's tone was one of shocked grief. "Truly, Paul, you're utterly mistaken."

"I don't want you to be mistaken about this one thing—if any fellow was to do any wrong to my sister, I'd kill him, just as sure as anything on earth."

"But Paul, I never dreamed of such a thing! Why, listen—I'll tell you—I'm in love with a girl—a girl in school. Oh, honest, Paul, I'm terribly in love, and I—I couldn't think of anybody else that way."

A quick blush had spread over Bunny's face as he made this confession, and it was impossible not to realize that he was sincere. Paul's voice became kinder. "Listen, son; you're not a child any more, and neither is Ruth. I don't doubt what you say—naturally, you'll pick out some girl of your own class. But it mightn't be that way with Ruth, she might get to be interested in you, and you ought to keep away."

Bunny didn't know what to say to that—the idea was too new to him. "I wanted to know about the strike," he explained; "and I've had no chance to talk with you at all. You can't imagine how bad I feel, but I don't know what to do." He rushed on, crowding all his grief into a few sentences; he was torn in half, between his loyalty to his father and his sympathy for the men; it was a trap he was in, and what could he do?

When Paul answered, his voice was hard again. "Your father is helping to keep these blackguards in the field, I understand."

"He's paying assessments, if that's what you mean. He's under contract with the Federation—when he joined—"

"No contract is valid that requires breaking the law! And don't you know these fellows are breaking a hundred laws a day?"

"I know, Paul; but Dad is tied up with the other operators; you don't understand—he's really having trouble financially, because his wells are shut down; and he's doing that entirely for the men."

"I know it, and we appreciate it. But now he says he's got to give up, and bring in scabs like the rest. They're driving us beyond endurance; they're making a dirty fight, and your father knows it—and yet he goes along with them!"

There was a pause, and Paul went on, grimly. "I know, of course; his money is at stake, and he won't risk it; and you'll do what he tells you."

"But Paul! I couldn't oppose Dad! Would you expect that?"

"When my father set up his will, and tried to keep me from thinking and learning the truth, I opposed him, didn't I? And you encouraged me to do it—you thought that was all right."

"But Paul! If I were to oppose Dad in such a thing— why, I'd break his heart."

"Well, maybe I broke my father's heart—I don't know, and neither do you. The point is, your father's doing wrong, and you know it; he's helping to turn these ruffians loose on us, and deprive us of our rights as citizens, and even as human beings. You can't deny that, and you have a duty that you owe to the truth."

There was a silence, while Bunny tried to face the appalling idea of opposing Dad, as Paul had opposed old Mr. Watkins. It had seemed so right in the one case, and seemed so impossible in the other!

At last Paul went on. "I know how it is, son. You won't do it, you haven't the nerve for it—you're soft." He waited, while those cruel words sank in. "Yes, that's the word, soft. You've always had everything you wanted—you've had it handed to you on a silver tray, and it's made you a weakling. You have a good heart, and you know what's right, but you couldn't bear to act, you'd be too afraid of hurting somebody."

And that was the end of their talk. Paul had nothing more to say, and Bunny had no answer. Tears had come into his eyes—and that was weak, wasn't it? He turned his head away, so that Paul might not see them.

"Well," said the latter, "I've got a pile of work to do, so I'll be off. This fight will be over some day, and your father will go on making money, and I hope it will bring you happiness, but I doubt it, really. Good-bye, son."

"Good-bye," said Bunny, feebly; and Paul turned on his heel and hurried away.

Bunny walked on, and there was a fever in his soul. He was enraged because of Paul's lack of understanding, his cruel harshness; but all the time another voice inside him kept insisting, "He's right! You're soft, you're soft—that's the word for it!" Here, you see, was the thing in Bunny which made his sister Bertie so absolutely furious; that Bunny subjected himself to Paul, that he was willing to let Paul kick him, and to take it meekly. He was so utterly without sense of the dignity which his father's millions conferred upon him!

IX

Bunny went back to school, and the oil-workers took a hitch in their belts, hanging on by their eye teeth, as the saying is. Meantime, America was in the war, and Congress was passing a series of measures—one providing for a vast "liberty loan," to pay the war costs, and another for the registering of all men of fighting age, and the drafting of a huge army.

And then began to come wild rumors of a truce with labor.

It came first in connection with the railway men, many of whom were on strike for a living wage and better conditions. The railways were absolutely vital to the winning of the war, and so Congress must authorize the Government to intervene in disputes, and make terms with the unions, and see that everybody got a square deal. If such steps were taken for the railway men, they would surely have to be taken for others; the oil workers might get those rights of which the Employers' Federation was endeavoring to deprive them! The labor press was full of talk about the new deal that was coming, and telegrams came from labor headquarters in Washington, bidding the men at Paradise stand firm.

It was like the "big scene" in the old "ten-twenty-thirty" melodrama that we used to see on the Bowery in our boyhood, in which the heroine is lashed to a log in the saw-mill, and being swiftly drawn to the place where she will be sliced down the middle; the hero comes galloping madly on horseback, and leaps from his steed, and smashes in the door with an axe, and springs to the lever and stops the machinery at exactly the critical instant. Or, if you want to be more high-brow and dignified, it was like the ancient Greek tragedies, in which, after the fates of all the characters have been tied into a hopeless knot, a god descends from the sky in a machine, and steps out, and resolves the perplexities, and virtue is triumphant and vice is cast down. You believe this, because it is in a Greek classic; but you will find it less easy to believe that the "open shop crowd" of California, the whole power of their industrial system, with all the millions of their banks, their political machine and their strike-breaking agencies, their spies and gunmen, and their state militiamen with machine-guns and armored cars in the background—that all this terrific power felt its hand suddenly grasped by a stronger hand, and drawn back from the throat of its victim! Another god descended from a machine—a lean old Yankee divinity, with a white goatee and a suit made of red and white stripes with blue stars spangled over it; Uncle Sam himself stretched out his mighty hand, and declared that oil workers were human beings as well as citizens, and would be protected in their rights as both!

The announcement came from labor headquarters in Washington, saying that the oil workers would get a living wage and the eight hour day; a government "conciliator" would be sent out to see to it, and meantime, they were to go back to work, so that the benevolent old gentleman with the white goatee and the red, white and blue suit might have all the oil he needed. The President of the United States was making speeches—oh, such wonderful, convincing speeches, about the war that was to end war, and bring justice to all mankind, and establish the rule of the people and by the people and for the people over all the earth. Such thrills as shook all hearts, such a fervor of consecration! And such rejoicing on the play-ground of the school-house at Paradise, when the news came that the gunmen would slink back into the slums from which they had come, and that work was to start up at once!

Dad got the news early in the morning, and Bunny danced all over the house, and made as much noise as if it were a foot-ball game; and Dad said he felt pretty good himself, it would sure be nice to get those wells on production again, he wouldn't have been able to hold on another week without them. And Bunny said he'd cut school in the afternoon, and they'd drive out and see the celebration, and make friends with everybody again, and get things started. The first thing they would do was to tear down that barbed wire fence that separated capital from labor! In the new world there would be no more barbed wire and no more bad feeling—the roses would bloom on the hedges in front of the workers' homes, and there would be a book of the President's speeches in the reading-room, and all the oil workers would have time to read it!

CHAPTER VIII

THE WAR

I

Eunice Hoyt was the daughter of "Tommy" Hoyt, of Hoyt and Brainerd, whose advertisements of investment securities you saw on the financial pages of the Beach City newspapers. Tommy you saw at racing meets and boxing events, and generally you noticed that he had with him a new lady, highly and artificially colored; sometimes she wore a veil, and you kept tactfully out of the way, understanding that Tommy was "playing the woman game." Mrs. Tommy you saw pictured among "the distinguished hostesses of the week"; she went in for art, and there would be a soulful young man about the house. The servants understood the situation, and so did Eunice.

She was dark and slender, a quick and impatient little thing, with an abundance of what was currently known as "pep." She was in two of Bunny's classes, and discovering that he was a serious youngster, she worried him by saying sharp and cutting things, that he was never sure whether she meant or not; he dared not ask, because then she would tease him worse than ever. There were always half a dozen fellows following her about, so it was easy to keep out of the way.

But one Saturday afternoon Bunny won the 220-yard run for the school team, and that made him a bit of a hero, and boys and girls swarmed about him, cheering and patting him on the back. Then, after he had had his shower and was dressed, he went out in search of his car, and there was Eunice just getting into her roadster, and she said, "Let me take you." He answered, "I've got my own car here," and she exclaimed, "Why, you horrid rude thing! Get into this car at once, sir!" So of course he did, a little rattled. When she said, "Are you afraid somebody will steal that cheap old car of yours?"—was it up to him to defend the newness and expensiveness of Dad's latest gift?

"Bunny," she said, "my mother and father are having a row at home, and it's horrid there."

"Well, what do you want to do?" said he, sympathetically.

"Let's go somewhere and have supper—away from everything. You come, and it'll be my party."

So they drove for an hour or so, and climbed by a winding road to the top of a hill, and there was a café, with a terrace looking out over a bay and a rocky shore-line that would have been famous if it had been in Italy. They ate supper, and chatted about school affairs, and Eunice told him about her home-life and how some one had written her mother a letter revealing that her father had paid a lot of money to some woman, and Mrs. Hoyt was furious, because why should men do things that made it necessary for them to pay money?

The sun set over the ocean, and the lights came out along the shore, and a big full moon behind the hills; and Eunice said, "Do you like me a little bit, Bunny?" He answered that of course he did, and she said, "But you don't show it ever." "Well," he explained, "I never know quite what to make of you, because you always kid me;" and to that she said, "I know, Bunny, I'm a horrid mean thing, but the truth is, I just do that to keep my courage up. I'm afraid of you, too, because you're serious, and I'm just a silly chatterbox, and I have to make a show." So after that Bunny was able to enjoy the party.

They got into the car and drove again. The road ran through a tangle of sand-dunes, high up above the ocean. "Oh, this is lovely!" said Eunice, and when they came to a place where the ground was firm she ran the car off the pavement and parked it. "Let's go and watch the ocean," she said. "There's a rug in the back." So Bunny got the rug out, and they walked over the dunes, and sat on top of one, and listened to the waves below; and Eunice smoked a cigarette, and scolded Bunny because he was a horrid little Puritan that wouldn't keep her company. Presently a man came walking by, and glanced at them as he passed, and Eunice said, "Have you got a gun?" And when he said that he hadn't, she remarked, "You're supposed to bring a gun nowadays when you go on a petting party." Bunny had not realized that this was exactly a petting party, but you can see that it would not have been polite of him to say so.

He listened while she told him about bandits who were making a business of holding up couples parked by the roadside; some were beastly to the girls, and what would Bunny do if one of them were suddenly to appear? Bunny said he didn't know, but of course he'd defend a woman the best he could. "But I don't want you to get shot," said Eunice. "We've a scandal already in our family." So she said, "Let's get lost, Bunny;" and he gathered up the rug and they wandered over the dunes—a long way from the road and from everything; and in one of the hollows, a still nest where the sand was soft and smooth, she told him to spread the rug again, and there they sat, hid from everything save the round yellow moon, which has looked down upon millions and millions of such scenes, and never yet betrayed a confidence.

They sat close together, and Eunice rested her head against Bunny's shoulder and whispered, "Do you care for me a little bit?" He assured her that he did, but she said, no, he must think she was a horrid bold thing; and when he declared that he didn't, she said, "Then why don't you kiss me?" He began to kiss her, but she wasn't satisfied—he didn't mean it, she said; and suddenly she whispered, "Bunny, I don't believe you've ever really loved a girl before!"

He admitted that he had not. "I've always known you were a queer boy," she said. "What is the matter?" Bunny said he didn't quite know; he was trembling violently, because he had never had anything like this happen to him, and several different emotions clamored at the same time, and which one should he follow? "Let me teach you, Bunny," whispered the girl; and when he did not answer at once, she put her lips upon his, in a long kiss that made him dizzy. He murmured faintly that something might happen, she might get into trouble; but she told him not to worry about that, she knew about those things and had taken the needed precautions.

II

Such was the way of Bunny's initiation into the adult life. Gone were the days of happy innocence when he could be content to sit holding hands with Rosie Taintor. "Holding hands" was now walking on a slippery ledge, over a dark abyss where pleasure and pain were so mingled you could hardly tell them apart. Bunny was frightened by the storm of emotion which seized upon him, and still more by the behavior of the girl in his arms; a kind of frenzy shook her, she clung to him in a convulsion of excitement, half sobbing, half laughing, with little cries as of an animal in pain. And Bunny must share this delirium, she would not have it otherwise, she was furious in her exactions, the mistress of these dark rites, and he must obey her will. The first time, the boy was overwhelmed by the realization of what he had done, but she clung to him, whispering, "Oh, Bunny don't be ashamed! No, no! I won't let you be ashamed! Why haven't we got a right to be happy? Oh, please, please, be happy!" So he had to promise, and do his best.

"Oh, Bunny, you are such a sweet lover! And we are going to have such good times." This was her crooning song, wrapped in his arms, there under the spring-time moon, which is the same in California as everywhere else in the world. And when the chill of the California night began to creep into their bones, they could hardly tear themselves apart, but all the way over the dunes they walked arm in arm, kissing as they went. "Oh, Bunny, it was bold and bad of me, but tell me you forgive me, tell me you're glad I did it!" It appeared to be his duty to comfort her.

Driving back to Beach City they talked about this adventure. Bunny hadn't thought much about sex, he had no philosophy ready at hand, but Eunice had hers, and told it to him simply and frankly. The old people taught you a lot of rubbish about it, and then they sneaked off and lived differently, and why should you let yourself be fooled by silly "don'ts"? Love was all right if you were decent about it, and when you had found out that you didn't have to have any babies, why must you bother to get married? Most married people were miserable anyhow, and if the young people could find a way to be happy, it was up to them, and what the old folks didn't know wouldn't hurt them.

Did Bunny see anything wrong with that? Bunny answered that he didn't; the reason he had been "such an old prude," was just that he hadn't got to know Eunice. She said that men were supposed not to care for a girl who made advances to them; therefore, she added with her flash of mischief, it would be up to Bunny to make some of the advances from now on. He said he would do so, and would have started at once, only Eunice was driving at forty-some miles an hour, and it would be better to hurt her feelings than to upset the car.

Were there other girls like Eunice, Bunny wanted to know, and she said there were plenty, and named a few, and Bunny was surprised and a little shocked, because some of them were prominent in class affairs, and decorous-seeming. Eunice told him about their ways, and it was a good deal like a secret society, without any officers or formal ritual, but with a strict code none the less. They called themselves "the Zulus," these bold spirits who had dared to do as they pleased; they kept one another's secrets faithfully, and helped the younger ones to that knowledge which was so essential to happiness. The old guarded this knowledge jealously—how to keep from having babies, and what to do if you got "caught." There was a secret lore about the art of love, and books that you bought in certain stores, or found stowed away behind other books in your father's den. Such volumes would be passed about and read by scores.

It was a new ethical code that these young people were making for themselves, without any help from their parents. Eunice did not know, of course, that she was doing anything so imposing as that; she just talked about her feelings, and what she liked and what she feared. Was it right to love this way or that? And what did Bunny think about the possibility of loving two girls at the same time? Claire Reynolds said you couldn't, but Billy Rosen said you could, and they were wrangling all the time. But Mary Blake got along quite happily with two boys who loved her and had agreed not to be jealous.—This was a new world into which Bunny was being introduced, and he asked a lot of questions, and could not help blushing at some of Eunice's matter-of-fact replies.

Bunny crept into the house at two o'clock in the morning, and no member of the family was the wiser. But he was equally as late the next night, and the next—had he not promised Eunice to "make the advances"? So of course the family realized that something was up, and it was interesting to see their reactions. Aunt Emma and Grandma were in a terrible "state," but they could not say why—such was the handicap the old generation imposed upon themselves. They both went to Dad, but could only talk about late hours and their effect on a boy's health. And Dad himself could not do much more. When Bunny said that he had been taking Eunice Hoyt driving, Dad asked about her, was she a "nice" girl? Bunny answered that she was the treasurer of the girls' basket-ball team, and her father was Mr. Hoyt, whom Dad knew, and she had her own car and had even tried to pay for the supper. So there could be no idea that Bunny was being "vamped," and all Dad said was "Take it easy, son, don't try to live your whole life in a couple of weeks."

Also there was Bunny's sister, and that was curious. Had some underground message come to Bertie, through connections with the "Zulus"? All that she said was, "I'm glad you've consented to take an interest in something beside oil and strikers for a change." But behind that sentence lay such an ocean of calm feminine knowledge! Bunny was started upon a new train of thought. Could it be that late hours meant the same thing for his sister that they had suddenly come to mean for him? Bertie was supposed to be dancing; and did she always come directly home, or did she also park by the waysides? Bunny had got over being shocked by the parking of Eunice's car, but it took him longer to get used to the idea of the parking of his sister's car. He began to notice, as he drove along the highways in the evening—what a great number of parked cars there were!

III

All this was near the end of the strike; and also it was while America was going to war. So the excitements of sex were mingled in Bunny's mind with those of patriotism. The two were not so far apart as you might think, for the youth of the country was preparing to march away to battle, and that loosened sexual standards. You might not come back, so it made less difference what you did in the meantime. The girls found their hearts softened toward the boys, and the boys were ready to snatch a bit of pleasure before it was too late.

Bunny was too young for the first draft, but he went to drilling at school, which cast the military halo about him. There was a high school corps, provided with old rifles of the state militia, and the athletic field was covered with groups of lads marching, "Hep, hep! Hep, hep! Squad right! Squad left!" —treading one on another's toes, but keeping the grim look on their young faces. Soon they would have uniforms, and so would the girls of the nurses' training corps. Boys and girls met in school assembly and sang patriotic songs with fervor.

Yes, it was war! Whole fleets of cargo vessels were taking supplies to England and France, and brigades of engineers and laborers to prepare the way for the army. The President was making speeches — wonderful, glowing, eloquent speeches.

There was a race of evil men, the Huns, who had risen up to threaten civilization, and now the might of democratic America was going to put them down. When this job had been done, there would be an end to all the world's troubles; so the duty of every patriot was to take his part in this last of all wars—the War to end War—the War for Democracy. Statesmen big and little took up the chorus, the newspapers echoed it a million copies every hour, and a host of "four minute men" were trained, to go into factories and theatres, and wherever crowds were gathered, to rouse America for this crusade.

The Ross family, like all other families, read, and listened, and argued. Bunny, the young idealist, swallowed every word of the propaganda; it was exactly what he wanted to believe, his kind of mental food. He would argue with his cool, slow-moving, quietly dubious father. Yes, of course, Dad would say, we had to win the war; we had to win any war we got into. But as to the future, well, it would be time to decide about that when we came to it. First, Dad was occupied with getting the strike settled, and after that, with selling oil on a constantly rising market. There was no sense giving it away, because the government wanted more wells drilled, and how were they to be financed, unless the product was paid for? The government was paying generously, and that was patriotism enough for Dad; he would see to the spouting of his wells, and leave the other kinds of spouting to the politicians.

Aunt Emma considered that a shameful way to talk to a boy, and she scolded vigorously, according to the privilege of "in-laws." Aunt Emma would go to the clubs and listen to the patriotic lady-orators, telling about Belgian babies with their hands cut off, and munition depots blown up by German spies, and she would come home in a blaze of militarism. Bertie was even worse, for her young man who took her to the jazz-parties was active in one of the defense societies, and knew the names of all the German agents in Southern California, and the villainies they were planning; so Bertie was full of dark hints, and a sense of awful responsibility.

You could never tell how this war excitement was going to hit any one person. For example, could you have imagined that a perfectly respectable old lady of way over seventy, brought up on a ranch, and supposed to be wrapped up in painting in oils, would suddenly blossom out as a Hun sympathizer? Such was Grandma, who declared that she had no use whatsoever for this war; the Germans were no worse than any of the other people concerned, they were all stained with blood, and all there was to the atrocity stories and spy rubbish was to make people hate the enemy. But Grandma wasn't going to hate anybody, no matter how much Emma and Bertie and the rest might rage; she proceeded to show her defiance by painting a picture of some Germans in old-time costumes drinking beer out of painted steins. She wanted to hang this in the dining-room, and there was a great row, with Aunt Emma and Bertie trying to persuade Dad to forbid it!

All this was part of Bunny's education; he listened and learned. From his quiet, steady old father he learned to smile amiably over the foibles of human nature, and to go on gathering in the dollars. Talk was all right, but after all, what was going to win the war was bullets and shells, and to get them to the battle-field you had to have transportation. The oil that Dad brought up out of the ground was driving big trucks that were carrying munitions up to the front; it was moving the biggest and fastest cargo-ships, and the swift destroyers that were protecting them; it was lubricating the machinery in the factories, and more and more was being called for. As soon as the strike was over, Dad proceeded to sign contracts with the government, and to put down a dozen new wells in the Paradise field. The one thing that was troubling him was that he could not make three times as many contracts and put down three times as many wells; the big fellows, who controlled the banks, would not let him have enough money—at least not unless he would go in with them and let them hog most of the profits. That was a different kind of war, one going on right at home, and there was no prospect of it's being ended by presidential speeches. Dad would explain that to Bunny, as a reason for the limitations in the "idealism" of a business man!

IV

Up at Paradise things were booming. All the men were back at work—even the blacklisted ones, at a dollar day more, and with another raise promised; a good driller was worth just about his weight in gold. Here too came the "four minute men," and were listened to gladly; the oil workers were patriotic, and would have enlisted to a man, but they were needed on this job—there was nothing more important than oil, and the way for them to serve their country was to keep the stuff flowing, and watch out for fires, and for obstructions dropped into the wells, and other acts of vandalism by enemy agents.

Paul was back as Dad's boss builder. But then came the first draft, and Paul had one of the lucky numbers. Dad offered to get him exempted, for obviously there had to be shacks to house the men who were to drill and operate the new wells. Dad had power to arrange matters—you can understand that, when you learn that the chairman of the exemption board was Mr. Carey, the rancher who had accepted money from Dad to get the road built for the drilling. But Paul said no, there were married men with families who knew as much about building houses as he did, so Paul would do his share in the field.

Paul and Bunny were friends again, and had no end of arguments. Paul wasn't nearly as keen for the war as Bunny thought he ought to be; he agreed that we had to win, since we were in, but he wasn't sure it was necessary for us to be in, so Bunny had to retell the arguments he heard from the orators at school. That made lively times at the Rascum cabin —because, strange as it may seem, Ruth was taking exactly the same attitude to the war as Grandma, whom Ruth had never met. Ruth declared that all wars were wicked, and she would never have anything to do with one. But of course you could see what she really meant, she didn't want Paul taken away and killed! When Paul read his number in the first draft-list, Ruth became quite frantic, and there was nothing that would pacify her. She clung to Paul, vowing he should not go, she would die of grief if he did; when she realized that he was actually going, she went about her work, pale and silent.

Paul went away to a training-camp, and after that paleness and silence became the dominant notes of Ruth's character. She went back to her father's home to stay at night, which meant that on Sunday's she had to go to church with them, and sit and bite her lips while Eli preached. For Eli was a prophet after the old testament model, calling down judgment upon the enemies of the Lord, smiting them hip and thigh, leaving not one alive, not even the little ones, the "spawns of the devil." Eli, being a preacher, did not have to do this killing himself; he was exempt, and so was his sister Meelie, who solved the war problem for herself by marrying a young derrick man and getting Dad to make him a foreman and have him kept at home. Meelie, who was a chatterbox and a fresh young thing, said to Bunny that Ruth ought to find herself a husband instead of mourning over Paul; maybe the day would come when Bunny would want to be exempted, and they might both solve the problem at the same time!

V

That was a feverish summer in Bunny's life, between the war and his raptures with Eunice. He spent a great deal of time at Beach City, because he had the excuse of the military work, and because the girl was so imperious in her demands. Indeed, the first rift in their happiness came because he would persist in paying visits to Paradise, where Eunice could not very well come. She took up Bertie's phrase that Bunny was a "little oil gnome." "What do you want with so much money?" she would argue. "My God, let me get some from Papa, if you need it!" Tommy Hoyt, it seems, had made a huge killing, buying old hulks down at the harbor just before the country entered the war; it was reported he had cleared a cool three million. There had been a lot about it in the papers —all very complimentary, since that was everybody's dream of glory.

How could Bunny explain that it wasn't the money, but the fact that the country had to have oil, and he wanted to do his share; what kind of preternatural solemnity was that for a youth of eighteen? He put the blame on Dad, who wasn't very well and needed his son; and so it became an issue, which did Bunny care for most, his Dad or his sweetheart? Eunice would grab him by the shoulders and shake him; she had to have some one to take her to a dance, and if he went off and buried himself in the desert, she would get another fellow.

She was insatiable, ravenous for pleasure; she never knew when to stop, whatever it might be. "One dance more! Just one!" she would plead; and then it would be one kiss more, or one drink. She was always pleading with Bunny to drink, and having her feelings hurt because he refused. How could he count his promise to his father more than his promise to be her pal? And how could she take him out with her crowd if he played the part of a skeleton at a feast?

Not for long was she content to lose themselves in the sand-dunes, and share their secret with the moon. Eunice loved the bright lights, the free and conspicuous spending of Papa's sudden wealth. They would drive to Angel City, where in fashionable hotels were palatial dining-rooms, with jazz-orchestras, and crowds of revellers, celebrating new contracts and new financial coups. The rooms were decorated with the flags of all the allies, and the men wore the uniforms of all the services. This was what the war meant to Eunice, to be in this shining company, and stand up while the orchestra played the "Star-spangled Banner," and after that to dance all night while it played, "Kiss me, honey-baby," or "Toodle-ums too," or whatever amorous cajolement the saxophone might present. She was an aggressive little dancer, clinging to her partner, her body fitted into his as if it had been moulded there. Bunny would not have thought it quite decent to behave like that in public, but it was the mood of the time, and no one paid any attention to them, especially after the hours had passed and the drinks had taken effect.

There was always the problem of getting Eunice away from these excitements. She never wanted to go, not even when she was exhausted; he would half carry her out, and she would fall asleep on his shoulder on the way home, and it was all he could do to keep from falling asleep himself. There was a boy in their crowd who would carry a broken nose about for the rest of his life, because he had dozed at the steering-wheel on a crowded boulevard; another had spent ten days in jail because, after a smash-up, the police had smelled liquor on his breath. It was the etiquette of parties that the man who had to drive must drink only gin—not because that would not make him drunk, but because it left no odor on his breath!

The time came when Eunice decided that it was silly to take that long drive to Beach City after dancing. She found a hotel where you could register as Mr. and Mrs. Smith of San Francisco and no one would ask any questions; you paid in advance, because of your lack of baggage, and in the morning you slipped out separately, and no one was the wiser. You told the folks at home that you had spent the night with a friend, and they did not pursue the matter—being afraid of what they might find out.

All this made a great difference in Bunny's life, and before long it began to show in his appearance; he was not quite so rosy, and Dad took notice, and was no longer embarrassed to speak. "You're making a fool of yourself, son; these late hours have got to stop." So Bunny would try to get out of going to some dance, and Eunice would fly into his arms, and sob, and cling to him, moulding her body into his in that terrible, breath-taking way she had; all Bunny's senses would be filled with her, the delicate perfume she used, the feeling of the filmy stuffs she wore, her tumbled hair, her burning, swift, persistent kisses. He would have to stand and argue and plead, trying to keep his reason while his head went round.

Sometimes there would be embarrassment mingled with his other emotions, because these scenes took place in the drawing-room of the Hoyt home, with either of the parents present. But what could they do? They had raised this wild young creature, giving her everything in the world, half a dozen servants to wait on her, to answer her every whim. She had always had what she wanted, and now she wanted her lover, and all that poor Mrs. Hoyt could say was, "Don't be hard-hearted, Bunny"—really seeming to blame him for these tantrums in her presence! As for poor "Tommy," when he happened in on a tantrum, there came a frightened look on his rosy, rather boyish face, and he turned and skedaddled. He had troubles enough of his own making, and the next time he met Bunny, he set forth his point of view in one pregnant sentence, "There's no such thing as a normal woman in the world!"

VI

Just before school opened, Bunny took the bit in his teeth and went to Paradise to spend a week with Dad, and found that Paul was there on a three day's furlough. Paul was not going to get overseas, it appeared; the army had put him to work at his old job—building barracks—only now, instead of ten dollars a day he was getting thirty a month "and beans." That was what it meant for a workingman to be patriotic! It was quite a contrast with Tommy Hoyt's three millions, and the hundred and twenty thousand a week of Dad's oil-contracts! But nobody thought about that, because of the eloquence of the President's speeches, and the concentrated ardor of the four minute orators.

Paul looked big and strong in his khaki uniform; and Ruth was happy, because Paul wasn't going to be killed. Meelie was happy, because there was a baby on the way, and Sadie because there was a young rancher "keeping company" with her. Dad was happy, because he had brought in another gusher, and proved up a whole new slope of the Paradise tract; he was putting in pipe-lines and preparing a colossal development—the bankers couldn't keep him down, he would finance himself with oil!

Everybody was happy except Bunny, who could think of nothing but the fact that Eunice was angry, and he was risking the loss of her. She had warned him, she would not be left alone; if he deserted her, she would punish him. He knew that she meant it; she had had lovers before him, and would have others after him. This "petting" was a daily necessity for her, and a girl could not get it unless she was willing to "go the limit." That was the etiquette prevailing in this smart and dashing crowd; the rich high school youths would go out hunting in pairs in their fancy sport-cars, and would pick up girls and drive them, and if the girls did not play the game according to their taste, they would turn them out on the road, anywhere, a score of miles from a town. There was formula, short and snappy, "Pet or walk!"

Bunny took long tramps, trying to shake off his cruel fever. He would come back to sleep, but instead he would think about Eunice, and the manifold intoxication of his senses would return; she would be there with all her allurements and her abandonments. Bunny tried haltingly once or twice to tell Paul about it; Paul being a sort of god, a firm and dependable moral force, to whom one might flee. Bunny remembered the scorn with which Paul had talked about "fornications," and Bunny had not known quite what he meant—but Bunny knew now, alas, only too well. He tried to confess, but was ashamed, and could not break down the barriers. Instead, he made some excuse to his father and drove back to Beach City, three days earlier than he had intended; and all the way as he rode he was hearing Paul's voice, those cruel words of the strike-days: "You're soft, Bunny, you're soft."

VII

The first rain of the season was falling, and Bunny got in fairly late, and found that Eunice was at home, and had not carried out her threat to get another lover. No, she was trying an experiment she had read about in a book of her mother's, a thing called "mental telepathy"; you sat and shut your eyes and "concentrated," "willing" that somebody should do something, and then they would do it, and the "new thought" doctrine would be vindicated. Eunice was trying it, and when she heard Bunny's step on the veranda, she sprang up with a little shriek of delight and rushed into his arms, and while she smothered him with kisses she told him about this marvelous triumph of experimental psychology. "Oh, Bunny, I just knew you couldn't be so cruel to me! I knew you'd come, because I'm all alone, Mamma has gone to raise money for the Serbian orphans. Oh, Bunny, come on!"—and she started to draw him toward the stairs.

Bunny didn't think that was quite the thing, and tried to hold back, but she smothered his protest in kisses. "You silly boy, are we going out and park in the rain? Or do you want to go to a hotel here in town, where everybody knows us?"

"But, your mother, Eunice—"

"Mother, bunk!" said Eunice. "Mother has a lover and I know it, and she knows I know it. If she don't know about you and me, it's time she was making a guess. So you come up to my room."

"But how'll I get out, Eunice?"

"You'll get out when I let you out, and maybe it'll be morning, and you'll be treated with decent hospitality."

"But Eunice, I never heard of such a thing!"

"Bunny, you talk like your grandmother!"

"But what about the servants, dear?"

"Servants, hell!" said Eunice. "You can run your home to please the servants, but that's not our way—at least, not tonight!" And to save Bunny any embarrassment, she kept him in her room in the morning while she broke the news to her mother; and if there were any mental agonies Bunny never knew it, because the patroness of the Serbian orphans breakfasted in bed, reading in the morning paper the account of her fashionable philanthropies.

After that, the ice was broken—as the French have observed, it is the first step that counts, thought it is doubtful if any parent in old-fashioned France has been compelled to take quite so long a step. The rainy season continued, making out-door petting parties uncomfortable, so whenever he was commanded, Bunny would stay in Eunice's home, and it was all quite domestic and regular according to advanced modern standards. In fact, there was only one small detail left, and

Bunny suggested that: "Eunice, why shouldn't we go and get married, and have it over with?"

He was surprised by the vehemence of the girl's reaction. "Oh, Bunny, we're having such a happy time, and why do you want to ruin it?"

"But why would that ruin it?"

"All married people are miserable. I know, because I've watched them. Mamma and Papa would give a million dollars—well, maybe not that much but certainly a couple of hundred thousand, if they could get loose without having to go through all the fuss in the courts, and the horrid things the newspapers would publish, and their pictures and all."

"But we won't have to do that, dear."

"How do you know we mightn't? If we got married, you'd think you had a right to me, and then you wouldn't do what I say any more, and I wouldn't be happy. Oh, let's do our own way, and not what other people try to make us. All my life other people have been making me do things, and I've been fighting them—even you, Bunny-bear." She had a score of such appellatives for him, because, as you can understand, his name was adapted to petting-party uses: they were dancing a contrivance known as the Bunny-hug, and he heard a lot about that.

You went about in this prosperous and fashionable society, and on the surface everything was decorous and proper, fitting the marital formulas laid down in the laws and preached in the churches. But when you got under the surface—anywhere, high or low—what you found was that human beings, finding themselves unhappy, had come to private understandings. Husbands and wives set one another free, they made exchanges of partners, they brought friends into their homes, who were in reality substitute husbands or wives; there were companions and secretaries and governesses and cousins who played such roles—and when the children found it out, they were in position to put pressure on their parents, a kind of informal family blackmail, good for motor-cars and fur-coats and strings of pearls, and most precious of all, the right to have your own way.

VIII

Early in the year, while America was getting into the war, the people of Russia had overthrown their Tsar and set up a republic. That had pleased most people in America; it was much pleasanter to be allied with a republic. But now, in the fall, came a terrifying event; there was another revolution, this time not made by respectable scholars and business men, but by wild-eyed fanatics called "Bolshevikis," who proceeded to confiscate property and smash things up. At once it became apparent what a calamity this was going to mean for the allies; Russia was going to desert them, and the mass of the Germans on the East would be set free to be hurled against the half-exhausted Western front. Already the Russian armies were going to pieces, the soldiers were deserting wholesale and swarming back to the cities or to their villages; at the same time the leaders of the new government were starting a world-wide propaganda attacking the allies and their war-aims.

Who were these leaders? It was enough for America to note that a horde of them, who had been hiding in Switzerland, were loaded into a sealed train by the German government and escorted across Germany and dumped into Russia to make all the trouble they could. That meant Lenin and his crowd were hired agents of the Hun; when they proceeded to attack what they called "allied imperialism," that was the Kaiser's voice speaking Russian, and when they published the secret treaties of the allies, taken from the archives of the Tsar, the newspapers in America dismissed the documents as obvious forgeries.

Dad, as a good American, believed his newspapers. He considered that this "Bolsheviki revolution" was the most terrible event that had happened in the world in his life-time; his face would grow pale as he talked to Bunny about it. America could get no army to France until next spring, and perhaps not till fall, and meantime the Germans had a million men they could move, only a few hundred miles across their country to the West front; they were jist a-goin' to roll over the British and French, and take Paris, and perhaps the whole of France, and we should have the job of driving them out again. The whole burden of the war now fell onto America's shoulders, and it would last years and years—neither Dad nor Bunny might live to see the end of it.

Dad would read paragraphs out of the papers, details of the horrors that were happening in Russia—literally millions of people slaughtered, all the educated and enlightened ones; the most hideous tortures inflicted, such obscenities as you could not put into print. Before long they began applying their Communist theories to the women of the country, who were "nationalized" and made into public property by official decree; the "commissars" were raping them wholesale. Lenin was killing Trotsky, and Trotsky was throwing Lenin into jail. It was a boiling up from the bottom of the social pit, such savagery as we had hardly dreamed existing in human nature. Bunny could see now the folly of that "idealism" he had been prattling, his idea of letting strikers have their way, and turning industry over to the mob. Here was the thing tried out in practice, and how did he like it? Bunny had to admit that he didn't like it so well, and he was crushed and sobered.

The problem came home to him, because he had to decide as to his own duty in this world crisis. This was his last year in school; then he would be old enough for the draft, and what was he going to do? He and his father talked it out in a solemn conference. Dad thought that he had responsibilities enough to entitle him to the help of one son; he didn't think he would be a slacker if he were to get Mr. Carey to release Bunny for service in the oil industry. But Bunny insisted that he must go to the front; he even talked of quitting school at once and enlisting, as a number of other boys had done. They finally agreed to compromise, waiting till Bunny was through school, and then see how matters shaped up. But meantime Bunny owed this much to his country, as well as to himself—he should give more time to his studies, and less to playing about. If a young fellow really understood this world crisis, he would surely stick to whatever work he was doing, and not throw himself away in dissipations. Bunny flushed and let his eyes fall, and said he guessed that was true, and he'd do better in future.

IX

He went to Eunice in his mood of high seriousness, to explain how the burden of the task of saving civilization had fallen upon their shoulders. She told him yes, she had been realizing it, she had just been getting a serious talk from her mother, who had explained that there was going to be a shortage of food and all kinds of materials, as a result of the war and the needs of our allies. The club-ladies had decided upon their duty—they would purchase only the most expensive kinds of food, so as to leave the lard and cabbage and potatoes for the poor; Mrs. Hoyt had given away all her clothing to the Salvation army, and spent a small fortune buying a complete outfit of the most costly things she could find. Eunice was of course quite willing to use only luxuries, but found it a little puzzling, because her Aunt Alice took just the opposite view, and had bought herself a lot of cheap things, in order to set an example to the working-classes. Which did Bunny think was right?

But this sober mood did not last long with Eunice. A couple of days later she was invited to a Belgian orphans' ball, and when Bunny insisted that he had to study, she threatened to go with Billy Chalmers, the handsome captain of last year's football team—there was no team this year. Bunny said all right, and so Eunice flaunted Billy in front of the whole school, and there were rumors that he was parking his car with her, and that Bunny's nose was out of joint. This went on for a week or two, until Bunny's heart-ache was more than he could stand. It was a Saturday night—and Dad had granted that it wouldn't be wrong to go to one dance a week; so he phoned Eunice, and they "made it up" with tears and wild gusts of passion, and she declared that she had never really really loved anyone but her Bunny-bear, and how could he have been so wicked as to refuse to please her?

But then came Christmas, and the shrewd and persistent Dad arranged a series of temptations—a big turkey, and Ruth to cook it, and two new wells coming in, to say nothing of the quail calling over the hills at sunset. Bunny promised, and simply had to go; and Eunice had the most terrible of all her tantrums, she grabbed Bunny by the hair and pulled him about her mother's drawing-room, with her mother standing helpless by; she vowed that Bunny was a four-flusher, and a wretch, and she would ring up Billy Chalmers, and they would go off on a joy-ride that very night, and not come back till the Christmas holidays were over and maybe not then.

Bunny went to Paradise, and studied the new wells, and the drawings for the new pipe-lines, and the "set-up" of the proposed refinery; he wandered over the hills with Dad and shot quail, and at night he lay in his lonely bed and writhed in misery. It seemed to him that he was turning into an old man —surely he would find all his hair grey in the morning! He was losing more sleep than if he had taken Eunice to the dances, and what was the sense of that? At school they were teaching him biology and nineteenth century English poets, and how was that going to help drive the Germans out of France? Eunice was so fragile, so beautiful, and she was going to be so unhappy! She was different from other girls, difficult to understand, and the next fellow would not be so good to her as Bunny had been! Also, the world that was trying to tear them apart was the same blind and stupid world that was killing millions of people; maybe Grandma was right after all, the whole thing was a chaos of cruelty, and it didn't matter what you did, or which side won.

Then in the morning there would be Dad, and the day's grinding of their tremendous big machine. Dad at least was dependable, Dad had something he was sure of. Also, he seemed to know all about Bunny without being told, he was gentle and sympathetic in a tactful way, not saying a word, but trying to entertain Bunny, and find things they could do together. Come to think of it, Dad had been through things like this himself! It would have been interesting to talk straight with him—only it would have embarrassed him so. Bunny thought of his "little Mamma," whom he had not seen for more than a year; she had gone to New York, and Bunny suspected that Dad had increased her allowance on condition that she would stay there. Bunny wished that he might talk with her about Eunice, and get her opinion on the subject of exchangeable lovers.

He stuck it out, and when he went back home, he did not go to see Eunice. Whenever he met her, his heart would give a jump that hurt, but he would turn the other way and walk a few miles to get over it. The news spread among the "Zulus" that the pair had broken for good, and several sprightly young ladies began making overtures to the young oil prince. But Bunny hardly saw them, his heart was dead within him, he told himself that he would never look at another girl. One of the nineteenth century poets was Byron, and in his romances Bunny found exactly the mood of aristocratic broken-heartedness to which he could respond. As for Eunice, she went on petting parties with her former football captain, and apparently managed to escape every one of the calamities which Bunny had feared for her.

CHAPTER IX

THE VICTORY

I

The first term of Bunny's school ended in February, and he passed his examinations with reasonable success; then there was a brief holiday, and Dad produced a wonderful scheme. He could not help feeling a little uncomfortable, with the Watkins family living right there on the tract, and he taking millions of dollars out of the ground for which he had paid them thirty-seven hundred. Dad had an impulse to do something, yet he was afraid to do too much, for fear he might "spoil" them, giving them the notion he owed them more. What he proposed was a family excursion; he would take Bunny and Ruth and Meelie and Sadie in the big limousine, and hire an extra car for old Mr. Watkins and his wife, and drive to the cantonment where Paul was working, and pay him a visit and see the new army in the making. They would stay a couple of days at some hotel nearby, and see all the sights, including the revival meetings which Eli was holding in a huge tent near the encampment.

The girls of course were wild with happiness. It was the first time they had ever had a long automobile trip in the whole of their unsophisticated lives. Bunny spoke to Ruth, who spoke to her mother, who in turn spoke to her husband, and obtained his promise that he would do his best to persuade the Holy Spirit not to send them any revelations or inspire any rolling or talking in tongues until they had got to the camp-meeting. As a matter of fact, the Holy Spirit had recently declared, through Eli as prophet of the Third Revelation, that these inspirational gymnastics had served their purpose and were to be dropped. No reason was vouchsafed, but there were rumors that the well-to-do people who were backing Eli in his evangelical campaigns were opposed to the rolling, and did not regard the speech of the archangels as having any meaning for mortal ears. One of these disciples was an eminent judge, and another was a proprietor of chain grocery-stores; their wives had taken Eli in hand and rubbed off the

212

rough spots and improved his grammar, explaining that because one said heathen, one did not necessarily say healen; also they had taught him where to get his clothes and how to hold a knife and fork, so that Eli was becoming a social success.

It was almost like going to see the war: this tremendous city of canvas and corrugated iron and redwood siding which had arisen as if by Arabian Nights magic, swarming with eager young men in khaki, all of them as busy as ants—yet never too busy to take note of the presence of three good-looking girls in a row! You could go through this city at certain hours, if you got the proper permit, and see a bit of the drilling; at certain other hours Paul could get off, and while the old folks and the girls went to hear Eli, Dad and Bunny and Paul sat on the hotel veranda and talked about the state of the world.

The Russians had just concluded a peace with Germany, withdrawing entirely from the war, and giving up a lot of territory to the enemy. Dad discussed this event, and repeated his opinion of the treacherous "Bolshevikis." Then Paul said how it seemed to him; Bunny saw that even here, with all the work he had to do, Paul had found time to read and to think his own thoughts. "Bunny," he said, "do you remember our oil-strike, and what we read about it in the papers? Suppose you had never been to Paradise, and didn't know the strikers, but had got all your impressions from the Angel City newspapers! Well, that's the way it seems to me about Russia; this is the biggest strike in history, and the strikers have won, and seized the oil-wells. Some day maybe we'll know what they're doing, but it won't be from newspaper stories made up by the allied diplomats and the exiled grand dukes."

That made Dad rather warm, because he had been reading this news for three or four months, and believing every word of it. He wanted to know if Paul didn't believe there had been any killing of the rich classes in Russia. Paul said he didn't doubt there had been some, because he had read about the French revolution. What you had to remember was the way the Russian people had been treated by their ruling classes, and the kind of government they were used to; you had to judge their revolution by their standards and not by ours. Paul smiled and added that it was a mistake for an American employer who had tried to give his men a square deal, to identify himself with those masters in Russia who had beaten their men

with knouts, and turned them over to the Cossacks if they
attempted any protest.

That pacified Dad a little, but he said the way it seemed
to him, these Bolshevikis were jist so many German agents.
He told about the train that had carried Lenin—Dad called him
Lee-nyne—through Germany. But Paul asked whether he had
watched the news that had come from the peace negotiations;
the Germans had apparently been as much afraid of the Russians as we were. These Bolsheviks were fighting the ruling
classes of both sides, and the Germans might find the peace they
had made more dangerous to them than the fighting; the revolutionary propaganda might spread in their armies, and even
to the Western front.

There was no use expecting Dad to see anything so complicated as that. He declared that if the Russians had really
wanted to help the cause of peace and justice, they should have
stood by the allies until the Kaiser was put out of business.
Then Paul asked whether Mr. Ross had read the secret treaties
of the allies, and Dad was obliged to confess that he had never
even heard of them. Paul explained how the Soviets, after
demanding that the allies should make known their war aims,
and having no attention paid to the request, had revealed to
the world all the secret agreements which the allies had made
with the Tsar, for dividing up the territories they meant to
take from the Germans and Austrians and Turks. Paul
declared that the text of these treaties, the most important
news of the day, had been suppressed by the American newspapers. If we were going into this war blindfolded, to help
Great Britain and France and Italy and Japan in their imperial-
ist aims, then our people were being deceived, and some day
they would have a bitter awakening.

Dad's answer to that was simple: Paul might rest assured,
those secret treaties would turn out to be Bolshevik forgeries.
Had not our government already given out a lot of documents
it had obtained in Russia, proving the Bolshevik leaders to be
German agents? Those were the true documents, and Paul
would find it out some day, and be ashamed of having doubted
our allies. How could he suppose that President Wilson would
let us be jockeyed?

Bunny sat, taking in every word of this discussion. It was
puzzling, and hard to be sure about, but it seemed to him that
Dad was right, what could a good American do, in war-time

like this, but trust his government? Bunny was a little shocked
to hear a man wearing the uniform of the army sit there and
express doubts about his superiors, and he considered it his
duty to get Paul off by himself, and tell him some of the things
the four minute men had said in school, and try to inspire him
with a more intense patriotism. But Paul only laughed, and
patted Bunny on the back, saying that they got any quantity
of propaganda here in the training-camp.

II

One evening they all went to hear Eli; in a great tent
such as would hold a three ring circus, with thousands of cars
parked in the fields about, and sawdust strewn in the aisles,
and hundreds of wooden benches, crowded with soldier boys
and ranchers and their wives and children. There was a platform with the evangelist, wearing a white robe with a golden
star on his bosom, for all the world like some Persian magus;
and there was a "silver band," with trumpets and bass-tubas
gleaming so that they put your eyes out. When those big
blarers started a hymn of glory, and the audience started to
rock and shout, "Praise the Lord!" the top of that tent would
bulge up!

Eli preached against the Hun, telling how the Holy Spirit
had revealed to him that the enemy was to be routed before
the year was by, and promising eternal salvation to all who
died in this cause of the Lord—provided, of course, that they
had not rejected their chance to be saved by Eli. In the middle
of the stage was a tank constructed, with steps descending into
it, and the converts sitting in rows on the platform, garbed
in white nighties; when that stage of the ceremonies arrived,
Eli descended into the water himself, and grabbed his victims
one by one by the backs of their necks, and in the name of the
Father and the Son and the Holy Ghost he swung them forward, souse! into the water. Thereby their sins were washed
from the very last hair of their bodies, and if from the holy
water they contracted any of those diseases which are the
penalty of sins, even among military crusaders—well, all they
had to do was to come back again and have themselves "healen"
by the prophet of the Third Revelation.

Next day the family drove home, and how much they had
to gossip about on the way, and for weeks thereafter! Bunny

was looking forward to living this camp-life the coming summer—except that, because of the preparation he was getting in school, and also because of Dad's influence, he was to be in an officer's training-camp. He was full of consecration, and working harder than ever at his duties.

Late in March began that long-dreaded onslaught on the Western front; one of those battles to which the world had grown accustomed, extending over a hundred miles of front, and lasting all day and all night for several weeks. Such a battle was not named from a town or a city, but from a province; this was the battle of Picardy. The German rush broke through the British line, and drove them back in rout for thirty or forty miles, and captured a hundred thousand men, and it seemed that Dad's worst forebodings were to be realized.

But neither the Germans nor the allies knew that in an obscure village amid the fruit orchards of California a mighty prophet was exercising his magic on their behalf. It chanced that Eli Watkins read a news item from the front, declaring that the only thing which could save the British armies was rain; and forthwith he assembled his hosts of prayer, and all night long they rocked upon their knees and wrung their hands unto the Lord, invoking storms in Picardy; and the Lord heard them, and the floodgates of heaven were opened, and the rain descended, and the feet of the Huns were stuck fast, yea, and their chariot wheels also, and their mighty men at arms were drowned in mud; but on the side where the hosts of the Lord were battling there fell no rain, but the ground was clean, and reinforcements came up, and the British line was saved, and back amid the California orchards the hosannas of the faithful shook the blossoms off the prune-trees.

III

Even amid such agonies and thrills, Bunny, being young, had his personal life. On his way home after drill he ran into Nina Goodrich, one of his class-mates, turning a corner in her car, clad in a bathing-suit with a cape over it. Upon such little things do one's life-destinies depend! She slowed up and called, "Come have a swim with me!" He hopped in, and she whisked him down to the beach in two minutes, and in five more he had hired a bathing suit and got into it, and the two of them were running a race along the sand.

Nina Goodrich was one of those lavish Junos, of whom California brings to ripeness many thousands every year. Her limbs were strong trunks, and her hips were built for carrying a dozen babies, and her bosom for the nourishing of them. She had fair hair and a complexion that had not come out of a bottle, and her skin was bronzed by hours in the surf, in those fragile one-piece bathing suits the girls were wearing, which revealed considerably more than fifty per cent of their natural charms. Never could a man who took himself a wife in Southern California complain that he did not know what he was getting!

The two swam down the shore, a long way, not troubled by the chill of the water; they ran hand in hand on the beach, and as they went back to the bath-house, Nina said, "Come have supper with me, Bunny; I'm tired of home." So Bunny slipped into his clothes, and she drove him back to her home, and while she changed he sat in the car and got up his next lesson in nineteenth century English poetry. The poet called attention to a chain of natural phenomena:

> The sunlight clasps the earth
>   And the moonbeams kiss the sea!
> What are all these kissings worth,
>   If thou kiss not me?

They drove to a cafeteria, an invention where California fish and California fruits and California salads are spread out before the eyes in such profusion as to trouble a nineteen year old Juno already struggling to "reduce." There was nothing so safe as celery, said Nina, it took both space and time; while she munched, they sat by the window, and watched the sun set over the purple ocean, and the slow fog steal in from the sea. Then they got into the car, and without saying a word she drove out of town and down the coast highway; one of her hands was in Bunny's, and he, searching the caverns of his memory, remembered having heard Eunice mention that Nina had had a desperate affair with Barney Lee, who had enlisted a year ago, and was now in France.

They stopped at a lonely place, and there was a rug in the

car, and pretty soon they were sitting by the noisy surf, and Nina was snuggled close to Bunny and whispering, "Do you care for me the least little bit?" And when he answered that he did, she said, "Then why don't you pet me?" And when he began to oblige her, he found his lips held in one of those long slow kisses which are sure fire hits on the silver screen, but which the censors cut to a footage varying according to geography—00 in Japan up to 8,000 in Algeria and the Argentine.

It was evident that this nineteen year old Juno was his to do what he pleased with, there and then; and Bunny's head had begun to swim in the familiar alarming way. He had never got the ache of Eunice out of his soul, and here at last was deliverance! But he hesitated, because he had sworn to himself that he would not get in for this again. Also from some of the English poets he had begun to hear about a different kind of love. He knew that he didn't really love Nina Goodrich, she was all but a stranger to him; so he hesitated, and his kisses diminished in ardor, until she whispered, "What's the matter, Bunny?"

He was rattled, but a sudden inspiration came to him. "Nina," he said, "it doesn't seem quite fair."

"Why not?"

"To Barney."

He felt her wince as she lay in his arms. "But Barney is gone, dear."

"I know; but he'll come back."

"Yes, but that's so far off; and I guess he's got a girl in France by now."

"Maybe so, but you can't be sure; and it don't seem quite right that a fellow should go risk his life for his country, and somebody else steal his girl away while he's gone."

So Bunny began to talk about the front, and what was happening there, and how soon the Americans would get in, and how he expected to go right after graduation, and about Paul and what he thought about Russia, and what Dad thought about Paul; and the young Juno continued to be in his arms, but with a more and more sisterly affection, until at last the fog began to chill even their young blood, and they got up to go, and the nineteen year old Juno put her arms about her escort and gave him an especially violent kiss, declaring, "Bunny, you're a queer fellow, but I like you an awful lot!"

IV

The Germans made another gigantic thrust at the British, and this time it was the Battle of Flanders. They captured a great stretch of the British lines, and if it had not been for a six day stand of laborers and chauffeurs and what not behind the lines, every man hiding in a hole and fighting for himself with any weapon he could pick up, the Germans would have taken the whole railway system in Flanders. A month or so later came another offensive, this time to the South, against the French, the battle of the Aisne and the Oise; it looked as if Paris was doomed, and people in America held their breath while they read the bulletins in the newspapers.

In the midst of that battle, covering nearly two hundred miles of front, an epoch-making thing happened; the hard-pressed French commander put in the first of the newly-arrived American troops. These boys had had only a few months training, and the French didn't think they would hold; but instead of giving way like the rest of the armies, they hit the German line and went forward a couple of miles over a three mile front. So more of them were rushed in, and a few days later came the battle of Belleau Wood, and all over America went a thrill of exultation. It was not national pride, but more than that, men felt—it was a victory of free institutions. When you ran over the lists of dead and wounded in these battles you found Horowitz and Schnierow and Samerjian and Samaniego, Constantinopulos and Toplitsky and Quong Ling; but they all fought alike, and it was a victory for that golden flood of eloquence that was being poured out from the White House.

In the midst of these excitements came Bunny's commencement time, and he had to make the great decision. He and his father had the most serious talk of their lives; Bunny had never seen the old man so deeply moved. What he said was, "Son, can't you possibly see your way to stay and help me with this job?" What Bunny answered was, "Dad, if I didn't get into the army, I'd never feel right the rest of my life."

Dad pointed out what it was going to mean to him person-ally. He was no longer able to carry this load alone. There had to be more and more wells, and every one was an added care. They simply had to have a big refinery, and that meant also a chain of service stations, you could not count on government contracts forever. This Paradise tract was Bunny's, but if he wanted to give it up, why then Dad would have to negotiate with some of the big people who had been sounding him out on the question of mergers. If Bunny went into the army there would be no use counting on him, because Dad was sure this war wasn't half over. "Those that go now aren't many of them coming back," was the way he put it; there was a catch in his voice, and with a little bit more they would have had to pull out their pocket-handkerchiefs, which would have been equally embarrassing to both. All that Bunny could do was to repeat, "I've just got to go, Dad; I've just got to go."

So Dad gave up, and a couple of weeks later Bunny got his notice to report to his training-camp. Aunt Emma spilled tears over him, while Grandma drew her withered old lips tight over her badly-fitting false teeth, and said it was a crime, and it ended her interest in life. Bertie made arrangements for a farewell party, and Dad reported that he had opened negotiations with Vernon Roscoe, the biggest independent oil operator on the coast, president of Flora-Mex and Mid-Central Pete, who had several times broached the project of a vast enterprise to be known as "Ross Consolidated."

V

They drove up to Paradise, to give Bunny a farewell look at things, and there they found that Paul was expected home for a furlough, preliminary to a journey across the Pacific Ocean. This war, Dad said, was like a fire in a "tank-farm," you could never tell which way things would explode, or what would go next. Here was Paul, with the bunch of carpenters he directed, ordered onto a transport to be shipped—of all places in the world—to Vladivostok in Siberia!

It appeared that when the Bolsheviks took charge of Russia they found themselves with a great army of war prisoners, among them a hundred thousand Czecho-Slovaks. This was a new name—you looked it up in the encyclopedias and couldn't find it, and had to have it explained to you that they were Bohemians, but this was a German word, and just as we had changed hamburger into liberty steak and sauerkraut into liberty cabbage, so the Bohemians became Czecho-Slovaks, which nobody knew how to spell when they heard it, or to pronounce when they saw it. The people of this race were revolting

against Germany, and the Bolsheviks had agreed that their
Czecho-Slovak prisoners would be shipped to Vladivostok,
where the allies might take charge of them, and bring them to
the fighting front if they saw fit. But on the way across Siberia
the Czecho-Slovaks got to fighting with the Bolsheviks and the
released German war prisoners, and had seized a great section
of the railroad.

So now into this weird mix-up the allies were intervening.
The newspapers explained the matter: the Bolshevik movement was an uprising of fanatics, imposed upon the Russian
people by the guns of hired mercenaries, Chinese and Mon-
golians and Cossacks and escaped criminals and general riff-
raff; it couldn't last very long, a few weeks or months at the
most, and what was needed was to supply a nucleus about
which the decent Russians might rally. The allies were now
undertaking to do that; American and Japanese troops were
to help the Czecho-Slovaks in Siberia; and American and
British troops were to organize the Russian refugees at Archangel in the far north. So here was Paul, going to build
barracks and Y. M. C. A. huts along the famous Trans-Siberian
railway, and see for himself those exciting events about which
he had been debating with Dad. Bunny was going to a training camp, and maybe when he got through they would send
him to the same front—that was a case where he would let Dad
use his influence! Bunny meant to work hard and rise in the
service, and maybe he would have Paul and his carpenters
under his command!

They had a hard time keeping their spirits up, because of
Ruth, who was utterly inconsolable. She would go about the
place with tears running down her cheeks, and now and then
would have to jump up and rush from the room. When the
time came for Paul to say his last farewell, Ruth almost went
out of her mind; she locked her arms about his neck, and he
had to pull her fingers away. It was sad for a fellow, to be
driven away with his sister lying in a faint in a chair. Old Mr.
Watkins had to come up and take her home, and send up
Sadie to do the housework for Dad. By golly, it made you
realize about war!

VI

Bunny went back to Beach City, to face a trial of the same
sort. Grandma did not cry out or faint, she just went up to

her studio-room and locked the door and did not appear, even for meals. When Bunny was ready to go, he went and knocked on the door, and Grandma let him into her laboratory of paints and oils and high art. Her face was drawn but grim, and only her withered red eyelids gave her away. "Little boy," she said —he was still that to her, he would never grow up—"little boy, you are a victim of the old men's crimes. That means nothing to you now, but remember it, and some day, long after I'm gone, you'll understand."

She kissed him without a sound, and he stole out, with tears running down his cheeks, and feeling somehow as if he himself were committing a crime. He felt still more that way when, a week later, he received a telegram saying that Grandmother Ross had been found dead in bed. He got a three day leave to come home and attend the funeral, and had to say his good-byes to the rest of the family all over again.

The training-camp was located in the South, a place of blazing sunshine and vigorous perspiration. It was crowded with boys from every part of the state, mostly high school and college fellows, with a sprinkling of others who had got into the officer class by having military experience. The sons of grape-growers and orange and walnut and peach and prune growers, of cowmen and lumbermen, and business and professional men in the cities—Bunny wanted to know what they were like, and what they thought about life and love and the war. He drilled until his back ached, and he studied, much the same as at school; but he lived in a tent, and ate ravenously, and grew in all directions.

Now and then he would explore the country with a companion, but keeping himself out of the sex adventures that occupied most of the army's free time. Here was a place where no bones were made about plain talk; your superiors took it for granted that when you went out of the camp you went to look for a woman, and they told you what to do when you came back, and had a treatment-station where you lined up with the other fellows and made jokes about where you had been and what it had cost you. Bunny knew enough to realize that the women in the neighborhood of this camp who were open to adventures must be pretty well debauched after a year, so he had little interest in their glances or the trim silk-stockinged ankles they displayed.

He had made application for the artillery, but they assigned him to study "military transportation," because of his knowledge of oil. He took this quite innocently, never realizing that Dad with his wide-spreading influence might have put in a word. Dad was quietly determined that Bunny was not going across the sea, no, not if this man's war lasted another ten years. Bunny was going to be among those who had charge of the army's supplies of gasoline and oil, seeing that the various products were up to standard and were efficiently and promptly shipped. Who could say—perhaps he might be among those who would have the job of working out contracts, and might be able now and then to put in a good word for Ross Consolidated!

VII

The new deal was going through, and Dad wrote long letters telling of the progress—letters which Bunny was to return when he had studied them, and not leave lying about in a tent. Also there were rumors in the papers, and then more detailed accounts, designed to prepare the public for the launching of a huge enterprise. Late in the summer Bunny got a furlough, and came home to get the latest news.

"Home" no longer meant Beach City; for Dad had only been waiting till Bunny had got through with school, and now he had moved to another moose. It was a palace in the fashionable part of Angel City, which he had leased through a real estate agent for fifteen thousand a year. It was all pink stucco outside, with hedge plants trimmed to the shape of bells and balls like pawn-broker's signs. It had a wide veranda with swings hanging by brass chains, and ferns planted in a row of huge sea shells, and big plate glass windows that did not come open. Inside was furniture of a style called "mission oak," so heavy that you could hardly move it, but that was all right, because Dad didn't want to move it, he would sit in any chair, wherever it happened to be, and the only place he expected comfort was in his den, where he had a huge old leather chair of his own, and a store of cigars and a map of the Paradise tract covering one whole wall. One thing more Dad had seen to, that Grandma's biggest paintings were hung in the dining-room, including the scandalous one of the Germans with their steins! The rest of the old lady's stuff, her easel and paints and a great stack of her lesser works, were boxed and stowed in the basement. Aunt Emma was now the mistress of the household, with Bertie as head critic when she was home.

On the desk in Dad's den was piled a stack of papers a foot high, relating to the new enterprise. He went over them one by one and explained the details. Ross Consolidated was going to be a seventy million dollar corporation, and Dad was to have ten millions in bonds and preferred stock, and another ten millions of common stock. Mr. Roscoe was to get the same for his Prospect Hill properties and those at Lobos River, and the various bankers were to get five millions for their financing of the project. The balance was to be a special class stock, twenty-five millions to be offered to the public, to finance the new development—one of the biggest refineries in the state, and storage tanks, and new pipe lines, and a whole chain of service stations throughout Southern California. This stock was to be "non-voting," a wonderful new scheme which Dad explained to Bunny; the public was to put up its money and get a share of the profits, but have nothing to say as to how the company was run. "We'll have no bunch of boobs butting in on our affairs," said Dad; "and nobody can raid us on the market and take away control."

A little farther on in the explanations, Bunny began to see the meaning of that perpetual and unbreakable hold which Dad and Mr. Roscoe were giving to themselves. In the prospectuses and advertisements of Ross Consolidated, the public would be told all about the vast oil resources in the Ross Junior tract at Paradise; but here it was being fixed up that Ross Consolidated was not to operate this tract, but to lease it to a special concern, the Ross Junior Operating Company, and nobody but Dad and Mr. Roscoe and the bankers were to have any stock in that! There was a whole series of such intricate devices, holding companies and leasing companies and separate issues of stock, and some of these things were to go into effect at once, and some later on, after the public had put up its money!

When Bunny, the "little idealist," began to make objections to this, he saw that he was hurting his father's feelings. Dad said that was the regular way of big money deals, and my God, were they running a soup-kitchen? The public would get its share and more—that stock would go to two hundred in the first year, jist you watch and see! But it was Dad and his

son who had done the hard work on the Paradise tract, and at
Prospect Hill and Lobos River too; and the government
wanted them to go on and do more such work, to drill a hundred new wells and help win the war, and how could they
do it if they distributed the money around for people to throw
away on jazz parties? Jist look at those "war-babies," and all
the mad spending in New York! Dad was taking care of his
money and using it wisely, in industry, where it belonged;
he was perfectly sincere, and hard set as concrete, in his conviction that he was the one to whom the profits should come.
He and Mr. Roscoe were two individuals who had fought the
big companies and kept themselves afloat through all the
storms; they were making an unbreakable combination this
time, and they were going to get the jack out of it, just you
bet!

VIII

Meantime, the Germans had begun another offensive against
the French, the most colossal yet; it was the second Battle of
the Marne, and they called it their "Friedensturm," because
they meant to capture Paris and win their peace. But now
there were large sectors held by the American troops, of whom
there were a million in France, and three hundred thousand
coming every month, with all their supplies, in spite of the
submarines. These troops were fresh, while all the others
were exhausted; and so where they stood, the line did not
give way, and the great German offensive was blocked and
brought to a standstill.

Then, a week or two later, began an event that electrified
the whole world; the allies began to advance! Attacking now
here, now there, they gained ground, they routed the enemy
out of intrenchments which had been years in building, and
were counted impregnable. All that mighty Hindenburg line
began to crumble; and behind it, the Siegfried line, and the
Hunding line, and all the other mythological constructions.
To people in America it was the breaking of the first sunrays
through black storm clouds. The "Yanks" were wiping out
the famous St. Mihiel salient, they were capturing the enemy
by tens of thousands, and even more important, the machine
guns and artillery which the Germans could not replace. All
through the early fall this went on; until the young officers-

to-be in Bunny's training camp began to fret because this man's war was going to be over before they got to the scene.

But all this time, not one word from Paul! Bunny received agonized letters from Ruth, "Oh, what do you think can have happened to him? I write him every week to the address he gave, and I *know* he would answer if he was alive." Bunny explained that it took six weeks for mail to go to Vladivostok and return; how much longer it took on the railroad no one could guess; and besides, there was a censorship, and many things might happen to letters in war-time. If Paul had been killed or wounded, the army would surely notify his parents; so no news was good news. There had been practically no fighting, as Ruth could see from the newspaper clippings which Bunny faithfully sent to her. The reports were scanty, but that was just because nothing much had happened; if there were any real fighting, or losses to the troops, the papers would get it, you might be sure.

In the month of July of this year of 1918, the American and Japanese troops had made a landing in Vladivostok, practically unopposed; they had spread along the Trans-Siberian railway, and were policing it, and in fact running it, all the way to Lake Baikal where they had met the Czecho-Slovaks. With the help of these intelligent men, the allies now controlled the country clean across to the Volga; the Bolsheviks had to keep back in the interior. Now and then the newspapers would report that admiral this or general that was setting up a stable Russian government, of course with the help of allied money and supplies. At the west end of the line it would be a Cossack ataman and at the east end a Chinese mandarin or Mongolian tuchun or other strange beast; thus new stretches of the earth's surface were being delivered from the wickedness of Bolshevism. Somewhere amid these picturesque and exciting events Paul Watkins of Paradise, California, was building army barracks and "Y" huts; and some day he would come back with a wonderful story to tell! So Bunny wrote, bidding Ruth keep cheerful, and have faith in the benevolence of her old Uncle Sam.

IX

The nights were growing cold in Bunny's cantonment, and from Europe the thrilling news continued to pour in, and spread across the front pages of the newspapers, six or eight editions every day. The allied advance was turning into a march, that long talked of march to Berlin! A march also to Vienna and to Sofia and to Constantinople—for everywhere the central powers were weakening, collapsing, surrendering. President Wilson issued his "fourteen points," on the basis of which the Germans were invited to quit. There were rumors of negotiations—the German leaders were suggesting a truce! There were two or three days of suspense, and then the answer, there would be no truce, only a surrender; the march to Berlin was on!

And then one day an amazing report; the enemy had capitulated, the surrender had been signed! As a matter of fact, it was a false alarm, due to the American custom of keeping one jump ahead of events. Each paper wants to beat the others, so they get everything ready in advance—speeches that have not yet been delivered, ceremonies that have not yet taken place. Some nervous reporter let his finger slip on the trigger, and the message came that set all America wild. Such a spectacle had never been witnessed since the world began; every noisemaking instrument conceivable was turned loose, and men, women and children turned out on the streets, and danced and sang and yelled until they were exhausted; pistols were shot off, and autos went flying by with tin-cans bouncing behind; newsboys and stock-brokers wept on one another's shoulders, and elderly unapproachable bank-presidents danced the can-can with typists and telephone girls. A day or two later, when the real news came, they turned out to do it all over again, but never could recapture their first fine careless rapture.

After that, of course, the fun had gone out of military training; all the young officers-to-be wanted to get back home, to go to college or to take up their jobs, and all who had any influence quickly got furloughs that were understood to be elastic. Such a favor came to Bunny, out of the blue void where Dad wielded his mysterious power, and he went home to watch the movements of "Ross Consolidated," which had been launched at an opening price of $108 per share for the "class B stock," and completely sold out in two days, and was now quoted in the market at 147¾. They had made the stock of "no par value"—another new device which Vernon Roscoe's fancy lawyers had recommended; there were certain taxes both

state and federal which could be dodged by this method, and
moreover there would never be need to issue "stock dividends"
to conceal the amount of the profit.   Mr. Roscoe was certainly
a wizard when it came to finance, jist about the smartest
feller Dad had met in the oil-game.

It was a tremendous load taken off Dad's shoulders, for
now the enormous Roscoe machine would market the oil and
collect the money.   Dad's job was new developments—the
part of the game he really liked.   He was a member of the
board of directors of the new concern, and also a vice-president, at a salary of a hundred thousand a year, with charge of
exploring and drilling; he would travel here and there and
lay out the tracts and select the drilling sites, and see that every
well was brought in properly, before turning it over to another
executive, the superintendent of operation.   It was Dad's idea
that Bunny should take a position under his father, to start
with say six thousand a year, until everybody was satisfied
that he knew the business; the two of them would have the
time of their lives, driving all over Southern California and
smelling out oil, jist like at Paradise!   Bunny said that sounded
good, but he'd want a little time to think it over and get used
to the idea that he wasn't going to Siberia or to France.   Dad
said all right, of course, he musn't jump into things in a hurry;
but Bunny could see that he was a little pained because his
son and namesake did not do that very thing!

X

They went up to Paradise to see the developments; and
one of the first developments they saw was Ruth, who had
their lunch ready in the Rascum cabin.   Bunny was shocked
by her appearance; she looked ten years older than when he
had seen her last, her face was pale, and her smile was forced.
She had given up all pretense of feminine charm, her hair
was drawn back tight and tied in a knot on top of her head,
and her skirts came to her ankles, which was half a leg longer
than the fashion.   Ruth was just setting out to be an old maid,
said Meelie, and all on account of grieving her heart out about
Paul.

"Oh, I know he's dead!" Ruth declared.   "Just think, it's
been five months since he went away, and don't you know Paul
would have written me a lot of letters in that time?"

It did seem strange; and Dad thought a bit and said, "Yes, we've waited long enough, and now we'll jist find out."

"Oh, Mr. Ross, how do you mean?" cried Ruth, clasping her hands together.

"Well, we ain't lost that army altogether in Siberia, and I guess there is some way to connect up with it."

Ruth had gone paler than ever. "Oh, I don't know as I'd dare find out! If I should hear he was dead—if I was really to know it—"

"Look here, child," said Dad, "the troubles you imagine is always a lot worse than the real ones. I want to know about my boss-carpenter, and I'm jist a-goin' to!"

So Dad went to the telephone, and called the hay and feed store of Mr. Jake Coffey in San Elido. "Hello, Jake. Yes, we're all fine here, how's your old man? Say, I understand you had the nominating—I fergit the feller's name, but the congressman from this district. Well, I never asked him a favor, but I guess I got a right to one, seeing all I put up to elect him. Well, now, you send him a telegram and tell him to toddle over to the War Department and put in an inquiry about the whereabouts and health of Paul Watkins. You got a pencil there?"

Dad turned to Ruth, "What is it now? Company B, Forty-seventh California Regiment, American Expeditionary Forces to Russia. I want the War Department to cable an inquiry and have the reply cabled; you wire the congressman twenty-five dollars to cover the cost, and if there's anything left over he can keep the change. I'll mail you my check today. You might explain, if you want to, a member of the family is ill, and it's a matter of life and death to get some word at once. And I'll be obliged, Jake, and if you need any gasoline for your car, jist drop round after we git this new refinery a-goin.' How'd you like that last dividend check from the company? Ha, ha, ha! Well, so long."

For two days Ruth waited on tenter-hooks, holding her breath every time the phone rang; and at last there was the voice of Jake Coffey—Bunny answered, and he turned from the receiver right quick, saying, "Telegram from Congressman Leathers, the War Department reports that Paul is at Irkutsk and well." Ruth gave a cry—she was standing by the dining table, and she grabbed at it and missed, and went swaying, and Bunny had to drop the receiver and catch her. And there she

was, by golly, white and cold and senseless, they had to lay
her out on the floor and sprinkle water on her face. And
when she came to, all she could do was to cry and cry like a
baby. Presently Bunny remembered the telephone receiver
hanging, and went and apologized to Mr. Coffey and thanked
him, and it was all Bunny could do to keep his own voice
straight; the truth was, he and Dad had been more worried
about Paul than they were willing to admit.

After Ruth was able to sit up and smile, Dad said, "Irkutsk,
where is that?" And the girl said at once, "It's on Lake Baikal,
in the middle of Siberia." Said Dad, "Hello, where did you
git your geography?" It turned out there was an old atlas
among Paul's books, and Ruth had the Siberia part clean by
heart—the names of every station on the Trans-Siberian Railway—Omsk, Tomsk, Tobolsk—Dad thought it was funny, and
made her say them off—by golly, if there had been a time-
table attached, she'd have known when the night-freight was
due at Vladivostok! She knew the physical geography of the
country, the races which inhabited it, the flora and fauna and
principal commercial interests, furs, lumber, wheat, dairy products.

The only trouble was, her information was twenty years
out of date! So now, what was she going to do but take the
stage to Roseville that afternoon, and in the library she would
find a big new atlas, and maybe some books on the subject.
Bunny said he'd drive her; so he did, and they found an atlas
with a picture of Irkutsk, a public square with some buildings,
churches or mosques or whatever they were called, with round
domes going up to a point on top; there was snow on the
ground, and sledges with big high harness up over the horses'
necks. It was dreadful cold there, Ruth said, Paul wasn't used
to such weather; but Bunny laughed and told her not to worry
about that, Paul would have plenty to wear, this was the best
taken care of army in history, and so long as they had the
railroad open, nobody would suffer.

But that was not enough for Ruth, what she wanted was
for Paul to come home. Surely, now that the war was over,
he ought to be on the way! But Bunny said she'd have to make
up her mind to wait, because an armistice wasn't the same as
a peace, there was a lot of negotiating to be done, and the army
would sit tight meantime. But when peace was declared, then
surely Paul would come back, because we certainly weren't

going on running the Trans-Siberian Railway after the war
was over. Bunny said that with a laugh, meaning it to be
funny, and Ruth smiled, because it sounded funny to her; so
innocent they were of the intricacies of world diplomacy, these
two babes in the California woods!

XI

Bunny spent a week hunting quail with Dad, or wandering
over the hills by himself, thinking things over. At last he sat
down to have it out. "Dad, I'm afraid you're going to be
disappointed in me, but this is the truth—I want to go to
college."

"College! Gosh, son, what's that for?" There was a look
of amazement on Dad's face; but he was an old hypocrite, he
had known perfectly well that Bunny was thinking about college, and he had thought about it a lot himself.

"I just don't feel I've got enough education, Dad."

"What is it you want to know?"

"Well, that's something you can't say; you don't know just
what you'll get till you've got it. But I have a feeling, I want
to know more about things."

Dad looked forlorn—pitifully, but quite innocently and unin-
tentionally. "It means you jist ain't interested in oil."

"Well, no, Dad, that's not quite fair. I can study for a
while and then come back to the business."

But Dad knew better than that. "No, son, if you go to
college, you'll get so high up above us oil fellers, you won't
know we're here. If you mean to be an oil man, the thing to
study is oil."

"Well, Dad, the truth is, I'm really too young to know what
I want to be. If I wanted to do something else, surely we've
got money enough—"

"It's not the money, son, it's the job. You know how I
feel—I like to have you with me—"

"I don't mean to go away," Bunny hastened to put in.
"There's plenty of colleges around here, and I can live at
home. And we can come up for week-ends and holidays, the
same as always. I'm not going to lose my interest in Paradise,
Dad, but I really won't be happy to buckle down to business
until I've had a chance to learn more."

Dad had to give way to that. There was that curious war

in his own mind, a mingling of respect for knowledge, of awe in the presence of cultured people, along with fear of "notions" that Bunny might get, strange flights of "idealism" that would make him unfit to be the heir and custodian of twenty million dollars worth of Ross Consolidated!

CHAPTER X

THE UNIVERSITY

I

Southern Pacific University had been launched by a California land baron as a Methodist Sunday school; its professors were all required to be Methodists, and it featured scores of religious courses. It had grown enormous upon the money of an oil king who had bribed half a dozen successive governments in Mexico and the United States, and being therefore in doubt as to the safety of his soul gave large sums to professional soul-savers. Apparently uncertain which group had the right "dope," he gave equally to both Catholics and Protestants, and they used the money to denounce and undermine each other.

If Dad had known that his son was to be educated by the donations of Pete O'Reilly, he would have been at once amused and reassured. Not knowing about it, he paid a visit to the place, to see at least the outside of Bunny's future environment. The university had started far out in the suburbs of Angel City, but now the community had grown around it—which meant another large endowment, contributed by all the rentpayers of the city. Its buildings were elaborate, which impressed Dad; the fact that they were crowded with five thousand young men and women impressed him still more, for when Dad saw a great number of people doing the same thing, he concluded it was something normal and safe.

Still more reassuring was his meeting with President Alonzo T. Cowper, D.D., Ph.D., LL.D. For Dr. Cowper was in the business of interviewing dads; he had been selected by his millionaire trustees because of his skill in interviewing trustees. Dr. Cowper knew how a scholar could be at the same time dignified and deferential. Our Dad, being thoroughly money-conscious, read the doctor's mind as completely as if he had been inside it: if this founder of Ross Consolidated is pleased with the education his son receives, he may some day donate a building for the teaching oil chemistry, or at least endow a chair of research in oil geology. And that

233

seemed to Dad exactly the proper attitude for a clergyman-educator to take; everybody in the world was in the business of getting money, and this was a very high-toned way.

Both Dad and Bunny took the university with the seriousness it expected. Neither of them doubted that money which had been gained by subsidizing political parties, and bribing legislators and executive officials and judges and juries—that such money could be turned at once into the highest type of culture, wholesale, by executive order. Bunny plunged into the excitements of courses and credits, he raced from English 5A to Spanish 2, and from there to Sociology 7 and Modern History 14, and accumulated a stack of text-books, and listened to lectures, and wrote notes, and stowed in his mind a mass of dates and other details.

It took him a long time to realize that the "English" was cruelly dull, and that the young man who taught it was bored to tears by what he was doing; that the "Spanish" had a French accent, and that the professor was secretly patronizing bootleggers to console himself for having to live in what he considered a land of barbarians; that the "Sociology" was an elaborate structure of classifications, wholly artificial, devised by learned gentlemen in search of something to be learned about; and that the Modern History was taught from text-books which had undergone the scrutiny of thousands of sharp eyes, in order to spare the sensibilities of Mr. Pete O'Reilly, and avoid giving to any student the slightest hint concerning the forces which control the modern world.

II

With equal seriousness Bunny took the social life of this enormous institution. It was the far-off wonderful goal to which all high school students had looked; a few lucky ones had got there, and he was among them. His sister's chum had a brother who was a senior, and belonged to the best possible fraternity; so the word was spoken, and Bunny was snapped up. They were a fast, free-spending crowd, aggressive, self-confident, slangy, voluble over the prospects of this year's track team. Bunny was a runner, so they had a reason for welcoming him that was more presentable than his old man's oil.

Like all Western universities, Southern Pacific was co-educational; so Bunny was exposed to the impact of a mass of feminity, the distilled and concentrated essence of allurement. Such swarms of graceful figures, trim ankles, dimpled white and brown arms, costumes the color of Brazilian butterflies; a kaleidescope of smiles and flashing eyes, a perpetual zephyr of soft scents, blown from lilac-bushes and jasmine vines and miles upon miles of California orange and lemon-orchards. Something was bound to happen to a young idealist in such an environment—especially when he had just spent the summer in a training-camp for men only!

Not all these bundles of feminine charm were accustomed to follow the market reports upon Ross Consolidated; yet somehow they managed to learn about the discoverer and heir-apparent of the Paradise oil field. Many sets of quick wits were concentrated upon him, he was invited to scores of dances and hundreds of fudge parties and thousands of motor-rides. Then a strange rumor spread; here was an unimaginable phe-nomenon, a young millionaire who would not "pet"! One by one the champion spell-weavers of Southern Pacific wove in vain; before long there were odds posted, and quite a trade in bets as to who would be the first girl that Bunny Ross would kiss! Researches were conducted in the Beach City High School, and word came that the young oil prince carried in his bosom a broken heart; which, of course, made him a romantic figure, and added enormously to his prestige.

These things go by contraries, and the girl who landed Bunny did so because she did not try. The family of Henri-etta Ashleigh had had money for generations, and so could afford to look down upon it, and all those who sought it. This was the way to impress Bunny, who was aware that his money was painfully new. Never would he attain to the aggressive self-assurance of his sister; he was looking for something better than himself, and for a while he found it in the Ash-leighs, with their perfect manners and well trained servants and mansion full of the debris of culture.

Henrietta was tall and slender, gentle, soft of voice, and reserved to the point of primness. Her mother had just died, and for a year she wore black, which of course was very con-spicuous. She was high church Episcopal, and on Sunday mornings wore long kid gloves and carried a little prayer-book and hymnal joined together, bound in black leather with a gold border. She took Bunny to church and he learned that one does not have to take ancient Hebrew mythology with vulgar

16

literalness, but may have its symbolic meaning explained by a white-haired old gentleman with a trace of English accent.

What Henrietta meant to Bunny was a refuge from the anguish and tumult of illegitimate desire. He fled to her as to a saint, a madonna alive and visible upon a college campus. She was so far above the glaring crudeness of the smart set; she did not use paint nor powder—nothing so common as perspiration would presume to appear on her delicately chiseled nose. You might dream of kissing her, but it would remain a dream; she would call you "Mr. Ross" during the first six months of your acquaintance, and after that she would call you "Arnold," finding it dignified, perhaps because of Matthew. So long as you knew and truly appreciated her, you would make the highest grades in class, and, as the little black and gold prayer-book phrased it, "honour and obey the civil authority, and submit yourself to all your governors, teachers, spiritual pastors and masters."

III

Bunny went up to Paradise for his Christmas holidays, and there was the first word from Paul; a plain card, bearing the stamp of the American Expeditionary Force, but no place; no picture post-card with "Scenes in Irkutsk" or "Camel-sleigh on the Volga," or anything like that! "Dear Ruth," it said: "Just a line to let you know that I am well and everything is all right. I have received three letters from you. Please write often. We are busy and I am having an interesting time. Give my love to all the family and to Bunny and Mr. Ross. Affectionately, Paul."

Ruth had had this treasure for several days, and there was no telling how many times she had read it, and studied every mark on both sides. It seemed to Bunny a cold and unsatisfactory note, but he did not say so to Ruth; he asked Dad about it, and Dad said there would necessarily be a great deal of censoring of soldier's mail, and Paul had probably written this bare message to make sure it got through. Why did there have to be so much censoring? Bunny asked; and Dad answered that these were ticklish times, and the army had to protect itself against enemy propaganda.

Dad had been reading a magazine article which explained what was happening in the world. The German and Austrian empires had come down with a crash, and that was a great triumph for democracy. But now the friends of democracy had a second big job to do, which was to crush the wild beast of Bolshevism. They were starving it by a blockade on every front, and wherever the well-behaved and respectable Russians had set up a government on the borders, the allies were helping them with money and supplies. General Denikin had taken possession of south Russia; on the west a lot of new states had been set up; on the north, at Archangel, an anti-Bolshevik group was making headway under British and American protection. As to Siberia, there had been a Socialist government, holding over from the Kerensky days; but these Socialists were a lot of talkers, and now they had been kicked out and replaced by a real fighting man, Admiral Kolchak, who had once commanded the Tsar's fleet. It was this he-admiral the allies were backing to run Siberia, and our troops were there to keep the railroad open for him. Of course the Bolsheviks, and their sympathizers in this country, were making a fuss about it, and telling all the lies they could; that was why we had to have a censorship, said Dad.

Bunny accepted this explanation without question. He had been in a training-camp for seven months, and had acquired the military point of view. He was keenly alert to the danger of Bolshevik propaganda, and determined that if ever he ran into any of it, he would hasten to denounce it. So innocent was he, and so little aware of the subtlety of the enemy—he never dreamed that he was at this time absorbing the poison; and—of all places in the world—in one of the class-rooms of his most Christian and conservative university!

It was hard on a poor overworked university president. Dr. Cowper's most trusted dean had engaged this young instructor, upon recommendation of high-up Y. M. C. A. authorities. The young man had been doing relief work in Saloniki, and was the son of a prominent Methodist pastor; he bore the name of Daniel Webster Irving, and how was anyone to imagine that a man with such a name might be suffering from political shell-shock?

This young instructor was subtle in his method; he did not say anything that could be pinned down on him, but would sow his seeds of doubt by asking questions, and advising students to "think for themselves." There are always in every college class one or more "sore-heads," the sons of unorthodox parents; one in Bunny's class was an avowed "rationalist," and another had a Russian name. All that a teacher had to do was to let these fellows ask questions, and quickly the whole group would be wandering in a maze, demoralized by what the Japanese government in its control of education describes as "dangerous thoughts."

President Wilson had gone to Europe, in order to bring about the reign of justice he had promised. He was having a triumphal progress through England and France, and our newspapers were full of the wonders of what he was about to achieve. But in Mr. Irving's class Bunny heard it pointed out that the President had dropped from mention the most important of his "fourteen points," the demand for "freedom of the seas." Could it be that this had been the price of British support for his program? And then, more startling yet, Bunny learned that the secret treaties which the allies had signed among themselves at the outset of the war were now laid on the peace table, and made the basis of jealous bickerings. Bunny had never forgotten about those treaties, how Dad had assured Paul that they would turn out to be Bolshevik forgeries. But here the allies were admitting them to be genuine, and furthermore, were setting out to enforce them, regardless of any promises of fair play which President Wilson had made to the Germans!

Bunny took this amazing news home with him to Dad; apparently Paul had been right, and the wicked Bolsheviks had been telling the truth! What did Dad make of it? Dad didn't know what to make of it; he was much disturbed, and could only say we couldn't judge, we'd jist have to wait. But the trouble was, the longer we waited, the worse things seemed to get; the more evident it became that our President had done the very thing that Dad had been sure he would never do—he had let himself be "jockeyed." Like water seeping underneath a dike, a subtle current of skepticism was creeping through those freshman classes in Southern Pacific University which were taking "Modern History 14."

Mr. Irving wasn't supposed to be discussing the peace conference at all; he was supposed to be seeing to it that his students memorized the names of battles and commanding generals in the Franco-Prussian war. But one theme led so easily to the other, and it was so difficult to keep the "soreheads" quiet! This same thing was happening in other class-rooms, and in other parts of the United States where men encountered their fellows, and thus became exposed to "dangerous thoughts." Before long the forbidden ideas were being voiced in Congress, and after that they could not be kept out of the newspapers. It was like a storm that burst over the whole country. A million idealists like Bunny woke up all at once to the cruel fact that their dolly was stuffed with sawdust.

IV

Yes, it was a trying time to be alive in the world. All those golden promises that had been made to us, those bright hopes we had cherished! All the blood of the young men that had been shed, three hundred thousand of them dead or wounded in France—and here were the allied statesmen, grim, cruel old men, sitting at the council-table and putting the world right back where it had been before! Perpetuating all the old hatreds, all the old injustices—with a thousand new ones to torment the future! Tearing Germans away from their own land and giving them to Frenchmen, giving Austrians to Italians, Russians to Poles—so on through a long list of blunders; condemning millions of people to live under governments which they feared and despised, and thus making certain they would revolt, and throw Europe into uproar again! Men could not realize these things all at once; they got them little by little, as details of the negotiations leaked out. Every country in the world was carrying on its own propaganda, thinking about its own selfish interests; and President Wilson was in the midst of the mess, being pulled and hauled about, this way and that, quite powerless for the good aims he had proclaimed. As the picture of this got back to America, there spread over the land such a wave of disgust as had never been known before.

And then the President himself came home, to declare that he had achieved a complete victory. In the name of "self-determination of all peoples" he was giving the German Rhineland to France, and German Africa to Britain, and the German Tyrol to Italy, and a Chinese province to Japan, and to the United States a mandate over Armenia! Also he had made a perpetual alliance with France and Britain, whereby we bound ourselves to maintain this brand of self-determina-

tion forever! When this program had been thoroughly realized, a tone of hilarious cynicism became the correct thing
among the young intellectuals of America; fashionable young
matrons took to deceiving their husbands in the name of
chastity, and college boys began toting hip-pocket flasks out
of loyalty to prohibition.

The thing was particularly hard upon Bunny, because he
had to go to Paradise every once in a while, and come face
to face with Ruth, and explain how self-determination for the
people of Siberia meant that her brother must stay there in
peace time and hold a bayonet at their necks. In elucidat-
ing this singular situation, Bunny became almost as skillful
a trickster as if he had had a regular diplomatic job with
extra-territorial immunity. For a month or two he managed
it, while the Germans were dragged to Versailles and made to
sign an agreement to pay an indemnity so vast that it could not
be named.

Then one day came a letter that made his task all but
impossible. It was an innocent-looking letter, written in a
crude hand on some sheets of cheap paper, postmarked Seattle,
and addressed to "Mr. Bunny Ross, Paridise, California." It
said:

"Dear Mr. Bunny: You dont know me but I am a returned soldier that used to punch cattle in Salinas valley.
Paul Watkins said I should write you because he cant get no
news by the censors. I am invalidded back, have had the
Asiatic dissenterry, am bleeding at the bowls three months
and you should wash your hands good when you have read
this letter, because it is an easy dissease to catch. I am in
issolation and this will be smuggled, for God's sake dont let
on I have wrote it they would sure put me in the can. But
Paul said your father might do something to get us boys out
if he knew what a hell it was. Mr. Bunny what are we
doing in that place and why do we have to stay? It is forty
below zero most of the winter and big storms a lot of the time
and you have to do sentry duty and in summer the muskee-
toes is big as flies and where they bite the blood runs. And
the Japs take shots at us, they are suppose to be our allies
but they are sure grabbing that country there is suppose to be
only seven thousand but there is seventy and why did we take
them in there? Our boys is not allowed to have no side arms
and the Japs have got bayonets and we have only fists. We

have zones that we are supposed to control but the Japs will not keep out of them and I have saw them put out with machine guns lined up, and if we have to have a war with them over Siberia there will sure be a lot of our boys massacreed at the startoff. And them Russian refugees and officers that we have orders to help I heard our colonel say, you give them money to start a government and they go on a bust and that night you have to pull them out of a sporting house. They have got one idea which is to shoot all the working-men they can get hands on and the women too and they torture them, Mr. Bunny I seen things that it would make you sick to read them. From General Graves down our army is sore on this job and some of them is gone crazy, there has been more than twenty in our regement and some has been sent home in a strait jacket. But the people at home is not allowed to know nothing, there is boys in our regement that is not had one line from their folks in half a year and they are crazy with worry. Why do we have to be there when the war is over, if you know I wish you would tell me. But Paul said not to tell his sister, because it is not so bad for himself, they move him a lot and he is always busy it is easy when you have a lot of carpenter work but for some fellers I seen them carry a stack of railway ties a hundred yards and then move them back to the old place just to keep us work-ing. Please send me some cigarettes that will be a way to say that you have got this letter and if you send two packages I will know that you want me to write some more. Yours re-spectfully, Jeff Korbitty."

V

Bunny took this letter to Dad, and it worried him very much, of course, but what could Dad do about it? He had three wells to bring in that week, and one of them broke loose and smeared up a couple of hundred acres of rocks. Also he and Mr. Roscoe had to deal with the amazing gyra-tions of the oil market. It seemed as if all the nations in the world had suddenly set themselves to buying up gasoline; perhaps they were making up for the shortage of the war, or perhaps they were getting ready for another war—anyhow, the price was up sky-high, and Southern California was being drained. It was truly amazing, the gas-stations were refusing to sell to any but their regular customers, and then only five gallons at a time; other stations were clean empty, and cars were stalled for days. Dad and Mr. Roscoe were making a tremendous killing; they were getting real money too, Dad said with a laugh, none of these foreign bonds for them!

Bunny shipped a dozen cartons of cigarettes to Jeff Korbitty; and day and night he worried over the problem of Paul. Somehow the putting down of Bolshevism took on quite a different aspect when it meant keeping Paul in Siberia! Also, Bolshevik propaganda seemed a different thing when it came from the pen of an ex-cowpuncher from Salinas valley! Bunny simply had to do something, and finally in desperation he sat himself down and composed a letter to his Congressman, Mr. Leathers, telling what he had heard about conditions in Siberia, and requesting that functionary to ascertain the War Department's reasons for censorship of soldiers' mail in peace time, also to urge an investigation by Congress of the reasons for keeping American troops in Siberia.

That letter was due to reach the Congressman five days later. Seven days after Bunny had posted it, a well-dressed and affable gentleman called at the Ross home in Angel City, stating that he was the owner of an oil concession in Siberia and wanted to interest Mr. Ross in it. Dad was up at Paradise, so Bunny talked with the gentleman, and finding him humane and catholic in his interests, told him all about Paul, and showed him Jeff Korbitty's letter. They discussed the situation in Siberia, and the gentleman said there had been no declaration of war against the Russians, so what right did we have fighting them? Bunny said it seemed the same way to him; and then the gentleman went away, and no more was heard about the oil concession, but a couple of weeks later Bunny received a second letter from the ex-cowboy soldier, bitterly reproaching him for having "throwed me down," as he must have done, because Jeff hadn't wrote to nobody else, but the army had got onto him, and they had throwed him into the can just like he had said, and he was smuggling out this letter to tell Bunny that he could go to hell and stay there. Which was one stage more in the education of a little idealist!

Bunny simply had to talk to somebody about this episode. Next day, as he was driving away from the university in his sporty new car, he noticed a young man walking with a slight limp, and it struck him as impolite for a student of the university to drive in a sporty new car, while an instructor of the university had to walk with a slight limp. Bunny slowed up, and inquired, "Will you ride with me, Mr. Irving?"

"If you're going my way," said the other.

"Whatever way you wish," was Bunny's reply. "As a matter of fact, I've been hoping for a chance to talk with you, and it would be a favor to me."

The young man got in, and stated the address to which he wished to go; then he said, "What is on your mind?"

"I want to ask you why you think it is that we are keeping an army in Siberia."

Mr. Daniel Webster Irving was a peculiar-looking person; his head came up a long way out of his collar, and with its quick alert movements it made you think of a quail sitting in a tree and looking out for you and your gun. He had a brown moustache, rather bristly and rebellious, and grey eyes which he fixed upon you sharply when you said something stupid in class. He fixed them now upon Bunny, demanding, "What makes you interested in that?"

"I have a friend with the troops there, nearly a year, and I've had some news that worries me. I don't understand what's going on."

Said Mr. Irving: "Are you asking me as a student, or as a friend?"

"Why," replied Bunny, a little puzzled, "I'd be glad to be a friend, if I might. What is the difference?"

"The difference," said the other, "might be the loss of my position in the university."

Bunny flushed, embarrassed. "I hadn't thought of anything like that, Mr. Irving."

"I'll put it to you bluntly, Ross. I spent all I had saved on relief work in Europe and came home broke. Now I am educating a young sister, and they are paying me the munificent salary of thirteen hundred a year. I am due to get a rise of two hundred next year, and the matter of contracts comes up this month. If it is reported that I am defending Bolshevism to my students, I won't get a contract, either here or anywhere else."

"Oh, but Mr. Irving, I wouldn't dream of reporting you!"

"You wouldn't need to. You'd only need to tell your parents or your friends what I think is the reason our troops are in Siberia, and they would consider it their moral duty to report me."

"Is it as bad as that?" said Bunny.

"It's so bad that I don't see how it could be worse," said Mr. Irving. "I will answer your question provided you agree that I am talking as a friend, and that you won't mention the conversation to anyone else." And you can see how deeply Bunny had fallen into the toils of Bolshevism, when he was willing to agree to a proposition such as that!

VI

What Mr. Irving said was that our troops were in Siberia because American bankers and big business men had loaned enormous sums of money to the government of the Tsar, both before the war and during it; the Bolshevik government had repudiated these debts, and therefore our bankers and business men were determined to destroy it. It was not merely the amount of the money, but the precedent involved; if the government of any country could repudiate the obligations of a previous government, what would become of international loans? The creditor nations—that is to say America, Britain and France—maintained that a government debt was a lien, not against the government, but against the country and its resources. The total amount of international loans was one or two hundred billions of dollars, and the creditor nations meant to make an example of Soviet Russia, and establish the rule that a government which repudiated its debts would be put out of business.

Bunny found this a novel point of view, and asked many questions. Mr. Irving said that in Washington was a Russian who had been the war-time ambassador to our country, and in that capacity had had the handling of the money loaned by our government, and used for buying guns and shells for Russia. At the time of the Bolshevik revolution, this ambassador had just got something like a hundred million dollars, and our government was allowing him to use it to set up a propaganda machine against the Soviet government, with a spy system as elaborate as the Tsar had ever known. Newspapers and newspaper men, government officials and legislators, all were on this ambassador's pay-roll. Moreover, there were in our state department officials who had married Rus-

sian wives of the old nobility, and these wives had lost everything in the revolution, and it was natural they should hate
the new regime. One official was a member of the banking-
house which had handled the loans and stood to lose a fortune;
other were tied up with banks and business concerns which
had vast sums at stake. So it came about that America was
at war with Soviet Russia, on the entire circumference of that
vast republic; and so it came about that an instructor in an
American university could not discuss the matter with one of
his students, even outside the class-room, without fear of losing his position.

Mr. Daniel Webster Irving denied that he had any sympathy
with Bolshevism, or wished to teach such doctrines in America;
and Bunny, in his innocence of soul, accepted this statement—
not knowing that all Bolshevik agents say that, until they
have got the minds of their victims thoroughly poisoned. Mr.
Irving expressed the view that what was happening in Russia was a great social experiment. Could a government of the
working class succeed? Was democracy in industry a possibility, or only a fanatic's dream? We ought to send disin-
terested people, experts of all sorts into Russia, to watch what
was happening and report it. Instead of that, we were helping France and Britain to starve the Russians out; we were
compelling them to spend all their energies resisting our armies,
and those which we subsidized; we were making it impossible for the experiment to succeed, and so, of course, its
failure would prove nothing.

Bunny, poor little propaganda victim, said that he was
beginning to change his mind about these matters. Yes, the
Russians surely had a right to work out their own problem
in their own way; and certainly we ought to know the truth
about what was happening—he wished there was some way
to get it. Thereupon Mr. Irving gave him the names of two
weekly magazines, which as it happened, had just been excluded from the library of the university, and from all the
high schools of Angel City, for "dangerous thoughts."

You can imagine what happened then. When you tell a
high-spirited lad that he must not read certain publications,
he becomes immediately filled with curiosity to know what
they contain. Bunny went home and sent in his subscription to
these papers; quite openly, in his own name. So there was
another entry in the card-indexes of the Military Intelligence

Department and the Naval Intelligence Department and the Secret Service Department; to say nothing of many organizations which were using these card-indexes as their own—several patriotic societies, and several militant newspapers, and several big private detective agencies, including, of course, the information service of the once-upon-a-time ambassador from a no-longer-existing Russian government.

Bunny, groping about for some way to help Paul, was next moved to write a letter to the Southern Pacific "Stude," telling what he had come to think about the Siberian situation; being careful, of course, not to refer to Mr. Irving, nor to name either Paul or Jeff Korbitty. His letter was returned to him by the student editor, with a note protesting against a man of his prominence in the university giving such aid to the enemies of his country. The news of this incident spread, and the wildest rumors took wing; Bunny was besieged by friends and others, who wanted to read the letter, and then to argue with him.

One member of the senior class declared that he agreed with Bunny—certainly the Russians had a right to run their own country. Billy George was this man's name, and his father was a wealthy manufacturer of iron pipe. Needless to say, Bunny was glad to have a little sympathy, and let his new friend read his letter to the "Stude," and Jeff Korbitty's letter to him, and told all his ideas and troubles; and thus the card-indexes in Angel City, New York and Washington were further enriched. Inasmuch as so many other people were allowed to inspect these indexes, it will surely not be unpatriotic for us to take a glimpse into the file. The cards were six by eight in size, neatly typed on both sides; and when one was full, another was started. Our young idealist's now stood as follows:

"Ross, James Arnold, junior, alias Bunny: 679 S. Mendocino Ave., Angel City, Calif., also Paradise, San Elido Co., Calif. Age 20, height 5' 9½", hair brown, eyes brown, features regular; photo attached. Son of J. Arnold Ross, v-pres. Ross Consolidated Oil Co., Vernon Roscoe Bldg., Angel City, also indept. oil interests, estimated worth $25,000,000. Graduate 1918 Beach City (Calif.) High School, school records good, reported sex susceptibility, report agent 11497 attached. Active sympathizer Paradise oil-strike 1916-17, intimate friend of Paul Watkins, strike leader, file 1272W17. Suspected intimate with Rose Watkins, sister of Paul. Training at Camp Arthur, 1917-18, record satisfactory. Wrote to Hon. H. G. Leathers, 49th California district, prompted by returned soldier Jeff. Korbitty, file 9678K30; see letter attached, also report agent 23,672 attached. Class of 1923, Southern Pac. Univ., member Kappa Gamma Tau fraternity, trackrunner, pupil of Daniel Washington Irving, file 327118. Sentimental sympathizer Bolsh. Subscriber Nation, New Republic. Futher reports from agent 11497, fellow student; also 9621, intimate with subject's sister, known as Birdie Ross."

<h1 style="text-align:center">VII</h1>

The elder Ross had another source of information as to world affairs, besides his morning and afternoon newspapers, and his idealist son. His associates in the oil game were thinking vigorously on the subject, and they held long conferences and studied elaborate reports. They also were dissatisfied with the diplomacy of President Wilson—not because he wasn't making the world safe for democracy, but because he wasn't making it safe for oil operators. In the territories being taken from the enemies were petroleum regions of wealth untold; and here, in the imbecile name of idealism, we were permitting France and Britain to grab this treasure, while all we got was the job of keeping the Turks off the Armenians!

So far as Dad personally was concerned, his interests were at home. It was Excelsior Pete and Victor Oil and the rest of the "Big Five" which were reaching out for foreign concessions, and if they got the prizes, the price of oil at home might drop, and cost Dad a good chunk of money. Nevertheless, he took the patriotic attitude; the country needed oil, and it was our business to get it. So you see, Dad also was an idealist; and it vexed him that his kind of idealism was so little appreciated by his son.

He was becoming convinced that the university was to blame. No matter what Bunny might say, it was this "education business" that was unsettling his mind, and spoiling him to deal with practical affairs. Several times Bunny realized that the shrewd old man was probing his mind; there must be some older person influencing Bunny's thought, and the most suspicious fact was Bunny's failure to mention such a person. Bunny realized that sooner or later the name of Daniel Webster Irving, alias Daniel Washington Irving, was bound to come into the open; so he hit on a shrewd idea—he would get Dad to meet his instructor-friend! It would never be possible for Dad to report a man whom he had received in his home!

"Dad, I want to bring one of my teachers up to see the field." And of course Dad was delighted; it would bring a bit of culture into his world, and give him a share in his boy's mental life. One fear which haunted Dad was that this "education business" might cause Bunny to become ashamed of his ignorant old father. Dad knew that there were "high-brow fellers," crazy enough to look down upon twenty-five million dollars—or at any rate to pretend to!

Mr. Irving was to teach in summer school, but he had ten days in between, and Bunny suggested that he might like to motor up to Paradise for a week-end, and the young instructor accepted with pleased surprise. So they set out, one morning in June, in that sunshiny weather which is so common in Southern California that you forget all about it. On the way they talked about events in Russia and Siberia; the progress being made by General Denikin and Admiral Kolchak, the desperate efforts of the Bolsheviks to organize a "red army," and the hope of the German ruling class to win back to respectability by serving the allies against the Russian revolution. Also Bunny told Mr. Irving his idea about this visit; Dad must be allowed to do most of the talking, and Mr. Irving should voice only such opinions as were proper for an elderly oil man to hear.

VIII

They arrived at Paradise, and the instructor was duly installed in the fine new Spanish "ranch-house" which Dad had erected on the tract for the use of himself and his guests. It was built around the four sides of a court, with a fountain splashing in the center, and date palms and banana plants and big shoots from the bougainvillea vine starting to climb the stucco walls. There was a Japanese who served the double function of butler and cook, and a boy who combined gardening with dish-washing, while Ruth had been promoted to be housekeeper and general boss. There were six guest-rooms, and when the executives and directors and geologists and engineers of Ross Consolidated came up to the tract, they were always Dad's guests, and it was one big happy family. They would settle around a green baize table in the living-room right after supper and start playing poker; they would pull off their coats and unhitch their suspenders, and ring for the Jap to bring more cigars and whiskey and soda, and they would fill the room with blue smoke and never move from their seats until the small hours of the morning. It was an amusing illustration of the double standard of morals, that Dad was glad his son preferred to stay in his own room and read, and not hear the stories which the oil men would tell when they broke loose.

But there was no gambling this time—this was to be a high-brow week-end, in honor of "the professor," as Dad persisted in referring to his guest. The elder Ross was naively proud to have a "professor" visiting him, and to show him the well that was spudding in, and the one that was bailing, and the score that were drilling. They inspected the new refinery, something really special, that had been exploited in the newspapers as the latest miracle in petroleum engineering; incidentally it was a work of art, buildings of concrete and shining, newly-painted metal, set in a regular pleasure park. Oil wells are black and greasy, incurably so, but a refinery is different; the stuff comes in underground pipes, and most of it is taken away in the same fashion, so a refinery can be laid out according to the taste of a young idealist, with neat fences of steel mesh covered with rose vines, and plots of grass with gravelled roads winding between. The Ross refinery was as big as a good-sized village, only most of its houses were tanks; big tanks and little tanks, high tanks and squat tanks, round tanks, oblong tanks and square tanks, black tanks, red tanks, and tanks with an infinite variety of colors inside where they did not show.

The main feature was an enormous battery of stills, set in a row and joined together with a tangle of pipes; each still big enough to have served the purposes of all the bootleggers of the United States. In the first still the crude oil was heated to a certain temperature, and it gave off one of its products; this was the "cracking" process. The remainder went on to the next still, where it got a little hotter, and gave off something else. So it went from still to still—the process known as "continuous" distillation. The product from each still was run into a big condenser, and from there into its own tank; so you got gasoline of several qualities, and kerosene and benzine and naphtha, and a dozen different grades of lubricating oil, and petrolatum, and thick, black lovely tar, and endless pans of smooth white paraffin wax.

You can see how in these processes there was room for no end of management, and the discovery of new methods. Dad had a chemist that he never tired of telling about—say, that fellow was a wonder! Dad paid him six thousand a year, and owned everything he discovered, and he had saved the company several millions since it had started. That McEnnis jist lived on carbon rings and chains—he would draw you diagrams on the black board, and it would be a purple dye, and then he would add another C-unit, and by golly, it was some green stuff that would cure tape-worms, and the name of it was longer than any tape-worm ever measured.

They must meet this wizard; so they went over to the laboratory, which was on a little hill-top away off by itself, so that the inmate might be free to blow himself up as many times as he wanted. McEnnis was pale, stoop-shouldered and partly bald, and peered at you through big spectacles. Dad was proud to introduce "Professor" Irving, and the chemist showed them a row of test-tubes and retorts, and explained that he was trying to ascertain why normal hexane and the more stable methyl cyclopentane are so much less stable to heat than saturated hydrocarbons of the same molecular weight. There was a chance here to effect the biggest saving in refining history, but the trouble was, the maximum percent of clefines demanded by the simple general equation—and here the chemist began to write on the blackboard—$RCH_2 — CH_2 — CH_2R_1 \longrightarrow RCH_3 + CH_2 = CH.R_1$—was seldom attained owing to polymerization of the clefines and the formation of naphthenes.

After learning which, they went back to the "ranch house" for a supper of fried chicken, with fresh green corn and honeydew melons from Imperial valley, and then they settled down for a chat. Mr. Irving behaved beautifully; they talked till midnight, and he answered a hundred of Dad's questions about world affairs, and told what he had seen of relief work in Greece and of diplomacy in France.

The young instructor had some relatives in high positions, so he knew things on the inside; they fitted in with what Dad knew—yes, it was awful, the way things were being bungled.

My God, here were we jist telling the Japs to help themselves to Saghalien, that had more oil perhaps than all the rest of the world; and the British of course were getting to work to repair the pipe-lines at Baku, and at Mosul they had the whole field, and the French were getting into Persia with the British, and the same in Syria, and where was your Uncle Sam? Vernon Roscoe was jist raising hell, because he had had some contracts at Baku, and what was the use of kicking out the Bolshevikis and putting in the Anglo-Dutch? Roscoe said this country needed a practical man for president and not a college professor—

Dad stopped, afraid that he had made a "break"; but Mr. Irving laughed, and said, "Don't worry, Mr. Ross, I am not entitled to that high honor, and don't expect ever to make it." So Dad went on with Roscoe's tirade; the oil men by golly had had their lesson, and were going to get together and have something to say about the next election—they were going to have a business man for president. Bunny and his Bolshevik instructor exchanged the faintest trace of a glance, but Dad suspected nothing. Afterwards, when he was alone with Bunny, he remarked, "Son, that's a bright young fellow. It's a pleasure to talk with a man that understands affairs like him." You see how the Bolshevik propaganda was spreading!

IX

Bunny spent that summer "playing about," as the phrase ran; he read a few books on the international situation, he studied some of the confidential reports of Vernon Roscoe's foreign agents, and watched the derricks climb over a couple more hills of the Ross Junior tract. Bertie telephoned, insisting that he should make his debut into society and meet some "eligible" girls; so he went with her to spend a week at the camp of the ultra-fashionable Woodbridge Rileys, located high in the mountains, in a "club" to which only the elect might attain. Here people boated and swam, but otherwise lived as complicated lives as in the city, tangled in the same web of social duties and engagements, and dressing several times a day. They drank a great deal at dinner, and danced to the music of a Negro jazz orchestra until daybreak, after which the young people would go horseback riding, and have a late breakfast, and sleep a couple of hours before keeping a luncheon engagement.

Here Bunny got to know Eldon Burdick, who had been his sister's favored suitor for a couple of years. Just what was their relationship Bunny was not sure. Dad had ventured a jest about an approaching wedding, but Bertie froze him; she would attend to her own engagements, with no parental meddling. Now Bunny discovered that the pair were quarreling; he could not help overhearing them, and seeing tears in his sister's eyes. She was angry because Eldon would only spend a week-end at the camp, and he was angry because she punished him by dancing too often with some other man. But neither of the pair offered any confidences to Bunny, and he did not seek them.

Eldon Burdick was the youngest son of a family of old California land-owners. Their holdings lay on the outskirts of Angel City, and every ten years or so they would sell off a chunk for "subdivisions," and this development would so increase the value of the remainder that the family grew richer all the time, despite the fact that forty people, young and old, spent money for everything they could think of. Eldon was a handsome, dashing sportsman with a tiny black moustache, after the fashion of a British army officer; he held himself erect and stiff, and Bunny discovered that he had a military mind. Bertie must have mentioned her brother's dangerous ideas, for Eldon invited the younger man for a horse-back ride, and proceeded to sound him out. Eldon himself was an amateur patriot, in the proper sense of the abused word amateur; he was letting his string of polo-ponies stay idle all summer, while he did his part to save society.

It did not take long for him to uncover the deeps of Bunny's peril. The boy had got by heart every one of the Bolshevik formulas: that the people of Russia had a right to run their own country in their own way; that our troops had no business shooting and killing them without a declaration of war by Congress; that people in this country had a right to express the above convictions without being beaten or tarred and feathered or sent to prison or deported. Eldon pointed out that all this was merely camouflage, the convenient formulas whereby criminal conspirators sought to cover themselves with a mantle of legality, "free speech" and "civil rights" and all the rest. The Soviet savages had repudiated all these principles, and it was our business to fight them with their own weapons.

Bunny listened politely while his companion explained the ramifications of the Bolshevik plot. Not merely had these traitors sought to give the victory to Germany, they were now organizing a propaganda machine to overthrow civilized government all over the world; they were stirring up Negroes, Hindoos, Chinese and Mohammedans to rise and exterminate the white race. They had secret organizations with hundreds of thousands of followers in this country, they published or subsidized some eight hundred papers, all preaching class hatred. How could any man of decent instincts make a truce with this monstrosity?

It was indeed terrifying, and difficult to answer; nevertheless, Bunny stuck it out, we had no right in Russia or Siberia, and if we would let the Bolsheviks alone, they couldn't hurt us. When we suppressed people's ideas, we made it seem that we couldn't answer them; when we smashed up meetings and threw hundreds of people into jail for trying to attend meetings, we simply advertised the ideas we were trying to suppress, we made lots of other people sympathize with the victims. Look at those Russian Jewish boys and girls that had been arrested in New York, all of them under twenty; they had done nothing but distribute a leaflet appealing to the American people not to make war on Russia, yet they had been tortured in jail until one of them died, and the rest had got sentences of twenty years! When Eldon Burdick discovered that Bunny was defending vermin such as these, he first became hot, and then he became cold; and soon Bunny noticed that others of the guests were cold, and his sister came to him with flashing eyes, declaring that he had ruined her social career.

X

So Bunny went to visit Henrietta Ashleigh, at the beach-home of her family; located on a beautiful blue lagoon, with little white sail-boats dotted over it, and yellow and gray cliffs covered with Spanish bungalows of many-tinted plaster. Here, gliding about in a canoe, Bunny tried to justify his ideas, but met no better success. Henrietta had an invincible prejudice against Bolsheviks, and Bunny suspected the reason—she had heard about the nationalization of women. He would have liked to hint to her that he doubted the truth of these stories; but if it had been possible to mention such a subject to Henrietta, she would not have been his ideal of feminine purity.

So Bunny had to motor up to Angel City and take Mr. Irving out to lunch, in order to have some one to tell his troubles to. But Mr. Irving made matters worse by giving him an article from a Socialist paper, written by an English journalist who had just come out of Russia, telling of the desperate efforts the Communists were making to defend their cause. The party had conscripted fifty per cent of its members to go to the front and die—that was what it amounted to, for even a slight wound was often fatal—there were no antiseptics anywhere in a country of more than a hundred million people. On twenty-six fronts the Russian workers were waging battle against a host of enemies. In Finland alone the counter-revolutionary general Mannerheim had slaughtered a hundred thousand people suspected of sympathy with Bolshevism; he had done it with American guns and American ammunition, and his troops many of them wearing American uniforms. In cases where the troops had been beaten by the Bolsheviks and forced to retreat, the American Red Cross had burned millions of dollars worth of medical supplies, for fear that they might be used to save wounded Bolshevik soldiers and Bolshevik women in child-birth. Somehow, when you knew that things like this were happening in the world, you did not enjoy drifting about in a canoe on a beautiful blue lagoon!

Bunny went back to Paradise, and studied and thought and waited. There came another post-card from Paul—just like the former one, cold and matter-of-fact; Paul was well and busy, and was being taken good care of; he had had another letter from Ruth; he hoped that the family was well, and also the Rosses. Bunny now knew the world-situation sufficiently to understand why Paul wrote such a card, and even to imagine the bitterness that Paul must feel to be compelled to write it.

Bunny thought that he also would try his hand at card-writing. He got a plain postal, and told Paul that they were all well and busy, and producing a lot of oil to help defeat America's enemies. "I am doing a lot of thinking," Bunny added; but then it occurred to him that this might suggest a forbidden procedure to troops, so he got another card and told how happy everybody was and how well things were going, and then added, "I am coming to agree with Tom Axton in everything." Bunny figured that the censor would hardly know, way out there in Siberia, how Tom Axton had organized the oil-workers in the Paradise field!

All this time Bunny was torn between two sets of emotions, both strong within him, and absolutely contradictory. He had been in the army as a prospective officer and had burned with patriotic loyalty; but now, only seven months later, here he was with a desire to "root" for the enemies of his country, and to cheer when the flag had to retreat! Yes, he was actually tempted to be glad when he read that the American troops at Archangel were checked, and their British commanders foiled in their objectives! He remembered the thrills that had stirred his soul in the training camp, when he had leaped from his tent at reveille, and seen "Old Glory" floating in the breeze of dawn; if in those days he could have seen himself as he was now, he would have called himself a black-hearted traitor!

XI

There were very few people in the world who thought the Russians would be able to defend themselves against the hosts of all the world. Yet somehow they were managing it. There was a peculiar thing to be noticed in the newspaper despatches from the various anti-Bolshevik fronts. The allied troops would win great victories; they would take Perm, or Ufa, or whatever city it might be, and capture vast thousands of the enemy. A month or two later they would win another victory, and again the patriots would be cheered up—until it occurred to them to get the map, and compare the location of the two places, and discover that the second place was one or two hundred miles farther back than the first one!

Later on Bunny found out what this meant. The peasants had a way of staying quiet while the allied forces advanced, and then rising up behind their lines and forcing them to retreat. So mighty was Bolshevik propaganda—it was working thus at Archangel, and all along the western front from the Baltic to the Crimea, and all over Siberia; no victory ever lasted. Admiral Kolchak got all the way across Siberia, General Denikin, in the Ukraine, got within a hundred and twenty-five miles of Moscow; but it all came to nothing.

Then, as summer turned into fall, and fall into winter, a still more terrifying thing began to happen. The armies of the great powers began to show signs of succumbing to the deadly propaganda poison! They were now in the second winter since the armistice, and the soldiers thought the war was over, and why couldn't they go home? The very worst of the prophesies of Eldon Burdick began suddenly to come true. The sailors of the French fleet in the Black Sea rose up and overthrew their officers and captured several battle-ships! German troops declined to win their way back to respectability by putting down Bolshevism for the allies! British soldiers at Folkestone refused to go onto the ships that were to take them to Archangel!

And most appalling of all, a mutiny in the American army! The first mutiny in the whole history of "Old Glory"! Michigan lumbermen and farmer-boys, shipped up there under the Arctic circle, put under the command of British officers, and ordered out to shoot half-starved and ragged Russian workingmen at fifty degrees below zero—these boys laid down their arms! The facts were hushed up in the newspapers—but not in the higher circles of the army and of world diplomacy, nor yet in the office-buildings where the gentlemen and lady-patriots planned the future of the world!

In the month of October the allies made their last military effort. They sent in the tsarist General Yudenich to take Petrograd; they gave him all the supplies he could use, and troops of many nations, and he got within a few miles of the city, so that the Soviets had to move their capital to Moscow. But the half-starved and ragged Communists drove back their foes, and Bolshevik propaganda proceeded to cause a revolution in Hungary and another in Bavaria!

Also at home there were portents. In spite of all the raids and jailings and deportations, great numbers of people could not be prevented from saying publicly and loudly that we had no business making war upon a friendly people. More and more there was discontent with the program of keeping our soldiers abroad after the war was over. "Radical" newspapers and magazines continued to be circulated, and in the big cities at any rate it was not possible to prevent mass-meetings.

It was a little difficult to make any protest effective, because of the peculiar condition into which the government had fallen. The President had set out on a tour, to convince the people that they should be satisfied with the peace settlement. He had come to Angel City, and Dad and Bunny had gone to hear him —in a vast hall where ten thousand people were marshalled, and taught to stand up and sit down again, and cheer at signal, all very reverently, quite like royalty. The great man's voice was strained, and his face had an unwholesome flush, and his arguments were as broken as his appearance. A few days later came word that his health had collapsed, and he was hurried back to Washington, where he had an apoplectic stroke. Now he lay, a helpless, half-conscious invalid, and the country was governed by a strange triumvirate—a Catholic private secretary, an army doctor, and one of the most fashionably dressed of Washington society ladies.

But somewhere, in the cabinet, perhaps, there was left a trace of intelligence, with which to realize the mounting dangers abroad and at home. At Christmas time, while Bunny was up at Paradise, hunting quail and watching the progress of Ross Consolidated, he went out one morning to meet the Ford car which brought the mail to the tract. He got his morning paper and opened it, and there on the front page was a despatch from Washington, announcing that the army authorities had decided it was no longer necessary for them to police the Trans-Siberian Railway; we were going to leave the Japanese in charge, and come home. Bunny gave a shout, and rushed into the house, calling for Ruth. "Paul is coming back! Paul is coming back!" And then he had to run quick and catch her by the arm and help her to a chair!

CHAPTER XI

THE REBEL

I

At Southern Pacific University the class lines were tacitly but effectively drawn, and in the ordinary course of events a man of Bunny's wealth, good looks and good manners, would have associated only with the members of fraternities and sororities. If some Negro boy were to develop eloquence as a debater, or if some one taking a course in millinery or plumbing were to display fleetness as a hurdler, the hurdler might hurdle and the debater might debate, but they would not be invited to tea-parties or dances, nor be elected to prominence in the student organizations; such honors were reserved for tall Anglo-Saxons having regular features, and hair plastered straight back from their foreheads, and trousers pressed to a knife edge and never worn two days in succession.

But here was Bunny Ross, persisting in fooling with "dangerous thoughts," that made his friends angry. Of course, as anyone would have foreseen, there were "barbs" and "goats," anxious to break in where they were not wanted, and perfectly willing to pretend to think that our country ought not to intervene in Russia, if by so professing they could get to know one of the socially élite. So Bunny found himself on talking terms with various queer fish. For example, there was Peter Nagle, whose father was president of a "rationalist society," and who seemed to have one dominating desire in life—to blurt out in class that what was the matter with the world was superstition, and that mankind could never progress until they stopped believing in God. In a university all of whose faculty were required to be devout Methodists, you can imagine how popular this made him. Peter looked just as you would expect such a boor to look, with a large square head and a wide mouth full of teeth, and a shock of yellow hair which he allowed to straggle round his ears and drop white specks onto his coat collar—his coat did not match his trousers, and he brought his lunch to the university tied with a strap!

And then there was Gregor Nikolaieff. George was all right, when you got to know him, but the trouble was, it was hard to know him, because his accent was peculiar, and at critical moments in his talk he would forget the English word. He had jet black hair, and black eyes with a sombre frown above them—in short, he was the very picture of what the students called a "Bolsheviki." As it happened, Gregor's father had belonged to one of the revolutionary parties whom the Bolsheviks were now sending to jail; but how could you explain that to a student body which dumped into one common garbage-can Socialists and Communists and Syndicalists and Anarchists, Communist-Anarchists and Anarchist-Syndicalists, Social Revolutionaries and Social Democrats, Populists, Progressives, Single-taxers, Nonpartisan Leaguers, Pacifists, Pragmatists, Altruists, Vegetarians, Anti-vivisectionists and opponents of capital punishment.

Also there was Rachel Menzies, who belonged to a people that had been chosen by the Lord, but not by the aforesaid student body. Rachel was rather good-looking, though in a dark, foreign way; she was short—what feminine enemies would have called "dumpy"—and made no pretense at finery, but came to the university in black cotton stockings and a shirt-waist that did not match her skirt. There was a rumor that her father worked in a clothing factory, and her brother was pressing students' pants for an education.

And here was the discoverer and heir-apparent of the Ross Junior oil field, letting himself be seen in public with these people, and even trying to introduce them to his fraternity brothers; excusing himself by saying that they believed in "free speech." As if it were not obvious that they would, having everything to gain and nothing to lose! Proletarians of all universities unite!

Poor Bunny got it from both sides. "Look here," said Donald Burns, president of the sophomore class, "don't you introduce me to any more of your Yid fairies." And then, "Look here," said Rachel Menzies, "don't you introduce me to any more of your male fashion-plates." Bunny protested, he had the idea that all kinds of people ought to know one another; but Rachel informed him that she thought too much of herself. "Probably you've never been snubbed in your life, Mr. Ross, but we Jews learn the lesson early in our lives—not to go where we aren't wanted."

Said Bunny, "But Miss Menzies, if you believe in ideas, you've got to teach people—"

"Thank you," she said; "I believe in my ideas, but not enough to teach Donald Burns."

"But how can you tell?" Bunny protested. "You're teaching me, and I don't belong to the working-class." He had learned that this girl was a member of the Socialist party, and it was "class consciousness," as well as Jewish consciousness.

Rachel insisted that Bunny was one person in a million, capable of believing what was contrary to his economic interests. But Bunny had no awareness of anything extraordinary about himself. Instead of being a conspicuous and shining leader, as his high destiny directed, he was always looking for some one he could lean on, some one who was positive, and whom he could trust. He found some of this in Henrietta Ashleigh, who knew exactly what was proper; and he found some more of it in Rachel Menzies, who knew exactly what was true, and said it with energy and frankness that were like flashes of lightning in the twilight of Southern Pacific culture.

The only trouble was, the contradiction between his two authorities; it appeared almost as if what was true was not proper and what was proper was not true! For Henrietta considered Rachel an impossible person, and was cold as a corpse in her presence; while Rachel's idea of being insulting was to tell Bunny that it was with Henrietta he really belonged, his Creator had made him to take her to church.

II

Amid this perplexity, Bunny found comfort in the backing of Billy George, who was Anglo-Saxon and broad-shouldered, and a senior besides. Billy assured him he was right, and suggested that they take some steps to make their ideas understood to the rest of the student body. Why not organize a little group, the Society for the Study of Russian Problems, or something of that sort? Bunny should ask Mr. Irving to advise them, and perhaps join them—it would be much better if they could have the backing of one of the teachers. So Bunny went to Mr. Irving, who said at once that he could not give any advice on the subject, for the reason that it would jeopardize his position to do so; the students would have to follow their own judgment. The young instructor did add this much, they ought surely not use the name "Russian," but take some inoffensive title, the "Liberal Club," or the "Social Problems Society."

Bunny took that advice to the others, meeting in one of the class-rooms after hours. Billy George said it didn't seem very "spunky" of Mr. Irving; whereupon Rachel Menzies flared up, he had no right to hint at such a thing, they all knew what the teacher's position was, and he had a perfect right to keep out of trouble. What business had Mr. George to be finding fault, when he himself had done nothing publicly?

The other demanded to know what he could do, and the girl was not backward in suggestions. Why not start a student paper, a little four-page sheet, once a week or even once a month? It would cost very little, and would make a hit, they could be sure; look how many people had wanted to read Mr. Ross's letter about Siberia! If they printed that letter they would set the campus on fire. Mr. George could have the honor of being editor, and Rachel would contribute her share of the cost. There was obvious irony in that, considering the quantity of iron pipe which Billy's father was known to be marketing in Angel City. But they discussed it gravely, and Billy didn't think he could take any responsibility; his old man would pull him out of college, and put him to work on a book-keeper's stool.

Then, automatically, the eyes of the group turned to Bunny. What did he think? Bunny found his cheeks growing red. He had wanted to explain his ideas to other people, but had thought of doing it in some dignified way, privately and quietly. A paper would make such a noise! Rachel Menzies apparently didn't mind a noise, but Henrietta would, she would be horrified by the bare idea. Also there was Dad—the "education business" would be damned forever by such a venture. So Bunny had to say no; and Rachel Menzies said that was all right, there were plenty of excuses, and she didn't blame anybody for finding the best one, but at least they had no business criticizing Mr. Irving for lack of courage!

III

Soon after that Bunny read in the paper that the transport "Bennington" had arrived in San Francisco with two thousand troops from Siberia. Paul's unit was listed; so Bunny called up Ruth on the telephone and told her the news, and said, be sure to let him know as soon as she got word. Two days later Ruth called him—Paul had arrived at Paradise. It was a Friday, so Bunny "cut" his afternoon courses, and jumped into his car. Dad had gone over to Lobos River, to see to a "fishing" job, and so missed this first meeting.

It was almost twenty months that Paul had been away, and Bunny was keyed up with eagerness. The first glance gave him a shock, for Paul looked quite terrible—gaunt and yellow, his khaki jacket hanging loose upon him. "You've been sick!" cried Bunny.

"Yes," said Paul; "but I'm getting all right now."

"Paul, tell me what happened!"

"Well, it was no picnic." And he seemed to think that would satisfy both his sister and his friend—after a year and a half!

They were over in the cabin on the Rascum tract, where Ruth and Paul had first begun house-keeping. It was supper-time, and the girl had prepared a bounteous repast; but Paul wasn't much on eating just now, he said—afraid to trust himself with good food. While they sat at table he told them about Manila, where they had stopped; and about a storm on the Pacific; but not a word about Siberia!

Of course that wouldn't do. After the meal they got Paul settled in an arm-chair, and Bunny said, "Look here, Paul, I've been trying to understand about this Russian business. I'm quarrelling with most everyone I know about it, and I counted on you for the truth. So please do tell us about it—just what happened to you."

Paul sat with his head lying back. His face had always been sombre, a prominent nose and wide mouth with a tendency to droop at the corners; haggard as he was, this tendency was accentuated, he looked like a mask of sorrow. "What happened to me?" he said, in his slow voice; and then he seemed to raise himself to the effort of recalling it. "I'll tell you what happened, son; I was kidnapped."

"Kidnapped!" The two of them echoed the word together.

"Yes, just that. I thought I went into the army to put down the Kaiser, but I was kidnapped by some Wall Street bankers, and put to work as a strike-breaker, a scab."

Ruth and Bunny could only sit and gaze at Paul, and wait for him to say what he meant by these strange words.

"You remember our oil strike, Bunny? Those guards the Federation sent up here—husky fellows, with plenty of guns, and good warm clothes, rain-coats and water-proof hats and everything. Well, that's what I've been doing for a year and a half—putting down a strike for Wall Street bankers. The guards here at Paradise got ten dollars a day, and if they didn't like it, they could quit; but I got thirty a month and beans, and if I tried to quit they'd have shot me. That was the cinch the bankers had."

Again there was a pause. Paul had closed his eyes, and he told a part of his story that way, looking at things he saw inside his mind.

"First thing, the allies took the city of Vladivostok. The strikers had that city, with a perfectly good government, everything orderly and fine. They didn't make much resistance—they were too surprised at our behavior. We shot a few longshoremen, who tried to defend one building, and the strikers had a big funeral with a procession; they brought the red coffins to the American consulate with banners that asked us why we had shot their people. It happened to be the Fourth of July, and we were celebrating our revolution; why had we overthrown theirs? Of course we couldn't answer; none of us knew why we had done it; but little by little we began to find out."

Paul paused, and waited so long that Bunny thought he wasn't going on. "Why, Paul?"

"Well, just outside that city, along the railroad track, there were fields—I guess there must have been ten or twenty acres, piled twenty feet high with stuff—guns and shells, railroad locomotives, rails and machinery, motor trucks—every kind of thing you could think of to help win a war. Some of it was in cases, and some without even a tarpaulin over it, just lying there in the rain, and sinking slowly—some of the heavy stuff two feet down in the mud. There was a hundred million dollars of it, that had been put off the steamers, intended to be taken across to Russia; but then the revolution had come, and there it lay. One of our jobs was to guard it. At first, of course, we thought it belonged to the government; but then little by little we got the story. Originally the British government had bought it for the Tsar's government, and taken bonds for it. Later, when we came into the war, the firm of Morgan and Company took over the bonds from the British government, and these supplies were Morgan's collateral, and we had overthrown the Vladivostok government to protect it for him."

Again there was a pause. "Paul," said Bunny, anxiously, "do you really know that?"

Paul laughed, but without any happiness. "Know it?" he said. "Listen, son. They sent out an expedition, two hundred and eighty men to run the railroad—every kind of expert, traffic men, telegraphers, linemen, engineers. They all wore army uniforms, and the lowest man had the rank of second lieutenant; of course we thought they were part of the army, like the rest of us. But they got fancy pay, and by God, it wasn't army pay, it was checks on a Wall Street bank! I've seen dozens of those checks. It was a private expedition, sent to run the railroad for the bankers."

"But why, Paul?"

"I've told you—to break the strike. The biggest strike in all history—the Russian workers against the landlords and the bankers; and we were to put the workers down, and the landlords and bankers up! Here and there were bunches of refugees, former officers of the Tsar's army, grand dukes and their mistresses, land-owners and their families; they would get together and call themselves a government, and it was our job to rush them supplies, and they would print paper money, and hire some adventurers, and grab a bunch of peasants and 'conscript' them, and that would be an army, and we'd move them on the railroad, and they'd overthrow another Soviet government, and slaughter a few more hundreds or thousands of workingmen. That's been my job for the past year and half; do you wonder I'm sick?"

"Paul, did you have to kill people?" It was Ruth's voice of horror.

"No, I don't think I killed anybody. I was a carpenter, and my only fights were with the Japs, that were supposed to be our allies. You see, the Japs were there to grab the country, so they didn't want either the 'white' Russians or the 'red' ones to succeed. The first thing they did was to counterfeit the money of the 'white' government; they brought in billions of fake roubles, and bought everything in sight—banks and hotels and stores and real-estate—they made themselves the capitalists, and broke the 'white' government with their fake money. They resented our being there, and the fact that we really tried to help the 'whites;' they butted in on our job, and there

were times when we lined up our troops and threatened to
fire in five minutes if they didn't move out. They were always
picking on our men; I was fired at three times in the dark—
got one bullet through my hat and another through my shirt."

Ruth sat there with her hands clasped together and her
face white. She could see those bullets going through Paul's
clothing right now! And be sure that she was not unlearning
any of her dislike for war!

"A lot of our fellows came to hate the Japs," said Paul;
"but I didn't. I got a philosophy out of this—the only thing I
did get. The ruling classes in Japan were grabbing half a
continent; but all the poor soldiers were grabbing was pay even
poorer than mine. They didn't know what they were there
for—they, also, had been kidnapped. There were some that
had been to America, and I got to talk with them, and we never
had any trouble in agreeing. That was true of Czecho-Slovaks,
and Germans—every nation I met. I tell you, Bunny, if the
private soldiers could have talked it over, there wouldn't have
been any war. But that is what is known as treason, and if
you try it you're shot."

IV

Paul and Bunny talked, that Friday night, and a lot of Saturday and Sunday, and Paul explained the Russian revolution.
There was an easy way for Bunny to understand it, Paul said;
if there was anything that puzzled him, all he had to do was
to remember their oil strike. "Ask yourself how it would have
been at Paradise, and then you know everything about Russia
and Siberia—yes, and Washington and New York and Angel
City. The Petroleum Operator's Federation, that fought our
strike, they're exactly the sort of men that sent our army
into Siberia—often they're the same individuals. I read in
the paper yesterday how a syndicate of oil men in Angel City
has got some concessions in Saghalien. I remember one name,
Vernon Roscoe. He's one of the big fellows, isn't he?"

Paul said this seriously, and Bunny and Ruth exchanged a
smile. Paul had been away so long, he had lost track of the
oil-game entirely!

Said Paul, "The operators are the same, and so are the
strikers. Do you remember that little Russian Jew, Mandel,
a roughneck that was in our strike? Used to play the bala-

laika, and sing us songs about Russia—we wouldn't let him make speeches, because he was a 'red.' Well, by jingo, I ran into him in Manila, on the way out. He'd been travelling steerage on a steamer, on the way to Russia, and they found he was a Bolshevik, and threw him ashore and took away everything he had, even his balalaika. I loaned him five dollars, and six months later he turned up at Irkutsk, in a 'Y' hut. Lying on a shelf there was a balalaika, and he said, 'Why, that's mine! How did it get here?' They told him a soldier had brought it, but didn't know how to use it. 'You can have it if you can play it,' they said, so he played it all right, sang us the Volga Boatman, and then the Internationale—only of course nobody knew what it was. A few days later there were orders to arrest him, but I helped him get away. Months after that we came on him out in the country, not far from Omsk; he had been a Soviet commissar, and the Kolchak people had captured him, and buried him alive, up to his nose, just so that he could breathe. When we found him the ants had eaten most of his eyes, but there was still some life in him, his forehead would wrinkle."

It was while Paul was alone with Bunny that he told this; and the younger man sat, speechless with horror. "Oh, yes," said Paul; "that's the kind of thing we had to see—and know we were to blame for it. I could tell you things much worse— I've helped to bury a hundred bodies of people that had been killed, not in battle, just shot down in cold blood, men and women, children, even babies. I've seen a 'white' officer shoot women in the head, one after another; and with our bullets, brought there by our railway men—I mean our bankers' railway men. A lot of our boys went plumb crazy with it. Out of the two thousand that came off our transport, I doubt if there were ten per cent quite normal. I said that to our surgeon, and he agreed."

V

All this was so different from what Bunny had been taught that it was hard for him to adjust his thoughts to it. He would go off and think it over, and then come back with another string of questions. "Then Paul, you mean the Bolsheviks aren't bad people at all!"

Paul answered, "Just apply the rule—remember Paradise!

They were workingmen, like any other workingmen on strike.
A lot of them have come from America—got their training
here. I used to meet them and have long talks—all kinds of
fellows, that had been all over this country. They are people
with modern ideas, trying to dig the Russians out of their
ignorance and superstition. They believe in education—I never
saw such people for teaching; everywhere, whatever they were
doing, they were always preaching, having lectures, printing
things—why, son, I've seen newspapers printed on old scraps of
brown butcher paper, or wrappings our army had thrown away.
I learned Russian pretty well—and it was just the sort of thing
our strikers printed at Paradise, only of course these people
have got farther in their struggle against the bosses, they see
things more clearly than we do."

Bunny was staring, a little frightened. "Paul! Then you
agree with the Bolsheviks?"

Paul laughed, a grim laugh. "You go up to Frisco and talk
with the men on that transport! That army was Bolshevik
to a man—and not only the privates, but the officers. I guess
that's why they brought us home. There was mutiny in
Archangel, you know—or maybe you don't."

"I heard something—"

"Let me tell you, Bunny—I've been there, and I know.
The Bolsheviks are the only people in that country that have
any faith or any solidarity; and they're going to run it, too—
mark my words, the Japs will get out, the same as we did.
You can't beat people that will die for their cause, the last
man and the last woman."

Said Bunny, timidly, "Then it isn't true what we've been
told—I mean about their nationalizing the women?"

"Oh, my Lord!" said Paul. "Is that the sort of rot you've
been thinking?"

"Well, but how can we know what to think?"

Paul laughed. "Come to think of it, I met some women
that had been nationalized by the Bolsheviks—as school-teach-
ers. They taught the men in their armies to read and write,
and made every man swear to teach ten others what he had
learned. I saw a couple of dozen such women in a cattle-
car on the Trans-Siberian railway, without a single blanket,
nothing but blocks of wood for pillows, not even a bucket
to serve for a toilet. They had several cases of Asiatic
cholera among them, and they'd been that way for ten or

twelve days—prisoners of war, you understand, waiting until they got to Irkutsk, where they'd be shot without a trial. And on the other hand, Bunny—here's the truth, I was in Siberia eighteen months, and never saw an atrocity committed by a Bolshevik, and never met a man in our army that had seen one. I don't say there weren't any; all I say is, I met men that had travelled all over Russia, our people as well as natives, and the only Bolshevik atrocity that anyone knew about was the fundamental one of teaching the workers they had a right to rule the world. You can set this down for a fact about the Russian revolution, all the way from Vladivostok to Odessa and Archangel—that where the 'reds' did any killing or executing, the 'whites' did ten, and a hundred times as much. You never hear about 'white' atrocities, because the newspapers don't report them—they are too busy telling how Lenin has murdered Trotsky, and Trotsky has thrown Lenin into jail."

VI

This meeting with Paul was the most exciting event of Bunny's life. It transvaluated all his values; things that had been wicked became suddenly heroic, while things that had been respectable became suddenly dull. Bunny, confronting the modern industrial world with its manifold injustices, had been like a man lost in a tangled forest. But here he had been taken up in a balloon, and shown the way out of the tangle. Everything was now simple, plain as a map. The workers were to take over the industries, and run them for themselves, instead of for the masters. Thus, with one stroke, the knot of social injustice would be cut!

Bunny had heard of this idea, and it had sounded fantastic and absurd. But now came Paul to tell him that it had actually been done! A hundred million people, occupying one-sixth of the earth's surface, had taken over their industries, and were running them, and would make a success of them— if only the organized greed of the world would stand off and let them alone!

Bunny took Paul in his car, to show him all the field. They investigated the new refinery, that wonderful work of art. Before them rose a great building, made entirely of enormous baking-pans set one inside another—a stack half way to heaven; the angels were making caramels for the whole world, dainties with a new, patented flavor, and sickish sweet odors that spread over the hills for miles and frightened the quail away!

It was twilight, and the white steam that rose from these pans had a faint violet tinge as it merged with the sky. Electric lights came on, white and yellow and red, until the place looked like a section of Coney Island. And this resemblance increased as you drove farther, and came to a building, long and low, in which forty-four Dutchmen sat hidden puffing on forty-four pipes, and doing it all in unison, like an orchestra; the most comical effect you could imagine—forty-four exhausts all keeping time, quick and sharp—puff-puff-puff-puff-puff-puff-puff!

Bunny felt his old embarrassment in connection with the Paradise tract; his title to these vast possessions was not clear, and Paul was bound to be jealous, realizing how his family had been tricked. But, then, in swift flashes of revelation, Bunny discovered how completely out of date these old feelings had become. Nevermore would Paul be jealous for his lost heritage; never would he consider the claims of the Watkins family—any more than the claims of the Ross family! The Paradise tract belonged to the Paradise workers; the beautiful new refinery was a ripe peach, hanging on a tree and waiting to be picked! All that was needed was for some one to point this out to the men. If Paul had not been weak and exhausted, he might have pointed it out that evening, and they could have taken over the plant, and had it ready for operation under the new management by morning! All power to the Soviets!

VII

Bunny went back to the university, charged with these electrical new thoughts; at one moment he would be trembling with excitement, and at the next he would be frightened to realize what he had been thinking. Some instinct warned him that the idea of expropriating the industries of Southern California would stand no chance with his class-mates; so he contented himself with telling the good tidings about Russia— that the revolution was not a blind outburst of ferocity, but the birth of a new social order. Bunny told this; and Peter

Nagle received the gospel with his large mouth wide open; while Gregor Nikolaieff said yes, but why had they got his cousin in jail; and Rachel Menzies said they had got thousands of Socialists in jail; and Billy George said, "Let's get a group of fellows together and have Paul come and talk to them."

The rumor spread with magical swiftness through the university, and the quick imaginations of Bunny's friends supplied all those details about which he had been silent. Bunny Ross knew a workingman who was an out-and-out Bolshevik, and had made Bunny into an out-and-out Bolshevik too; "the millionaire red" became his future designation. Men and women gathered round to question and argue with him; the arguments often broke up with furious word rows, but all the same it was interesting, and they came back for more. Bunny was made into a centre of Soviet propaganda; for, when they drove him to the wall with their arguments, what could he do but go to Paul for more facts, and then come back and hurl them at his adversaries' heads? His fraternity brothers sat up half the night with him, wrangling over his challenge to everything they considered good.

With rest and home cooking Paul picked up considerably, and in a couple of weeks came down to Angel City to meet a friend. Bunny joined him, and had another adventure, in the person of Harry Seager. This man, ten years older than Paul, was the head of a small business college, who had put his affairs into a partner's hands and gone in for "Y work" during the war. They had sent him to Siberia, to help those two hundred and eighty railway men whom the bankers were paying. He had travelled up and down the line, seeing everything there was to see, and now he had "kicked over the traces," and was telling the truth about the situation, in spite of the protests of the "Y" authorities, and the army, and the state department, and the Merchants' and Manufacturers' Association, and everybody that could put pressure on the head of a business college in Angel City.

Dad was up to the ears just then in work, on account of some wild-catting they were planning on the Bandy tract. But Bunny insisted he must meet Harry Seager, and lured the two of them to lunch, and Paul also, and before the soup was eaten they had got Dad so stirred up that he did not eat any more. Of course he was horrified at their story; but

there was no use expecting his mind to work the same as
Bunny's. Dad couldn't straighten out all the tangles in the
world, and didn't feel the impulse to try. What worried him
was that the Japs were in Siberia; and that our diplomacy
was so unaware of oil; and most of all, that his son was falling under the spell of wild and dangerous ideas.

This fellow Seager, for example—a big six-foot Westerner,
handsome as a Viking, and picturesque because of hair turned
prematurely grey by his labors; you couldn't deny the fellow's facts, you couldn't think he was lying—but good Lord,
there was no use being thrown off your base, and going round
the country raising a public disturbance, attacking the government because it had made a blunder in the confusion of war-
time, and then hadn't known how to get out.

Bunny dragged his father to a Socialist meeting at which
Harry Seager was to speak. It was in a big hall, with two
or three thousand people packed into it, and Dad thought
he had never seen so many dangerous people in all his life
before: foreign faces, dark and sinister, intense-looking intellectuals with hair over their collars, women with short hair
and big spectacles, workingmen, sullen and dull, or sharp-
faced, bitter—oh, terrible, terrible people! And this man
Seager, lashing them to frenzy! Telling about the "death-
train" he had seen on the Trans-Siberian—more than two
thousand men and women packed into cattle cars, prisoners
of the "Whites," who did not know what to do with them,
but ran the train here and there, shunting it onto sidings
for weeks, while the victims perished of hunger, thirst and
disease. And American troops standing by, feeding such mur-
derers, supplying them with money, protecting them with guns!
Yes, and it was still going on! Right now Polish troops
were invading Russia, wearing American uniforms, killing
Russian workingmen with American ammunition! What did
the people of America have to say?

What the people of America had to say was a roar that
sent shivers down the spine of J. Arnold Ross. He looked
about him at this human ocean tossed by a storm—hands waving, fists clenched, heads bobbing up and down with excitement; and he knew what it meant—nobody could fool him.
When presently the crowd burst into cheering at the name
of Lenin, they were not cheering for what the Russian Lenin
had done, but for what some American Lenin meant to do.

"Hands off Russia!"—that was mere camouflage; what they meant was, "Hands on Ross Consolidated!"

And then, out of the corner of his eye, Dad stole a glimpse at his son. Bunny apparently did not feel one particle of his father's fear! Bunny was like the rest of the mob, his face shining with excitement. Bunny was shouting for "Hands off Russia!"—and either he did not know what this mob meant to do to Ross Consolidated, or else—worse yet—he did not care!

VIII

The little bunch of "reds" from the university had attended this Seager meeting, and next day were all a-thrill with it. Most of Bunny's fraternity brothers had refused to go; and now they proceeded to criticize an argument they had not heard! Bunny's feelings boiled over as he listened to them. All this rubbish about nationalization of women, these faked figures concerning millions of victims of Bolshevism! It was a disgrace to a university that such stuff should pass for knowledge, and no effort made to contradict it. Bunny voiced this idea to Peter Nagle, and Peter went home and talked to his father about it, and came back announcing that he was willing to serve as editor for a student paper to present the truth.

There was another meeting of the conspirators, and thirty dollars was quickly subscribed, and it was voted to publish a four-page weekly sheet of all kinds of truth-telling, to bear the name of "The Investigator." It was agreed that the best approach to the Russian problem was Harry Seager, because he had been a "Y" worker in good standing; therefore Rachel Menzies was requested to write a two thousand word interview with Mr. Seager. Another young rebel was to collect facts and rumors concerning secret payments made out of an alumni fund to bring promising athletes to Southern Pacific. Bunny, as social light of the crowd, was assigned the theme of college snobbery, apropos of the fact that a Hindoo student with high scholarship records had been black-balled for the "Lit."

And then Peter Nagle brought up his favorite hobby, in the form of a poem mildly satirizing God. There was some question as to the wisdom of bringing in the religious issue, but Peter asserted his prerogatives as editor; either he was or he wasn't, and if he was, then he took his stand upon the Russian formula, "Religion is the opium of the people." Billy George backed him up, insisting that the new paper should cover the whole field of modern thought.

Well, "The Investigator" was written, and edited, and set up into galleys, and pasted on a "dummy," and then cut up and pasted differently. At last it was printed; there lay the sheets, fresh from the press, soft and damp, like locusts newly emerged from the chrysalis. Next day they would be dry; and meantime, "Ssh! Not a word!"

How were the papers to be distributed? There had been much discussion. Bunny, with his lordly ideas, wanted to give them away. But Rachel brought word from her father, the tailor, who was also literature agent for Local Angel City of the Socialist party, that the papers must be sold; people wouldn't respect them otherwise. "What they pay good money for they will read," said Papa Menzies, with proper Jewish insight; and his daughter added, with proper Socialist fervor, "If we really believe in our cause, we won't mind a little ridicule." It was a call to martyrdom, and one after another they responded—though not without qualms.

So, promptly at eight-thirty next morning, the campus in front of the Assembly building beheld a sight, the like of which had never thrilled the student-body of S. P. U. since the first days of the Methodist Sunday-school. The discoverer and heir-apparent of the Ross Junior oil field turned into a newsboy! Standing on a bench, with an armful of papers, shouting gaily, "The Investigator! First issue of the Investigator! Five cents a copy!"

Did they buy them? Oh, ask! They crowded around Bunny three deep, he couldn't make the change fast enough; as the excitement spread, they crowded six deep, ten deep— it was a mob, a riot! Everywhere, all over the campus, men and women, seeing the throng, came running. An accident? A fight? What was the matter? People who got their copies and drew out of the crowd, became centres of minor disturbances, others trying to see over their shoulders, asking questions.

For just about ten minutes this went on; until from the Administration building there emerged, portly and dignified, with gold nose-glasses and a roll of fat around his neck— just such a personage as you would meet in any big real estate office or bank in the city—Reginald T. Squirge, Ph. D., Dean of Men. Quietly and masterfully he penetrated the throng, and quietly and masterfully he took charge of the millionaire newsboy, and conducted him into his private office, still clutching his armful of papers. "Wait here," he commanded, and again went out, and returned with Peter Nagle; a third time he went out, and his prey was Gregor Nikolaieff; while at his heels came deputy deans, appointed ad hoc, escorting the other criminals.

How many copies had been sold no one could say; the unsold copies were stacked in a corner of the Dean's office, and if they were ever counted the result was not made known. But enough had been distributed to set the campus ablaze. "Have you read it?" "Have you got a copy?"—that was all anybody heard that day. The price of "The Investigator" leaped to one dollar, and before night-fall some had sold for two or three times that price.

One reason was that a copy had reached the Angel City "Evening Booster," most popular of newspapers, printed in green, five editions per day. The second edition, on the streets about noon, carried a "streamer head" across the front page:

RED NEST AT UNIVERSITY!

Bolshevik Propaganda at S. P. U.

There followed a two-column story, carried over to page fourteen, giving a lurid account of "The Investigator's" contents, including the most startling of the facts about the hiring of athletes for the university, and the whole text of the satiric poem about God—but alas, only a very brief hint as to what Harry Seager had told about Siberia. A little later in the day came the rivals of the "Evening Booster," the "Evening Roarer" and the "Evening Howler"; they had been scooped one whole edition, but they made up for it by a mass of new details, some collected by telephone, the rest made up in the editorial offices. Said the "Evening Roarer":

RED COLLEGE PLOT UNEARTHED

and it went on to tell how the police were seeking Russian agents who had made use of Southern Pacific students to get their propaganda into print. The "Evening Howler," which went in especially for "human interest stuff," featured the ring-leader of the conspiracy:

MILLIONAIRE RED IN COLLEGE!

Son of Oil Magnate Backs Soviets!

And it scooped its rivals by having a photograph of Bunny, which it had got by rushing a man to the Ross home, and informing Aunt Emma that Bunny had just been awarded a prize for the best scholarship record in ten years. The good lady was so excited, she sent the butler out to the corner drug-store three times, to see if the "Evening Howler" had arrived with the story of that prize!

IX

In the ordinary course of events this newspaper excitement would have lasted thirty-two hours. Next afternoon's papers would have recorded the fact that the university authorities had banned "The Investigator," and on the following day their streamer-heads would have proclaimed, "Film Star Divorces Champ," or "Magnate's Wife Elopes with Cop."

But fate had prepared a fantastic torment for the "parlor reds" of S. P. U. On the morning after their flyer in publicity, it chanced that a wagon loaded with blasting material, making its way through Wall Street with customary indifference to municipal ordinances, met with a collision and exploded. The accident happened in front of the banking offices of Morgan and Company, and about a dozen people were killed. A few minutes after the accident, the bankers called in America's sleuth-celebrity to solve the mystery; and this able business man, facing the situation that if it was an accident it was nothing, while if it was a Bolshevik plot it was several hundred thousand dollars, took three minutes to look about him, and then pronounced it a plot.

And forthwith throughout the world a horde of spies and informers went to work, knowing that if he or she could find or invent a clue, it was fame and fortune for him or her. A wave of witch-hunting swept the country, and other countries—for two or three years thereafter new discoveries would be made, and new "revelations" promised, and poor devils in Polish and Roumanian dungeons would have their arms twisted out of joint and their testicles macerated, while eager newspaper readers in New York and Chicago and Angel City waited ravenously for promised thrills.

As for the Angel City "Evening Booster" and "Evening Howler" and "Evening Roarer," the situation confronting them was this: if they could connect the Bolshevik conspiracy in Southern Pacific University with the bomb explosion in Wall Street, they would have several hundred dollars' additional sales; while if they failed to make the connection, they would lose this amount to some more clever rival. This being the case, it took the "Evening Howler" about one hour to remember that "The Investigator" had featured Harry Seager, and to ascertain from the agents of the American Defense League that at a recent mass-meeting this Seager had fiercely denounced the firm of Morgan and Company, and predicted a dire fate for them. So, in its third edition, on the streets about one o'clock, the "Evening Howler" told the world:

BOMB FORETOLD BY RED AID

Police Seek Soviet Agent Here

That was taking a chance, as the headline writer of the "Evening Howler" would have admitted with a grin; but he knew his business, and sure enough, before the day was by, a war veteran came into the editorial office with confirmation. Two days ago he had ridden on a public stage with Harry Seager, and had got into conversation, and heard the sentence: "You mark my words and watch the papers, within three days you will read that the House of Morgan has paid for its crimes in this war." It is only fair to the shell-shocked soldier to add that he may have been sincere in his statement, for it happened that the two men in their conversation had touched upon the Polish invasion of Russia, then at its height, and Seager had uttered the sentence, "You mark my words and watch the papers, within three days you will read that the Poles are back of where they are now."

Prior to this incident, the office door of the Seager Business College had been chewed to a ragged edge by the chisels of detectives and other patriots breaking their way in at night; but on the night after this "bomb expose" they used an axe, and when Seager arrived in the morning he found every desk-drawer in the place, not merely his own, but the students', dumped onto the floor, and trampled beneath the hob-nailed boots of patriotism. They had carted off, not merely Seager's notes for his orations, but likewise the typewriting exercises of his students—and most damaging evidence they afforded, too, for Seager did not make his students write, "The quick brown fox jumps over the lazy dog,"—no, siree, he gave them revolutionary propaganda that would send shivers down the spine of any patriot: "All men are created free and equal," or, more desperate yet, "Give me liberty or give me death!"

X

Not many in Southern Pacific University seriously believed that their "student reds" had any responsibility for or even guilty knowledge of the Wall Street bomb explosion. But they knew that these silly fools had been misled by sinister men who quite possibly did have part in the plot, or anyhow were bad enough to have it. Also they knew that the fools had got the university in for a lot of hideous publicity. So the fools were badgered and browbeaten on every hand; they were summoned to the Dean's office one by one and there racked and cross-questioned—and not merely by President Cowper and Dean Squirge, but by various stern gentlemen representing the district attorney and the city prosecutor and the federal secret service and the patriotic newspapers and the defense societies and the information service of the once-upon-a-time ambassador of a no-longer-existing Russian government.

When Bunny Ross realized that this was happening, there was another explosion. Being a rich man's son, he was accustomed to having his rights, and more. So of the first of his questioners he demanded, "Who are you, and what brings you into this?"

"Now, Ross," said Dean Squirge, "if there are evil men threatening our country's welfare, you certainly do not wish to protect them."

"It depends on what you mean by evil," retorted Bunny. "If you mean men who are trying to tell the truth, I wish to protect them all I can."

"All we want to know is, what you know about a man called Paul Watkins."

So there it was; either Bunny must submit to being cross-questioned by detectives, or else he must have everybody decide that he was hiding some dark secrets about Paul. Said he: "Paul Watkins is my best friend. I have known

him for seven or eight years. He is the straightest man I
have ever known, bar none. He has come home sick, after a
year and a half in the army in Siberia. He could claim an
allowance from the government if he wasn't too proud. What
he did to me was to tell me what he saw with his own eyes,
and I believe every word of it. And I am going to tell it to
other people, inside the university or out, and no one is going
to stop me."

So that was that, and Bunny was excused for the present.
They would tackle the less wealthy conspirators—beginning
with Peter Nagle, most guilty of all, because his name had
appeared on the paper as editor. Peter was commanded forthwith to recant his impoliteness to God, and he swore by
God that he wouldn't; so the "Evening Howler" carried a two-
column head:

STUDENT RED LET OUT

And Peter grinned and said for the rest of the bunch not to
worry, he was going into the plumbing business and get his
revenge on society; and when he had made some money he
would publish a paper of his own and kid the life out of
God every week.

And then came the turn of Rachel Menzies. She had
been warned by Bunny as to the secret agents, and had promised to give them a piece of her mind; but they had a way
to break her nerve. Just what had been her father's share
in this conspiracy? They had ascertained that Papa Menzies
had been born in Poland, and under the new deportation
laws it didn't matter what you believed or what you had
done, they would cancel your naturalization papers, and grab
you and ship you away, leaving your family behind to starve,
if it so happened. You had no trial, and no recourse of any
sort. And furthermore, if a man was dumped into Poland
with the red tag on him these days, no trial was held and
no questions were asked—he was stood against a wall and
shot.

So there was Rachel, bursting into tears before these
strangers and declaring that her father was a Socialist and
not a Communist—as if that meant anything to any patriot!
Hadn't the Socialists been opposing the war right along? And
wasn't it a fact that the country had an attorney-general who
was intriguing to get the nomination for president at the next

Democratic convention, and was basing his claim to that distinction upon his valiant campaign to put down the red menace?

Rachel telephoned to Bunny, and he hopped into his car and paid a call on President Alonzo T. Cowper, D.D., Ph.D., LL.D., at that worthy's private residence in the evening, contrary to the established etiquette of the university. He began by stating his own decision—he was willing to agree to make no more public "propaganda" during his stay in the university; but he wanted to add this, if the authorities permitted Mr. Menzies to suffer deportation as punishment for his daughter's having written a review of a lecture—then he, Bunny Ross, was going on the war-path, and use some of his father's money to blow things wide open before he quit Southern Pacific.

The reverend doctor's round clerical face had grown rosy to the roots of his snow-white hair as he listened to this scarcely veiled blackmail. "Young man," said he, "you seem to overlook the fact that the university authorities have nothing to do with the decisions of the United States government."

"Dr. Cowper," responded the young man, "I learned from my father to go to headquarters when I want things done. I know that if you tell these defense idiots that you want this matter dropped, they will drop it. And I want to say that while I have never met Mr. Menzies, I know his daughter, and she brought us his ideas at different times, and he believes in democracy and in educating the people—every bit of advice he sent us was along that line. He belongs to the right wing group among the Socialists, and is opposing the Bolsheviks in the movement. You must know enough about the situation to realize that that is not the sort of people we are supposed to be deporting."

It turned out that Dr. Cowper really didn't know that much, but was willing to learn. It was rather comical; underneath the indignation he was officially obliged to feel, the old gentleman had an unholy curiosity about these strange new ideas that had seduced his prize millionaire sophomore. So here was Bunny telling him about Paul Watkins, and about Harry Seager, what sort of people they were, and what they had seen in Siberia, and what they thought about it, and what Bunny thought. The doctor asked the most naive and childish questions, but he did try to understand, and Bunny gave him a complete lecture on Bolshevism versus Socialism lasting two hours.

At the end the prize millionaire sophomore was sent away with a pat on the back, and the assurance that Papa Menzies would not be deported so long as he behaved himself; plus a solemn warning that whereas mature minds such as Dr. Cowper's were equipped to deal with these dangerous new thoughts, the immature minds of the students were not to be trusted with them!

XI

There was an interview to be had with Henrietta Ashleigh. It was not so painful as Bunny had feared, because she hid her grief under a cloak of dignity. "I am sorry, Arnold, but I am beginning to fear there is something in you that enjoys this crude notoriety." Bunny tried to be humble and accept this rebuke, but he couldn't; there was something in him that was bored by Henrietta's ideas; and when you are bored, you can no longer keep up romantic imaginings about a girl.

And then the folks at home! First, Aunt Emma, horrified, tearful, and completely muddled. Bunny had not got that prize after all! Aunt Emma had somehow got it fixed in her head that there had been a prize, and that Bunny might have got it if it had not been for the reds. This awful peril of Bolshevik agents, right in one's home! Aunt Emma had heard hair-raising stories from lecturers to her club-ladies, but had never dreamed that these emissaries of Satan might be seducing her darling nephew! "Watch out, auntie!" said the nephew. "You may be next!"

And then Bertie. Bertie was just wild! She had been invited to a house-party of the very desirable Atherton-Stewarts, but now she would be ashamed to show her face among decent people. That was the way every time, no sooner did she achieve a social triumph, than Bunny came along and made one of his stinks. It was the most disgusting thing that could have happened, it showed his tastes were naturally low. Bertie and Bunny were quite fond of each other, and called each other violent names with true brotherly and sisterly frankness.

Finally Dad, who was a perfect brick; never said a word, nor asked a question, and when Bunny started to explain, he said, "That's all right, son, I know just how it happened." And that was true; he knew Paul and Harry Seager, he had been inside his boy's mind. And he knew the tragedy of life, that each generation has to make its own mistakes.

The uproar died away surprisingly soon. In a few days Bunny's classmates were "joshing" him, it was all a joke. There was only one serious consequence, that Mr. Daniel Webster Irving received a letter from President Cowper, advising him in advance, as a matter of courtesy, that his contract with Southern Pacific University would not be renewed for next year. The instructor showed it to Bunny, with a dry smile; and Bunny was enraged, and wanted to blackmail the reverend doctor a second time. But Mr. Irving said to forget it, there were too many ways to make life miserable for a teacher who wasn't wanted. He would file his references with the employment agencies, and write a lot of letters, and move on to pastures new. "That is," he added, "assuming I can get something. They have a pretty tight organization, and I may find I'm blacklisted for good."

"How do you suppose they got on to you, Mr. Irving?"

"It was bound to happen," said the other. "They have so many spies."

"But we have been so careful! We've never mentioned your name, except among our own little group!"

"They've probably got a spy right among you."

"A student, you mean?"

"Of course." And smiling at Bunny's incredulity, Mr. Irving reached into his desk and pulled out a mimeographed sheet of paper. "This was handed to me by a business friend of mine," he said.

It was one of the weekly bulletins of the "Improve America League," a propaganda organization of the business men of Angel City. It explained how they had their agents at work in colleges and high schools, training students to watch their teachers and fellow students, and report any signs of the red menace. The league boasted its fund of a hundred and sixty thousand dollars a year for the next five years. So here was another chunk of reality, falling with a dull sickening thud upon the head of a young idealist! Bunny sat, running over in his mind the members of the little group. "Who could it be?"

Said Mr. Irving: "Some one who was very 'red,' you can be sure. That is how it works—a man is looking for something to report, and when it's too slow making its appearance, he's tempted to help it along. So the spy almost always becomes a provocateur. You can tell him by the fact that he talks a lot and does nothing—he can't afford to have it said that he was a leader."

"By God!" cried Bunny. "He promised to help us sell those papers, and then he didn't show up!

"Who is that?"

"Billy George. We never could be red enough to suit him! He was the cause of that fool poem of Peter Nagle's going into the paper. And now he's dropped clean out—he wasn't mentioned in the scandal."

Mr. Irving smiled. "Well, Ross, you've seen the white terror in action! You'll find it helps you to understand world history. Fortunately, you're rich, so it was just a joke. But don't forget—if you'd been a poor Russian Jew in the slums, you'd be in jail now, with ten thousand dollars bail, and ten or twenty years in state's prison for your destiny. If you had happened to live in Poland or Finland or Roumania, you and all your little bunch would have been buried in one muddy trench a week ago!"

CHAPTER XII

THE SIREN

I

Springtime had come again, and Bunny was finishing his second year at Southern Pacific. But the bloom was now worn off the peach; he no longer took the great institutiton at its own valuation. He knew that the courses were dull, and that they taught you masses of facts of little importance, and were afraid of new and original thinking. The one thing he had got was a clue to some worthwhile books; he wanted to read them —but you could do that better at home. He was debating whether he would come back next year.

Things were freer at Paradise, it seemed. Paul had gone back to work as a boss carpenter for the company; he had recovered a part of his strength, and was making good money— building labor was scarce, because the country was making up for the lost construction of war-time. Ruth was happy again; at least three of the oil workers were in love with her, but she would think of no one but her wonderful brother. Paul was studying again; but not the biology books, all his money now went for magazines and pamphlets and books that dealt with the labor struggle. There were a good many returned soldiers with the company, some of whom had come to think about the war just as Paul did; twice a week they had regular classes, reading aloud a chapter from a book and discussing it.

So the Rascum cabin became what the Angel City news-papers were accustomed to describe as a "Bolshevik nest." Much as these workingmen might differ about tactics, they were a unit on the proposition that capital and labor had noth-ing in common but a fight. And they made no bones about saying it; they would start an argument on the job, or while a bunch of the men were eating their lunch; the echoes would spread all over the place. There were "wobblies" in the field also, you would find their literature in the bunk-houses. Dad must have known about it, but he did nothing; his men had always been free to say what they pleased, and he would take his chances. Indeed, he could hardly do anything else, while every man on the place knew that the discoverer and heir-apparent of the field was one of the "reddest" of the bunch!

Ever since the war, the union of the oil workers had been recognized and dealt with, as the government had decreed. But now the hand of Uncle Sam was beginning to relax; the idealistic President was a semi-invalid in Washington, and in Angel City the "open shop" crowd were getting ready to bring back the good old days. At least that was the rumor among the union officials, and how were they going to meet the employers' move? The wage agreements expired towards the end of the year, and this was the issue to which all the arguments of the oil workers led, whether among the "reds" in Paul's cabin, or among the rank and file. Over Bunny's head the prospect of another strike hung like a black shadow of doom.

Dad never gave up longing to have his son take an interest in the company and its growing activities. And Bunny, always aware of this loving bond, would study monthly reports of production, and cost sheets and price schedules, and go out to the wells that were drilling, and take part in long consultations with the foremen. Only a few years ago, an oil well had been to him the most interesting thing in the world; but now cruel fate had brought it about that one oil well seemed exactly like another oil well! Number 142 had brought in six hundred thousand dollars, whereas Number 143 had brought in only four hundred and fifty thousand. But what difference did it make, when all you would do with the extra hundred and fifty thousand was to drill another well?

Dad's answer was kept in stock on the shelves of his mind: "The world has got to have oil." But then, you looked at the world, and saw enormous crowds of people driving to places where they were no better off than at home! But it would annoy Dad to have you say that—it was a step outside the range of his thinking. To Bunny he now seemed like an old horse in a treadmill; he climbed and climbed, all day long, and at night he climbed in dreams. But if you should let him out of the treadmill, he would die—for lack of any reason for living.

So Bunny learned more and more to keep his traitor doubts to himself; those theories of the "class struggle" that he learned from Paul and his fellows, and the rumors of a strike that he read in the oil workers' journal. Instead, he would take Dad fishing, and they would pretend they were just as happy as of

old in the bosom of their mother Nature—though the sad truth
was that Dad was too heavy and too stiff in the joints to get
much fun out of scrambling over the rocks.

II

Bunny spent his Easter holidays at Paradise, and it happened that Vernon Roscoe paid a visit to the tract. He had
been there before, but only while Bunny was away; their
meetings so far had been brief ones at the office, amid the
press of business. Bunny had got a general impression of a
big face and a big body and a big voice. Dad said that
"Verne" had also a big heart; but Bunny's only evidence was
that Mr. Roscoe had patted him on the back, and called him
"Jim Junior," with great gusto.

Now he came; and it happened that a desert wind came
with him, and made a funny combination. As a rule the heat
of the day was endurable at Paradise, and the nights were
always cold and refreshing; but three or four times in a year
the place would be struck by a wind off the desert, and it
would be like a hot hand reaching out and holding you by the
throat. "A hundred and fourteen in the shade and their ain't
any shade," was the way the oil workers put it, as they went
on working in the sun, drinking barley water by the quart.
The worst of it was, the hot wind blew all night, and the
houses, which had heated up like furnaces, stayed that way for
three or four days.

The "oil magnate," as the newspapers called Vernon Roscoe, left Angel City after dinner, and reached the tract just
before midnight. Dad and Bunny were expecting him, sitting out on the veranda, and he saw them, and his voice started
before the engine of his car stopped. "Hello, Jim! Hello,
Jim Junior! By Jees, what's this you're doing to me! Christ
amighty, man, I never felt such heat. Is it going to be
like this tomorrow? By Jees, I think I'll turn my tail
and run!"

He was out of the car, and coming up the path, his face as
round as the moon that shone down on his half-bald head. He
had taken off his coat and shirt, and was in a pink silk under-
shirt; no perspiration, of course, because you were always dry
when you drove in this desert heat—you might stop at a filling
station and stand under a hose and soak yourself, and the wind

would dry everything but your sitting down place in a couple of minutes.

"Hello, Verne," said Dad; and Bunny said, "How are you Mr. Roscoe?" He was careful to get a grip on the magnate's paw before the magnate got a grip on his—for he would make the bones crunch with his mighty grasp. He had been a cattle-puncher back in Oklahoma, and it was said that he had grabbed a Mexican horse-thief with his two hands and bent him backwards until he broke. He still had that strength, in spite of his rolls of fat.

"I'm hot as hell," he said, answering Bunny's polite inquiry. "Say, Jim, do you think I'd better stay?"

"You've got to stay," said Dad. "I'm not going ahead with development on that Bandy tract till you've looked the field over. We'll sit you on ice."

"Has my beer come? Hey, there, Kuno"—this to the Jap, who was grinning in the door-way. "Bring me some of my beer! Bring me a bucketful—a tubful. By Jees, I brought some in my car—I wouldn't take a chance. Did you hear what happened to Pete O'Reilly? Damn fool tried to come across the border with a crate of whiskey in his car; told me it cost him a hundred dollars a quart before he got through! Christ amighty, Verne, how do you stand this?"

"Well, for one thing, I drink lemonade instead of beer." This was a reform which Bunny had imposed upon his father, and now Dad was very proud of it.

"No pop for me!" said Verne. "By Jees, I'll have my suds in the bath-tub. Any women about, Verne?" And Mr. Roscoe kicked off his shoes and his trousers, and sat himself under an electric fan. "The damn thing blows hot air!" he said; and then he looked at Bunny. "Well, here's our boy Bolsheviki! Where's the red flag?"

Now Bunny was expecting to reach the impressive age of twenty-one in a month or two, and he had heard all possible variations on this "Bolsheviki" joke. But he was host, and had to smile. "I see you read the papers."

"Say, kiddo, you made the front page all right! It did me a lot of good in some negotiations. Come down to the office and I'll introduce you to a Soviet commissar in disguise; they're trying to sell me a concession in the Urals. 'Where the hell is that?' I says; but it seems there is really such a place, unless they have forged some atlases. The guy started to pull this brotherhood of man stuff on me, and I says, 'Sure, I'm great on that dope,' I says. 'The junior member of our firm is in the business! Look at this, by Jees,' and I showed him the papers, and we've been 'Tovarish' ever since!"

III

Well, Tovarish Roscoe went to bed, in Nile green silk pajamas on a cot out in the court alongside the fountain; and at five in the morning they woke him, so that he might go out with Dad and the geologist and the engineer, to O. K. the plans for the Bandy tract. He came back with the sunrise in his eyes, puffing and snorting, and yelling for beer instead of breakfast, and how would he get some more when this gave out? They persuaded him that he must not try to cross the desert until the sun went down, so he and Dad and Bunny retired into the living-room, and shut all the doors and windows, to stick it out as best they could.

Well, the sun got to work on the roof and walls of that house, and every ten minutes the great man would get up and look at the thermometer and emit another string of mule-skinner's technicalities. By the middle of the morning he was frantic; declaring that surely there must be some way to cool a house. By Jees, let's get a hose and soak this room! But Bunny, who had studied physics, said that would only shift them from the climate of the desert to the climate of the Congo river. Mr. Roscoe suggested turning the hose on the veranda and the roof; and Bunny called the gardener boy, and pretty soon there were half a dozen sprinklers going, a regular rain-storm over the doors and windows of the living-room.

But that was not enough, so Dad went to the phone and called up the foreman of the sheet metal shop, and he said sure thing, he could design a refrigerator; and Dad said to drop everything else and build one, and he'd pay the men a dollar apiece extra if they finished it inside an hour. So here came four fellows with a truck and a big metal box with double walls all the way from the floor to the ceiling; and they cut a hole in the floor for a vent-pipe, and brought in about half a ton of cracked ice from the ice-plant, and a couple of sacks of salt, and in a few minutes the thermometer showed a zero wind blowing out from the bottom of that

box. The great man moved over close to it, and in a little
while he began to sigh with content, and in half an hour he
gave a loud "Kerchoo!" and they all roared with laughter.

After that he was sleepy, with all the beer he had drunk,
and had a nap on the lounge, while Dad went out to see to the
drilling. And then the party had lunch, and Mr. Roscoe had
another nap, after which he felt fine, and did a lot of talking,
and Bunny learned some more about the world in which he
lived. "Jim," said the "magnate," "I want two hundred thousand dollars of your money."

"Where's your gun?" said Dad, amiably.

"You'll get it back many times over. It's a little fund
we're raising, me and Pete O'Reilly and Fred Orpan. We
can't talk about it except to a few."

"What is it, Verne?"

"Well, we're getting ready for the Republican convention,
and by Jees, it's not going to be any god-damn snivelling long-
faced college professor! We're going to get a round-faced
man, like you and me, Jim! I'm going on to Chicago and pick
him out."

"You got anybody in mind?"

"I'm negotiating with a fellow from Ohio, Barney Brockway, that runs the party there. He wants us to take their
Senator Harding; big chap with a fine presence, good orator
and all that, and can be trusted—he's been governor there,
and does what he's told. Brockway thinks he can put him
over with two or three million, and he'll pledge us the secretary of the interior."

"I see," said Dad—not having to ask what that meant.

"I've got my eye on a tract—been watching it the last ten
years, and it's a wonder. Excelsior Pete put down two test
wells, and then they capped them and hushed it up; there
was a government report that mentioned it, but they had
it suppressed and you can't get a copy anywhere—but I
had one stolen for me. There's about forty thousand
acres, all oil."

"But how can you get it away from Excelsior?"

"The government has taken the whole district—supposed
to be an oil reserve for the navy. But what the hell use will
it be to the navy, with no developments? The damn fools think
you can drill wells and build pipe-lines and storage tanks
while Congress is voting a declaration of war. Let us get in

there and get out the oil, and we'll sell the navy all they want."

That was Dad's doctrine, so there was nothing to discuss. He laughed, and said, "You'd better be on the safe side, Verne, and get the attorney-general as well as the secretary of the interior."

"I thought of that," said the other, not noticing the laugh. "Barney Brockway will be the attorney-general himself. That's a part of his bargain with Harding."

And then all at once Mr. Roscoe recollected Bunny, sitting over by the window, supposed to be reading a book. "I suppose our boy Bolsheviki will understand, this ain't for use on the soap-box."

Dad answered, quickly, "Bunny has known about my affairs ever since he was knee-high to a grass-hopper. All right, Verne, I'll send you a check when you're ready."

IV

The sun went down, and it was time for Mr. Roscoe to make his get-away. But first he had dinner; and when he was through with his ice cream and coffee, he pushed his plate away, and took his napkin out of his neck, and leaned back in his chair with a sigh of content; and while he was unrolling his cigar from its gold foil, he fixed his shrewd eyes upon Bunny across the table, and said, "Jim Junior, I'll tell you what's the matter with you."

"All right," said Jim Junior, receptively.

"You're a nice kid, but you're too god-damn serious. You take life too hard—you and your old man both. You got to get a little fun as you go along, and I know what you need. You got a girl, kid?"

"Not right now," said Bunny, blushing a trifle.

"I thought so. You need one, to take you out and cheer you up. Mind you, I don't mean one of these jazz-babies— get a girl that's got some sense, like my Annabelle. You know Annabelle Ames?"

"I've never met her. I've seen her, of course."

"Did you see her in 'Madame Tee-Zee'? By Jees, that's what I call a picture—only one I ever made any money out of, by the way! Well, that girl takes care of me like a mother—if she'd been up here, I wouldn't 'a drunk all that beer, you bet! You come up to my place some time, and Annabelle'll find you a girl—lots of 'em up there, with the ginger in 'em, too, and she's a regular little match-maker—never so happy as when she's pairing 'em off, two little love-birds in a cage. Why don't you drive back with me now?"

"I've got to go to college the day after tomorrow," said Bunny.

"Well, you come some time, and bring the old man along. That's what he needs too, a girl—I've told him so a dozen times. You got a girl yet, Jim? By Jees, look at him blush, the old maid in pants! I could tell the kid some things about you that would bust the rouge-pots in your cheeks—hey, old skeezicks?" And the great man, who had been getting out of his chair as he discoursed, fetched Dad a couple of thumps on the back and burst into a roar of laughter.

It was things like that that made you know Vernon Roscoe had a "big heart." He seemed to have really taken a fancy to Bunny, and was concerned that he should learn to enjoy life. "You come see me some time, kiddo," he said, as he was loading himself into his big limousine. "Don't you forget it now, I mean it. I'll show you what a country place can be like, and you make the old man get one too." And Bunny said all right, he would come; and the engine began to purr, and the car rolled off in the moonlight, and the big laughing voice died away among the hills. "So long, kiddo!"

V

Bunny came back into the house, and followed Dad into his study and shut the door. "Dad, are you really going to put up that money with Mr. Roscoe?"

"Why, sure, son, I got to; why not?" Dad looked genuinely surprised—as he always did in these cases. You could never be sure how much of it was acting, for he was sly as the devil, and not above using his arts on those he loved.

"Dad, you're proposing to buy the presidency of the United States!"

"Well, son, you can put it that way—"

"But that's what it *is*, Dad!"

"Well, that's one way to say it. Another is that we're protecting ourselves against rivals that want to put us out of business. If we don't take care of politics, we'll wake up after election and find we're done for. There's a bunch of big fellows in the East have put up a couple of millions to put General Leonard Wood across. Are you rooting for him?"

Bunny understood that this was a rhetorical question, and did not answer it. "It's such a dirty game, Dad!"

"I know, but it's the only game there is. Of course, I can quit, and have enough to live on, but I don't feel like being laid on the shelf, son."

"Couldn't we just run our own business, Dad?" It was, you may remember, a question Bunny had asked before.

"There's no such thing, son—they're jist crowding you all the time. They block you at the refineries, they block you at the markets, they block you in the banks—I don't tell you much about it, because it's troubles, but there's jist no place in the business world for the little feller any more. You think I'm a big feller because I got twenty million, and I think Verne is a big feller because he's got fifty; but there's Excelsior Pete—thirty or forty companies, all working as one—that's close to a billion dollars you're up against. And there's Victor, three or four hundred million more, and all the banks and insurance company resources behind them—what chance have we independents got? Look at this slump in the price of gas right now—the newspapers tell you there's a glut, but that's all rot—what makes the glut, but the Big Five dumping onto the market to break the little fellers? Why, they're jist wiping 'em off the slate!"

"But how can public officials prevent that?"

"There's a thousand things that come up, son—we got to land the first wallop—right at the sound of the bell! How do we get pipe-line right-o'-ways? How do we get terminal facilities? You saw how it was when we came into Paradise; would we ever 'a got this development if I hadn't 'a paid Jake Coffey? Where would Verne and me be right now, if we didn't sit down with him and go over the slate, and make sure the fellers he puts on it are right? And now—what's the difference? Jist this, we got bigger, we're playin' the game on a national scale—that's all. If Verne and me and Pete O'Reilly and Fred Orpan can get the tracts we got our eyes on, well, there'll be the Big Six or Big Seven or Big Eight in the oil-game, that's all—and you set this down for sure, son, we'll be doin' what the other fellers done, from the day that petroleum came into use, fifty years ago."

They were on an old familiar trail now, and Bunny knew the landscape by heart.

"It's all very well for a feller to go off in his study and figure out how the world ought to be; but that don't make it that way, son. There has got to be oil, and we fellers that know how to get it out of the ground are the ones that are doing it. You listen to these Socialists and Bolshevikis, but my God, imagine if the government was to start buying oil-lands and developing them—there'd be more graft than all the wealth of America could pay for. I'm on the inside, where I can watch it, and I know that when you turn over anything to the government, you might jist as good bury it ten thousand miles deep in the earth. You talk about laws, but there's economic laws, too, and government can't stand against them, no more than anybody else. When government does fool things, then people find a way to get round it, and business men that do it are no more to blame than any other kind of men. This is an oil age, and when you try to shut oil off from production, it's jist like you tried to dam Niagara falls."

It was a critical moment in their lives. In after years Bunny would look back upon it, and think, oh why had he not put his foot down? He could have broken his father, if he had been determined enough! If he had said, "Dad, I will not stand for buying the presidency; and if you go in with Mr. Roscoe on that deal, you've got to know that I renounce my inheritance, I will not touch a cent of your money from this day on. I'll go out and get myself a job, and you can leave your money to Bertie if you want to." Yes, if he had said that, Dad would have given way; he would have been mortally hurt, and Mr. Roscoe would have been hurt, but Dad would not have helped to nominate Senator Harding.

Why didn't Bunny do it? It wasn't cowardice—he didn't know enough about life as yet to be afraid of it. He had never earned a dollar in his life, yet he had the serene conviction that he could go out and "get a job," and provide for himself those comforts and luxuries that were a matter of course to him. But the trouble was, he couldn't bear to hurt people. It was what Paul meant when he said that Bunny was "soft." He entered too easily into other people's point of view. He saw too clearly why Dad and Mr. Roscoe wanted to buy the Republican convention; and then, a few hours later, he would go over to the Rascum cabin, and sit down with Paul and "Bud" Stoner and "Jick" Duggan and the rest of the "Bolshevik bunch," and see too clearly why they wanted the oil workers to organize and educate themselves, and take over the oil wells from Dad and Mr. Roscoe!

VI

Bunny went back to Southern Pacific, and just as he was finishing his year's work, the convention of the Republican party met in Chicago, a thousand delegates and as many alternates, and as many newspaper correspondents and special writers, to tell the world about this mighty historic event. The convention listened to impressive "key-note" speeches, and smoked enormous quantities of tobacco, and drank enormous quantities of bootleg liquor; and meantime, in a room in the Blackstone Hotel, the half-dozen bosses who controlled the votes sat down to make their deals.   In the millions of words that went out over the wires concerning the convention, the name of Vernon Roscoe was never mentioned; but he had his suite adjoining that hotel room, and he made exactly the right offers, and paid his certified checks to exactly the right men, and after a long deadlock and the taking of eight ballots, amid wild excitement on the convention floor, the support of General Leonard Wood began suddenly to crumble, and on the ninth ballot Warren Gamaliel Harding of Ohio became the Republican party's standard-bearer.

College was over; and Gregor Nikolaieff went up to San Francisco to ship on one of the vessels of the "canning fleet," which went up to Alaska to catch and pack salmon.   Rachel Menzies and her brother joined three other Jewish students who had equipped themselves with a battered Ford car, to follow the fruit-picking; moving from place to place, sleeping under the stars, and gathering apricots, peaches, prunes and grapes for the canners and driers. Bunny was the only one of the little group of "reds" who did not have to work all summer; and he was the only one who didn't know what to do with himself.

In the old days, when he and Dad were drilling one well at a time, Bunny would pitch in and help at anything there was to do; he was only a "kid" then, and the men liked it.

But now he was of age, and supposed to be dignified; the company was of age, too, a huge machine in which every cog had its place, and must not be interfered with. Bunny could not even cultivate the plants at home without trespassing on the job of the gardener! He had resolved to study some of Paul's books; but he had never heard of anyone studying eight hours a day, and he couldn't take Paul's job for part of the time, because he wasn't a good enough carpenter!

It was a world in which some people worked all the time, and others played all the time. To work all the time was a bore, and no one would do it unless he had to; but to play all the time was equally a bore, and the people who did it never had anything to talk about that Bunny wanted to listen to. They talked about their play, just as solemnly as if it had been work: tennis tournaments, golf tournaments, polo matches—all sorts of complicated ways of hitting a little ball about a field! Now, it was all right, when you needed exercise and recreation, to go out and hit a little ball; but to make a life-work of it, to give all your time and thought to it, to practice it religiously, read and write books about it, discuss it for hours on end—Bunny looked at these fully grown men and women, with their elaborate outfits of "sport clothes," and it seemed to him they must be exercising a kind of hypnosis upon themselves, to make themselves believe that they were really enjoying their lives.

VII

Bertie came along, making one more effort to drag her brother out into this play world, to which by right of inheritance and natural gifts he belonged. Bertie had broken off her affair with Eldon Burdick. He was a "dud," she told Bunny, and always wanting to have his own way. There was another affair on, a very desperate one, Bunny gathered, since his sister exposed her feelings even to him. It was the only son of the late August Norman, founder of Occidental Steel; the boy's name was Charlie, and he was a little wild, Bertie said, but oh, so fascinating, and rich as Croesus. He had nobody to take care of him but a rather silly mother, who was still trying to be young and giddy, dressing like a debutante, and having surgical operations performed on her face it keep it from "sagging." They had a most gorgeous yacht down at the harbor, and had asked Bertie to bring her brother, and why wouldn't he go and help her, as he so easily could, with his good looks and everything?

Bunny thought his sister must indeed be hard hit, if she was counting upon his reluctant social charms! But he went; and as they drove to the harbor Bertie coached and scolded him—he must not talk about his horrible Bolshevik ideas, and if they mentioned his disgrace at Southern Pacific, he must make a joke of it. Bunny had already learned that that was the thing to do; and so he did it, and found that it was very easy, for Charlie Norman was one of those brilliant young persons who found something funny to say about everything that came up; if he couldn't do any better, he would make a bad pun out of your remark.

Here was the "Siren," a floating mansion, all white paint and shining brass, finished in hand-carved mahogany, and upholstered in hand-painted silk. The sailors who shined and polished, and the Filipino boys who flitted here and there with trays full of glasses, were spick and span enough for the vaudeville stage. The party of guests would step into a launch, and from that into several motor-cars, and be transported to a golf-links, and from there to a country club for luncheon; they would dance for an hour or two, and then be whirled away to a bathing-beach, and then to a tennis-court, and then back to the "Siren" to dress for dinner, which was served with all the style you would have expected at an ambassador's banquet. There would be many-colored electric lights on the deck, and an orchestra, and friends would come out in launches, and dance until dawn, while the waves lapped softly against the sides of the vessel, and the tangle of lights along the shore made dim the stars.

These people talked about the appearance and peculiarities and adventures of all their acquaintances, and it was hard to follow their conversation unless you were one of their set; they even had slang words of their own, and the less possible it was for an outsider to understand them, the funnier they seemed to themselves. They talked about clothes, and what was going to be the newest "thing." They talked about their bootleggers, and who was reliable. For the rest of the time they talked about the hitting of little balls about a field; the scores they had made that day and previous days, and the relative abilities of various experts in the art. Was the tennis-champion going to hold his own for another year? How were the American golf players making out in England? Was the polo team coming from Philadelphia, and would they carry off the cup? There were beautiful silver and gold-plated trophies with engraved inscriptions, which helped to hypnotize you into thinking that the hitting of little balls about a field was of major importance!

VIII

Sitting on the deck of this floating mansion, Bunny read about the famine on the Volga. The crops had failed, over huge districts, and the peasants were slowly starving; eating grass and roots, eating their dead babies, migrating in hordes, and strewing their corpses along the way. It was the last and final proof of the futility of Communism, said the newspaper editors; and if Charlie Norman did not take the occasion to do some "joshing" of Bunny, it was only because Charlie never read a newspaper.

Bunny had talked with Harry Seager, and got a different view of famines in Russia. They were caused by drought, not by Communism; they had been chronic ever since the dawn of history, and their occurrence had never been taken as evidence of the futility of Tsarism. Conditions were bad now, because of the breakdown of the railroads. But people who blamed that on Communism overlooked the fact that the railroads had broken down before the revolution; and that under the Soviet administration they had had to stand the strain of three years of civil war, and of outside invasion on twenty-six fronts. Newspapers which had incited these invasions, and applauded the spending of hundreds of millions of American money to promote them, now blamed the Bolsheviks because they were not ready to cope with a famine!

You can understand how a young man with such thoughts in his mind would not fit altogether into this play party. He tried his best to be like the others, but they found out that he was different; and presently Charlie's mother took to sitting beside him. "Bunny," she said—for you were Bunny or Bertie or Baby or Beauty to this crowd as soon as you had played nine holes of golf and had one drink out of anybody's hip-pocket flask—"Bunny, you go to the university, don't you? And I'm sure you study some."

"Not very much, I fear."

"I wish you would tell me how to get Charlie to study some. I can't get him to do anything but play and make love to the girls."

Bunny wanted to say, "Try cutting off his allowance," but he realized that that would be one of those "horrid" things for which Bertie was always rebuking him. So he said, "It's quite a problem"—in the style of a diplomat or politician.

"The young people are too much of a problem for me," said Charlie's mother. "They want to race about all day, and they just insist on dragging you with them, and it's getting to be more than I can stand." So then Bunny was sorry for Charlie's mother—he had supposed that she did all this "gadding" because she enjoyed it. To look at her, she was a nautical maid, plump but shapely, clad in spotless white and blue, with fluffy brown hair that the breeze was always blowing into her bright blue eyes. Bunny stole a glance now and then, and judged that the surgical operations upon her face must have been successes, for he saw no trace of them.

"I've devoted my whole life to that boy," the nautical maid was saying, "and he doesn't appreciate it a bit. The more you do for people the more they take it as a matter of course. This afternoon I think I'll go on strike! Will you back me up?"

So when the golfing expedition was setting out, Charlie announced, in a tone loud enough for the whole company, "Mumsie's not going—she's got a crush on Bunny!" At which they all laughed merrily, and trooped down the ladder, secretly relieved to be rid of one of the old folks, who insisted on "tagging along," and trying to pretend to be one of the crowd, when it was perfectly evident that they were not and could not.

IX

So Bunny and Mrs. Norman sat on the deck of the "Siren," in two big canvas chairs under a striped canvas awning, and sipped fruit juices and chatted about many things. She wanted to know about his life, and his family; Bunny, having heard something about the ways of "mumsies," guessed that she was investigating Bertie as a possible daughter-in-law, so he mentioned all the nice things he could. Assuming that she would not be entirely indifferent to practical matters, he told about the Ross tract, how he and Dad had discovered it, and how the wells continued to flow. And Mrs. Norman said, "Oh, money, money, always money! We all of us have too much, and don't know how to buy happiness with it!"

She went on to reveal that she was Theosophist, and how there was a great mahatma coming, and we were all going to learn to live on a different astral plane. She had noticed that Bunny, when he stood against a dark background at night, had a very decided golden aura—had anyone ever mentioned it to him? It meant that he had a spiritual nature, and was destined for higher things.

Then she began to ask about his ideas; she had heard nothing about his "disgrace" at the university, apparently, and he gave her just a hint as to his conviction that there was something wrong with our social order, the world's distribution of wealth. The nautical maid, leaning back among her silken cushions, replied, "Oh, but that's all material! And it seems to me we're too much slaves to material things already; our happiness lies in learning to rise above them."

That was a large question, and Bunny dodged it, and presently Mrs. Norman was talking about herself. Her life was very unhappy. She had married when she was very young, too young to know what she was doing, except obeying her parents. Her husband had been a bad man, he had kept mistresses and treated her cruelly. She had devoted her life to her son, but it all seemed a disappointment, the more you gave to people the more they would take. Charlie was always in love, but he didn't really know anything about love, he wasn't capable of unselfishness. What did Bunny think about love?

This was another large question; and again Bunny ducked. He said he didn't know what to think, he saw that people made themselves unhappy, and he was waiting, trying to learn more about the matter. So Mrs. Norman proceeded to tell him more. The dream of love, a really true and great love, never died in the soul of a man or woman; they might become cynical, and say they didn't believe in it, but they were always unhappy, and secretly hoping and waiting, because really, love was the greatest thing in the world. It made Mrs. Norman happy to know that among this loud and noisy generation there was one young man who was not making himself cheap.

The loud and noisy generation came back to the "Siren,"

and cut off these intimacies. Charlie's "mumsie" went below, and when she reappeared, it was in the dining-saloon, with painted panels of Watteau nymphs and shepherds, and seventeenth century ladies reclining to the lascivious pleasing of a lute. The hostess was no longer the nautical maid, but instead a great lady of many charms, a shimmer of pale blue satin, and a gleam of golden hair, and snowy bosom and shoulders, and a double rope of pearls. It was a striking transformation, and Bunny, who had watched Aunt Emma at work, ought to have understood, but his mind had been on other matters.

Mrs. Norman had the young oil-man next to her at table; and when they danced, she asked him would he dance with her—these horrid young fellows neglected their hostess quite shamelessly. They danced, and Bunny discovered that she was a good dancer, and she said that he was an exquisite dancer, she just adored it, and would he dance some more with her? Bunny was willing; there was no one else he particularly wanted to dance with. She had a faint elusive perfume, and he might have learned about that also from Aunt Emma, but he had the vague impression that women somehow naturally smelled that way, and it was very sweet of them. The steel-widow's bosom was bare most of the way, and her back was bare all the way, down to where he put his hand.

Charlie teased them, and the rest of the company giggled. But next morning, when they took a long walk about the deck, Bunny realized that it took these young people less than twenty-four hours to get used to anything, and after that it was a bore. So he sat with Mrs. Norman, and drove with her, and danced with her, and played golf with her, while Charlie did all these things with Bertie, and it suited at least three of them completely.

X

Then one evening there was something in a magazine that Bunny wanted to read, and towards midnight he slipped away to his own cabin, and settled himself in his gold-plated bed, with hand-embroidered pink silk pillows, and a gold-plated, or possibly solid gold lamp-stand at his head, and presently was far away—in Russia seeing the famine stragglers dying by the roadside, or maybe in Hungary, where they were putting down the social revolution by the simple plan of slaughtering everybody who believed in it; using, as always, machine-gun bullets made in American steel mills, and purchased with an American loan. Bunny was so much absorbed in these unhappy far-off things, that he did not hear the door of his cabin very softly opened, nor the key very gently turned on the inside. The first thing he noticed was the faint elusive sweet odor, and he gazed upon a vision standing by his bedside, clad in a purple kimono with huge red hibiscus flowers. The vision looked timorous, and had its two hands clasped in front of it, and it whispered in a voice he could hardly hear, "Bunny, may I talk to you a little?"

Of course Bunny had to say that it might; and the vision sank down on its knees by the bed, and gently one of the soft hands touched his, and the soft voice trembled, "Bunny, I'm so lonely and so unhappy! I don't know if you can understand what it means to a woman to be so lonely, but you are the first man I've wanted to trust for a long, long time. I know I shouldn't come like this, but I have to tell you, and why shouldn't men and women be frank with each other?"

Bunny didn't know any reason why they shouldn't, and so they were. The substance of the frankness was that the dream of love had stirred once more in the soul of a woman who was utterly bewildered about life. He must not think that she was shallow or light, she had never done anything like this before, and it was honest—the tears came into her eyes as she said it, and oh, please, please not to despise her, she wanted to be happy, and there were so few people you could love. "Bunny, tell me, are you in love with any other woman?"

It might have been a kindness to tell her that he was; but this was his first adventure of the sort, and he told the truth, and it was like sunlight after an April shower, as the smile shone through her tears. There was a little catch in her voice, as she whispered, "I'm being silly, the tears will come, and they make a woman look so ugly, let me put out the light." So she pulled the little golden chain, and was no longer the least bit ugly, but only sweet-smelling, as she clung to his hand with her two hands, and whispered, "Bunny, do you think you could love me just a little?"

He had to say it, somehow or other. "Mrs. Norman," he began—but she stopped him: "Thelma." He stammered, "Thelma—I hadn't thought—"

"I know, Bunny, I'm older than you; but look at these flappers, how empty their heads are! And believe me, I really do care for you, I would do anything for you, give you anything you wanted."

Bunny learned something from this incident. He knew that he had only to stretch out his arms and take her; and he knew what to do—Eunice Hoyt had taught him how to love a woman. He could have swept her into ecstacy, and from that hour forth she would have been his slave, he could have had everything she owned; he might have mistreated her, used her money to keep other women, but still she would have been his slave. So now he could understand things that went on under his eyes, in this world that was a gamblers' paradise. There were men who would not share Bunny's lofty indifference to luxury and power, but would go in deliberately to seduce Dame Fortune; turning their bodily charms and social graces into weapons of prey—there were many names for them, lounge lizards, parlor snakes, tame cats, Romeos, sheiks. How many years had old August Norman slaved to build a great steel plant, and a floating mansion in the ocean, and a ten times bigger one on the shore; and here all these treasures were magically incorporated in one feminine body, clad in— well, the kimono had slid off, and there was a night-dress so filmy that it was nothing, and a faint sweet odor, and a pair of soft caressing arms, and lips pressing hot, moist kisses. "Bunny," whispered the voice, "I would marry you if you wanted me to. I would give you everything you asked for."

Bunny had learned from Eunice that when you are disposed to love, the lips can be seductive; he now learned from Mrs.—no, Thelma—that when you are not so disposed, they are repellant. "You know, Thelma," he pleaded, "I don't happen to need anything."

"I know, and I'm a horrid vulgar thing. But I'm trying in my poor blundering way to make you understand that I do care for you, and you mustn't think ill of me!"

That gave him his lead, and he explained to her that he would never think ill of her; but he did not love her, he had thought of her as a friend. And so gradually her clasp relaxed, and she sank down in a pitiful heap by the bedside, sobbing that he would be sure to loathe her, he would never want to see her again. He pleaded that that was not so, there was no disgrace about it, there was no reason to quarrel because you did not happen to love. She was so abject, he was sorry for her, and put out his hand to comfort her; but he saw at once that this would not do, she had caught his hand and was kissing it, and he was being tempted by his sympathy. Away back in the eighteenth century, one of the English poets had announced the discovery that pity moves the soul to love.

One has to think these matters out in advance, and have a standard of conduct. Bunny had made up his mind that the next time he embraced a woman, it would be one he truly loved; and now the clear cold voice of his reason told him that he did not love Charlie Norman's mother, it would only be an intrigue, and neither of them would be happy very long. So he said, gently, that he thought she had better go; and slowly and sadly she gathered up the kimono from the floor, and rose to her feet. "Bunny," she said, "people have nasty minds. If they hear about this they will make it horrid."

"Don't think of that," he answered. "I shall not tell."

He heard the door softly opened, and softly closed again; and he turned on the light, and locked the door—never again would he fail to take that precaution at a house-party! For a while he paced the floor, thinking over this alarming experience. He told himself, with becoming modesty, that it wasn't because he was irresistibly fascinating; but in this new pagan civilization women were so startled by an encounter with chastity, it struck them as something colossal, superhuman.

Next morning the nautical maid had her first natural blush in many years when she encountered the young Adonis on deck. But she soon got over it, and they talked about Theosophy, as spiritually as ever, and were perfectly good friends; he called her Thelma, and Charlie did not even make a joke. But on the way home Bertie wanted to know all about it, had Mrs. Norman made love to him, and how much? And when Bunny blushed, she laughed at him, and was provoked because he was silly and wouldn't tell. She decided that of course they had had an affair. That was all right, there had been other affairs on board the "Siren"—the lights were dim in the central hall-way, so that you needn't be recognized as you flitted from door to door. "But don't imagine she'll ever marry you," added Bertie, sagely. "She talks a lot of reincarnation bunk, but she hangs onto her Occidental Steel bonds for this incarnation!"

XI

Occidental Steel had a bad slump in the market a few days after this, and Bertie was worried—taking a proprietary interest in the concern. She asked Dad about it, and he said it was "jist manipulation." But right away a lot of other stocks went tumbling, including Ross Consolidated, and then Dad said there were fools who would gamble and bid stocks up, and then they had to come down. But the trouble continued to spread over the country, and there were reports of big concerns, and even banks, in trouble. There was panic in the air, and Dad and "Verne" held anxious consultations, and stopped all their development work, and laid off several hundred men; "pulling in their horns," as Dad phrased it. There was plenty of money in the banks, Dad said, but only the big fellows had the use of it; "Verne" was in a rage with Mark Eisenberg, the banker, who had "thrown him down." It was the "Big Five," at their old tricks of trying to freeze out the independents. Wouldn't they jist like to get Ross Consolidated in a hole, and buy it up for five or ten millions!

Bunny had a talk with Mr. Irving, who told him that it was the Federal Reserve system at work; a device of the big Wall Street banks, a supposed-to-be government board, but really just a committee of bankers, who had the power to create unlimited new paper money in times of crisis. This money was turned over to the big banks, and in turn loaned by them to the big industries whose securities they held and must protect. So, whenever a panic came, the big fellows were saved, while the little fellows went to the wall.

In this case it was the farmers who were being "deflated." They were unorganized, and had no one to protect them; they had to dump their crops onto the market, and the prices were tumbling—literally millions of farmers would be bankrupt before this year was by. But the price of manufactured goods would not drop to the same extent, because the big trusts, having the Wall Street banks behind them, could hold onto their stocks. Bunny took this explanation to his father, who passed it on to Mr. Roscoe, who said it was exactly right, by Jees; he knew the bunch that had their fingers in the till of the Federal Reserve bank here on the coast, and they were buying up everything in sight, the blankety-blank-blanks, but they weren't going to get the Roscoe-Ross properties.

Money was so scarce, Bertie could not have a new car, despite the fact that she had damaged hers in a collision; and Dad talked economy at meal-times, until Aunt Emma took to feeding them on hash made from yesterday's roast! Shortage everywhere, and worry in people's faces, and hints of bankruptcy and unemployment in the newspapers—they tried their best to hide it, but it leaked out between the lines.

Then a funny thing happened. A big limousine with a chauffeur drove up before the Ross home one summer evening, and out stepped a stately personage in snow white flannels; a tall young man with yellow hair and a solemn visage— Eli Watkins, by heck! He shook hands all round—he had developed the manners of an archbishop—and then asked for a private conference with Dad. He was taken into the "den," and half an hour later came out smiling, and bowed himself away; and Dad said nothing until he was alone with Bunny, and then his face expanded into a grin and he chuckled, by Judas Priest, Eli had gone into the real estate business. He had found a block on the outskirts of the city which was exactly the size for the temple which the angel of the Lord had commanded him to build; or rather he had found some real estate subdividers who had a pull with the city board of supervisors, and had got permission to create a block of this unprecedented size. So the word of the Lord had been vindicated, and the golden temple was to arise. But for some reason unknown the Lord had failed to tip off Eli to the panic, and here he was "stuck," just like any common, unholy business man, with a payment on his hundred and seventy-five thousand dollar tract nearly a month overdue. The collections at the revivals had fallen off, and the Lord had made it manifest that He desired Eli to employ some other method of raising funds.

"What did he want of you, Dad?"

"The Lord had revealed to him that I would take a second mortgage on the property. But I told him the Lord had failed to reveal where I was to get the cash. I gave him five hundred to help him over."

"Good God, Dad! I thought we were economizing!"

"Well, Eli pointed out that he had blessed that first well on the Paradise tract, and that was why we had got all the oil. You can see, it would 'a been sort of blasphemy if I'd denied it."

"But Dad, you know you don't believe in Eli Watkins' bunk!"

"I know, but that fellow has got a tremendous following, and we might need him some day, you can't be sure. If there should come a close election, here or at Paradise, we might get our money back many times by getting Eli to endorse our ticket."

XII

Bunny thought this over, and then summoned his nerve, and went back to his father. "Look here, Dad! If you've got five hundred for a joke with Eli Watkins, I want five hundred for something serious."

Dad looked alarmed right away. He should not have told Bunny about that money! "What is it, son?"

"I've been to see Mr. Irving, Dad, and he's in trouble, he can't get a teaching job anywhere. They've got him black-listed. You see, he has to mention that he's been teaching at Southern Pacific the last two years, and the people write to enquire about him, and he's convinced that somebody in the university is telling them he's a red."

"I shouldn't wonder," said Dad. "But that's not your fault."

"Yes, it is, Dad! I was the one that dragged him out and made him talk to me. I thought I could keep it to myself, but they had some one spying on us."

"Well, son, is he trying to borrow money from you?"

"No, I offered him a little, but he wouldn't take it. But I know he needs it, and I've been talking about it with Harry Seager, and with Peter Nagle—they know some of the labor men in the city, and they think there is a possibility of starting a labor college here. We all agree that Mr. Irving is the ideal man to run it."

"A labor college?" said Dad. "That's a new one on me."

"It's to educate the young workers."

"But why can't they go to the regular schools, that are free?"

"They don't teach them anything about labor. At least they don't teach them anything that's true. So the labor men are founding places where bright young fellows can be fitted to take their part in the labor struggle."

Dad thought it over. "You mean, son, it's a place where a bunch of you reds teach Socialism and such stuff."

"No, that's not fair, Dad; we don't propose to teach any doctrines. We want to teach the open mind—that has always been Mr. Irving's idea. He wants the labor men to think for themselves."

But that kind of talk didn't fool Dad for a moment. "They'll all turn into reds before they get through," he said. "And see here, son—I don't mind your giving five hundred to Mr. Irving, but it's going to be kind of tough on me if I'm to spend my life earning money, and then you spend it teaching young people that I haven't got any right to it!"

And Bunny laughed—that was the best way to take it. But he thought it over—more and more as the years passed—and he realized how that shrewd old man looked into the future and read life!

CHAPTER XIII

THE MONASTERY

I

Bunny was studying and thinking, trying to make up his mind about the problem of capital versus labor. It had become clear to him that the present system could not go on forever—the resources and wealth of the country thrown into an arena, to be scrambled for and carried off by the greediest. And when you asked, who was to change the system, there was only one possible answer—the great mass of the workers, who did not have the psychology of gamblers, but had learned that wealth is produced by toil. In the very nature of their position, the workers could only prevail by combining; and so, whether they would or not, they had to develop solidarity, an ideal of brotherhood and co-operation.

Such was the fundamental faith of all "radicals," and Bunny accepted the doctrine joyfully, as a way of escape from the tangle of commercialism and war. Labor was to organize, and take over industry, and rebuild it upon a basis of service. The formula was simple, and worthy of all trust; but alas, Bunny was being forced to admit that the reality was complicated. The makers of the new society were not able to agree upon plans for the structure, nor how to get the old one out of the way. They were split into a number of factions, and spent a good part of their energies quarreling among themselves. Bunny would have thought that here in Southern California at least, the labor movement had enemies enough in the federations of the employers, with their strike-breaking and spy agencies, their system of blacklist and persecution, and their politicians, hired to turn the law against the workers. But alas, it did not seem so to the young radicals; they had to make enemies of one another!

Just now they were in a fever over the Russian revolution; a colossal event that had shaken the labor movement of the whole world. Here for the first time in history the workers had got possession of a government; and what were they making of the chance? The capitalist press of the world was, of course, portraying Russia as a nightmare; but the Soviets continued to survive, and every day of survival was a fresh defeat for the newspaper campaign. The workers *could* run a government! The workers *were* running a government! Just look!

So, in every country of the world, the labor movement became divided into two factions, those who thought the workers in their country could follow the example of the Russians, and should organize and prepare to do it; and those who thought that for one reason or another it couldn't be done, and the attempt was madness. This great division showed itself in every faction and school of thought. The Socialists split into those who wanted to follow Russia and those who didn't; the Anarchists split in the same way, and so did the "wobblies"; even the old line labor leaders divided into those who wanted to let the Soviet government alone, and those who wanted to help the capitalists to put it down!

For Bunny this struggle was embodied in the Menzies family. Papa Menzies was an old-time Social-Democrat from abroad, active in the clothing workers' union. Of his six children, two daughters had followed their mother—an old-time, orthodox Jewess who wore a dirty wig, and kept all the feast days in the home, and wept and prayed for the souls of her lost ones, stolen from the faith of their fathers by America, which had made them work on Saturdays, and by the radical movement, which had made them agnostics and scoffers. Rachel and the oldest boy, Jacob, were Socialists like their father; but the other two, Joe and Ikey, had gone over to the "left wing," and were clamoring for the dictatorship of the proletariat.

II

Bunny received a letter from Rachel. "Dear Mr. Ross"— she always addressed him that way, alone of his class-mates; it was her way of maintaining her proletarian dignity, in dealing with a person of great social pretensions. "We are home after picking all the prunes in California, and next week we begin on the grapes. You said you wanted to attend a meeting of the Socialist local, and there is to be an important one tomorrow evening, at the Garment-workers' Hall. My father and brothers will be there, and would be glad to meet you."

Bunny replied by a telegram, inviting one old and four

young Jewish Socialists to have dinner with him before the meeting. He took them to an expensive restaurant—thinking to do them honor, and forgetting that they might feel uneasy as to their clothes and their table manners. Verily, it is easier for a camel to pass through the eye of a needle, than for a rich man to enter into the feelings of the disinherited.

Bunny found Rachel quite altered from the drab, hard-working girl he had known. She belonged to that oriental type which can pick fruit in the sun for several weeks without worrying about complexions; she had sunset in her cheeks and sunrise in her spirit, and for the first time it occurred to Bunny that she was quite an interesting-looking girl. She told about their adventures, which seemed to him extraordinarily romantic. Most people, when they indulged in day-dreaming, would picture themselves as the son and heir of a great oil-magnate, with millions of dollars pouring in upon them, and a sporty car to drive, and steel widows and other sirens to make love to them. But Bunny's idea of a fairy-story was to go off with a bunch of youngsters in a rattle-trap old Ford that broke down every now and then, and camp out in a tent that the wind blew away, and get a job picking fruit along side of Mexicans and Japanese and Hindoos, and send home a post-office order for ten or twelve dollars every week!

Papa Menzies was a stocky, powerful-looking man with curly yellow hair all over his head, and a deep chest—though most of it seemed to be in back instead of in front, so much was he bent over by toil. There were certain English letters he could never pronounce; he would say, contemptuously, "Dis talk about de vorld revolution." His son Jacob, the Socialist one, Bunny knew as a stoop-shouldered, pale student, and found him much improved by outdoor life. The other two boys, the young "left wingers," were talkative and egotistical, and repelled the fastidious Bunny, who had not insight enough to guess that they were meeting a young plutocrat for the first time in their lives, and this was their uneasy effort to protect their working-class integrity. Nobody was going to say that they had been overawed! In addition to this, they were hardly on speaking terms with the rest of the family, because of the bitter political dispute going on.

They went to the hall, which was crowded with people, mostly workers, all tense with excitement. There had been a committee appointed to deal with the policy of the "local," and this committee brought in a report in favor of expelling the "left wingers"; also there was a minority report, in favor of expelling everybody else! So then the fat was in the fire; and Bunny listened, and tried valiantly to keep from being disillusioned with the radical movement. They were so noisy, and Bunny had such a prejudice in favor of quiet! He wouldn't expect working people to have perfect manners, he told him-self, nor to use perfect English; but did they need to shriek and shake their fists in the air? Couldn't they debate ideas, without calling each other "labor fakers" and "yellow skunks" and so on? Bunny had chosen to call upon Local Angel City of the Socialist party at a critical moment of its history; and decidedly it was not putting on company manners for him!

Here was Papa Menzies, clambering onto the platform, and shouting at his own sons that they were a bunch of jack-asses, to imagine they could bring about mass revolution in America. "Vy did de revolution come in Russia? Because de whole country had been ruined by de var. But it vould take ten years of var to bring de capitalist class in America to such a breakdown; and meanvile, vot are you young fools doing? You vant to deliver de Socialist party over to de police! Dey have got spies here—yes, and dose spies is de mainspring of your fool left ving movement!"

That seemed reasonable enough to Bunny. The business men of Angel City would want the radical movement to go to extremes, so that they might have an excuse to smash it; and when they wanted something to happen, they did not scruple to make it happen. But to say this to the young extremists was like waving a red rag before a herd of bulls. "What?" shouted Ikey Menzies at his own father. "You talk about the police? What are your beloved Social-Democrats doing now in Germany? They have got charge of the police, and they are shooting down Communist workers for the benefit of the cap-italist class!"

"Yes, and they will do the same thing in California!" cried the other brother. "You are a bunch of class-collaborators!" That was a new word, and a dreadful one, it appeared. The question was whether the tottering capitalist system could be propped up for another ten years or so; and the "right-wingers" would take office under the capitalists, and help to save them. "You make yourself their agent," proclaimed Joe Menzies, "to bribe the workers by two cents more wages per hour!"

And so there was a bust-up in Local Angel City, as everywhere else in the world; the "reds" withdrew, and presently split into three different Communist groups; and Joe and Ikey Menzies left home, and set up house-keeping with two girl-workers of their own way of thinking. So Bunny was more perplexed than ever; life appeared so complicated, and happiness so hard to find!

III

One Saturday the telephone rang, and it was Vernon Roscoe calling Dad. Bunny happened to answer, and heard the jovial voice, "Hello, how's the boy Bolsheviki? Say, Jim Junior, I thought you were coming up to my place! Eventually—why not now? Annabelle is resting from 'Pangs of Passion'—she'll be glad to see you. Vee Tracy is there, and Harvey Manning —quite a bunch of people over Sunday. Sure, I'll be up! You go ahead, your old man will tell you the way."

Bunny told Dad he had accepted the invitation, and Dad said that Mr. Roscoe's domestic arrangements were such that Bunny ought to be told about them in advance. Annabelle Ames, the moving picture actress, was what people called his mistress, but it wasn't really that, because she was devoted to him, and all their friends knew about it, and it was just the same as being married; only, of course, there was Mrs. Roscoe, who lived in the house in the city, with her four sons. Mrs. Roscoe went in for society and all that, and had tried to drag Verne in, but he wasn't cut out for that life. Sometimes Mrs. Roscoe would go out to the Monastery, as the country place was called, but of course not when Miss Ames was there; Dad said they must have some system to keep from running into each other. Miss Ames had her own house, near to the studio, and the Monastery was a "show-place," where they took their friends over week-ends.

You drove up behind a chain of mountains that lined the coast: another of those wonderful roads, a magic ribbon of concrete laid out by a giant's hand. The engine purred softly and you raced ahead of the wind, up long slopes and down long slopes, and winding through mazes of hills; there were steep grades and vistas of tumbled mountains, and broad sweeps of valley, and stretches of shore with fishermen's huts, and boats, and nets drying in the sun; then more hills and mountain grades—for hours you flew, as fast as you pleased, for you were twenty-one now, and Dad no longer expected you to obey the speed-laws.

There was a road that branched off towards the ocean, and after climbing ten miles or so, you came to a high steel fence, and steel gates, and a sign: "Private: Turn Back Here."—and a wide place in the road, made especially so that you might obey! The gate was open, so Bunny drove on, and climbed another hill, and came over the brow, and then, oh, wonderful!—a great bowl of yellow and green, two or three miles across, with one side broken out towards the ocean, and in the center of the bowl the grey stone towers of the Monastery! Mountains on every side, and the oil magnate owned everything in sight, both the land and the landscape; if the public wanted to see his retreat, it would have to get a row-boat, or swim.

You rolled down the winding drive, through tumbled masses of rocks and clumps of live oaks a century or two old, and came to a fork in the road, and one way said "Delivery," and the other said, "Guests." If you were so fortunate as to be a guest, your road led under a porte-cochere big enough for half a dozen double-decker stages; a footman appeared, and summoned a chauffeur to take your car to the garage, and you were escorted into a living-room—well, it was like going into a cathedral, your eyes would follow the arches overhead, and you might trip yourself on the skin of an aurochs or a gnu or whatever the dickens it was. What grim sardonic architect had played this jest of Gothic towers and steeples and crenellations and machicolations—here in the midst of a new pagan empire, and called by such a very suggestive name! Assuredly, the Monastery would need to be of pre-reformation style, to fit the ways of the monk who occupied it!

The transept of the cathedral concealed an elevator, Bunny discovered; and out of it tripped suddenly a diminutive vision in lemon-colored chiffon, with lemon-colored stockings and shoes, and a big lemon-colored hat such as shepherdesses used to wear when having their portraits painted. It was complete and costly enough for a fancy-dress ball; and no introduction was needed, for Bunny was one of that ninety percent of all males in the civilized world, and perhaps seventy percent in Madagascar, Paraguay, Nova Zembla, Thibet and New Guinea, who could have told the number of lashes in each of Annabelle Ames's eyelids, or drawn a diagram of her dimples, and the exact course of a tear down her cheek. He had seen her as the "wild" daughter of a Pittsburg steel king, duly chastened and brought to faith in mother, home and heaven; as the mistress of a French king, dying elegantly to expiate elegant sins; as the mistreated and eloping heiress of a Georgian manor-house; as a bare-legged "mountainy-girl" in the Blue Ridge—"Howdy, stranger, be you-all one of them revenooers?" All this in the "movies"; and now here she was in the "speakies!"

"So this is Mr. Ross!" Her "speakie" was a queer little high treble. "Papa has told me so much about you!" (Papa was Mr. Roscoe.) "I'm so glad to have you here, and do make yourself at home. Do whatever you please, for this is liberty hall." Bunny recalled the caption—but was it from "Hearts of Steel," or from "The Maid of the Manor?"

"And here is Harve," the mistress of the manor was saying. "Oh, Harve, come here, this is Bunny Ross; Harvey Manning. It's the first time Mr. Ross has been here, and please be nice to him so he'll come back. He's going to college, and reads a lot and knows everything, and we're going to seem so ignorant and frivolous!"

Harvey Manning was coming in through one of the French windows which took the place of the stations of the cross in this cathedral. He was walking slowly, and did not increase his pace; he talked slowly also, a dry sort of drawl—having never had to hurry, because he came of one of the old families of the state. He had a queer, ugly face, with a great many wrinkles, and Bunny never was clear whether he was old or young. "Hello, Ross," he said, "pleased-to-meecher. I got an uncle that's spending a hundred thousand dollars to put you in jail."

"Is that so?" said Bunny, a trifle startled.

"Sure thing! He's nuts on this red-hunting business, and the pinks are worse than the reds, he says. I've been worried about you."

"Never mind," said Bunny, perceiving that this was a "josh," such as helps to make life tolerable for idle men, young and old. "Dad will spend two hundred thousand and get me out again."

"Come to think of it, I guess Verne would chip in—wouldn't he, Annabelle?"

"None of my guests ever stay in jail," replied the star.

"They phone to Papa, and he phones to the chief of police, who lets them out right away."

She said this without smiling; and Harvey Manning remarked, "You see, Ross, Annabelle has a literal mind."

IV

Yes, that was the truth about this bright luminary of the screen, as Bunny came to observe it; she had a literal mind. All the poetry and romance the public imagined about her—that was in the public's eye, so to say. All that Annabelle had to contribute was a youthful figure and a pliable face; the highly paid directors did the rest. She produced pictures as a matter of business, and her talk was of production costs, and percentages on foreign sales, just as if it had been an oil well. That was why she got along with Vernon Roscoe, who also had a literal mind. A primrose by the river's brim a yellow primrose was to him, and to Annabelle it was a decoration for an "interior," or a back-ground on "location."

There was a certain grim honesty about this, as Bunny discovered; it was Annabelle's desire to be an actress rather than a mistress. "By Jees," Verne would proclaim to his guests, "it's cost me eight million dollars to make a movie queen out of this baby." And the thirty year old baby had the dream that some day she would achieve a masterpiece, that would earn this eight million and vindicate her honor. Meantime, she paid installments by taking care of Verne—so publicly that it was quite touching, and respectable according to the strictest bourgeois standards If the oil magnate had ever had the idea that in taking to his bosom a movie star he was going to lead a wild and roystering life, he had made a sad mistake, for he was the most hen-pecked of all "butter and egg men."

"Now, Papa," Annabelle would say, "you've had enough to drink. Put that down." She would say it before a company assembled in their gladdest rags for a dinner party; and Verne would protest, "My God, baby, I ain't got started yet!"

"Well, you stop before you start tonight. Remember what Doctor Wilkins says about your liver."

Verne would bluster, "To hell with livers!" and the answer would be, "Now, Papa, you told me to make you obey! Have I got to make you ashamed before all this company?"

"Me ashamed? I'd like to see anybody make me ashamed!"

"Well, Papa, you know you'll be ashamed if I tell what you said to me the last time you were drunk."

Verne paused, with his glass half way in the air, trying to remember; and the company burst into clamor, "Oh, tell us! Tell us!"

"Shall I tell them, Papa?" It was a bluff, for Annabelle was very prim, and never indulged in vulgarity. But the bluff went, and the great man set down his glass. "I surrender! Take the stuff away." Whereat everybody applauded, and it gave the party a merry start.

Strange as it might seem, Annabelle was a pious Catholic. Just how she managed to fix things up with her priests Bunny never knew, but she gave freely to charity, and you would find her featured at benefits for Catholic orphan asylums and things of that sort. At the same time her little head was as full of superstitions as an old Negro mammy. She would not have started a picture on a Friday for the whole of Vernon's eight million dollar endowment. When you spilled the salt, she not merely advised you to throw some of it over your shoulder, she did it for you, if necessary. Once, at luncheon, she made a girl friend eat at a side table, because otherwise there would have been thirteen, and this girl, being the youngest, would have fallen the victim.

At the same time she was very good. She really liked you, and liked to have you around, and when she begged you to come back, she meant it. Nor would she make unkind remarks about you after you were gone. Along with the ecstasies of the artistic temperament, she had escaped its gnawing jealousies; she was one of the few lady-stars before whom it was safe to praise the work of other lady-stars, Bunny found. Also, she had an abiding respect for him, because he had read books, and had ideas about public questions. The fact that Bunny had got his name on the front pages of the newspapers as a dangerous "pink," served to lend him that same halo of mystery and romance, which the public assigned to Annabelle as a luminary of the screen world, and the mistress of a monastery!

V

"Harve," said Annabelle, "there's time for you to show Mr. Ross over the place before dinner." And so Bunny got to see what a country place could be like, so that he could make his father give him one. But Harvey Manning did not make a very good escort. To show off a show-place you need some one of an admiring disposition, whereas "Harve" had seen too many places, and was inclined to patronize them all.

There were almost as many buildings on this estate as there were tanks at the Paradise refinery; only these were Gothic tanks, with miniature towers and steeples and crenellations and machicolations. There was no chapel or place of worship, nor tombs of ancient abbots; but there was a gymnasium, with a swimming pool of green marble, and a bowling alley, and squash courts and tennis courts, and a nine hole golf course, and a polo field—everything you would find at the most elaborate country club. There was a stable with saddle horses ridden mostly by grooms, and a library read only by motion picture directors looking up local color—or at any rate that was Harvey's tale about it.

Also there was a regular menagerie of local creatures. The hired men and their youngsters had discovered that such gifts pleased the master, so they brought in everything they could capture. There was an enclosed park with deer and mountain sheep, and heavily barred dens with grizzly bears shambling over the rocks, and wild cats and coyotes and mountain lions dozing in the shade. There was a giant dome covered with netting, with a big dead tree inside, and eagles seated thereon. An eagle in his native state, sailing with supreme dominion through the azure deep of air, has been a thrilling theme for poets; but sitting in a cage he is a melancholy object. "Some of your red friends in jail!" Harvey Manning remarked in passing.

But even the most blasé man of the world has something in which he is interested, so Bunny found. Presently his guide took out his watch and remarked that it was nearly six-thirty, and they must get back to the house. He was "on the water wagon" until that hour of each day, and when it drew near, he was about ready to jump out of his skin. So they strolled back, and a Chinese boy clad in white duck had evidently learned to expect him, and was on hand with a tray. Harvey took two drinks, to make up for lost time, and then he sighed contentedly, and revealed that he could talk without a drawl.

When Bunny came down for dinner there was quite a company assembled—some in evening dress and some in golf clothes and some in plain business suits like the host—it was "liberty hall," according to the caption. Roscoe was talking politics to Fred Orpan—the drubbing they were going to give the Democratic party. Roscoe did the talking, for the other was a queer silent creature, tall and lean, with a tall, lean face, like a horse. He had the strangest grey-green eyes, that somehow looked absolutely empty; you would decide that his head was empty too, when he would listen and say nothing for an hour—but this would be a mistake, for he was the directing head of a great chain of oil enterprises, and Dad said he was sharp as a steel trap.

Also there was Bessie Barrie, because good form required that she be invited wherever Orpan went. He had backed her in several pictures, and she was "paying the price," as the current phrase ran; but it wasn't quite the same respectable arrangement as in the case of Roscoe and his Annabelle, because Bessie had been in love with her director, and he was still in love with her, and the attitude of the two men was far from cordial. This was explained to Bunny by Harvey Manning, gossip-in-chief, who had now had several more drinks, and got his tongue entirely loosened. Bunny noted that the hostess had tactfully placed the rival males at opposite ends of the table.

They were in a smaller cathedral now, known as the "refectory"; and Bunny was in the seat of honor, at the right of the charming Annabelle, transformed from a lemon-colored shepherdess to a duchess in white satin. On her left sat Perry Duchane, her director, telling about the cuts in the first two reels, which he had brought along for a showing. Next to him was a vacant seat; some lady was late, and Bunny was too young in the ways of the world to know that this is how great personages secure importance to themselves. It was his first meeting with actresses, and how should he know that they sometimes act off-stage?

VI

You remember in that colossal production, "The Emperor of Etruria," the Scythian slave girl who is brought in from the wilds to serve the pleasures of a pampered sybarite, and the scene where the fat eunuchs lay hands upon her? With what splendid fury she claws them and knocks their heads together!

Her clothing is torn to shreds in the struggle, and you have glimpses of a lithe and sinewy body—the extent of the glimpses depending upon the censorship laws of the state in which you see the picture. The scene made a hit with the public, and many producers competed for Viola Tracy—pronounce it Vee-ola, please, with the accent on the first syllable. She displayed her magnificent fighting qualities next in "The Virgin Vamp," and thereafter escaped dishonor by a hair's breadth in many palpitating scenes. Of late she had acquired dignity, and was now regal on all the bill-boards of Angel City in "The Bride of Tutankhamen," an alluring figure, with deep-set mysterious black eyes, and a smile fathomless as four thousand years of history.

Well, here she was, stepping out of the billboards, and into the refectory of the Monastery; her Egyptian costume changed for a daring one of black velvet, fresh from Paris, and with black pearls to match. The footman drew out her chair, and she rested one hand upon it, but did not take her seat; her hostess said, "Miss Tracy, Mr. Ross"—and still she paused, smiling at Bunny, and he smiling at her. It was a striking pose, and Tommy Paley, her director, who had taught her the stunt, and watched it now from the other end of the table, suddenly called, "Camera!" Everybody laughed, and "Vee" most gaily of all—revealing two rows of white pearls, more regular than the black ones, and worth many times as much to a movie star.

Annabelle Ames got along in the world without ever saying anything unkind about anybody, but that was not "Vee" Tracy's style; she had a fighting tongue, as well as fighting fists, and her conversation gave Bunny the shock of his innocent young life. They happened first to be discussing a lady vamp, recently imported from abroad with much clashing of advertising cymbals. "She dresses in very good taste," said Annabelle, mildly. "Oh, perfect!" said Vee. "Absolutely perfect! She selected her dog to match her face!" And then presently they were talking about that million dollar production, "The Old Oaken Bucket," which was just then waking home memories and wringing tears from the eyes of millions of hardened sinners. Dolly Deane, who played the innocent country maiden seduced by a travelling salesman, was so charmingly simple, said Annabelle. "Oh, yes!" replied Vee. "For the chance to be that simple, she slept with her producer, and two angels, and the director and his assistant; and all five of them told her how an innocent virgin says her prayers!"

Bunny, who was a rebel in his own line, sat up and took notice of this conversation; and you may be sure that Vee did not fail to take notice of the young oil prince, flashing him mischief with her sparkling black eyes. The footman brought her a plate of soup in a golden bowl, and she took one glance and cried, "Oh, my God, take it away, it's got starch in it! Annabelle, are you trying to drive me out of the profession?" Then, to Bunny, "They say that nobody can eat a quail a day for thirty days; but Mr. Ross, what would you say if I told you I have eaten two lamb chops and three slices of pineapple every day for seven years?"

"I would ask, is that an Egyptian rite, or maybe Scythian?"

"It is the prescription of a Hollywood doctor who specializes in reducing actresses. We public idols are supposed to be rioting in luxury, but really we have only one dream—to buy enough Hollywood real estate so that we can retire and eat a square meal!"

"Don't you really ever steal one?" asked Bunny, sympathetically.

She answered, "Ours are the kind of figures that never lie. You can ask Tommy Paley what would happen if they were to see any fat on me when the gentleman heavy tears my clothes off! They would put me into the comics, and I'd earn my living being rolled down hill in a barrel!"

VII

Conversation at this dinner-party, as at most dinner-parties in America at that time, resembled a walk along the edge of a slippery ditch. Sooner or later you were bound to slide in, and after that you could not get out, but finished your walk in the ditch. "Mr. Ross," said Annabelle, in her capacity as hostess, "I notice you aren't drinking your wine. You can trust what we have—it's all pre-war stuff." And so they were in the ditch, and talked about Prohibition.

The law was two years and a half old, and the leisure classes were just realizing the full extent of the indignity which had been inflicted upon them. It wasn't the high prices —they were all of them seeking ways to spend money rapidly; but it was the inconvenience, and the difficulties of being sure what you were getting. People escaped the trouble by pinning their faith to some particular bootlegger; Bunny noticed it as an incredible but universal phenomenon that persons otherwise the most cynical, who made it the rule of their lives to trust nobody, would repeat the wildest stories which men of the underworld had told them, about how this particular "case of Scotch" had just been smuggled in from Mexico, or maybe stolen from the personal stock of a visiting duke in Canada.

They discussed the latest developments in the tragedy which had befallen Koski, one of the emperors of their screen-world, who had had a priceless stock in the cellar of his country place, and had taken the precaution to have it walled in with two feet of brick, and guarded by doors such as you would find on a bank vault; but thieves had come during the owner's absence, and bound and gagged the caretaker, and cut through the floor of the drawing room, above the cellar, and hauled out everything with rope and tackle, and carted it away in trucks. Since then Koski had been raising a row with the authorities; he charged that they were standing in with the thieves, and he had brought in an outside detective agency, and threatened a scandal that would shake the pants off the police department. By this means he had got back the greater part of his casks and bottles; but alas, the real stuff was gone, they had all been emptied and refilled with synthetic. And so, after that, there was a convincing story for your bootlegger to tell you; this was some of the original Koski stuff! Millions of gallons of original Koski stuff were being drunk in California, and even in adjoining states.

Suddenly Vee Tracy clapped her hands. "Oh, listen! I have one on Koski! Him and some others! Has anybody heard The Movie's Prayer?"

There was a silence. No one had.

"This is something for all of us to teach our children to recite every night and morning. It is serious, and you mustn't joke."

"Let us pray," said the voice of Bessie Barrie.

"Fold your hands, like good little children," ordered Vee, "and bow your heads." And then with slow and solemn intonation she began:

"Our Movie, which art Heaven, Hollywood be Thy Name. Let Koski come. His Will be done, in studio as in bed."

There was a gasp, and then a roar of laughter swept the

table; no explanations were needed, they all knew their emperor, master of the destiny of hundreds of screen actresses. "Go on!" shouted voices; and the girl continued to intone an invocation, which echoed in outline and rhythm the Lord's prayer, and brought in the names of other rulers of their shadow world, always with an obscene implication. It was a kind of Black Mass, and performed the magic feat of lifting the conversation out of the ditch of Prohibition. They talked for a while about the sexual habits of their rulers; who was living with whom, and what scandals were threatened, and what shootings and attempted poisonings had resulted. There were thrilling crime mysteries, which would provide a topic of conversation for hours in any Hollywood gathering; you might hear half a dozen different solutions, each one positive, and no two alike.

VIII

They adjourned to the larger cathedral, where the lights were dim, and there appeared, very appropriately in place of the altar, a large white screen. At the far end of the room was a projecting machine, and the guests distributed themselves in lounging chairs, prepared to pay for their entertainment by watching the first two reels of Annabelle's new picture, and giving their professional judgments on the "cutting." "Pangs of Passion" you may recall as a soul-shaking story about a society bud whose handsome young husband is led astray by a divorcee, and who, in order to make him jealous, begins a flirtation with a bootlegger, and is carried off in a rum-running vessel, and made the victim of the customary pulling and hauling and tearing of feminine costumes. "My God," said Vee Tracy, in an aside to Bunny, "Annabelle has been playing these society flappers since before they were born, and in all that time she's never had a story above the intelligence of a twelve year old child! You'll think it's a joke, but I know it for a fact that Perry Duchane gets a bunch of school children together and tells them the scenario, and if there's anything they don't like, he cuts it out."

And then to Annabelle she said, "It's up to standard, my dear; it will sell all right." And to Bunny, "That's one good thing about Annabelle, you can say that and she's satisfied—she doesn't ask you if it's a work of art. But others do, and

I've made mortal enemies because I won't lie to them. I say, 'Leave art out of it, dearie; we all know our stuff is trash.'"

There was technical discussion, and Bunny had an opportunity to learn about the tricks of "cutting." Also he learned what had been the gross business on a number of Annabelle Ames' pictures, and the inside figures on other successes. Tommy Paley had recently indulged in the luxury of making an artistic and beautiful picture, which the papers had called a "classic"; he and a group of friends had come out something over a hundred thousand in the hole, and he had charged it up to education, and said, "Let the Germans do the art stuff after this!"

All this time there had been a silent spectral figure flitting about the cathedral, clad in white duck coat and trousers and padded purple slippers; the Chinese boy, bearing a tray with little glasses full of pink and yellow and purple and green liquid. He would move from guest to guest, offering his tray, and they would put down empty glasses and take up full ones, and during the entire course of the evening the spectre never made one sound, nor did anyone make a sound to it. Some three hundred years ago an English poet, long since forgotten by the movie world, had asked the question why a man should put an enemy into his mouth to steal away his brains; but here at the Monastery, the anxiety appeared to be that some one might forget to put the enemy into his mouth—hence this Chinese spectre to save the need of recollecting.

There were a few who did not drink; Annabelle was one, and Vee Tracy another. The spectre had apparently been instructed not to go near Vernon Roscoe, and if Vernon tried to approach the spectre, there would be a sharp warning, "Now, Verne!" But others drank, and tongues were loosened, and hearts poured out as the evening passed. Even Fred Orpan came to life, and revealed a tongue! It was Vernon Roscoe's habit to "josh" everybody, and now he got paid back, as the one-time rancher from Texas sat up in his chair and opened his long horse's face and demanded, in a falsetto voice which sounded as if it came from a ventriloquist: "Anybody here know how this old shyster got his start in life?"

Apparently nobody did know; and Orpan put another question: "Anybody ever seen him in swimming? I bet you never! When it's out-doors, he'll tell you the water is too cold, and when it's indoors he'll tell you it's dirty or something. The reason is, he's got one toe missing, and he's afraid to have it proved on him. When he was drilling his first well, he ran out of money and was clean done for; so he went and took out an accident insurance policy, and then went rabbit-hunting and shot off one of his big toes. So he got the cash to finish the well! Is that true, old socks, or ain't it?"

The company laughed gleefully and clamored for an answer; and Vernon laughed as much as anyone. He didn't mind the story, but you could never get him to tell. Instead, he countered on his assailant, "You ought to hear about this old skeezicks, how he got rich leasing oil lands from Indians. They tell this about a dozen oil men, but Fred was the real one that done it, I know because I was there. It was Old Chief Leatherneck, of the Shawnees, and Fred offered him one-eighth royalty, and the old codger screwed up his eyes and said, 'No take one-eighth, got to have one-sixteenth!' Fred said he couldn't afford that, and begged him to take one-twelfth, but he said, 'One-sixteenth or no lease.' So they signed up for a sixteenth, and now it's the Hellfire Dome, by Jees! Is that so, old skeezicks, or ain't it?"

Said Fred Orpan, "You might complete the story by telling what the old chief does with his royalties. He's got a different colored automobile for each day of the week, and he figures to get drunk three times every day."

"Oh, take me to the Hellfire Dome!" wailed the voice of Harvey Manning. "They won't let me get drunk but one time in a night, and none at all in the day-time!"

IX

There was a large organ in this cathedral, a magic organ of the modern style, which played itself when you put in a roll of paper and pressed an electric switch. It played the very latest jazz tunes from Broadway, and the company danced, and Vee Tracy came to Bunny and said, "My doctor allows me only one drink in an evening, and I want a sober partner." Bunny was glad to oblige, and so the time passed pleasantly. He danced with his hostess, and with the blonde fairy, Bessie Barrie. In between dances they chatted, and the Chinese spectre continued to flit about, and the deeps of the human spirit were more and more unveiled.

In front of Bunny stood Tommy Paley, super-director,

handsome, immaculate if slightly ruffled, flushed of face, and steady upon his legs if not in his thoughts. "Look here, Ross," he said, "I want you to tell me something."

"What is it?"

"I want to know what it's all about."

"What, Mr. Paley?"

"Life! What the hell are we here for, and where do we go when we get through?"

"If I knew," said Bunny, "I would surely tell you."

"But, lookit, man, I thought you went to college! I never got any education, I was a newsboy and all that. But I thought when a fellow's read a lotta books and goes to college—"

"We haven't got to it yet," said Bunny. "Maybe it comes in the last two years."

"Well, by God, if they tell you, you come tell me. And find out, old son, what the hell we going to do about sex? You can't live with 'em and you can't live without 'em, and what sort of a mess is it?"

"It's very puzzling," admitted Bunny.

"It's the devil!" said the other. "I'd pay anybody ten year's salary if they'd teach me to forget the whole damn business."

"Yes," said Bunny; "but then, what would you direct?"

And the super-director looked at him, bewildered, and suddenly burst out laughing. "By God, that's so! That's a good one! Ho, ho, ho!" And he went off, presumably to pass the good one on.

His place was taken by Harvey Manning, who was no longer able to stand up, but sprawled over a chair, and in a voice of the deepest injury declared, "I wanna know whoze been tellin bout me!"

"Telling what?" asked Bunny.

"Thaz what I wanna know. What they been tellin?"

"I don't know what you mean, Harvey."

"Thass it! Why don't you know? Why don't you tell me? Mean say I ain't askin straight? You think I'm drunk—that it? I say, I wanna know whoze been talkin bout me an what they been sayin. I gotta take care my reputation. I wanna know why you won't tell me. I'm gonna know if I have to keep askin all night." And accordingly he started again, "Please, ole feller, what they been tellin you?"

But just then the Chinese spectre flitted past, and Harvey

got up and made an effort to catch him, and failing, caught hold of a lamp-stand, slightly taller than himself. It was not built like the lamp-posts that he was used to clutching on street-corners; it started to fall, and Bunny leaped and caught it, and Harvey cried, in alarm, "Look out, you're upsettin it!"

Then a funny thing happened. Bunny had noticed at the dinner-table a well-groomed man of the big Western type, polite and unobtrusive; the superintendent of the estate, and one of the few who kept sober. Now it appeared that among the duties of superintendent at a monastery was that of the old-fashioned "bouncer" of the Bowery saloon. He came up, and quietly slipped his arm about Harvey Manning; and the latter, evidently having been there before, set up an agonized wail, "I d'wanna go to bed! I woan go to bed! Dammit, Anderson, lemme lone! If I go to bed now I wake up in the mornin an I can't have a drink till evenin an I go crazy!"

Against that horrible fate poor Harvey fought frantically; but apparently the material inside the shoulders of Mr. Anderson's dresscoat was not the ordinary tailor's padding, and the weeping victim was helpless as in the grip of a boa-constrictor. He went along, even while proclaiming loudly that he wouldn't. "I'll get up again, I tell you! I woan be treated like a baby! I woan come this damn place again! It's an outrage! I'm a grown man an I got a right get drunk if I wanna—" and so his weeping voice died into the elevator!

"Mr. Ross," said Vee Tracy, "there are two cries that one hears at Hollywood parties. The first is, I don't want to go to bed; and the second is, I do."

X

When Bunny made his appearance on Sunday morning, he had the Monastery all to himself. He breakfasted, and read the papers, which had been delivered from the nearest railroad station; then he went for a stroll, and renewed his acquaintance with the "reds" in the eagle cage. He walked down towards the ocean, and discovered a combination of fire-break and bridle-path, leading over the hills along the coast. He followed this for a couple of miles, until it led down to a long stretch of beach. The owner of the Monastery had erected a barrier here, with signs warning the public to keep out; there was a gate with a spring lock, and on the inside a

board with keys hanging on it, and instructions to take one
with you, so that you could return. Bunny did this, and continued his walk down the beach.

Presently he came upon a Rhine castle, set upon one of
these lonely hills; and in front of it, coming down to the water,
a series of terraces and gardens. There were paths, and water-
courses, "bridal-veil" falls, and fountains with stone-carved
frogs and storks and turtles and tritons—all suffering from
drought, for the water was shut off. You could guess that
the owner was away, because the window-shades in the Rhine
castle were drawn, and here and there throughout the gardens
were great lumps of white sheeting, evidently wrapped about
statues. Some of these were on pedestals, and some perched
on the stone walls; and directly over the head of each hung
an electric light.

It was such a curious phenomenon that Bunny took the
trouble to climb into the garden, and lift up the hem of one of
these sheets, and was embarrassed to discover the entirely
naked round limbs of a large marble lady—presumably a Lore-
lei, or other kind of German lady, because you could tell by
the shape of the cloth, and by feeling through it, that she had
a goblet uplifted in one hand, and behind her head a thick
marble rope, made by her braided hair. With golden comb
she combs it, you remember, and sings a song thereby, das hat
eine wundersame gewaltige Melodei; and Bunny was the
fisher-boy whom it seized with a wild woe. He peered under
half a dozen of the sheets, and counted the rest, establishing
the fact that the gardens contained no less than thirty-two
large, fat marble ladies with braided hair hanging down their
backs. An amazing spectacle it must have afforded, at night
when all the lights were turned on—and no one to behold it
but seals! Yes; Bunny looked out over the sea, and there was
not a sail in sight, but close to the shore were clusters of rocks,
and on these the seals sat waiting to see if he were going to
unveil the statues, and bring back the merry days before prohibition ruined America!

He returned to the beach, and walked on. The sun was
high now, and the water tempting; there were more rocks with
seals on them, and green-white breakers splashing over them,
not high enough to be dangerous, but just enough to be alluring.
Bunny made sure he was alone, and then undressed and waded
into the water.

The attention of the seals became riveted upon him, and with each step that he took, one of them would give a hump, hump, and get nearer to the water's edge. Some of them were yellow, and some a dark brown, little ones and big ones, each of them enormously fat—having consumed his own weight in fish in the course of a day. As Bunny swam near, they slid silently off the rocks, politely yielding place to him; when he clambered onto the rocks, they would bob up and form a circle a few yards away, yellow heads and brown heads sticking out of the water, whiskers bristling and mild eyes staring. They were strangely human, a circle of foreign children, watching some visitor who does not know their language and may or may not be dangerous.

California water is always cold, but California sunshine is always warm; so Bunny would swim for a while, and then approach a cluster of rocks, and watch the silent company hump themselves into the water. Whatever he wanted, they would yield to him, the superior being, and content themselves with the places he had left. The green-white seas splashed over him, and underneath their surface was a garden of strange plants, with anemones and abalones clinging, too tightly to be pried off by fingers. White clouds drifted by, making swift shadows over the water, and far out at sea a streak of smoke showed where a steamer was passing.

The world was so beautiful, and at the same time strange, and interesting to be alive in! What must it be like to be a seal? What did they think concerning this arrogant being who commandeered their resting places? Did they see the Rhine castle on the shore, or did they see only fish to eat, and how did they understand so clearly that they must not eat a man? Embarrassing if one of them should be a "red," and rebel against the genial customs of the phocidae! Thus Bunny—just the same at the age of twenty-one as when first we met him, driving over the Guadalupe grade and speculating about the feelings of ground-squirrels and butcher-birds. He had completed in the meantime a full course at the Beach City High School, and half a course at Southern Pacific University, but neither institution had told him what he wanted to know!

XI

The young philosopher decided that he had had enough, and started to swim in; but then he noticed someone on horseback, galloping down the beach towards him. The figure was bare-headed and clad in knickerbockers, and appeared to be a man; but you never could be sure these days, so he swam and waited, and presently made out that it was Vee Tracy. She saw him, and waved her hand, and when she was opposite, reined up her horse. "Good morning, Mr. Ross."

"Good morning," he called. "Is this part of the doctor's prescription?"

"Yes, and it also includes swimming." There was laughter in her face, as if she guessed his plight. "Why don't you invite me to join you?"

"It would embarrass the seals." He swam in slowly, and stood with the waves tumbling about his shoulders.

"It is the morning of the world," said Vee. "Come out, and let us enjoy it."

"Look here, Miss Tracy," he explained, "it so happens that I wasn't expecting company. I am the way the Lord made me."

"O ye sons of men," she chanted, "how long will ye turn my glory into shame?" And she explained, "I once acted in 'King Solomon'—a religious pageant. We had three real camels, and I was Abishag the Shunammite, the damsel who cherished the king and ministered unto him; and he sang to me, Rise up my love, my fair one, and come away. For lo, the winter is past, and the rain is over and gone; the flowers appear on the earth, the time of the singing of birds is come, and the voice of the turtle is heard in our land. The fig-tree putteth forth her green figs, and the vines with the tender grape give a good smell. Arise, my love, my fair one, and come away. Oh my dove, that art in the cleft of the rocks—"

He was near enough to see the imp of mischief dancing in her black eyes. "Young woman," he said, "I give you fair notice. I have been in this water an hour, and I am cold. I was on my way out."

She continued, "Thy neck is like the tower of David builded for an armoury, whereon there hang a thousand bucklers, all shields of mighty men."

He took a few steps, until the breakers barely reached his waist. "I am on the way," he said.

"Who is this that cometh out of the water? My beloved is white and ruddy, the chiefest among ten thousand. His head is as the most fine gold, his locks are bushy—"

"Fair warning!" he announced. "One—two—three!" And when she gave no sign of yielding, he strode out from the waves.

"His legs are as pillars of marble, set upon sockets of fine gold; his countenance is as Lebanon, excellent as the cedars."

He stood confronting her, the water playing about his feet.

"Thou are beautiful, O my love, as Tirzah, comely as Jerusalem, terrible as an army with banners. Turn away thine eyes from me, for they have overcome me!"

"If that's in the Bible, I suppose it's all right," said Bunny.

" 'King Solomon' lost a fortune," said the lady on horseback, "so it's the only pageant I was ever in, and it's the only poetry I can recite. But I dare say if I had been in a Greek pageant I could quote something appropriate, for I read they used to run naked in the games, and it did not embarrass them. Is that true?"

"So the books say," said Bunny.

"Well then, let's be Greek! You are a runner, I have heard. Are you in training?"

"Partly so."

"My beloved's lips are blue and he's got goose-flesh, so let's have a race, you and my horse, and it'll be a Greek pageant."

"Anything to oblige a lady."

"Ready! Set!" she called sharply—and then, to his great surprise, pulled a little revolver from under her jacket, and fired it into the air. It was to be a real race!

He started at the rate of twenty miles an hour, or a little better, and heard the horse loping on the sand behind him. He did not know how long the race was to last, so presently he settled down to a long distance gait. He was warm again, and willing to investigate being a Greek. The sky was blue, and the clouds white, and the sea green, and the sand sparkling cold; truly, as the girl had said, it was the morning of the world!

They came to a place where wagon-tracks came down to the beach, and there were fishermen's boats, and three men had just shoved out through the breakers. They rested on their oars, to stare at this amazing spectacle, an entirely naked youth running a race on the beach with a woman on horseback. Their swarthy Italian or Portuguese faces wore broad grins, with white teeth showing. They knew about the Monastery, and this was the latest freak of the idle rich!

But then came a place where the highway came near to the beach. There were tents ahead, and automobiles parked, with canvas covers to protect them from the sun. There were people on the beach; and these, Bunny knew, would not be primitive foreigners, but ranchmen from the interior, having brought their families to spend Sunday away from the baking heat. They would have no toleration for the freaks of the idle rich, neither would they know about the customs of the ancient Greeks; they were sober, church-going people, the sort who formed the Ku Klux Klan, and punished fornications and adulteries by tarring and feathering and riding on a rail. But Vee had challenged Bunny, and he said to himself that it was up to her. Did she really want to be pagan and take the consequences?

He ran on and on. The tents came near, and he saw women stare, and then dive into shelter; he saw the men, not running away, nor turning their heads, but glaring with menace in their faces. What would they do? Seize the obscene intruder, and wrap him perforce in a blanket, and deliver him over to the police? Bunny's quick mind leaped to the outcome—a streamer-head across the front page of the "Angel City Evening Howler"—

STAR RACES NUDE OIL RED!

Then suddenly he heard a voice behind him: "I give up! I'm going back!" So he whirled, and the horse whirled, and away they went, even faster than they had come, and both of them shaking with laughter in the morning of the world!

XII

The Greeks had never worn either trousers or shirts, and the process of getting into these garments did not lend itself to romantic or esthetic interpretations. Therefore Vee Tracy rode down the beach while Bunny dressed; and when he rejoined her, she was no longer Greek, but an American young lady upon her dignity, and it would have been bad taste to have referred to her crazy prank.

She was leading the horse with the bridle over its head,

and Bunny walked by her side. "Did you notice that night-mare?" she said, as they passed the thirty-two Loreleis in their grave-clothes. "That was one of the dreams of old Hank Thatcher. You've heard of 'Happy Hank,' the California Grape-king?"

"So that's his place!" exclaimed Bunny.

"He dreamed of orgies, and kept half a dozen harems; his wife refused him a divorce to punish him, and when he died she covered up his dream as a kind of public penance."

"Nobody seems to see it but the seals."

"Oh, the papers were full of it; they would never pass up any news about the Thatchers. They send out a reporter once in a while. One time they had a scream of a story—the reporter had worn a suit of chain mail under his trousers, and the dogs had torn at him in vain!"

"She sets dogs on them?"

"That's why nobody dares go up there to peek at the statues."

"Good Lord!" exclaimed Bunny. "I peeked at half a dozen of them."

"Well, you were lucky. That's why I carried this revolver along; they sometimes come onto the beach, and the neighbors make war on them."

"Why doesn't she put up a fence?"

"She's in a dispute with the county. She claims to own the beach, and every now and then she puts a barrier across it, and the county sends men at night to tear it down. They've been fighting it out for the past ten years. Also the state is trying to put a highway through the tract—it would save several miles of the coast route—but she has spent a fortune fighting them; she lives in that castle like a beleaguered prin-cess in the old days—all the shades drawn, and she steals about from room to room with a gun in her hand, looking for burg-lars and spies. Ask Harve about it—he knows her."

"Is she insane?"

"It's a reaction from her life with her husband; he was a profligate, and so she's a miser. They tell a story about him, he used to pay his hands in cash, and would drive about the country in a buckboard with little canvas bags, each containing a thousand dollars in gold. One time he dropped one bag and didn't miss it; one of his hands brought it to him, and old Hank looked at the man with contempt, and put his hand into

22

his pocket and pulled out a half dollar. 'Here,' he said, 'here's the price of a rope; go buy one and hang yourself'!"

"So now she's taking care of the money!"

"Exactly. She pays all her bills by registered mail, and preserves the receipts, and insists on having a return receipt from the post office, and when that comes she files the two together, and when the receipted bill comes back, she files and indexes that. She won't let a book-keeper do it, because you can't find any employees who can be trusted to attend to things properly. She spends hours poring over her business papers, and discovering other people's carelessness and incompetence. She employs lawyers, and then she employs other lawyers to check them up, and then a detective agency to find out how the lawyers are selling her out. She's convinced the county authorities are persecuting her, and that they're all a lot of crooks—she mayn't be so wrong in that. She's lean and haggard, and wears herself to a skeleton roaming about the house, dusting the furniture and nagging at the servants because they won't take care of things."

The two walked on down the beach. "Up over that hill," said Vee, "lives old Hank's sister; he left her part of the estate, and the two women have quarrelled about the boundary line and the water-rights. Tessie Thatcher's an old rake—hires men to work for her, and makes them her lovers, and writes them tootsie-wootsie letters, and then they try to blackmail her, and she tells them to go to hell, and they bring suit for unpaid salaries, and sell the letters to the newspapers, and they're all published; but Tessie doesn't care, she knows that nothing can hurt her social position, she's too rich; and besides, she's an old booze-fighter, and knows how to forget her troubles."

"My God!" exclaimed Bunny. "What property does to people!"

"To women especially," said Vee. "It's too much for their nerves. I look at the old women I meet, and think, which of them do I want to be? And I say, Oh, my God! and jump into my car and drive fifty miles an hour to get away from my troubles, and from people who want to tell me theirs!"

"Is that what you were doing when the judge sent you to jail for a week?" laughed Bunny.

"No," she answered, "that was a publicity stunt, the bright idea of my advertising man."

CHAPTER XIV

THE STAR

I

Bunny went back to Angel City, and discovered that if he wanted to follow Vee Tracy's program of dodging other people's troubles, he had made a fatal mistake to get interested in a labor college! He went to see Mr. Irving, and found the young instructor up to his ears in the growing pains and disputes of the labor movement. All summer long his job had been interviewing leaders and sympathizers, and trying to get them together on a program. He had managed to get the college started, with three teachers and about fifty pupils, mostly coming at night; but it was all precarious—the difficulties seemed overwhelming.

There were a handful of progressive and clear-minded men and women in the labor movement; and then there was the great mass of the bureaucracy, dead from the ears up; also a little bunch of extreme radicals, who would rather have no bread at all than half a loaf. The old-line leaders would have nothing to do with the college if these "reds" got in; on the other hand, if you excluded the "reds," they would set up a clamor, and a lot of genuine liberals would say, what was the use of a new college that was so much like the old ones?

The labor movement had its traditions, having to do with getting shorter hours and more pay for the workers; and the old officials were bound by that point of view. The average union official was a workingman who had escaped from day-labor by the help of a political machine inside the union. Anything new meant to him the danger of losing his desk job, and having to go back to hard work. He had learned to negotiate with the employers and smoke their cigars, and in a large percentage of cases he was spending more money than his salary. Here in Angel City, the unions had a weekly paper, that lived by soliciting advertising from business men—and what was that but a respectable form of graft? When you took any fighting news to an editor of that sort, he would say the dread word "Bolshevism," and throw your copy into the trash basket.

And the same thing applied to the movement in its national aspects. The American Federation of Labor was maintaining a bureau in Washington, for the purpose of combatting the radicals, and this bureau was for practical purposes the same as any patriotic society; its function was to collect damaging news about Russia from all over the world, and feed it to the American labor press. And of course, if any labor man was defiant, and insisted upon telling the other side, he would incur the bitter enmity of this machine, and they would throw him to the wolves. There would be a scare story in the capitalist press, telling how the Communists had got possession of the plasterers' union, or maybe the button workers, and the grand jury was preparing action against a nest of conspirators. The average labor leader, no matter how honest and sincere, shivered in his boots when such a club was swung over his head.

II

Also there was Harry Seager and his troubles. The Seager Business College had turned out a class of young men and women, thoroughly trained to typewrite, "All men are created free and equal," and also, "Give me liberty or give me death." And now these young people were going about in the business offices of Angel City, and discovering that nobody wanted employes to typewrite anything of that sort! In plain words these young people were being told that the Seager Business College was a Bolshevik institution, and the business men of the city had been warned not to employ its graduates. The boycott was illegal in Angel City, and if any labor men tried to apply it, they would be whisked into jail in a jiffy. But imagine Harry Seager asking the district attorney to prosecute the heads of the Merchants' and Manufacturers' Association, whose campaign contributions had put the district attorney into office!

Bunny went up to Paradise, and there was another bunch of grief. In preparation for the coming struggle over the wage scale, the oil operators were weeding out the "trouble-makers," which meant the active union men. And now for the first time, Ross Consolidated was following the policy of the rest. Ben Riley, one of the fellows who met in the Rascum cabin, had been told that he was no longer needed. They had too many men, the foreman had said, but that was a plain lie, because he had taken on half a dozen new men since. No, Ben was a Socialist, and had talked at meetings in Paradise, and distributed Socialist papers that showed the monstrous wastes in the oil industry, and the world-rivalry for oil which was to cause the next great war.

It was Ruth who told Bunny about this; very seriously, with distress in her gentle eyes. "It's a shame, Bunny, because Ben has got no place to go. And here he's got a home, and a wife and two little girls."

Bunny was worried too; Dad had promised this kind of thing should not happen!

"Can't you do something about it?" pleaded Ruth.

"Well, but Ben was a pumper, and that's in the department of operation, and Dad only has to do with the development work. He wouldn't butt in on the superintendent of operation."

"But then, ask him to give Ben a job on development."

"I'll ask him, Ruth, but I know what he'll say. If he undertook to make jobs for men that other departments want to get rid of, he'd make bad feeling. You know what a lot of fuss he makes about good feeling inside the organization."

"Yes, Bunny, but then, what about Ben's feeling, and all the men?" Ruth persisted, with that surprising force that gentle people sometimes display. Ruth did not understand abstract questions, she had no theories about the "class struggle;" but when it came to a human fact, a grievance, then she was possessed by it, and as determined as Paul. These men who came to the cabin to argue and discuss, they were all her friends, and if they did not get a square deal, something must be done!

So here was Bunny, in his old tormenting position, watching a fight which he was powerless to stop, or even to mitigate! Ben Riley managed to get work on a ranch; he had to put in twelve hours a day, but all the same, he would come onto the tract at night and distribute his Socialist literature—and of course with a burning sense of bitterness, shared by his friends.

Tom Axton was back in the field, at his organizing job, and he and Paul and Bunny had long discussions. Here in the oil workers' union, just as in the labor college, there was the problem of what to do about the "reds." You could never have any big group of workers without Socialists and Communists and

I. W. W. among them—and all busily "boring." Paul was endorsing the position of Axton, that the one thing in the oil industry was to save the union; all the workers must concentrate on that, and avoid every cause of division. To this the Socialists and the Communists made answer, all right, they would help; but as the struggle developed, the bosses would call in the police and the courts, and the oil workers, like all other workers, would find they could not stay out of politics, they would have to master the capitalist state. So far the Socialists and Communists would agree; but then would come the question, how was this mastering to be accomplished—and at once the two groups would be imitating the Menzies family!

The "Industrial Workers of the World," as they called themselves, were a separate group, men who had been revolted by the corruption and lack of vision in the old-line unions, and had formed a rival organization, the "One Big Union," that was some day to take in all the workers. They were hated by the regular labor leaders, and the newspapers represented them as criminals and thugs. When Bunny met one, he found a young fellow clinging to an ideal in the spirit of the early Christian martyrs. These "wobblies" were now being hunted like wild beasts under the "criminal syndicalism act" of California; every one who came into a labor camp or industrial plant was liable to be picked up by a constable or company "bull," and the mere possession of a red card meant fourteen years in state's prison. Nevertheless, here they were in Paradise; half a dozen of them had a "jungle" or camping place out in the hills, and they would lure workingmen out to their meetings, and you would see the glare of a camp-fire, and hear the faint echo of the songs they sang out of their "little red song book." To Bunny this was romantic and mysterious; while to Dad and Mr. Roscoe and the managers of Ross Consolidated, it was as if the "jungle" had been located in the province of Bengal, and the sounds brought in by the night wind had been the screams of man-eating tigers!

III

From these and all other troubles Bunny now had a way of swift escape, the Monastery. Nobody up there had troubles—or if they did, they didn't load them onto him! "Make this your country club," Annabelle had said; "come when you please and stay as long as you please. Our horses ought to be ridden, and our books ought to be read, and there's a whole ocean—only watch out for the rip-tides!" So Bunny would run up to this beautiful playground; and sometimes Vee Tracy was there, and when she wasn't she would turn up a few hours later—quite mysteriously.

She was several years older than he, and in knowledge of the world older than he would be at a hundred. Nevertheless, she was a good playmate. It was her business to be young in both body and spirit—it was the way she earned her living, and she practiced the game all the time. She had to live hard, like an athlete in training, a pugilist before a battle. Who could tell what strange freak might next occur to the author of a novel, or to a "continuity man," or a director dissatisfied with the progress of a melodrama? She would find herself tied upon a wild horse, or to a log in a saw-mill, or dragged by a rope at the end of a speed-boat, or climbing a church steeple on the outside. In ages past, in lands barbarian and civilized, the hardships of the ascetic life have been imposed upon women for many strange reasons; but was there ever one more freakish than this—that she might appear before the eyes of millions in the aspect of a terror-stricken virgin tearing herself from the hands of lustful ravishers!

Anyway, here she was, a playmate for a young idealist running away from other people's troubles. They would take Annabelle's unused horses, and ride them bareback over the hills to the beach, and gallop them into the surf and swim them there, to the great perplexity of the seals; or they would turn the horses loose, and run foot-races, and turn hand-springs and cart-wheels—Vee would go, a whirlwind of flying white limbs and flying black hair, all the way into the water, and the waves would be no wilder than her laughter. Then they would sit, basking in the sun, and she would tell him stories about Hollywood—and assuredly the waves were no wilder than these. Anything might happen in Hollywood, and in fact had happened—and Vee knew the people it had happened to.

Bunny would go away, and find himself haunted by a figure in a scanty one-piece bathing suit, a figure youthful, sinewy but graceful, vivid, swift. It was evident that she liked him, and Bunny would wake up from his dreams and realize he liked her. He would think about her when he ought to be studying; and his thinking summed itself up in one question, "Why not?"

Echo, in the form of Dad and Mr. Roscoe and Annabelle Ames
and their friends, appeared to be answering, "Why not?" The
one person who would have answered otherwise was Henrietta
Ashleigh, and Henrietta, alas, was now hardly even a memory.
Bunny was not visiting the blue lagoon, nor saying prayers out
of the little black and gold books.

Bunny would call Vee Tracy on the telephone, at the studio
or at her bungalow, and she was always ready for a lark. They
would go to one of the restaurants where the screen folk dined,
and then to one of the theatres where the same folk were pictured, and she would tell him about the private lives of these
people—stories even stranger than the ones made up for them.
Very soon the screen world was putting one and one together
in its gossip. Vee Tracy had picked up a millionaire, an oil
prince—oh, millions and millions! And it was romantic, too,
he was said to be a Bolshevik! The glances and tones of voice
that Bunny encountered gave new echoes of the haunting
question—"Why not?"

IV

Sitting on the beach, half dug into the sand, and staring out
over the blue water, Vee told him something about her life.
"I'm no spring chicken, Bunny, don't imagine it. When I
came into this game, I had my own way to make, and I paid
the price, like every other girl. You'll hear them lie about it,
but don't be fooled; there are no women producers, and no
saints among the men."

Bunny thought it over. "Can't they be satisfied with finding
a good actress?"

"She can be a good actress in the daytime, and a good
mistress at night; the man can have both, and he takes them."

"It sounds rather ghastly," said the other.

"I'll tell you how it is, there's such fierce competition in
this game, if you're going to get ahead, nothing else matters,
nothing else is real. I know it was that way with me; I hung
round the doors of the studios—I was only fifteen—and I
starved and yearned, till I'd have slept with the devil to get
inside."

She sat, staring before her, and Bunny, watching her out of
the corner of his eye, saw that her face was grim.

"There's this to remember too," she added; "a girl meets

a man that has a wad of money, and can take her out in a big car, and buy her a good meal, and a lot of pretty clothes, and set her up in a bungalow, and he's a mighty big man to her, it's easy to think he's something wonderful. It's all right for moralists to sniff, that don't know anything about it; but the plain truth is, the man that came with the cash and offered me my first real start in a picture—he was just about the same as a god to me, and it was only decent to give him what he wanted. I had to live with him a few months, before I knew he was a fat-headed fool."

There was a silence. "I suppose," said Vee, "you're wondering why I tell you this. I'm safe now, I've got some money in the bank, and I might set up for a lady—put on swank and forget the ugly past. If I'd told you I was an innocent virgin, how would you have known? But I said to myself, 'By God, if having money means anything to me, it means I don't have to lie any more.'"

Said Bunny: "I know a man that says that. It made a great impression on me. I'd never known anybody like it before."

"Well, it makes you into a kind of savage. I've got an awful reputation in the picture world—has anybody told you?"

"Not very much," he answered.

She looked at him sharply. "What have they told you? All about Robbie Warden, I suppose?"

"Hardly all," he smiled. "I heard you'd been in love with him, and that you'd sort of been in mourning ever since."

"I made a fool of myself twice over a man; Robbie was the last time, and believe me, it's going to stay the last. He put up the money for the best picture I ever made, and he was handsome as a god, and he begged me to marry him, and I really meant to do it; but all the time he was fooling with two or three other women, and one of them shot him, so that was the end of my bright young dream. No, I'm not in mourning, I'm in rejoicing because I missed a lot of trouble. But if I'm a bit cynical about love, and a bit unrefined in my language, you can figure it out."

And Vee shook the mountain of sand off her bare legs and stood up. "Here's how I keep off the fat," she said, and put her hands down on the sand where it was wet and firm, and stood the rest of herself upon them, her slender white limbs going straight up, and her face, upside down, laughing at

Bunny; in that position she walked by slow handsteps down to the water, and then threw herself over in the other half of a handspring, and lighted on her feet and dashed into the breakers. "Come on in! The water's fine!"

V

Bunny thought over this conversation, and learned from it his usual lesson of humility. Vee had had to fight for her success; whereas he had never had to fight for anything. If he wanted a moving picture career, Dad would arrange it for him, the studio doors would fly open. And the same with any other sort of career he could think of. How could he afford to pass judgment on anybody?

Also, while he listened to Vee Tracy, he had the memory of Eunice Hoyt to keep him humble. No, people didn't know what was right about sex; or at any rate rate, if they did, they didn't make it clear. It was disagreeable to have to think about so many other men; but then, too, it helped to clear the atmosphere. She wouldn't expect to marry him right off; there were marriages among the screen people, but apparently not until they had made sure they were happy. Also, it enabled Bunny to be certain that Vee would not be shocked by the knowledge that she was haunting his dreams.

They were at the Monastery, and had been dancing, and went out upon one of the loggias, or platforms, or terraces, or whatever you call the outside of a cathedral. There was a moon shining down—the same that shone on Bunny and Eunice, and on Bunny and Ethel Goodrich. There was organ music inside, and the scent of flowers outside, and Bunny was thinking to himself, "What am I going to do about this?" It couldn't go on, that was certain; he had got so that he was trembling all over. And yet, somehow, he seemed to be tongue-tied. So far, all the girls had had to propose to him, and it was quite absurd. What the dickens was the matter with him?

In a faltering voice he suggested, "Let's dance." Vee stood up, and he stood up; they had danced out onto this loggia, or terrace or platform, and now they would dance back, and he would be, literally, just where he had been before. No, that wouldn't do! He had a sudden fit of desperation; and instead of the particular kind of embrace which has to do with dancing, he put his arms about her in a way that made it impossible for her to dance. This was a crude procedure, no credit to a junior classman and leader of fashion in a high-toned university. Bunny knew it, and was in a panic. She would not understand—she would be angry, and send him away!

But no, she was not angry; and somehow, she was able to understand. There is an old saying, that fingers were made before forks, and in the same way it is true that embraces were made a long time before words. Bunny became aware that his clasp was being returned—and by a pair of capable arms, that were able to hold a girl upside down in the air and carry her into the surf! It was all right! "Oh, Vee!" he whispered. "Then you do care for me!" Her lips met his, and they stood there in the moonlight, locked together, while the organ music rose to a shout.

"Vee, I was so scared!" And she laughed. "You silly boy!" But suddenly she drew back her head.

"Bunny, I want to talk to you. There's something I must say. Let me go, and sit down, please—no, in that chair over there! I want us to talk quietly."

There was fear in her voice, and he did what she asked. "What is it, Vee?"

"I want us to be sensible, and know what we're doing. It seems to me hardly anybody I know can be happy in love, and I swore to God I never would get into it again."

"You'll have to get a new God!" Bunny had managed to recover the use of his tongue.

"I want us to promise to be happy! Any time we can't be happy, let's quit, and not have any fuss! Let's be sensible, and not go crazy with jealousy, and torment each other."

"You'll be a plenty for me," declared Bunny. "I surely won't make you jealous!"

"You don't know what you'll do! Nobody ever knows! It's the devil's own business—oh, you've no idea what I've seen, Bunny! You're nothing but a babe in arms."

"You'll be good to me, Vee, and raise me up!"

"How do you know what I'll do? How do you know anything about me? You want me, without really knowing what I am or what I'll do! I could have told you a million lies, and how would you have known? The next woman that comes along will tell you a million and one, and how will you know about her?"

"That's too easy, Vee—you'll tell me!"

He sank down on his knees before her, and took one of her hands, intending to comfort her; but she pushed it away. "No, I don't want you to do that. I want you to think about what I'm saying. I want us to decide in cold blood."

"You make my blood cold," he laughed, "telling about the vamps of Hollywood!"

"Bunny, a man and a woman ought to tell each other the truth—all the time. They ought to trust each other that much, no matter how much it hurts. Isn't that so?"

"You bet it's so."

"If that means they give each other up, all right—but they've no business holding each other by lies. Will you make that bargain, Bunny?"

"I will."

"And I want you to know, I don't want any of your money."

"I haven't got any money, Vee—it's all Dad's. That is the first painful truth."

"Well, I don't want it. I've got my own, and I'll take care of myself. I've got a job, and you'll have yours, and we'll let each other alone, and meet when it makes both of us happy."

"That's too easy for a man, Vee!"

"It'll be a game, and those are the rules, and if we break the rules, it's cheating."

Bunny could assure her that he had never cheated in a game, and would not cheat in this one. So he overcame her fears, and she was in his arms again, and they were exchanging those ravishing kisses, of which for a time it seems impossible ever to have enough. Presently she whispered, "Some one will come out here, Bunny. Let me go in, and I'll dance a bit, and then make my excuses and get away, and you come up to my room."

VI

Had anybody seen them in the moonlight? Or had Vee whispered the secret to Annabelle? Or was it just the light of happiness radiating from the eyes of the young couple? Anyhow, it was evident next day that the truth was out, and there was an atmosphere of festivity about the Monastery. Nobody went so far as to sprinkle rice on the pair, or to throw old shoes at them, or tie white ribbons to their cars; but there were friendly smiles, and sly jests, enough to keep the play spirit alive. Annabelle, of course, was enraptured; she had planned this from the beginning, she had picked this young oil prince for her friend from the day that Verne had told her about him. And Verne—well, you can imagine that when he started to make jokes on such a subject, nobody was left in doubt as to what had happened!

Strangely enough, when Bunny got home, he found this spirit of orange blossoms and white ribbons in some mysterious way communicated to Dad. Could it be that Verne, the old rascal, had taken the trouble to telephone the news? Here was Dad, shining with satisfaction, and Bunny could read his every thought. Dad had met Vee Tracy, and liked her fine. A motion picture star—by golly, that was something to brag about! That was the right sort of career for a young oil prince—quite in the aristocratic tradition! Bunny would have something else in his mind now but this fool Bolshevik business!

Presently here was Dad trying to drop hints—with about as much tact as you would expect from a full grown rhinoceros! Had Vee Tracy been up at the Monastery this time? Say, that was a live wire, that girl! Verne said she got as high as four thousand a week; and that was no press agent money either. She had more brains than all the male dolls put together; she had money salted away, owned lots all over Hollywood. She'd come to Verne to ask his advice about Ross Consolidated, and he had told her to go the limit, and by golly, she had brought him a cashier's check for fifty thousand dollars, and had got a block of the stock at the opening price, and now it was worth three times that, and Vee said that Verne had saved her from six rapings! Then the old rhinoceros went on and explained what Vee had meant—that she wouldn't have to act in six pictures!

And then there was Bertie, who got the news at once because it happened that Charlie Norman's bootlegger was in love with Annabelle Ames' sister. Right away Bertie was curious to meet Vee Tracy, and ordered Bunny to bring her to lunch. Vee was uneasy about this—declaring that sisters always poisoned men against sweethearts. But Bunny laughed and said he had plenty of antitoxins against Bertie. So they met, and everything went off beautifully; Vee was humble, and anxious to please, and Bertie was the great lady, supremely gracious. That was according to the proprieties, for Vee was only an actress, while Bertie was in real "society," her doings appearing in a sanctified part of the newspaper, where the

screen people seldom broke in. After the luncheon, Bertie
told her brother that Vee was all right, and maybe she would
teach him a little sense; which, from a sister, was the limit of
cordiality.

So there they were, everything hunkydory. Bunny's sleep
was no longer disturbed by dreams; the dream had become a
reality, and it was his. When they visited the Monastery, they
were placed in connecting rooms; and when he went to visit
Vee at her bungalow, the discreet elderly lady who kept house
for her would quietly disappear. As for the moving picture
colony, it said nothing more—having already said everything
there was to say.

Bunny would call Vee on the telephone, and if it was a
Saturday or holiday, they would make a date; but if it was a
week-day, Vee would say, "No, Bunny, you ought to stay home
and study."

He would answer, "Oh, bosh, Vee, I'm a whole week ahead
of my classes."

"But Bunny, if I make you neglect your work, your father
will get down on me!"

"Dad's more in love with you than I am! He thinks you're
the brightest star in the movie zodiac."

"We just mustn't overdo it, Bunny! Your conscience will
get to troubling you, and you'll blame it on me."

"Dog-gone-it, Vee, you boss me worse than if we were
Annabelle and Roscoe."

"Well, let me tell you, if I manage to keep my oil prince as
long as Annabelle has kept her's, I'll count myself a lucky
woman!"

VII

Gregor Nikolaieff was back from his trip to Alaska, with
more troubles for the conscience of a young idealist. Gregor
was gaunt and hollow-eyed, like Paul returned from Siberia.
Poor unsuspecting foreign youth—he had shipped on what the
sailors call "the hell fleet of the Pacific," and had found himself trapped in a desolate bay, walled in by mountains on one
side and ocean on the other, housed in barracks whose floors
were wet by the tides, sleeping in vermin-ridden bunks, and
eating food like that fed to the inmates of county jails. No
way of escape, save on ships that would not take you! While

Bunny had been romping in the Pacific with Vee and the seals, Gregor had been near to drowning himself in the same ocean.

Also Rachel Menzies had come home, with more troubles; there was a strike of the clothing workers! Quite unforeseen and spontaneous—hundreds of workers, driven beyond endurance by petty oppressions, had walked out in the middle of a job; the movement had spread all over this Angel City, paradise of the "open shop." The workers were crowding into the union offices and signing up, and a regular mass-struggle was under way. But Papa Menzies, one of the intellectuals among the strikers, a man of force and insight—Papa Menzies was sitting at home, with his frantic Hebrew wife clinging to his coat-tails and wailing that if he went out and took part in the strike, the police would get him and ship him off to Poland to be shot, and never to see his family again!

As a result of this strike, Rachel was not going to be able to come to college. Bunny, elegant young gentleman of leisure, who had never known what it was to need money in his life, could not understand this, and had to be told in plain words that Rachel's family had been making sacrifices to get her an education, and all these plans were knocked out. Then of course Bunny wanted to get Dad to help; what was the use of having a rich father, if you couldn't serve your friends in a pinch? But Rachel answered no, they had always been independent, and she would not think of such a thing; she would have to skip a term in the university.

"But then you won't be in my class!" exclaimed Bunny—realizing suddenly how much he needed an antitoxin for the dullness of Southern Pacific culture!

"It's very kind of you, Mr. Ross," she answered, sedately. "But perhaps you will come to the meetings of the Socialist local."

"But see here, really, I can get the money without the least trouble; and you don't have to consider it a gift, you can pay it back when you want to. Won't it be easier to earn money if you have a college degree?"

Rachel admitted that; she had meant to get a position as a social worker—she had come to this university because there were special courses which would make such a career possible. Bunny pleaded, why not take Dad's money, with no strings to it whatever, and pay him back ten or twenty dollars a month out of her future salary. But Rachel was stubborn

—some strange impulse born of her "class-consciousness."

He felt so keenly about it that without saying anything to her, he got into his car and drove to the home of the Menzies family. He had the address in his notebook, and it did not occur to him that she or her family might be embarrassed to have him see the way they lived—in a wretched slum district, crowded into a little three-room house on the back of a lot, without a shred of a green thing in sight. It was a rented place, Papa Menzies having put his money into Socialism, instead of into real estate and shrubbery. Bunny found him in a crowded front room, with furniture and books, and a job of sewing, and the remains of a meal of bread and herring, and the proofs of an article which he was getting ready for a strike bulletin, and a fat old Jewish lady rushing about in a panic, trying to put things away from the sight of this alarmingly fashionable visitor.

None of that bothered the old man; he was used to confusion, and all wrapped up in the strike. He told Bunny about it, and read his article, a bitter statement of the grievances of the clothing workers. And then Bunny got down to the question of Rachel and her education, insisting that Chaim Menzies should persuade his daughter not to give up her career. Mrs. Menzies sat. staring with her large dark eyes, trying to understand; and suddenly she broke into a torrent of excited Yiddish, of which it was just as well that Bunny could not make out a word. For Mamma Menzies placed no trust in this handsome young goy, and put the worst possible construction upon his visit; he was trying to lure their daughter into sin, and maybe he had already done so—who could tell what sort of life she was living, with all these atheist and Socialist ideas in her head, and going to a college run by a lot of Krists!

Papa Menzies bade her sternly to hold her tongue, which according to the Hebrew law she was supposed to do; but apparently she took her Hebrew law with as many allowances as the Krists took their's. In the middle of her torrents of Yiddish, Chaim thanked Bunny for his kindness, and explained that what was worrying Rachel was the hard time the family would have during the strike. If Bunny would help the family, then it would be easy for Rachel to help herself. So they shook hands, and Bunny went home to report to Dad that he had acquired the responsibility of supporting half a dozen Jewish clothing workers!

VIII

Bunny was back at Southern Pacific. It was the line of least resistance; a nice, clean occupation, honorific and easy on the nerves. One who was good-looking and wealthy, and knew how to charm the professors, could get by with almost no work at all, and have abundant time to read Bolshevik propaganda, and watch strikes happen; also to sport about town with a moving picture star, to drive and dine and dance with her, and escort her to week-end parties of the Hollywood élite.

He might even have found time to visit the studio and watch her at work on her new picture; but she would not let him do this. She was too much in love with him, she could not concentrate with him looking on. Moreover, she said, her work was horrid, all pictures were horrid; Bunny wouldn't like what she was doing. It was just a way she earned her living, and she had to do what other people told her; it was without any relation to life, and Bunny, who was serious and educated, would think it childish, or worse. She liked him to be serious, he was a dear and all that, and one of the few men who really could tell her something about the world; he must go on being like that, and not pay any attention to her pictures.

It struck Bunny as a little mysterious; she protested too much. And before long he discovered the reason—in some of the gossip about the screen world which filled pages upon pages of the newspapers. Vee Tracy was working on a picture about Russia! She was to be a beautiful princess of the old regime, caught in the storm of the revolution, falling into the hands of the Bolsheviks, and making one of her famous "get-aways" with the aid of a handsome young American secret service man! Vee had been working on this picture for the past six months; and right in the middle of it, she had gone and got herself a "parlor Bolshevik" for a lover, and now was afraid to let him know what she was doing!

Poor Bunny, he was making such earnest and devoted efforts to ride on two horses at once! And the horses kept getting farther and farther apart, until he was all but split in the middle! Here was this strike of the clothing workers, breaking in upon the peace of America's premier "open shop" city. It was the climax of a series of disorders—first a walk-out of the street railwaymen, and then of the carpenters; it was evident that the program of the reds, "boring from within," was having a terrifying success, and the thing had to be stopped, once for all. The city council passed an anti-picketing ordinance, which forbade anyone to even make an ugly face in front of a place where there was a strike. Since not all the clothing workers had faces of natural beauty, there was much infringement of this law, and very soon the papers were full of accounts of riots, valiently put down by the police. A part of Bunny's curriculum at the university consisted of having Rachel Menzies describe to him and the rest of the "red bunch" how girls who were doing nothing but walking up and down the street in pairs, were being seized by the police and having their arms twisted out of joint.

Then one morning Rachel did not show up in class; next day came a note for Bunny telling him that Jacob Menzies had been clubbed almost insensible on the picket-line. Jacob was the "right wing" brother, the pale, stoop-shouldered one who had been earning his education by pressing students' pants; and Bunny had so far departed from the safe rule of dodging other people's troubles that he felt it his duty to drive over to the Menzies' home, and have his feelings harrowed by the sight of Jacob Menzies in bed, pale as the sheets, and with a Hindoo turban wound about his head. There was Mamma Menzies, with tears streaming down her cheeks, wailing over and over one Yiddish word that Bunny could understand—"Oi! Oi! Oi!" Chaim Menzies, the father, was nowhere to be seen, because he had torn his coat-tails loose from his wife's fingers, and was over at strike headquarters, doing his duty.

The next afternoon, coming out from his classes, Bunny saw on a newsstand the familiar green color of the "Evening Booster," and his eye was caught—as it was meant to be caught —by flaring headlines:

POLICE RAID RED CENTER

So Bunny purchased a paper—as it was meant that he should do—and read how that morning a squad from police headquarters had invaded the rooms of the clothing workers' union, and taken off nearly a truck-load of documents which were expected to prove that the disturbance in the city's industry was being directed and financed by the red revolutionists of Moscow. The officials of the union were under arrest, one of those apprehended being Chaim Menzies, "self-confessed socialistic agitator."

IX

So there was another job for Bunny. He didn't know quite how to set about it, and Dad was on the way to Paradise, and could not be consulted. Bunny went to see Dad's lawyer, Mr. Dolliver, a keen-witted, soft-spoken gentleman who had no sympathy with reds, but, like all lawyers, was prepared for any weird trouble his wealthy clients might bring along. He called up police headquarters and ascertained that the self-confessed socialistic agitator was to be arraigned the following day; bail would be set at that time, and it would be up to Bunny to have the cash on hand, or real estate to twice the amount. Bunny said he wanted to see the prisoner, and Mr. Dolliver said he knew the chief of police, and might be able to arrange it.

He wrote a note, and Bunny went over to the dingy old building which had been erected to serve a city of fifty thousand, and was now serving one of a million. The chief proved to be a burly person in civilian clothing, smelling strongly of civilian whiskey; he requested Bunny to sit down, and summoned a couple of detectives, and began an obvious effort to find out all that Bunny knew about Chaim Menzies, and Bunny's ideas, and Chaim's ideas. And Bunny, who was growing up fast in an ugly world, gave a carefully phrased exposition of the difference between the right and left wings of the Socialist movement. Finding that he could not be trapped into indiscretions, and knowing that he was a millionaire's son, and could not be thrown into a cell, the chief gave him up, and told one of the detectives to take him in to see the prisoner.

So Bunny got a glimpse of his city's jail. The old building was cracked, and had been condemned as a menace to life by half a dozen successive commissions; nevertheless, here it was, a monument to the greed of real estate speculators, who cared nothing about a city's good name, provided only its tax-rate were low. The mouldy old place stank, and if you looked carefully, you might see vermin crawling on the walls. The prisoners were confined in a number of "tanks," which were steel-barred cages holding thirty or forty men each, with no ray of daylight, and not enough artificial light to enable anyone to read. This city, so oddly named "Angel," appeared anxious to cultivate all possible vices in its victims, for it provided them no reading matter, and no exercise or recreation, but permitted them to have cards, dice and cigarettes—and the jailers secretly smuggled in whiskey and cocaine to such as had money for bribes.

In one of these tanks sat Papa Menzies—on the floor, since there was no other place to sit. He appeared quite contented, having gathered round him the entire congregation of the cell, to hear about the struggle of the clothing workers, and how it was up to the toilers of the world to organize and abolish the capitalist system. When Bunny appeared, the old man jumped up and grabbed him by the hand; and Bunny said quickly, "Mr. Menzies, you should know that this gentleman with me is a detective."

Papa Menzies grinned. "Sure, I got notting to hide. I been a member of de Socialist party for tventy years. I believe in de ballot box—dey vill find notting to de contrary, unless dey make it. I have been telling dese boys vat Socialism is, and I vill tell dis gentleman, if he vants to listen. I have been helping de cloding vorkers stand togedder for decent conditions, and I am going on vid it de day I git out again." So that was that!

And in the evening Bunny phoned to his father and told him the situation. Bunny had been accustomed to sign his father's name to checks of any size, and had been careful not to abuse the privilege; but now he was proposing to draw fifteen thousand dollars, because they would probably fix the bail very high, in the hope of keeping the old man in jail until the strike had been broken. There was no risk involved, Bunny declared, for Menzies was the soul of honor, and would not run away.

Dad made a wry face over the telephone—but what could he do? His dearly beloved son was ablaze with indignation, and insisted that he knew all about it, there was no possibility whatever that this old clothing worker might be a secret agent of the Soviet government, deliberately planted in Angel City to destroy American institutions. How Bunny could know such things Dad couldn't imagine, but he had never known his boy to be so wrought up, and finally he said all right, but to have Mr. Dolliver send somebody to court with the money, so that Bunny would not get his name into the newspapers again.

X

The matter was handled as Dad ordered; the lawyer's clerk went to court, and came back and reported that the prisoners had appeared, but Chaim Menzies had not been among them. His case had been taken over by the Federal authorities, because it had been discovered that he was born in Russian Poland, and it was proposed to cancel his naturalization papers and deport him. Chaim had been transferred to the county jail, another condemned structure, fully as dingy and filthy as the city jail. There was no longer anything you could do about it, because in these deportation cases the courts were refusing to intervene, holding them to be administrative matters. The Democratic attorney-general had failed in his effort to get the nomination for president by his campaign against the reds, but the machinery he had set going was still grinding out misery for guilty and innocent alike.

So here was some real trouble for Bunny! Over at the Menzies home was Rachel, white-faced and pacing the floor, and Mamma Menzies wailing and tearing her clothing. It was impossible even to get word to poor Chaim—he was "incommunicado"; indeed, he might already have been put onto a train for the east. After that there would be no chance for him whatever—he would be dumped onto a steamer for Dantzig, and there turned over to the Polish "white terror."

Bunny insisted that something must be tried, and so Mr. Dolliver called in a couple of still more expensive lawyers—at Dad's expense— and they debated habeas corpuses and injunctions and other mystical formulas, and made out a lot of papers and tried this court and that, all in vain. Meantime, in response to frantic commands from his son, Dad broke the speed laws from Paradise; and when he arrived, there were Bunny and his Jewish girl-friend waiting on his front porch. They dragged him into his den and made him listen to a disquisition on the difference between the right and left wings of the Socialist movement, with a complete description of the activities of a literature agent of the Socialist party. In the middle of it Rachel burst into tears, and sank down upon the sofa; and Dad, who was really no more able to stand a woman weeping than was Bunny, went over and patted her on the shoulder, and said, "There, there, little girl, never mind! I'll get him out, even if I have to send a man to New York!"

So Dad stepped out and sped away in his car. That was about lunch-time—and a little before three o'clock of that same day, who should emerge from a taxi-cab in front of the Menzies tenement but Chaim himself, dirty and unshaven, but smiling and serene, and ready to continue his labors for his "cloding vorkers"! He hadn't the least idea how it had happened; the keepers of the county jail had volunteered no information as they turned him loose, and Chaim had not stopped for questions. He never did know, and neither did his daughter, for what Dad told Bunny was strictly confidential, a bit of oil men's secret lore.

"What did I do? I called in an old friend of ours, Ben Skutt."

"Ben Skutt!" Bunny had not thought of their "lease hound" for years.

"Yes, Ben is high up in this defense business now, and he did it for me."

"What did you tell him?"

"Tell him? I told him one grand."

"One what?"

"That's bootlegger's slang. I gave him five hundred dollars, and said, 'Ben, go and see the man that's got that old kike in jail and tell him to turn him loose, and then come back to me and I'll give you another five hundred!'"

"My God!" said Bunny.

And Dad took a couple of puffs at his big cigar. "Now you see why we oil men have to be in politics!"

XI

Besides completing Bunny's political education, this incident was important to him in another way; it was the cause of Vee Tracy's taking over the management of his life. Ross senior got the moving picture lady on the telephone that very evening, and he said, "Look here, Vee, you're laying down on your job!"

"How do you mean, Mr. Ross?"

"My name is Dad," said the voice, "and what I mean is that you're not taking care of my son like I wanted you to do. He's been a-gettin' into trouble with these Bolshevikis again, and it's all because you don't see enough of him."

"But Mr.—Dad—I've been trying to make him study—I thought that was what you wanted."

"Well, you forget about him studyin', that's all bunk, it ain't a-goin' to do him no good, and besides, he don't do it; he jist goes off to Socialist meetin's, and he'd better be with you."

"Oh, Dad!" There was a little catch in Vee's voice. "There's nothing I'd like better! I'm just crazy about that boy!"

"Well, you take him under your wing and keep him there, and if you can get him loose from these reds, I'll remember you in my will."

So after that Bunny found that he could have a date with his beloved at any hour of the day or night. She never told him the reason—no, her idea of truth-telling did not go that far! She let him think it was because of his overwhelming charms, and his male egotism was satisfied with the explanation. She would make feeble pretenses at resistance. "Oh, Bunny, Dad will think I'm wasting your time, he'll call me a vamp!" And Bunny would answer, "You goose, he knows that if I'm not with you, I may be off at some Socialist meeting."

They were so happy, so happy! The rapture of fresh young souls and fresh young bodies, eager, quivering in every nerve! Their love suffused their whole beings; everything became touched with magic—the sound of their voices, the gestures of their hands, even the clothing they wore, the cars they drove, the houses they lived in. They flew together—the telephone girls were overworked keeping them in touch. Bunny became what in the slang of the time was known as a "one-arm driver"; also he studied the arts of cajoling professors and cutting lectures. His conscience was easy, for had he not done his duty by the Socialist movement, with that "one grand" of Dad's? Besides, the strike was over, and the clothing workers had won a few concessions; the leaders had been released, and the promised "Moscow revelations" forgotten by the newspapers, and therefore by everybody else.

Vee would still not let Bunny come to the studio where she was working. For the next picture, perhaps, but not this one; he and his Bolsheviks wouldn't like it, and he must put off seeing it as long as possible. But all the rest of her time was his—every precious instant! The elderly housekeeper received a five dollar bill now and then, and was deaf, dumb and blind. Vee's room in the bungalow was upstairs, the only second-story room, open on all four sides, and with ivy wreathing its windows; inside it was all white, a bower of loveliness. Here they belonged to each other; and tears of ecstasy would come into Vee's eyes. "Oh, Bunny, Bunny! I swore I'd never do this; and here I am, worse in love than I ever dreamed! Bunny, if you desert me, I shall die!" He would smother her fears in kisses; it was a case for the application of another old saying, that actions speak louder than words!

There was no cloud in the sky of their happiness; except just one little cloud, no bigger than a man's hand! Bunny did not see it at all; and the woman saw it for an instant or so, and then looked the other way. Oh, surely the rose will bloom forever!

XII

The hands of destiny, turning upon the face of the movie clock, had brought Vee's hour of glory again. The great picture was ready, and once more she was on all the billboards of the city: "Schmolsky-Superba presents Viola Tracy in the twelve-reel Superspecial, 'The Devil's Deputy, Million Dollar Heart Drama of the Russian Revolution.'" The scene which ornamented the billboards disclosed Vee, as usual with her lingerie torn, crouching in the arms of the ineffably handsome young American secret service agent, and the agent presenting a revolver to a mass of tangled black whiskers, behind which hideous foreign faces lurked.

Also there was publicity in the newspapers, columns and columns about the picture, the authors of the book, the continuity man and the director and the writer of the titles and the artists and the decorators and the costumers and the musicians; but most of all about the star. Was it to be expected that the publicity man should drop no hint to the reporters about the fascinating young oil prince who had now become Miss Tracy's most intimate friend? It had been expected by Bunny, and maybe by Dad, but assuredly not by anyone else. The reporters laid siege to the young prince, and sweet, sentimental sob-sister ladies sought to lure him into revealing how it felt to be the very, very dearest dear friend of such a brilliantly scintillating star of the movie heavens. One day it was rumored they were engaged to marry, and the next day they were not; and if they said nothing, the reporters knew what they ought to have said. And when Bunny would not give his picture, they snapped him on the street, and when he turned his face away, they gave it a jolly caption: "Oil Prince Is Shy!"

"The Devil's Deputy" was to have its "world premiere" at Gloobry's Million Dollar Melanesian Theatre; and these "world premieres" are, as you may know, the great social events of Southern California. Searchlights search the clouds and bombs boom in the sky; red fire makes an imitation Hades in the streets, and kleig lights make day in the arcade which the million dollar Melanesians hold upright upon their naked shoulders. The crowds pack the streets, and swarms of burglars invade the city, because all the police department is required to make a pathway for the movie stars as they move in their appointed courses, from their shining ten thousand dollar limousines, across the sidewalk and through the arcade and under the million dollar portals. The kleigs glare upon them, and a dozen moving picture cameras grind, and flashlights boom, and the crowd surges and quivers and murmurs with ecstasy.

Never in all human history has there been such glory; never have the eyes of mortals beheld such royal pageantry! Trappers and hunters have perished in the icy wastes of the arctic to bring the ermines and sables in which these queens are robed; divers have been torn by sharks to bring up their pearls from the depths of tropic seas, and miners have been crushed in the deep earth to dig their blazing diamonds; chemists have blown themselves up in search for their cosmetics and dyes, and seamstresses have grown blind embroidering the elaborate designs which twinkle upon their silken ankles. All this concentrated in one brief glory-march—do you wonder that heads are high and glances regal? Or that the crowd surges, and rushes wildly, and women faint, and ambulances come clanging?

Inside the theatre, over the head of one of the million dollar Melanesians, is a huge megaphone; and as the great ones descend from their cars, a giant's voice acquaints the audience with their progress. "Mr. Abraham Schmolsky is coming through the arcade. Mr. Schmolsky is accompanied by Mrs. Schmolsky. Mrs. Schmolsky wears a blue satin opera cloak trimmed with chinchilla, made by Voisin, just brought by Mrs. Schmolsky from Paris. Mrs. Schmolsky wears her famous tiara of diamonds. Mr. and Mrs. Schmolsky are now entering the theatre. Mr. and Mrs. Schmolsky have stopped to talk with Mr. and Mrs. Jacob Gloobry."

And so on and on, thrill after thrill—until at last, exactly at the sacred hour of eight-thirty, the supreme, the superthrill of the evening:

"Miss Viola Tracy is descending from her car. Miss Tracy is accompanied by her friend, Mr. J. Arnold Ross, junior, discoverer and heir-apparent of the Ross Junior oil field, of Paradise, California. Miss Tracy and Mr. Ross are coming through the arcade. Miss Tracy wears a cloak of gorgeous ermine furs; her slippers are of white satin, trimmed with pearls. She wears a collar of pearls and a pearl head-dress, presented to her by Mr. J. Arnold Ross, senior. Miss Tracy and Mr. Ross junior are in the lobby, shaking hands with Mr. and Mrs. Schmolsky and Mr. and Mrs. Gloobry"—and so on, until Miss Tracy and Mr. Ross junior are in their seats, and history is at liberty to begin.

XIII

So Bunny saw the Russian picture. His beloved was the beautiful bride of a grand duke; the gestures, the kisses, the raptures of love, which had been rehearsed upon himself, were now lavished upon a magnificent, sharp-whiskered personage in a military uniform with many stars and orders. This personage was haughty but high-minded, and his grand duchess was the soul of charity; and oh, such lovely gentle peasants as she had to exercise her charity upon! How sweetly they courtsied, how charmingly they danced, and gathered to cheer and throw flowers after the grand ducal carriage! It was a beautiful, almost idyllic world—one was tempted really to doubt whether any world so perfect ever had existed on earth.

There was only one thing wrong with it, and that was a secret band of villains with twisted, degenerate faces, some of them with wild hair and big spectacles, others with ferocious black whiskers and knives in their boots. They met to concoct anarchist manifestoes, intended to seduce the sweet innocent peasants; and to make dynamite bombs to blow up noble-minded grand dukes. They drank in booze-dens, and grabbed women by the arms and man-handled them, right out before one another. There was no wickedness these creatures did not do, and their leader, with the face of a rat and the arms of a gorilla, made evident to the dullest mind why the picture was called "The Devil's Deputy."

Then came the young secret service man, clean-cut, smooth-shaven, quick on the trigger. His job was to get messages from the American embassy to the American fleet, and later on to save the treasure of the embassy from the Bolsheviks. For of course you know what happened in Russia—how this band of villains with twisted faces rose up and overthrew the government, and killed the haughty but just grand duke with cruel tortures. It was, of course, the grand duchess that the Devil's Deputy especially wanted; and first he chased her about the castle, and battered in the doors, and the young secret service hero dashed with her from room to room. Blood ran down his face from a bullet wound, but he carried her out of a window of the castle, and away they flew on horseback, over hills and dales covered with the familiar Russian eucalyptus trees.

And then presently they were trapped in St. Petersburg, and the Devil's Deputy laid his foul hands on Vee, and tore her lingerie to shreds, as the billboards had promised you he would. But here came the hero with his automatic, and he held the mob at bay, while Vee behind her back made signals to a friend of the hero who was preparing one of the villains' own bombs to throw at them—could you imagine more poetic justice than that? Vee and her savior fled, this time in a motor-car, over roads of the well-known Russian concrete, through the well-known mountains of the suburbs of St. Petersburg, and came to the River Neva, with its eucalyptus groves concealing a speed-boat. There was another mad chase, which ended in the capture of the agonized pair, and more tearing of Vee's lingerie by the Devil's Deputy.

But—don't be worried—at the most critical instant came the American Navy, that whole glorious flotilla which we kept in the River Neva during the war. Old Glory floated in the breeze, and the band played "The Stars and Stripes Forever," and the million dollar audience burst into enraptured cheering. A launch from a battleship came dashing up, the Devil's Deputy leaped into the water with one of his own bombs in his mouth, and Viola Tracy and the secret service man stood clasped in an attitude which was familiar to Bunny, and hardly less so to the million dollar audience.

All the time this story was unfolding, Bunny was privileged to sit and hold the heroine's hand. Once she leaned to him and whispered, "Is it so very bad?" His answer was, "It is up to standard. It will sell." It was the formula she had used with

Annabelle Ames; and Bunny felt a tight pressure of his hand. It was clever of him, as well as kind!

XIV

The screen was dark, and the cheering died away, and the lights came up, and the moving picture world crowded about Vee Tracy, and Mr. Schmolsky, the producer, and Tommy Paley, the director, and all the rest of the personages whose services had been faithfully catalogued on the film. There was hand-shaking and chatter; and meantime the crowds stood about, gaping at the celebrities—it was hard to get the theatre empty after a "world premiere." The throngs in the lobby, and outside in the arcade, were still held back by the police— many had stood for three hours, in order to see their favorites emerge.

Vee and her lover went out among the last, greeting this one, greeting that one, the observed of all observers. Bunny saw many he knew, and among them one face he had not expected—Rachel Menzies! She saw him, and he saw that she saw him; and straightway it became a point of honor with a young idealist, he must not fail to treat her as well as any-body else. Rachel, a poor working-girl, and class-conscious, pitiful in a dingy, worn coat and a faded, out-of-fashion hat— Rachel must not think that he would slight her in this expensive company! He went straight to her. "How do you do, Miss Menzies? I didn't know you were a movie fan."

"I'm not," she answered. "But I wanted to see what they would do to the Russian revolution."

"There wasn't much in it for us," said Bunny; and she answered, grimly, "No, there was not."

He would have liked to talk with her, but not in this place. "Can I help you out?" he asked; and turned as if to seek a way through the crowd.

But at that moment came Vee! With all the throngs of the great ones about her, with all the praise they poured upon her, there was one thing she really cared about, and that was Bunny—she did not want to be separated from him! And straightway, of course, the honor of a young idealist was still more deeply involved. He must not be unwilling to introduce his dingy working-girl friend to the gorgeous lady of the ermines and pearls! "Meet Miss Viola Tracy," he said. "Vee, this is Miss Rachel Menzies, a class-mate of mine at the university."

Equally, it was a point of honor with Vee to be cordial. "Oh, how do you do, Miss Menzies?" And she held out her hand. Rachel did not move to take the hand, but stood very stiff and straight, and answered, "How do you do, Miss Tracy." To Bunny, who knew her, the voice sounded strange and dead; but of course Vee had no means of knowing what her voice ought to be, and the withheld hand might easily be shyness at meeting the most important person in all Hollywood that night. Vee was still cordial as she inquired, "And how did you like the picture?"

Bunny heard that question—more dangerous than any bomb ever made by a Devil's Deputy! He groped in his bewildered mind for something to say—"Miss Menzies is a Socialist, like me"—anything of that playful sort; but before he could get his tongue to move, Rachel had answered, swift and deadly, "I think it's the most poisonous thing I ever saw on the screen."

There was no mistaking that for shyness, or anything else. And Viola Tracy stared at this amazing creature. "Oh, indeed, Miss!"

"Yes, and people who helped to make it will someday have on their conscience the blood of millions of young men."

Bunny broke in, "You see, Vee—"

But she put out her hand to stop him. "Wait! I want to know what you mean!"

"I mean that this picture is part of the propaganda to get us into a war with Russia, and a woman that lends herself to such work is a disgrace to her sex."

Vee glared, and fury leaped into her face. "You bitch!" she cried, and her hand shot out, and smack! she landed a blow across Rachel's cheek.

For one horrible moment Bunny stood numb; he saw the red start to Rachel's face, and the tears start to her eyes; then he sprang between them, and caught Vee's hand to stop another blow. "No, Vee, no!" A burly policeman completed the job of blocking the way between the two antagonists, and Rachel faded back into the crowd—something it was easy enough to do, since everybody was pushing to the front. In the confusion Bunny became aware of one hideous thing—a young man jabbing at them and demanding, "What is it? What is the matter? What happened, Miss Tracy? What was the trouble, officer?" Bunny whispered into Vee's ear, "Quick! It's a reporter!" He grasped her arm, and they fled through the crowd.

XV

Sitting in their car, with Bunny driving, Vee whispered, "Who is that woman?"

"Her family are Jewish clothing workers. Her father's the man who got arrested—don't you remember I told you?"

"Oh! That girl!"

"Yes. You see, you stepped on her class-consciousness." Vee's teeth were clenched. "Oh, the odious creature!"

"But Vee! Don't forget you asked her what she thought."

"Oh, so insolent! Outrageous!"

"But dear, you take the liberty of saying what you think. Don't you grant her the same right?"

"Bunny! You are going to defend her!" And before he could reply, she cried, in a voice of fury, "I hate those people, I hate them! They're nasty, they're low, they're jealous—they haven't an idea but to take away things from people who've slaved to earn them."

There was a long silence. Bunny drove; and when Vee spoke again, it was to ask, "Where are you going?"

"Don't forget the Schmolsky's supper party."

"No, I won't go to any supper party, it would choke me. Take me home—right away."

He obeyed; and when she was in the bungalow, she fled to her room. He followed, and found the ermine cloak on the floor, and Vee in a heap on the bed, without regard to the costliest of embroidered silk gowns. She was convulsed with sobbing, and he made out the words, "It's going to ruin us!"

Suddenly she sat up, blinded by her tears, and stretched out her arms. "Oh, Bunny, Bunny, don't let's have our love killed! Don't let's quarrel like all the others! Bunny, I don't care about those people, they can say anything they please to me, I'll never mind again! I'll apologize to that girl, I'll let her walk on me, I'll do anything you say! But oh, please don't let's stop loving each other!"

It was the first time he had ever seen Vee break down; and of course it always produces a great impression upon the protective male. He took her in his arms, tears and all, without regard to the costliest of broadcloth evening suits. Their love flamed up, and their troubles were melted in the fire, and they swore that nothing, nothing should ever, ever tear them apart.

Long afterwards, as they lay in each other's arms, Vee whispered, "Bunny, that girl is in love with you!"

"Oh, absurd, Vee!"

"Why do you say so?"

"She's never given the least sign of such a thing."

"How would you know a sign?"

"But dear—"

"Of course she's in love with you! How could anybody fail to be in love with you, Bunny?"

It was not worth while to try to argue. It appeared to be a peculiarity of women, they were always sure that all other women were in love with their man. When he had told Vee about Henrietta Ashleigh, she had been sure that Henrietta was desperately enamored, and that only her pride of caste had kept her from trying to hold him. Likewise, when he told her about Ruth, she was sure this poor country lass was pining her heart out. That was the reason she was so indifferent to the charms of oil-workers, and not because she was wrapped up in Paul. Sisters didn't make so much fuss over brothers—no, that was rubbish! Bunny remembered that Bertie said this same thing; and strangely enough, Eunice Hoyt had said it also—it had been one reason why she hated to have him go up to Paradise. Bunny decided that it was better not to tell women about one another; and especially not to introduce them, if it could possibly be avoided!

Morning came, and the newspapers were outside the door of their room. Sitting up in bed in silken garments they devoured—no, not the elaborate accounts of the world premiere with details of the gowns worn by the women—that would come later. First, their eyes leaped to the headline:

STAR SLAPS RIVAL IN LOBBY

There it was! The reporter, having been unable to get the real story, had made the inevitable romantic assumption. Another triangle of the screen world! He had written a highly playful article about the world-famous star, emerging in the hour of her glory upon the arm of the young oil prince—about whom so many interesting rumors were being circulated. Seeing him leave her side and join some other woman, the star had rushed over in a fit of jealous fury and smacked the other woman in the face. There was an interview with Officer Tony Reber of the Angel City police department, who had stepped between the enfuriated combatants. The star had called her rival an awful name, which the officer's modesty would not permit him to repeat. "But I'll say this," he told the world, "She certainly packs an awful punch, that lady. If I was to hit anybody as hard as that I would sure get canned."

XVI

Bunny met the other combatant on the campus that same day, and her face was pale and her dark eyes sombre. "Mr. Ross," she began, quickly, "I want to tell you I'm ashamed for what I said."

"You don't have to be ashamed," he replied. "It was true."

"I know, but I had no right to say it to a friend of yours, and after all you have done for me. It was just that I was so wrought up over that picture."

"I understand," Bunny said. "Miss Tracy wishes me to tell you she is truly sorry for what she did."

"I know, you'd make her sorry. But I don't care about that—we Jews have been struck many times, and we workers also, and there'll be more of it before the class war is over. The real harm is one she can never atone for—that hideous picture that's going out to poison the people's minds—millions upon millions of them. For that she can never apologize."

It was an aspect of the matter that had somehow fallen into the background of Bunny's consciousness during all the excitement. "I've nothing good to say about the picture," he replied, "but I think you must make allowances for Miss Tracy. She doesn't know as much about Russia as you and I."

"You mean she doesn't know there were hideous cruelties in old Russia—that the Tsardom was another word for terror?"

"Yes, but then—"

"She doesn't know that the men she portrays as criminals have most of them been in the dungeons of the Tsar for the sake of their faith?"

"She may not know that, Miss Menzies. It's hard to realize how ignorant people can be, when they read nothing but American newspapers and magazines."

"Well, Mr. Ross, you know that I'm not a Bolshevik; but

we have to defend the workers of Russia from world reaction. That picture is a part of the white terror, and the people that made it knew exactly what they were doing—just as much as when they beat my brother over the head and started to deport my father."

"Yes," said Bunny, "but you must understand, an actress does not write the story, and she's not always consulted about the parts she plays."

"Ah, Mr. Ross!" Rachel's face wore a pitying smile. "She would tell you that, and you're so anxious to believe the best about people! Well, I'm going to tell you what I think, and maybe you won't ever speak to me again. A woman who makes a picture like that is nothing but a prostitute, and the fact that she's highly paid makes her all the more loathsome."

"Oh, Miss Menzies!"

"I know, it sounds cruel. But that's a murder picture, and that woman knew it perfectly well. They paid her money and jewels and fur cloaks and silk lingerie, and her face on the billboards and in all the newspapers; and she took the price—as she's done many times before. I don't know one thing about her private life, Mr. Ross, but I'll wager that if you investigate, you'll find she's sold herself, body as well as mind, all the way from the bottom up to the pedestal she's on now!"

And so Bunny decided that he had better postpone for a while the plan he had had in mind, of having Vee Tracy and Rachel Menzies meet and understand each other!

CHAPTER XV

THE VACATION

I

All this summer and fall, Dad and Mr. Roscoe had been carrying a heavy burden—they were helping to make over the thinking of the American people. A presidential campaign was under way; and the oil men, having made so bold as to select the candidate, now had to finish the job by persuading the voters that he was a great and noble-minded statesman. Also they had to pay a part of the expense, which would come to fifty million dollars, so Bunny learned from the conversations at Paradise and at the Monastery. This was several times as much as would get recorded, since the money went through local and unofficial agencies. It came from the big protected interests, the corporations, the banks—everyone that had anything to get out of the government, or could be squeezed by politicians; the process was known as "frying out the fat." The oil men, having grabbed the big prize, were naturally a shining mark for all campaign committees, county, state and national. Dad and Mr. Roscoe received visits from Jake Coffey, and from the bosses of the state machine, and listened to hair-raising stories about the dangers of the situation.

It was necessary to persuade the American people that the Democratic administration for the past eight years had been wasteful and corrupt, ignorant and fatuous—and that was easy enough. But also it was necessary to persuade them that an administration by Senator Harding was likely to be better—and that was not so easy. Naturally, the chairmen of campaign committees wanted to make it appear as difficult as possible, for the more money that passed through their hands, the larger the amount that would stick. As the campaign drew to its close, Bunny had the satisfaction of hearing his father swearing outrageously, and wishing he had taken his son's advice and left the destinies of his country to the soap manufacturer who had put up the millions for General Wood!

The Senator from Ohio was a large and stately and solemn-faced person, and conducted what was called by the newspapers

a "front-porch campaign." That is to say, he did not put himself out to travel on trains and meet people, but received deputa-
tions of the Hay and Feed Dealers of Duluth, or the Morticians
of Ossawotomie. They would sit in camp-chairs upon his lawn,
and the statesman would appear and read an imposing discourse, which had been written by a secretary of Vernon
Roscoe's selection, and given out to all the press associations
the day before, so that it could be distributed over the wires
and published simultaneously on fifty million front pages.
That is a colossal propaganda machine, and the men who run
it have to lose a lot of sleep. But the majestic candidate lost
no sleep, he was always fresh and serene and impassive; he
had been that way throughout his career, for the able business
men who groomed him and paid his way had never failed to
tell him what to do.

Bunny now dwelt upon an Olympian height, looking down
as a god upon the affairs of pitiful mortals. Dad and Mr.
Roscoe let him hear everything—being sure that common sense
would win in the end, and he would accept their point of view.
They had a philosophy which protected them like a suit of
chain-mail against all hesitations and doubts. The affairs of
the country had to be run by the men who had the money and
brains and experience; and since the mass of the people had not
sense enough to grant the power freely, the mass of the people
had to be bamboozled. "Slogans" must be invented, and hammered into their heads, by millions, yes, billions of repetitions.
It was an art, and experts knew how to do it, and you paid
them—but by Jees, the price made you sweat blood!

The tremendous campaign came to an end, and it was
revealed that 16,140,585 Americans had been successfully bamboozled. Senator Harding had seven million more votes than
the Democratic candidate, the greatest plurality ever polled in
American history. So there were shouting mobs on the streets,
and in the expensive restaurants and clubs where the rich celebrated, everybody got hilariously drunk. Yes, even Vernon
Roscoe got drunk, because Annabelle was too drunk to stop
him; Vee Tracy defied her doctor, and Dad forgot his resolu-
tions, and even Bunny drank enough to make him fear for his
idealism. Man is a gregarious animal, and it is hard not to do
what everybody you know is doing!

II

Christmas had come, and the quail were calling from the hills at Paradise. There were not so many on the tract, but there was plenty of adjacent land over which an oil prince and his royal sire were welcome to shoot. And once you were out of sight of the derricks, and out of smell of the refinery, it was the same beautiful country, with the same clear sky and golden sunsets, and you could get the poisons of bootleg liquor out of your blood, and the embarrassing memories out of your soul. Tramping these rocky hills, drawing this magical air into your lungs, it was impossible to think that men would not some day learn to be happy!

This visit corresponded with a great historic event, which put Paradise upon the map of California. Eli Watkins, prophet of the Lord, had completed the payments for the land upon which his tabernacle in Angel City was to stand, and he celebrated this event by coming back to the scenes of his boyhood, the little frame temple where the Third Revelation had been handed down to mankind, and there holding a novel and interesting performance of his own invention, known as a "Bible Marathon." You see, Eli had read in the papers about Marathon races, and though he didn't know what the word meant, it was romantic-sounding, and he had a fondness for strange words. So the disciples of the First Apostolic Church of Paradise announced that a "Bible Marathon" consisted in reading the Lord's Holy Word straight through without a single pause; they would be told off in relays, and day and night there would be a little group in the church, and one voice after another would take up the sacred task, regardless of oil wells "on the pump" just outside the door.

This was Big Magic. Not only did it thrill the believers, and bring swarms of people to town, but it caught the fancy of the newspapers, and they rushed reporters to write up the event. Many new miracles were wrought, and many crutches hung up; and in the midst of the excitement the Lord vouchsafed a fresh sign of His mercy—Eli, preaching to the throngs outside, announced in the Lord's name that if the reading were completed, Divine Omnipotence would cause the rest of the money to be offered, and the Angel City tabernacle would be erected within a year. After that, of course, nothing could stop the "Marathon," and the epoch-making feat was accomplished in the time of four days, five hours, seventeen minutes, and forty-two and three-quarter seconds—glory hallelujah, praise the Lord!

Bunny saw the shouting thousands with their heads bared, their faces uplifted and a searchlight playing upon them; for Eli had money now, and used it for spectacular effects. His "silver band" was mounted upon a platform with electric lights shining upon the instruments; and the prophet would exhort, and then wave his hand, and the musicians would blare forth an old gospel tune, and the crowd would burst into a mighty chorus, and sway and stamp, their souls transported to glory, the tears running down their cheeks.

There were many wives of oil workers among the audience, and these would plead and pray, and persuade their husbands to attend. There is not much for a man to do out in a lonely place like Paradise; a third-rate movie was the only form of amusement—and here were the bright lights and the silver trumpets and the heavenly raptures, all free—and with a gambler's chance of heaven thrown in! No wonder many of the men "fell for it"; and Paul and his little bunch of rebels insisted that the employers had hired Eli to come there at this critical time, while the struggle to save the union was impending. Bunny would have thought the idea exaggerated—but then he remembered that five hundred dollars his father had given to Eli! Also, he remembered a remark of Vernon Roscoe at the Monastery—"They can have their pie in the sky, so long as they let me have the oil." Annabelle had given a frightened exclamation, "Hush, Verne! What a horrid thing to say!" For Annabelle knew that the heavenly powers are jealous, and liable to cruel whims.

The "wobblies" also were trying to stir the revival spirit in their members, and use the power of song. But feeble indeed was the singing in the "jungles," compared with the mighty blast of Eli's silver trumpets, and the hosannas of his hosts. The operators were not subsidizing the "wobblies," you bet! They had sent their sheriff, and a score of deputies, carrying shotguns loaded with buckshot, and raided the camping place of the rebels, and loaded eleven of them into a motor truck and locked them up in the county jail. There they were now, and Bunny had to hear the tragic tale of Eddie Piatt, one of Paul's friends, who had gone down to San Elido to find out what the bail was, and had been locked up on suspicion of being a member of the outlaw organization. He wasn't, but how could he prove it?

Ruth, who told Bunny about it, wanted to know if Dad wouldn't put up the money to bail him out. Did Bunny remember him, a dark-haired young fellow, very quiet, determined-looking? Yes, Bunny remembered him. Well, he was as trust-worthy as a Jewish garment worker, and the food they gave you in that terrible place was full of worms, and the boys hadn't even a blanket to cover them. It was planned to railroad them all to San Quentin, and Paul knew one of the "politicals" who had just come out of there, and oh, the most horrible stories—the tears came into Ruth's eyes as she told how they put the men to work in the jute mill, and the brown stuff filled their lungs, and presently they were coughing, it was the same as a death-sentence. When they could not stand the labor, they were beaten and thrown into the "hole"—and think of fellows that you knew and cared for having to go through such things!

Bunny knew the sheriff of San Elido County, and also the district attorney, and knew that Dad had named these officials, and could give them orders. But would Dad butt in on their efforts to protect the oil companies? Would he go against the wishes of all the other directors, executives and superintendents of Ross Consolidated? No, assuredly he would not! All that Bunny could do was to give Ruth a couple of hundred dollars, with which to get food for the prisoners. He went back to take up his work at the university; and inside himself there was a "hole," and his conscience would drag him to it, protesting and resisting in vain, and throw him in, and shut a steel door behind him with a terrifying clang. Yes, even when Bunny was up in the snow-white room with the ivy vines wreathing the window, even while he held in his arms the eager body of his beloved—even then the prison door would clang, and he would be in a tank of the county jail with the "class-war prisoners"!

III

Under the arrangements which had kept peace in the oil industry during the war, a government "oil board" would listen to grievances of the workers, and decide what was fair. But now the war was fading in men's memories, and the operators were restive under this "outside" control. Was it not the fundamental right of every American to run his own business in his own way? Was it not obvious that war-time wages had been high, and that "deflation" was desirable? Here and there some operator would refuse to obey the orders of the "oil board"; there would be long arguments, and resorts to the courts, and meantime the workers would be protesting, and threatening, and everyone could see that a crisis was at hand.

In the old days, J. Arnold Ross had 'been one of the little fellows, and all that Bunny could do was to await events. But now he dwelt among the Olympians, and saw the fates in the making. The Petroleum Operators' Federation, by its executive committee, of which Vernon Roscoe was a member, came to a decision to brush the Federal Oil Board aside, ignore the unions, and announce a new schedule of wages for the industry. A copy of this schedule was in Dad's hands, and it averaged about 10 per cent under the present scale.

It was going to mean a bitter struggle, and Bunny was so much concerned that, without saying anything to his father, he made an appeal to Mr. Roscoe. This being a business matter, the proprieties suggested a visit to the office, so Bunny called up the secretary and asked for an appointment in the regular way.

The great man sat at his flat mahogany desk, as clear of papers as the prevailing superstition required. It appeared as if a captain of industry had not a thing to do but grin at a college boy, and gossip about the boy's mistress and his own. But then Bunny remarked, "Mr. Roscoe, I came to see you here because I want to talk to you about the new wage-scale." And in a flash the smile went off the magnate's face, and it seemed as if even the fat went off his jaws; if you have thought of him as a mixture of geniality and buffoonery, this is the time for you to set yourself straight, along with Bunny, and all other rebels against the American system.

Bunny started to tell about the way the men felt, and the trouble that was brewing; but Mr. Roscoe stopped him. "Listen here, Jim Junior, and save a lot of breath. I know everything the men are saying, and everything that Bolshevik bunch up there is teaching them. I get a confidential report every week. I know about your friend, Tom Axton, and your Paul Watkins, and your Eddie Piatt, and your Bud Stoner and your Jick Duggan—I could tell you all you know, and a lot that would surprise you."

Bunny was taken aback, as the other had intended. "Jim Junior," he continued, "you're a bright boy, and you'll get over this nonsense, and I want to help you over it—I might save you a lot of suffering, and also your father, that's the salt of the earth. I've been in this world thirty or forty years longer than you, and I've learned a lot that you don't know, but some day you will. Your father and the rest of us that are running the oil industry, we got here because we know how, and that's a real thing, by Jees, and not just a lot of words. But some other fellers want to kick us out, and think all they got to do is to make speeches to oil workers and set them to raising hell—but let me tell you, kiddo, it's going to take a lot more than that!"

"Yes, Mr. Roscoe, but that's not the point—"

"Pardon me, but it is. Let's cut out the hokum—just say to yourself that I've been sitting in at the arguments of that Bolshevik bunch of yours. Do they mean to take the industry away from me and your old man, or don't they?"

"Well, they may think that ultimately—"

"Yes, exactly. And so far as I'm concerned, the time to stop the ultimately is now. And I tell you that if any sons-of-bitches imagine they're going to live off my wages while they're getting ready to rob me, they're mistaken; and if they find themselves in the jute-mill at San Quentin, they're not going to get my money to bail them out!"

That was a centre shot, and Vernon Roscoe was looking Bunny straight in the eye. "Jim, Junior, I know all the fine idealistic phrases them fellers use on you. It's all lovely and sweet and for the good of humanity—but they know that's all bait for suckers, and if you could hear them laughing at you behind your back, you'd realize how you're being used. What I tell you is, you better get on your own side of the fence before the shooting begins."

"Is there going to be shooting, Mr. Roscoe?"

"That's up to your Bolshevik friends. We've got what we want, and they're going to take it away from us."

"We needed the oil workers during the war, Mr. Roscoe, and we made them promises—"

"Pardon me, kiddo—we didn't make any promises at all! A god-damn long-faced snivelling college professor made them for us, and we're done with that bunk for good! We've got a business man for president, and we're going to run this country on business lines. And let me tell you for one, I'm god-damn sick of having to buy labor leaders, and I can think of cheaper ways to manage it."

Bunny was startled. "Is that really true, Mr. Roscoe? Have you been able to buy the oil workers' officials?"

Verne hitched himself a few inches across the desk, and stuck a large finger at Bunny's face. "Kiddo," he said, "get this straight: I can buy any officials, just the same as I can buy any politicians, or anybody else that a bunch of boobs can elect to office. And I know what you're thinking—here's an old cow-puncher, without any fine ideals, and he's got a barrel o' money and thinks he can do anything he pleases with it. But that ain't the point, my boy—it's because I had the brains to make the money, and I got the brains to use it. Money ain't power till it's used, and the reason I can buy power is because men know I can use it—or else, by Jees, they wouldn't sell it to me. You get that?"

"Yes, but what are you going to do with the power, Mr. Roscoe?"

"I'm going to find oil and bring it to the top of the ground and refine it and sell it to whoever's got the price. So long as the world needs oil, that's my job; and when they can get along without oil, I'll do something else. And if anybody wants a share in that job, let him do like I done, get out and sweat, and work, and play the game."

"But Mr. Roscoe, that's hardly practical advice for all the workers. Everybody can't be an operator."

"No, kiddo, you bet your boots they can't—only them that's got the brains. The rest have to work; and if they work for me, they'll get fair wages, and the money will be there every Saturday night for them, no matter how much worrying and planning I got to do. But when some feller comes along with the gift of the gab, and sticks himself in between me and my men, and says I can't deal with them except by paying him a rake-off, why then I say, 'The jute-mill for him!'"

IV

The thing that Bunny carried away from this interview was Vernon Roscoe's final appeal. "Can't you see, boy, that your father's a sick man? You're not going to have him with you many years more, and some day when it's too late you're going to wake up and realize what you done to him. That old man ain't had a thought in the world but to make things easier for you; you can say he shouldn't if you want to, but all the same, that's what he lived for. And now—now you're spittin' on his life! Yes, just that, and you might as well face it. Everything he's done has been no good, it's all crooked and dirty, and the only people with any ideals or any rights on their side are a bunch of ne'er-do-wells that hate him because he's made good and they never will. And if you think the old man don't feel that, if you don't know it's eating his heart out—well, you take it from me, and get your eyes open before it's too late. If you got to despise your father's money, for Christ's sake wait till he's dead, and the money's your own."

So when Bunny went out from the office, he was not thinking about the troubles of the oil-workers. Was it true that Dad's health was so bad? And wasn't there some way he could be got to stop working so hard? Was it necessary for him to be on hand and see every new well that Ross Consolidated brought in, whether it was at Lobos River or Paradise or Beach City? And what was going to happen to Dad when this labor struggle actually came to a head?

Early in the spring the union leaders held a conference, and served notice on the oil board that the defiance of government authority by the operators was beyond endurance; either the board must assert its authority, or else the workers would take matters into their own hands. The board did nothing; and when the union officials addressed letters to the operators' committee, the letters were ignored. A strike was inevitable; and the longer it was postponed, the worse for the men.

Then a peculiar thing happened. Vee Tracy came to Bunny; she had just completed another picture—no propaganda this time, no, she had laid down the law to Schmolsky, she would never again have anything to do with Russia, or with strikes, or anything that might wound the sensibilities of her oil prince. This time the billboards announced Viola Tracy in "An Eight Reel Comedy of College Capers, entitled 'Come-hither Eyes.'" Vee was glorious as the flirt of the campus, breaking hearts of football stars by the eleven at a time, and incidentally foiling the plot of a band of bookmakers, who had bet a million dollars on the outcome of the big game, and sought to paralyze the team by kidnapping its mascot and darling. Bunny having no sympathy with either bookmakers or kidnappers, it had been all right for him to watch this picture in the making, and supply local color out of his experience with college capers.

The "world premiere" of "Come-hither Eyes" was to take place in New York, and the star had to attend. "Bunny," she said, "why not come with me, and have a little fun?"

Now Bunny had never been east, and the idea was tempting. He had two weeks' Easter vacation, and if he missed a bit of college, it could be made up. He said he would think it over; and later in the day—this was at the Monastery—Annabelle opened up on him, "Why don't you go with Vee, and take Dad along? The change would be the very thing for him."

He studied her ingenuous countenance, and a grin came over his own. "What's this, Annabelle—you and Verne trying to get us out of the way of the strike?"

She answered, "If your friends really care for you, they'll wish you to be happy." And when he said something about it's being cowardly to run away, she made a striking reply. "We're going to have roast spring lamb for dinner, but you didn't consider it necessary to visit the slaughter-house."

"Annabelle," he replied, "you are a social philosopher." And she told him that people went to universities to learn long names for plain common sense!

Evidently the plot was deeply laid; for when Bunny got back home, there was Dad, inquiring, "Did Verne say anything about what he wants me to do?"

"No, Dad, what's that?"

"There's a conference in New York that somebody's got to attend, and he wanted to know if I could get away. I was wondering if it would break you up at the university if you were to take a bit of vacation."

Bunny debated with himself. What could be accomplished by staying? In the first strike, he had managed to keep the workers in their homes, but he couldn't do even that much now, for Verne would be in charge, and would not budge an inch. Annabelle's simile of the spring lamb appeared to fit exactly the position of the oil workers' union. The job of slaughtering might take weeks, or even months, but it would be done—and all that Bunny could do would be to torment his poor father.

And then Bertie was called into the conspiracy. Bertie wanted him to go. She was to visit the fashionable Woodbridge Riley's, and after that to be on Thelma Norman's yacht, and

she didn't want her brother getting mixed up in an oil strike
and perhaps making another stink in the newspapers! Wouldn't
he think about Dad for once, and get the old man to take a
rest? Bunny was tired of arguing, and said, all right.

V

The proposed trip brought up a curious problem. How
did one travel with one's mistress, in this "land of the pilgrim's
pride?" Bunny remembered vaguely having heard of people
being put out of hotels, because of the lack of marriage certificates. Would he and Vee have to meet clandestinely? He
asked her about it, assuming that her experience would cover
the question; and it did. On the trains one took a compartment, and no questions were asked. As for hotels, you went
to the most fashionable, and let them know who you were,
and they made no objection to putting you in adjoining suites,
with a connecting door. Look at Verne and Annabelle, said
Vee; when it suited their convenience they stayed quite openly
at the most high-toned of Angel City's hotels, and there was
never a peep from either the management or the newspapers.
It had happened more than once that Mrs. Roscoe had been
stopping at the same hotel, and the papers would report her
doings on the society page, and Annabelle's on the dramatic
page, so there was never any clash.

In truth the land of the pilgrim's pride no longer existed;
in its place was the land of the millionaire's glory. When a
moving picture star went east, with or without a paramour,
she always left by daylight, and her publicity man saw to it
that the newspapers published the time and place. There
would be shouting thousands, and policemen to hold them back,
and cameras clicking, and armfuls of flowers to let everybody
on the train know who was who. There would be crowds at
every station, calling for a glimpse of their darling; and if she
had an oil prince travelling in the same compartment, that was
not a scandal, it was a romance.

And when they got to New York, there was another crowd,
conjured into being by the efficient publicity machine of
Schmolsky-Superba. At the hotel there were people waiting,
and more armfuls of flowers, and a dozen reporters demanding
interviews. And with all that free advertising for the hotel,
was any officious clerk or house detective going to concern him-

self with the question of whether or not the connecting door between two suites was kept locked? And with a personage of such magnificent authority as J. Arnold Ross travelling along, and beaming his approval on the situation? Dad's face was as good as a dozen marriage certificates at any hotel in the land!

For the old man this journey was just peaches and cream all the way; a vicarious jag, with no "hang-over" the next morning. He insisted upon paying all the bills; and he had his secretary along, so everything just happened by magic—train accommodations, hotel suites, taxicabs, flowers, candy, theatre tickets—you had only to hint a wish, and the thing was there. What more could there be to add to mortal bliss? Only that Vee would have liked to eat a square meal now and then; and to have spent the morning in bed, instead of having to keep an appointment to "reduce" at a gymnasium!

They saw the world premiere of "Come-hither Eyes." Possibly you have never been to college in America, and do not understand our lively ways of speech; so let it be explained that sometimes the eyes of "co-eds" have been observed to possess, whether from natural endowment or by practice acquired, a certain quality suggestive to the male creature of an impulse to proximity. A delicious title, you see; and a delicious picture, transporting tired and bored millions into that very same world of glorious money-spending to which Vee and Bunny had been lifted up. The mechanic who had been screwing up nut number 847 in an automobile factory all day, the housewife who had been washing baby-diapers and buying shoddy goods in a five and ten cent store—these were placed in the same position as Dad, enjoying a vicarious jag with no hang-over the next morning!

The scenes at the New York premiere were the same as in Angel City; the crowds as great, and the cheering as enthusiastic. And Vee and Bunny, sitting up in bed in their silken garments, while black-clad robots silently and mechanically served breakfast on silver trays—Vee and Bunny read the accounts of their triumph, and who had attended and what they had worn. And then, turning over the paper, Bunny read a dispatch from Angel City—ten thousand oil workers had walked out on strike, and the industry was tied up tight. The operators announced that they were no longer willing to recognize the oil board, and issued a new wage-scale that was to be taken or left. Trouble was feared, added the newspapers, because it was known that radical agitators had for some time been active among the men.

VI

Bunny was on a holiday, and must enjoy himself; if he failed to do so, the enjoyment of his two companions would be marred. He must smile and escort them to a theatre, and afterwards send Dad home in a taxi, and go with Vee to a supper-party with some of the screen people, and gossip about their productions and their profits, and see them drink too much, and know that there would be an hour's talk about prohibition and bootleggers, starting as soon as he and Vee refused to drink. Were they "on the wagon"? Or were they afraid of this liquor? This was something special—the original Koski stuff, or whatever it might be in New York.

Then in the morning the pair would go to the "gym," and practice stunts together, making themselves a quite competent pair of gymnasts—Vee said that if ever Dad went broke, and she got "kleig eyes" and had to quit the movies, they could earn several hundred a week on the "big time circuit." They would have lunch, and then maybe there would be a matinee, or somebody calling, or reporters or special writers; or Vee would go shopping, and absolutely insist upon having her darling Bunny along, because he had such exquisite taste, and why did she dress but to please him? Bunny met other rich young men in his position, and learned that such remarks were preliminary to the man's ordering the bill sent to him. But there was nothing of the "gold-digger" about Vee—when she gave the invitation, she paid.

What she wanted was her Bunny-rabbit. She adored him, and wanted to be with him every moment, and to show him off to all the world, including the newspapers. They had been together long enough for Bunny to know her thoroughly, and to realize the drawbacks as well as the advantages of the alliance. That she was sensual did not trouble him, for he was young, and his ardors matched hers. The arts that he had learned from Eunice Hoyt were combined with those Vee had learned from many lovers, and they were dizzy with delight; the impulse that drew them together was impossible to resist. But intellectually they were far from being mated. Vee would listen to anything he wanted to talk about, but how little she really cared about serious things would be comically revealed by her sudden shifting of the conversation. She had her own life, one of speed and excitement and show. She might jeer at the movie world and its works, but nevertheless, she was of that world, and applause and attention were the breath she lived by. She was always on the stage, playing a part—the world's professional darling; always bright, always fresh, young, beautiful, sprightly. Such a thing as thoughtfulness was suspect, a cloak for dangerous enemies stealing into your mind. "What's the matter, Bunny-rabbit? I believe you're thinking about that horrid strike!"

Sitting down and reading a book was a thing quite unknown to this world's darling. A newspaper, yes, of course, or a magazine—one had them lying about, and a man would pick them up and glance over something, but always ready to stop to look at a new dress or listen to a bit of gossip. But to become absorbed in reading and not want to be interrupted—well, it didn't seem quite polite, did it? As for spending a whole after-noon or evening reading a book—Vee had simply never heard of such a thing. She did not put it into words, but Bunny could understand that a book was cheap; anybody could get one and sit off in a corner, but few could have a box at the theatre, presented by the management, and sit there, almost as important as the play.

One of the young fellows who had taught at Dan Irving's labor college was in New York, and Bunny met him, and they talked about what was going on in the labor movement all over the world. Bunny would have liked to meet him again, and to go to meetings—there were so many exciting things in this great city, headquarters of the radical movement as of every-thing else. But Vee found out about this, and set out to save him—just as if he had wanted to smoke opium or drink absinthe! She would make engagements for him, and claim his time, and question him, with an anxious, "Where is my wandering boy tonight?" sort of an air. Bunny knew, of course, that she was doing it for his soul's salvation, and doubt-less at Dad's direct request; but all the same it was a bore.

He had one other acquaintance, to whom Vee made no objection—his mother. She had married again some time ago, and her husband was rich, and she had a lovely home, so she had written. Bunny went to see her, and had to make an extreme effort not to reveal his consternation at her appearance. A dreadful example of what happened when a woman yielded to her craving for a square meal! Mamma had filled out till she was round as a ball of butter, and so soft that it was hard to keep together on a hot day like this. "Fair, fat, and forty" runs the saying; the surgeons add, "and a bad gall bladder," but Bunny didn't know that, and neither did Mamma. She was dressed like a queen in his honor, and had a poodle dog— selected, as Vee would have said, to match her figure. Her husband was a dealer in jewelry, and apparently he used his wife instead of a safe. She insisted on giving Bunny a diamond ring, and when he told her about the strike, she gave him another to be sold for the strikers' relief fund. Oil men were cruel, said Mamma—she knew!

VII

Dad was attending to the business which had brought him east. He didn't say much about it, and that was unusual, so Bunny knew it was something off color. Presently he wormed it out of his father, it had to do with those naval reserve leases they were planning to get. President Harding had been inaugurated, and had made Barney Brockway his attorney-general, according to schedule, and appointed Vernon Roscoe's man as secretary of the interior. This was Senator Crisby, an old party hack who had served Roscoe and O'Reilly when they were occupied in turning out one Mexican administration and putting in another; they had held over the Mexicans' heads the threat of American intervention, and this Crisby, as senator from Texas, had clamored for war and almost got it. He couldn't let women alone, Dad said, and so he was always busted, and ready for any new job that came along.

Now he was to give the oil men a whole string of valuable leases for practically nothing; but he had to have more money, there were a lot of fellows that had to have a lot more money. That was the trouble in dealing with politicians; you bought them before election, and then you had to buy them again after election, they wouldn't "stay put," like business men. What Dad had come on here for was to consult a lawyer that Verne considered the greatest in the country, and fix up a little corporation for the purpose of buying government officials legally.

Of course Dad didn't put it in those crude words, but that was what it amounted to, Bunny insisted, and how could it be done? Dad answered that a real good lawyer could do anything. This was going to be a Canadian corporation, so that it wouldn't have to obey United States laws; and the men that took stock in it were to get their leases in the end. But the trouble was, nobody could be sure just what the leases would be worth, and Pete O'Reilly and Fred Orpan were trying to make Dad and Verne put up too big a share of the money. Verne was mad and said they could go to hell, and he wanted Dad to settle down and wait a while in New York, and bluff them out. Could Bunny make up his mind to skip the rest of his college term, and maybe do some studying with a tutor, and pass his examinations in the fall?

Bunny said he didn't care about college, but this worried him—what was Dad getting in for with this Canadian corporation? Dad insisted it was perfectly all right, he had the best lawyer in the country. But Bunny said, "Are you sure Verne isn't putting something over on you?" Dad was shocked at that, how could Bunny have such an idea, why Verne was the best friend Dad had ever had in business, he was straight as they made them. "Yes, Dad, but they don't make them so very straight in the oil game. And why doesn't Verne do his own bribing? Why didn't he come to New York?"

"But son, Verne has got to handle the strike—you know he couldn't get away now. He's taken that off my shoulders, and you ought to be glad." Dad added a naive remark, the oil men wouldn't let him deal with labor, he was "too soft." The phrase sounded familiar.

It turned out that Vee and Dad had been putting their heads together. Vee wanted a vacation, also; they would go up to Canada to complete Dad's business, and then they would find a camp, and instead of tiresome "gym" work, she and Bunny would tramp the forests and swim in a beautiful lake. So Dad sent a telegram to President Alonzo T. Cowper, D.D., Ph.D., LL.D., explaining that urgent business compelled his son to remain in the east, and could it be arranged that Bunny might return and take his examinations in the fall? Dr. Cowper wired that the authorities would be very pleased indeed to grant this favor.

And then, the very morning after it was all settled, a telegram came for Bunny, and he opened it and read the signature,

Ruth Watkins. With swiftly flying eyes he took in the sense of it—Paul and Eddie Piatt and Bud Stoner and Jick Duggan and four others of their group had been arrested, charged with "suspicion of criminal syndicalism," and were lodged in the San Elido county jail with ten thousand dollars bail demanded for Paul and seventy-five hundred for each of the others. "They have done nothing and everybody knows it," declared the telegram, "merely scheme to lock them up during strike. Jail is horrible place Paul's health will not stand it implore you for sake our old friendship obtain needed bail for all surely no need assure you no money will be lost on our boys."

VIII

At first Bunny had a cruel suspicion—that his father had known of this arrest, or at any rate that it was pending, before his latest effort to keep Bunny away from California. But he realized, it was enough to believe that Vernon Roscoe, intending to break up the "nest of Bolshevism" in the Rascum cabin, had made plans to get both Dad and Bunny away and keep them away. Anyhow, the scheme would not work, for Bunny was not going to permit his friend to be treated in that crude fashion!

Dad happened to be out, and Bunny showed the telegram to Vee, and talked it out with her. She wanted to know what he meant to do, and he answered that Dad would have to put up the bail for Paul, at least.

"But Bunny, you know he can't do that—he wouldn't cross Verne in regard to the strike."

"He's simply got to do it, Vee! I'd be a dog to let a man like Paul be locked up in that filthy hole."

"But suppose Dad won't, Bunny?"

"Then I've got to go back, that's all there is to it."

"What could you do when you got there?"

"I'll hunt around till I find somebody that's got a sense of decency and also a little cash."

"The combination isn't so easy to find, dear—I know, because I've tried it. And it's going to make Dad dreadfullly unhappy, to say nothing of spoiling our vacation. I have just learned of the loveliest place—a camp that Schmolsky bought up in Ontario, and he's never been there, he's too busy. And, oh, Bunny, I thought we were going to have such a marvelous time."

She put her arms about him, but he hardly knew she was there, so cruelly was his spirit wrung by the vision of Paul in jail. And he, Bunny, running away from the trouble, loafing about and pretending it was a "vacation"! He that thought he understood the social problem, and had an ideal, at least a glimpse of what was kind and fair! He broke loose from Vee's arms and began to pace the floor, storming half at himself for a renegade and half at the dirty crooks that ran the government of San Elido county, and stole the funds that were supposed to keep the jail clean and feed the prisoners. Bunny was twisting his hands together in his misery, and Vee watched him, startled; it was a new aspect of her Bunny-rabbit, that she had thought so sweet and soft and warm!

"Listen, dear!" she broke in, suddenly. "Stop a minute and talk to me quietly. You know, I don't know much about these things."

"What is it?"

"How can you be sure that Paul hasn't broken any law?"

"Because I know him. I know all his ideas. I've talked the thing out with him from A to Z—all about this strike, and how it's to be handled, the importance of getting the men to stand as a unit, how everything else must be subordinated to that. That's what he's been doing, and that's why Verne has thrown him into jail."

"You're quite sure Verne has done it?"

"Of course—he and the rest of the operators' committee. What are those officials in San Elido, but office-boys for the oil men? Before Verne came in there, Dad ran that county; I've seen him pay the money with my own eyes, and more times than one."

"And you don't think they may have evidence that Paul has been conniving at violence?"

"I don't know what evidence they've got. Verne as good as told me he had spies on that bunch, and I don't know what those spies may have planted—and neither does Verne know, for that matter. That's one of the damnable things about it. Another is—you see that charge, 'suspicion of criminal syndicalism'! What they call 'criminal syndicalism' means that you advocate overthrowing the government, or changing the social system by force; but you notice they don't arrest you for that— they arrest you for 'suspicion' of it! In other words, you advocate some idea that some ignorant cop or some crook in office chooses to think may be dangerous, and then they throw you into jail, and there you stay—the courts are crowded, and they can keep you a year without a trial or any chance at all."

"Oh, surely they can't do that, Bunny!"

"They're doing it right along. I know fellows it's been done to. They put the bail high on purpose, so that workingmen can't get it. And they think they're going to do it to Paul Watkins, the best boy-friend I ever had, the straightest fellow I ever knew—yes, by God, and he went to Siberia and served in that war, and came out sick—that boy was as tough as a hickory nut before that, a country fellow, simple and straight, and with no vices. And this is the reward he gets for his services to his country—by Jesus, I'd like to see them get me to fight for a country like that!"

Bunny had to dash a tear out of his eyes, and he began to pace the floor again, and stumbled against a chair. Vee put her arms about him and whispered, "Listen, dear, I know some people that have got money, and I may be able to help you. Leave it to me for a few hours, and don't say anything to Dad about it—what's the use of worrying him to no purpose? If I can arrange it, he'll be able to tell Verne that he knew nothing about it, and that'll be so much better all round."

She went off, and a couple of hours later came back. Bunny was to wire Ruth that neither he nor his father could do anything, but a friend had taken an interest in the case, and the money had been deposited with the American Bonding Company, and their office in Angel City would obtain Paul's release. Bunny said, "How did you do it?" and she answered, "The less you know about it the better. I know somebody that owns some real estate in Angel City, and has a salary coming to them, and employers that are anxious to keep them happy and contented." Bunny said it must have cost a good deal, and he ought to pay it back, and Vee said, "Yes, it cost a pile, and you're going to pay in love and affection, and you can start right now." She flew to his arms, and he covered her with kisses, and it was like an orchestra that went surging up in their hearts. It is an extremely unsettling thing to have a whole orchestra inside you!

IX

Well, Paul got out, and Bunny was supposed to be satisfied. To be sure, seven other fellows were in, and Bunny knew them all; but it would have cost fifty-two thousand five hundred dollars to release them, and that would certainly be carrying idealism to unreasonable extremes. So Bunny let Vee carry him and Dad off to that "camp" on a lake with a long Indian name, and there they swam, and canoed, and fished, and tramped the forests, and took pictures of moose in the water; they had Indian guides, and everything romantic—and at the same time hot and cold water in their bed-rooms, and steam-heat if they wanted it; all the comforts of Broadway and Forty-second Street.

Here, if ever, they had a chance to get enough of each other; there were no distractions, no social duties, no visitors dropping in, no dressing to be done; they were together all day and all night. What Bunny found was that they were perfectly happy so long as they were doing physical things: canoe trips to other places, new fishing stunts, hunting with the camera, shooting rapids, learning to make camp, to start a fire like the Indians—anything it might be. But they must be playing all the time, otherwise a great gulf opened between them. If Bunny wanted to read, what was Vee to do?

Once a day a little steamer came the length of the lake and put off supplies and a packet of mail. There were papers from Angel City, and also, once a week, the strike bulletin of the oil workers, which Bunny had very unwisely subscribed for. What was the use of running three thousand miles away from trouble, and then having it sent to you in a mail sack? Reading of the scenes that he knew so well—the meetings, the relief work, the raising of funds, the struggles with the guards, the arrests, the sufferings of the men in jail, the beating up of strike pickets, the insolence of the sheriff and other officials, the dishonesty of the newspapers—it was exactly the same as if Bunny were in Paradise. Paul was one of the executive committee, Paul had become Tom Axton's right-hand man, and his speeches were quoted, and his experiences in the San Elido county jail—when Bunny had finished that little paper, he was so shaken he was not the same all day. Vee found out about it, of course, and began trying to persuade him to stop reading it. Had he not done his share by giving the strikers back their leader? And had he not promised to repay her, his darling Vee-Vee, with love and affection for a whole summer?

Bunny wrestled it out with his own soul, in such free moments as he could get. He told himself that it was to help his father—a more respectable excuse than entertaining a mistress! But did his father have a right to expect so much? Did any one person have a right to replace all the rest of humanity? If it was the duty of the young to sacrifice themselves for the old, how could there ever be any progress in the world? As time passed, and the struggle in the oil fields grew more tense, the agony of the workers more evident, Bunny came to the clear decision that his flight had been cowardly.

He tried to explain his point of view to Vee, but only to run into a stone wall. It was not a subject for reasoning, it was a matter of instinct with her. She believed in her money; she had starved for it, sold herself, body and mind, for it, and she meant to hang onto it. Bunny's so-called "radical movement" meant to her that others wanted to take it away. He discovered a strange, hard streak in her; she would spend money lavishly, for silks and furs and jewels, for motor-cars and parties—but that was all professional, it was part of her advertising bill. But, on the other hand, where no display was involved, where the public did not enter—there she hated to spend money; he overheard her wrangling with a washer-woman over the amount to be charged for the ironing of her lingerie, and those filmy night-dresses in which she seduced his soul.

No, he could never make a "radical" out of this darling of the world; he would have to make up his mind to that. She would listen to him, because she loved him, even the sound of his voice talking nonsense; she would make a feeble pretense at agreeing, but all the time it was as if he had the measles and she waiting for him to get cured; as if he were drunk and she trying to get him "on the wagon." She had apologized to Rachel, and had got Paul out of jail, but merely to please him, and in reality she hated both these people. Still more did she hate Ruth, with a cold, implacable hatred—an intriguing minx, pretending to be a simple country maiden in order to win an oil prince! No women were simple, if you believed Vee, and damn few of them were maidens.

Nor would Ruth ever stop being a nuisance. In the midst of one of their happiest times, she sent Bunny another telegram—her brother was in jail again, this time it was contempt of court. Bunny considered it necessary to paddle down to the nearest telegraph office and wire Mr. Dolliver, the lawyer, to investigate and report. The answer came that nothing could be done—Paul and others of the strike leaders had disregarded an injunction forbidding them to do this and that, and there was no bail and no appeal, neither habeas corpusses nor counter-injunctions, and Paul would have to serve his three months' sentence.

Bunny was bitter and rebellious against judges who issued injunctions, and Vee was afraid to speak, because it seemed obvious to her that somebody had to control strikers. Of course after that there was a shadow over their holiday—Bunny brooding upon his friend shut up in the county jail. He sent Ruth five hundred dollars, to take care of all the prisoners; and in course of time got a letter, saying that the prisoners had refused the money, and Ruth had turned it over to the strike relief. It was a terrible thing to see children without enough to eat; terrible also that men who had power should use it to starve children! Thus the "simple" Ruth—not meaning any hint at Dad!

X

Bunny had to study for his fall examinations, and that looked like a problem, for what was Vee going to do? But fate provided a solution—Dad telegraphed to Harvard University, which sent up a young instructor to do tutoring, and he was the solution. He was tall, and had the loveliest fair blue eyes, and a softly curling golden moustache, and soft golden fuzz all over him like a baby; he wore gold nose-glasses, and had a quiet voice and oh, so much culture—one of those master minds which can tutor you in anything if you give them a week's start!

Coming as he did from an old Philadelphia family, and having been trained in the haughtiest centre of intellectual snobbery, you might have thought he would look down upon an ex-mule driver and his son, to say nothing of an actress who had been raised in a patent medicine vender's wagon, and had never read a whole book in her life. But as a matter of fact, young Mr. Appleton Laurence just simply collapsed in the presence of the situation he found at this Ontario camp; it was the most romantic and thrilling thing that a young instructor had encountered since Harvard began. As for the patent medicine vender's daughter, he could not take his eyes off her, and when she came near, the tutoring business was scattered as by a hurricane.

Vee of course had put her sparkling black eyes to work at once; all those stunts which Tommy Paley had taught her she now tried out on a new victim, and Bunny, as audience, was in position to study them objectively. Vee would wait till Mr. Laurence had set Bunny his morning's work, and then she and the tutor would go for a walk in the woods, and Bunny would sit with one half his mind on his books, while the other half wondered what was happening, and what he had reason to expect from one who had had so many lovers.

She did not leave him long in doubt. "Bunny-rabbit," she said, "you aren't going to be worried about my Appie, are you?"—for the hurricane that struck the tutoring business had swept all dignity away, and Mr. Appleton Laurence was "Appie," except when he was "Applesauce."

"I won't worry unless you tell me to," Bunny answered.

"That's a dear! You must understand, I'm an actress, that's the way I earn my living, and I simply have to know all about love, and how can I learn if I don't practice?"

"Well, that's all right, dear—"

"Some of the men they give you in Hollywood are such dubs, it makes you sick, you would as soon be in the arms of a clothing dummy. So I have to tell them how to act, and I have to know how a real gentleman behaves—you know what I mean, the highbrows and snobs. Oh, Bunny, it's the cutest thing you ever saw, he falls down on his knees, and the tears come into his eyes, and you know, he can recite all the poets by heart; I never saw anything like it; you'd think he was an old Shakespearean actor. And it's really a great opportunity for me, to cultivate my taste and get refined."

"Well, yes, dear, but isn't it a little hard on him?"

"Oh, rubbish, it won't hurt him, he'll go off and put it into sonnets—he's doing it already, and maybe he'll get to be famous, and it'd be great publicity! Don't you bother about him, Bunny, and don't bother about me; there's nobody in the world for me but my Bunny-rabbit—all the rest is just a joke." And she put her arms about him. "I know what it is to be jealous, dear, and I wouldn't cause you that unhappiness for anything in the world. If you really mind, you can send old Applesauce packing, and I won't be cross."

Bunny laughed. "I can't do that, I've got to be tutored."

Vee told Dad about it, too—lest he should be having any vicarious pangs. When Dad heard about the falling on the

knees and the tears, he chuckled. Bunny would get the contents of the tutor's mind, and Vee would get the contents of
his heart, and they would send him home like a squeezed
orange. It appealed to Dad as good business. Back in Paradise, you remember, he was hiring a chemical wizard, paying
him six thousand a year, and making millions out of him!

XI

There came another development, to protect Vee from the
possibility of boredom. Schmolsky sent her up the "continuity"
of the new picture upon which she was to start work in the
fall. And then suddenly it was revealed that the world's darling knew how to read! For a whole hour she sat buried in it,
and then she leaped up, ready to start rehearsing—and all the
hurricanes that ever swept the province of Ontario were as
nothing to the one that came now. Clear the way for "The
Princess of Patchouli"!

It was a popular musical comedy which was to be made into
a moving picture. "Patchouli" was one of the little Balkan
kingdoms, though it looked and acted very much like Vienna
of the Strauss waltzes. A young American engineer came in
to build a railroad, and found himself mistaken for a con-
spirator, and presently he was rescuing the lovely princess from
a revolutionary band—no Bolsheviks, these were aristocratic
army conspirators, so Bunny wouldn't have his feelings hurt,
would he? Of course the hero carried her off, married her for
love only, and then got the kingdom thrown in—the bankers
who were financing the railroad bought it for him.

So here was Vee, being a princess all over the place. It
was amazing to watch her work—Bunny suddenly came to
realize that her success hadn't been all money and sex, after all.
She pounced onto the role like a tiger-cat, and when she got
going the rest of the world ceased to exist—except to the extent
that she needed it for a foil. "Now, Dad, you're the king; you
walk in here—no, no, for God's sake, kings don't walk so fast!
And I have to fall at your feet, and plead for his life, 'Oh,
mercy sire, and so-and-so, and so-and-so, and so-and-so!'"

It is one of the peculiarities of motion picture acting that it
doesn't matter what you say, so long as you are saying something; so Vee would weep, "And so-and-so," and she would
croon "And so-and-so" in passionate love-accents to either

Bunny or Appie, and she would shriek "And so-and-so" in deadly terror to an executioner with uplifted axe. And if in the course of the scene the other person didn't do it right, then scolding and commands would serve equally well for a love-song, "Hold it, now, you idiot, I adore you, darling"—or maybe it might be, "Take your hands off me, foul beast—don't let go, you goose, grab! That's better, you don't have to be polite when you're a murderer."

If Bunny had wanted to rehearse tempestouous emotions, and shriek and scream and tear his hair, he would have sought refuge in the woods, where only the chipmunks could have heard him. But Vee was utterly indifferent to the existence of other humans. That is something one learns on "the lot"; for there will be camera-men and scene-shifters, and property-boys, and carpenters working on the next set, and some visitors that have managed to break in despite the strictest regulations—and you just go on with your work. The first time the executioner lifted his axe and Vee started screaming, the Indian guides came running in alarm; but she hardly stopped even for a laugh, she went on with the scene, while they stood staring with mouths wide open. She and her two lovers would come in from swimming, and suddenly she would call for a rehearsal of some royal pageantry—she could be a princess just as well in a scanty bathing suit, with a carpet of pine-needles under her bare feet.

Mr. Appleton Laurence had never met any princesses, but he had read a great deal of history and poetry, and so he was an authority, and must criticise her way of walking, her gestures, her attitudes, her reaction to the love-advances of a handsome young American engineer. "Just imagine you're in love with me yourself, Appie," she would say—and so his emotions became sublimated into art, and he could pour out his soul to her, right before Bunny and Dad and Dad's secretary and the Indians! "You're much better at it than Bunny," she would declare. "I believe he's got used to me, it's as bad as if we were married."

So the time passed pleasantly. Until at last Vee had got to feel perfectly at home in her Appie's conception of royalty; she no longer had to ask questions, nor to stop and think, but knew instantly what to do—and forever after, in all her entrances to and exits from Hollywood society, she would be a little of a Harvard instructor's Princess of Patchouli. She was

impatient now, wanting to see the sets, and to hear Tommy
Paley call, "Camera!" Bunny also was loaded up with answers
to all possible exam questions, and ready to get back and unload
them onto his professors. Dad had run down to Toronto, and
signed the last of the papers for his Canadian corporation;
he had telegrams from Verne almost every day—the strikers,
having held out for nearly four months, had learned their lesson, and the Federal Oil Board had written them a letter, advising them to go back to work as individuals, and promising there
would be no discrimination against union men.

Then one day the steamer brought a telegram signed Annabelle, addressed to Bunny, and reading, "Spring lamb for dinner
come on home." He explained what that meant, the strike was
over; and so the occupants of the camp packed up, and Mr.
Appleton Laurence went back to his fair Harvard, with woe
in his heart and a packet of immortal sonnets in his suit-case,
while Vee Tracy and Dad and Bunny and the secretary made
themselves luxurious in compartments on a Canadian-Pacific
train bound West.

CHAPTER XVI

THE KILLING

I

Bunny passed his examinations, and was duly established as a "grave old senior" in Southern Pacific University. And then he hunted up his friends—and such a load of troubles as fell onto his shoulders! Literally everybody had troubles! Rachel and Jacob Menzies had come back from their summer's fruit-picking, to find their two younger brothers, the "left wingers," in the county jail! The police had raided a Communist meeting and arrested all the speakers, and the organizers, and the literature sellers, and all who had red badges in their buttonholes. They had raided the Communist headquarters—determined, so the newspapers announced, to root every Moscow agent out of the city. They had sorted the prisoners, and fined a few, and were holding the rest, including the Menzies boys, under that convenient universal charge, "suspicion of criminal syndicalism."

These foolish boys had made their own trouble, said Rachel; but still it was an outrage to arrest people for their beliefs; and it was tormenting to think of your own flesh and blood shut up in those horrible cages. Bunny asked the bail—it was two thousand dollars per brother. He began explaining his troubles with his father, and his own impotence; and Rachel said of course, she understood, they couldn't expect him to bail out the whole radical movement. And yet that did not entirely restore his peace of mind.

Then Harry Seager, whose business college was on the rocks. The boycott had wrecked it, and Harry was trying to sell the debris. He was going to buy him a walnut ranch; it would be harder to boycott walnuts, you couldn't tell the "red" ones from the "white"!

And then Dan Irving, whose labor college was in almost as bad a way. The orgy of arrests had frightened the old line labor leaders completely off. The college was still going, but it was in debt, and the head of it hadn't had any salary for several months. Bunny wrote a check for two hundred dollars, and went away debating the question that never would be set-tled—to what extent had he a right to plunder his father for the benefit of his father's enemies?

From Dan Irving he learned that Paul had got out of jail, and was in Angel City, together with Ruth. It was a dirty deal the oil workers had got, said Dan; the operators had made one last use of the oil board, to trick the men into a complete sur-render. They had promised the oil board there would be no discrimination against union men, but they had never had the least intention of keeping this promise. They had kept all the strike-breakers at work, and taken back just enough of the strikers to make up their needs. All the active union fellows were begging jobs, and the oil industry was a slave-yard of the "open shop."

II

Bunny went at once to call on Paul and Ruth at the address which Dan Irving gave him. It was a mean and dingy lodging-house, in a part of the city given up to Mexicans and Chinese. An old woman sent him up to the second floor, and told him which door to knock on, but he got no response. He came back later, and found that Ruth had just got in. They were crowded into one little room, with a gas plate and a sink in an unventilated alcove, and another alcove with a curtain before it, and a cot on which Paul slept. Ruth was ashamed to have Bunny see them in such a place, but explained that it wouldn't be long, just till Paul got a job; he was out looking for one now. She herself had got work in a department store, and as soon as they could get ahead, she was going to study trained nursing. She looked pale and worn, but smiled bravely; she didn't really mind anything, so long as Paul was out of jail.

Bunny wanted to know all the news, and plied Ruth with questions. Just what had Paul done to get arrested? The first time, Ruth said, the sheriff had raided the Rascum cabin, with a lot of rough, hateful men, who had torn everything to pieces and carried off all of Paul's books and papers—they had them still. They had done the same thing to all the other fellows that used to come to the cabin—they were going to prove them "reds," but what evidence they had or claimed to have was a secret the sheriff or the district attorney or whoever it was was keeping to himself. They had had a lot of spies on the bunch—one fellow was known to be a spy, and two others had disappeared, and would no doubt turn up as witnesses—but who could tell what they would testify? All the other boys were still locked up in those horrible tanks, so dark and dirty, and nothing to do all day or night. The trial was set for next February, and apparently they were to stay there meantime. Paul was free, thanks to Bunny's ten thousand dollars; Ruth could never express her thanks—

Never mind about that, Bunny said—what about the second arrest? And Ruth told how Judge Delano had issued an injunction forbidding anyone to interfere with Excelsior Pete in the course of its business, the production and marketing of oil. That meant that you mustn't advocate or encourage the strike; and of course Paul had done that, so the judge had sent him to jail—that was all. Judges were getting so they did that all the time, and what were union men going to do? It had been a fearful ordeal for Paul, he was not very well, and of course he was terribly bitter. He would never go back to Paradise again, it wasn't the same place at all. Ruth smiled a wan smile, "They've cut down all those lovely trees that we planted, Bunny. They needed the room for tanks."

Bunny hauled out his check-book, and sought to salve his conscience by making a present to his friends. But Ruth said no, she was sure Paul wouldn't let him do that. They were going to get along all right. Paul was a good carpenter, and sooner or later he would find some boss that didn't mind his having been in jail. Bunny argued, but Ruth was obdurate; even though she were to take the check, Paul would send it back.

Bunny did not wait till Paul came home; he made some excuse, and went away. He just did not have the nerve to sit there, in his fashionable clothes which Vee had selected for him in New York, and with his new sport car waiting downstairs, and see Paul come in, half sick, discouraged from seeking work in vain, and with all the black memories of injustice and betrayal in his soul. Bunny could make excuses, of course. Paul did not know that he had been spending the summer at play with the world's darling, Paul would believe that he had gone away on his father's account. But nothing could change the fact that it was on money wrung from the Paradise workers that Bunny was living in luxury; nothing could change the fact that it had been to increase the amount of this money, to intensify the exploitation of the workers, that Paul had spent three months in jail, and the other fellows were to spend nearly a year in jail. So long as that was the truth, there was nothing Bunny could do but just run away from Paul!

III

Money! Money! Money! It was pouring in upon Dad and Verne. Never had oil prices been so high, never had the flow at Paradise been so rapid. Millions and millions—and they were scheming to make it tens of millions. It was a game, marvelous, irresistible; everybody was playing it—and why could not Bunny be interested? Why did he have to go sneaking around in the dressing-rooms and behind the grand-stands, finding out dirty and disreputable facts about the players of this game and their methods?

It seemed as if the fates had it in for Bunny. Just as sure as he made some pitiful effort to be like his father and his father's friends, some new development would come along and knock him down! Here he had gone to a university, a solemnly respectable university, trying to improve his mind and make a gentleman of himself; he had turned over his young and eager mind to the most orthodox and regular authorities—and surely they would know how to make him good and honest and happy, surely they would teach him wisdom, dignity, and honor! Such things were being taught to all students in this great institution, which had begun as a Methodist Sunday-school, and still had more courses on the religion of Jesus Christ than on any other subject whatever! Oh, surely yes!

The university had grown great on the money of Pete O'Reilly, the oil king; and Pete O'Reilly's son was a graduate, and the two of them, "Old Pete" and "Young Pete," were the gods of the campus. When they came to commencement, the faculty bowed down before them, and in all the stories which the university's publicity man sent to the newspapers, the names of Pete O'Reilly, father and son, never failed to be featured. The son was the most active of the alumni, and their god; when they had banquets, he was toasted and flattered and cheered; he was the patron saint of all the teams, the bounteous friend of all athletes. And of course, if you know anything about American universities, you know that this is what counts in the molding of the students' minds; this is the thing they do for themselves, and into which they put their hearts.

At first it seemed all right. You knew that S. P. U. was a glorious college, and had splendid teams, and won victories that resounded up and down the coast. And presently there was a stadium, and a vast business of athletics, that resulted in infinite applause and free advertising for your alma mater. Of this you were proud, the whole student body was made one by it—the thing called "college spirit." Bunny, a track-runner, had had his share of cheering; and here was a "game" he could play with all his heart!

But now he was a senior, and on the inside of things, just as with the oil game, and with strikes, and with political campaigns. And what did he find? Why, simply that all the football and track and other athletic glory that had come to Southern Pacific had been stolen, and "Young Pete" O'Reilly was the thief! The oil king's son had put up a fund of fifty thousand dollars every year, for the purpose of turning the game of college athletics into a swindle! The fund was administered by a secret committee of alumni and students, and used for the purpose of going out into the market and buying athletes, to come and enroll themselves under false pretenses and win victories for S. P. U. Husky young truck-drivers and lumbermen and ranch-hands and longshoremen, who could not speak correct English, but could batter down "interference" and crash through to a goal! And the pious Methodists who constituted the faculty were conniving at the procedure, to the extent of permitting these young huskies to pass farcical examinations— well knowing that any professor who presumed to flunk a promising quarterback would soon be looking for some other university to presume in. Was not "Young Pete" showing what he thought of professors, by paying a football coach three times the salary of the best?

And of course these hired athletes were hired to win, and did not bother about the rules of the game; they slugged and fouled, and the rival teams paid them back, and there was a nasty mess, with charges and countercharges, bribery and intimidation—all the atmosphere of a criminal trial. Along with secret professionalism, came its accompaniments of the underworld, bootleggers and bookmakers and prostitutes. Study was a joke to hired gladiators, and quickly became a joke to students who associated with them. The one purpose was to win games, and the reward was two hundred thousand dollars in gate receipts; and when it came to distributing this prize,

there were just as many kinds of graft as if it had been a
county government: students putting in bills for this and that,
students looking for easy jobs, students and alumni building
up a machine, and paying themselves and their henchmen with
contracts and favors. Such was the result of an oil king's
resolve to manufacture culture wholesale, by executive order!

IV

Bunny went to see the young lawyer whom the oil workers'
union had engaged to defend the eight "political prisoners."
The union had since become practically extinct, and the young
lawyer had been wondering where he was going to get his pay.
When Bunny came to question him, it was a great relief—for
surely this young oil prince would put up something for the
defense of his friends! Or could it be that he was sent as an
emissary from the other side, to feel out the situation?

Young Mr. Harrington talked freely about the case. The
thing which the state was doing to these eight men was without precedent in our law, and if it could stand, it meant the end
of American justice. Every prisoner was supposed to know
the charges against him, the specific acts he was alleged to have
committed. But in all these "criminal syndicalism" cases, the
state simply alleged violation of the law in its vague general
terms, and that was all. How could you prepare a defense in
such a case? What witnesses would you summon—when you
didn't know the time, or the place, or the particular things a
man was alleged to have done, or said, or written, or published?
You were taken into court blindfolded, bound and gagged. Yet,
so completely were the courts terrorized by the business crowd,
no judge would order the district attorney to make a detailed
statement of the charges!

Bunny went away, and in his desperation played a dirty
trick on Vernon Roscoe—he went to see Annabelle Ames.
Annabelle was kind and gentle, and he would wring her soul,
and see if in that way he could not get under the hide of the
old petroleum pachyderm! He told her about these boys, what
they looked like, what they believed, what they were suffering
in the jail. Annabelle listened, and the tears came into her
eyes, and she said it was horrible that men could be so cruel.
What could she do? Bunny told her that the strike was over,
the spring lamb had been slaughtered and eaten, and Verne

ought to be willing to cry quits. It would be of no use for him
to plead that he couldn't do anything, that the law must take
its course; that was all rubbish, because the district attorney
had the right to ask for the dismissal of the cases, and he would
surely do it if Verne said the word.

Well, Bunny got under the hide of the old petroleum pachyderm! The way Bunny heard about it, Dad came in in a terrible state, Verne had jumped on him, Verne was mad as the
very devil, Bunny sneaking into his home and plotting against
his domestic peace! He wanted it understood, by Jees, if Dad
couldn't control his son, Verne would. Bunny wanted to know
what Verne meant to do, spank him? Or have him locked up
with the others?

Bunny had made up his mind, and stood his ground—he had
a perfect right to talk to Annabelle, she was a grown woman,
and there was no way Verne could stop him. He was going to
do more talking before he got through—he was sorry enough
to make his father unhappy, but here was the fact, if that case
ever came to trial, he, Bunny Ross, was going to take the stand
as a witness for the eight defendants, and not merely a character witness, but one with first-hand knowledge of the facts;
he had sat in the Rascum cabin night after night, and heard
them discuss the problems of the strike, and their own attitude
to it, and he could testify that every man of them had agreed
on workers' solidarity as the way to victory, and acts of violence as a trap the operators would try to lure them into. If
there was no other way to get money for the defense of these
boys, Bunny would sell the car that Dad had given him—"I
suppose Verne won't have any right to keep me from walking
to the university!"

Poor Dad, he couldn't stand talk like that from his darling
son; he began to give way, and revealed that he and Verne
had discussed the possibility of a compromise with the rebels.
Would they agree to get out of the state, or at least to keep
their hands off the oil industry? And Bunny said, by God, if
Vernon Roscoe wanted to make any such proposition, he could
be his own messenger boy! Bunny knew what Paul's answer
would be—Paul had a right to try to organize oil workers,
and he would never quit while he lived. Bunny was sure the
whole eight would respond with a unanimous shout, they would
rot in jail the rest of their lives before they would make such a
bargain!

Then, having said that very magnificently, the young ideal-ist who was gradually and painfully evolving into a man of the world, went on to point out that as a matter of fact none of the eight would have much chance to bother Verne. His efficient blacklist system would see to it that they didn't get work in the oil fields; and any organizing they could do would be of a pitiful sort. On the other hand, Verne must realize that if he per-sisted in trying to railroad these fellows to jail, there was going to be a long trial, and a lot of publicity of a kind the operators might find troublesome. The testimony would have to be "framed"; and Bunny would do everything in his power to expose it, and to see that the public got the facts. What if it should occur to the defendants' lawyer to subpoena Mr. Vernon Roscoe and ask what he knew about the planting of spies on the Paradise workers?

"Oh, son!" cried Dad, "You wouldn't do a dirty thing like that!"

Bunny answered, "Of course I wouldn't. I said the lawyer might do it. Wouldn't you, if you were in his place?" And Dad, very uncomfortable, said to let the matter ride, and he would see what he could do with Verne.

V

One outcome of these negotiations, Dad appealed to Vee Tracy: couldn't she possibly do more to keep Bunny out of the hands of these awful reds? Why, he wasn't thinking about a thing else! Vee said she would try, and she did, and it was a further strain upon their love and affection. For Bunny was beginning to know what he wanted now, and he didn't want to be kept from it.

Vee was hard at work on "The Princess of Patchouli." It was a silly story, she would freely admit; yet her whole being was concentrated upon making it real and vivid. If you asked her why, the answer would be, it was her profession; which meant that she was getting four thousand a week, with the possibility of increasing it to five thousand a week if she "made good." But what did she want with the five thousand a week? To buy more applause and attention, as a means of getting more thousands for more weeks? It was a vicious circle—exactly like Dad's oil wells. The wobblies had a song about it in their jungles: "We go to work to get the cash to buy the food to get the strength to go to work to get the cash to buy the food to get the strength to go to work—" and so on, as long as your breath held out.

Vee wanted to talk about the picture and the problems that arose day by day, and the various personalities and their jealousies and vanities, their loves and hates. Bunny, who loved her, would pretend to be interested, because it would hurt her if he wasn't. And it was the same with the Hollywood parties; once they had been new and startling, but now they all seemed alike. Everybody was making a new picture, but it would always be like the old pictures. Nobody did anything original, but everybody followed fashions; the public's taste ran to society pictures, and nobody would look at a war picture—but presently the public would want war pictures, and after that costume pictures, and then sea pictures, and then back to society pictures. Vee's friends changed their bootleggers, but it was always the same stuff they drank. Also they changed their lovers; a certain man slept with a certain woman, and then presently it was a different woman—but the more it changed, the more it was the same thing.

Bunny and Vee loved each other, just as passionately as ever. At least, they told themselves it was as ever, but all the while the subtle chemistry of change was at work. Men and women are not bodies only, and cannot be satisfied with delights of the body only. Men and women are minds, and have to have harmony of ideas. Can they be bored with each other's ideas, and still be just as much in love? Men and women are characters, and these characters lead to actions—and what if they lead to different actions? What if the man wants to read a book, while the woman wants to go to a dance?

Vee had been so considerate in the matter of her adoring "Applesauce," so careful lest Bunny should be jealous; and now Bunny made the irritating discovery that it was his turn to be careful! Vee had two enemies among women—and Bunny persisted in keeping them as his intimates. That Socialist girl at the university—of course he had to see her there, but did he have to make dates to go to Socialist meetings with her? Vee was ready to believe that he wasn't in love with a common little sweatshop Jewess; but what if Vee wanted to be taken to a "world premiere" on the evening of the Socialist lecture?

And then—that Ruth Watkins! Of course Bunny wouldn't be in love with an ignorant country girl, without any education;

but all the same, she was setting her snares for him, and Vee had seen enough of men to know that a woman can always get what she wants, if she keeps after it. Bunny kept going to that lodging-house room, and plotting and scheming with Paul to worry his father, and make trouble with Verne and Annabelle, so that pretty soon they wouldn't welcome Bunny any more at the Monastery, which was practically Vee's country club, and where you met the most important people. It wasn't just the social life, it was the business connections, that meant everything in the career of an actress. In the screen world promotion goes by favor, and Vee simply couldn't afford to give up her intimacy with Verne and Annabelle. She tried to convey this tactfully to Bunny, but when he failed to heed it, she had to keep insisting, until it began to sound like nagging. Bunny remembered her playful remark to her Applesauce, "It's as bad as if we were married!"

VI

Dad and Verne had a lot of negotiating to do with Pete O'Reilly, concerning the new leases they were putting through, and Dad was invited to spend a week end at this famous man's country place. Bunny was included in the invitation, and Dad said he ought to come; Dad was always nourishing the hope that something in this "great" world that so impressed him would impress his fastidious son. Besides, he added with a grin, the O'Reillys had a marriageable daughter.

Bunny had already met "Young Pete" at the university in connection with athletic events. Bunny had been singled out for attention, because he also was a scion of oil; some day he and "Young Pete" would be running the government of the United States, as their two fathers were running it now. "Young Pete" was a perfectly colorless business man, of the nationally advertised brand; but the father was the real thing—an old Irishman who had wandered over the deserts leading a burro loaded with a pick, a blanket, a sack of bacon and beans, and a skin full of water. This had continued up to middle age—he delighted to tell how, when he had come to Angel City to print a prospectus about his find, the printshop would not trust him for a thirteen-dollar job! Now, nobody could guess his millions; but he was plain as an old shoe, a likeable old fellow who wanted to sit in his shirt in hot weather, but was not allowed to.

The boss of the family was Mrs. Pete, who had risen from a section foreman's daughter to this high station in Southern California society. She was large and decisive; when she went into a department store she did not fool with the clerks, but strode at once to the floor-walker and announced, "I am Mrs. Peter O'Reilly, and I wish to be waited on promptly." The functionary would hit the floor with his forehead, and tear three clerks loose from their duties and set them rushing about at the great lady's behest.

Mrs. Peter it was who had summoned the architects and ordered the royal palace in a park, and set the high bronze fence all about, and the bronze gates; she it was who had caused the name of the owner of the estate to be graven on the gates. She had negotiated for the yacht of a fallen European monarch, and then torn it all out inside, and made it over to be fit for an Irish-American oil prospector—finished in Circassian walnut and blue satin, and with the owner's name in plain sight. Also there was a private car finished in Circassian walnut and blue satin, and with the owner's name on a brass plate. It was as fine as a haberdashery shop.

Now Mrs. Peter had Dad and Bunny to practice "society" upon; to shake hands high up in the air, and remark the early cold weather and the snow upon the mountains. And then to introduce Patricia, and to watch while Patricia did the stunts which her director had taught her, and which gave Bunny an impulse to say "Camera!" Miss Patricia O'Reilly was tall like her mother, and had a tendency to grow stout too early, so she was taking reducing medicine, which was injuring her heart and making her pale and aristocratic. She had learned every motion and every formula so carefully that she was as interesting as a large French doll, and her mother beamed upon the young couple—a possible union between two great dynasties, and there would be a wedding in Holy Name Church, and fifty thousand people outside, and pictures on the front pages of all the newspapers. Bunny's thoughts went even further—the "yellows" would interview Vee Tracy, and she would be cold and haughty, and in secret she would weep, and then catch a glimpse of her face in the mirror, and the thought would come, "Hold it!"

There were other guests, including Dr. Alonzo T. Cowper, D.D., Ph.D., LL.D., than whom it was not possible to imagine a human being radiating more cordiality. He was delighted that Bunny had passed his examinations successfully, and charmed to have been able to oblige his father, and again delighted that Dad was pleased with his son's progress. When they were alone, he ventured some playful remark about Bunny's red measles, and was much distressed to learn that the patient had not yet recovered; he took occasion to question the young man—was it really true that the reds were making such alarming progress in Angel City. Dr. Cowper wanted to talk about these shocking doctrines, in the same way that a small boy wants to read a naughty book!

Bunny was not called in to the conference between Old Pete and his father, but on the way home Dad told him about it. They were having the devil's own time; buying a government was not so simple a matter as they had thought. Everybody had to have a "rake-off," all the way down the line; by golly, the very office boy that brought you a letter about the matter expected a ten-dollar bill! Bunny took the occasion to plead, why not get out of the thing, surely they had enough money! But Dad said they were in too deep, the thing had cost him personally nearly six hundred thousand dollars, and it was real money, and it had hurt. No, they would go through with it, and when they had got the leases, it would be all hunky-dory.

Two troubles had arisen. The naval reserve lands had been under the control of the navy department, and it had been necessary to get them shifted to the control of Secretary Crisby. There had been question whether this could be done by executive decree, or did it require an act of Congress. The officials had made a lot of delay, but of course it was just a hold-up; they wanted more money for this one and that. Old Pete had sent his son on to Washington to act as paymaster. The other difficulty was that some little oil company had got onto the Sunnyside tract—the one that Verne and Dad were to get—and had started drilling under an old lease. They would have to be ejected, and it must be done quietly, they must fix matters up with the newspapers somehow. Verne wanted Dad to go up there and look the ground over, and maybe he and Bunny might make a trip of it. Sunnyside was going to be the world's wonder of an oil field—it would beat Paradise many times over, and when they had got it safely tucked away, Dad would take a good long rest.

VII

There was a telephone call for Bunny—he was to call "long distance" in a city a hundred miles up the state. When he did so, there was a nurse in a hospital, with a message from Bertie; she wanted him to come to her. She was not in any danger, and there was no use worrying the family, therefore she wished him to say nothing about the matter. Bunny of course jumped into his car and made all haste. His sister had been visiting the Normans, a long way from this hospital.

When he got there, the attendants told him that Bertie had had an operation for appendicitis, and was doing well. He was taken up to her room, and there she lay, pale, and strange-looking, because he had never seen her without her colors. Everything about her was spotlessly clean, a lacy white night-gown, and soft white pillows in which she lay sunken—nun-like, and pathetic in her gladness to see him. "Gee whiz, Bertie! How did this happen?"

"It came quite suddenly. It was pretty bad, but I'm all right now. Everybody's been so good to me." There was a nurse in the room, and Bertie waited until she had gone out and closed the door. Then she fixed her tired eyes on her brother, and said, "We call it appendicitis, because that's the conventional thing, and what you'll have to tell Dad and Aunt Emma. But you might as well know the truth—I was going to have a baby."

"Oh, my God!" Bunny stared at her, aghast.

"You needn't begin acting up—you're no spring chicken, Bunny."

"Who is the man?"

"Now, don't start any melodrama. You know it might happent to anybody."

"Yes—but who was it, Bertie?"

"I want you to get this straight at the beginning—it wasn't his fault. I did it on purpose."

Bunny didn't know what to make of that. "You might as well tell me, Bertie."

"Well, I want you to behave yourself. I'm my own boss, and I knew what I was doing. I wouldn't marry him now for a million dollars—not for all his millions, because he's a yellow pup, and I despise him."

"You mean Charlie Norman!"

She nodded in assent; and as she saw Bunny's hands clench, she said, "You don't have to do any heroics. There can't be a shot-gun wedding when the bride refuses to attend."

"Tell me about it, Bertie."

"Well, we were in love quite desperately for a while, and I thought he was going to marry me. But then I saw he wouldn't lay off other women, and I thought it over, and I decided, if I had a baby, he'd have to marry me, so I tried it."

"Good God, Bertie!"

"You needn't make faces. Thousands of women do it—it's one of our tricks. But Charlie's a yellow cur. When I told him about it, he behaved so disgustingly, I told him to go to hell. I got the name of a doctor that would fix me up, and Dad will have a thousand dollars to pay, and that's all the damage."

"Bertie," he whispered, "why in the world do you have to do things like that?"

"Don't worry, I'll not do it again. I had to learn, like everybody else."

"But why did you have to do it once? Trying to trap a rich man into marriage! Doesn't Dad give you enough money?"

"That's very easy for you to say, Bunny, you're satisfied to get off in a corner and read some old book. But I'm not like that, I have to have a little life. Dad gives me pocket money, but that's not what I want. I want a career—something of my own. And don't start preaching at me, because I'm weak as a kitten and can't stand anything just now. I wanted what every woman wants, a home of my own, and I didn't want a bungalow, I wanted a place I could invite people to, and make some use of my talents as a hostess. Well, I fell down, and now I want somebody to be kind to me for a few minutes, if you've possibly got that in you."

It looked as if the tears were coming into her eyes, so Bunny hastened to say, "All right, old girl, I'll lay off. But naturally I was taken aback."

"You needn't be. The doctor says it's done a million times a year in the United States. I amused myself figuring that out—it's about once every thirty seconds. Life is a messy business. Let's talk about something else!"

It was a time for confidences, and she wanted to know about him and Vee—was he going to marry her? He said he didn't know if she would have him. Bertie laughed—she would have him all right, she was playing her cards cleverly. But Bunny told how many times she got irritated at him, and why, and that gave Bertie occasion for a discourse. She was the same old Bertie; she might weaken for a few minutes, and ask him to be kind, but she still believed in money, and the things money bought. She discussed Vee from that point of view; it would be more dignified, and safer in the long run, for him to marry a lady, rather than an actress; but all the same, Vee had a lot of sense, and he might do worse. To go and wreck their happiness for the sake of his fool Bolshevik notions—that was just sickening!

Then she wanted to know about Dad's affairs, and how that deal in Washington was going; would they really get the leases? And was it true that Dad had any real pull with the administration in Washington? Bunny was sure he had; and Bertie revealed what she had in mind. "I've been thinking it over— I've had a lot of time to think, lying here. I believe that what I'll do is to go back to Eldon Burdick. He's a good deal of a dub, but you always know where to find him, and that seems to me a virtue right now."

"Would you tell him about this?" asked Bunny, wonderingly.

"No, why should I? He's made his mistakes, I guess, and he doesn't advertise them. He knows I've been living with Charlie, but I think he's still in love with me. What I have in mind is that I could make a career for him; I'd get Dad or Verne to pull some wires and get him a good diplomatic post. I believe I'd like to live in Paris, you meet all the important people there, and it's very good form. We're going to have to take charge of Europe, Eldon says, and I think he's the sort of man they'll need. How does that strike you?"

"Well, if it's what you want, I've no doubt you can get it. But it'll be rather tough on Eldon to have me for a brother-in-law."

"Oh, you're going to behave yourself," said Bertie, easily. "This is just a sort of children's complaint that you'll get over."

VIII

The navy department ousted the little company which had started drilling on the Sunnyside naval reserve. It sent in a bunch of marines to do it, and this unprecedented move attracted a lot of attention, which worried Dad and Verne. The latter had a man up there, to fix matters with the newspaper correspondents; and "Young Pete" was in Washington, seeing to things there. You began to notice in the newspapers items to the effect that the navy department was greatly worried because companies occupying lands adjoining the naval reserves were drilling, and draining the navy's oil; this would be a calamity, and the authorities were of the opinion that in order to avoid it the reserves should be turned over to the department of the interior, which would lease them upon terms advantageous to the government.

Bunny didn't need to ask his father about that propaganda; he knew what it meant, and he waited, wondering—was it possible to get away with anything so crude? Could anybody fail to see that the government could have taken the adjoining lands, under the same powers which had set aside the present reserves? Or that the navy could have put down offset wells on its own property, exactly as any oil man would have done? But no, this administration was not thinking about the navy—it was thinking about Dad and Verne! When the oil men had bought the Republican convention, they had also got the machinery of the party, and that included the press, which now accepted meekly the "dope" sent out from Washington, and commended the prompt measures of the administration to protect the navy's precious oil.

Then a peculiar thing happened. Dan Irving called Bunny on the phone, and made a date for lunch. The first thing he said, "Well, the labor college is flooey—naa poo!" He went on to declare, it was a waste of time to try to keep such an enterprise alive, so long as the present labor leaders were in power; they didn't want the young workers to be educated—it wouldn't be so easy for the machine to control them. Last week somebody had raided the college at night, and taken most of its belongings, except the debts; Dan had decided to pay these out of his savings and quit.

"What are you going to do?" asked Bunny. And Dan explained he had been sending in news to a little press service which a bunch of radicals were maintaining in Chicago, and he had got a lot of information from Washington that had attracted attention. He had some friends there on the inside, and the upshot of it was that Dan had been offered fifteen dollars a week to go to the national capital as correspondent of this press service. "I can exist on that, and it's the best job I can do."

Bunny was enthusiastic. "Dan, that's fine! There's plenty of rascals that need to be smoked out!"

"I know it; and that's what I want to see you about. One of the things I've got my eye on is these naval reserve oil leases. They look mighty fishy to me. Unless I'm missing my guess, the people behind it are Vernon Roscoe and Pete O'Reilly, and there's bound to be black wherever their hands have touched."

"I suppose so," replied Bunny, trying to keep his voice from going weak.

"There's talk in Washington that that's how Crisby came into the cabinet. The deal was fixed up before Harding got his nomination. General Wood says the nomination was offered to him if he'd make such a deal, and he turned it down."

"Good Lord!" said Bunny.

"Of course I don't know yet, but I'm going to dig it out. Then I remembered that Roscoe is an associate of your father's, and it occurred to me, it would be awkward as the devil if I was to come on anything — well, you know what I mean, Bunny—after your father was so kind to me, and you put up money for the college—

"Sure, I know," said Bunny. "You don't have to worry about that, Dan. You go ahead and do your job, just as if you'd never known us."

"That's fine of you. But listen—I was afraid maybe some day there might be a misunderstanding, unless I got this clear, that I never got any hint on this subject from you. My recollection is positive, you've never mentioned it in my hearing. Is that right?"

"It's absolutely right, Dan."

"You've never discussed your father's business with me at all—except the strike; and you haven't discussed Roscoe's or O'Reilly's, either."

"That is true, Dan. There'll never be any question about that."

"There will be, Bunny, rest assured—if I should bust loose in Washington, nothing would ever convince Roscoe and O'Reilly that I hadn't wormed it out of you. I'm afraid nothing would convince your father, either. But I want to be sure that your own mind is clear, I haven't been dishonorable."

Bunny gave him his hand on it; and not one of the veteran poker-players who sat all night in the smoke-filled living-room of the "ranch-house" at Paradise could have acted more perfectly the part of impassivity. Bunny even made himself finish lunch, and he wrote a check to cover part of the debt of the labor college, and gave his friend a hearty farewell and best wishes for his new job. Then he drove off in his car, and was free to look as he felt, which was quite unhappy!

He decided that it was his duty to tell his father about this conversation. It couldn't make any difference to Dan Irving's work, and it might yet be possible to keep Dad out of the mess. But when the elder Ross got home that evening, Bunny had no time to get in a word. "Well, son, we got those leases!"

"You don't say, Dad!"

"They've been approved, and Verne left for Washington today. They'll be signed next week, and you and me are going to take a trip and have some fun!"

IX

Joe and Ikey Menzies had been out of jail for a couple of months, their comrades of the Workers' party having scraped together the bail. Now came their trial, with several other members of the party. The state was undertaking to show that this organization was nothing but the Communist party under a camouflage; it was the "legal" part of the organization, but the real direction was in the hands of an "underground" group, which received funds and took orders from Moscow. It advocated the forcible overthrow of the "capitalist state," and the setting up of a "dictatorship of the proletariat," after the Russian pattern. On the other hand, the indicted men claimed that they had organized a legitimate working-class political party, and their attitude to violence was purely defensive. They believed the capitalists would never permit the power to be taken from them peaceably; it was the capitalists who would overthrow the constitution, and the workers would have to defend themselves.

The prisoners were all tried at once, and the procedure took three weeks and was quite an education in contemporary problems—or would have been, had the newspapers reported both sides. To get the workers' side, you had to sit in the court room; and Bunny went whenever he could get loose from the university. He was there when the prosecution sprung a "sur-

prise" witness, and it was a surprise to Bunny also—his boyhood friend, Ben Skutt! Ben, it appeared, had grown a moustache and taken a course in the Moscow dialect, and had turned
up as an oil worker out of a job, and been admitted to the
Workers' party, and before long had got a job in the office.
Now he had harrowing stories to tell of the criminal things he
had heard said, and of efforts the party had made to incite the
oil workers to rise and destroy the wells. On the other hand,
so Bunny was told by Ikey Menzies, the Communists were
ready to swear that Ben Skutt had himself done all the proposing of destruction—at the crisis of the strike he had spent his
time insisting that the only way to save the situation was to get
a bunch of real fighting men and burn up half a dozen oil fields.

Bunny went home to his father. "Dad, just what was it
made you get rid of Ben Skutt?"

"Why, I found he'd been taking commissions from the
other feller. He'd been up to other rascalities, too."

"Just what?"

Dad laughed. "He had a scheme that was a wonder. You
know, down there at Prospect Hill, people were in a crazy
hurry to drill; the owner of the next lot was getting his well
down first, and draining all the oil away. Ben and another
feller would find a bunch of lot owners jist on the point of
making a good lease; and Ben would have his pal give him a
quit-claim deed to one of those lots. Ben would record the
deed, and of course, when the title company come to report
on the property, there was that cloud on the title. The owner
would come hustling after Ben Skutt in a panic, what the hell
was this? And Ben would look shocked, and tell how he had
bought the lot from some feller in good faith. Who was the
feller? Well, the feller had disappeared, and nobody could find
him. But there Ben had the lease tied up, and the drilling
couldn't start. The lot owner would rage and swear—all the
lot owners in the lease was all tied up together, and nobody
could do anything with their property till that one lot had got
free. To go into court and clear the title would take six months
or so, and meantime the chance to lease would be gone; so the
owners would have to chip in and pay Ben five thousand or so—
whatever he claimed he had paid to the other man."

"I should think that trick would have been tried a lot of
times," remarked Bunny; and Dad answered, it would be tried
jist long enough for the news to git round, and then some lot

owner would stick a gun under Ben's nose, and settle it that way. What had happened in his case was the usual thing, a woman had got hold of him and plucked him clean, and that was why he was doing spy work for the patriotic societies. Bunny knew that his father didn't owe anything to this slippery rascal, and wouldn't mind his being exposed, provided Bunny's name was not dragged in. It would be easy to trace the matter down, by looking up Ben's real estate transactions in the county records; he would have given a quit-claim deed to the lot owners whom he had held up, and if these men were still in the neighborhood, no doubt they would testify, or could be made to. Bunny saw Rachel at the university next morning and told her the story, and gave her a hundred dollar bill to cover the costs of a title search. She passed it on to Joe or Ikey, and two days later Ben was confronted by half a dozen infuriated citizens, male and female, who did a good deal to shake the jury's faith in his testimony as to secret conspiracies in the Workers' party! The jury disagreed in the case of all but two men, the leading party directors; these got six years apiece, but the Menzies boys got off, and the party held a celebration, which was described in the newspapers as an orgy of red revolutionary raving.

X

Dad was not so much troubled by the news which Bunny told him, that Dan Irving was on the trail of Vernon Roscoe in the national capital. There was bound to be gossip about the lease, of course; there were always "soreheads," trying to make trouble, but everybody would understand it was jist politics. It was the biggest "killing" of Dad's life-time, and of Verne's, too; they would go ahead and drill the land and get out the oil, and nothing else would count. You had to be a sort of hard-shell crab in this game; it was too bad Bunny wasn't able to grow the necessary shell. Also, it was too bad that a nice young feller like "the professor" couldn't find anything better to do with himself than to go smelling round Verne's out-house.

There had been a new company formed, to develop this greatest oil field in America, and Dad was part owner of the stock, and a vice-president, with another hundred thousand a year for directing the development work. But he wasn't going to wear himself out with detail, he promised Bunny; he had trained some competent young fellers by now, and all he had to do was direct them. It was a wonderful job, and he was all wrapped up in putting it through, working harder than ever, in defiance of his doctors.

A telegram came from Verne; the leases had been signed. Bunny arranged to get a week off from his studies—such favors could be had by a grave old senior, especially when there was hope that his father might endow a chair of research in petroleum chemistry. They took a long drive to Sunnyside, a remote part of the state, grazing country, with very few settlers, and poor roads. They stayed in a crude country hotel, and inspected the new fields, riding horseback part of the time. Dad's geologists were there, and the engineers and surveyors; they decided upon the drilling sites, and the roads, and the pipe-lines, and the tank-farm—yes, even a town, and how the streets were to run, and where the moving picture theatre and the general store were to be! The necessary wires had been pulled, and the county was to start work on a paved road next week. It was all hunkydory!

Bunny ought to have been interested in all this; he ought to have been proud of the "killing," like any loyal son. Instead of that, here he was as usual, "smelling round the out-house" to use the ex-mule-driver's crude phrase. The fates which willed that Bunny should be always on the wrong side of his father's work followed him here to this country hotel, and brought him into contact with an old ranchman, a feeble-faced, pathetic old fellow with skin turned to leather by sixty years of baking heat and winds. Anxious watery blue eyes he had, and a big case of papers under his arm, which he wouldn't leave in his room for fear they would be stolen. He wanted Dad to consider a lease, and of course Dad had no time to fool with little leases, and told him so, and that settled it. But the old man found out somehow that Bunny lacked the customary hard-shell of the big oil-crabs, and succeeded in luring the young man to his room and showing his documents. It was a certified file from the department of the interior, all fixed up with impressive red seals and blue ribbons—but all the same it wasn't complete, the old man declared; somebody had stolen the essential documents from the government files, which showed how "Mid-Central Pete" had done him out of his homestead. "It's a feller named Vernon Roscoe, one of the big crooks in this game."

The old man, Carberry, had set out to homestead a claim to some lands nearby; and oil had been discovered, and Mid-Central Pete had just come in and shoved him out, paying him not a cent for his twenty-two hundred dollars of improvements. They could do this—the old man had a copy of the law to show how it read, excluding "mineral lands" from homestead rights; there were thousands in this part of the state who had been caught in that trap. But Carberry had actually got a patent on his land, and so had a valid claim; but somebody had managed to doctor the government records, and now for several years he had been struggling for redress. With pathetic trustfulness he had written to his congressman, to get a lawyer in Washington to represent him, and the congressman had recommended a lawyer, and Carberry had sent him money several times with no result—and then, going to Washington, had discovered that the alleged lawyer was simply a clerk in the congressman's office, plundering land claimants and presumably dividing the graft with his employer!

A pitiful, pitiful story—and the worst part of it, you could see it wasn't a single case, but a system. One more way by which the rich and powerful were plundering the poor and weak! Carberry had with him a government document he had managed to get in Washington, the report of a congressional investigation of California land cases. Bunny spent an evening glancing through it—a thousand pages of wholesale fraud and stealing in close print. For example, the seizure of oil rights by the railroads! The government land grants had turned over to the railroads every other section of land along their right of way, but had specifically exempted all "mineral lands." Wherever minerals might be discovered, the roads were bound to surrender these sections and take other sections. Under the law, the word "minerals" included petroleum; but were the railroads paying any attention to that law? The Southern Pacific alone had California oil lands to a value of more than a billion dollars; but every effort to recover these properties for the state had been blocked by cunning lawyers and purchased politicians and judges. As they drove home, Bunny tried to tell his father about this; but what could Dad do? What could he do about old Carberry, who had been robbed of his home by "Mid-Central Pete"? You could be sure that Dad wasn't going "smelling round Verne's out-house"!

CHAPTER XVII

THE EXPOSURE

I

All that fall and winter the quail had been calling from the hills of Paradise unheeded. Bunny didn't want to go there. But now it chanced that Dad had some matters to see to, and his chauffeur had got sent to jail for turning bootlegger in his off hours. Dad was having spells of bad health, when he did not feel equal to driving; and this being a Friday, his son offered to take him.

The Ross Junior tract had nothing left of Bunny but the name. There was a strange woman as housekeeper in the ranch-house, and the Rascum cabin had been moved, and the bougainvillea vine replaced by a derrick. Every one of the fellows who had met with Paul was gone, and there were no more intellectual discussions. Paradise was now a place where men worked hard at getting out oil, and kept their mouths closed. There were hundreds of men Bunny had never seen before, and these had brought a new atmosphere. They patronized the bootleggers and the pool-rooms, and places for secret gambling and drinking. "Orange-pickers" was the contemptuous name the real oil-workers applied to this new element, and their lack of familiarity with their jobs was a cause of endless trouble; they would slip from greasy derricks, or get crushed by the heavy pipe, and the company had had to build an addition to the hospital. But of course that was cheaper than paying union wages to skilled men!

A deplorable thing happened to Bunny; his reading of a book was interrupted by a visit from the wife of Jick Duggan, one of the men in the county jail. The woman insisted on seeing him, and then insisted on weeping all over the place, and telling him harrowing tales about her husband and the other fellows. She begged him to go and see for himself, and he was weak enough to yield—you can see how imprudent it was, on the part of a young oil prince who was trying to grow his hard shell, so that he could be a help to his old father, and enjoy life with a darling of the world. Bunny knew that he was doing wrong, and showed his guilt by not telling his father where he was going that rainy Saturday afternoon.

They let him into the jail without objection; the men who kept the place being used to it, and unable to foresee the impression it would make upon a young idealist. The ancient dungeon had been contrived by an architect with a special genius for driving his fellow beings mad. The "tanks," instead of having doors with keys, like other jail cells, were designed as revolving turrets, and whenever you wanted to put a prisoner in or take one out, you revolved the turret until an opening in one set of bars corresponded with an opening in another set. This revolving was done by means of a hand-winch, and involved a frightful grinding and shrieking of rusty iron. There were three such tanks, one on top of the other, and the revolving of any one inflicted the uproar on everybody. In the course of the jail's forty years of history, scores of men had gone mad from having to listen to these sounds at all hours of the day and night.

Have you ever had the experience of seeing some person you know and love shut behind bars like a wild beast? It was something that hit Bunny in the pit of his stomach, and made him weak and faint. Here were seven fellows, all but two of them young as himself, crowding together like so many friendly and affectionate deer, nuzzling through the bars and expecting lumps of sugar or bits of bread. Their pitiful clamor of welcome, the grateful light on their faces—just for a visit, a few minutes of a rich young man's time!

These were all ranch-fellows, out-door men, that had worked in the sun and rain all their lives, and grown big and bronzed and sturdy; but now they were bleached white or yellow, dirty and unshaven, with sunken cheeks and hollow eyes. Jick Duggan was coughing, just as his wife had said, and there was not one healthy-looking man in the bunch. If Bunny had been able to say to himself that these men had done some vile deed, and this was their atonement, he might have justified it, even while he questioned what good it would do; but they were there because they had dared to dream of justice for their fellows, and to talk about it, in defiance of the "open shop" crowd of big business men!

Bunny had sent them some books—they were allowed to have books that didn't look radical to very ignorant jailers, and provided the books came direct from the publishers, so that they would not have to be searched too carefully for concealed objects such as saws and dope. Now they wanted to tell him how much these books had helped, and to ask for more. And what did Bunny know about their prospects of getting a trial? Had he seen Paul, and what did Paul think? And what about the union—was there anything left of it? They were not allowed any sort of "radical" paper, so they were six or seven months behind the news of their own world.

II

Bunny came out into the sunshine with a fresh impulse of desperation. His father was half sick, but even so, his father must have this burden of pain dumped onto him! The last time they had discussed the matter, Dad had said to wait, Vernon Roscoe would "see what he could do." But now Bunny would wait no longer; Dad must compel Verne to act, or Bunny would take up the job himself.

He drove his father back to Angel City, and learned that the radicals had organized a "defense committee," and there was to be a mass meeting of protest, at which funds would be raised for the approaching trial. Paul was to be the principal speaker —despite the fact that it might cause his bail privilege to be cancelled. When Bunny got that news, he served an ultimatum on his father; the meeting was to take place the following week, and unless Verne had acted in the meantime, Bunny was going to be one of the speakers, and say his full say about the case.

Dad of course protested. But it was one of those times when his son surprised him by failing to be "soft." Bunny went farther than ever in his desperation. "Maybe you'll feel I haven't any right to behave like this while I'm living on your money, and perhaps I ought to quit college and go to work for myself."

"Son, I've never said anything like that!"

"No, but I'm putting you in a hole with Verne, and it would be easier if you could say I'm not living on you."

"Son, I don't want to say any such thing. But I do think you ought to consider my position."

"I've considered everything, Dad—considered till I'm sick at heart. I just can't let my love for any one person in the world take the place of my sense of justice. We're committing a crime to keep those men in jail, and I say Verne has got to let them out, and if he don't, then I'm going to make it hot for him."

Verne was on his way back from the east; and Bunny demanded that he should phone the district attorney his wishes; he might phone the judge, too, if he thought necessary—it wouldn't be the first time, Bunny would wager. If he didn't do it, then Bunny's name would be announced as one of the speakers at that mass-meeting. Upon Dad flashed the memory of that terrible meeting of Harry Seager's; he saw his beloved son publicly adopting that same ferocious mob, clasping that sea of angry faces and uplifted hands and lungs of leather!

Also Bunny renewed his threat about Annabelle. "You tell Verne with my compliments, I'm going to lay siege to his girl, and take her to that meeting. I'll tell her he's trying to keep her in a golden cage, and that'll make her go; and if ever she hears the full story of those political prisoners, she'll make Verne wish he'd known when to quit!" Dad could hardly keep from grinning. Poor old man, in his secret heart he was proud of the kid's nerve!

Whether Dad used the argument about Annabelle, or what he said, this much is history—two days after Vernon Roscoe arrived from Washington in his private car, carrying in his own hands the precious documents with the big red seals of the department of the interior, the district attorney of San Elido County appeared before Superior Judge Patten, and entered a "nolle pros" in the eight criminal syndicalism cases. So Vee Tracy got back her ten thousand dollars, and the seven oil workers were turned out half-blinded into the sunshine, and Bunny postponed his premier appearance in the role of that ill bird—whatever may be the name of it—which is reputed to foul its own nest.

III

Bunny got the news before it was in the papers, and he hastened to take it to Paul and Ruth. Paul had got work as a carpenter, and they had rented a little cottage on the rear of a lot. Ruth had started her nurse's course in one of the big hospitals, and Paul had got some books, and there was a little of Paradise transported to a working-class part of Angel City. And oh, the happiness that shone in Ruth's face when Bunny came in with the news! And then the strange mixture of anguish and pride, as Paul spoke: "It's good of you, son, to have taken so much trouble, and I do appreciate it; but I'm afraid you won't think me very grateful when you hear what I'm going to do with my freedom."

"What is it, Paul?"

"I've decided to join the Workers' party."

"Oh, Paul!" Bunny's face showed dismay. "But why?"

"Because I believe in their tactics. I always have, ever since my time in Siberia. I waited, because I didn't want to hurt the strike; and after I got arrested, I couldn't do anything without compromising the other fellows. But now it won't hurt anyone but myself, so I'm going to say what I know."

"But Paul! They'll only arrest you again!"

"Maybe so. But this time they'll arrest me as a Communist, and they'll try me that way."

"But they've already convicted so many!"

"That's the way an unpopular cause has to grow—there's no other way. Here I am, an obscure workingman, and nobody pays any attention to what I think or say; but if they try me as a Communist, I make people talk and think about our ideas."

Bunny stole a look at Ruth: a pitiful sight, her eyes riveted upon her brother, and her hands clasped tight in fear. It was so that she had looked when Paul was going off to war. It was her fate to see him go off to war!

"Are you sure there's nothing more important you can do, Paul?"

"I used to think I was going to do a lot of great things. But the last few years have taught me that a workingman isn't very important in this capitalist world, and he has to remember his place. A lot of us are going to jail, and a lot more are going to die. The one thing we must be sure of is that we help to awaken the slaves."

There was a pause. "You're quite sure it can't come peaceably, Paul?"

"The other has to say about that, son. Do you think they were peaceable during the strike? You should have been there!"

"And you've given up hope for democracy?"

"Not at all! Democracy is the goal—it's the only thing worth working for. But it can't exist till we've broken the strangle-hold of big business. That's a fighting job, and it can't be done by democracy. Look at the boobs that Eli has got in his tabernacle, and imagine them setting out to get the best of Vernon Roscoe!"

Bunny could not avoid a smile. "That's exactly Verne's own statement."

"Well, he's a practical man, and I've a great respect for him. He wants to do something, and he finds out the way, and he does it. He doesn't let the government get in his way, does he? No, he overthrows the government by bribery. By the way, son, have you seen Dan Irving's Washington letter this week?"

"The paper's at home, but I didn't stop to look at it."

"Well, you'll be interested. Dan says it's known to all the newspaper men in Washington that Roscoe and O'Reilly made a deal with the attorney-general to buy the nomination for Harding, on condition they were to get these naval reserve leases. They've been buying government officials right and left, and newspaper men also. There's a clamor for an investigation, but the gang won't let it happen."

There was a pause. Paul, watching his friend's face, saw an uneasy look, and added, "Don't talk to me about it, son—I don't want to know anything I'm not free to tell. But you and I both understand—that is capitalist government, and what has it got to do with democracy?"

Again Bunny didn't answer; and Paul said, "I think about Verne, as you call him, because I've just had a run-in with him, and he's the system to me. I want to take his powers away from him; and how am I going to do it? I've boxed the compass, trying to figure how it can be done legally. He's got the courts, and they'll call anything legal that he says; they'll wind you up in a spider's web of technicalities. He's got the machinery for reaching the masses—you can't tell them anything but what he wants them to hear. He's got the movies—people say he has a movie star for a mistress—maybe you know about that. And you've been to college—O'Reilly attends to that, I'm told. We could never get a majority vote—because Verne has the ballot-boxes stuffed; even if we elected anybody, he'd have them bought before they got into office. The more I think of the idea that he would give up to paper ballots— the crazier it seems to me."

"But then, Paul, what can you hope for?"

"I'm going to the workers! Verne's oil workers are the basis of his power, they produce his wealth, and they can be reached, they're not scattered all over. They have one common job, and one common interest—they want the wealth that Verne takes from them. Of course they know that only dimly; they read his newspapers, and go to his movies. But we're going to teach them—and when they take the oil wells, how can Verne get them back?"

"He'll send troops and take them, Paul!"

"He won't send troops, because we'll have the railwaymen. We'll have the telegraphers, and they'll send our messages instead of his. We'll have the men in all the key industries—we're going out to organize them, and tell them exactly how to do it—all power to the unions."

Bunny was contemplating once more the vision which his friend had brought back from Siberia. And Paul went on, with that condescending air that had always impressed Bunny, and infuriated his sister. "It seems dreadful to you, because it means a fight, and you don't want to fight—you don't have to. The men for this job are the ones that have had the iron in their souls—men that have been beaten and crushed, thrown into jail and starved there. That's how Verne makes the revolution, he throws us into jail and lets us rot. We lie there and have bitter, black thoughts. All the Bolsheviks got their training in dungeons; and now the masters are giving the same course in America. It's not only that we're tempted and made hard—it's that we become marked men, the workers know us; the poor slaves that don't dare move a hand for themselves, they learn that there are fellows they can trust, that won't sell them out to Vernon Roscoe! I'm going back to Paradise, son, and teach Communism, and if Verne has me arrested again, the Moscow program will go into the court records of San Elido county!"

IV

The newspapers announced a social event of the first importance, the engagement of Miss Alberta Ross, only daughter of Mr. J. Arnold Ross, to Mr. Eldon Burdick, a scion of one of the oldest families of the city, and recently chosen president of the California Defense League. A few days later came the announcement that Mr. Burdick had been appointed a secretary to the American embassy at Paris; and so the wedding was a state occasion, with more flowers than were ever seen in a church before, and Bunny all dolled up for a groomsman, and Dad looking as handsome as the ringmaster of a circus, and Aunt Emma, who considered that she had made this match, assuming the mental position of the bride's mother, with the proper uncertain expression, half elation and half tears. "Mrs. Emma Ross, aunt of the bride, wore pink satin embroidered in pastel colored beads and carried pink lilies"— thus the newspapers, which set forth the importance of the Burdick family, and all about the Ross millions, and never mentioned that the father of the bride had once been a mule-driver, nor even that he had kept a general store at Queen Center, California!

And when the excitement was all over, and bride and groom had set out for their post of duty, then a funny thing happened; Aunt Emma, uplifted by her success as match-maker, turned her arts upon Bunny! The occasion was the world premiere of "The Princess of Patchouli," a sort of family event. Had not Dad and Bunny been present at the inception of this sumptuous work of art? Had not Dad been king? By golly, he had, and he had told Aunt Emma about it at least a dozen times—and so, what more natural than that he should escort her upon his arm, following immediately behind the star of the occasion and her Bunny-rabbit? And what more natural than that Aunt Emma should meet Vee Tracy, and fall in love with her at first sight, and tell her darling nephew about her feelings?

In short, Bunny became aware that he was being manipulated by the proverbial tact of woman to think that Vee Tracy made a perfect princess on the screen, she was a natural-born aristocrat in both appearance and manner. It is part of the proverbial intuitive powers of woman, that she will be able to say exactly how an aristocrat will look and act, even though she has never been outside the state of California, and never laid eyes upon a single aristocrat in all her fifty years.

Bunny said, yes, Vee was all right; she was a good-looker. With the proverbial unresponsiveness of the selfish male, he did not warm up to his aunt's hints and tell about his love affair. In fact he was rather shocked, because he thought she was too old to know about anything improper. So Aunt Emma had to come right out with it, "Why don't you marry her, Bunny?"

"Well, but Aunt Emma, I don't know that she'd have me."
"Have you ever asked her?"
"Well, I've sort of hinted round."

"Well, you stop hinting, and ask her plain. She's a lovely girl, and you're getting old enough to be serious now, and I think it would make a very distinguished marriage, and I know it would please your father—I believe he'll propose to her himself if you don't." Aunt Emma was quite charmed with this naughtiness, giving the younger generation to understand that they needn't be laying the old folks away on the shelf quite yet!

Bunny always liked to oblige; so he went off and thought it over, and half made up his mind to talk it over with Vee. But alas, the next time they met they got into one of those disputes that were making it so hard for them to be happy. Vee had just come from Annabelle Ames, and reported that Annabelle was in distress, because some rascal journalist was writing letters from Washington, accusing Verne of having bought the presidency of the United States, denouncing the Sunnyside lease as the greatest steal of the century, and demanding that Verne be prosecuted for bribery. Some thoughtful friend had cut out a copy of this printed article, and marked it all with red pencil and mailed it to Annabelle's home, marked "Personal." The article was most abusive, and the name of the writer sounded familiar to Vee—Daniel Webster Irving, where had she heard of Daniel Webster Irving? Of course Bunny had to tell her at once—because she'd be bound to find it out, and would think he was hiding it from her: Dan Irving was his former teacher at the university, and head of the labor college that had failed.

So then Vee went up into the air. This fellow had been worming secrets out of Bunny! And when Bunny stated firmly that he had never mentioned the matter to Dan or to any other of his radical friends, Vee cried, "Oh, my God! My God! You poor, naive, trusting soul!" She went on like that, it was proof positive of the cunning of these dangerous reds, that they should be able to keep him in ignorance while they used him for an oil well and pumped him dry! In Vee's view of the matter, it now became of the utmost urgency that Annabelle and Verne should not find out that Bunny knew this rascal journalist, and had actually helped to support him. If they found out, it would be all over with their friendship, they would be sure they had been basely betrayed, or at least that Bunny was such a scatter-brain that it was unsafe to have him about. Vee wanted to be loyal and romantic and melodramatic, just like one of her "continuities." And Bunny was bored, and told her that Dad had probably told Verne all about the matter, at the time that he, Bunny, had told his father.

So the young oil prince did not ask the "natural-born aristocrat" to marry him. No, he went off and was wretchedly unhappy; because he ached for Vee whenever he was away from her, and yet they seemed to be always having violent emotional crises, and having to make it up with tears. There was no way for him to avoid trouble, except to give up the radical movement; and it was a fact that intellectually nothing else appealed to him. He wanted to see Paul, and argue with him, and present a score of new objections to the Workers' party! He wanted to take Rachel to meet Paul and Ruth, and hear the arguments that would fly fast and furious, when Rachel set forth her opinion of the left wing insanity! He wanted to go to the meetings of the "Ypsels," the Young Peoples' Socialist League, of which Rachel had recently taken on the duties of secretary—here was real education, young folks who actually wanted to use their minds, and took ideas with the seriousness that other students reserved for football and fraternity politics!

V

Of all the people Bunny knew, it appeared just now that only one was perfectly successful and completely happy, and that was Eli Watkins, prophet of the Third Revelation. For the Lord had carried out to the letter the promise revealed to the runners of the Bible Marathon; he had caused a great banker, Mark Eisenberg, who ran the financial affairs of Angel City, to reflect upon the importance of Eli's political influence, and to put up a good part of the money for the new tabernacle. Now the structure was completed, and was opened amid such glory to the Lord as had never been witnessed in this part of the world.

Southern California is populated for the most part by retired farmers from the middle west, who have come out to die amid sunshine and flowers. Of course they want to die happy, and with the assurance of sunshine and flowers beyond; so Angel City is the home of more weird cults and doctrines—you couldn't form any conception of it till you came to investigate. To run your eye over the pages of performances advertised in the Sunday newspapers would cause you to burst into laughter or tears, according to your temperament. Wherever three or

more were gathered together in the name of Jesus or Buddha
or Zoroaster, or Truth or Light or Love, or New Thought or
Spiritualism or Psychic Science—there was the beginning of a
new revelation, with mystical, inner states of bliss and esoteric
ways of salvation.

Eli had advantages over most of these spiritual founders.
In the first place, he had been a real shepherd of flocks and
herds, and there are age-old traditions attaching to this profession. Also it was symbolically useful; what Eli had done to
the goats he was now doing to the human goats of Angel City,
gathering them into the fold and guarding them from the cruel
wolf Satan. He had taken to carrying a shepherd's crook on
the platform, and with his white robes and the star shining in
his yellow hair, he would call the flocks, just as he had done
upon the hills, and when he passed the collection plate, they
would do the shearing of themselves.

Eli possessed a sense of drama and turned it loose in the
devising of primitive little tableaux and pageants, which gave
rapture to his simple minded followers. When he told how he
had been tempted of the devil, the wicked One came upon the
scene, hoofs, horns and tail, and with a red spotlight on him;
when Eli lifted up the cross on high, the devil would fall and
strike his forehead on the ground, and the silver trumpets
would peal, and the followers would burst into loud hosannahs.
Or perhaps it would be the command, "Suffer little children to
come unto me"; there would be hundreds of children, all robed
in white, and when Eli lifted his shepherd's crook and called,
they came storming to the platform, their fresh young voices
shouting, "Praise the Lord!" And of course there was the
regular mourners' bench, and the baptisms in the marble
tank. You were never allowed to forget that you had a soul,
and that it was of supreme importance to you and to Jesus,
and that you were having it saved by Eli's aid. You were
always being called upon to do something—to stand up for the
Lord, or to clap your hands for salvation, or to raise your right
hand if you were a new-comer to the tabernacle.

But the great advantage Eli had over the other prophets
was the pair of leathern bellows he had developed out on the
hills of Paradise. Never was there such an electrifying voice,
and never one that could keep going so long. All day Sunday
it bellowed and boomed—morning, afternoon, evening; there
were week-day services every evening but Saturday, and in the

mornings and afternoons there were prayer meetings and Bible schools and services of song and healing blessings and baptismal ceremonials and thank offerings and wholesale weddings and Bride of the Lamb dedications—you just couldn't keep track of all that was going on in the many rooms and meeting-halls of this half million dollar tabernacle.

Science had just completed a marvelous invention; the human voice became magnified a hundred million fold, it could be spread over the whole earth. The population of America had gone wild over radio, and everybody had rushed to get a set. The first great public use made of this achievement in Angel City was to open a new three million dollar hotel for the pleasure of the very rich, and the opening ceremonies were broadcasted, and the newspapers were full of the wonder of it; but it proved to be dreadful, because everybody in the hotel got drunk, and the manager of the institution placed himself in front of the microphone and poured out a stream of obscenities such as farmers' wives from Iowa had never dreamed in all their lives. So it was felt that the new invention needed to be sanctified and redeemed, and Eli proceeded to install one of the biggest and most powerful broadcasting stations. Through the Lord's mercy, his words were heard over four million square miles, and it was worthwhile to preach to audiences of that size, praise Jesus!

Eli's preaching had thus become one of the major features of Southern California life. You literally couldn't get away from him if you tried. Dad had been told by his doctor that he needed more exercise, and he had taken to walking for half an hour before dinner; he declared that he listened to Eli's sermons on all these walks, and never missed a single word! Everybody's house was wide open in this warm spring weather, and all you had to do was to choose a neighborhood where the moderately poor lived—and 90 per cent of the people were that. You would hear the familiar bellowing voice, and before you got out of range of it, you would come in range of another radio set, and so you would be relayed from street to street and from district to district! In these houses sat old couples with family bibles in their hands and tears of rapture in their eyes; or perhaps a mother washing her baby's clothes or making a pudding for her husband's supper—and all the time her soul caught up to glory on the wings of the mighty prophet's eloquence! And Dad walking outside, also exalted—because, don't forget that he was the man who had started this Third Revelation—he had invented all its patter, that day he had tried to keep old Abel Watkins from beating his daughter Ruth!

VI

Bunny received a letter from Dan Irving, telling about his new job. It was a simple matter to be a radical press correspondent in Washington these days; the regular newspaper fellows were loaded up with material they were not allowed to handle. All but a few of the "hard guys" were boiling over with indignation at what they saw, and when they met Dan, they boiled over on him. The only trouble was, his labor press service had so little space, and only a score or two of radical papers that would look at its material.

President Harding had brought with him a swarm of camp followers, his political bodyguard at home; the newspaper men knew them as "the Ohio gang," and they were looting everything in sight. Barney Brockway had given one of his henchmen a desk in the secret service department; this was the "fixer," and if you wanted anything, he would tell you the price. The Wilson administration had grown fat by exploiting the properties seized from enemy aliens; and now the Harding administration was growing fat out of turning them back! Five per cent was the regular "split"; if you wanted to recover a ten million dollar property, you turned over half a million in liberty bonds to the "fixer." Bootlegging privileges were sold for millions, and deals were made right in the lobbies of the Capitol. Dan heard from insiders that more than three hundred millions had already been stolen from the funds appropriated for relief of war veterans—the head of that bureau was another of the "Ohio gang." And the amazing fact was, no matter how many of these scandals you might unearth, you couldn't get a single big newspaper or magazine in the country to touch them!

Bunny took that letter to his father, and as usual it meant to the old man exactly the opposite of what it meant to Bunny. Yes, politics were rotten, and so you saw the folly of trusting business matters to government. Take business away from the politicians, and turn it over to business men, who would run it without graft. If those oil lands had been given to Dad and Verne in the beginning, there wouldn't have been any bribing—

wasn't that clear? Dad and Verne were patriots, putting an end to a vicious public policy!

Did Dad really believe that? It was hard for Bunny to be sure. Dad had lies that he told to the public; and perhaps he had others that he told to his son, and yet others that he told to himself. If you laid hold of him and tore all those lies away, he would not be able to stand the sight of his nakedness.

His enemies, the "soreheads" in Congress, were busily engaged in depriving him of these spiritual coverings. There was one old senator in Washington by the name of LaFollette— his head had been sore for forty years, and no way could be found to heal it. Now he was denouncing the oil leases, and demanding an investigation. The Harding machine had blocked him, but it couldn't keep him from making speeches—he would talk for eight hours at a stretch, and the galleries would be full, and then he would mail out his speeches under government frank. Dad would grumble and growl—and then in the midst of it he would realize that his own dear son was on the side of these trouble-makers! Instead of sympathizing with his father's lies, Bunny was criticizing them, and making his father ashamed!

Then a painful thing happened. There was a newspaper publisher in a western city, one of those old pirates of the frontier type, who had begun life as a bartender, and delighted to tell how he would toss a silver dollar up to the ceiling, and if it stuck it belonged to the boss and if it came down it belonged to him. By this means he had got rich, and now he owned a paper, and he got onto this scandal of the oil leases. There came to him a man who had some old claim to part of the Sunnyside lease, and the publisher made a deal with this man to go halves, and then he served notice on Verne that they had to have a million dollars. Verne told him to go to hell, and the result was, this newspaper opened up with front page exposures of the greatest public steal in history. And this was no obscure Socialist sheet, this was one of the most widely read newspapers in the country, and copies were being mailed to all members of Congress, and to other newspapers—gee, it was awful! Dad and Verne and the rest held anxious conferences, and suffered agonies of soul; in the end they had to give up to the old pirate, and paid him his million in cold cash—and the great newspaper lost all its interest in the public welfare!

When Bunny was a youngster, he had read the stories of

Captain Mayne Reid, and he remembered one scene—a fish-
hawk capturing a fish, and then a swift eagle swooping down
from the sky and taking the prize away. Just so it was in the
oil game—a world of human hawks and eagles!

VII

Bunny no longer felt comfortable about going to the
Monastery. But Vee would not let him quit, she argued and
pleaded; Annabelle was so kind and good, and would be so
hurt if he let horrid political quarrels break up their friendship!
Bunny answered—he knew Verne must be sore as the dickens;
and imagine Verne being tactful or considerate of a guest!

When you went out into society and refused to take a drink,
you caused everybody to begin talking about prohibition. In
the same way, when you did not join in denunciation of the
"insurgent" senators in Washington, you caused some one to
comment on your sympathy for bomb-throwers. The little
bunch of "reds" in Congress were interfering with legislation
much desired by the rich, and they were denounced at every
dinner table, including Vernon Roscoe's. The great Schmolsky
said, what the hell were they after, anyhow? And Verne replied
"Ask Jim Junior—he's chummy with them." Annabelle had
to jump in and cry, "No politics! I won't have you picking on
my Bunny!"

Then, later in the evening, when Harvey Manning got drunk,
he sat on Bunny's knee, very affectionate, as he always was,
and shook one finger in front of Bunny's nose and remarked,
"You gonna tell 'm bout me?" And when Bunny inquired,
"Tell who, Harve?" the other replied, "Those muckrakin
friends o yours. I aint gonna have 'em tellin on me! My ole
uncle fines out I get drunk he'll cut me out o his will." So
Bunny knew that his intimacy with the enemy had been a
subject of discussion at the Monastery!

There had been a series of violent outbreaks in Angel City.
The members of the American Legion, roused by the "red
revolutionary raving," had invaded the headquarters of the
I. W. W. and thrown the members down the stairs, and thrown
their typewriters and desks after them. Since the courts
wouldn't enforce law and order, these young men were going
to attend to it. They had raided bookstores which sold books
with red bindings, and dumped the books into the street and

burned them. They had beaten up newsdealers who were selling radical magazines. Also they were taking charge of the speakers the public heard—if they didn't like one, they notified the owner of the hall, and he hastened to break his contract.

John Groby, one of Verne's oil associates from Oklahoma, was at the dinner-table, and he said, that was the way to handle the rattle-snakes. Groby may not have known that one of the snakes was sitting across the way from him, so Bunny took no offense, but listened quietly. "That's the way we did the job at home, we turned the Legion loose on 'em and cracked their heads, and they moved on to some other field. You're too polite out here, Verne."

Annabelle had put Bunny beside her, so that she might protect him from assaults. Now she started telling him about her new picture, "A Mother's Heart." Such a sweet, old-fashioned story! Bunny would call it sentimental, perhaps, but the women would just love it, and it gave her a fine part. Also Vee had a clever scenario for her new picture, "The Golden Couch." Quite a fetching title, didn't Bunny think? And all the time, above the soft murmur of Annabelle's voice, Bunny heard the loud noise of John Groby blessing the Legion. Bunny longed to ask him what the veterans would say to the "Ohio gang," stealing the funds from their disabled buddies.

Someone mentioned another stunt of the returned soldiers— their setting up a censorship of moving pictures. One Angel City theatre had started to show a German film, "The Cabinet of Dr. Caligari," and this Hun invasion had so outraged the Legion men, they had put on their uniforms and blockaded the theatre, and beaten up the people who tried to get in. Tommy Paley laughed—the courage of each of those veterans had been fortified by a five dollar bill, contributed by the association of motion picture producers! They didn't want foreign films that set them too high a standard!

Then Schmolsky. He was too fat to comprehend such a thing as irony, and he remarked that the directors were mighty damn right. Schmolsky, a Jew from Ruthenia, or Rumelia, or Roumania, or some such country, said that we didn't want no foreign films breaking in on our production schedules. An hour or so later Bunny heard him telling how the Hollywood films were sweeping the German market—it wouldn't be three years before we'd own this business. "Vae victis!" remarked Bunny; and Schmolsky looked at him, puzzled, and said, "Huh?"

VIII

From such a week end Bunny would return to Angel City, and accompany Rachel to a meeting of the Young People's Socialist League.   In an obscure hall twenty-five or thirty boys and girls of the working class met once a week, and read papers, and discussed problems of politics and economics, the labor movement and the Socialist party.   Rachel had grown up with this organization, and had prestige with it because she had got a college education, and because she brought "Comrade Ross" with her.   The most thoroughly "class-conscious" young people could not help being thrilled by a spectacle so unusual as a millionaire who sympathized with the workers and had helped to bail out political prisoners.

With these young Socialists, as with the old ones, it was right wing versus left; everybody argued tactics, and got tremendously excited.   The Communists also had an organization, the Young Workers' League, and the two rivals carried on sniping operations; sometimes they held formal debates, and young people would jump up and down in their seats, and carry on the controversy in their homes and working places for weeks afterwards.   It was Moscow versus Amsterdam, the Third International versus the Second, the "reds" against the "pinks," as the mild Socialists were called.   And this same struggle was going on in the soul of Bunny.   Paul Watkins would pull him forward, and then Rachel Menzies would haul him back; and his trouble seemed to be, he was of the opinion of the one he talked with last.   He was so prone to see the other fellow's point of view, and lose himself in that!   Why couldn't he have a mind of his own?

Theoretically it was possible to bring about the change from Capitalism to Socialism by peaceable, one-step-at-a-time methods.   Anyone could lay out the steps.   But when you came to take the first one, you confronted the fact that the capitalists didn't want to be evolved into Socialism, and wouldn't let you take any step.   It was a fact that so far they had outwitted the workers at every turn; they had even forced the government to retrace the steps which had been taken in the emergency of war. It was also true, as Paul contended, that the capitalists would not permit the workers to be peaceable; they resorted to violence every time, and set aside the laws and the constitution when it suited their convenience.

To Bunny that seemed a pathetic thing about the Socialists. Take a man like Chaim Menzies; he had the long vision, the patience of the elderly worker; with ages of toil behind him, and ages ahead of him, he did not shrink from the task of building an organization. But he was never allowed to finish the building, the masters would knock it down overnight; they sent in spies, they bribed the officials and sowed discord, and in time of strikes their police and gunmen raided the offices, and jailed the leaders, and drove the workers back into slavery. So here was a curious situation—the masters in their blindness working as allies of the Communists! Verne and his oil operators and the rest of the open shop crowd saying to the working people, "No, don't listen to the Socialists, they are a bunch of old fogies. The Communists are the fellows who can tell you what we are like, and how we are going to behave!"

One thing Bunny had felt certain about—the workers ought to determine their tactics without bitterness and internal strife. But now he was beginning to doubt if even that were possible. The quarrel between the two factions was implicit in the nature of the problem. If you believed in a peaceable transition, your course of action would be one thing, and if you didn't so believe, it would be another thing. If you thought you could persuade the masses of the voters, you would be cautious and politic, and would avoid the extremists, whose violent ways would repel the voters. So you would try to keep the Communists out of your organization, and of course that would make them hate you, and denounce you as a compromiser and a "class collaborator," and insist that you were in the pay of the bosses, who hired you to keep the workers under their yoke.

And then the Socialists would counter with the same charge of bribery. Chaim Menzies never failed to declare that some of the Communists were secret agents, paid by the bosses to split the movement, and expose it to raids by the police. Bunny knew, from talk he heard among his father's associates, that these big business men had elaborate secret agencies for the disrupting of the labor movement. And these agencies would work either way; they would hire old line leaders to sell out the workers, calling off strikes, or calling premature strikes that couldn't win; or they would send in spies to pose as reds, and split the organizations and tempt the leaders into crime.

Incredible as it might seem, the government secret service, under that great patriot, Barney Brockway, was up to the neck in such work. At the trial of one group of Communists the federal judge presiding remarked that apparently the whole direction of the Communist party was in the hands of the United States government!

IX

Bunny was always having the beautiful dream that his friends were going to be friends with one another. Now he took Rachel to call on Paul and Ruth; he liked them so, and they must share his feelings. But alas, they didn't seem to! Both sides were reserved, and avoided talking politics as carefully as if they had been visiting at the Monastery! But Bunny wanted them to talk politics, because he was trying to settle his own inner debate, and he felt that they were qualified, they were members of the working class, while he was only an outsider. Perhaps one might convert the other; but which one he wanted to be the converter, and which the converted, it would have been hard for him to say!

Bunny questioned Paul, and learned that he had given up his carpentry job—the Workers' party was paying him a small salary to give all his time to organizing. Paul had met Joe and Ikey Menzies, the young "left wingers"; and Bunny told about how he and Rachel had helped to put Ben Skutt out of business at the trial. How he wished the Socialists and the Communists might work together like that, instead of making things easier for the enemy!

Thus led on, Rachel said that she would be interested to understand the ideas of Comrade Watkins. (Whenever a Socialist wanted to be very polite to a Bolshevik, she called him by that old term, which had applied before the family row broke out!) How could a mass uprising succeed in America, with the employing class in possession of all the arms and means of communication? They had poison gas now, and would wipe out thousands of the rebel workers at a time. The one possible outcome would be reaction—as in Italy, where the workers had seized the factories, and then had had to give them up because they couldn't run them.

Comrade Watkins replied that Italy had no coal, but was dependent on Britain and America, which thus had the power to strangle the Italian workers. As a matter of fact the Fascist reaction in Italy had been made by American bankers— Mussolini and his ruffians had not dared to move a finger till they had made certain of American credits. We had played the same role there as in Hungary and Bavaria; all over the world, American gold was buttressing reaction. Paul had seen it with his own eyes in Siberia, and he said, with his quiet decisiveness, that nobody could understand what it meant unless he had been there. Paul didn't blame Comrade Menzies for feeling as she did, that was natural for one who had been brought up under peace conditions; but Paul had been to war, he had seen the class struggle in action.

"Yes, Comrade Watkins," said Rachel, "but if you try and fail, things will be so much worse!"

"If we never try," said Paul, "we can never succeed; and even if we fail, the class consciousness of the workers will be sharpened, and the end will be nearer than if we do nothing. We have to keep the revolutionary goal before the masses, and not let them be lured into compromise. That is my criticism of the Socialist movement, it fails to realize the intellectual and moral forces locked up in the working class, that can be called out by the right appeal."

"Ah, said Rachel, "but that is the question—what is the right appeal? I want to appeal to peace rather than to violence. That seems to me more moral."

Paul answered, that to make peace appeals to a tiger might seem moral to some, but to him it seemed futile. The determining fact in the world was what the capitalist class had done during the past nine years. They had destroyed thirty million human lives, and three hundred billions of wealth, everything a whole generation of labor had created. So Paul did not enter into discussions of morality with them; they were a set of murderous maniacs, and the job was to sweep them out of power. Any means that would succeed were moral means, because nothing could be so immoral as capitalism.

When Bunny went out with Rachel, she said that Paul was an extraordinary man, and certainly a dangerous one to the capitalist class. He was a case of shell-shock from the war, and those who had made the war would have to deal with him. Then Bunny asked about Ruth, and Rachel said she was a nice girl, but a little colorless, didn't Comrade Ross think? Bunny tried to explain that Ruth was deep, her feelings were intense, but she seldom expressed them. Rachel said Ruth ought to think for herself, because she would have a lot of suffering if she followed Paul through his Bolshevik career. Bunny suggested that Rachel might help to educate her, but Rachel smiled and said that Comrade Ross was too naive; surely Paul would not like to have a Socialist come in and steal his sister's sympathy from him. In spite of all Bunny could do, his women friends would not be friends!

Then later on Bunny saw Paul, and got Paul's reaction to Rachel. A nice girl, well-meaning and intelligent, but she wouldn't keep her proletarian attitude very long. The social revolution in America was not going to be made by young lady college graduates doing charity work for the capitalist class! What she was doing among the "Ypsels" was mostly wasted effort, according to Paul, because these Socialist organizations spent their efforts fighting Communism. The capitalists ought to be glad to hire her to do such work!

But somehow it wasn't that way, Bunny found; the capitalists were narrow-minded, and lacking in vision! A few days later Bunny learned that Rachel was facing a serious dilemma. She had taken her four years course at the university with the idea of making a career as a social worker; but now a woman friend, upon whose advice she was acting, had warned her that she was throwing away her chances by her activity with these "Ypsels." It was hard enough for a Jewish girl, and one from the working-classes, to have a professional career, without taking on the added handicap of Socialism. Rachel should at least wait till she had got a position, and got herself established.

So there were more troubles! What was Rachel going to do? The answer was that she was not going to desert her beloved young Socialists. It was all very well to say wait, but that was the way all compromising began; once you started, you never knew where to stop. No, Rachel would take her chances of the "Ypsels" being raided by the police, or placarded in the newspapers as a conspiracy to undermine the morals of youth! If it turned out that her friend was right, and the bourgeoisie wouldn't have her as a dispenser of their charities, she would find some sort of job in the labor movement. And Bunny went off to keep an engagement to a dinner party with Vee Tracy; he went with a sober face and a troubled conscience, neither of which he was clever enough to hide!

X

Graduation time was at hand, and all the grave old seniors had the job of choosing their future careers. Dad asked Bunny if he had made up his mind, and Bunny answered that he had. "But I hate to tell you, Dad, because it's going to make you unhappy."

"What is it, son?" A look of concern was upon the old man's round but heavily lined features.

"Well, I want to go away for a year, and take another name, and get myself a job as a worker in one of the big industries."

"Oh, my God!" A pause, while Dad gazed into his son's troubled eyes. "What does that mean?"

"Just that I want to understand the working people, and that's the only way."

"You can't ask them what you want to know?"

"No, Dad they don't know it themselves—except dimly. It is something you have to live."

"Good Lord, son, let me help you! I've been there. It means dirt and vermin and disease—I thought I was saving you from it, and making things easier for you!"

"I know, Dad, but it's a mistake; it doesn't work out as you thought. When a young fellow has everything too easy for him, he gets soft, he has no will of his own. I know what you've done, and I'm grateful for it, but I have to try something different for a time."

"You can't possibly find anything hard enough for you in the job of running an oil industry?"

"I might, Dad, if I could really run it. But you know I can't do that. It's yours; and even if you gave it to me, Verne and the operators' federation wouldn't let me do what I'd want to do. No, Dad, there's something vitally wrong with the oil industry, and I can never play the game with the rest. I want to go off and try something on my own."

"You mean to go alone?"

"There's another fellow has the same idea, and we're going together. Gregor Nikolaieff."

"That Russian! Couldn't you possibly find an American to associate with?"

"Well, it just happens, Dad, that none of the Americans are interested."

There was a long pause. "And you really mean this seriously?"

"Yes, Dad, I'm going to do it."

"You know, son, the big industries are pretty rough, most of them. Some of the men get badly hurt, and some killed."

"Yes; that's just the point."

"It's pretty hard on a father that has only one son, and had hopes for him. You know, I've really thought a lot about you— it's been the main reason I worked so hard."

"I know, Dad; and don't think I haven't suffered about it; but I just can't help doing it."

Another pause. "Have you thought about Vee?"

"Yes."

"Have you told her?"

"No, I've been putting it off, just as I did with you. I know she won't stand for it. I shall have to give her up."

"A man ought to think a long time before he throws away his happiness like that, son."

"I have thought, all I know how. But I couldn't spend my life as an appendage to Vee's moving picture career. I should be suffocated with luxury. I have convictions of my own, and I have to follow them. I want to try to help the workers, and first I have to know how they feel."

"It seems to me, son, you talk like one of them—I mean the red ones."

"Maybe so, Dad, but I assure you, it doesn't seem that way to the reds!"

Again there was a silence. Dad's supply of words was running short. "I never heard of such a thing in my life!"

"It is really quite an old idea—at least twenty-four hundred years." And Bunny went on to tell about that young Lord Siddhartha, in far off India, who is known to the western world as Buddha; how he gave up his lands and his treasures, and went out to wander with a beggar's bowl, in the hope of finding some truth about life that was not known at court. "The palace which the king had given to the prince was resplendent with all the luxuries of India; for the king was anxious to see his son happy. All sorrowful sights, all misery, and all knowledge of misery were kept away from Siddhartha, and he knew not that there was evil in the world. But as the chained elephant longs for the wilds of the jungle, so the prince was eager to see the world, and he asked his father, the king, for permission to do so. And Shuddhodana ordered a jewel-fronted chariot with four stately horses to be held ready, and commanded the roads to be adorned where his son would pass." And then Bunny, seeing the bewildered look on Shuddhodana's face, began to laugh. "Which would you rather I became, Dad—a Buddhist or a Bolshevik?"

And truly, Dad wouldn't have known what to decide!

XI

There has been during the present century a new universe opened up to knowledge—the subconscious mind—and many strange things are told about it. It is accustomed to make determined efforts to have its own way; and sometimes when it is balked it will go to such lengths as to make the body ill. A jealous wife will suffer nervous collapse, a quite genuine case, thus retaining the attentions of her husband; and so on through a catalog of strange phenomena. But the Freudian theories, not being consistent with Methodist theology, had not yet penetrated into Southern Pacific. So Bunny was entirely unsuspicious when it happened, just after his graduation, and before he set out with Gregor Nikolaieff, that Dad came down with a severe attack of the flu. Of course Bunny had to postpone his leaving, and was able to find all the trouble he needed at home. There were several days when it was not certain if Dad would live; and Bunny felt all the remorse that Vernon Roscoe had foretold. Also he faced the alarming prospect, he might have to take over control of all those millions of Dad's money!

The old man pulled through; but he was very weak, and pitiful, and the doctor warned his family that the flu was apt to leave the heart in bad condition, and he would have to be guarded and kept from shock. Down in the deeps of Dad there must have been a merry chuckling, for now it was impossible for Bunny to go away. The father clung to his boy's hand like a child, and Bunny must sit and read to him the sad and tender story of the young Lord Siddhartha. Had Dad said something to Vee about the plot, or was it a telepathic contact between two subconscious minds? She came frequently to the house, and was so kind and sympathetic—the wild elephant in Bunny's spirit was tied down with a million silken cords.

And then, when Dad was able to be about, and to sit on the porch in the sunshine, his shrewd conscious mind started work, and presently he had a scheme. "Son, I've been thinking about your problem, and I realize that you have a right to express your ideas. I've been wondering if we mightn't work out a compromise, and let me help."

"How, Dad?"

"Well, you might have some money that you could use in your own way, and wouldn't feel you were taking from mine. Of course, I wouldn't feel it was right to help you do anything that was against the law; but if there is some kind of education that isn't for violence, why, that would be all right, and if you had an income of a thousand dollars a month that you might use for such propaganda—would that help?"

A thousand dollars a month! Gee whiz! Bunny forgot the standards of his own class, according to which a thousand dollars a month would not keep a string of polo ponies or a small racing yacht; he thought according to the standards of the radicals, to whom a thousand dollars a month meant a whole labor college or a weekly paper! Nothing was said about Bunny's staying at home, but he understood that the offer was a bribe; he would have to administer the fund! He yielded to the temptation, and hastened to phone Rachel—he had a job in sight for her!

He invited her to lunch; and all the way as he drove to the place, his busy mind was flying from scheme to scheme. Rachel would remain secretary of the "Ypsels," and be paid a salary for her work, the same as she would have got as a social worker. The young Socialists would hire a larger hall, and would publish a weekly paper, aimed at the high schools and colleges of Angel City. Bunny was now free from the promise he had made to Dr. Cowper, not to make propaganda in Southern Pacific. And he was going to make it, you bet! The students of that university and all others would learn something about modern thought, and about the labor movement, and about Socialism, and—well, not too much about Communism, of course, because Dad would call that violence, and it might be breaking the law!

CHAPTER XVIII

THE FLIGHT

I

This summer of 1923 was a pleasant one for Bunny. To be one of the editors of a little paper, and be able to say what you thought, and print it week by week and distribute it, with no Dean Squirge to take it away from you, and no police or patriots to raid your office! To mail it to every one you knew, and flatter yourself with the idea that they were reading it, and being cured of their prejudices! Bunny had put all his former classmates on the mailing list of "The Young Student," and in the fall the "Ypsels" were going to sell it on the college campuses, and maybe trouble would begin then, and they would get some advertising free!

Dad was slowly picking up. He read the little paper every week, a sort of loving censorship. But it wasn't needed, because Rachel, orthodox Socialist party member, was wasting no space on the left wingers. When these extremists got hold of Bunny and cajoled him into thinking that both sides ought to have a hearing, Rachel would say, what was the matter with their getting out a paper of their own? So here was Bunny, being "bossed" as usual—and by a woman! It was almost as bad as being married!

Another source of relief—Vee was not quarreling with him so much. She had been so shocked by his mad proposal to go off and get himself killed in heavy industry, that she was glad to compromise and take half his time, and let Rachel and "The Young Student" have the other half. Vee was working hard on her new picture, "The Golden Couch," telling about an American darling of luxury who fell into the toils of a fake prince from some Balkan country. To play the part they had got a real Roumanian prince, who had most charming manners, and was willing to devote himself to Vee at all times when Bunny was busy with his Socialist Jewess.

Also they were getting agreeable letters from Bertie, who had been transported to heaven. Such a brilliant world, with such important things going on! She had lunched with the

Prince de This, and dined with the Duchesse de That. Why wouldn't Dad and Bunny come over and visit them—Bunny might make a really brilliant marriage. Dad chuckled; the idea of him going to Paree and trying to polly voo Francy!

The blackmailers were busy, of course; but since his illness Dad had left all that trouble to Verne. Congress was on vacation, which meant a partial respite; the senatorial reds might denounce the oil leases in their home states; but the papers no longer had to print what they said. A curious superstition, that when things were said in Congress, even the most respectable newspapers found it necessary to mention them. Such things brought politics into disrepute with business men.

The drilling of the Sunnyside tract was under way. A dozen wells were flowing, and justifying all that had been expected of them. Sometimes Dad was driven to the office, but most of the time the bright young executives would come out to his home, and sit in the den and get their orders. Such clean-cut efficient young men, with all their faculties concentrated upon getting oil out of the ground! No visions tormenting them, no strains of music haunting them, no hesitations, no uncertainties, never a doubt that to get oil out of the ground was the purpose of man's life! So they kept their wits about them, and mastered their departments, and increased their prestige and their salaries; and when any one of them had taken his departure, there was an unuttered sadness between Dad and his son. Why couldn't Bunny have been like young Simmons, or young Heimann, or young Bolling?

II

The doctor had said that Dad must not think about business more than two hours a day; so Bunny would tempt him for a stroll, a very slow one, and perhaps they would hear a sermon of Eli's as they walked along the street, and that never failed to divert Dad's mind and set him to chuckling. He took a kind of malicious delight in watching the glory sweep of the Third Revelation; by proving that the masses were boobs, you made it all right to take their naval reserves! Dad subscribed to a little paper issued by one of the rival religious showmen of the town, full of denunciations of Eli and exposures of his trickery.

The regular churches were jealous of this new Revelation, which had burst so rudely upon them. Eli was an upstart and a mountebank, and Tom Poober, the clerical rival, declared that he faked a lot of his alleged cures, he hired people to stand up and tell how their crippled limbs had healed and their cancers had disappeared. Also, Eli's followers had not been willing to give up their customs of rolling and talking in tongues, and Eli had had to build for them a number of sound-proof rooms in the Tabernacle, where these rites were carried on. "Tarrying rooms," they were called, because you went there to "tarry with Jesus"; and when things got going, you would see a hundred men and women rolling on the floor, pawing one another, tearing off their clothing; you would see a woman jerking her head back, or leaping several feet at a time, here and there, exactly like a chicken with its head cut off. The orgies would end with a mass of human creatures piled into a heap, wriggling and writhing, amid a smell of sweat that would make you ill.

The Reverend Poober would print such things, and send newsboys to sell the paper in front of the Tabernacle; the newsboys would be fallen upon and beaten, and the police would fail to arrest the assailants, or having arrested them, would turn them loose. Were the politicians of Angel City afraid of the power of this stuffed prophet? Tom Poober would ask in large capital letters, and Dad would chuckle—in the mood of that Western pioneer who came home and found his wife in a hand-to-hand conflict with a bear, and rested his gun upon the fence and took a seat and called, "Go it, woman! Go it, bear!"

There was another charge—the prophet was said to be fond of the company of handsome young women. That was a cruel thing to hint, because Eli was strenuous in denouncing fornications and adulteries, as much so as any Hebrew prophet of the First Revelation. Dad chuckled and speculated; until it happened one day that he and Bunny took a long drive, and stopped at an unfrequented beach, looking for a place for Bunny to get a swim. There was a cheap hotel on the waterfront, and coming out of the door, whom should they run into but Eli Watkins, with an indubitably handsome young woman! The young woman walked quickly on, and Eli exchanged greetings with Dad and Bunny, and then excused himself. Dad stood for a minute, looking after the couple and saying, "By golly!"

Then he turned and went into the hotel, and to the man at the desk remarked, in a casual tone, "I met that gentleman, but his name has slipped my memory—the one that just went out."

"That's Mr. T. C. Brown, of Santa Ynez."

"Is he staying here"?

"He just checked out."

Dad began to glance over the hotel register, and there he read, as big as life, "T. C. Brown and wife, Santa Ynez." And in the crude scrawly handwriting of Eli Watkins, which Dad had at home upon several business letters! It was all Dad could do to keep from bursting out laughing. By golly, if he were to tip off Tom Poober to the contents of that hotel register, he would knock the Third Revelation as high as a kite!

III

President Harding died; and Dan Irving wrote Bunny the gossip from Washington. The old gentleman had been reluctant to take the oil men's money, so Barney Brockway and his "fixer" had fixed things for him—they had "carried an account" in a Wall Street brokerage, a method whereby business men make life comfortable for statesmen. Every now and then they would bring the old gentleman a bundle of liberty bonds which they had "won" for him. And now his widow had found several hundred thousand dollars of these bonds in a safe deposit box, and become convinced that he had meant them for another woman, and was in such a fury about it that she was telling all her friends, and giving great glee to Washington gossip.

And then the new president: a little man whose fame was based upon the legend that he had put down a strike of the Boston policemen, when the truth was that he had been hiding in his hotel room, with a black eye presented to him by the mayor of the city. His dream in life, as reported by himself, was to keep a store, and that was the measure of his mentality. He didn't know what to say, and so the newspapers called him a "strong silent man."

Bunny didn't publish much of this, because Rachel didn't approve of gossip. But they did publish some of the inside facts about professionalism in college athletics, and when this was offered for sale on the campuses, the athletic students mobbed the "Ypsels." But even the mobbers read the paper, and Bunny was having the time of his life.

In December the new Congress assembled, and an alarming state of affairs was revealed; the "insurgents" had the balance of power in the Senate, and their first move was to combine with the Democrats and order an investigation of the oil leases. This news fell upon Dad and Verne like a thunderbolt—their scouts in Washington had failed to foresee such a calamity, and Verne had to jump into his private car and hurry to Washington, to see what a last-minute expenditure of cash might do. Apparently it didn't do much, for the committee proceeded to put witnesses on the stand and "grill" them—a terrifying newspaper phrase, but really it was not so much a culinary operation as an explosion, with the debris scattered all over the front pages of the press.

The thing was too sensational to be held down any longer. It didn't read like politics, but like some blood and thunder movie. Secretary Crisby hadn't had the sense to put his oil money into liberty bonds and hide them in a safe deposit box —he had gone like a fool and paid off a big mortgage on his Texas ranch, and bought a lot of stuff that everybody could see; he had even told the foreman of his ranch that he had got sixty-eight thousand dollars from Vernon Roscoe, and the foreman had told one of the ranch-hands. Now the senators put the badly rattled foreman on the witness stand, and he had to explain that it was all a misunderstanding—what he had said was not "sixty-eight thousand dollars," but "six or eight cows." You can see how easy it was for such a mistake to happen!

But then it was shown that Secretary Crisby had deposited a hundred thousand dollars in his bank one day; and where had he got that? A great Washington newspaper publisher came forward to declare that he had loaned his dear friend the secretary that little sum for no particular reason. The great publisher then went off to Florida to spend the winter, and he was sick and couldn't possibly be disturbed. But the perverse committee sent one of its members to Florida and put the publisher on the witness stand, and in the presence of half a hundred newspaper reporters pinned him down and made him admit that his story had been a friendly fairy-tale.

Where had the hundred thousand come from? The scandal-mongers were busy, of course—fellows like Dan Irving running to the committee with tales of what Washington gossip was saying. So the committee grabbed "Young Pete" O'Reilly, and "grilled" him, and made him admit that he had carried the trifling sum of a hundred thousand dollars to Secretary Crisby in a little black bag—more stuff right out of a movie! And then they grabbed "Old Pete," and he claimed it was just a loan—he had got a note, but he couldn't recollect where the note was. He finally produced a signature which he said had been cut off the note, but he couldn't tell what had become of the rest of it; he was very careless about notes, and thought he had given this one to his wife, who had misplaced all but the signature. And these scandalous details about the leaders of the most fashionable society in Washington and Angel City! The newspapers published it, even while they shivered at their own irreverence.

IV

Every day Dad was getting long telegrams from Verne, not coming direct, of course, but addressed to Mrs. Bolling, the wife of the trusty young executive; they were signed "A. H. Dory"—a play upon Dad's favorite formula, "All hunkydory." They were not the sort of telegrams that a doctor would have picked out for the soothing of his patient's nerves; no, they kept the patient in a fever of anxiety—how many, many times he wished that he had listened to the warnings of his young idealist, and kept clear of this mess of corruption! But of course Bunny couldn't say that now; he could only read the news and wait and wonder at what hour the thunderbolt would descend upon them.

Annabelle's new picture was done, "A Mother's Heart," and there was going to be an especially grand premiere, and Bunny was to take Vee, of course, and Dad was to take Aunt Emma, and everything would be all hunkydory for that one night at least. Bunny came home from reading the proofs of the next issue of the paper, and there in the entrance hall he found his aunt waiting for him, her hands shaking with excitement, and her teeth chattering. "Oh, Bunny! The most dreadful thing! They're trying to arrest your father!"

"Arrest him?"

"Men are after him—right in front of the house! You've got to get away without being seen—they'll follow you—oh, I'm so frightened—oh, please, please, be careful! Don't let them catch your father!"

He managed to get the story, and it was really almost as melodramatic as her wild words conveyed. Young Bolling, the trusty executive, had been to the house a few minutes ago, looking for Bunny with a message from Dad of the utmost urgency; he had written it out, and Bunny read it: he was to drive in his car, and make absolutely certain that he was not being followed —there would be men trying to follow him, in order to trail Dad. As soon as he had shaken off these men, he must leave his car, which of course had his name on the license; he must go to some automobile place where he was not known, and buy a closed car under an assumed name; it must not be a new car, because they might have to do very fast driving. Still making sure that he was not being followed, Bunny must proceed to the suburban town of San Pasqual, and at a certain corner Dad would join him. Mr. Bolling had given Aunt Emma five thousand dollars in bills, and then had gone away, hoping that the men who were watching the house would follow him.

Bunny said a few words to comfort the poor old lady. Nobody wanted to put Dad into jail, they just wanted to get him on the witness stand, the way they had done the "Petes," young and old. Bunny threw a few clothes into an old suit-case, that had no name or initials on it, and hurried out to his car. Sure enough, there was another car just down the street, and when Bunny started, this other started also. Bunny swung round half a dozen corners, but the other car kept on his trail. He bethought himself of the traffic jam in the heart of the city, which was at its worst right now, between five and six in the evening. The traffic was controlled by signals, with two or three officers at the crowded corners, and it would be possible by dodging here and there to get several cars between you and a pursuing car, and sooner or later to get across just as the bell rang and compelled your pursuer to wait.

Bunny worked the trick, and shook off the other car; then he left his own in a public garage for storage, and made the purchase of a two-passenger closed car under the name of "Alex H. Jones." The dealers' receipt would serve for a license temporarily, and Bunny counted out eighteen of his hundred dollar bills, and drove away. Half an hour later he was in the town of San Pasqual, driving past the corner specified. He passed it twice, and the second time Dad stepped out of a hotel, and Bunny slowed up, and then away they went! "Anybody following you?" were Dad's first words, and Bunny said, "I don't think so, but we'll make sure." They swung round several corners, and Dad kept watch through the rear window.

"All hunkydory," he said, at last, and Bunny asked, "Where are we going?" The answer was, "To Canada"; and Bunny, who had been prepared for anything, took the boulevard that led North out of San Pasqual.

While he drove, Dad told him the news. The first thing, Verne had skipped to Europe; at least, his steamer was sailing today, and it was hoped he had not been caught. "A. H. Dory" had telegraphed to Mrs. Bolling, advising her that it was absolutely necessary for Mr. Paradise—that was Dad's code name—to meet his friends in Vancouver immediately, and he must start tonight, otherwise he would be too late for the appointment. Dad hadn't needed any further hint; he had learned yesterday —though he had kept the painful news from Bunny—that the Senate investigators had got wind of that Canadian corporation, and were planning to subpoena all its organizers. Undoubtedly the subpoenas had been issued that day, and telegraphed to Angel City, with instructions to the United States marshal to serve them at once. Dad and young Bolling had made their getaway from the office by means of a fire-escape—more movie stuff, you see! And here they were, Alex H. Jones and Paul K. Jones, driving all night on a rain-battered highway, not daring to stop at any hotel, because a United States marshal might be lurking in the lobby; not daring even to pass through the big cities, for fear the all-seeing eye of their irate Uncle Sam might be spying from a window!

V

They got to Vancouver in a heavy snow-storm; and immediately dropped their uncomfortable aliases, and put up at the best hotel. Straightway, of course, the newspaper reporters came running; and Dad said with his quiet dignity that it was all rubbish about their being fugitives from the Senate investigation, they were American business men who had come to British Columbia to consider investments. That scandal in Washington was nothing but cheap and silly politics, the leases had been most advantageous to the government, and as for the Canadian corporation, it had been an enterprise of great benefit to Canada. Did Mr. Ross and his son plan to explore for oil in British Columbia? asked the reporters, eagerly; and Dad said that he had nothing to communicate as yet.

Here they were: comfortable in the physical sense, but mentally not at all so, in a city which to them was a frontier place, with cold weather and nothing of interest. Yet Dad was likely to be in exile for a long time; the new Congress would be in session half a year, and the trouble-makers would certainly keep the oil-scandal going, so as to have something to use in next fall's presidential election. Dad sent telegrams to his office, and wireless messages to Verne on board ship; and presently came a reply from Verne requesting Dad to meet him in London immediately.

Dad had to go; and then, what about Bunny? He had his sweetheart at home, and also his paper, so perhaps he should return to Angel City. But Bunny said nonsense, it was out of the question for Dad to cross a continent and an ocean in winter-time alone. His son would go with him, and after they had talked things out with Verne, they could go over to Paris, and spend a while with Bertie, and meet those swell diplomatic friends of hers. Then, if necessary, Bunny might come back alone—they would see about that later.

The old man was pitifully glad of this decision. Bunny was all he had to care about now. In his secret heart he must have been humiliated before his son, but he had to go on with the pretense that he was a dignified business man, persecuted by unscrupulous political enemies. He talked about the matter very little with Bunny, but to other people he would discourse for hours; this sudden talkativeness about his affairs was the most pitiful of all signs of his weakening.

Bunny wrote long letters to Vee, telling her the situation and pledging his love; and to Rachel, turning over the paper to her, and arranging for the thousand dollars a month to be paid to her. Dad wrote long letters to his efficient young executives—thank God for their efficiency right now! They would keep in touch with him and Verne by cable; and Verne's agents in Washington would send the "low down" on the investigation. Bunny arranged to get Dan Irving's weekly letter, and the various radical papers he was reading; so father and son would be in position to carry on their controversy in Europe!

They spent four days on a train crossing the snowy plains of Canada. It was bitter cold outside, but snug and warm within, and on the rear of the train was an observation car, made use of by a score or two of business men, American and Canadian. In an hour or two they had learned that the great J. Arnold Ross was among them, and after that Dad held court, and told his troubles to all and sundry. It was curious to Bunny to see the class-consciousness of these men, an instant, automatic reaction; every one of them was with Dad, every one knew that the exposure was the work of malicious political disturbers, and that the leases had been a good bargain for the public. The savings that intelligent business men effected always made up many times over for what profits the business men took.

When they got to Montreal, there was a palatial steamer waiting, with several hundred wage-slaves of various sorts prepared to serve them in return for a few hundred barrels of the stolen oil. They went on board, and the steamer proceeded down the St. Lawrence river; it stopped at Quebec, and there were newspapers, and Bunny read that Federal agents had raided a secret convention of the Workers' party, and arrested all the delegates. It was a highly sensational event, and the Canadian papers gave full particulars—they too had this problem! Their account gave the names of the criminals who had been trapped, and one of them was Paul Watkins!

VI

Not all the oil money in the world could make the winter passage to England other than cold and stormy. Dad proved to be a poor sailor, and so he was a forlorn object when he got to Vernon Roscoe's hotel in London. But Verne cheered him up; yes, truly, Dad began to revive with the first thump upon the back and the first boom of Verne's voice in the hotel lobby. "By Jees, the old skeezicks! I believe the reds have got his nerve!"

Nobody had got Verne's nerve, you bet; he was sitting on the top of the world! That investigation—shucks, that was a circus stunt to entertain the yokels. It would blow over and be forgotten in a few months—Verne quoted a chieftain of Tammany Hall who had been up against the same kind of racket, and said, "Dis is a nine day town. If yez kin stand de gaff fer nine days, ye're all right." No, by Jees—and Verne gave his partner another thump—they were getting the oil out of Sunnyside, and the money was going into their bank accounts, and not into anybody's else, and they were going to have one hell of a lark spending it. What was more, they were going to turn the tables on those blankety-blank red senators—just let

Dad wait a few days, and he'd see some stuff that would get on the front pages of the papers, even here in England!

Jim Junior got his due share of back-slapping. The boy Bolsheviki must take his old man around and show him some of the sights of London; hadn't he learned about 'em in the history books—the places where men had had their heads chopped off five hundred years ago, and such cheerful spectacles? After the old man had got rested up, then Verne would show him some oil propositions that would make his eyes pop open. Verne hadn't been losing any time—not he! He had put five million into a project that was to reopen a great oil field in Roumania that had been burned during the German invasion, and it was a deal that would beat Sunnyside, and Verne had got fifty-one per cent and full control, and was going to bring over a complete American outfit, and show those gypsies or whatever they were what a real oil job looked like. And now he was fighting with some of the British oil men over the Persian situation, and Verne and the state department between them were waking old John Bull from a long sweet dream.

It was a curious situation that was unveiled to Bunny here. Vernon Roscoe was a fugitive from the oil investigating committee of the Senate, but at the same time he was master of the foreign policy of the United States government concerning oil, and the ambassadors abroad and the secretary of state at home behaved as his office boys. Of course there were other oil men; Excelsior Pete and Victor and the rest of the Big Five all had their agents, hundreds of them, abroad; but Verne was so active, and had so much the best word in Washington, that the rest had come to follow his lead. President Harding might be dead, but his spirit lived on, and Verne and his crowd had bought and paid for it.

The American magnate came among these Britishers with as much tact and grace as one of his long-horned steers from the southwestern plains. He wasn't going to put on any society flummery, he was an old cattle-puncher from Oklahoma, and if "Old Spats and Monocle," as he called Great Britain's leading oil magnate, didn't like him, by Jees he could lump him! Bunny attended a banquet at which a group of the rivals sat down together, and it seemed to Bunny that Verne was more noisy and more slangy than even at his own dinner-table at the Monastery. There was method in it, the younger man suspected; Verne frightened these strangers with his wild western airs, and that was the proper mood for negotiations! They had needed our navy damn bad a few years ago, and had got it free of charge, but they weren't going to get it that way again, and Verne was the feller to tell them so. The next time, it would be the oil crowd's say about the battle-ships—and the same with the dollars, by Jees.

There was a new deal in American diplomacy since the war. The state department had taken charge of foreign investments made by our bankers, and told them where to go and where to stay away from. The bankers had to obey, because they never knew when they might need the help of the marines to collect their interest. What it meant in practice was that a few fighting men like Vernon Roscoe could go to foreign business men and say, let me in on this and give me a share of that, or you can whistle for the next loan from Wall Street. The procedure is known to all cattle men, they call it "horning in"; and after a few of the Britishers had been "horned in on," they learned what the little fellows had learned back home—who were the real masters of America!

VII

Dad of course had no trace of interest in seeing the place where men had had their heads chopped off five hundred years ago; and Bunny tried it, and found that he didn't have much either. What Bunny wanted was to meet the men who were in danger of having their heads chopped off now. There was a great labor movement in England, with a well developed system of workers' education, supported by the old line leaders; also a bunch of young rebels making war on it because of its lack of clear revolutionary purpose. "The Young Student" had been exchanging with the "Plebs," and now Bunny went to see these rebels, and soon was up to his ears in the British struggle —a wonderful meeting at Albert Hall, and labor members of Parliament and other interesting people to meet.

A couple of papers published interviews with the young oil prince who had gone in for "radicalism," as the Americans called it. And this brought an agonized letter from Bertie. She had been begging them to come over to Paris and meet the best people; but now, here was Bunny, six thousand miles away from home, still making his stinks! Couldn't he for God's sake stop to think what he was doing to his relatives? Eldon just about to get a promotion, and here his brother-in-law coming in and queering it all! You could see Bertie making a strong moral effort on paper, controlling herself and patiently explaining to her brother the difference between Europe and California. People really took the red peril seriously over here, and Bunny would find himself a complete social outcast. How could Eldon's superiors trust him in delicate matters of state policy, if they knew that members of his family were in sympathy with the murderous ruffians of Moscow?

Bunny replied that it was very sad indeed, but Bertie and her husband had better repudiate him and not see him, for he had no intention of failing to make acquaintance with the labor and Socialist movements of the countries he visited. Having got that off his chest, Bunny sat down to write for "The Young Student" an account of all the red things he had seen and the red people he had met so far.

The little paper was coming, and Bunny was reading it from the upper left hand corner of page one to the lower right hand corner of page four, and finding it all good. Yes, Rachel Menzies was going to make a real editor—a lot better one than Bunny himself, he humbly decided. She had started a series of papers called "Justice and the Student," discussing the problems of the younger generation. She saw it all so clearly, and was so dignified and persuasive in manner—not angry, as the young reds so easily got! Even Dad was impressed, yes, that was a clever girl; you wouldn't think it to look at her—but those Jews were always smart.

Also the labor press service was coming, with Dan Irving's Washington letter and other news from the oil scandal. And very soon Bunny saw what Verne had meant by predicting the collapse of the investigation. The whole power of the attorney general's office had been turned against the insurgent senators. Barney Brockway, backed against the wall, was fighting for the life of himself and his "Ohio gang." Secret service agents had raided the offices of the senators conducting the investigation and rifled their papers; they were raking up scandals against these men, sending women to try to "get" them, preparing a series of "frame-ups" in their home states—every trick they had rehearsed on the Communists and the I. W. W. now applied to the exposers of the oil steal. Presently they had one of the senators under indictment; and just as Verne had predicted, the big newspapers came to their senses, and took the crimes of the oil men off the front page, and put the crimes of the reds in their place.

There was quite a bunch of "magnates" now in exile; Fred Orpan, and John Groby, and all those who had formed the Canadian corporation, and distributed two million dollars of bribes in Washington. Dad and Bunny would lunch with them, and they would have confidential telegrams, and it was curious to watch their reactions. They all made a joke of it—"Hello, old jailbird!" would be their greeting; but underneath they were eaten with worry. Among other developments, the new President was preparing to throw them overboard, in anticipation of next fall's elections. He, Cautious Cal, had never had any oil stains on him—oh, no! oh, no! The oil men would jeer—the little man had sat in the cabinet all the time the leases were being put through, he had been the bosom friend of all of them. The first time any of Verne's crowd enjoyed the exposures was when the Senate committee began digging into a file of telegrams which showed the immaculate one as heavily smeared as the other politicians; he had been sending secret messages, trying to stave off the exposure, trying to save this one and that. But now he was getting ready to kick their agents out of the cabinet, and how they did despise him! "The little hop-toad," was Verne's regular description of the Chief Magistrate of his country!

VIII

Dad didn't get well as quickly as they had hoped. Apparently the cold damp darkness of London was not good for him, so Bunny took him to Paris. Bertie relented, and met them at the station; even her husband risked his diplomatic career, and everything was polite and friendly for a few hours. But then the brother and sister got to arguing; Bertie wanted Bunny not to investigate the Socialist movement of France, at least, and Bunny said he had already promised Rachel an article about it. There was a "youth" paper here that was on their exchange list, and there was to be a Socialist meeting that very week which Bunny was going to attend. Bertie said that settled it, he would never meet the Prince de This and the Duchesse de That, and Bunny was so ignorant, he didn't know what he was missing.

Paris was wet and cold also, and Dad had a cough, and sat around in a hotel lobby and was so forlorn it made your heart ache. He would let you drive him around, and would look at public buildings—yes, it was very fine, a beautiful city; people had been working on it a long while, we hadn't had time to get anything so good at home. But all the while you could see that Dad didn't really care about it; he didn't like this strange people with their jabber, the men looked like popinjays and the women immoral, and people were always trying to pass off lead money on you, and the food had fancy fixings so you couldn't tell what it tasted like, and why in the world Americans wanted to come chasing over here was beyond Dad's power to imagine.

It was decided to take him to the Riviera till spring. And here they were settled in a villa looking over the Mediterranean, and there was sunshine at last, a pale copy of California. Bertie came for a visit, and then Aunt Emma to keep house for them, and it was a sort of a home. Aunt Emma and Bertie got along beautifully, because the elder lady never failed to admire the right things—oh, how perfectly lovely, how refined and elegant, the most magnificent buildings, the most life-like paintings, the most fashionable costumes! Aunt Emma would meet the Prince de This and the Duchesse de That, and never injure the diplomatic career of her nephew-in-law!

Bunny got himself a tutor, and rapidly unlearned the French he had acquired at Southern Pacific. Of course he had to pick out a Socialist tutor, a weird-looking, moth-eaten young man who did not seem to have had a square meal in many years— a poet, he was reported to be. Other Socialists came round, and a few Communists and Anarchists and Syndicalists and hybrids of these; they wore loose ties, or none at all, and hair hanging into their eyes, and looked to Dad and Aunt Emma as if they were spying out the premises with intentions of burglary. Even here there were radical meetings, on this Coast of Gold, where the rich of Europe gambled and played; and poor devils dangling always on the verge of starvation roused the pity of a young American millionaire, who lived in luxury and had a guilty conscience. When it was ascertained that he would lend money, there were some to ask, and most of them were frauds—but how was a young American millionaire to know?

Aunt Emma had been escorted from Angel City by Dad's private secretary, bringing two big brief cases full of reports and letters. And so Dad was busy and happy for a while, he studied these papers, and wrote long instructions, and sent cablegrams in code, and fretted because some of the replies were not clear. Yes, it was a hard matter to carry on an oil business six thousand miles away. They were putting down test wells in the north half of Sunnyside, and you wanted to be there to examine the cores. Why, the damn fools had even failed to send the full text of the geologists' reports!

Dad wasn't well enough to go into the big new deals with Verne; he must rest first. But the rest didn't help him, because he fretted for something to do, and for his secretary to do. To go driving up and down the same coast was monotonous; while to sit at tea-parties and chatter with fashionable idlers—Dad had unutterable contempt for these people, they weren't even crude and healthy, like the rich in California, no, they were rotten to the core, vicious and terrible people. The ex-mule-driver took one look into their gilded gambling palace, that was famed all over the world, and he went outside and spit on the steps—faugh! He was even willing to consider Bunny's argument, that such people were made by generations of hereditary privilege; let things go as they were going in California, and Dad's grand-children would be giving this crowd lessons in depravity. For that matter, some of them were giving it now right here on the Riviera—rich Americans setting the pace in frivolity and ostentation.

Anyhow, said Dad, give him Americans! He wandered out and found a retired department store proprietor from Des Moines, just as desperately bored as himself, and the two would sit for hours on the esplanade and tell about their business and their troubles. Presently there was added a banker from South Dakota, and then a farmer who had struck oil in Texas. The women folks insisted on these fool European tours, and all the fathers could do was to get off by themselves and grumble at the bills. But here were four of them, and they gave one another courage, and fixed up a little place to pitch horseshoes—and in their shirtsleeves, by heck, just as if they had never made the mistake of making too much money and ruining their family-life!

IX

The weather grew hot, and they went back to Paris. Dad liked it better now, he could stroll on the boulevards, and sit in those outdoor cafes, where you sipped things to drink; there was always a waiter who understood English, and maybe he had been in God's country and would chat about it. There were numbers of Americans to meet; Dad found the express company office where they got their mail, and he even ran into people from Angel City there! The newspapers from home came twice a week, and lasted a long time.

Also, friends turned up—Annabelle Ames, for example, to attend the London premiere of "A Mother's Heart," and to visit Roumania with Verne, and also Constantinople. It appeared that Verne was backing the Turkish government, as a means of squeezing a bigger share of the Mosul oil out of the British. A funny thing—Excelsior Pete, Verne's bitterest rival at home, had offered to take him in on these concessions. Yes, you were getting something when you bought the leading cabinet members of the United States government! Excelsior Pete's action showed how much real importance they attributed to the oil scandals, and to the new President's public attitude.

Annabelle was a business woman, and understood these matters, which made her a comfort to Dad. She pleaded with Bunny, in her gentle, loving way—it was all right for him to set up new standards in business, but was it fair to judge his father by them? Certainly no big business men followed such standards. And surely America was entitled to its share of the world's oil; but there was no way to take it from these greedy foreign rivals, except to mass the power of the government against them.

Annabelle had lots of news from home. Not gossip, she didn't tell mean things; but there was one story she couldn't help telling, it was so funny, and it caused Dad many a chuckle. A sudden fit of modesty had struck the O'Reilly family; they had taken down all those bronze and brass signs that had announced their progress about the world! No name on their front gates, none on the "Conqueror," their yacht, none on the private car with its Circassian walnut and blue satin upholstery! No longer was it a glorious thing to be an oil magnate's wife— some fanatic might throw a bomb at you!

Congress had adjourned for the summer, and Verne was going back. But he wanted Dad to stay for a while, because that Canadian corporation was the most vulnerable of all the oil men's actions; it had never done anything except to distribute that two million dollars of bribes. It was more than ever important to keep the story down, because the government was proceeding to bring suits for the return of all the naval reserves. That would tie up the profits in the courts—all that good money, by Jees, it was terrible!

Dad would stay, of course; and Bunny would have to stay with him. To make matters easier, the great Schmolsky came along, fresh from the job of buying most of the great German moving picture stars—another step in the process of taking over the industry. Annabelle appealed to him, and he was a good sport, he said yes, it was a damn shame the way old Jim had been treated, and it was fine of the kid to stick by him— the Jews are strong for the family; so Schmolsky would arrange several premieres for "The Golden Couch" in Europe, and Vee might spend a long holiday with her Bunny-rabbit. Lest Schmolsky should forget about the matter, Annabelle made him dictate a cablegram right then; so Bunny saw a demonstration of what it means to have influential friends! It was good business as well as good nature, of course; because, when the world's darlings have these glory-progresses, a publicity man precedes them from one great capital to the next, and the news of the crowds and the clamor is cabled back to the United States, and takes the front page every time.

Bunny could salve his conscience, because nobody needed him at home. The magazine was getting along all right. Fifty-two issues had been published, more than half of them of Rachel's own editing; it was something to count upon, the same as the sunrise—and it was the most interesting paper in the world!

Also Paul was out of immediate trouble. One of the nineteen men arrested at the Communist convention had been convicted and had appealed; the cases of the rest were held up until that one was decided, and meantime Paul and the others were out on bail. Ruth wrote Bunny the news; it was a torment to have a twenty year jail sentence hanging over you, but they were getting used to it. Ruth was going on with her nurse's work, and getting along fine. Paul had gone on a long journey—she was not at liberty to say where.

But the capitalist press was at liberty, and did so. From time to time you would read in the French papers items of news about Russia, made, of course, to sound as hateful as possible. Soon after getting Ruth's letter, the papers reported that there had been a dispute among the American Communists as to tactics, and the two factions had carried their case to the chiefs of the Third International. There were half a dozen leaders of the American party now in Moscow, and one of those named was Paul Watkins, under indictment at home for participation in an illegal convention.

X

Several interesting events came along, to keep them busy in their exile. First, Aunt Emma fell in love; yes, by golly, when it comes to such things, you jist never can tell what will happen to either ladies or gentlemen! It was a respectable elderly hardware merchant from Nebraska, who was occupying his leisure collecting cameos. Maybe Aunt Emma reminded him of one; anyhow, after beauing her around for several months, he suddenly popped the question, and they had a quiet family wedding, and went off on a honeymoon—to Nebraska!

It left Dad quite lonesome; but presently he hunted up an adventure for himself, and that was stranger still—you couldn't have guessed it in a million years. SPOOKS!! It happened that Bunny went off one evening to a meeting at which the Socialists and the Communists engaged in violent warfare, as appeared to be their custom in Paris; and when he got back, he found that Dad was not in his room. Next morning the old man told about it—hesitatingly, with not a little embarrassment. Just what did Bunny think about Spiritualism? Bunny said he didn't think at all, he didn't know; and Dad revealed that he had had an amazing experience—a long talk last night with grandma!

Holy smoke! said Bunny; and Dad said yes, he might well be surprised, but there was jist no getting away from it. She had told him all about his childhood, described the ranch where they had lived, and asked all about her paintings, what had he done with that one of the Germans drinking out of steins, and did he still have the one of the mansion with the fountain in front and the carriage with the two horses and the lady and gentleman sitting in it? She had called him "Little Jim," and it was all so real, it had made tears come into Dad's eyes.

Bunny wanted to know, where had this happened, and Dad told him, there was a lady living in this hotel, Mrs. Olivier—she was a lady from Boston who had been married to a Frenchman, and her husband had died a year or two ago. Dad had got to talking with her, and she had told him about being a Spiritualist, and how she had a famous medium who gave seances in her rooms here in the hotel, and she had invited Dad to attend, and that was the way of it. Most amazing things had happened, there had been horns floating in the air, and voices coming out of them, and lights flickering about; then the ghosts had appeared, and finally this old lady ghost, who had asked for "Little Jim," and started right off to tell these things that had taken Dad's breath away. How could a medium possibly have known such things?

Well, here was Dad with something to occupy his time! Of course he went to the next seance, and the next; very soon he was learning all the patter of the Spiritualists, taking it as seriously as a religion. You could see how it was—he had got along without any religion, so long as he was well and busy, but now that he was old and tired and sick, he craved something to lean on. He was shame-faced about it, afraid his son would ridicule him. But after all, did Bunny know any reason why the soul might not survive after death? Bunny didn't, and thereupon Dad invited him to go to a seance. Obviously, this was something more important than Socialism. If it was really true that we lived forever, why then it would be easy to endure any temporary discomfort, it was hardly worth arguing about such things as money. This from J. Arnold Ross!

Bunny, who always tried to oblige, went to a seance, and witnessed the strange phenomena. He knew that such things can be done by sleight of hand, and that he had no way of telling the difference; no chance was given in this company, made up of believers in a state of emotional exaltation. So one session was enough, and he went back to the Socialists. But let Dad be a Spiritualist if it made him happy!

Not so Bertie, who found out about it, and went into a regular tantrum. What did Bunny mean by letting his father fall into such hands? It was the worst kind of swindling in the world! And that woman, Mrs. Olivier, it was perfectly obvious what her scheme was—she wanted to marry Dad! Here Bertie and Bunny had worked all their lives to help him accumulate a fortune and save it—and a designing adventuress would jump in and grab the money, and Bunny hadn't even sense enough to know what was happening! Never had he seen his sister so mad in her whole life—she called him a fool seven times running—when he said that the Spiritualist widow might have her share, if only she could help the poor old man to find happiness.

XI

Then another strange affair for them to discuss: one you would have found still harder to guess! The American newspapers in Paris published a despatch from Angel City, setting forth that Eli Watkins, self-styled prophet of religion, was believed to be drowned. He had gone swimming at the beach, leaving his clothing in a hotel room, and had never been seen since; a search was being made for the body. That was all the news for a time; and Dad shook his head, and said, golly, what a strange thing—a man whose God had saved so many others, but couldn't save His own prophet! What would become of that big Tabernacle, that had been Eli's personal property?

Then the New York papers came; and later on, the papers from Angel City, with the story spread all over the front page day after day. The body of Eli could not be found. The people of the temple employed divers—they had searchlights sweeping the water at night, and thousands of the faithful patrolling the sands, holding revival services there, weeping and praying to God to give them back their beloved leader in his green bathing-suit. This went on for a week, for two weeks; and it was puzzling, because the longest time a body could stay in the sea without floating was nine days, and never before had it happened that a drowned body had failed to be washed ashore.

Then, more and more amazing, there began to be rumors in the papers—they were afraid to say anything direct, but they hinted, and quoted others who hinted—Eli was possibly not drowned; Eli had been seen here, he had been seen there—and always in the company of a certain young woman, whom rumor declared to have been the keeper of the sacred robes in the Tabernacle. Of course, the first time Dad saw one of these hints, he remembered what he and Bunny had seen that day at the beach hotel, and he went up into the air. "By God, that fellow's playing a trick! He's gone off on a spree with a woman!"

There was a thrill for you! Dad talked about it for hours—it almost drove the spooks out of his mind! It was no joking matter, because in the course of the search for Eli's body two men had lost their lives—one diver had been taken with pneumonia, and a member of the Tabernacle, seeing what he thought was a body, had swam out too far and gone down. And here was Dad with the key to the mystery! Was it his duty to cable the facts to the Reverend Poober?

More sensations yet—the people at the Tabernacle began getting letters from kidnappers, who alleged that they had taken Eli in his green bathing-suit, and had him in hiding, and demanded half a million dollars ransom for him! What was that? Nobody in Angel City could be sure. Had the prophet really been kidnapped? Or was it true that he was driving over the state, in company with Miss X, as the newspapers referred to the former keeper of the sacred robes? One of the funniest aspects of the scandal was that various young couples who had gone off on love-expeditions in motor-cars— a favorite diversion of the well-to-do—now found themselves in an embarrassing situation; all over the state newspaper reporters and police officials were looking for Eli and Miss X, and woe to any tall blond man who happened to register at a hotel with a girl and no marriage certificate!

The denouement, when it finally came, was so sensational that it got itself cabled, and thus spared Dad a tedious wait. Thirty-five days after Eli's disappearance, some fishermen, rowing in a harbor several hundred miles from Angel City, encountered a man swimming to shore, and picked him up; and behold, it was a tall blond man in a green bathing-suit—in short, it was the prophet! The story he told was that, finding himself being carried out to sea, he had prayed to the Lord, and the Lord had heard his prayer, and had sent three angels to hold him up in the water. The name of one of these angels was Steve, and the second was a lady angel, whose name was Rosie, and the third was a Mexican angel, and his name was Felipe. These angels had taken turns holding onto the shoulder-straps of Eli's green bathing suit; and when he grew faint, one of them would fly away and bring him food. They had upheld him, even while he slept, quite peacefully in the water. For the entire period of thirty-five days Eli had been thus alternately swimming and sleeping. The devil had come, with wings of flame, and driven the good angels away, and bound Eli's hands behind him so that he had nearly drowned. But he had prayed to the Lord, and the angels had floated him to a rusty old can, and held it while he rubbed his bonds against the sharp edges, and severed the bonds and was able to swim again.

So here was the prophet, none the worse for his adventure; and when he had landed on the shore, and got some clothing,

here came the reporters hot-foot—for there have not been so
many miracles in these skeptical recent days, and this was an
indubitable one. Crowds of people swarmed about the prophet,
they sang hosannas, and strewed his path with flowers, and
when he got back to Angel City, you just couldn't imagine the
excitement—fifty thousand people at the railroad station, it
beat anything that even the greatest movie stars had achieved.
And when he got to the Tabernacle, there were his followers
falling on their knees and weeping for joy, because the Lord
had answered their prayers and given them back their prophet;
six times a day the vast auditorium was packed, and outside a
park was filled with people, and Eli's mighty bellow was conveyed by a dozen loud-speakers, and men and women fell down
at the sound and shouted "Praise the Lord!"

Of course there were skeptics, people with the devil in their
hearts who refused to believe Eli's story, and persisted in talking about a blue-colored automobile driven by a good-looking
girl, having a heavily veiled man wearing goggles in the seat
beside her. They talked about signatures on hotel-registers,
and hand-writing experts, and other such obscenities; but all
that made no difference to the glory-shouters at the Tabernacle,
which was packed all day and all night, as never before in the
history of religions. Over and over Eli would tell his story, full
of the most convincing details—why, he even told how the
angels' wings had swished, and sometimes splashed water into
his face; he told the very words the angels had spoken to him.
Said the prophet, if God in His Omnipotence could keep Jonah
three days in the belly of a whale, and Shadrach, Meshach and
Abednego in the burning fiery furnace, why could he not keep
Eli Watkins afloat on the sea? It is obvious that no one could
answer that.

And then came an incident which settled the matter, completing the glory of the Third Revelation. Eli happened to look
inside his green bathing suit, and what should he find but a
snow-white feather! He recognized it, of course—a proof of
his story, left there by the mercy of the Lord! When this
fresh miracle was announced, the hosannas of the faithful shook
the roof; and presently the angel's feather was mounted in a
glass case, and set up behind the place where Eli preached, and,
such was the Lord's mercy, whoever even looked upon this relic,
was instantly cured of all his ailments and had his sins forgiven
—yes, even the most deadly sin of fornication!

CHAPTER XIX

THE PENALTY

I

The billboards of Paris broke into universal ecstasy: "Schmolsky-Superba Présente l'Etoile Américaine, Viola Tracy, dans La Couche d'Or, Cinéma-Mélodrame de la Société en Huit Reels." There were pages in the newspapers, "Premiere Production sur le Continent d'Europe"—Schmolsky was doing the job in style. "L'Etoile" herself was coming, all the way from California; and Bunny motored to Havre to meet her, and oh, how happy they were, a second honeymoon, with the old disharmonies forgotten. He drove her back to Paris—no, almost to Paris, she must board a train outside the city and make her entrance according to schedule announced in the newspapers. There were the shouting thousands, the cameras, and the reporters, including those whose duty it would be to cable the stirring news back to New York and Angel City.

The world grows one, and it is the "cinéma-mélodrame de la Société" that is doing it—which is to say the world grows American. The premiere here in Paris was the same as a premiere in Hollywood, except that the crowd made more noise, and sought to embrace its idol, actually imperilling the idol's life. There was a double reason for excitement, because the man who had played the leading part was no common movie actor, but a real prince from Roumania, who had been visiting in Southern California, and had yielded to the wiles of Schmolsky and become a star for a night. Now here he was in person, on his way home to Roumania—having traveled on the train and the steamer with Vee, so Bunny learned. A tall, lean young man, not very handsome, but used to attention; courteous, but easily bored, wearing a quizzical smile, and reluctant to be serious—until he heard Bunny express some sympathy with the murderous and blasphemous reds! After that, he preferred the company of Bunny's sister.

When the Paris premiere was over, Dad got him a touring car of royal proportions, and they motored to Berlin, Bunny driving, with Vee by his side, and Dad on the back seat with his secretary and a chauffeur for emergencies. It was all just as grand as their tour to New York; perfect roads, beautiful scenery, humble peasantry standing cap in hand and awe-stricken, servants rushing to wait upon them at every stop. All Europe owes us money, and this is how it pays.

And then Berlin—"Erste Auffuehrung in Deutschland, Schmolsky-Superba ankuendigt," etc. And the crowds and the cameras and the reporters—the world was one. This had been enemy country less than six years ago; but did any ex-soldiers in uniform take station at the theatre entrance, and forbid American films to set too high a standard for the native product? They did not; and Bunny smiled, remembering his remark to Schmolsky, "Vae victis!" and the latter's reply, "Huh?"

They went on to Vienna. It is a poor city now, and hardly repays the advertising; but there is still magic in the name, and it counts with the newspapers. So here was another premiere, less noisy but more genial. Vee and her lover were a little bored now; she had had the last great "kick" that she could get out of life. When a star has had her continental tour, and has got tired of it, she is an old-timer, blasée and world-weary, and life from then on is merely one thing after another.

The person with gift of perennial childhood was Dad. He enjoyed each premiere as if he had never seen the others, and he would have liked to go on to Bucharest, where her majesty the queen—herself a genius at advertising—was to attend the first showing, in honor of Prince Marescu. But another attraction kept Dad in Vienna—the spooks had followed him! His friend, Mrs. Olivier had given him a letter to a wonderful medium, and they went to a seance, and Vee was told all about the patent medicine vendor who had raised her in a wagon—the very phrases this man had used to the crowd. By golly, if it was a trick, it was certainly a clever one!

II

There was only one cloud on this second honeymoon, and Bunny kept it hidden in his own soul. There were "youth" papers in both Berlin and Vienna, and he considered himself bound to call at their offices and invite the rebel editors to lunch, and send home letters for Rachel to publish. In Vienna was a paper in the English language devoted to the defense of political prisoners; it was a Communist paper, but so well camouflaged that Bunny didn't realize the fact, and anyhow, he would have wished to meet the editors. He was still making his pitiful attempt to understand both sides—even here in Central Europe, where the Socialists and the Communists had many times been at open war.

In this obscure office in a working class part of the city Bunny came upon a ghastly experience. There was exhibited to him a creature that had once been a young man, but now was little more than a skeleton covered with a skin of greenish-yellow. It had only one eye and one ear, and it could not speak because its tongue had been pulled out or cut off, and most of its front teeth had been extracted, and its cheeks were pitted with holes made by cigarettes burned into it. Likewise all the creatures' finger-nails had been torn out, and its hands burned with holes; the men in the office bared its shirt, and showed Bunny how the flesh had been ripped and torn by lashes this way and that, like cross-hatchings in a pen and ink drawing.

This was a prisoner escaped from a Roumanian dungeon, and these scars represented the penalty of refusal to betray his comrades to the White Terror. Here in this office were photographs and letters and affidavits—for this kind of thing was being done to thousands of men and women in Roumania. The government was in the hands of a band of ruling class thugs, who were stealing everything in sight, selling the natural resources of the country; one of the biggest of Roumanian oil fields had just been leased to an American syndicate, possibly Comrade Ross had heard of that? And Comrade Ross said that he had. He didn't add that his father was in on the deal!

This victim of the White Terror was from Bessarabia, a province taken from Russia under the blessed principle of self-determination. It was inhabited by Russian peasants, and the natural struggles of these people for freedom were met by slaughtering or torturing to death not merely everyone who revolted, but everyone who expressed sympathy with the revolt. Nor was this a sporadic thing, it was the condition prevailing all along the Russian border, a thousand miles from the Baltic to the Black Sea. All these provinces and countries, inhabited by Russian peasants, had been taken from the reds and given to the whites. And so you had this situation—on the Eastern side of the line the peasants had the land and the government, they were free men and women, making a civilization of workers; while on the other side they were serfs at the mercy of landlords, robbed of the fruits of their toil, and beaten or shot if they ventured a murmur. It was impossible to prevent peasants from one side crossing to the other; and the contrast between the two civilizations was so plain that no child could fail to understand it. So the class struggle went on all the time, a hideous civil war, of which no word was allowed to leak to the outside world.

Left to themselves, this landlord aristocracy could not survive a year. But they had world capital behind them; they got the munitions with which to do the slaughtering, or the money to make the munitions, from American big business. Yes, it was America which kept alive this White Terror, in order to collect interest on the debts, and to come in and buy up the country—the railroads, the mines, the oil fields, even the great castles and landed estates. Would not Comrade Ross tell the American people what bloody work their money was doing?

Bunny went away with the question on his conscience. Would he tell, or wouldn't he? Would he begin by telling his darling of the world? Would he mention that the young Prince Marescu, whom she so greatly admired, was the son of one of the bloodiest of these ruling class thugs?

All the time Bunny was driving his darling through winding passes amid the glorious snow-covered mountains of Switzerland, he was not happy as it was his duty to be. He would have long periods of brooding, and she would ask, what was the matter, and he would evade. But then she would pin him down —being shrewd, like most women where love is concerned. "Is it those reds you've been visiting?" He said, "Yes, dear, but let's not talk about it—it isn't going to make any difference to us." She answered, ominously, "It is going to make all the difference in the world to us!"

III

Back in Paris, and there were long letters from Verne; the government had filed suit for the return of its oil lands, and the Sunnyside tract was in the hands of a receiver, and all the development stopped. But they were not to worry—their organization would be put to work on the various foreign concessions, and as for the money, what they were getting out of Paradise would keep them in old age.

Strange to say, Dad worried scarcely at all. Mrs. Olivier
had discovered a new medium, even more wonderful than the
others, and this Polish peasant woman with bad teeth and
epilepsy had brought up from the depths of the universal consciousness the spirit of Dad's grandfather, who had crossed the
continent in a covered wagon and perished in the Mohave
desert; also there was the spirit of an Indian chief whom the
old pioneer had killed during the journey. Most fascinating
to listen while the two warriors told about this early war
between the reds and the whites!

Bertie was furious, of course; she didn't dare say much to
Dad, for the old man was still the boss, and would tell her
"where to get off." She took it out on Bunny, storming at
him, because he was the one who might have saved Dad from
this dangerous vamp. Bunny couldn't help laughing, because
Mrs. Olivier was so far from the type which the Hollywood
directors had taught him to recognize: a stoutish, elderly lady,
sweet and sentimental, with a soft, caressing voice—it was too
funny to listen to her coo to the fierce and surly Indian chief,
"Now, Red Wolf in the Rain, are you going to be nice to us
this evening? We are so glad to hear you again! Captain
Ross's little grandson is here, and wants you to tell us if the
faces of the redmen are white in your happy world."

Bunny was taking Vee about to see Paris; a city which was
exhibiting to the world the moral collapse of capitalist imperialism. In the theatres of this culture centre you might see a
stage crowded with naked women, their bodies painted every
color of the rainbow; some of them died of the poisoning which
this treatment inflicted upon the system, but meantime the war
for democracy was justified. While Bunny was there, the
artists of the city took offense because the managers of the
underground railway objected to an obscene advertisement; to
express their scorn of censorship, some hundreds of men and
women emerged at dawn, having torn off their clothing in
drunken orgies, and invaded the subway cars entirely naked.
These beauty-creators and guides of the future held a festival
once every year, the Quatres Arts Ball, a famous event to which
Vee, as a visiting artist, was welcome; and here, when the
revels were at their height, you might stroll about a vast hall,
and see, upon platforms set against the walls, the actual enact-
ment of every variety of abnormal vice which human degeneracy had been able to conceive.

With the time he had left from such diversions, Bunny was preparing for "The Young Student" a moving protest against the Roumanian White Terror. He left this nearly completed manuscript on the writing table in his hotel room, and when he came back it was gone, and inquiries among the hotel staff brought no information. Two days later Bertie came to him with another tantrum; she knew all the contents of his manuscript, and what shame he was bringing upon their heads! "So Eldon's been setting spies on me!" exclaimed Bunny, ready to get hot himself; but Bertie, said rubbish, Eldon had nothing to do with it, it was the French secret service. Did he imagine for a moment the government was failing to keep track of Bolshevik propaganda? Or that they would let him use their country as a centre of plotting against the peace of Europe?

Bunny wanted to know, were they so silly as to imagine they could keep him from writing home what he had learned in Vienna? He would do the article over, and find ways to get it to America in spite of all the spies. Then Bertie actually broke down and wept; of all countries for him to pick out— Roumania! Here she had been pulling wires to get Eldon appointed to a high diplomatic post, with the combined influence of Verne in Washington and Prince Marescu in Bucharest; and now Bunny came along and smeared them with his filth!

And more than that! Blind fool, couldn't he see that Marescu was interested in Vee? Did he want to give her up to him? The prince would of course hear about this matter through the French government, which was arming Roumania against Russia. Suppose he were to come back to Paris and challenge Bunny to a duel? The young smart-aleck answered, "We'll fight with tennis rackets!"

IV

Matters came to a climax. A letter for Bunny, bearing a French stamp, but in a familiar handwriting that made his pulses jump. He tore it open and read: "Dear Son, I am in town for a few days and would you like to meet me? Yours for old times, Paul Watkins."

Bunny was twenty-four years old now, but it was just the way it had been eleven years ago, there in Mrs. Groarty's back yard, when he had left his father and run shouting, "Paul! Paul! Where are you? Please don't go way!" Bunny had a date with Vee, but he got out of it—his sister would invite her to one of those diplomatic tea-parties where you met the Prince de This and the Duchesse de That. Then Bunny hurried off to the obscure hotel where his friend was staying.

Paul was haggard; one does not take a trip to Moscow to get fat. But his sober face was shining with a light of fanaticism—the same thing which his brother Eli called the glory of the Lord! Dad would have said there were two of them, equally crazy; but it didn't seem that way to Bunny, who mocked at Eli's god, but believed in Paul's—at least enough to tremble in his presence. Paul had been living under a workers' government again—and this time not as a wage-slave, a strike-breaker in army uniform, but as a free man, and master of the future. So now in this dingy hotel room Bunny was sitting opposite an apostle; Paul, with his sombre, determined features and toil-accustomed figure, the very incarnation of the militant working class!

And the miracles of which he had to tell were real. First of all a spiritual miracle—a hundred million people proclaiming their own sovereignty, and the downfall of masters and exploiters, kings, priests, capitalists, the whole rabble of para-sites. It was a physical miracle, too, because these hundred million people controlled one-sixth of the earth's surface, and were building a new civilization, a model for the future. They were poor, of course; they had started with a country in wreck. But what were a few years, and a little hunger, compared with the ages of torment they had survived?

Paul described the sights of Moscow. First of all, the youth movement; a whole new generation being taught to be clear-eyed and free, to face the facts of nature, and to serve the working-class, instead of climbing out upon its face and founding a line of parasites! You saw those young Com-munists in class-rooms, on athletic fields, in the streets—march-ing, singing, listening to speeches—Paul himself had talked to tens of thousands, in his little bit of Russian, and nothing had ever meant so much to him. He had but one interest for the rest of his life, to tell the young workers of America about the young workers of Russia. He began by telling Bunny!

He talked about the councils he had attended, the interna-tional gatherings where the future of the parties all over the world was charted out. Bunny of course made his protest against this. Did Paul really think it was possible for an

American political party to have its course determined in a
foreign country? Paul smiled and said it was hard enough—
the Russian leaders couldn't understand how far back in history America stood. But what else could you do? Either you
meant to have world order, or you didn't? If you left the
party in each country to determine its own course, you were
right back where you were before the war, with men calling
themselves Socialists, and holding power in the name of
Socialism, who were in reality patriots, ready to back the
exploiters of their own land in wars against the exploiters of
other lands.

That was the thing which threatened to destroy the human
race; and the only way to end it was to do what the Third
International was doing—have a world government and enforce
its orders. The workers' world government was located in
Moscow, because elsewhere the delegates would be thrown into
prison, or assassinated, as in Geneva. But before many years
the Third International would hold a Congress in Berlin, and
then in Paris and London, and in the end in New York. The
workers of the world would send their representatives, and
that Congress would give its orders, and the nations would stop
their fighting, just you bet! Thus Paul: and Bunny, as usual,
was swept along upon a wave of enthusiasm.

V

There were so many things Bunny wanted to know about.
He took Paul to dinner, in an outdoor cafe, and they spent a
good part of the evening, French fashion, conversing there.
Paul told about the schools; all the new educational discoveries
that had been made in America, but could only be applied in
Russia. And the papers and books—the modern, progressive
writers being translated and spread over the half of two con-
tinents. And industry—the colossal labors of a people to build
a modern world out of nothing, with no capital and no help
from the outside. Paul described the oil industry under this
Soviet system; a state trust, in which the workers' unions were
recognized, and given a voice in labor affairs. The workers
published papers, they had clubs and dramatic societies, a new
culture, based upon industry instead of exploitation.

Then, of course, Bunny wanted to know about Ruth, and
about Paul's arrest and his trial, and what was he going to do

now. He was on his way back to America, and would probably be put to organizing in California, because that was the place he knew best. He had been in Paradise and held secret meetings with the men; until at last he had been found out and put off the tract—the place where he had been born, and had lived nearly all his life! But that was all right, the party had a "nucleus," as it was called, in the field, and literature was being distributed and read.

Bunny told what he had learned in Vienna, and how his article on Roumania had been stolen; Paul said that in every European capital there were more spies than there were lice. Very probably there was some agent sitting at one of these tables, trying to hear what they said. His baggage was rifled every few days. The imbecile governments, trying to crush the workers' movement—and at the same time piling up their munitions, getting ready for the next war, that would make Bolshevism as inevitable as the sunrise!

"You really think there'll be another war, Paul?"

The other laughed. "Ask your eminent brother-in-law! He'll know."

"But he wouldn't tell me. We barely speak."

Paul answered that armaments produce wars automatically; the capitalists who make the armaments have to see that they are used, in order to get to make more. Bunny said that the idea of another war seemed too horrible to think about; and Paul replied, "So you don't think about it, and that makes it easy for the business men to get it ready."

He sat for a bit in thought, and then went on, "Since I've been travelling in Europe, I find myself remembering that night when you and I met for the first time. Do you recollect it, son?"

When Bunny said that he did, Paul went on, "I wasn't in my aunt's living room, and I didn't see those people that had come to lease their lots; but I listened outside and heard the wrangling; and now, as I go about Europe I say to myself, that is world diplomacy. A wrangle over an oil lease! Every nation hating every other one, making combinations and promising to stick together—but they've sold each other out before night, and there's no lie that any one hasn't told, and no crime they haven't committed. You remember that row?"

How well Bunny remembered! Miss Snypp—he hadn't known her name, but her face rose before him, brick-red with wrath. "Let me tell you, you'll never get me to put my signature on that paper—never in this world!" And Mr. Hank, the man with the hatchet-face, shouting, "Let me tell you, the law will make you sign it"—only there was no law in European diplomacy! And Mrs. Groarty, Paul's aunt, glaring at Mr. Hank and clenching her hands as if she had him by the throat. "And you the feller that was yellin' for the rights of the little lots! You was for sharin' and sharin' alike—you snake in the grass!"

Said Paul: "Those people were so blind with greed, they were willing to throw away their own chances for the satisfaction of beating the others. They did that, I think you told me—threw away the lease with your father. And everybody in the field behaved the same way. I wonder if you happen to know, it's government statistics on that Prospect Hill field— more money was spent in drilling than ever was taken out in oil!"

"Yes, of course," said Bunny. "I've seen derricks there with platforms actually touching."

"Each one racing to get the oil, and spending more than he makes—isn't that a picture of capitalism? And then the war! You remember how we heard the racket, and ran to the window, and there was one fellow hitting the next fellow in the nose, and the whole roomful milling about, shouting and trying to stop the fight, or to get into it!"

"One said, 'You dirty, lying yellow skunk!' And the other said, 'Take that, you white-livered puppy!' "

"Son, that was a little oil war! And a year or two later the big one broke out, and if there's anything you don't understand about it, all you need is to think about what happened in my aunt's home. And remember, they were fighting for a chance to exploit the oil workers, to divide the wealth the oil workers were going to produce; in their crazy greed they killed or injured seventy-three per cent of all the men they put to work on Prospect Hill—that's government statistics also! And don't you see how that's the world war exactly? The workers doing the fighting, and the bankers getting the bonds!"

VI

So many things to talk about! Bunny told the story of Eli, concerning which Paul had heard no rumor. The latter said it was easy to understand, because Eli always had been a chaser after women. It was one reason Paul had been so repelled by his brother's preaching. "I wouldn't mind his having his girl," he said, "only he denies my right to my girl. He preaches a silly ideal of asceticism, and then goes off secretly and does what he pleases."

Here was an opportunity for which Bunny had been seeking. He took a sudden plunge. "Paul, there's something I want to tell you. For the past three years I've been living with a moving picture actress."

"I know," said Paul; "Ruth told me."

"Ruth!"

"Yes, she saw something about it in the papers." And then, reading his friend's thought, Paul added, "Ruth has had to learn that the world is the way it is, and not the way she'd like it to be."

"What do you think about such things, Paul?"

"Well, son, it's a question of how you feel about the girl. If you really love her, and she loves you, why, I suppose it's all right. Are you happy?"

"We were at first; we still are, part of the time. The trouble is, she hates the radical movement. She doesn't really understand it, of course."

Paul answered, "Some people hate the radical movement because they don't understand it, and some because they do." After Bunny had had time to digest that, he went on, "Either you'll have to change your ideas, or you'll have a break with the girl. That's something I'm sure about—you can't have happiness in love unless it's built on harmony of ideas. Otherwise you quarrel all the time—or at least, you're bored."

"Have you ever lived with a woman, Paul?"

"There was a girl I was very much attracted to in Angel City, and I could have had her, I guess. But it was a couple of years ago, when I saw that I was going Bolshevik, and I knew she wouldn't stand for it, so what was the use? You get yourself tangled up in a lot of emotions, and waste the time you need for work."

"I've often wondered about you and such things. You used to think the way Eli talks, when we first met."

Paul laughed. "I'd hardly keep my Christian superstitions when I became a Communist organizer. No, son; what I think is, find a woman you really love, and that wants to share your work, and that you mean to stick by; then you can love her, you don't need any priest to give you permission. Some day I suppose I'll meet a woman comrade—I think about it a good deal, of course—I'm no wooden post. But I'll have to wait and see what happens at my trial. I'd be little use to a girl if I've got to spend twenty years in Leavenworth or Atlanta!"

VII

Paul was going to speak at a meeting of Communists the next evening, and Bunny must go to that meeting, of course. But what was he to do with Vee? She would not be interested in hearing Paul tell about Russia; she had learned all about it from her friend, Prince Marescu. Bunny bethought him of Dad and the seances, and by tactful manipulation he caused the old gentleman to call up Vee and tell her about an especially interesting seance they were going to have that evening. Vee promised to come, and Bunny thought he was free.

But then about lunch-time Bertie called him on the phone. "So your old Paul is in Paris!"

Bunny was startled; having thought he was keeping a secret. Then he laughed. "So your old secret service has been at work!"

Said his sister, "I just thought you might be interested to know—your old Paul is not going to speak tonight. The police have arrested him."

"Who told you that?"

"They've just notified the embassy. He's to be expelled—in fact he's on his way now."

"My God, Bertie, are you sure?"

"Of course I'm sure. Did you think they'd let him make Bolshevik speeches in France?"

"I mean—are you sure they're going to expel him?" Bunny had learned so much about the treatment accorded to the reds—all Europe had adopted the sweet custom of the American police, to beat their prisoners with rubber hose, which leaves no marks upon the skin. So there began a wrangle over the phone, Bunny in a panic, insisting upon knowing what official had given the information to Eldon; and Bertie insisting that Bunny should not make another of his stinks in Paris, and maybe get himself deported, and his brother-in-law ruined in the eyes of all Europe.

In the end Bunny hung up, and called the office of the Communist newspaper. Did they know about the arrest of Comrade Puull Votkan—so it was necessary to say it. No, they knew nothing about it, they would endeavor to find out. And Bunny jumped into a taxi-cab and hastened to the office of the Prefet de Police, where he was received with a lack of that courtesy which police officials usually display to young gentlemen properly tailored. They had no information to give about the American, Puull Votkan, but they would like to receive information about an American named Zhay Arnoll R-r-osss feess, and how long he expected to abuse the hospitality of the French government by giving sums of money to enemies of public safety.

Meantime Bertie, in her desperation, was appealing to Vee Tracy, begging her to make one more effort to get Bunny out of this hideous entanglement. Vee answered that she would make one more, and only one. She turned from the telephone and ordered her maid to pack her belongings, and when Bunny came back from his visit to the police, he found a note in his mail-box:

"Dear Bunny: I have just learned why I was to be put off with a spiritualist seance tonight, instead of going to the opera with you! The time has come when you have to choose between your red friends and me, and I have moved to another hotel until you make up your mind. Please give me your decision by letter. Do not try to see me, because I will not speak to you again until this matter has been settled. If it is to be all over between us, a quick clean cut is the way I choose. I will no longer endure the humiliation of being associated with dangerous criminals; and unless you can say that you love me enough to change your associates, I mean that you are never to see me again. Take time to think it over, but not too much time. Yours, Vee."

As a matter of fact, Bunny did not need any time. Even while he was reading the letter, a voice was telling him that he had known it was coming. After the first shock of pain had passed, he sat himself down and wrote:

"Dear Vee: We have had great happiness together. I have suffered for a long time, because I knew it had to end. I won't waste your time arguing in defense of my ideas; I have some, and cannot give them up, any more than you can yours. I wish you every happiness that can come to you in life, and hope you will not cherish bitterness in your heart, because it is something I truly cannot change. If ever the time comes that I can aid you, I will be yours to command. With just the same affection, Bunny-rabbit."

VIII

Bunny must not stop to nourish his grief, but must hurry to call upon the French Communists and offer to pay the costs of a lawyer to institute legal proceedings and find out what was happening to Paul. But as a matter of fact the effort was not necessary, for next morning all the newspapers had the story: a notorious American Bolshevik agitator had been escorted by the authorities to Havre and placed on board a steamer to sail that day. The Communist paper in its report commented sarcastically; this was one Bolshevik agitator whom the American government could not very well refuse to admit, since they had him under bond of twenty thousand dollars to make his appearance in court! Bunny had so little confidence in the French authorities that he took the precaution to wireless Paul to the steamer with reply prepaid; and a few hours later he got the words, "On the way to Paradise"—a code message from Paul!

Three days later came a message from his sweetheart—no code this time, but a proclamation to the whole world. The newspapers of Paris and all other capitals—of Madagascar, Paraguay, Nova Zembla, Thibet and New Guinea—announced the engagement of Viola Tracy, American screen actress, to Prince Marescu of Roumania; the wedding was to take place in the great cathedral of Bucharest, and Queen Marie herself would attend. The efficient publicity organization of Schmolsky-Superba had contrived many a stunt in its time, but never one so effective as this which fate handed to it, free, gratis, and for nothing!

And so there was a chapter closed in Bunny's life. The door which had led from his suite in the hotel to Vee's suite was locked, and a piece of furniture moved in front of it. But there was no piece of furniture that could be moved in front of the memory in Bunny's mind! Nothing could shut out that slender white figure, so vivid and eager, and the memory of the delights she had brought to him. He was maimed in soul, as the victims of the White Terror were maimed in body—and in the same cause!

There were women here, of all kinds and sizes, native and American, young ladies of the highest fashionableness, willing to receive the attentions of a young oil prince. They knew about his romance and his broken heart; and their shrewd mammas told them an ancient formula, known to the feminine world since the dawn of coquetry—"Catch him on the rebound!" Bunny was besought to attend tea-parties and dances, but mostly he went to Socialist meetings; and when he thought about girls, it was to Angel City that his fancy fled. Ruth Watkins was so gentle and quiet, yet brave—not giving up her brother because he turned into a Bolshevik! And Rachel Menzies was so steady, so grim in her determination to send him a four-page paper, as regular as the calendar, and always telling him everything he wanted to know! Once every month she sent an itemized statement of receipts and expenditures, typed with her own fingers, and always exactly right—whatever dollars were left over went for sample copies, so he was never troubled by either surplus or deficit!

IX

September, and Dad came bringing an announcement that caused him to hesitate, and turn fiery red after he got going. "You know, son, I have got to be very good friends with Alyse, we—that is, we are interested in the same ideas, and we realize that we can help each other."

"Yes, Dad, of course."

"Well, the fact is—you know how it is—I've been imposing on you for so long, but now you will be free, because I've asked Alyse to marry me, and she consents."

"Well, Dad, I've been expecting that for quite a while. I'm sure you will be happy."

Dad looked very much relieved—had he feared a tantrum, after the fashion of Bertie? He hastened to say, "I want to tell you—Alyse and I have talked the matter over, and we agree—she is fond of you, and appreciates your standing by me and all, and she wants you to know that she's not marrying me for my money."

"No, Dad, I don't think that."

"Well, you know Bertie, and what she thinks. Bertie is mercenary—I suppose she got it from her mother. Anyhow, I'm not a-goin' to say anything to her about this, it is none of her business; we'll jist get married on the quiet, and Bertie can read about it in the papers. What I'm a-goin' to do is this—Alyse says she hasn't had anything to do with helping me make my money, and she don't want my children to hate her, as they will if she comes in and takes a big share."

"Oh, but I won't, Dad!"

"We've agreed that I'm to make a will, and leave a million dollars to her, and the rest will go to you and Bertie, and Alyse will be satisfied with that—it will give her enough to carry on the psychic work she's interested in. You understand, she wants to do that—"

"Yes, of course, Dad. I am a propagandist too!"

"I know son; and what I've been thinking—you have a right to express your ideas. And while I don't agree with that little paper, I can see that it's honest, it says what you think; so I'm a-goin' to make over a million dollars worth of Ross stock to you, and you can jist go ahead and do what you please with that. I hope you won't turn into a Bolsheviki like Paul, and I hope you won't find it necessary to get into jail."

"It would be pretty hard to keep me in jail if I had a million dollars, Dad."

The old man grinned; the mediums and the spirits had not yet driven the old devil entirely out of him. He went on to say that of course they weren't going to have as much money as he had once thought. Those government suits were a-goin' to dig a big hole in it—no doubt the politicians would fix it so Dad and Verne would lose. Of course they might get a pile out of these new deals abroad, but that was speculative—not the sort of thing Dad fancied, but he was leaving it to Verne.

"What are you and Mrs.—Alyse going to do, Dad?"

"Well, we want to have a sort of—you might call it a Spiritualist honeymoon. We'll go see that medium in Vienna, and there's another in Frankfort that we've heard about. It'll depend for one thing on what you want. Maybe you'll go back to California."

"I think I will, Dad, for a while—if you are sure you can spare me."

Yes, Dad said he and Alyse would get along all right; his secretary had learned enough French for practical purposes, and they would have a courier or interpreter for their stay in Germany. He hoped the climate there would agree with him;

he didn't seem ever to be strong now. That flu had sort of done him up.

The preliminary steps were taken, and Bunny and his father and the secretary and Mrs. Alyse Huntington Forsythe Olivier all put on their best glad rags and appeared before the maire of one of the small towns on the outskirts of Paris and were duly wedded, and Bunny kissed his new stepmother on both cheeks, and the maire did the same, and also kissed Bunny and Dad on both cheeks. And then Dad took his son to one side and placed an envelope in his hands. It was an order on Verne to turn over thirty-two hundred shares of Ross Consolidated Class B stock; a little more than a million at the market. They were "street certificates," Dad explained—he had already signed them and left them with Verne, in case they wished to market them. "And now, son," said the old man, "have a little sense— this is a pile of money, and don't throw it away. Take your time, and be sure what you want to do, and don't let yourself be plucked by grafters that will come round jist as soon as they smell it!"

The same old Dad! They gave each other hugs and squeezes; there were tears in everybody's eyes, even the secretary, and the maire and his clerks, who had never heard of such fees for a wedding—marvelous people, ces Americains! And Bunny said for Dad to write all the news, and Dad said for Bunny to write all the news; and Bunny said he would return to France next summer if Dad were not able to come to America, and Dad said he was sure Verne would have it all fixed up before that. And then Bunny kissed his stepmother again, and then he hugged Dad again, and then shook hands with the secretary— a regular debauch of the sweet sorrows of parting, with the officials and a crowd of street urchins standing by on the sidewalk, staring at the grand rich car and the grand rich Americans. Bunny was glad to look back on it in after years—at least that once the old man had been happy! All the chatter, and the messages, and the flowers, the baggage to be seen to and the robes to be tucked in—and then at last they were rolling down the street, amid waving of hands and cheers—headed for a Spiritualist seance in Frankfort-am-Main!

Bunny took a train back to Paris, and wrote out two messages announcing that he was sailing for home; one to Ruth Watkins and one to Rachel Menzies—playing no favorites! Then he bought a paper, and read a brief despatch—"Great

California Oil Fire." A bolt of lightning had struck one of the storage tanks of the Ross Consolidated Oil Company at Paradise, California, and as a high wind was blowing, it was not thought possible to save any portion of the tank-farm, and possibly the whole field might be destroyed.

When Bunny got back to the hotel, there was a cablegram from Angel City. It was impossible to make any guess what the damage would be, but they were fully insured and nothing to worry about, "A. H. Dory"—still Verne's signature when he wanted to be playful. Bunny forwarded the message to his father, and asked if he should wait; but Dad's answer was, no, whatever he had to say could be said by letter or cable, and he would be glad to have Bunny on the scene to report. "Love and best wishes," were the concluding words—the last that Dad was ever to say to his son, except through the channel of the spirits!

X

A steamer took Bunny out to sea—one of those floating hotels, like the one he had left in Paris, fitted in the style of a palace, mahogany finish and silken draperies and cushions, and the most elegant society, flashing jewels and costly gowns— five thousand dollars per female person would have been a modest estimate for evenings in the dining saloon. And very soon the tongues of gossip began to buzz—"His father's the California oil man, they say he owns whole fields out there, but one of them is burning up, according to the papers. The Ross that was in the scandal, you remember, he's hiding abroad, been there nearly a year, but the son can come back, of course. They say he was one of the lovers of Viola Tracy, but she chucked him and married the Roumanian prince. Catch him on the rebound, my dear!"

So everybody was lovely to Bunny; so many charming young things to dance with, until any hour of the morning; or to stroll on deck and be lost in the darkness with, if one preferred. All day they flitted about him, casting coy and seductive glances: they were interested in everything he was interested in, even the book he was reading—provided he would talk about it instead of reading it. There were some who would say that they were interested in Socialism, they didn't know much about it, but were eager to learn. Until the second morning out, when the young Socialist received a wireless which entirely removed him from fashionable society:

"Your father very ill with double pneumonia have obtained best medical attention will keep you informed deepest sympathy and affection Alyse."

So then Bunny walked the deck alone, and suffered exactly those torments of remorse which Vernon Roscoe had predicted for him. Oh, surely he could have been kinder, more patient with that good old man! Surely he could have tried harder to understand and to help! Now fate was taking him away, five or six hundred miles every day—and at any moment might snatch him to a distance beyond calculation. His father himself had felt it—Bunny went over what he had said, and realized that Dad had faced the thought of death, and had been giving his son such last advice as he could.

At first nothing but remorse. But then little by little the debate—the old, old dispute that had torn Bunny's mind in half. Was it possible for men to go on doing what Dad had been doing in the conduct of his business? Could any civilization endure on the basis of such purchase of government? No, Bunny told himself; but then—he should have tried harder, more lovingly, and persuaded his father to stop it! But at what stage? Dad had been purchasing government ever since Bunny could remember, as a little boy. All the oil men purchased government, all big business men did it, either before or after election. And at what stage of life shall a boy say to his father, your way of life is wrong, and you must let me take charge of it?

There was no new thought that Bunny could think about all this; any more than in the case of Vee Tracy. Just the grief, and the ache of loneliness! Old things going; they kept going—and where did they go? It was a mystery that made you dizzy, at moments like this; you stood on the brink of a precipice and looked down into a gulf! The most incredible idea, that his father, who was so real, and had been for so long a part of his being—should suddenly disappear and cease to be! For the first time Bunny began to wonder, could Alyse be right about the spirits?

Another message in the evening. "Condition unchanged will keep you advised sympathy and affection." These last words never failed in the messages; the next day, when Dad's condition was the same and the crisis expected tomorrow; and then tomorrow, when Dad was sinking; and then, the morning after, when Alyse wired, "Your father's spirit has passed from this world to the next but he will never cease to be with you he spoke of you at the last and promises that if you will communicate with a good medium in Angel City he will guide your life with love and affection as ever Alyse." And then a message from Bertie: "I was with Dad at the end and he forgave me will you forgive me also." When Bunny read that, he had to hurry to his stateroom, and lie there and cry like a little child. Yes, he would forgive her, so he wired in reply, and might whoever had made them forgive them all!

CHAPTER XX

THE DEDICATION

I

Bunny was alone in the roaring city of New York—six or seven millons of people, and not many known to him. There were reporters, of course—it made a "human interest" story, fate snatching one of the oil magnates away from the Senate inquisitors. The country was near the end of a bitter presidential campaign, and the smallest item about the oil scandal was of importance. Also Bunny had cablegrams and telegrams of sympathy—from Verne and Annabelle, from Paul and Ruth, from Rachel and her father and brothers; yes, and one from the Princess Marescu, signing herself, with old-time nearness, "Vee-Vee."

He purchased his ticket home, by way of Washington, and on the train he read the back newspapers, with the day by day account of what happened to his boyhood dream of a great oil field: enormous oceans of flame rolling over the earth, turning night into day with the glare, turning day into night with thunder clouds of smoke; rivers of blazing oil rushing down the valleys, and a gale of wind sweeping the fire from one hill to the next. A dozen great storage tanks had gone, and the whole refinery, with all its tanks, and some three hundred derricks, licked up and devoured in that roaring furnace. It was the worst oil fire in California history, eight or ten million dollars loss.

In Washington was some one for Bunny to tell his troubles to—Dan Irving! They took a long walk, and the older man put his arm about Bunny and told him that he had done everything possible in a difficult situation. Dan could assure him that he didn't have to think of his father as a bad man; Dan had made it his business to know, and could confirm Bunny's judgment, American big business men all purchased government, they all justified the purchase of government. It was something that had shocked Dan in the beginning, but he had come to realize now that it was a system; without the purchase of government, American big business could not exist. You

480

saw it written plain in the instinctive reaction of the whole business world to the oil scandals, the determinaton to damp them down, to make nothing of them, to indict and prosecute, not the criminals, but the exposers of the crime.

So they got to talking politics, which was the best thing for Bunny, to divert his mind and get him back to his job. Dan had been doing what he could in this presidential campaign, but he was sick with the sense of impotence. The whole capitalist publicity machine had been set to work on a new job, to glorify "Cautious Cal" to the American people—this pitiful little man, a fifth-rate country politician, a would-be store-keeper, he was the great strong silent statesman and the plain people's hero! One thing, and one only, the business men expected of him, to cut down their income taxes; in everything else he would be a cipher. The newspaper men were disgusted by their job, but all were helpless, their papers at home would take only one kind of news. And here was poor Dan with his labor press service, a score or two of obscure papers, perhaps a hundred thousand circulation in all, and most of the time not enough money for the office rent.

"That's what I want to talk to you about," said Bunny. "Before I left France, Dad gave me a million dollars in Ross Consolidated stock. I don't know what it'll be worth since the fire, but Verne says there's full insurance. I'm not going to touch the principal till I have time to think things over, but I'll put a thousand dollars a month of the income into your work, if that will help."

"Help? My God, Bunny, that's more money than we've ever thought of! I've been trying to raise an extra hundred a month, so as to mail free copies where they would count."

Said Bunny, "I'll turn the money over to you with only one provision—that you're to have two hundred a month salary. There's no reason why you should run yourself into debt financing the radical movement."

Dan laughed. "No reason, except that there wouldn't be any radical movement if some didn't do that. You're the first really fat angel that has appeared in my sky."

"Well, wait," said Bunny, "till I find out just how fat I'm going to be. I've an idea my friend Vernon Roscoe will do what he can to keep me lean. He knows that whatever I get will go to making trouble for him."

"My gosh!" said Dan. "Have you seen the things we've

been sending out about Roscoe's foreign concessions, and what the state department is doing to make him rich? That story would beat the Sunnyside lease, if we could get the Senate to investigate it!"

II

Chicago, and more messages for Bunny. He had cabled Dad's secretary to ascertain if there was any will among Dad's papers. The secretary replied that nothing had been found, and neither the widow nor the daughter knew of such document. They were proceeding to Paris after the funeral, and the secretary would cable if anything was found there.

So then to Angel City, and more cablegrams; the secretary advised that no will was among Mr. Ross's papers in Paris, and Bertie cabled, "I believe that infamous woman has destroyed will. Have you anything in Dad's writing or hers." From which Bunny made note that death-bed repentances do not last very long—at least not when it's another person's death-bed! Bunny had nothing from Dad, except the order for the Ross stock, and that wouldn't bring much satisfaction to Bertie. He cabled to Alyse, at her Paris hotel, reminding her that his father had stated the terms of their marriage to be that she was to receive one million dollars from the estate, and no more, and asking her to confirm that agreement. The reply which he received was from a firm of American lawyers in Paris, advising him on behalf of their client, Mrs. Alyse Huntington Forsythe Olivier Ross, that she knew of no such agreement as he had mentioned in his cablegram, and that she would claim her full rights in the estate. Bunny smiled grimly as he read. A clash between Spiritualism and Socialism!

Also a clash between Capitalism and Socialism! Bunny went to call on his father's partner, at the office, where both could speak frankly; and they did. Verne's first statement was a knockout—Bunny's father had been mistaken in thinking that he had any Ross Consolidated Class B stock, and therefore his order upon Verne was worthless. All those street certificates had been sold some time ago at Dad's order; Dad's memory had evidently been failing since his illness—or perhaps he had not been watching his affairs since taking up with Spiritualism. His business was in a bad way. In the first place, the Ross Consolidated Operating Company, which had been Dad's choicest holding, was practically bankrupt. Verne had that day been notified by the fire insurance companies involved that they would not pay the claims, because they had evidence that the fires had been of incendiary origin; they didn't quite say it in plain English, but they implied that Verne or his agents had started the fires, because the company had an oversupply of oil and was caught with a failing market.

"Good God!" said Bunny. "What's that, a bluff?"

"No," said Verne, "that's a scheme of Mark Eisenberg, who runs the banking business in this city for the Big Five, to knock one of the independents out. They'll tie us up in the courts for Christ knows how many years. Ross Operating won't have the cash to develop that burned over field, and if it has to assess its stockholders for the money, your father's estate won't be able to finance its share without help. The Lobos River wells are played out, and the Prospect Hill field is filling with water. Of course your father's got shares in my foreign undertakings, but none of them will realize anything for a long time; so it looks as if you'll have to sell them out."

"Who is to handle all this?"

"Here's a copy of Jim's will—you can take it home and study it at your leisure. The executors are you and me and Fred Orpan, and you and Bertie are to divide the estate. Of course that's been knocked out by his marriage; unless he's made another will, the widow gets one half, and you and Bertie a quarter. I promised your father I'd do the executor's work, so I suppose it's up to me. Let me say this right away— that Paradise field bears your name, and if you want to take it over and run it, I won't stand in your way. You can sell some of your other holdings and buy me out at the market price and run the business for yourself. Do you want to be an oil man?"

"No," said Bunny, promptly. "I do not."

"Well, then, I'll have to buy out your father's stock; because the company is bankrupt, and I won't carry it unless I have control. You and me couldn't work together, Jim Junior—your ideals are too high." Verne laughed—but without his usual jollity. "If I hadn't promised your old man to do this job, I'd like to dump Ross Operating onto you and let it go bankrupt on your hands, and see what you'd do. You didn't agree with your father about business men controlling the courts. Well, by Jees, you just be an upright public-spirited young citizen, and let the courts appoint a receiver for Ross Operating, without any bribery or undue influence of any sort—not pulling any political wires or making any threats or improper promises—and see how much you'd have left of the eight or ten millions, or whatever will be collected from the insurance companies a few years from now!"

III

From these ugly problems Bunny had a refuge—his little paper. He had arrived on a Sunday, and Rachel had met him at the train, with a dozen of the Ypsels, their faces shining. There was a cheer at sight of him—just as if he had been a moving picture star! There were handshakes all round—he and Rachel had several extra shakes, they were so glad to be together. The young people knew that Bunny would be sad over his father's death, and possibly also the burning of his oil field; so they crowded round, and told him all the news at once, and Rachel produced the proofs of a new issue of "The Young Student," also last week's issue, and several others that he might not have received.

The little office was home—the only home Bunny had, because the mansion his father had rented had been subleased, and their personal belongings put in storage before Aunt Emma came to Europe. The office was only one room, but quite impressive with files and records accumulating; they had a subscription list of over six thousand now, and were printing eight thousand this week. But Rachel still had only one assistant—the Ypsels did the wrapping and addressing, evenings and Saturdays and Sundays. They hadn't got mobbed or arrested any more; the Socialists were supporting LaFollette for president, and that gave them the right to be let alone for a while.

And then Ruth. Bunny went to call on her, in the same little cottage. Paul had not got home yet; he had stopped in Chicago for a party conference, and now was coming by way of the northwest, speaking every night. He was having good meetings, because of the prominence his arrests had given him. The story of his expulsion from France had been in the papers all over the country, and Ruth showed Bunny letters telling about this and other adventures with police and spies. Ruth had made Paul promise to write her a postcard every single day; and when she didn't get one, then right away she began to imagine him in some police dungeon, getting the third degree.

Bunny watched her face as she talked. Her words were cheerful—she was a graduate nurse now, and able to earn good money, and save some if Paul should be in need. But she was pale, and her face was strained. There were Communist papers and magazines on the table, and Bunny could see at a glance what was happening. These papers came for Paul; and Ruth, sitting here alone many and many an evening, had read them, looking for news about her brother; so she had absorbed all the horrors about the torturing and maiming and shooting of political prisoners, and it had been exactly as if Paul had been in battle.

Ruth hadn't what you would call a theoretical mind; you never heard her talk about party tactics and political developments and things like that. She was instinctive, yet with class consciousness all the more intense and passionate for that. She had been through two strikes, and the things she had seen with her own eyes had been all the lessons in economics she would ever need. She knew that the workers in big industry are wage slaves, fighting for their very lives. And this war was not like capitalist wars—this one had to be, because the masters made it. But even thus believing in Paul's work, Ruth could not help being in a tension of anxiety.

Also—a strange and perplexing thing—Ruth was angry with Rachel and "The Young Student"! It appeared that the Socialists had been getting up meetings all over the country for a so-called Social-revolutionary from Russia, a lecturer who made the imprisonment of his partisans in Russia the pretext for attacks on the Soviet Government. The Social-revolutionaries were the people who had tried to assassinate Lenin, and who had taken the money of capitalist governments to stir up civil war inside Russia. How could Bunny's paper give support to them?

Bunny went back to Rachel and the Ypsels, who declared that this man was a Socialist, opposing the partisans of violence; the Communists had come to the meeting and tried to howl him down, and there had been almost a fight. So here was poor Bunny, facing with dismay the same internal warfare in the movement, which had so distressed him in Paris and Berlin and Vienna! He had been so profoundly impressed by Paul and his account of Russia, but he found that Rachel had not moved an inch from her position. She would defend the right of the Russians to work out their own destiny, she would defend their right to be heard in America—even though they would not defend her right. But she would have nothing to do with the Third International, and no talk about dictatorships—unless it was her own dictatorship, that was going to see to it that "The Young Student" didn't give the post office authorities or the district attorney's office any pretext for a raid! No, they were going to stand for a democratic solution of the social problem; and Bunny, as usual, was going to be bossed by a woman!

It was a curious thing—the nature of women! They seemed so gentle and impressionable; but it was the pliability of rubber, or of water—that comes right back the way it was before! From the very first—look at Eunice Hoyt, so set upon having her own way! And even little Rosie Taintor—if he had married her, he would have discovered that she had a fixed religious conviction as to the proper style of window curtains, and how often they had to be laundered! And Vee Tracy, who had given up her happiness—she would not be happy with a Roumanian prince, Bunny knew. And Ruth and Grandma, in the matter of the war! And Bertie, so hell-bent upon getting into fashionable society, in spite of having been born a mule-driver's daughter! And now here was Rachel Menzies, and Bunny knew exactly the situation—it would break her heart to give up the little paper, she had adopted it with the passion of a mother for a child; but she would walk out of the office in a moment, if ever Bunny should fall victim to the Communist process of "boring from within."

IV

Bertie arrived in Angel City a week behind her brother, and afforded him still more evidence of the unchangeable nature of femininity. Bertie had come to get her share of the estate, and she went after it with the single-mindedness of a rabbit-hound. Bertie knew a lawyer—her kind of lawyer, another rabbit-hound—and she saw him the day of her arrival; and then Bunny must come to this lawyer's office, and with the help of Bertie and a stenographer have the insides of his mind turned out and recorded: exactly what Dad had said about his arrangements with Mrs. Alyse Huntington Forsythe Olivier—Dad hadn't said a word about it to Bertie, alas, nor to anyone else; he had made a will, of course, and that infamous woman had destroyed it—Bertie knew that with the certainty of God.

And then, everything else about Dad's affairs that Bunny could recall; where he had kept his money and his papers, what secret hiding-place for stocks and bonds he may have had, what he had spent, so far as Bunny could guess, who had been in his confidence. And then the statements which Vernon Roscoe rendered; and all the files of Dad's correspondence with Verne; and the trusted young executives—Bolling and Heimann and Simmons and the rest; and the bankers and their clerks; and Dad's secretary whom Bertie had brought back from Paris with her—a veritable mountain of detail, and Bunny was required to attend all the sessions, and be just as much a rabbit-hound as the rest. He told himself that it was his duty to the movement, which so badly needed the aid of a "fat angel"!

Right at the outset, there was one bitter pill that Bertie had to swallow. Her lawyer advised her that there was no chance of depriving Mrs. Alyse Ross of her half of the estate. Bunny's testimony was worth, in law, precisely nothing; and so, unless there should be found another will, they must accept the inevitable, and combine with the widow to get as much as possible out of Vernon Roscoe. Mrs. Ross's Paris lawyers had named some very high priced lawyers in Angel City as their representatives, and Bertie had to swallow her rage and admit these men to their counsels.

There were troubles enough to need the very highest-priced lawyers. Accountants were put to work on the books of J. Arnold Ross, and on the statements rendered by his partner, and in a few days there began to emerge out of the tangle one colossal fact: over and above all the money that Dad had put into new business ventures with Verne and others, above all the cash which he had handled through his bank, there was more than ten million dollars' worth of stocks and bonds which had disappeared without a trace. Verne declared that these securities had been taken by Dad, and used by him for purposes unknown; and Bertie declared that was idiocy, and that Vernon Roscoe was the biggest thief in all history. Having access to Dad's safe deposit box, he had simply helped himself to the contents. And with rage Bertie turned upon her brother, asserting that he was to blame—Verne knew that Bunny would use his money to try to overturn society, and so it was only common sense to keep him down.

Nor could Bunny deny that this sounded reasonable. It was easy to imagine Verne saying to himself that Bunny was a social danger, and Bertie a social waster, and the widow a poor half-wit, while he, Verne, was a capable business man, who would use those securities for the proper purpose—to bring more oil out of the ground. Learning of Dad's death, Verne had quietly transferred the securities from Dad's strong box to his own, before the state inheritance tax commissioner came along to make his records! Verne wouldn't consider that stealing, but simply common sense—the same as taking the naval reserves away from a govermnent which hadn't intelligence enough to develop them.

Now Bertie wanted to start a law-suit against her father's partner, and put him on the stand and make him tell everything about his affairs; and Bunny, with the help of the lawyers, had to argue with her, and bear the brunt of her rage. So far, Verne had been careful to put nothing into writing; and when he took the stand, he would have a story fixed up to leave them helpless. He could say that Dad had given him the securities, and how could they disprove it? He could say that Dad had taken the securities, unknown to his partner, and lost the money on the stock market—how could they disprove that? Even if they traced the sales of Dad's securities through Verne's brokers, they would gain nothing, because Verne could say that he had turned over the money to Dad, or that he had been authorized to invest it, and had lost it—a hundred different tales he could invent! "Then we've simply got to take what that scoundrel allows us!" cried Bertie; and the lawyers agreed that was the situation. Being themselves on a percentage basis, their advice was sincere!

Then an incident that multiplied the bitterness between Bertie and her brother. Bunny went to the storage warehouse where his belongings had been put away, and in an atlas that his father had occasionally consulted he came upon five liberty bonds for ten thousand dollars each. It was some money Dad had been keeping handy—possibly to bribe the officers in case he should be caught; anyhow, here it was, and Bunny would have been free to consider it a part of the million which Dad had tried to give him in Paris. But he haughtily decided that he would not join in plundering the estate; he would turn the bonds in, to be counted as part of the assets.

But he made the mistake of telling Bertie about it—and oh, what a riot! The imbecile, to make Alyse and her lawyers a present of twenty-five thousand dollars! Instead of quietly dividing with his sister, and holding his mouth! That twenty-five thousand became to Bertie a thing of more importance than all the millions that Verne had got away with; these bonds were something tangible—or almost tangible—until Bunny took them out of her reach, and made them a present to those greedy vultures! And right when both of them needed cash, and were having to go to one of their father's bankers to borrow money on the basis of their claims to the estate.

Bertie raved and stormed, and Bunny, to get it over with, took the bonds to the bank and turned them in; and after that Bertie never forgave him, she would mention his imbecility every time they were alone. She was making herself ill with all this hatred and fuming; she would sit up half the night poring over figures, and then she couldn't sleep for excitement. Like all young society ladies, she set much store by the freshness of her skin and its freedom from wrinkles; but now she was throwing away her charms, and making herself pale and haggard. In after years she would be going to beauty specialists and having the corners of her mouth lifted, and the skin of her face treated with chemicals and peeled off—because now she could not control her fury of disappointment, that she was to get only a paltry one or two million, instead of the glorious ten or fifteen million she had been confident of some day possessing.

V

Rachel had published a brief article about Bunny's return from abroad, quoting him as saying that he intended to use his inheritance for the benefit of the movement. And this statement had attracted the attention of a bright young newspaper woman, who had written a facetious article:

MILLIONAIRE RED TO SAVE SOCIETY

And now it appeared that there were a great many people who had ideas as to how to save society, and they all wanted to see Bunny, and waited for him in the lobby of his hotel. One had a sure cure for cancer, and another a perpetual motion machine actually working; one wanted to raise bullfrogs for their legs, and another to raise skunks for their skins. There were dozens who wanted to prevent the next war, and several who wanted to start colonies; there were many with different ways of bringing about Socialism, and several great poets and philosophers with manuscripts, and one to whom God had revealed Himself—the bearer of this message was six-feet-four and broad in proportion, and he towered over Bunny and whispered in an awe-stricken voice that the Words which God had spoken had been set down and locked in a safe, and no human eye ever had beheld them, or ever would. Several others wrote that they were not able to call because they were unjustly confined to asylums, but if Bunny would get them out they would deliver their messages to the world through him.

There was one more "nut," and his name was J. Arnold Ross—no longer "junior." He had a plan, which he had been turning over and over in his mind; and now he gathered his friends to get their reaction. Old Chaim Menzies, who had been a long time in the movement, and watched most of its mistakes; Chaim was working in a clothing shop, as usual, and giving his spare time to getting up meetings. And Jacob Menzies, the pale student—Jacob had got a job teaching school for a year, but then he had been found out, and now was selling insurance. And Harry Seager, who was growing walnuts, and escaping the boycotts. And Peter Nagle, who was helping his father run a union plumbing business in an open shop city, and spending his earnings on a four page tabloid monthly ridiculing God. And Gregor Nikolaieff, who had done his Socialist duty working for a year in a lumber camp, and was now assistant to an X-ray operator in a hospital. And Dan Irving, who had come from Washington at Bunny's expense—these six people sat down with Rachel and Bunny at a dinner party in a private dining room, to discuss how to save society with a million dollars.

Bunny explained with becoming modesty that he was not putting forth his plan as the best of all possible plans, but merely as the best for him. He wasn't going to evade the issue by giving his money away, putting off the job on other people; he had learned this much from Dad, that money by itself is nothing, to accomplish anything takes money plus management.

Moreover, Bunny himself wanted something to do; he was tired of just looking on, and talking. He had thought for a long time about a big paper, but he had no knowledge of journalism, and would only be a blunderer. The one thing he did know was young people; he had been to college, and knew what a college ought to be, and wasn't.

"What we're doing—Rachel and Jacob and the rest of us Ypsels—is trying to work on young minds; but the trouble is, we only get them a few hours in the week, and the things that count for most in their lives are the enemy's—I mean the schools, the job, the movies—everything. So I want to get some students together for a complete life, twenty-four hours a day; and see if we can't build a Socialist discipline, a personal life, with service to the cause as its goal. Rachel will agree with me in this—I don't know if anyone else will—I think one reason the movement suffers is that we haven't made the new moral standards that we need. Our own members, many of them, are personally weak; the women have to have silk stockings and look like the bourgeoisie, and their idea of freedom is to adopt the bad habits of the men. If the movement really meant enough to Socialists, they wouldn't have to spend money for tobacco, and booze, and imitation finery."

"Dat let's me out!" said old Chaim Menzies, who had already lighted his ten-cent cigar.

The substance of what Bunny wanted was a labor college on a tract of land somewhere out in the country; but instead of spending his million on steel and concrete, he wanted to begin in tents, and have all the buildings put up by the labor of the students and teachers. Everybody on the place was to have four hours' manual labor and four of class work daily; and they were all to wear khaki, and have no fashionable society. Bunny had the idea of going out among the colleges and high schools, and talking to little groups of students, and here and there seducing one away from football and fraternities to a new dedication. Also the labor unions would be invited to select promising young men and women. It was a thing that should grow fast, and take little money, because, with the exception of building materials, everything could be produced on the place; they would have a farm, and a school of domestic arts— in short, teach all the necessary trades, and provide four hours' honest work of some sort for all students who wanted to come.

VI

What did they think about it? Chaim Menzies was, as always, the first to speak. Perhaps his feelings had been hurt by the reference to tobacco; anyhow, he said it looked to him like it vas anodder colony; you didn't change a colony by calling it a college, and a colony vas de vorst trap you could set for de movement. "You git people to go off and live by demselves, different from de rest of de vorkers, and vedder dey are comfortable or vedder dey ain't—and dey von't be!—all de time dey are tinking about someting else but de class struggle out in de vorld."

"That's quite true," said Bunny. "But we shan't be so far from the world, and the purpose of our training will be, not the colony, but the movement outside, and how to help it."

"De people vot are going to help de movement has got to be in it every hour. You git dem out vun mont' and dey are no good any more; dey have got some sort of graft den, someting easy, dey are no longer vorkers."

"But this isn't going to be so easy, Comrade Chaim——"

"Listen to him! He is going to git nice young college ladies and gentlemen to come and live lives dat vill not seem easy to de vorkers!"

"You might as well admit it, Bunny," put in Harry Seager. "You'll have a nice polite place, with all the boys and girls wearing William Morris costumes. They'll work earnestly for a while, but they'll never be efficient, and if you really have any buildings put up, or any food raised, you'll have regulation hard-fisted workingmen to do it. I know, because we're picking walnuts now!"

"I don't want a polite place," said Bunny. "I want a gymnasium where people train for the class struggle; and if we can't have discipline any other way, how about this as part of the course—every student is pledged to go to jail for not less than thirty days."

"Attaboy!" cried Peter Nagle. "Now you're talking!"

"Vot is he going to do—break de speed laws?" inquired Chaim, sarcastically.

"He's going into Angel City and picket in a strike. Or he's going to hold Socialist meetings on street corners until some cop picks him up. You don't need me to tell you how to get arrested in the class struggle, Comrade Chaim."

"Yes, but he might run into some judge dat vould not understand de college regulation, and might give him six mont's."

"Well, that's a chance we'll have to take; the point is simply, no senior student is in good social standing until he or she has been in jail for at least thirty days in a class struggle case."

"And the teachers?" demanded Gregor Nikolaieff.

"Once every three years, or every five years for the teachers."

"And the founder! How often for the founder?" Peter clamored in glee; but Dan Irving said the founder would have to wait until he had got rid of his money.

They argued back and forth. Could you interest young people in the idea of self-discipline? Would your danger be in setting the standard too easy, so that you wouldn't accomplish much, or in setting it too high, so that you wouldn't have any students? Bunny, the young idealist, was for setting it high; and Harry Seager said that people would volunteer more quickly to die than they would to get along without tobacco. And he wanted to know, what were they going to do about the Communists. Harry was no politician any more, he was a social revolutionist, and only waiting for the day of action. Regardless of what Socialist party members might wish, they couldn't keep Bolshevik students out of a college, and even if they did, the ideas would bust in.

Bunny answered by setting forth his ideal of the open mind. Why couldn't the students do their own educating, and make their own decisions? Let the teachers give the information they were asked for: and then let the students thresh it out— every class room an open forum, and no loyalty except to research and freedom? They were all willing to admit that there would be no use starting a sectarian institution, to advocate one set of doctrines and exclude the others. Also, it took a partisan of each doctrine to set it forth fairly. So then, here was Bunny pinning them down: "Chaim, would you be willing for Harry to explain his ideas to your class? Harry, would you give Chaim a chance to talk?" Bunny could see his own job— the arbitrator who kept these warring fractions out of each other's hair!

Then said Chaim, the skeptic, "I vant to know, vot are you going to do about sex?"

Bunny admitted that this worried him. "I suppose we'll have to conform to bourgeois standards."

"Oh, my God!" cried Peter Nagle. "Let the bourgeoisie begin!"

Jacob Menzies, the student, had just been reading a book about Ruskin, the old time Socialist colony in Tennessee. It was the sex problem which had broken up that colony, he declared; and his father chimed in, "It vill break up any colony dat ever exists under capitalism! Dere is only vun vay you can make vun man live vit vun voman all his life, and dat is to shut dem up in a house togedder and never let dem out. But if you let dem get vit odder couples, den right avay vun man finds he vants some odder voman but de right vun."

"But then," said Dan Irving, "according to bourgeois standards, they get a divorce."

"Sure ting!" said Chaim. "But not in a Socialist colony! If dey vould do it in a colony, it vould be a free love nest, and you vould be on de front page of de papers, and de American Legion come and bust you in de snoot!"

VII

The upshot of the debate was that no one of them was sure the enterprise would be a success, but all the young ones were willing to pitch in and help, if Bunny was determined for a try. And Bunny said that he had already been looking about for a site, with good land and plenty of water, somewhere about fifty miles from Angel City; he was going to make a first payment on land as soon as he could get the cash, and meantime they would work out the details. He would give his own time for three years to getting the institution on its feet, and if it proved possible to develop the right discipline and morale, he would make the institution self-directing, and furnish whatever money could be used effectively. They would need teachers, organizers, and business managers, so there were jobs for all.

And meantime, Bunny must go back to the interviews with lawyers, to try to save as much as possible of the estate. It meant long wrangles with Bertie, for their affairs were in a snarl, and getting worse every day. Verne insisted that Ross Operating must have funds to meet its current expenses; and did they want him to assess the stock, and force the estate to raise the money, or did they want him to buy the lease to the

Ross Junior tract, the only asset of Ross Operating, except the claims against the insurance companies? Verne could do what he pleased, because the directors of the concern were himself and his trusted young executives. He was proposing to form another concern, the Paradise Operating Company—with other trusted young executives as directors, and sell himself the lease, which had twenty years still to run, and was worth nobody could tell how many millions of dollars, for the sum of six hundred thousand!

All right then, said Verne, let the estate do better. Bertie took up the challenge, and exchanged long cables with her husband in Paris, and went out among her rich friends—to make the embarrassing discovery that people who have six hundred thousand dollars in cash do a lot of investigating before they spend it, and then want to hog the whole thing for themselves. Bertie spent much worry and hard work—and what made her most furious was that she couldn't do it for herself alone, but had to do it for the whole estate, giving the incompetent Bunny and the infamous Alyse the benefit of her labors. She got a proposition; and then the lawyers of the infamous Alyse turned up with another proposition; and Bertie declared they were bigger thieves than Verne.

And then Ross Consolidated needed money, and Verne was going to assess that stock—meaning to drive the estate to the wall and plunder it of everything. Presently he made a proposition—there was the Roumanian oil venture, into which Dad had put a million and a quarter in cash. Verne offered to purchase this back for the same amount, and the necessary papers were prepared—the heirs all had to consent to the sale, and they did so, and then the court must approve the proposal. This meant delay, and meanwhile the estate was delinquent in the assessment on the Ross Consolidated stock, and this stock was to be sold out. The money from the Roumanian deal was to save it, but to the consternation of the lawyers, the court refused its consent to this deal. There were technical points involved— the court questioned the authority of Mrs. Alyse Ross' lawyers, and demanded her personal signature, attested in France. In short, the estate couldn't get the money in time for the sale, and it was Vernon Roscoe who bought the Ross Consolidated stock at a bargain.

Oh, how Bertie raved and swore—the veritable daughter of a mule-driver! Verne, the filthy swine, had put that trick over on them! Not content with having stolen Dad's papers, he had diddled them along like this, and got one of his crooked judges to hold up the order, so that he might grab another plum! Bertie threatened to take a gun to Verne's office and shoot him down like a dog; but what she really did was to abuse her brother, who had been such a fool as to make a mortal enemy out of the most powerful man they knew.

It taught them a lesson. They would get themselves out of Verne's clutches, get rid of everything that he controlled. Dad had put nearly a million into a concern called Anglo-California, which was to develop the big Mosul concession; and the lawyers of Alyse got an offer for that stock, but it included time payments, and Bertie wouldn't agree to that, and the lawyers wouldn't agree to Verne's cash offer, and Bertie was in terror lest Verne would do some more hocus-pocus—organize an Anglo-California Operating Company, and lease the Mosul tract to it, and swipe all the profits!

Amid which wrangling came a letter from Alyse to Bunny. She was sure that he would not let horrid money troubles come between him and her, and break their sacred bond, the memories of dear Jim. Alyse had gone to consult her favorite medium, immediately upon her arrival in Paris, and at the third seance Jim had "manifested," and ever since then Alyse had had his words taken down by a stenographer, and here was a bulky record, big as the transcript of a legal trial, and tied with blue ribbons of feminine elegance. Alyse hoped that Bunny had not failed to consult a medium, and would send her whatever dear Jim had had to say in his old home.

Bunny went through the record, and it gave him a strange thrill. There were pages and pages of sentimental rubbish about this happy shore and this new state of bliss, with angel's wings and the music of harps, and tell my dear ones that I am with them, but I am wiser now, and my dear Bunny must know that I understand and forgive—all stuff that might have come out of the conscious or subconscious mind of a sentimental elderly lady or of a rascally medium. But then came something that made the young man catch his breath: "I want my dear Bunny to know that it is really his father who speaks to him, and he will remember the man who got all the land for us, and that he had two gold teeth in the front of his mouth, and Bunny said that somebody would rob his grave." How in the name of all the arts of magic was a medium in Paris to know about a joke which Bunny had made to his father about Mr. Hardacre, the agent who had bought them options on ranches in Paradise, California?

By golly, it was something to think about! Could it really be that Dad was not gone forever, but had just disappeared somewhere, and could be got hold of again? Bunny would go for a walk to think about it; and through the streets of Angel City he would hear the voice of Eli Watkins booming over the radio. Eli's Tabernacle was packed day and night, with the tens of thousands who crowded to see the prophet who had been floated over the sea by the angels, and had brought back a feather to prove it; all California heard Eli's voice, proclaiming the ancient promise: "Behold, I shew you a mystery; we shall not all sleep, but we shall all be changed, in a moment, in the twinkling of an eye, at the last trump; for the trumpet shall sound, and the dead shall be raised incorruptible, and we shall be changed."

CHAPTER XXI

THE HONEYMOON

I

Bunny was looking for a site for the labor college. It was a much pleasanter job than seeking oil lands; you could give some attention to the view, the woods and the hills, and other things you really cared about; also it wasn't such a gamble, because you could really find out about the water supply, and have a chemical analysis of the soil. It meant taking long rides in the country; and since Rachel was to be one of the bosses, it was good sense for her to go along. They had time to talk—and a lot to talk about, since they were going to take charge of a bunch of young radicals, boys and girls of all ages—twenty-four hours a day.

They had looked at a couple of places, and there was another farther from the city, and Bunny remarked, "If we go to that, we'll be late getting home." Rachel answered, "If it's too late, we can go to some hotel, and finish up in the morning." Said Bunny, "That would start the gossips." But Rachel was not afraid of gossips, so she declared.

They drove to the new site. It was near a village called Mount Hope, in a little valley, with the plowed land running up the slopes of half a dozen hills. It was early November, and the rains had fallen, and the new grain had sprouted, and there were lovely curving surfaces that might have been the muscles of great giants lying prone—giants with skins of the softest bright green velvet. There were orchards, and artesian water with a pumping plant, and a little ranch-house—the people had apparently gone to town, so the visitors could wander about and look at everything, and make a find—a regular airdrome of a barn, gorgeous with revolutionary red paint! "Oh, Bunny, here's our meeting place, all ready made! We have only to put a floor in and we can have a dance the opening night!" Imagine Rachel thinking about dancing!

They climbed one of the slopes, and here was a park, with dark live oaks and pale grey sycamores, and a carpet of new grass under foot. The valley opened out to the west, and the sun had just gone down, in a sky of flaming gold; the quail were giving their last calls, and deep down in Bunny's heart was an ache of loneliness—because quail meant Dad, and those beautiful hills of Paradise, and happiness he had dreamed in vain.

Now it was Rachel dreaming. "Oh, Bunny, this is too lovely! It's exactly what we want! Mount Hope College—we couldn't have made up a better name!"

Bunny laughed. "We don't want to buy a name. We must take samples of the soil."

"How many acres did you say?"

"Six hundred and forty, a little over a hundred in cultivation. That's more than we'll be able to take care of for quite a while."

"And only sixty-eight thousand! That's a bargain!" Rachel had learned to think on Bunny's imperial scale, since she had been racing over the state in his fast car, inspecting millionaire play-grounds and real estate promoters' paradises.

"The price is not bad," said Bunny, "if we are sure about the soil and water."

"You could see the state of the growing things, before it got dark."

"Maybe so. We'll come back in the morning, and have a talk with the ranchman. Perhaps he's a tenant, and will tell us the truth." Not for nothing had Bunny spent his boyhood buying lands with his shrewd old father!

II

Twilight veiled this valley of new dreams, and across the way the hills were purple shadows. Bunny said, "There's just one thing worrying me about our plan now: I'm afraid there's going to be a scandal."

"How do you mean?"

"You and me being together all the time, and going off and being missing at night."

"Oh, Bunny, what nonsense!"

"No, really, I'm worried. I told Peter Nagle we'd have to conform to bourgeois standards, and we're beginning wrong. My Aunt Emma is a bourgeois standard, and she would never approve of this, and neither would your mother. We ought to go and get married."

"Oh, Bunny!" She was staring at him, but it was too dark to reveal any possible twinkle in his eyes. "Are you joking?"

"Rachel," he said, "will you take that much trouble to preserve the good name of our institution?"

He came a step nearer, and she stammered, "Bunny, you don't—you don't mean that!"

"I don't see any other way—really."

"Bunny—no!"

"Why not?"

"Because—you don't want to marry a Jewess!"

"Good Lord!"

"Don't misunderstand me, I'm proud of my race. But all your friends would think it was a mistake."

"My friends, Rachel? Who the devil are my friends—except in the radical movement? And where would the radical movement be without the Jews?"

"But, Bunny—your sister!"

"My sister is not my friend. Neither did she ask me to pick out her husband."

Rachel stood, twisting her fingers together nervously. "Bunny, do you really—you aren't just speaking on an impulse?"

"Well, I suppose it's an impulse. I seem to have to blurt it out. But it's an impulse I've had a good many times."

"And you won't be sorry?"

He laughed. "It depends upon your answer."

"Stop joking, please—you frighten me. I can't afford to let you make a mistake. It's so dreadfully serious!"

"But why take it that way?"

"I can't help it; you don't know how a woman feels. I don't want you to do something out of a generous impulse, and then you'd feel bound, and you wouldn't be happy. You oughtn't to marry a girl out of the sweat-shops."

"Good God, Rachel, my father was a mule-driver."

"Yes, but you're Anglo-Saxon; away back somewhere your ancestors were proud of themselves. You ought to marry a tall, fair woman that will stay beautiful all her life, and look right in a drawing-room. Jewish women bear two or three children, and then they get fat, and you wouldn't like me."

He burst out laughing. "I have attended the weddings of some of those tall, fair Anglo-Saxon women; and the priest pronounces, very solemnly, 'Into this holy estate the two persons now present come now to be joined. If any man can show just cause, why they may not lawfully be joined together, let him now speak, or else hereafter forever hold his peace.' "

"Bunny," she pleaded, "I'm trying to face the facts!"

"Well, dear, if you must be solemn—it happens that I never loved a fair woman. The two I picked out to live with were dark, the same as you. It must be nature's effort to mix things. I suppose you know about Vee Tracy?"

"Yes."

"Well, Vee had the looks all right, and she'll keep them— she makes a business of it. But you see, it didn't do me any good, she threw me over for a Roumanian prince."

"Why, Bunny?"

"Because I wouldn't give up the radical movement."

"Oh, how I hated that woman!"

There was a note of melodrama in Rachel's usually serene voice, and Bunny was curious. "You did hate her?"

"I could have choked her!"

"Because she struck you?"

"No! Because I knew she was trying to take you out of the movement; and I thought for sure she would. She had everything I didn't have."

Bunny was thinking—by golly, it was queer! Vee had known it—and he hadn't! Oh, these women! Aloud he said, politely, "No, she didn't have quite everything."

"What is there that I have, Bunny? What do I mean to you?"

"I'll tell you—I'm so tired of being quarreled with. You can't have any idea—my whole life, since I began to think for myself, has been one wrangle with the people who loved me, or thought they had a right to direct me. You can't imagine what a sense of peace I get when I think of being with you; it's like settling down into nice soft cushions. I've hesitated about it, because of course I'm not very proud of the Vee Tracy episode, and I didn't know if you'd take a man second-hand—or third-hand it really is, because there was a girl while I was in high school. I'm telling you my drawbacks, to balance your getting fat!"

"Bunny, I don't care about the other women—they will always be after you, of course. I was heartsick about Miss Tracy, because I knew she was a selfish woman, and I was afraid you'd find it out too late, and be wrecked. At least, I told myself that was it—I suppose the truth is I was just green with jealousy."

"Why, Rachel! You mean that you love me?"

"As if any woman could help loving you! The question is, do you love me?"

"I do—yes, truly!"

"But Bunny—" there was a little catch in her voice. "You don't show it!"

So then he realized that he had been wasting a lot of time! He had to take only one more step, and put his arms about her, and there she was, sobbing on his shoulder, as if her heart would break. "Oh, Bunny, Bunny! Can I believe it?"

So to make her believe it, he began to kiss her. She had been such a sedate and proper little lady, such a manager in the office and all that, he had been in awe of her; but now he made the discovery that she was exactly like the other women who had been in love with him; as soon as she was sure that she might let herself go, that it was not some blunder, or some crazy dream—why, there she was, clinging to him in a sort of daze of happiness, half laughing, half weeping. As he kissed her, there was mingled in his emotion the memory of how brave she had been, and how loyal, and how honest; yes, it was worth while making a girl like that happy! To mingle love with those other emotions, that appeared to be safe! And she was just as passionate as either Eunice or Vee had been, not a particle more sedate or reticent! "Oh, Bunny, I love you so! I love you so!" She whispered it in the darkness, and her embraces said more than her words.

"Dear Rachel!" he said, with a happy little laugh. "If you feel that way, let's go find a preacher or a justice of the peace."

She answered, "Foolish Bunny! I want to know that you love me, and that I'm free to love you. What do I care about preachers or justices?"

So then he caught her tighter, and their lips met in a long kiss. If she tried to voice any more doubts, he would stop the sounds, he would find a way to convince her! And what better place for their love than this mysterious grove, the scene of their future labors? Yes, they would have to buy this ranch now, regardless of soil deficiencies! It would be a haunted place; in after years, while the young folks had their games and pageants in this grove, Bunny and Rachel would look on with a secret thrill. Had it not been in ancient oak-groves that mystic rites had been celebrated, and pledges made, and holy powers invoked!

III

They found the justice of the peace next morning; and then they finished the inspection of the ranch, and drove back to Angel City and made arrangements for a first payment on the purchase price. After which they had the thrills of telling all their friends about having got married—strictly in the interest of the college, of course, and to avoid scandals in the bourgeois press!

Bunny went to see Ruth, and tell her; and strange to say, this embarrassed him. Bertie and Vee had planted in his mind the idea that Ruth had been in love with him for the past ten years; and now Rachel was certain of it; and these women had all proved to be right about each other every time! Also, there was a fact which he had not mentioned to Rachel: there had been a while on the way back from Paris, when he was debating in his mind whether it was Rachel or Ruth he was going to invite to become his wife! He had a deep affection for Ruth, the same still quiet feeling that she herself manifested. But the trouble was, there was Paul. Ruth was bound by steel chains to her brother—and that meant the Communist movement, and so Bunny had to wrestle over that problem some more.

Sooner or later you had to decide, and take your place with one party or the other. Were you going to overthrow capitalism by the ballot or by "direct action"? This much had become clear to Bunny—the final decision rested with the capitalist class. They were getting ready for the next war; and that meant Bolshevism in all the warring nations, at the end of the war, if not at the beginning. The Socialists would try to prevent this war; and if they failed, then the job would be done in Paul's way, by the Third International. But meantime, Bunny was drawn to the Socialists by his temperament. He could not call for violence! If there was to be any, the other side must begin it!

Whatever Ruth may have thought or felt about the news of his marriage, she gave no sign but of pleasure. She had expected it, she said; Rachel was a fine girl, who agreed with his ideas, and that was the main thing. Then she told him that Paul was expected back tomorrow, and was to speak at a meeting—his supporters had got him into the Labor Temple by much diplomacy, and he would have a chance to tell the workingmen about what he had seen in Russia. Bunny and Rachel must come and hear him; and Bunny said they would.

This was the Sunday before election day, the end of a long political campaign. The workers had heard no end of appeals for their votes—but here was something different, more important than any election issues. However hostile the leaders of labor might be, it was impossible for the rank and file to resist the contagion of this miracle that was happening on the other side of the world—a vast empire where the workers ruled, and were making their own laws and their own culture. Paul was fresh from these scenes; his words were vivid, he brought the things before your eyes: the red army, and the red schools, and the red papers, the white terror, and the resistance to capitalist siege on ten thousand miles of front.

Oh, the fury of the capitalist press next day! They didn't report the meeting, but they published protests about it, and stormed in editorials. The LaFollette "reds" were bad enough, but this was an intolerable outrage—an avowed Moscow agent, who had been expelled from France, permitted to hold a meeting in Angel City and incite union labor to red riot and insurrection! What was our police department for? Where were our patriotic societies and our American Legion and our other forces of law and order?

Bunny called up Ruth next morning; he wanted to see Paul, to talk about the proposed college. Ruth said that Paul had gone down to the harbor, to see about addressing meetings of the longshoremen. These men had had a big strike while Bunny was abroad, and had taken their full course in capitalist government. Six hundred of them had been swept up off the street, for the crime of marching and singing, and had been packed into tanks with all ventilation shut off, to reduce them to silence. A score of the leaders had been sent to state's prison for ten or twenty years for "criminal syndicalism"; so the rest ought to be ready to listen to the Communist doctrine, that the workers had to master the capitalist state. There was to be an entertainment that night in the I. W. W. hall at the harbor; there would be music and refreshments, and Paul thought it would be a good chance to get acquainted with the leaders. Bunny said that he and Rachel were going down to

Beach City, and they might run over and bring Paul back with them.

IV

Bunny had yielded to the importunities of his sister: wouldn't he have the decency to help out the estate in at least one way—look into those reports which Vernon Roscoe had rendered concerning the Prospect Hill field? Verne asserted that more than half the wells were off production, and Bertie suspected one more trick to rob them. Bertie wouldn't know an oil well off production from a hen-coop; but Bunny would know, and couldn't he go down there, and snoop around a bit, and find out what other oil men thought about the field and its prospects? Bunny took Rachel with him—she went everywhere with her new husband, of course. They had got one of the oldest of the Ypsels to run the magazine office, and Rachel was just manager and editor, very high and mighty. Bunny was a one-arm driver again, and the automobile was lopsided, and Rachel was nervous when he drove fast, because the gods are jealous of such rapture as hers.

Rachel had never seen an oil field at close range. So Bunny took her to the "discovery well," and told how Mr. Culver had had his ear-drums destroyed, trying to stop the flow with his head. He showed her the first well that Dad had drilled, and on which Bunny had helped to keep the mud flowing. That had been the beginning of Dad's big wealth; he and perhaps a score of others had got rich, and to balance it, there were in Beach City many thousands of people who had their homes plastered with mortgages, representing losses from the buying of "units." That was the way most of the money had been made in Prospect Hill—selling paper instead of oil. It was a fact, as Paul had cited, that more money had been put into the ground than had been taken out of it. Here had been a treasure of oil that, wisely drilled, would have lasted thirty years: but now the whole field was "on the pump," and hundreds of wells producing so little that it no longer paid to pump them. One sixth of the oil had been saved, and five-sixths had been wasted!

That was your blessed "competition," which they taught you to love and honor in the economics classes! Another aspect of it was those frightful statistics, that of all the thousands of men who had worked here, seventy-three out of every hundred had been killed or seriously injured during the few years of the field's life! It was literally true that capitalist industry was a world war going on all the time, unheeded by the newspapers.

Bunny did his checking up of the Ross wells; he couldn't do any "snooping," because some of the old hands knew him, and came up to greet him. He talked with a number of men, and found their reports about the same as Verne's. Then, towards evening, as he and Rachel were getting ready to leave, they came to a bungalow, dingy and forlorn, black with oil stains and grey with dust, with a storage-tank in the back yard, and a derrick within ten feet on the next lot, and on the other side a shed which had housed the engine of another derrick. Bunny stopped, and read the number on the front of the bungalow, 5746 Los Robles Blvd. "Here's where Mrs. Groarty lives! Paul's aunt—it was in that house we had the meeting about the lease, and I first heard Paul's voice through the window there!"

He told the story of that night, describing the characters and how they had behaved. Paul said it was a little oil fight, and the world war had been a big oil fight, and they were exactly the same. While they were talking, the door opened, and there emerged a stout, red-faced woman in a dirty wrapper, and Bunny exclaimed, "There's Mrs. Groarty!" Out he hopped— "Hello, Mrs. Groarty!" How many years it had been since she had seen him; he had to tell her who he was, that little boy grown up, and with a wife—well, well, would you believe it, how time does fly! And so Mr. Ross was dead—Mrs. Groarty's husband had read the sad news out of the paper. She knew that he had got to be very rich, so she was thrilled by this visit, and invited them in, but all in a flutter because her house wasn't in order.

They went in, because Bunny wanted Rachel to see that staircase, and to have a laugh on her afterwards, because she wouldn't notice anything, but would think the staircase led to a second story—in a one-story bungalow! There was the room—not a thing changed, except that it seemed to have shrunk in size, and the shine was all gone. There was the window where Bunny had stood while he listened to Paul's whispered voice. And. by golly, there was "The Ladies' Guide, a Practical Handbook of Gentility," still on the centre table, faded and fly-specked gold and blue! Along side was a stack of what appeared to be legal papers, a pile at least eight inches high, and fastened with ribbons and a seal. Mrs. Groarty caught his glance at it; or perhaps it was just that she was longing for someone to tell her troubles to. "That's the papers about our lot," she said. "I just took them away from the lawyer, he takes our money and he don't do nothing."

So then she was started, and Rachel continued her education in oil history. The Groarty's had entered a community agreement, and then withdrawn from it and entered a smaller one: then they had leased to Sliper and Wilkins, and been sold by those "lease hounds" to a syndicate; and this syndicate had been plundered and thrown into bankruptcy; after which the lease had been bought by a man whom Mrs. Groarty described as the worst skunk of them all, and he had gone and got a lot of claims and liens against the property, and actually, people were trying to take some money away from the Groartys now, though they had never got one cent out of the well—and look at the way they had had to live all these years!

Here was the record of these transactions, community agreements and leases and quit claim deeds and notices of release and notices of cancellation of lease, and mortgages, and sales of "percents," and mechanic's liens and tax receipts and notices of expiration of agreement—not less than four hundred pages of typewritten material, something like a million and a half of words, mostly legal jargon—"the undersigned hereby agrees" and "in consideration of the premises herein set forth," and "in view of the failure of the party of the first part to carry out the said operations by the aforesaid date," and so on—it made you dizzy just to turn the pages. And all this to settle the ownership of what was expected to be ten thousand barrels of oil, and had turned out to be less than one thousand! Here you saw where the money had gone—pale typists shut up in offices all day transcribing copies of this verbiage, and pale clerks checking and rechecking them, or looking them up, or recording them—there were men up in Angel City who had become mighty magnates by employing thousands of men and women slaves, to transcribe and check and recheck and look up and record literally millions of documents like these!

V

Bunny and Rachel had dinner, and then strolled on the water front; it was one of those warm nights that come now and then in Southern California; there was a moon on the sea, and a long pier with gleaming lights, and the sound of an orchestra drawing the lovers. At the entrance to the pier was a big bare hall, owned by the city, where very proper dancing was chaperoned by a religious city government. Bunny and his bride danced—oh, surely it was all right to dance a little bit, in this well chaperoned place on what ought to have been their honeymoon!

But in between the dances, while the orchestra was still, something shook the hall, a dull, sombre blow, like distant thunder, making the windows rattle, and jarring your feet. "What's that?" exclaimed Rachel. "An earthquake?"

"The guns," answered Bunny.

"Guns?" And he had to explain, the fleet was practicing. There were a score or so of battleships stationed at the harbor, facing some unnamed enemy; and now they were at night target-practice. You heard them now and then, day and night, if you lived near the coast.

So Rachel couldn't dance any more then. Each time she heard that dull boom, she saw the bodies of young men blown into fragments. The capitalists were getting ready for their next war; what business had the Socialists to be dancing?

They drove along the boulevard which follows the harbor-front. It is fifteen or twenty miles, and there are towns and docks and bridges and railroad tracks and factories, and inland the "subdivisions" for the homes of working people. It is one of the world's great ports in the swift making; and those who have charge of the job, the masters of credit, see rearing before them that monstrous spectre known as "direct action" or "criminal syndicalism." The "Industrial Workers of the World" had a headquarters, where they met to discuss this program; and the masters made incessant war upon them.

The address which Ruth had given to Bunny was an obscure street in a working-class quarter. There was a fair-sized hall, with lights in the windows, and the sound of a piano and a child's voice singing. Among the cars parked along the curb Bunny found a vacant space, and backed into it, and was just about to step from his car, when Rachel caught him by the arm. "Wait!" There came rushing down the street a squadron of motor-cars, two abreast and blocking the way entirely; and from them leaped a crowd of some fifty men, carrying weapons of various sorts, clubs, hatchets, pieces of iron pipe. They made a rush for the entrance, and a moment later the music ceased, and there came the sound of shrieks, and the crash of glass and battering of heavy blows.

"They're raiding them!" cried Bunny, and would have run to the scene; but Rachel's arms were flung about him, pinning him to his seat. "No! No! Sit still! What can you do?"

"My God! We must do something!"

"You're not armed, and you can't stop a mob! You can only get killed! Keep still!"

The sounds from within had risen to a bedlam; the hall must have been crowded, and everyone inside yelling at the top of his lungs. And that horrible drumming of blows—you couldn't tell whether they were falling on furniture or on human bodies. Bunny was almost beside himself, struggling to get loose, and Rachel fighting like a mad thing—he had never dreamed that she had such strength. "No, Bunny! No! For God's sake! For my sake! Oh, please, please!" She knew in those dreadful minutes the terror that was to haunt the rest of her life—that some day in this hideous class war there would come the moment when it was her husband's duty to get himself killed. But not yet, not yet! Not on their honeymoon!

It was like the passing of a tornado, that is gone before you have time to realize it. The attacking party emerged from the hall, as quickly as they had entered. They were dragging half a dozen prisoners, and threw these into the cars, of which the engines were still going; then down the street they went roaring, and silence fell.

It was permissible for Bunny to get out now, and run into the hall, with Rachel at his heels. He had one thought, the same as on that night when he had run over Mrs. Groarty's place, crying, "Paul! Paul!" They were certain to have taken Paul away on that lynching party; and how could Bunny save him?

The first thing he saw, in the doorway, was a man with a great gash across his forehead, and the blood streaming all over him; he was staggering about, because he couldn't see, and crying, "The sons-o'-bitches! The sons-o'-bitches!" Near him was another man whose hand had been slashed across, and a woman was tearing her skirt to make a bandage. A little girl lay on the floor, screaming in agony, and some one was pulling off her stockings, and the raw flesh was coming with them. "They threw her into the coffee!" said a voice in Bunny's ear. "Jesus Christ, they threw the kids into the boiling coffee!"

Everywhere confusion, women in hysterics, or sunk upon the floor sobbing. There was not a stick of furniture in the place that had not been wrecked; the chairs had been split with hatchets; the piano had been gutted, its entrails lay tangled on the floor. Tables were overset, and dishes and crockery trampled, and the metal urn or container in which the coffee had been boiling had been overset, and its steaming contents running here and there. But first they had hurled three children into it, one after another, as their frantic parents dragged them out. The flesh had been cooked off their legs, and they would be crippled for life: one was a ten years old girl known as "the wobbly song-bird;" she had a sweet treble, and sang sentimental ballads and rebel songs, and the mob leader had jerked her from the platform, saying, "We'll shut your damned mouth!"

What was the meaning of this raid? According to the newspapers, it was the patriotic indignation of sailors from the fleet. There had been an explosion on one of the battleships, and several men had been killed, and the newspapers had printed a story that one of the wobblies had been heard to laugh with satisfaction. It is an ancient device of the master press. In old Russia the "Black Hundreds" were incited by tales of "ritual murders" committed by the Jews, Christian babies killed for sacrifice. In Britain now the government was forging letters attributed to the Soviet leaders, and using them to carry an election. In America the deportations delirium had been sanctified by a great collection of forged documents, officially endorsed.

It was a spontaneous mob, said these law and order newspapers. But this fact was noted: on all other occasions there had been policemen at these wobbly meetings, to take note of criminal utterances; but this night there had been no policeman on hand. Nor were there any afterwards; Bunny and the other "reds" might besiege the police department and the city government, and offer the names of the principal mob leaders, but there would be no step taken to punish anyone for this murderous raid!

VI

Bunny didn't expect to find Paul, but there he lay, flat on his back, with several people bending over him. His left eye was a mass of blood, and seemed as if destroyed by a blow;

he lay, limp and motionless, and when Bunny called his name he did not answer. But he was alive, gasping with a kind of snoring sound.

A doctor! A doctor! There were several in the neighborhood, and people rushed away to look for them. From the days of Bunny's residence in Beach City he knew the name of a surgeon, and hurried to a phone, and was so fortunate as to find the surgeon at home. Bunny told what had happened, and the other said he would come at once; in the case of injury to skull or other bones, X-ray pictures would be needed, so he gave the name of doctors who did such work, and Bunny did more telephoning, and arranged for one of these to be at his laboratory and await developments. Also he ordered an ambulance from a hospital.

Then back to the hall, where Paul lay in the same condition. Rachel had laid a clean handkerchief over the battered eye, and put a pillow under his head. The other victims had been carried away, and the door of the wrecked hall shut against the curious crowd.

The surgeon came, and said it was concussion of the brain. There was evidence of a heavy blow at the base of the skull—either Paul had been struck in the eye, and had hit the back of his head in falling, or else he had been knocked down by a blow from behind, and later struck or trampled over the eye. The first thing was a picture; so the unconscious body was taken to the X-ray laboratory, and pictures were made, and the surgeon showed Bunny and Rachel the line of a fracture at the base of the skull, running to the front above the oral cavity. There was nothing to be done, it was impossible to operate in such a place. It was a question of how the brain had been affected, and as to that only time could tell. They must keep the patient quiet.

There was a private hospital in the town; so before long Paul was lying on a bed, with a bandage over his eye, and his head in a sling to avoid pressure on the injured place; and Bunny and Rachel were sitting by the bedside, gazing mournfully. Womanlike, Rachel was reading his thoughts. "Dear heart, are you going to blame yourself all your life because you didn't rush in and get your skull broken, too?" No, he couldn't have prevented the harm, he knew it; but oh, why did it have to be Paul's brain—the best brain that Bunny had ever known! He sat with a horrified, brooding stare.

But there was another ordeal to be faced. Rachel reminded him, "We've got to tell Ruth." She offered to attend to it, to spare his feelings. She got her brother Jacob on the phone—he had just got home from a committee meeting, and now he must call a taxi, and drive to Ruth's home and bring her to the harbor.

Two hours later Ruth came running up the stairs, her face like a mask of fright. "How is he? How is he?" When she entered the room, and saw Paul, she stopped. "Oh, what is it?" And when they told her—"Is he going to live?" She drew nearer, never taking her eyes off his face. Her hands would stretch out to him, and then draw back, because she might not touch him; they would go out again, as if they had a will of their own. Suddenly her knees gave way, and she sank to the floor, and covered her face with her hands, sobbing, sobbing.

They tried to comfort her, but she hardly knew they were there. She was alone, in the dreadful corridors of grief. Bunny, watching her, felt hot tears stealing down his cheeks. It wasn't natural for a girl to feel that way about a brother, Vee had said; but Bunny knew how it was—Ruth was back in those childhood days on the lonely hills of Paradise, when Paul had been her only friend, a refuge from a family of fanatics, with a father who beat her to make her think like him. Back there she had known that Paul was a great man, and had followed him all these years; she had watched his mind unfolding, and learned everything she knew from it—and now, to see it destroyed by a brute with a piece of iron pipe!

VII

It was long after midnight; and Rachel sought to draw Bunny away. There was nothing more they could do, either for Paul or his sister. There was a small hotel a few doors away, they would get a room there, and rest, and the hospital nurse would notify them if there were any change. And Bunny yielded: he must not be unfair to Rachel. He knew there was something unnatural about his own devotion to Paul, the subjection of his mind to everything that Paul thought, the exactness of his memory of everything Paul had said. Yes, Bertie had told him that, and then Vee—and now Rachel!

He could not sleep. So, lying a-bed in the hotel-room, he explained it to her; how Paul had come when Bunny was groping for something different and better in his life. Paul had given him an ideal—something stern and hard—self-sufficiency, independence of judgment, determination to face life and understand it, and not be drawn away in pursuit of money or pleasure. Bunny had not been able to follow that ideal—no, he had lived in luxury, and gone chasing after women; but he had had the vision, the longing to be like Paul.

And then, at each new crisis in his life, Paul would come along, a sort of standard by which Bunny could measure himself and what he was doing, and realize how little success he was having. Paul had taught him about the workers, and how they felt; Paul had been the incarnation of the new, awakening working-class. Paul's mind had been a searchlight, illumining the world-situation, showing Bunny what he needed to know. Now the light was out, and Bunny would have to see by his own feeble lantern!

"Dear, he may get well," Rachel whispered; but Bunny moaned, no, no, he was going to die. Like a jagged flash of lightning before his mind was that X-ray picture of the crack at the base of Paul's skull. The light was out, at least from this world; a brute with a piece of iron pipe had extinguished it.

Rachel put her arms about him and sought to beguile him with caresses. And she succeeded, of course; he could not refuse her love. So presently he slept a little. But Rachel did not sleep, she lay holding him in her arms, because he would jump and start in his sleep, his limbs would quiver—just the way she felt when the great guns went off!

What was Bunny doing? Fighting those brutes with their clubs and hatchets and iron pipe? Or back in the old days, when he had hovered over Paul and Ruth, watching events that wrung his soul? Watching Dad deprive the family of their land; watching the oil operators crush the first strike; watching the government tear Paul away and make him into a strike-breaker for Wall Street bankers; watching Vernon Roscoe throw Paul into prison; watching capitalism with its world-wide system of terror drive Paul here and there, harry him, malign him, threaten him—until at last it hired the brute with the iron pipe!

VIII

Morning came, and they went back to the hospital room. Nothing was changed. Paul still lay, breathing hoarsely; and

Ruth sat in a chair by the bedside, her eyes fixed upon him,
her hands clasped tightly. She was whiter, that was all, and
her lips were quivering, never still. The hospital nurse begged
her to lie down and rest, but she shook her head. No, she
was used to watching the sick; she was a nurse too. The other
answered that all nurses slept when they could; but no, please—
Ruth wanted to stay right here.

The surgeon came again. There was nothing he could do,
time would have to tell. Bunny took him aside and asked what
were the chances. Impossible to say. If Paul were going to
get well, he would return to consciousness. If he were going
to die, there might be a meningitis, or perhaps a blood clot on
the brain.

Rachel said the family ought to be notified. So Bunny
sent a telegram to Abel Watkins at Paradise, telling him to
engage an auto and bring the family at Bunny's expense. He
debated whether it was his duty to telegraph Eli, and decided
not to. Old Mr. Watkins might do it, but Bunny would be
guided by what Paul would have wished. Then he got the
morning papers, and read their exultant account of the night's
events: the reds had been taught a much-needed lesson, and
law and order were safe at the harbor.

It was the morning of election day: the culmination of a
campaign that had been like a long nightmare to Bunny. Senator LaFollette had been running, with the backing of the
Socialists, and the great issue had been the oil steals; the
indicted exposers of the crime against the criminals in power.
At first the exposers had really made some headway, the
people seemed to care. But the enemy was only waiting for
the time to strike. In the last three weeks of the campaign
he turned loose his reserves, and it was like a vast cloud of
hornets, the sky black with a swarm of stinging, burning,
poisoning lies!

It was the money of Vernon Roscoe and the oil men, of
course: plus the money of the bankers and the power interests
and the great protected manufacturers, all those who had something to gain by the purchase of government, or something to
lose by failure to purchase. Another fifty million dollar campaign; and in every village and hamlet, in every precinct of
every city and town, there was a committee for the distribution
of terror. The great central factories where it was manufactured were in Washington and New York, and the product was

shipped out wholesale, all over the land, and circulated by every agency—newspapers and leaflets, mass meetings, parades, bands, red fire and torchlights, the radio and the moving picture screen. If LaFollette, the red destroyer, were elected, business would be smashed, the workers would be jobless; therefore vote for that strong silent statesman, that great, wise, noble-minded friend of the plain people known as "Cautious Cal." And now, while Paul Watkins lay gasping out his life, there was a snow-storm of ballots falling over the land, nearly a thousand every second. The will of the plain people was being made known.

IX

It was a day like midsummer, and the windows of the hos-pital room were open. Next door, some twenty feet away, was an apartment house, and in the room directly across this space, by the open window, was one of the two hundred thousand radio sets which are in use in the state of California. The occupant of the apartment was one of those two hundred thousand housewives who are accustomed to perform their domestic duties to the tune of "Jesus, Lover of My Soul," or else of "Flamin' Mamie, Sure-fire Vamp." There are a dozen broadcasting stations within range, and some are always going, and you can take your choice. This housewife had catholic tastes, and the watchers at Paul's bedside were beguiled by snatches from the Aloha Hawaiian Quartette, and the Organ Recital of the First Methodist Church, and the Piggly Wiggly Girls' Orchestra, and Radio QXJ reporting that a large vote was being cast in the East, and Radio VZW offering second-hand automobiles for sale, and an unidentified orator exhorting all citizens to hurry to the polls, and Miss Elvira Smithers, coloratura soprano, singing, "Ah loves you mah honey, yes Ah doo-oo-oo-oo."

There came telephone calls from the Workers' party, and from the wobblies at the harbor. And newspaper reporters, who politely listened to Bunny's indignation at the raid, and made a few notes, but published nothing, of course. The news-papers of Angel City have a policy which any child can under-stand—they never print news which injures or offends any business interest.

A telephone call from Paradise; Meelie Watkins, now Mrs. Andy Bugner, calling. Her father and mother, with Sadie, had gone to attend a revival meeting. Meelie didn't know just where it was, but would try to locate them. How was Paul? And when Bunny told her, she asked had they summoned Eli. Whether they believed in him or not, it was a fact that Eli was a great healer; he had cured all sorts of people, and surely should have a chance with his own brother! So Bunny sent a telegram to Eli at the Tabernacle, telling him of Paul's condition; and two hours later a large and expensive limousine stopped at the hospital door.

Eli Watkins, Prophet of the Third Revelation, wore a cream white flannel suit, which made his tall figure conspicuous. He had adopted a pontifical air in these days of glory and power. He did not shake hands with you, but fixed you with a pair of large, prominent, bright blue eyes, and said, "The blessings of the Lord upon you." And when he was in the presence of his brother, he stood gazing, but asking no questions; he was not interested in X-ray pictures of skulls, the Lord knew all that was needed. Finally he said, "I wish to be alone with my brother." There was no evident reason for denying that request, so Bunny and Rachel and Ruth went out.

It didn't make any difference to Ruth where she was—there was nothing to do but stare in front of her, with that terrible quivering of her lips, that wrung your heartstrings. A picture of dreadful grief! The doctor of the hospital begged her to drink a little milk, and the nurse brought a glass, and Ruth tasted, but she could not swallow it. There came a rush of tears to her eyes. You couldn't talk to her, or do anything with her at all.

Eli went away without saying a word; the ways of the Lord being not always understandable by common mortals. There was no apparent change in Paul's condition. Ruth went back to her vigil; but now the doctor gave an order, she must take a sleeping powder and lie down; he would not permit her to kill herself in his establishment. Being trained to take the orders of doctors, Ruth was led away, and Bunny and Rachel kept the vigil.

X

Night fell. The householder who occupied the apartment opposite their window came home and had his supper, and now, comfortable in his shirtsleeves, with pipe in mouth, he sat in a deep wicker chair in front of his radio set, and proceeded to explore the circumambient ether. So the watchers by Paul's bedside got the news of the election without leaving their posts. Owing to difference in time, California gets returns from the east before it gets its own; but it was all the same this Tuesday evening, east and west, the fifty million dollar campaign fund had done its work, and wherever you listened, you learned that more voters had cast their ballots for the strong silent statesman than for all his opponents put together. And since that was the thing ardently desired by the broadcasting stations, and the great newspapers and churches and temples and tabernacles which own them, there was a tone of jocularity in the announcements, and after you had learned that Massachusetts was going three to one for her favorite son, you would hear the Six Jolly Jazz Boys proclaiming, "Got a hot little gal in a railroad town!"—or perhaps the Chicago Comet, chuckling, "My cutie's due at two-to-two!" It made a cheerful atmosphere to die in; but unfortunately Paul wasn't hearing it.

The Tabernacle of the Third Revelation on the air. Eli's followers were not concerned with elections, being soon to wing their way to celestial regions which are conducted upon the monarchical principle. They opened with an organ recital, and the householder didn't care for that, but preferred Radio VKZ, program sponsored by the Snow Baby Soap Company, introducing the first appearance in Angel City of the Pretty Pet Trio, singing their latest popular melody hit, "My Little Jazz-baby, Razz-baby Coon." But later the householder tried the Tabernacle again, and there was the bellowing voice of Eli, that all California householders love. So Bunny and Rachel learned what had been the meaning of Eli's visit.

"Brethren, the Lord has vouchsafed a wonderful proof of His mercy to me. Glorious tidings He gives to the world tonight! I have an older brother, the helpmate of my boyhood, Paul by name, and he was brought up in the fear of the Lord; the voice of the Most Highest was familiar to him on the lonely hills where we tended our father's flocks together. Shepherd boys we were, sitting under the stars, awaiting a sign of the Lord's mercy, and praying for the lost ones of this world to be saved from the devices of the great Tempter.

"Brethren, this brother grew up, and he strayed from the faith of his childhood, he fell into evil company, and became a scoffer at the Lord's Word. The love of our Savior Jesus

Christ was no longer in his heart, but hatred and strife and jealousy of those to whom the Lord has revealed His Truth. And, brethren, the ruin which this misguided brother sought to bring upon others has fallen upon his own head, and tonight he lies dying, struck down by the evil passions which he himself incited. It was my painful task to go to his bedside, and see him lying in a stupor.

"But oh my friends, who can foresee the Wisdom of the Lord? Who can understand His ways? It was His Will to answer my prayers, and permit my lost brother to open his eyes, and hear the voice of the Lord speaking by my lips, and to answer, and confess his transgressions, and repent, and be healed, and washed in the Blood of the Lamb. Glory hallelujah! Glory! Though thy sins be as scarlet they shall become as white as snow, blessed be the name of the Lord! Brethren, rejoice with me; for I have found my sheep which was lost. I say unto you that likewise joy shall be in heaven over one sinner that repenteth, more than over ninety and nine just persons, which need no repentance. Hallelujah! Hallelujah!"

All through this discourse you were aware of the murmur and stir of a great crowd. They would break into ejaculations at every pause in the prophet's words; and now at the end they drowned him out with a chorus of rejoicing, "Glory! Glory, hallelujah!" And in the doorway of the hospital room stood Ruth Watkins, having awakened from her sleep. She was staring at Bunny with horrified eyes, and whispering, "Oh, what a lie!"

Yes, Bunny suspected that it was a lie; but he could not prove it; and even if he could, what then? The radio is a one-sided institution; you can listen, but you cannot answer back. In that lies its enormous usefulness to the capitalist system. The householder sits at home and takes what is handed to him, like an infant being fed through a tube. It is a basis upon which to build the greatest slave empire in history.

XI

The householder shifted his dial. The returns from California were beginning to come in. "Radio VXZ, the Angel City Evening Howler, Angel City, California." The announcer had a soft, caressing voice, worth a thousand dollars a month to him; it had a little chuckle which caused the children to

adore him—he went by the name of "Uncle Peter," and told
them bed-time stories. Now he was applying his humor to the
returns. "Rosario, California. Hello! The home town of
Bob Buckman, secretary to the Chamber of Commerce! Let's
see what Bob's been doing! Rosario, 37 precincts out of 52
give LaFollette 117, Davis 86, Coolidge, 549. Well, well! If
Bob Buckman is listening in on VXZ, congratulations from
Uncle Peter—you're a great little booster, Bob!"

And then, startling the watchers by the bedside—"Paradise,
California. Now what do you think of that? The location of
the Ross Junior oil field, owned by Bunny Ross, our parlor
Bolshevik! Bunny's the boy that bails out the political prisoners, as he calls them; he publishes a little paper to dye our
college boys and girls pink. Let's see what Little Bunny's
town has to say to him. Paradise, California, 14 precincts
out of 29 give LaFollette 217, Davis 98, Coolidge 693. Well,
well, Bunny—you've got some more boring from within
to do!"

The householder shifted again. "Radio QXJ, the Angel
City Evening Roarer, banjo solo by Bella Blue, the Witch
of Wicheta." Plunkety-plunkety—plunkety-plunkety—plunk-
plunk-plunk-plunk!

Paul's lips were beginning to move. There was a trace of
sound, and Ruth bent close to him. "He's coming back to life!
Oh, call the doctor!" The hospital doctor came, and listened,
and felt Paul's pulse; but he shook his head. It was merely
a question of what areas of the brain were affected; the speech
areas might be uninjured. The sounds were incoherent, and
the doctor said Paul didn't know what he was saying. He
might stay that way for days, even for a week or two.

But Ruth continued to listen, and try to catch a word. Paul
might be there, somehow, trying to speak to her, to convey
some request. She whispered, in an agony of longing, "Paul,
Paul, are you trying to talk to me?" The sounds grew louder,
and Rachel said, "It's a foreign language." Bunny said, "It
must be Russian"—the only foreign language Paul knew. It
was strange, like a corpse talking, or a wax doll; the sounds
seemed to come from deep in his throat. "Da zdrávstvooyet
Revolútziya!" over and over; and Bunny said, "That must mean
revolution." And then, "Vsya vlast Soviétam!"—that must
have something to do with the Soviets!

For an hour that went on; until suddenly Ruth exclaimed,

"Bunny, we ought to find out what he's saying! Oh, surely we ought to—just think, if he's asking for help!"

Rachel tried to argue with her; it was just a delirium. But Ruth became more excited—she didn't want Rachel to interfere. Rachel had saved her man, and what did she know about suffering? "I want to know what Paul's saying! Can't we find somebody that knows Russian?" So Bunny got Gregor Nikolaieff on the phone, and asked him to jump on the car and come down here.

When Bunny returned to the room, Paul was talking louder than ever, but still moving only his lips. The Angel Jazz Choir were shouting, "Honey-baby, honey-baby, kiss me in the neck!" And Paul was saying again and again, "Nie troodyáshchiysia da nie yest!"

"Oh, Bunny," pleaded Ruth, "We ought to write down what he says! He might stop—and never speak again!" Bunny understood—Ruth had been brought up to believe in revelations, in words of awful import spoken on special occasions, in strange languages or other unusual ways. The doctors might call it delirium, but how could they be sure? Things that were hidden from the wise were revealed to babes and sucklings. So Bunny got out his notebook and fountain-pen, and wrote down what Paul's words sounded like, as near as he could guess. "Hliéba, mira, svobódy!" And when Gregor came in, an hour or so later, he was able to say this meant, "Bread, peace, freedom," the slogan of the Bolsheviks when they took possession of Russia: and "Dayesh positziyu!"—that was a war-cry of the red army, commanding the enemy to give up the position. The other things Paul had been saying were phrases of the revolution, that he had heard first in Siberia, and then in Moscow. No, Paul was not trying to talk to his sister; he was telling the young workers of America what the young workers of Russia were doing!

XII

"Radio VXZ, the Angel City Evening Howler, Winitsky's orchestra, in the main dining-room of the Admiralty Hotel, broadcasting by remote control." And then presently "Radio QXJ, the Evening Roarer," giving election returns—big figures now. "Republican Campaign Headquarters in New York, in a bulletin issued at 1 A. M., estimates that Calvin Coolidge has

carried Massachusetts by 400,000 plurality—hooray for the
Old Bay State! And New York by 900,000—three cheers for
the Empire State—ray, ray, ray! And Illinois by—wait a
minute there, somebody's knocked my glasses off—they're pulling the rough stuff in this studio. Behave yourselves, girls,
don't you know the world's listening in on QXJ tonight? Illinois by 900,000. Whoopee! That noise you hear is the Chicago
Comet yelping for his home state! It's time we heard the
Chicago Comet again—sing us a hot one, Teddy—that little
warble about the street car comin' along. You know what I
mean?" A broad, jolly Negro voice answered, "Yessah, Ah
knows! Yessah, hyar Ah goes!" Plunkety-plunk—

"Ah had some one befoah Ah had you
     An' Ah'll have someone aftah you's gone,
A street car or a sweetheart doan' mattah to me,
     There'll be another one comin' along!"

Six or seven years ago the people of the United States in
their sovereign wisdom had passed a law forbidding the sale of
alcoholic liquor for beverage purposes. But the advocates of
law and order reserve to themselves the privilege of deciding
which laws they will obey, and the prohibition act is not among
them. All ruling class America celebrates its political victories
by getting drunk. Bunny knew how it was, having got drunk
himself four years ago when President Harding had been
elected; he could smile appreciatively when the announcer of
QXJ tripped over his syllables—"Thass not polite now, Polly,
quit your shovin' this micro-hiccrophone!"

The householder next door was a workingman, or clerk, or
such humble being, denied the royal privilege of breaking the
law at ten dollars a quart for gin and thirty for champagne.
But he could sit here till after midnight, and turn from one
studio to another, and enjoy a series of vicarious jags. "Radio
VXZ, the main diningroom of the Admiralty Hotel." A
chanteuse from the Grand Guignol in Paris was singing a
ballad, and you could hear the laughter of those who understood the obscenity, and those who pretended to understand it,
and those who were too drunk to understand anything but how
to laugh. Bunny was there in his mind, because it was in this
diningroom that he had been drunk, and Dad had been drunk,
and Vee Tracy and Annabelle Ames and Vernon Roscoe—and
Harvey Manning sound asleep in his chair, and Tommy Paley

trying to climb onto the table, and having to be kept from fighting the waiters. There were three hundred tables in that hall, all reserved a month in advance, and all with occupants in the same condition; the tables stacked with hip-pocket flasks and bottles, strewn with the ashes of cigarettes, the stains of spilled foods, flowers and confetti, and little rolls of tissue-paper tape thrown from one table to another, covering the room with a spider's web of bright colors; toy balloons tossing here and there; music, a riot of singing and shouting, and men sprawling over half naked women, old and young, flappers, and mothers and grandmothers of flappers.

There would be election returns read, more of those triumphant, glorious majorities for the strong silent statesman; and a magnate who knew that this victory meant several million dollars off his income taxes, or an oil concession in Mesopotamia or Venezuela won by American bribes and held by American battleships—such a man would let out a whoop, and get up in the middle of the floor and show how he used to dance the double shuffle when he was a farm-hand; and then he would fall into the lap of his mistress with a million dollars worth of diamonds on her naked flesh, and the singer from a famous haunt of the sexual perverts of Berlin would perform the latest jazz success, and the oil-magnate and his mistress would warble the chorus:

> What do I do?
> I toodle-doodle-doo,
> I toodle-doodle-doodle-doodle-doo!

XIII

Paul moved one hand: and again Ruth cried in excitement—he was coming back to life! But the nurse said that meant nothing, the doctors had said he might move. They must not let him move his head. She took his temperature, but told them nothing.

Paul's hands were straying over the sheet that covered him; aimlessly, here and there, as if he were picking at insects on the bed. His voice rose louder—Russian, always Russian, and Gregor would tell what the words meant. They were in the red square, and saw the armies marching, and heard the working masses shouting their slogans: they were on the playing fields with the young workers; they were in Siberia, with Mandel playing the balalaika, and having his eyes eaten out by ants. "Da zdrávstvooyet Revolútziya!"—that meant "Long live Revolution!" "Vsya vlast Soviétam!—All power to the Soviets!"

And from there they would be swept to the ballroom of the Emperor Hotel, Angel City, Radio RWKY, the Angel City Patriot broadcasting by direct control. Or was it to the heart of the Congo, where the naked savages danced to the music of the tomtom, their black bodies, smeared with palm oil, shining in the light of blazing fires? For a hundred centuries these savages had paddled the river, and never to the mind of one of them had come the thought of an engine; they had stood on the shores of mighty lakes, and never dreamed a sail. The weight of nature's blind fecundity rested upon them, stifling their minds. And now capitalist civilization, rushing to destruction with the speed of its fastest battle-planes, cast about to find a form of expression for its irresistible will to degeneracy, and chose the tomtom of the Congo for its music, and the belly-dances of the Congo for its exercise, and so here was America, Land of Jazz.

A voice from the megaphone, raucous, shrill, and mocking:

"There's where mah money goes,
Lipsticks and powderpuffs and sucha things like that!"

And Bunny was in that great "Emperor" ball-room, where he had danced so many a night, first with Eunice Hoyt and then with Vee Tracy. All his friends would be there tonight—Verne and Annabelle and Fred Orpan and Thelma Norman and Mrs. Pete O'Reilly and Mark Eisenberg—the cream of the plutocracy, celebrating their greatest triumph to date. There would be American flags and streamers on the walls, and some would wave little flags—a great patriotic occasion—nothing like it since the Armistice—ray for Coolidge, keep cool with Cal! The room would be crowded to suffocation, and by this hour nine-tenths of the dancers would be staggering. Large-waisted financiers with crumpled shirt-fronts, hugging stout wives or slender mistresses, with naked backs and half-naked bosoms hung with diamonds and pearls, red paint plastered on their lips and platinum bangles in their ears, shuffling round and round to the thump of the tomtom, the wail of the saxophone, the rattle and clatter of sticks, the banging of bells and snarl of stopped trumpets. "She does the camel-walk!" shrilled the

34

singer; and the hip and buttock muscles of the large-waisted financier would be alternately contracted and relaxed, and his feet dragged about the floor in the incoordinate reactions of locomotor ataxia and spastic paraplegia.

XIV

Paul had begun to thresh his arms about: it was necessary to hold him, and when they tried it, he began to fight back. Did he think the strike-guards at Paradise had seized him? Or was it the jailors at San Elido? Or the Federal secret service agents? Or the French gendarmes? Or the sailors of the fleet? Or the thugs with hatchets and iron pipe? He fought with maniacal fury, and there was Bunny holding down one arm and Gregor the other, with Ruth and Rachel each clinging to one foot, while the nurse came running with a straight jacket. So with much labor they tied him fast. He would make terrific efforts; his face would turn purple, and the cords would stand out in his neck; but the system had got him, he could not escape.

Meantime, through the open window, Radio VXZ, the main dining room of the Admiralty Hotel; a blended sound of many hundreds of people, shouting, singing, cheering, now and then smashing a plate, or pounding on the table. Some one was making a speech to the assembly, but he was so drunk he could hardly talk, and they were so drunk they could not have understood anyhow. One got snatches—"glorish victry—greatesh country—soun instooshns—greatesh man ever in White Housh —Cautioush Cal—ray for Coolidge!" A storm of cheers, yells, laughter—and the voice of the announcer, drunk also: "Baby Belle, hottes' lill babe, sing us hot one, right off griddle. Go to it, Babe, I'll hold you!"

Yes, the announcer was drunk, the very radio was drunk, the instruments would not send the wave-lengths true, the ether could not carry them straight, they wavered and wiggled; the laws of the physical universe had gone staggering, God was drunk on His Throne, so pleased by the election of the greatesh man ever in White Housh. Bunny, dazed with exhaustion, saw the scene through a blur of sound and motion, the shining mouths of trumpets, the waving of flags, the flashing of electric signs, the cavorting of satyrs, the prancing of savages, the jiggling of financiers and their mistresses simulating copulation.

Baby Belle was unsteady before the microphone, you lost parts of her song at each stagger; but snatches came, portraying the nymphomania of "Flamin' Mamie, sure-fire vamp—hottes' baby in the town—some scorcher—love's torture—gal that burns 'em down!"

"Oh, God! Oh, God!" cried Ruth. "He's trying to speak to me!" And so for an instant it seemed. Paul's one eye had come open, wild and frightful; he lifted his head, he made a choking noise—

"Comes to lovin'—she's an oven!" shrilled the radio voice.

"Paul! What is it?" shrieked Ruth.

"Ain't it funny—paper money burns right in her hand!"

Paul sank back, he gave up, and Ruth, her two hands clasped as if praying to him, seemed to follow with her soul into that far-away place where he was going.

"Flamin' Mamie, workin' in a mine, ate a box o' matches at the age o' nine!"

"He's dead! He's dead!" Ruth put her hand over Paul's heart, and then started up with a scream.

"Flamin' Mamie, sure-fire vamp," reiterated the chorus, "hottes' baby in the town!"

And Ruth rushed to the window, and threw herself—no, not out, because Bunny had been too quick for her; the others helped to hold her, and the nurse came running with a hypodermic needle, and in a few minutes she was lying on a cot at the side of the room, looking as dead as her brother.

And the householder turned to Radio RWKY, the Angel City Patriot broadcasting from its own studio. "Latest bulletin from New York, the Republican Central Committee claims that Calvin Coolidge will have the greatest plurality ever cast in American history, close to eighteen million votes. Good-night, friends of Radioland."

XV

The Communists wanted to have a "Red funeral," to make a piece of propaganda out of Paul's death. But Eli interposed his majestic authority; since Paul had repented his evil ways and come back to Jesus, he should be buried according to the rites of the Third Revelation.

So three days later a little pageant wound its way to the top of one of the hills of Paradise. There was a crowd on hand, and a truck with the necessary radio apparatus—never were any of the precious words of Eli lost nowadays; the two hundred thousand radio housewives of California had been notified by the newspapers, and a hundred and ninety thousand of them had put off their marketing to hear this romantic funeral service. Bunny and Rachel and a handful of the reds stood to one side, knowing they were not welcome. Ruth stood near the grave with the weeping family, having on each side of her a sturdy oil worker—her two brothers-in-law, Andy Bugner and Jerry Black—because she had been violent on occasions, and no one knew what she might do. She was white and fearful in looks, but seemed not to realize the meaning of the big hole dug in the ground, or of the long black box covered with flowers. While Eli was preaching his fervid sermon about the prodigal son who returned, and about the strayed lamb which was found, Ruth stood gazing at the white clouds moving slowly behind the distant hill-tops.

She would make them no more trouble. All she wanted was to wander over these hills, and call now and then for the sheep which were no longer there. Sometimes she called Paul, and sometimes she called Bunny, and so they let her wander; until one day she went calling Joe Gundha. The oil workers who were putting up the new derricks and cleaning out the burned wells to put them back on production were new men to the Ross Junior tract—it is the Roscoe Junior tract now, by the way, one of Vernon Roscoe's four sons being in charge of the job. These new men had never heard about the "roughneck" who had fallen into the discovery well, so they paid no attention to the unhappy girl who wandered here and there calling his name.

It was not till late that night, when Ruth was missing, and the family making a search, that some one told of hearing her call Joe Gundha. Meelie remembered right away, and they put down a hook in the discovery well, which was having to be drilled again, and they brought up a piece of Ruth's dress; so they put down a three-pronged grab, and brought up the rest of her, and Eli came again, and they buried her alongside Paul, and with Joe Gundha not far away.

You can see those graves, with a picket fence about them, and no derrick for a hundred feet or more. Some day all those unlovely derricks will be gone, and so will the picket fence and the graves. There will be other girls with bare brown legs running over those hills, and they may grow up to be happier women, if men can find some way to chain the black and cruel demon which killed Ruth Watkins and her brother—yes, and Dad also: an evil Power which roams the earth, crippling the bodies of men and women, and luring the nations to destruction by visions of unearned wealth, and the opportunity to enslave and exploit labor.

THE END